2499

THIS EARTHLY PILGRIMAGE

Books by Walter Wangerin Jr.

The Book of God: The Bible as a Novel
Paul: A Novel
The Book of the Dun Cow
The Book of Sorrows
Preparing for Jesus
Reliving the Passion
Little Lamb, Who Made Thee?
The Manger Is Empty
Miz Lil and the Chronicles of Grace
Mourning into Dancing
The Orphean Passages
Ragman and Other Cries of Faith
Whole Prayer
In the Days of the Angels
As For Me and My House
The Crying for a Vision

For Children

Mary's First Christmas
Peter's First Easter
The Book of God for Children
Probity Jones and The Fear-Not Angel
Thistle
Potter
In the Beginning There Was No Sky
Angels and All Children
Water, Come Down
The Bedtime Rhyme
Swallowing the Golden Stone
Branta and the Golden Stone
Elisabeth and the Water Troll

Expanded Editions of Ragman and Other Cries of Faith; Little Lamb, Who Made Thee?; & Miz Lil and the Chronicles of Grace

WALTER WANGERIN JR.

THIS
EARTHLY

TALES AND OBSERVATIONS ON THE WAY

PILGRIMAGE

ZONDERVAN™

GRAND RAPIDS, MICHIGAN 49530 USA

HARPERCOLLINS

ZONDERVAN™

This Earthly Pilgrimage
Copyright © 2003 by Walter Wangerin Jr.

Ragman and Other Cries of Faith
Copyright © 1984, 2003 by Walter Wangerin Jr.

Miz Lil and the Chronicles of Grace
Copyright © 1988, 2003 by Walter Wangerin Jr.

Little Lamb, Who Made Thee?
Copyright © 1993, 2003 by Walter Wangerin Jr.

Requests for information should be addressed to:

Zondervan, *Grand Rapids, Michigan 49530*

Library of Congress Cataloging-in-Publication Data

Wangerin, Walter.
   This earthly pilgrimage : expanded editions of Ragman and other cries of faith, Little
lamb, who made thee? and Miz Lil and the chronicles of grace / Walter Wangerin Jr.
      p. cm.
   ISBN 0-310-24970-8
   1. Christian fiction, American. I. Title: Ragman and other cries of faith. II. Title: Little
lamb, who made thee?. III. Title: Miz Lil and the chronicles of grace. IV. Title.
   PS3573.A477 T48 2003
   813'.54 — dc21

                                                                                    2002013640

Published in association with the literary agency of Alive Communications, Inc., 7680
Goddard Street, Suite 200, Colorado Springs, CO 80920.

Interior design by Susan Ambs

Printed in the United States of America

02 03 04 05 06 07 08 09 /❖ DC/ 9 8 7 6 5 4 3 2 1

To David McFadzean
Artist of Sacred Hilarities
and My Friend

And which of yow that bereth hym best of alle,
That is to seyn, that telleth in this caas
Tales of best sentence and moost solaas,
Shal have a soper at oure aller cost
Heere in this place, sittynge by this post,
Whan that we come agayn from Caunterbury.

Geoffrey Chaucer
Canterbury Tales
"The General Prologue," 11, 795–801

[And the one among you who performs best of all,
That is to say, who tells in this affair
Tale of high teaching and best entertainment,
Shall have a supper at everyone else's cost,
Here, in this place, sitting by this very post,
When we have come back from Caunterbury.]

CONTENTS

INTRODUCTION
11

BOOK ONE:
Ragman and Other Cries of Faith

Part 1: The Christ of God

Part 2: The Servant of Christ

PART 3: THE BODY OF CHRIST

BOOK TWO:

LITTLE LAMB, WHO MADE THEE?

PART 1: THE CHILD OF HIS PARENTS

PART 2: THE PASTOR OF CHILDREN AND PARENTS TOGETHER

PART 3: THE PARENT OF HIS CHILDREN

PART 4: THE PARENT OF HIS PARENTS

PART 5: THE GRANDPARENT, FINALLY, OF MANY

BOOK THREE:
MIZ LIL AND THE CHRONICLES OF GRACE

JUST BEFORE THIS VOLUME was published, I entered the fifty-ninth year of my age. For a short while yet, I shall live just shy of my sixtieth—which, when I have arrived at it, shall constitute the three-score part of the Psalmist's measurement: "The years of our life are threescore and ten," which "come to an end like a sigh."

I am considering endings. *Blessed* endings, let me assure you, and thereby the wholeness of things. For a blessed ending is never an interruption. It is, rather, the rounding of the fullness of one's life. The blessed ending announces, without anguish but with the convictions of Christ, *"Consummatum est"*: the whisper of the Savior in our innermost ear, "It is, you know, my dear one, finished." And so, at the word of the Lord, it is.

Finished. Made complete. And by its ending rendered whole. Fulfilled. Filled up. Ahhhh.

Such blessings are not reserved for the old alone. Even the girl-child who meets her ending young is not different from an old man dying; for both lives are made equally *whole* by the call of the King of Heaven.

Both the girl-child and the old man have completed their earthly pilgrimages, each in her and his own way—though they are more similar than not. It isn't the length of life that distinguishes us, but the life itself.

The beginnings and the endings of the faithful are the same: we come from the Eden of our mothers' wombs. Will we, nill we, there is no help for it: all children next are sent from Eden to make an earthly pilgrimage toward the highest shrine of all. We walk. We wind through the terrible and marvelous complexities of this human existence. We stop at ten times ten thousand places on the way. These *become* the journey. All our stoppings become all our memories, and memory is the map of all our previous days, and that map for each of us is the shape of our individual lives. It is what we have been and what we are.

But at some point, early or late, at some point for all the faithful, our various ways and all our myriad faces are set upon the single most perfect ending of this earthly pilgrimage: Jerusalem.

We, with Abraham, "look forward to the city which has foundations, whose builder and maker is God." With all our wandering ancestors we confess that we are "strangers and pilgrims on earth." We desire a better country than the ones which we have left behind, a better country than all the countries of this earth, that is, a heavenly one: Jerusalem, that city without a temple, for its temple is the Lord God, the Almighty, and the Lamb.

"The years of our life are threescore and ten," says the writer of the ninetieth Psalm, adding, "or even by reason of strength, fourscore!" Unaware of the sciences and the medicines of this latter age, the Psalmist puts our limits at seventy years. Nor is seventy an unreasonable figure for the great majority of the peoples. But my father has already reached his eighty-fifth year, my mother her eighty-fourth. And my wife's parents lived into their nineties. *Or even fourscore!*

There is among us the chance of serious longevity.

A few more experiences of human complexities, then. Another thousand stopping places, to be sure. But it would be foolish to demand those extra years, and perilous to *depend* upon them.

I depend upon the promises of my Redeemer, Jesus.

Therefore I contemplate my personal ending without fear or despair, but with a happy gratitude and in the dearest trust.

For having seen the ending of my pilgrimage (it is but a stone's throw ahead of me), and having recognized my destination and all my conclusions as Jerusalem the Golden, I am already at peace.

At peace, then, I'm free to review the pilgrimage itself and all the places where I stopped along the way.

At peace, dear friends, I am also at sweet liberty to tell the stories of these stoppings: confessing sins where I have sinned; announcing glory where I have been blinded; touching upon the human relationships we all experience, and the various ages at which we experience them; and, under the tutelage of Rabbi Jesus, offering some instruction to others regarding our common complexities.

I tell you all this in order to describe the volume you now hold in your hands: it is a loose account of this earthly pilgrimage. It is a kind of journal of my own pilgrimage from its beginning east of Eden, even from my boyish days through youth and marriage and fatherhood and ministry and laughter and anger and sorrow and reconciliation and sin and blessed atonements again.

The pieces are as various as all our countless experiences. But there will be found, finally, a unified pattern here, and a wholeness that weaves everything together.

My stories, perhaps. But stories, you know, make cousins of us all. And more than laws or cities or governments, it is the *story* that creates and preserves deepest community. My stories, then, I hope to make *your* stories before we are done and come to the ends of the journey.

If we enter together the good community of our sacred stories, then each of our lives will be illuminated by the light of the others. My reader, your eyes shine light upon my writing—you give my words a mind and a heart in which to abide—while my words and my insights may enlighten your reading and your whole trek through.

Come. Sit. Be still.

And I will tell you, in this cause, tales of best sentence and most solace.

Walter Wangerin Jr.

BOOK ONE:

RAGMAN AND OTHER CRIES OF FAITH

THE CHRIST OF GOD

I SAW A STRANGE SIGHT. I stumbled upon a story most strange, like nothing my life, my street sense, my sly tongue had ever prepared me for.

Hush, child. Hush, now, and I will tell it to you.

Even before the dawn one Friday morning I noticed a young man, handsome and strong, walking the alleys of our City. He was pulling an old cart filled with clothes both bright and new, and he was calling in a clear, tenor voice: "Rags!" Ah, the air was foul and the first light filthy to be crossed by such sweet music.

"Rags! New rags for old! I take your tired rags! Rags!"

"Now, this is a wonder," I thought to myself, for the man stood six-feet-four, and his arms were like tree limbs, hard and muscular, and his eyes flashed intelligence. Could he find no better job than this, to be a ragman in the inner city?

I followed him. My curiosity drove me. And I wasn't disappointed.

Soon the Ragman saw a woman sitting on her back porch. She was sobbing into a handkerchief, sighing, and shedding a thousand tears. Her knees and elbows made a sad X. Her shoulders shook. Her heart was breaking.

The Ragman stopped his cart. Quietly, he walked to the woman, stepping round tin cans, dead toys, and Pampers.

"Give me your rag," he said so gently, "and I'll give you another."

He slipped the handkerchief from her eyes. She looked up, and he laid across her palm a linen cloth so clean and new that it shined. She blinked from the gift to the giver.

Then, as he began to pull his cart again, the Ragman did a strange thing: he put her stained handkerchief to his own face; and then *he* began to weep, to sob as grievously as she had done, his shoulders shaking. Yet she was left without a tear.

"This *is* a wonder," I breathed to myself, and I followed the sobbing Ragman like a child who cannot turn away from mystery.

"Rags! Rags! New rags for old!"

In a little while, when the sky showed grey behind the rooftops and I could see the shredded curtains hanging out black windows, the Ragman came upon a girl whose head was wrapped in a bandage, whose eyes were empty. Blood soaked her bandage. A single line of blood ran down her cheek.

Now the tall Ragman looked upon this child with pity, and he drew a lovely yellow bonnet from his cart.

"Give me your rag," he said, tracing his own line on her cheek, "and I'll give you mine."

The child could only gaze at him while he loosened the bandage, removed it, and tied it to his own head. The bonnet he set on hers. And I gasped at what I saw: for with the bandage went the wound! Against his brow it ran a darker, more substantial blood—his own!

"Rags! Rags! I take old rags!" cried the sobbing, bleeding, strong, intelligent Ragman.

The sun hurt both the sky, now, and my eyes; the Ragman seemed more and more to hurry.

"Are you going to work?" he asked a man who leaned against a telephone pole. The man shook his head.

The Ragman pressed him: "Do you have a job?"

"Are you crazy?" sneered the other. He pulled away from the pole, revealing the right sleeve of his jacket—flat, the cuff stuffed into the pocket. He had no arm.

"So," said the Ragman. "Give me your jacket, and I'll give you mine."

Such quiet authority in his voice!

The one-armed man took off his jacket. So did the Ragman— and I trembled at what I saw: for the Ragman's arm stayed in its sleeve, and when the other put it on he had two good arms, thick as tree limbs; but the Ragman had only one.

"Go to work," he said.

After that he found a drunk, lying unconscious beneath an army blanket, an old man, hunched, wizened, and sick. He took that blanket and wrapped it round himself, but for the drunk he left new clothes.

And now I had to run to keep up with the Ragman. Though he was weeping uncontrollably, and bleeding freely at the forehead, pulling his cart with one arm, stumbling for drunkenness, falling again and again, exhausted, old, old, and sick, yet he went with terrible speed. On spider's legs he skittered through the alleys of the City, this mile and the next, until he came to its limits, and then he rushed beyond.

I wept to see the change in this man. I hurt to see his sorrow. And yet I needed to see where he was going in such haste, perhaps to know what drove him so.

The little old Ragman—he came to a landfill. He came to the garbage pits. And then I wanted to help him in what he did, but I hung back, hiding. He climbed a hill. With tormented labor he cleared a little space on that hill. Then he sighed. He lay down. He pillowed his head on a handkerchief and a jacket. He covered his bones with an army blanket. And he died.

Oh, how I cried to witness that death! I slumped in a junked car and wailed and mourned as one who has no hope—because I had come to love the Ragman. Every other face had faded in the wonder of this man, and I cherished him; but he died. I sobbed myself to sleep.

I did not know—how could I know?—that I slept through Friday night and Saturday and its night, too.

But then, on Sunday morning, I was wakened by a violence.

Light—pure, hard, demanding light—slammed against my sour face, and I blinked, and I looked, and I saw the last and the first wonder of all. There was the Ragman, folding the blanket most carefully, a scar on his forehead, but alive! And, besides that, healthy! There was no sign of sorrow nor of age, and all the rags that he had gathered shined for cleanliness.

Well, then I lowered my head and, trembling for all that I had seen, I myself walked up to the Ragman. I told him my name with shame, for I was a sorry figure next to him. Then I took off all my clothes in that place, and I said to him with dear yearning in my voice: "Dress me."

He dressed me. My Lord, he put new rags on me, and I am a wonder beside him. The Ragman, the Ragman, the Christ!

MEDITATION ON A NEW YEAR'S DAY

MIGHTY GOD!

Creator unbegun, unending!

Your works, when I think that they are yours, dazzle me to silence and to awe and aweful prayer.

For I am thrice removed from the knowledge of them, and each remove diminishes me until I am near nothing by your greatness. Yet you love me.

For I may know some little something of the sun, may take its temperature, may track its travels relative to other stars, may date its age, predict its death, observe the windy rage of its digestion in the time between. But what do such solar figures do to the size of me? And what are my own travels and my age and my death beside this brutal fire in the universe? Tiny, tiny, insignificant. My God, the little that I know of your sun, and this but one among a sea of suns, belittles me. How is it that you love me?

Yet this is but the first of the levels of knowledge of your creation. Of the second level, I am ignorant and left to guess, conjecture only.

For who can say, of those who did not see it, how first you bulged that sun into its place, and hammered its brazen face, and shocked it at the heart and set it afire? Who knows the word wherewith you commanded the sun to be? Who knows the beginning of the things which we *can* know? Theory! Theory! We chirp theories like chickadees, because ignorance is a terrifying thing and we need the noise. But when I can with courage know I do not know; when I admit that I stand with my back to a void, that I am indeed blind to the beginning of things, then I am silenced. Then I am chilled by my own triviality— some dust at the edge of a desert. Nevertheless, you kneel down, and find me, and tell me that you love me.

Yet there is a final level of knowledge from which I am shut altogether. Of this I cannot even guess. I gape alone, and wonder.

For you who made the sun, the metagalaxies, and the hairs on the head of my daughter Mary, you first of all created space in which these things could be. Ah, mighty God! Space, where there had been no space? Dimension, where none had been before? Not just the *things* do I now consider, but the room that contains them. Nor just this room or that, but *room itself.* My Lord, I haven't the language any more, not the least imagination of the act you acted *before* the beginning of things. For someone might imagine a space in which nothing is; but no one can imagine a nothing in which not even space is.

Thou Deity, holy, mighty, and immortal!

Panto Krator! From whom the cosmos, on whom the founding of all things, by whom existence!

Ah, my Father, how can you love me so?

For even as you created space in which things are, so also you created time in which events occur. These two creations, space and time, are each as elemental as the other.

And even as I am dust in space, so am I but an instant in time— always an instant, never more than this particular instant: the end of the year that ended yesterday, the beginning of the year that begins today, the first day of that year, the morning of that day, the minute, the second that ticks for me *now.* How insignificant, small, and pipping this moment! How like a rat's tooth, unworthy of any memory. Yet it is me. And behold! You enter from the other side of time; you stride from timelessness to this sole moment, to the ragged stretch of my existence, to me, to love me. How can such a kindness be?

For you who made time are not bound by time—except you choose to be.

You embrace me, my dribble of moments. Right now you are standing at my birth, receiving me an infant into this created world. Yet right now you are present for this prayer of mine, prayed between the years. But right now you are establishing the answers of our prayers in our futures, in your present. And right now, right now, dear God, you are waiting at my death, your hands extended, ready to receive me to your kingdom—not only the same God as hears me now, but in the same eternal moment as now I pray!

Ah, Lord, who, before Abraham was, *is!*

Eternal God, such thoughts are too wonderful for me. They are high: I cannot attain unto them.

For you are wonderful beyond describing it. And yet you love me. And still you choose to notice me. And nonetheless, you bend your boundless being, your infinity, into space and time, into things and into history, to find me, to preserve my life.

Abba, Abba, Father!

How is it that you care for me?

I whisper, amazed that you should care to hear it; I whisper, astonished that it could make a difference to the Deity; I whisper here, now, the truth of my heart and the wholeness of my being:

I whisper, God, I love you, too.

I LOVE A CHILD.

But she is afraid of me.

I want to help this child, so terribly in need of help. For she is hungry; her cheeks are sunken to the bone; but she knows little of food, less of nutrition. I know both these things. She is cold, and she is dirty; she lives at the end of a tattered hallway, three flights up in a tenement whose landlord long forgot the human bodies huddled in that place. But I know how to build a fire; and I know how to wash a face.

She is retarded, if the truth be told, thick in her tongue, slow in her mind, yet aware of her infirmity and embarrassed by it. But here am I, well-traveled throughout the universe, and wise, and willing to share my wisdom.

She is lonely all the day long. She sits in a chair with her back to the door, her knees tucked tight against her breasts, her arms around these, her head down. And I can see how her hair hangs to her ankles; but I cannot see her face. She's hiding. If I could but see her face and kiss it, why I could draw the loneliness out of her.

She sings a sort of song to pass the time, a childish melody, though she is a woman in her body by its shape, a swelling at her belly. She sings, "Puss, puss." I know the truth, that she is singing of no cat at all, but of her face, sadly, calling it ugly. And I know the truth, that she is right. But I am mightily persuasive myself, and I could make it lovely by my love alone.

I love the child.

But she is afraid of me.

Then how can I come to her, to feed and to heal her by my love? Knock on the door? Enter the common way?

No. She holds her breath at a gentle tap, pretending that she is not home; she feels unworthy of polite society. And loud, imperious bangings would only send her into shivering tears, for police and bill collectors have troubled her in the past.

And should I break down the door? Or should I show my face at the window? Oh, what terrors I'd cause then. These have happened before. She's suffered the rapings of kindless men, and therefore she hangs her head, and *therefore* she sings, "Puss."

I am none of these, to be sure. But if I came the way that they have come, she would not know me different. She would not receive my love, but might likely die of a failed heart.

I've called from the hall. I've sung her name through cracks in the plaster. But I have a bright trumpet of a voice, and she covers her ears and weeps. She thinks each word an accusation.

I could, of course, ignore the doors and walls and windows, simply appearing before her as I am. I have that capability. But she hasn't the strength to see it and would die. She is, you see, her own deepest hiding place, and fear and death are the truest doors against me.

Then what is left? How can I come to my beloved? Where's the entrance that will not frighten nor kill her? By what door can love arrive after all, truly to nurture her, to take the loneliness away, to make her beautiful, as lovely as my moon at night, my sun come morning?

I know what I will do.

I'll make the woman herself my door—and by her body enter in her life.

Ah, I like that. I like that. However could she be afraid of her own flesh, of something lowly underneath her ribs?

I'll be the baby waking in her womb. Hush: she'll have the time, this way, to know my coming first before I come. Hush: time to get ready, to touch her tummy, touching the promise alone, as it were. When she hangs her head, she shall be looking at me, thinking of *me,* loving me while I gather in the deepest place of her being. It is an excellent plan! Hush.

And then, when I come, my voice shall be so dear to her. It shall call the tenderness out of her soul and loveliness into her face. And when I take milk at her breast, she'll sigh and sing another song, a sweet Magnificat, for she shall feel important then, and worthy, seeing that another life depends on hers. My need shall make her rich!

Then what of her loneliness? Gone. Gone in the bond between us, though I shall not have said a word yet. And for my sake she shall wash her face, for she shall have a reason then.

And the sins that she suffered, the hurts at the hands of men, shall be transfigured by my being: I make good come out of evil; I *am* the good come out of evil.

I am her Lord, who loves this woman.

And for a while I'll let her mother me. But then I'll grow. And I will take my trumpet voice again, which once would kill her. And I'll take her, too, into my arms. And out of that little room, that filthy tenement, I'll bear my mother, my child, alive forever.

I love a child.

But she will not fear me for long, now.

Look! Look, it is almost happening. I am doing a new thing—and don't you perceive it? I am coming among you, a baby.

And my name shall be Emmanuel.

TO A LADY WITH WHOM I'VE BEEN INTIMATE, WHOSE NAME I DO NOT KNOW

You. I saw you in the Great Scot Supermarket tonight, and now I can't sleep on account of you—thinking that, perhaps, you're not sleeping either.

Ah, you! You count your coins with bitten nails, not once but again and again. This is the way you avoid the checker's eyes, as though ashamed of the goods you buy, as though they declare your loneliness at midnight:

Two six-packs of Tab, because your buttocks, sheathed in shorts, are enormous and hump up your back as you shift your weight from foot to foot. You sigh. I think that you do not know how deeply you sigh, nor yet that I am behind you in the line.

Four frozen dinners whose cartons assure you that there is an apple dessert inside. Swiss steak, roast beef in gravy, chicken drumsticks, shrimp. Which one will you save for Sunday dinner? Do you dress up for Sunday dinner? Do you set the table neatly when the dinner thaws? Or do you eat alone, frowning?

Liquid breakfasts, a carton of Marlboros, five Hershey bars, Tampax, vitamins with iron, a *People* magazine, Ayds to fight an appetite, two large bags of potato chips. At the very last minute you toss a Harlequin paperback on the counter. Is this what you read at Sunday dinner? Is this your company?

What private wars are waged between your kitchen and your bathroom? Here I see an arsenal for both sides: the *She* who would lose weight against the *She* who asks, "Why?" and "So what?"—the *She* whose desires are fed too much, even while they're hardly fed at all. "It's your own fault," the first accuses; "two tons were never tons of love." But the other cries, "If I were loved I would not need to eat."

Ah, you.

Rubber thongs on your feet. The polish on your toenails has grown a quarter inch above the cuticle. I notice this because when

29

the checker rings your bill, you drop a quarter which rolls behind me in the line. I stoop to pick it up. When I rise, your hand is already out and you are saying, "Thanks," even before I have returned it to you.

But I do a foolish thing, suddenly, for which I now ask your forgiveness. I didn't know how dreadfully it would complicate your night.

I hold the quarter an instant in my hand; I look you in the eyes— grey eyes of an honest, charcoal emotion—and I say, "Hello." And then I say, "How are you?" I truly meant that question. I'm sorry.

Shock hits your face. For one second you search my eyes; your cheeks slacken, then, as though they lost their restraint and might cry. That frightens me: what will I do if you cry? But then your lips curl inward; your nostrils flare; the grey eyes flash; and all at once you are very, very angry.

Like a snake your left hand strikes my wrist and holds it, while the right scrapes the quarter from my hand. I am astonished, both by your strength and by your passion.

You hissed when you hurt me. I heard it and remember it still. Then you paid, crunched the sacks against your breast, and walked out into the night, the thongs sadly slapping at your heels.

Ah, you. You.

How much I must have hurt you by my question. Was that mild commonplace too much a probe, too lethal, too threatening for the delicate balance your life has created for itself? Does kindness terrify you because then, perhaps, you would have to do more than dream, more than imagine the Harlequin, but then would have to *be?*

I think so.

To cross the gulf from Life Alone to Life Beloved—truly to be real, truly to be worthy in the eyes of another—means that you are no more your own possession. You give yourself away, and then games all come to an end. No longer can you pretend excuses or accusations against the world; nor can you imagine lies concerning your beauty, your gifts and possibilities. Everything becomes what it really is, for you are *seen* and you know it. "How are you" triggers "Who are you." And it wasn't so much that I said it, but rather that I *meant* it and that I awaited an answer, too—this caused the lonely *She* to know her loneliness, even in the moment when I offered you the other thing: friendship.

It's frightening, isn't it?

To be loved, dear lady, you must let all illusions die. And since, between the bathroom and the kitchen, between *People* magazine and the Harlequin, your Self was mostly illusion—at least the acceptable self—then to be loved meant that your very Self had to die—at least the acceptable self.

Instead, you attacked, and my wrist is still bruised tonight. Ah, you.

A rich young ruler came to Jesus, desiring eternal life. He announced that he had kept all the commandments and wondered whether that weren't enough. But Jesus told him he lacked one thing. He ought, said Jesus, to sell all that he had and give the money to the poor. Upon these words, two were made sorrowful: the rich, because he could not lose his riches, which were his identity and his Self; he turned away. And Jesus, because he loved and could not love this man, for the man had turned away.

Riches. O my dear and lonely lady, how rich are you in your illusions. Ironically, you cling to the very loneliness which you despise. It feels safe. But love—God's love—always comes in light. That's what scares you. Light illumines truth: obesity, the foolish game between Ayds and potato chips, between cigarettes and vitamins. These things are the truth. These you hide. Yet it is only truth that Jesus can love. He cannot love your imaginings, your riches. Sell all that you have. Undress—

Not me, after all. It is Jesus who asks, "How are you?" And if you would then sell the false self by which you sustain the contemptible Self and die; if you would answer truly, "I'm fat, helpless and alone, unlovely," then he would love you. No: then you would *know* that he has loved you all along. To see one truth is to discover the other—which is that he loves you not because you are lovable, but because he is love. And here is the power of his love, that it makes ugliness beautiful! To be loved of God is to be lovely indeed.

All night long I keep a quarter back and ask, "How are you?" I can't sleep, waiting for the truth: "I'm just terrible." For then I would cry, "Good! Now there's a confession I can love!"

And the mighty God, the trumpet-voiced, cries, "I love a child. But she is afraid of me. Then how can I come to her, to feed and to heal her by my love?—"

Signs! Signs! A singular star
    Outblazing constellations
Inscribed the sky in this regard:
    "A King for all the nations."
The Magi read the word,
      And sought the Lord,
      And found the Lord.

Signs! Signs! A thundering dove
    Descended to creation
Itself a symbol, Sacred Love,
    Its cry a consecration:
"Beloved Son, with Thee
      Am I well pleased,
      Am I well pleased.

Signs! Signs! Consignments of wine
    Surpassing sixty gallon
Renewed a wedding in decline
    When lesser spirits failed them.
And who had done this? Who?
      Disciples knew.
      Disciples knew.

Signs! Signs! A face was inflamed,
    The noonday sun descending;
Both Moses and Elijah came;
    The cloud cried out, commending
To Peter, James and John
      "A Son, my Son,
      Beloved One!"

Signs! Signs! The world is a book,
    And what is not the writing?
The world is charged, for those that look,
    With grandeur, God's reminding:
    In all things near to thee
        Oh, read and see
        Divinity!
Then name these mysteries
        Epiphanies!
        Epiphanies!

STILL THE LORD, the Lord God, merciful, gracious, long-suffering and good, whispers on the side of his holy mountain: "I love a child. But he is stone in the palm of my hand. Then how shall I make him to know me, how crack his heart with the hammer, forgiveness?—"

The water had no right to be wine.

Six jars stood empty; that was demonstrable. Then Jesus issued a command, and the servants heard it, and the servants, prepared by Mary's ministration, obeyed; that sequence, too, was clear, evident, and reasonable. Soon water brimmed in the six jars, and no one wondered at that. Fill a jar, and water will brim in a jar: it was the natural result of servants' obedient labor, and thus far the process was properly consequential, each detail proceeding from a former constellation of details. Cause and effect. This was common and in the order of things.

Jesus issued a second command, and again the servants heard, and again they obeyed. They dipped liquid and served it to the master of ceremonies, and he drank. But he swallowed wine. *That* was not reasonable! The wine had no right to be there. Somewhere a breach had broken the sequence. Some *un*demonstrable cause had cracked the logic; some invisible force had a very visible, manifest effect, and tasty: wine. According to natural processes, the wine had no right to be there.

So something unnatural, something most uncommon was present in that place. The disciples stared at Jesus—deep, deep, deeper than his brow and down the hallways of his eyes. Rabbi, who are you? Water has no right to be wine—except that God be in you.

For the moment the disciples surrendered logic. They accepted that a door had opened in the universe. They took the impossible production as a sign and worked backward to a cause they had not seen, for flesh and spirit abide on different planes, and their eyes were flesh: "We see the light, even if we cannot see the source of light." Light and source together they called the Glory of God— and they believed on him.

Even so did Jesus reveal himself.

Even so he does.

Listen: here is a story historically true.

My son Matthew has always been borderline hyperactive. This is a very exhausting condition for all concerned, and unnerving. The kid leaped before he crawled and played football before he talked. He watched the televised games with his whole body—that is, he ran every play in the living room, dropping back for the quarterback, shooting forward for the wide receiver, making magnificent dives for bullet-balls, and then managing even to tackle himself against glass hutches and expensive china. Matthew was the whole damn team, at the age of four, in a poor man's living room.

Now, I am a patient man. I'm a pastor; I'm paid to be patient. I spent many a Sunday afternoon in painful patience, practicing this virtue, this fruit of the Spirit—and sometimes I would slip, suddenly delivering myself of a stentorian sermon in a living room before one wide-eyed four-year-old, damping his enthusiasm for a while; but I would generally regain my patience again, presenting my son with an admirable example of Christian restraint. *Restraint,* Matthew. Self-control! See? This is how it's done.

Through my teeth: Ssssee? *This* is how it's done.

But Matthew heard other drums. Matthew took other examples, each of them more vigorous than the last, and terrifying to a father's heart.

He watched what he called "the Six Millions Dollar Man" with worshipful attention. But that which he watches he believes in. And that which he believes in he becomes. The completeness of this kid's loyalty is an inspiration to all the faithful anywhere. No better disciple existed. Let him teach the saints of sainthood. But for God's sake, let him believe in the meek—not the Six Millions Dollar Man!

For the Six Millions Dollar Man, having indestructible right extremities, destroyed things.

There came the day when, in order to find some peace for my work, I commanded my son to his bedroom then bowed my head over my typewriter and trembled for a moment in the cool silence. Silence is a blessed thing. And patience is a virtue. I raised my head and began to type a sentence, tentatively. Another sentence followed, and soon a paragraph developed. It was wonderful. I found my stride; I was on the way to a full page, entertaining visions of a possible chapter before the day was through—when an almighty *crash* erupted from Matthew's bedroom. No, it was more like a *bang!* together with splintering wood.

Up on my poor legs, flying to the bedroom, my fingers still crooked to typewriter keys—

The bedroom door was still shut. No matter. I could read instantly what the Six Millions Dollar Boy had done—for his foot stuck *through the door* two and a half feet above the floor. When I opened it in the proper fashion, I dragged a child out, smiling, on his back. "Hi, Dad," he said. "I tried to come out—"

Through my teeth: strangled screams and very heavy judgment upon a child's head. I soon took the smile from his face, even before we took his foot from the door. The flying boy.

At the age of eight, Matthew ran away from home.

This is the cause-effect sequence, as best as I can remember it; there is a bleak, reasonable logic to every successive step, and I can understand that he should have run away:

At night we prayed a regular prayer, certain portions of which I italicized for the edification of my son. We prayed, "Jesus Savior, wash away/ all that has been wrong today/ Help me every day to be / *good and gentle*/ more like thee."

And then sons Matthew and Joseph were to close their eyes in a fine and tired obedience and go to sleep.

But on a particular night particular energies sizzled in my Matthew.

I folded my hands, standing between their beds. We were a picture of familial devotion.

"Jesus Savior / wash away / all that has been wrong today / Help us every day—Matthew! What are you doing?"

Dear Matthew had slipped from covers and concentration, was sitting on the floor, emptying a cardboard box of some 3000 football cards. "Sorting my cards," he said. "Terry Bradshaw—" He's a Steelers fan.

"No you're not." Through my teeth. "We're praying. It's time to go to sleep. In bed, please. Fold your hands, please. Now: Jesus Savior, wash away/ all that has been wrong today/ Help us— *Matthew! What are you doing?*"

He was trotting out of the room. He was going toward the bathroom. "To brush my teeth."

Jesus! Savior! Well, but tooth-brushing is my rule, after all; and the boy is obeying a rule, grant him that. And I shouldn't countermand rules which earlier I had extolled with wonderful proofs of importance. Patience is a virtue. I let him go. I bowed my head and waited. Patience is a virtue, yes; but Vesuvius is a volcano.

When he returned, broad-grinning, white-toothed, content with himself, we made white-knuckled folds of our hands again, and again we drove into our prayer: "Jesus / Savior / Wash / Away! All that has been / wrong—MATTHEW! WHERE ARE YOU GOING?"

To the bathroom. To the bathroom. To pee!

And what was I to do? If he did not go to the bathroom to pee, the kid would pee in his bed, and then his mother and my wife would find good reason to become his protector and my adversary, herself defeated by wet, stinking sheets.

When he bounced back into the bedroom and back into his bed; when he folded his hands so sweetly, he noticed a certain smolder in my countenance.

"Aren't we going to pray?" he said.

"Tomorrow!" I roared. "We wore the prayer out tonight."

"Aren't you going to hug me?" he said.

"Tomorrow!" I thundered, and left.

Tomorrow.

Breakfast.

My wife called the children, four of them, to wash their hands to eat. Three of them washed their hands. One of them didn't budge, was reading the sports page in the living room.

I was no longer a patient man. "Matthew," I said, "didn't you hear your mother?"

"Yes," he said, "I heard her."

"What did she say?"

"She said, Wash your hands."

"And why haven't you washed your hands?"

In perfect innocence the child looked up at me from the floor. With perfect rationality, lifting two fingers, he answered me: "Because she didn't ask me twice."

All my rhetorical skills, honed these ten years in the pulpit, flashed in the living room, slammed the walls, damned a child for a no-account and withered his soul to nothing. In round and echoing terms I did condemn the boy. In the language of Moses and the prophets, I sinned against my son.

That afternoon he ran away.

Clarence Fields, Cub Scout leader, called from Church. "Isn't Matthew coming today?" he said.

"He should have come straight from school," I said.

"That's an hour ago. He isn't here yet," said Clarence.

I covered the mouthpiece and spoke to Joseph in the kitchen. "Do you know where Matthew is?"

His brother said, "Yes." Then he said, "No."

"What does that mean?" I asked.

Joseph's eyes were wounded and near tears. "He ran away," said Joseph. "But I don't know where he went."

"From home?"

"He said he wasn't worth nothing. He said he wasn't coming back."

Then Joseph cried.

And a hammering began in my own chest. It was no easy thing to tell Clarence that Matthew ran away. This was my son. This was my doing.

The Cub Scouts immediately deployed, all leaping into Mr. Fields' car and good-deeding it through the city at high speeds, crying, "Matthew!" out the windows.

For my own part, I didn't know what to do. There was water in me that threatened to drown my soul—and I could have been glad to die, or to weep, one. Lord, how I have mishandled my son, my son, my busy, exuberant, vulnerable son!

I went out the front door. I wandered into Bayard Park and began to cross it through trees. Oh, my son, what have I done to you?

Guilt is a very real pain, thick in the chest, sharp in the gut, and almost intolerable. The guilty man will hunch and cup his belly in order to hold the pain; but a broken posture does not ease it: there is no one to blame but himself.

Then I saw him—Matthew, dragging his little self across Powell and into the park, coming home.

I didn't touch him. I hadn't the right. I held my distance and fell in step beside him.

"You ran away?" I asked, to be talking, to hear him talk.

"Yes."

"But you came home." I said that as brightly as I could, as though things were made right thereby.

He said, "I saw a man. I thought he was going to kidnap me. I was afraid. So I came home."

Ah, Matthew! The home that I made for you is only the lesser of two fears—a place to hide in, not to live in. Ah, Matthew! Tiny child at my side.

I had no more words to say, a wretched father. We went home in silence, he to his room, I to my study, where I sat in my chair and could not move. I faced the open door and grieved for the past and the future together. Earth stood still.

I think it was a half hour later that Matthew passed that door toward the stereo, glanced in, saw me, and stopped.

"You okay?" he said.

"No," I said.

"Are you sick?"

"No. Yes."

He gazed at me a moment, perplexed, and I dropped my eyes. Without a sound, neither sobbing nor sighing, I cried.

"Oh-h-h," said Matthew softly. "No, Dad," he said, "don't worry." He came into the study and put his hand on my knee. "I love you," he said. He smiled briefly. And he left.

That child! *That child had no right to forgive me so!* Where did he get the knowledge? Where did he get the maturity, the might of an ageless mercy, the transfiguring power to make me *his* son, and to make his son *free?* No, this was not logical. The sequence, somewhere between my sin and his charity, was breached; some other cause had cracked into the process: he was wine! And I—sweetly limp in my chair—whispered, "Except God be in you."

A door had opened in the universe, and through my son, and in my face. The Glory of the Lord had burst from a little child. Not Sunday school lessons, nor all the sermons he had heard me preach, nor the smattering of Bible reading that the child had done, but Jesus Christ himself was the cause of this most dramatic and real wonder. Matthew didn't speak the Christ; for an instant Matthew *was* the Christ—or rather, Christ abode in him, and I saw it; not with my eyes, for that was his own short-fingered hand on my knee, but with my soul, to which the Word had penetrated, changing it. He had done so casually what in fact he could not do. Only God could do that. But I was most certainly done: I was forgiven indeed.

Even so did Jesus reveal himself and sign my soul.

Even so he does.

And I believe on him.

The first of the first day's dawn was white,
That detonation of Time, white;
That primal verb and the birth of being,
Fiat! from the yawp of God,
Was a shout of light,
Was a perfect howl of progenitive light—white!
 And in between,
  The whole earth's springing green.

Then this shall be the evening
End of Time's long westering—
When the phenomenal noun dispredicates
And the growl of God has closed debate
And the light descends in separates—
This: universal purple gloom.
 But in between,
  The whole earth's springing green.

And the Christ's intrusion in Time was white,
The re-murmuring of the First Word, white;
So that advent requires a swaddling white.
 But the King's conclusion's imperial,
 For the Judge shall conjugate us all.
 Oh, *that* advent demands a purple pall.
  Yet in between—
  All in between—
  The whole earth's springing green. . . .

Wheat, and the young vine, green;
Shoots, and the small stalk, sweetly green;
And the tree unfolds and flattens high
A gang of hands to weave the sky,
An audience, applauding light—
And green! Ten thousand leaves are busy green!
    For the grace of the spacious Time between
    Is the whole earth, springing green.
    All in between,
    The good earth's springing green.

MODERN HEXAMERON: *DE ARANEA*

THE SPIDER'S THE SPINNER, the spinster, the busy web-weaver, often a widow—for embarrassing reasons—and a homemaker generally careless of her children. Most commonly, she swaddles her eggs together with a stunned bit of food against the day of the children's emergence, and then she takes her leave before she has taken their measure, or seen their faces, or named them.

Little of love in most of the spinsters. Personal survival, rather, and a life, though lasting, lonely: suitors and visitors alike fast become corpses. Her dining room's a morgue.

Plainly: she eats them that come to her.

She's very much like the rest of us: she allows a little fly his shape and the illusion of wholeness; but she has drunk his insides, and he is hollow, in fact; has become his own casket, as it were; his own memorial.

It is a neat, deceptive way to eat. But she has no stomach of her own, you see. She can digest nothing within her. Therefore her prey must also *be* her stomach. Through tiny punctures she injects into a bounden fly digestive juices; inside *his* body his organs and nerves and tissues are broken down, dissolved, and turned to warm soup. This soup she swills—

—even as the most of us swill souls of one another after having cooked them in various enzymes: guilt, humiliations, subjectivities, cruel love—there are a number of fine, acidic mixes. And some among us are so skilled with the hypodermic word that our dear ones continue to sit up and to smile, quite as though they were still alive. But the evidence of eating is in our own fatness. Neither we nor the spinster can conceal fatness.

But (and this *but* is no ordinary conjunction: it is graceful altogether!) there is one species of spider different from all the others.

Not that she has a stomach. She is a spider, after all, with all the external properties of her genus; with them, she lacks a stomach.

No, it is her manner that makes her wonderful. A man might almost weep to see how she *behaves.*

For this one does not leave her eggs to chance.

She stays. She protects the eggs in incubation. By the hundreds she gathers her brood upon her back so that she seems a grotesque sort of lump, rumpled and swollen. But such is love: it makes the lover ugly.

And when the children emerge, she feeds them. Her juices soften the meat to their diminutive snorkels. Yet even this care, peculiar among the spinsters, does not give her a name above all other names. Many mothers mother their children; that is not uncommon. Rather, it is the last supper which she reserves against necessity that astonishes the watcher and makes him wonder to see heaven in a tiny thing. . . .

Sometimes food grows scarce, and no amount of netting can snare the fly that isn't there. Sometimes tiny famine descends upon the mother and her spiderlings, and then they starve, and then they may die, if they do not eat.

But then, privately, she performs the deed unique among the living.

Into her own body this spinster releases the juices that digest. Freely they run through her abdomen while she holds so still, digesting not some other meat, but her own, breaking down the parts of her that kept her once alive, until her eyes are flat.

She dies.

She becomes the stomach for her children, and she herself the food.

And Jesus said to those who stood around him, "I am the bread of life. I am the living bread which came down from heaven; if any one eats of this bread, he will live forever; and the bread which I will give for the life of the world is my flesh."

Take—and eat.

This one was different from all the rest of us: cooked on a cross.

My Lord! My Lord, how can this be? All the world did shiver and teach me to despise the spider. Yet it was in her that I heard your voice.

THE CRY OF THE WHOLE CONGREGATION

THE FOLLOWING DRAMA TAKES place on the Sunday of the Passion. Its purpose is to allow each worshiper suddenly to discover (pitifully, intensely, truly to discover) his own rootedness in the drama which is Christ's—so that the Passion Story may no longer be mere story for observance, analysis, learning or history; so that it embrace the worshiper, name him, and become his own story indeed: the shape of his being.

Therefore, all senses are enlisted: sight, sound, the rhythm of both—music and motion—and the feel of the worshiper's voice in his throat and his emotion in his breast. This drama has no audience. All are actors. None objective. All subjective—or else the objects *of* the driving love of God.

There are four readers:

1. The Narrator, responsible both for narrative material and for the words of Jesus.

2. The Judas figure, who also represents the unrepentant criminal.

3. The Peter figure, who also represents that criminal who repents and receives the promise of the Lord—thus, forgiveness follows sin.

4. The Pilate figure, who also reads the Pharisee's lines during the entrance into Jerusalem and later represents Joseph of Arimathea—by which device, again, forgiveness is signaled.

The congregation as a whole shifts its identity so that it suffers the common conversion of the Christian, which is often an extended, dramatic process: that is, it begins with the ignorant praise of the multitude who knew not what sort of Messiah this Jesus was; next, it is the disciples, loving but failing the Lord; next, it plays the neutral role of the watchers, the questioners who disturb Peter by their curiosity; next, it descends to the sinful shrieks of manipulated people crying, "Crucify." This is the congregation's deepest level. Next, it arises to play out an internal conflict: men and women divide in their speaking, and some lament the deed, praying forgiveness, while others clearly participate in the deed. In "Crucify" they sinned; in this passage, though they continue in sin, yet they are conscious of it, too; and that is the more painful state, to be sure, but it is also the better, being the beginning of confession. Next, with the repentant criminal, the congregation recognizes the kingdom, power, glory of the Lord; and finally it is the women, blessedly separated from the event, yet witnesses unto it. Witnesses!

In the congregation's shifting role, the Lord's Prayer plays a constant harmony to the Lord's passion, again and again thrusting the people (by their connotative memory of these significant words) into a worshipful attitude—making real not only to the mouth and the mind but also to the soul what is taking place today.

There is a dancer. She is female. She alone takes the chancel, in which no furniture is but the rail and the altar. Nor does she enter the rail and approach the altar until that moment when Jesus is crucified—and then her feet are rooted and motion appears in her upper body only. At death her head and body sag. At burial she crumples altogether. Before then she may use the passages of music—particularly when the congregation sings—for sweeping steps and speed. But she will also vary her presentation so that sometimes it closes in on mime; for example, during the words of the Last Supper, "This is my body," she will seem to draw from her very abdomen the invisible gift which then she proffers; and at the right moments she will turn her head through sad degrees to look at Judas, to gaze upon the Peter figure.

The congregation, as it busies itself in reading and singing, shall catch fleeting images of this dancer—and so shall she effect a metaphorical communication. Since they shall not see her whole and lineal, they will find themselves unconsciously filling in the blanks; and what they give to her by imagination shall be diverse among them and mighty indeed.

Please note that she does not play Christ. Rather, she represents, as best as possible, the moods, the changes he must have passed through. She represents both his suffering and his love.

There is a drummer. He teaches the congregation its rhythm, beginning very slowly and softly, but increasing speed and impact as the drama unfolds, nipping the people's heels like a sheepdog, driving them, making them restless and thumping thunder to their cries of "Crucify! Crucify!" In the last passages of the cross, just before Jesus dies, his beat becomes the death march, funereal and impossibly sad. At death he falls silent altogether—and that silence shall be *heard*. It shall be deep space and a dangerous thing. I promise you: at that moment not a member of the congregation shall move, for death will be very present against their hearts.

There is a soloist—a male and tenor, if possible. He may be accompanied on piano for the first three verses of his piece. But the last verse must be sung a cappella, for it must be very lonely. For the first three verses—as for the passages which the congregation sings—the drummer and the dancer fall in rhythm.

There is a children's choir. They, together with all the other principals, process during the first hymn and take positions ready to sing; their still presence there will draw the attention of the congregation and its anticipation. But when their piece is finished, they take their seats. They should be versed in reading the congregational role, for they will lend dear credulity to the sound; moreover, the children ought *never* to be forgotten! They know better than we how to hear a story and how to discover the value of it. The theology shall escape them; but the drama shall catch them up. And isn't that the better thing anyway? Isn't theology simply the drama's interpretation?

Finally, this drama, as written, is essentially Lucan. But the author has sometimes been free with the text.

Oh, and this is not considered extracurricular. This is worship indeed.

Worship for the Way of the Cross

1. The Entry into Jerusalem

(Four readers' stands are visible before the chancel and empty. All is emptiness. A gentle flurry on the drum draws the congregation's attention, out of which rhythm a slow two-note fanfare of the organ rises and lowers again. Before it is silenced, while yet it holds last notes long, long, the narrator begins to read from the back of the church. His voice is clear and declarative.)

NARRATOR: When Jesus drew near to Bethphage and Bethany, at the mount that is called Olivet, he sent ahead two of his disciples, saying, "Go into the village opposite. There you will find a colt tied, on which no one has ever yet sat; untie it and bring it here. If any one asks you, 'Why are you untying it?' you shall say, 'The Lord has need of it.'"

(During the next portion of the narrator's reading, let the Peter and the Judas figures walk forward to their stands.)

NARRATOR: So those who were sent went away and found it as he had told them. . . .

PEOPLE: AND AS THEY WERE UNTYING THE COLT, ITS OWNERS SAID TO THEM, "WHY ARE YOU UNTYING THE COLT?"

PETER: And they said, "The Lord has need of it." And they brought it to Jesus, and throwing their garments on the colt, they set Jesus upon it.

(As the narrator reads the next portion, the organist plays once through the music of the coming hymn, swelling so that the narrator must raise his voice louder and louder.)

NARRATOR: *(Processing slowly, the whole company of presenters and the children's choir following with good space between each.)* And as he rode along, they spread their garments on the road. As he was now drawing near, at the descent of the Mount of Olives, the whole multitude of the disciples began to rejoice and to praise God with a loud voice for all the mighty works that they had seen, saying:

PEOPLE: *(Singing this or another hymn of high praise, preferably one with messianic titles, certainly one they know well; an excellent choice would be the traditional Sanctus, if the people know it and can be lusty about it. Then it would be sung through twice, the organist pedaling down between verses—as here—for the shouted exchange between the Pharisee and Jesus.)*

Refrain:
ALL GLORY, LAUD AND HONOR TO THEE REDEEMER KING,
TO WHOM THE LIPS OF CHILDREN MADE SWEET HOSANNAS RING.
THOU ART THE KING OF ISRAEL, THOU DAVID'S ROYAL SON,
WHO IN THE LORD'S NAME COMEST, THE KING AND BLESSED ONE.

Refrain.

THE COMPANY OF ANGELS ARE PRAISING THEE ON HIGH,
CREATION AND ALL MORTALS IN CHORUS MAKE REPLY.
Refrain.
THE MULTITUDE OF PILGRIMS WITH PALMS BEFORE YOU WENT;
OUR PRAISE AND PRAYER AND ANTHEMS BEFORE THEE WE PRESENT.

PHARISEE: *(Shouting.)* And some of the Pharisees in the multitude cried to him, "Teacher, rebuke your disciples! They're calling
you the Christ. Tell them to shut up!"

NARRATOR: *(In strong voice over the organ.)* He answered, "I tell
you, if these were silent the very stones themselves would cry out."

PEOPLE: *(Singing with the swell of the organ.)*

Refrain—and then:

TO THEE BEFORE THY PASSION THEY SANG THEIR HYMNS OF PRAISE;
TO THEE WE TOO REPEAT THEM AND MELODIES WE RAISE.
Refrain.
THOU DIDST ACCEPT THEIR PRAISES; ACCEPT THE PRAYERS WE
BRING,
WHO IN ALL GOOD DELIGHTEST, THOU GOOD AND GRACIOUS KING.

*(All now are in position, the children facing the congregation and
prepared to sing.)*

NARRATOR: And when he drew near and saw the city he wept
over it, saying, "Would that even today you knew the things that
make for peace! But now they are hid from your eyes. O Jerusalem!
The days shall come upon you, when your enemies will cast up a
bank about you and surround you, and hem you in on every side,
and dash you to the ground, you and your children within you, and
they will not leave one stone upon another in you; because you did
not know the time of your visitation."

*(Piano introduction to the children's piece begins before the nar-
rator is through, timing it so that there is but a beat or two and the
children sing.)*

CHILDREN: O Jerusalem, you missed your time to sing,
You missed your loving king

When he came to bring
You healing in his name
And wholeness to the lame;
You were blinded to his reign,
So the children sang:
Hosanna to the Son of David! Hosanna! Hosanna! Hosanna!
Hosanna to the Son of David! Hosanna! Hosanna! Hosanna,
To the King, to the King, to the King, to the King.*

(This song begins wistfully, rises to joy, ought to be sung at a quick pace, but delivers its last phrases sadly once again. If the children can, they might go to their seats while singing the final phrases; it will give the effect of a dying echo and loneliness.)

2. The Preparation and the Eating of the Last Supper

NARRATOR: Now, the feast of Unleavened Bread drew near, which is called the Passover. And the Temple Priests were seeking how to put Jesus to death; for they feared the people.

JUDAS: Then Satan entered into Judas called Iscariot, who was of the number of the Twelve; he went away and conferred with the temple priests and officers how he might betray him to them. And they were glad, and engaged to give him money. So he agreed, and sought an opportunity to betray him to them in the absence of the multitude.

NARRATOR: Then came the day of Unleavened Bread, on which the Passover lamb had to be sacrificed. So Jesus sent Peter and John, saying, "Go and prepare the Passover for us, that we may eat it."

PEOPLE: THEY SAID TO HIM, "BUT WHERE, LORD? WHERE WILL YOU HAVE US PREPARE IT, AND WHAT ARE WE TO DO?"

NARRATOR: He said to them, "Behold, when you have entered the city, a man carrying a jar of water will meet you; follow him into the house which he enters, and tell the householder, 'The Teacher says to you, Where is the guest room, where I am to eat the Passover with my disciples?' And he will show you a large upper room furnished; there make ready." And they went and found it as he had told them; and they prepared the Passover.

*"Hosanna to the Son of David" from *Kids of the Kingdom,* words and music by Anne Herring, © 1979 Latter Rain Music. All rights reserved. Used by permission.

(The dancer enters the chancel simply: Jesus at the Last Supper. Quietly, the organist plays "Let Us Break Bread Together on Our Knees" until the narrator has read through the institution of Holy Communion, falling silent immediately before the words, "But behold the hand of him who betrays—" The dancer serves slowly and with clean simplicity.)

NARRATOR: And when the hour came, he sat at table, and the apostles with him. And he said to them, "I have earnestly desired to eat this Passover with you before I suffer. *(Dancer signifies awareness of the congregation:* with you!) For I tell you, I shall not eat it until it is fulfilled in the kingdom of God." And he took the cup, and when he had given thanks he said, "Take this and divide it among yourselves; for I tell you that from now on I shall not drink of the fruit of the vine until the kingdom of God comes." And he took bread *(the dancer draws this from her abdomen)* and when he had given thanks he broke it and gave it to them, saying, "This is my body which is given for you. Do this in remembrance of me." And likewise the cup after supper, saying, "This cup which is poured out for you is the new covenant in my blood. *(Dancer: round with slow fire.)* But behold the hand of him who betrays me is with me on the table. For the Son of Man goes as it has been determined: but woe to that man by whom he is betrayed!"

PEOPLE: AND THEY BEGAN TO QUESTION, "WHO, LORD? WHO IS TO BETRAY YOU? IS IT I? IS IT I?"

NARRATOR: He answered, "He who has dipped his hand in the dish with me will betray me. Oh, it would have been better for that man if he had not been born."

JUDAS: Judas, who betrayed him, said, "Is it I, Master?"

NARRATOR: Jesus said to him, "You have said so."

(Silence a moment while the Judas figure withdraws from his stand and walks to the back of the church.)

PETER: *(With lunging impetuosity, even before Judas is fully gone.)* Simon Peter was indignant. "But not I!" he said. And he declared, "Though they all fall away from you, I will never leave you."

NARRATOR: "Peter, truly I say to you, this very night, before the cock crows, you will deny me three times."

PETER: Peter said to him, "Even if I must die with you, I will never deny you!"

PEOPLE: AND SO SAID ALL OF THE DISCIPLES, OVER AND OVER AGAIN.

(Let these exchanges follow with a tense speed.)

3. The Agony in the Garden

PEOPLE: *(Singing, after the organist has played through the melody once, simply. Let the dancer's motion show the journey and then sorrow.)*

GO TO DARK GETHSEMANE, YE THAT FEEL THE TEMPTER'S POWER;

YOUR REDEEMER'S CONFLICTS SEE, WATCH WITH HIM ONE BITTER HOUR;

TURN NOT FROM HIS GRIEFS AWAY:

LEARN OF JESUS CHRIST TO PRAY.

NARRATOR: And he came out and went, as was his custom, to the Mount of Olives; and the disciples followed him. And when he came to the place he said to them, "Pray that you may not enter into temptation."

PEOPLE: LEAD US NOT INTO TEMPTATION, BUT DELIVER US, DELIVER US.

NARRATOR. And he withdrew from them about a stone's throw, and knelt down and prayed, "Father, if thou art willing, remove this cup from me; nevertheless, not my will, but thine be done."

PEOPLE: OUR FATHER WHO ART IN HEAVEN, HALLOWED BE THY NAME. THY KINGDOM COME; THY WILL BE DONE. THY WILL BE DONE. THY WILL BE DONE—

NARRATOR: And when he rose from prayer, he came to the disciples and found them sleeping for sorrow, and he said to them, "Why do you sleep? Rise and pray that you may not enter into temptation."

PEOPLE: LEAD US NOT INTO TEMPTATION, BUT DELIVER US FROM EVIL, EVEN THE EVIL WITHIN OURSELVES.

JUDAS: *(While coming from the back of the church; the dancer signifies awareness of his approach and reacts to him from her distance, especially during the words of the Lord—but none of the readers attempt interaction with the dancer; she's in her world alone, using readers and people as foci.)* While he was still speaking, there came a crowd, and the man called Judas, one of the Twelve, was leading them. He drew near to Jesus to kiss him *(this facing the congregation),*

NARRATOR: But Jesus said to him, "Judas, would you betray the Son of Man with a kiss?"

JUDAS: Judas said, "Hail, Master."

PEOPLE: WHEN THE DISCIPLES SAW WHAT WOULD FOLLOW, THEY SAID, "LORD, SHALL WE STRIKE WITH THE SWORD?"

PETER: And one of them struck the slave of the high priest and cut off his right ear.

NARRATOR: But Jesus said, "No more of this!" And he touched his ear and healed him.

PEOPLE: FORGIVE US OUR TRESPASSES AS WE FORGIVE THOSE WHO TRESPASS AGAINST US.

NARRATOR: Jesus said to those who had come out against him, "When I was with you day after day in the temple, you did not lay hands on me. But this is your hour, and the power of darkness." *(The organist should begin, during this passage, the music to indicate the next hymn verse, so that the congregation begins to sing immediately after the narrator's next words.)* Then they seized him—

4. The Judgment

PEOPLE:

FOLLOW TO THE JUDGMENT HALL, VIEW THE LORD OF LIFE ARRAIGNED;

OH, THE WORMWOOD AND THE GALL! OH THE PANGS HIS SOUL SUSTAINED!

SHUN NOT SUFFERING, SHAME OR LOSS;

LEARN FROM HIM TO BEAR THE CROSS.

NARRATOR: Then they seized him and led him away, bringing him to the high priest's house.

PETER: Peter followed at a distance; and when they had kindled a fire in the middle of the courtyard and sat down together, Peter sat among them.

PEOPLE: THEN A MAID, SEEING HIM SIT IN THE LIGHT, SAID, "THIS MAN ALSO WAS WITH HIM."

PETER: But he denied it, saying, "Woman, I do not know him."

PEOPLE: AND A LITTLE LATER SOMEONE ELSE SAW HIM AND SAID, "YOU ALSO ARE ONE OF THEM."

PETER: But Peter said, "Man, I am not."

PEOPLE: AN HOUR LATER ANOTHER INSISTED, SAYING, "CERTAINLY THIS MAN ALSO WAS WITH HIM; FOR HE IS A GALILEAN."

PETER: But Peter said, "Man, I do not know what you are saying!"

NARRATOR: And immediately, while he was still speaking, the cock crowed. And the Lord turned and looked at Peter. *(Let the dancer turn!)*

PETER: And Peter remembered the word of the Lord, how he had said to him, "Before the cock crows today, you will deny me three times." And he went out and he wept bitterly.

(Silence for Peter—while he walks to the back of the church, precisely as Judas did before him!)

NARRATOR: Now the men who were holding Jesus mocked him and beat him; they blindfolded him and demanded:

PEOPLE: "PROPHESY! WHO IS IT THAT STRUCK YOU?"

NARRATOR: And they spoke many other words against him, reviling him. *(Pause, head down; continue in subdued yet audible voice, with peace facing the congregation: there should be contrast between Jesus' presentation and the accusers', and contrast between this short scene and the driving one to come. The rhythm is all of a piece, now, till Pilate releases him to the enemies.)* When the day came, the assembly of the elders of the people gathered together and led him to their council;

PEOPLE: AND THEY SAID, "IF YOU ARE THE CHRIST, TELL US."

NARRATOR: But he said to them, "If I tell you, you will not believe; and if I ask you now, you will not answer. But from now on the Son of man shall be seated at the right hand of the power of God—"

PEOPLE: AND THEY SAID, "ARE YOU THE SON OF GOD, THEN?"

NARRATOR: And he said to them, "You say that I am."

PEOPLE: AND THEY SAID, "BLASPHEMY! WHAT FURTHER TESTIMONY DO WE NEED? WE HAVE HEARD IT OURSELVES FROM HIS OWN LIPS. BLASPHEMY! OH, *BLASPHEMY!*"

(Boom! *One hard knock on the drum signals its presence; a good space of time before the second beat, much softer, and then the third, immediately after which the narrator begins the next scene, the drum's rhythm established. It will continue, now, at first far away, but coming louder, faster, nearer as the scene continues, until it beats a dreadful climax on the first syllable of the two words, "Crucify! Crucify!" Let the rhythm be simple—beat, beat, beat—and continual.*)

5. Dawn Friday: Jesus Before Pilate

NARRATOR: Then the whole company of them arose, and brought him before Pontius Pilate.

PEOPLE: AND THEY BEGAN TO CURSE HIM, SAYING, "WE FOUND THIS MAN PERVERTING OUR NATION, AND FORBIDDING US TO GIVE TRIBUTE TO CAESAR, AND SAYING THAT HE HIMSELF IS CHRIST THE KING!"

PILATE: And Pilate asked him, "Are you the King of the Jews?"

NARRATOR: And he answered him, "You have said so."

PILATE: And Pilate said to the Chief Priests and the multitudes, "I find no crime in this man."

PEOPLE: BUT THEY WERE URGENT, SAYING, "HE STIRS UP THE PEOPLE, TEACHING THROUGHOUT GALILEE EVEN TO THIS PLACE."

PILATE: And when Pilate heard that he was a Galilean, of Herod's jurisdiction, he sent him to Herod,

NARRATOR: Where he was vehemently accused, and treated with contempt and mocked, and arrayed in gorgeous purple, and then sent back again.

PILATE: Pilate said to the rulers of the people, "You brought me this man as one who was perverting the people; and after examining him, behold, I did not find him guilty of any of the charges against him. Behold, *nothing* deserving death has been done by him. I will therefore chastise him and release him—"

PEOPLE: BUT THEY ALL CRIED OUT TOGETHER, "AWAY WITH THIS MAN! AWAY! AWAY! RELEASE TO US BARABBAS—"

NARRATOR: Barabbas!—a man who had been thrown into prison for insurrection and for murder—

PILATE: Pilate addressed them once more, desiring to release Jesus—

PEOPLE: BUT THEY SHOUTED OUT, "CRUCIFY HIM! *CRUCIFY HIM!*"

PILATE: "Why? What evil has he done? I've found no crime in him deserving death. I'll chastise him. I'll release him—"

PEOPLE: BUT THEY WERE URGENT, DEMANDING WITH LOUD CRIES THAT HE SHOULD BE CRUCIFIED.

NARRATOR: And their voices prevailed.

PILATE: So Pilate gave sentence that their demand should be granted. He released the man who had been jailed for murder. But Jesus he delivered up to their will.

6. Friday Morning: Crucifixion

(The organist plays the melody of the following hymn through once with a single, keening note—a reed?—and makes the people's singing subdued.

The drummer has tempered his passion for a while, playing with rather than against the people's voice rhythm and inclination, and so shall he echo them through the first part of this scene, sadly scoring the soloist's words for two verses. But when the exchange begins between women and men at the foot of the cross, he must teach them the tension of that, the pain of the conflict between sinning and seeking forgiveness; therefore, for the first time he breaks his single-beating rhythm and creates a frenetic one, that their words be pitched back and forth with harder and quicker impact: they find themselves stepping on each others' verbal toes, and distressed.

The dancer, with the processional to the cross and the crucifixion itself, enters the rail for the first time and then faces the congregation, standing immediately before the altar, arms extended, yet motion in the upper body, thus showing both the severe restriction upon our Lord and the pain. But do not overdramatize this agony! Head and shoulders may roll; yet half-an-action doubles its force; the whole of an action, a mimicked depiction, halves it!)

PEOPLE: CALVARY'S MOURNFUL MOUNTAIN CLIMB. THERE ADORING AT HIS FEET, MARK THAT MIRACLE OF TIME, GOD'S OWN SACRIFICE COMPLETE. "IT IS FINISHED!" HEAR HIM CRY. LEARN FROM JESUS CHRIST TO DIE.

NARRATOR: But Jesus he delivered over to their will.

ALL MEN: AND AS THEY LED HIM AWAY, THEY SEIZED ONE SIMON OF CYRENE, WHO WAS COMING IN FROM THE COUNTRY, AND LAID ON HIM THE CROSS, TO CARRY IT BEHIND JESUS.

ALL WOMEN: AND THERE FOLLOWED HIM A GREAT MULTITUDE OF WOMEN WHO BEWAILED AND LAMENTED HIM—

(The contrast of men- to women-voices will strike a sudden, new dimension: us, but us at odds with ourselves.)

NARRATOR: But Jesus turning to them said, "Daughters of Jerusalem, do not weep for me, but weep for yourselves and for your children. For behold, the days are coming when they will say, 'Blessed are the barren, and the wombs that never bore, and the breasts that never gave suck!' For if they do this when the wood is green, what will happen when it dries!"

SOLO: *(A pause; the piano lightly plays an introduction; the soloist sings with infinite gentleness, and sings this particular piece not only for its familiarity, but also to stress You are there, now!)* Were you there when they crucified my Lord? Oh, sometimes it causes me to tremble, tremble—Were you there when they crucified my Lord?—

(The accompanist plays quietly the chorus while the narrator reads the next passage, so that words and music, the crucifixion, all comes as one single event, unbroken.)

NARRATOR: Two others also, who were criminals, were led away to be put to death with him. *(At this point the Peter figure returns up the aisle of the church, quietly.)* And when they came to the place which is called the Skull, there they crucified him, and the criminals, one on the right and one on the left.

SOLO: *(Immediately.)* Were you there when they nailed him to the tree? Oh, sometimes it causes me to tremble, tremble—Were you there when they nailed him to the tree?

(Drummer: the new rhythm. Establish it under these next words.)

NARRATOR: And Jesus said, "Father, forgive them; for they know not what they do."

ALL WOMEN: FORGIVE US OUR TRESPASSES.

ALL MEN: AND THEY CAST LOTS TO DIVIDE HIS GARMENTS.

ALL WOMEN: FORGIVE US OUR TRESPASSES.

ALL MEN: AND THE PEOPLE STOOD BY, WATCHING. BUT THE RULERS SCOFFED AT HIM, SAYING, "HE SAVED OTHERS; LET HIM SAVE HIMSELF, IF HE IS THE CHRIST OF GOD!"

ALL WOMEN: FORGIVE US OUR TRESPASSES.

ALL MEN: THE SOLDIERS ALSO MOCKED HIM, COMING UP AND OFFERING HIM VINEGAR.

ALL WOMEN: THERE WAS AN INSCRIPTION OVER HIM: "THIS IS THE KING OF THE JEWS."

ALL MEN: FORGIVE US OUR TRESPASSES. FORGIVE US, O LORD, OUR TRESPASSES!

JUDAS: One of the criminals who were hanged with him railed at him, saying, "Are you not the Christ? Save yourself and us!"

PETER: But the other rebuked him, saying, "Do you not fear God, since you are under the same sentence, and we justly? But this man has done nothing wrong." And he said, "Jesus, remember me when you come into your kingdom."

PEOPLE: FORGIVE US OUR TRESPASSES. DELIVER US FROM EVIL. THINE IS THE KINGDOM—

NARRATOR: And Jesus said to him—

PEOPLE: AND THE POWER—

NARRATOR: "Truly, truly, I say to you—"

PEOPLE: AND THE GLORY—

NARRATOR: "Today you will be with me in Paradise."

PEOPLE: FOREVER AND EVER. AMEN!

SOLO: *(Immediately, the intro having been played over previous words):* Were you there when he cried out at the end? Oh, sometimes it causes me to tremble, tremble—Were you there when he cried out at the end?

(Drummer: during that verse you almost disappeared. Now you return with rapidly increasing force, beating a death-march, louder and louder and louder until the word "spirit" at which you bang your last tormented bang and be still.)

(Narrator: read this passage with grave pauses, but lift your voice more and more until, when Jesus cries with loud voice, you are roaring at the top of your lungs, but slowly; do not look at the congregation; look at your script. On "Spirit" you, too, shut up totally, tomb-like,

and allow the silence to be a shocking, lasting thing. Then speak the death words quietly, as though the thing hath truly just occurred. Again, pause before you give words back to the people. This is a grievous moment; they need the time to grieve.)

NARRATOR: It was now about the sixth hour—and there was darkness over the whole land until the ninth hour, while the sun's light failed.... And the curtain of the temple was torn in two, from the top to the bottom.... Then Jesus, crying with a loud voice, said, "Father, into thy hands I commend my spirit!" *(Silence. Damnable, deafening silence.)*

And having said this, he breathed his last.

(Pause. The dancer loses the taut position of the last cry, sags gently to death.)

And all the multitudes who had assembled to see the sight,

PEOPLE: WHEN THEY SAW WHAT HAD TAKEN PLACE, RETURNED HOME BEATING THEIR BREASTS.

ALL WOMEN: AND ALL HIS ACQUAINTANCES AND THE WOMEN WHO HAD FOLLOWED HIM FROM GALILEE STOOD AT A DISTANCE AND SAW THESE THINGS—

7. Late Friday Afternoon: Burial

SOLO: *(No piano—the naked voice alone: a cappella, lonely)* Were you there when they laid him in the tomb? Oh, sometimes it causes me to tremble, tremble—Were you there when they laid him in the tomb?

PILATE: Now there was a man named Joseph from the town of Arimathea, a good man, a righteous man, one looking for the kingdom of God. This man went to Pilate and asked for the body of Jesus. Then he took it down and wrapped it in a linen shroud, and laid him in a rock-hewn tomb, where no one had ever yet been laid.

NARRATOR: It was the day of Preparation, and the Sabbath was beginning.

ALL WOMEN: THE WOMEN WHO HAD COME WITH HIM FROM GALILEE FOLLOWED, AND SAW THE TOMB AND HOW HIS BODY WAS LAID. THEN THEY RETURNED, AND PREPARED SPICES AND OINTMENTS—

NARRATOR: On the Sabbath they rested according to the commandment.

(Silence. Sit. And done.)

An excellent hymn with which to conclude this piece is "Rock of Ages," since it both takes and transfigures the imagery of this story, making it cleansing and finding the Good News in this Bad Event. A parish might reverently prepare for Holy Communion at this point, the organist using "Let Us Break Bread Together"; but little else should be required of the people. They will want to be still with their grieving.

LILY

THREE SISTERS LIVED ON the edge of a wood, an older, a middle, and a younger. They caught the summer sunlight all day long, since their dwelling was on the south side of that wood; and each did something different with the day and the light.

Few took notice when the eldest was born. She had been a plain sort, a simple, skinny sprout growing at a busy pace. But she'd been born with a will, and she said "I'll *make* them notice me!" So she tied up her hair and went to work. She produced a flower that looked like a purse, pale and small and forgettable, and no one noticed, and she said, "Just wait. They'll notice me." She went to work. She made ten of these flowers and more, twenty, fifty, a hundred and more, and she hung them like socks in the sunlight, and still no one noticed, but she said, "You'll see. They'll notice me." Each of her flowers filled up with the sunlight, and then this was the stuff that she worked with. All day long she ground the sunlight, as though it were meat, and she kneaded and squeezed it and pushed and she patted until her stem and her pedicels ached. Water she added and sugars and vitamins, valuable ingredients, basically healthy, though nothing so tasty as spice: this sister knew nothing of spice or excitement. Of the sunlight, then, and of an uncommon amount of work, she produced a food, long like a sausage, moisty green and crisp if you ate it now, nutty and hard and wholesome if you waited till later.

This sister's name was Bean Plant. Soon everyone noticed her. Several hundred members of the Family Fowl made her acquaintance and praised her labor by eating it. And Squirrels, who ate the nut sitting up, gnawing politely and silently, took dinner with her. And before that the Host of Rabbits had praised her salad. Everyone noticed her. Of sunlight and labor she fed a thousand stomachs.

And so it was that she could draw herself up very high and say, "See? I'm a very important person. How could all of these do without me? They couldn't at all, at all. They need me."

The middle sister, on the other hand, produced nothing. She had no desire to weave or whittle, to cook or sew, to hammer or dig or work at a thing. "I," she said, "am important just as I am." And she smiled exquisite smiles on all around her, and all said, "To be sure!"

For when Marigold was born, *everyone* took notice. She was simply beautiful. And when she grew, her blossoms burst forth *like* the sunlight itself, golden-yellow, full and glowing, beatific altogether. The Grandmother Elms said, "Oh." The Willows, her aunts, and all of them spinsters, wept to see such brightness in the world. A hundred suitors stood behind her, tall and handsome, dark and green, named Spruce; and when she danced with the Wind and whirled in his rhythm and trembled to his breath, the Spruce, to a man, made moans because she wasn't dancing with them. And what did she do with the sunlight? Why, she stood in it, was all. She let it shine on her, to everyone's gratification. Happy the souls who saw her, she thought; happy the sun to touch her; and happiest *she* to receive such attentions.

But wasn't she grander than the sun after all? "Of course," she sighed, patting her hair. "I am a knockout. What would the world do without me?"

Bean Plant and Marigold would sometimes discuss their sister. Nor did they lower their voices when they did. They talked about her as though she weren't there, for she was a fool, they thought, and somewhat dim in her brains and helpless, and how could she mind?

"What of Lily?" they said, and they shook their heads.

"What of Lily, indeed." Lily, the youngest of the three.

The child had nothing whatever to recommend her, neither beauty nor skill. She was fat, flat and green, her tongue stiff and thick; she could not dance to the wind nor produce a single kernel of food; she looked like a walking-stick stuck in the ground and forgotten, no reason to be there, no reason at all. Why, even *she* said, "What of Lily?" when they had said it; for she had searched through her whole being herself and had found nothing of worth.

But what bothered her sisters the most was her habit of talking to the sun. The child was addled, dreamy, and deluded; and who was to say how poorly that might reflect upon two sisters so up in the world? They had their reputations to consider.

"The sun is good for food," Bean Plant told her, "but the sun can't talk."

"Maybe not, and maybe so," said Lily, exasperating the busy sister.

"The sun is good for radiance," Marigold told her, "but the sun can't talk."

"Maybe not, and maybe so," said Lily, irritating the beautiful sister.

But it seemed to Lily that the sun *did* talk. Oh, not in words that anyone could hear, actually. But what he *did* was his talking. To rise in the morning and to peep at her from the greening east and to warm her to the root was his way of saying, "Good," and she said, "Morning," and together, then, they said, "Good morning." And when he did not pause one second in the sky, but crossed it slowly, certainly, surely in such a way as might be trusted absolutely, it seemed to her that he was saying, "Good," and she said, "Day," and together they said, "Good day." And when he laid him down in a purple, westerly bed and grew very big just before he shut out the light, as though he were stretching and yawning, that was how he said, "Good"; and then she never, never said, "Bye," for she would be sad if he went away forever. No, she said, "Night," and so they said, "Good night" together.

This is what Lily did with the sun: she had conversations with him. And always his word was, "Behold, it is very good"; and always her word said *what* was very good—and that was something, since her sisters' words were, "Useless and ugly, idle and plain, and worthless altogether." But Lily never stopped listening to him however they scorned her, because she thought that one day he might say to her, "I love you," which would be a very important thing not to miss, since she knew in her soul that she was a very *un*important person, but loving might make a difference.

"The sun is not a somebody," said Bean Plant and Marigold.

And Lily said, "Maybe not, and maybe so."

And her sisters said, "Ugh! You are impossible."

And Lily said, "That's true."

Then it came to pass that a sadness settled on Lily, and that was further aggravation to her sisters. Lily stupid was one thing. Lily sad was another and noxious altogether.

Dew, it seemed, on the poor child's leaf, dewdrops at the tip end of her spears. These were her tears.

"Be busy," said Bean Plant, "and you'll have no time for moping."

"A fine how-do-you-do," said Marigold. "By bright smiles I can make all the world happy—except my sister, except my own small sister. How do you think that looks to my suitors? It could cause talk, you know."

Bean Plant said, "All right, all right! What *is* the matter with you anyhow?"

Lily sobbed. Then Lily whispered the sorrow of her heart. "I think," she said, "that the sun is dying."

"The *sun!*" cried the sisters together. "Lily, you dream up the strangest things!"

"The sun does its duty," said Bean Plant.

"The sun shines on beauty," said Marigold.

"What makes you think it would die?" they demanded.

"He told me so," said Lily.

"The sun doesn't talk!" shrieked the sisters.

"Maybe not, and maybe so," said Lily. "But he is weaker today than yesterday and lower in the sky than a week ago and he doesn't last as long from the east to the west, and this is how he said, 'I'm dying, Lily, dying!'" Poor Lily could barely say the words, and she bowed her head and she wept.

The sisters cast uncertain glances to the heavens, and squinted, and measured, and had to agree. Facts were facts, after all: the sun was in decline.

"Well," said the sisters, "So what? So what if the old bald-head wears out? We'll do right well without him."

"But," said Lily, "I love him. He watches me. Oh, Bean Plant, how could I live without him?"

"Lily, don't be a nincompoop!" said Bean Plant. "The sun is not a somebody, and that's that. Now, you'll excuse me; I've work to do."

And work she did.

Bean Plant began to preserve her abundance. She dried it and packaged it, wrapped it in tough skins of tan and yellow as long as witch's fingers and hung it on branches above the ground, and these were her pods. "Because," she said, "I don't need the sun after all. I've got my wit and my work and my health. All on my own I am a very important person. It's neither here nor there to me, if the sun should go away." Busy Bean Plant! She stored her goods in bigger barns and waited and wished that her sister wouldn't cry.

Marigold, on the other hand, did nothing.

She checked her brilliant golden blossoms. She looked behind her on the ground and perceived a shadow there and said, "I made that." She took note of the posture of the grass, all brown and all bowed down—to her, as it seemed to her—and she said, "I did that." She touched her cheek and found it warm. And upon all the evidence she concluded that she did herself shine as brightly as the sun, that she was her own burnished light, "and therefore," she said, "tut-tut to the sun. It's time that I were radiant alone and free from competition. I am a very important person." Beautiful Marigold! She patted her hair and waited for all the wood to acknowledge that she was a knockout indeed, and she wished that her sister wouldn't cry.

It cast a shadow on their repute.

But Lily was helpless to stop her tears. For the sun sighed daily, daily weaker than the day before. And when the sun sagged into bed on a distant horizon, saying, "Good," poor Lily whispered, "Bye." They said "Good-bye" together. Lily knew the truth.

And the deepest truth of all she knew, for the sun was very great, and the sun had told her: all would die in his passing. Not one would be left alive. And as strange as it may sound, Lily accepted her death right readily, even gladly, thinking that then she would not be lonely when he left.

It was a murderer coming, said the sun, as cold a killer as ever roamed the earth, stark terrible in his deeds.

For this reason alone could Lily make herself say "Bye" when the sun had said "Good."

But when she told the sorrowful news to her sisters, they said, "Tittle-tattle, Lily," completely unmoved, because they said, "No one would kill the one who does her duty as well as I," and they said, "No one would dare destroy such beauty," and they said, "We are very important persons after all."

So Bean Plant labored righteously.

And Marigold primped most blithely.

And Lily wept for what was to come; poor Lily wept alone.

Once more before he left her, the sun spoke a word to Lily. It was a word of the morning and one that he had been speaking all along, but it had never been so important to Lily as it was now, and she had not heard it so clearly before. Perhaps she had been too young before and innocent; perhaps she had not yet hurt enough to *need* to hear it. Truly, it made her no less sad, for the sun was dying indeed. But it stilled her heart in the middle of sadness, and she ceased her tears and she fell silent. The word was "Again."

But Lily was always different from her sisters, untimely, so they thought, and stupid.

For now that she was quiet, they were shrieking.

The Family Fowl that fed from Bean Plant were thinning drastically. And when she asked them what had become of their relatives, her good friends, they rose on the wind crying, "Murderer! Murderer!" and flew south as swiftly as wings could take them. And when they ceased to come altogether, then poor Bean Plant believed them, and she began to shriek.

The wind that once had dallied with Marigold, dancing round her blossom, now ripped from the north at a terrible speed, frightened by something, snatching the petals from her headdress, stripping her to a most embarrassing bare, careless altogether of his sometime lover. "Look out!" screamed Marigold, trying to catch her colors. "Why don't you stop any more? Why don't you care to look at me?" "The Murderer," moaned the wind, "so close behind me! Ah, the Murderer!" And when the wind, in his speed, had broken her stem, then poor Marigold believed him, and she began to shriek.

"It's not fair!" shrieked Bean Plant, gone wonderously skinny and shivering. "I've worked all my life, brought bumper crops to everyone, been good, been good, Lord, I've been good! Oh, that should count for something. Not I! I shouldn't have to die!"

"It's okay," said Lily, yearning to comfort her sister.

Poor Bean Plant pleaded, "Then I *won't* have to die?"

"No, you will die," said Lily, "and I am so sad about that—"

And then she wanted to tell her sister what the sun had said, but Bean Plant shrieked, "Then it's *not* okay! It's a *cheat* to someone who's paid her dues—"

But Marigold—with brazen lips—could shriek louder than anyone.

"I don't want to die!" she screamed, as though this made a difference. "Spinster Willows, let them die! Grandma Elms are old and ought to die. But I, I am a knockout! *I don't want to die!*"

"It's okay," said Lily, unhappy for this sister, too.

"Oh, you!" cried Marigold. "What do *you* know?"

"That the sun said 'Again,'" said Lily.

"Your sun is vindictive and jealous!" cried Marigold.

Lily whispered, "He's coming back again—"

But her sisters raised such a loud lamentation that her whisper was lost, and Lily bowed her head, sad, sad, and hating the killer to come, yet very still at the center of her.

And so he came.

The murderer came grey as they said he would—out of the north with terrible robes all around him. And this is how he killed: he killed by kissing.

He kissed Bean Plant in the middle of a shriek and cut it off so that her bones alone stood up above the ground, quivering in death.

Marigold saw and Marigold hid her face in the earth. No matter. He sank into the soil and rose around her roots, froze those, and touched her pretty head, and she was still shrieking "No—" when he silenced her with a kiss. No, nothing stopped him, and nothing protected the living, for he was complete. His name was Winter, dead-white and mighty, hugging the Willows to death, petrifying the waters and rolling the sky in smoke.

Only Lily looked directly at him when he came, hating him, but silently. Only Lily held her peace before he sucked the life from her.

For she had heard the sun to say, "Again."

Come Easter the following year, there grew a plain, white Lily in the field south of the wood.

For the sun had come and kissed her corpse, and that was how he said, "I love you."

Then the flower had burst a white bonnet.

That was how *she* said, "I love you, too."

THE POET AND HIS CONGREGATION
TO CHRIST:
OUR BELOVED, AND OUR SWEET COMMUNION
(JOHN 6:35–59)

Come, touch my lips, my Lord, caress
  With flesh the flesh of me;
One mortal morsel and my "Yes!"
  Shall make me one with thee.
  Come, kiss thee into me.

Suffuse my breathing and my soul
  With sweetness of the wine;
No blood runs hotter nor more whole,
  No scent more sweet, than thine.
  I burn, thy breath in mine.

Then hold me, Christ, a hard embrace,
  The holy arms round me!
Hold, hold me in your body's grace;
  Your Church's unity
  Is my security.

"The Lord be with you." "And with you"—
  What salutations here!
But since he melts into us two,
  We can, nor do we fear,
  Breathe out such spells, my dear.

Oh, all my people, laugh with me!
    We have been loved by Christ—
We move, one nuptial company,
    His bride by sacrifice,
    From here to paradise.
Oh, what a wedding feast will greet
    The bride and pride of Christ!

THE SERVANT OF CHRIST

THEN JESUS SAID TO THEM, "These are my words which I spoke to you, while I was still with you, that everything written about me in the law of Moses and the prophets and the psalms must be fulfilled." Then he opened their minds to understand the scriptures, and said to them, "Thus it is written, that the Christ should suffer and on the third day rise from the dead and that repentance and forgiveness of sins should be preached in his name to all nations, beginning from Jerusalem. You are witnesses of these things. And behold, I send the promise of my Father upon you; but stay in the city, until you are clothed with power from on high."

Then he led them out as far as Bethany, and lifting up his hands he blessed them. While he blessed them, he parted from them, and was carried up into the heaven. And they returned to Jerusalem with great joy, and were continually in the temple blessing God. (Luke 24:44–53)

To those of you who are graduating,* those responsible for my invitation to speak in this place, thank you. Sincerely. Great gratitude comes of great humility, and I am humbled now—for what could one so close to you have new to say to you? I could wish that I had years on my shoulders, silver in my hair, and wisdom upon my head for an occasion like this. Lacking these, I will give you myself.

And I will let the final lines of Luke's Gospel shape my words to you: how the disciples had, before their Lord's ascension, one moment of burning purity; and a gift; and a command.

Pure, for the nonce, was their immediate relationship with Jesus, who stood face-to-face with them one final time. The long struggle of that relationship had come to a sort of climax: hereafter they would not so much witness as *be* witnesses.

Pure, before departure, was the fellowship of those who had learned under the Lord's bright, demanding tutelage. They were

---

*These words were first delivered as the commencement address for the graduating class of Christ Seminary-Seminex, St. Louis, 1981.

yet *they* in the moment; but in the days to come they would scatter as preachers of assorted names, vocations, histories, and deaths.

Pure, too; pure, finally, was the fine conclusion of their education; for now their minds were opened to the Scriptures and to the Christ and to his deeds and to the purpose of their preaching. Exegetes on the edge, they were. Well—it was sort of graduation.

And then—then!—the Lord gave them a gift. Please be careful that you distinguish clearly the gift then given. It was not the power from on high; rather, it was the *promise* of power from on high. The *promise* they might take with them; by the *promise* they might comfort themselves; in the *promise* they might boldly begin to act, because it assured them of the power's coming in its own right time. But they would, nevertheless, go and live and act all with a profound sense of personal weakness, because the promise was not itself the power.

Oh, and the place where they were to go—to stay and to wait in weakness—was also identified by the Lord, for that was his command: in the city. After the fine moment of purity, but before the power yet to come, wait in the city. . . .

My face burned when I was ordained. This is historical truth, no image, no metaphor. My face became bright red and burned.

I suppose the people might have said, "Walt's excited. Look at him blush." It was the end of my two year's education at Redeemer Church in Evansville, under a man named David Wacker. That church had been my school, that man my teacher, and here was the ceremony of endings and beginnings, with music and preaching, lights, flowers, rites, noise, my seat center-front, my self the single excuse for the gathering. "Walt's excited—"

But I knew even then that the excitement of the ceremony was not cause enough for the fire in my face. This was more than mere blush.

Rather, the burning came of this: for once in my long and vigorous struggle with the Lord Jesus Christ, the struggle itself had ceased. For a moment, the relationship had reached a certain purity. At that instant my faith was not being ripped between yes-and-no, nor my calling ripped between yes-and-no, as both had been for years. My Lord was Lord and Mine, my calling exquisitely clear—

My faith, you see, was the flame in my face.

And the burning came of this: I sat in the midst of a people with whom I had learned and laughed, talked, failed, and cried; a people against whom I had sinned, from whom had experienced forgiveness, among whom had roared, lived, and loved. And in that instant our fellowship had reached a certain purity, a quiescence of joy. There stood Joselyn Fields—a woman of deep, dark, penetrable skin and flashing white eyes—directing the choir in "Isaiah, Mighty Seer in Days of Old." By her music, her love and her solemnity she touched my lips with hot coals from the altar—

My face burned, you see, with the vital love of the people around me.

And the burning came of this: my education had come to a climax; my knowledge was being validated. My mind had been opened to the Scriptures, and the teacher much responsible was at that moment grinning down upon his charge. To David Wacker, when my vows had been pronounced, to that rangy man at the right of the chancel I walked; and we fell upon each others' shoulders; and we wept; and my face burned.

Three loves brightened my face. The love of my Lord so near. The love of the people so dear. And the love of the knowledge of Christ in words, in Word, and in the holy frame of my teacher.

And still there was more.

Somehow I received that facial heat as a sign from God that he would send his Spirit upon my ministry. This is the truth. I said to myself, "I will remember that my face burned. I'll save this sign." The promise of power from on high. I was content.

But then came Monday, and the ceremony passed; and the music, the moment, the light and the brightness of my face all faded, resolving themselves into a memory. I began my ministry at little Grace church, inner city, twenty pews, a tiny study but twice the size of the desk in it, and plaster cracked and dusting that desk.

It was a good thing that I had promised to remember the promise. I was about to need it, because instead of experiencing power, I experienced, more than anything else, The City.

My first sermons seemed to me possessed of a certain nascent power. I preached, I thought, with vigor. And I was particularly gratified to note that Sunday after Sunday bold Joselyn Fields would bow her head behind the organ, nodding, rubbing her chin, meditating. This was a lady of stark determinations, an ebony will, and a forthright honesty. What she did not like, she did not pretend to like. What she liked received her nod and her attention. And if I had captured the organist with my preaching, why, then there was no one I had not captured.

Yet, curiously, she never mentioned my sermons to me when the service was done.

There came the Sunday when I chose to direct my preaching altogether to her. I mean, I looked at her where she nodded behind the organ. I sidled toward her, away from the pulpit. I smiled. I peeped overtop her organ—and behold! The woman was reading music—nodding, meditating, selecting the offertory.

Preachers can feel very lonely for want of an ear.

"Mrs. Fields," I said at the end, "what did you think of the sermon?"

She sized me with a narrow eye and decided to state an opinion. "I know preachers," she said, "who make loud noises to the Lord. Please do the same. I can't hear you."

I was in The City.

Grace was an all-Black congregation, except for me. During that first summer of my ministry racial tensions ran high in Evansville, and higher, until riots broke out around the church. I suffered anguish at the news because I lived, then, at some distance, but my own people were caught in the turmoil, cordoned behind police barricades. Worse, I wavered at what to do; they hadn't taught us Riot in the Seminary. Finally, I clapped my collar to my throat—some sort of a badge, at any rate—and prepared to drive to the thick of the threat, to be Pastor in the crisis or else lose my rights of pastoring altogether.

But the telephone rang. It was Joselyn Fields.

She said, "You're not coming, are you?"

I said, "I have to."

She said, "Stay home."

"Why?" I said. My ministry, don't you see? My ministry was at stake.

"You'll get cut," she said.

And I asked, "Why?"

"Man," she said, "because you white," and hung up.

I was in The City.

I was in the common lives of common people: *that* was The City. And I had not yet earned the right to speak an effectual, respected word to the people in their communities, according to their most worldly affairs. That was a higher degree yet to be earned; and it took time.

Neither had I learned the language of The City or its laws, its history, traditions, the triggers of its power, its manner of marketing not only goods, but goodly emotions, ideas, anger, love, complaints, and compliments. That was an education yet to be obtained; and it took time.

But The City was a cold shock for one whose face had burned. For The City reduces the witness. No longer glorying in fine fellowship, the witness is one alone. No longer glorying in knowledge, the witness feels a very stupid sort. In a word, the witness comes up most power-*less*.

How terribly, terribly important, then, that the witness sent into The City remember the promise of the power to come!

And now you.

This is a blessed night, a right holy ceremony, your graduation.

Glory is warm in this place. And I don't know; some of your faces are burning. Surely, you are not wrong to smile, or to laugh lightheaded in the occasion, to glow!

Because three loves have come, tonight, to a certain climax and to a moment of unwonted purity.

Your minds have been opened to the Scriptures, to the acts of God in his Christ, to an understanding of the drama of repentance and forgiveness. Your education is at plateau and judged by this very ceremony as Good! Your teachers sit behind me, smiling. The whole process of learning stands still an instant, pure. It is a good thing.

And look at you! You sit center-front among community: class-mates among classmates, who have suffered, studied, laughed, talked, and grown together, who have hurt and healed one another; graduates among family and friends, a vast, supporting fellowship of the saints. Pure are all relationships in this peculiar moment. It is, after all, a glory to make a face to burn.

And your faith! After so much rising and falling in the past; after so much struggle with your Christ, denying him and crying after him; after the days when the only thing certain about your calling was that it was uncertain, now comes a moment of sweet truce and unalloyed purity. Jesus sits beside you, and you by him most confident. So lovely is the moment that you want to bark with laughter. Do! It is the right response to glory in this place.

And then, remember it.

For these three loves—your education, fellowship and faith—are strings. And God himself doth play upon the strings sweet music. He strums them now, right now, to sing to you a song; and by that song he whispers you a gift. *Not power!* That is not yet the gift. But the promise of power, the promise that power will come in its own right time.

Please, people, remember that it is but the promise of power to come—so that when, by the Lord's direction, you enter The City tomorrow you shall not despair over a creeping sense of powerless-ness. Rather, you will say, "This is right. This was to be expected." For the glory of this evening shall tomorrow seem no brighter than a match flame in the common light of day.

But also, please remember that you do *have* the promise, so that you may draw from it both patience and the motivation to do what must be done with your time in The City:

Two assignments by which to earn your higher degrees.

1. Learn The City. Learn the languages of its people, its secular means of communication, the flicker of eyes, the gesture of hands, the postures of contempt, servility, pride, protection, love. Learn The City. Learn the laws that shape it, both hidden in society and open in the books of government. So was Israel shaped at Sinai. Learn The City. Learn its hierarchy, the levels of its power. Learn

to read what hurts are real and what their symptoms are. Discover first the human dramas already being enacted in The City before your arrival—for the Holy Spirit is ahead of you, already establishing his work, already directing his purposes. Learning The City, you begin to learn of him.

2. Earn your right to be heard by The City. This is not bequeathed you with your graduation nor even with an ordination. It comes of a very specific labor. It comes when you—to your own sacrifice—commit your ways to the people of The City; and they shall believe that commitment only over a period of time. Stand with them in the courtroom, if that's where their lives take them; sit with them in hospitals, in jails, in the streets, in their places of business, in their bitter and their brighter moments. It's a hard thing to do, when you feel one and dumb and singularly lacking in the manifestations of faith; but it shall earn you the right to speak when that Spirit gives you the power to speak. It's a hard thing to do; but it is eased and enabled by the promise. You shall have the promise to support you. Remember the promise of power from on high.

For it shall surely happen! By the grace of God, someone's hurt shall find healing in you. And someone's hunger shall, by God's good grace, be satisfied in you. And someone's need shall in you meet solution, all by the grace of God! That moment, that blinding, incandescent, most surprising moment shall be the power come, the Pentecost toward which a long, laborious ministry was tending all along. It shall be. I tell you, it shall be!

In the second year of my ministry at Grace, Joselyn Fields fell sick.

In spring they diagnosed a cancer. In summer they discovered that it had metastasized dramatically. By autumn she was dying. She was forty-seven years old.

Spring, summer, and autumn, I visited the woman.

For most of that time I was a fool and right fearful to sit beside her; but I visited the woman.

Well, I didn't know what to say, nor did I understand what I had the *right* to say. I wore out the Psalms; Psalms were safe. I prayed often that the Lord's will be done, scared to tell either him or Joselyn what the Lord's will ought to be, and scared of his will anyway. I bumbled.

One day when she awoke from surgery, I determined to be cheerful, to enliven her and to avoid the spectre that unsettled me—the death. I chattered. I spoke brightly of the sunlight outside, and vigorously of the tennis I had played that morning, sweetly of the flowers, hopefully of the day when she would sit again at the organ, reading music during my sermon—

But Joselyn rolled a black eye my way. She raised one bony finger to my face. And she said, "Shut up."

God help me!—I learned so slowly. But God in Joselyn taught me with an unutterable patience. I, who had thought to give her the world she did not have, was in fact taking away the only world she *did* have. I had been canceling her serious, noble, faithful and dignified dance with death.

I shut up. I learned.

I kept visiting her. I earned my citizenship.

And then the autumn whitened into winter; and Joselyn became no more than bones; her rich skin turned ashy; her breath filled the room with a close odor which ever thereafter has meant dying to my nostrils. And the day came when I had nothing, absolutely nothing to say to my Joselyn.

This is as true as the fact that once my face had burned.

I entered her room at noon, saying nothing. I sat beside her through the afternoon, until the sun had slanted into darkness, saying nothing. She lay awake, her eyelids paper-thin and drooping, watchful eyes—we, neither of us, saying anything. The evening took us, and no artificial light went on when the sun went out; but with the evening came the Holy Spirit. For the words I finally said were not my own.

I turned to my Joselyn. I opened my mouth and spoke as a Pastor. I spoke, too, as a human. More than that, I spoke as a man to a woman.

I said, "I love you."

And Joselyn widened her ebony eye. And that lady, she put out her arms. As a parishioner, I suppose; as a woman, to be sure. She hugged me. And I hugged those dying bones.

She whispered, "I love you, too."

And that was all we said. But that, dear people, people, was the power from on high, cloaking both of us in astonished simplicity, even as Jesus had said it would. For in a word that I did not know I knew, a need had found not only its expression, but its solution, too. How dear, finally to hold my Joselyn!

And she died. And I did not grieve.

For God's sake, people! When you find yourselves inside The City, know the promise. Remember it. It is true! Not always and always, but in the right moment, in the fullness of its own time, the power shall be given unto you. Let this be peace in your weakness, and purpose in your long routine: it shall be. It shall most surely be, for the mouth of the Lord hath spoken it.

I WISH TO MEMORIALIZE ARTHUR FORTE, dead the third year of my ministry, poor before he died, unkempt, obscene, sardonic, arrogant, old, old, lonely, black, and bitter—but one whose soul has never ceased to teach me. From Arthur, from the things this man demanded of me, and from my restless probing of that experience, I grow. This is absolutely true. My pastoral hands are tenderized. My perceptions into age and pain are daily sharpened. My humility is kept soft, unhardened. And by old, dead Arthur I remember the profounder meaning of my title, minister.

It is certainly time, now, to memorialize teachers, those undegreed, unasked, ungentle, unforgettable.

In memoriam, then: Arthur Forte.

Arthur lived in a shotgun house, so-called because it was three rooms in a dead straight line, built narrowly on half a city lot.

More properly, Arthur lived in the front room of his house. Or rather, to speak the cold, disturbing truth, Arthur lived in a rotting stuffed chair in that room, from which he seldom stirred the last year of his life.

Nor, during that year, did anyone mourn his absence from church and worship. I think most folks were grateful that he had turned reclusive, for the man had a walk and a manner like the toad, a high-backed slouch and a burping contempt for fellow parishioners. Arthur's mind, though mostly uneducated, was excellent. He had written poetry in his day, both serious and sly, but now he used words to shiv Christians in their pews. Neither time nor circumstance protected the people, but their dress and their holiness caught on the hooks of his observations, and pain could spread across their countenance even in the middle of an Easter melody, while Arthur sat lumpish beside them, triumphant.

No: none felt moved to visit the man when he became housebound.

Except me.

I was the pastor, so sweetly young and dutiful. It was my job. And Arthur phoned to remind me of my job.

But to visit Arthur was grimly sacrificial.

After several months of chair-sitting, both Arthur and his room were filthy. I do not exaggerate: roaches flowed from my step like puddles stomped in; they dropped casually from the walls. I stood very still. The TV flickered constantly. There were newspapers strewn all over the floor. There lay a damp film on every solid object in the room, from which arose a close, moldy odor, as though it were alive and sweating. But the dampness was a blessing, because Arthur smoked.

He had a bottom lip like a shelf. Upon that shelf he placed lit cigarettes, and then he did not remove them again until they had burned quite down, at which moment he blew them toward the television set. Burning, they hit the newspapers on the floor. But it is impossible to ignite a fine, moist mildew. Blessedly, they went out.

Then the old man would sharpen the sacrifice of my visit. Motioning toward a foul and oily sofa, winking as though he knew what mortal damage such a compost could do to my linens and my dignity, he said in hostly tones: "Have a seat, why don't you, Reverend?"

From the beginning, I did not like to visit Arthur Forte.

Nor did he make my job (my ministry! you cry. My service! My discipleship! No—just my job) any easier. He did not wish a quick psalm, a professional prayer, devotions. Rather, he wanted acutely to dispute a young clergyman's faith. Seventy years a churchgoer, the old man narrowed his eye at me and debated the goodness of God. With incontrovertible proofs, he delivered shattering damnations of hospitals (at which he had worked) and doctors (whom he had closely observed): "Twenty dollars a strolling visit when they come to a patient's room," he said. "For what? Two minutes' time, is what, and no particular news to the patient. A squeeze, a punch, a scribble on their charts, and they leave that sucker feeling low and worthless." *Wuhthless,* he said, hollowing the word at the center. "God-in-a-smock had listened to their heart, then didn't even tell them what he heard. Ho, ho!" said Arthur, "I'll never go to a hospital. That cock-a-roach is more truthful of what he's about. Ho, ho! I'll never lie in a hospital bed, ho, ho!" And then, somehow, the failure of doctors he wove into his intense argument against the goodness of the Deity, and he slammed me with facts, and I was a fumbling, lubberly sort to be defending the Almighty—

When I left him, I was empty in my soul and close to tears, and testy, my own faith seeming most stale, flat, unprofitable at the moment. I didn't like to visit Arthur.

Then came the days of his incontinence, both physical and religious.

The man was, by late summer, failing. He did not remove himself from the chair to let me in (I entered an unlocked door), nor even to pass urine (which entered a chair impossibly seamy). The August heat was unbearable and dangerous to one in his condition; therefore, I argued that Arthur go to the hospital despite his criticisms of the place.

But he had a better idea, ho, ho! He took off all his clothes.

Naked, Arthur greeted me. Naked, finally, the old man asked my prayers and the devout performance of private worship—and we prayed. Naked, too, he demanded Communion. Oh, these were not the conditions I had imagined. It is an embarrassing thing, to put bread into the mouth of a naked man: "My body, my blood," and Arthur's belly and his groin—he'd raised the level of my sacrifice to anguish. I was mortified.

And still he was not finished.

For in those latter days, the naked Arthur Forte asked me, his pastor, to come forward and put his slippers on, his undershorts, and his pants. And I did. His feet had begun to swell, so it caused him (and me!) terrible pain in those personal moments when I took his hard heel in my hands and worked a splitbacked slipper round it. He groaned out loud when he stood to take the clothing one leg at a time. And he leaned on me, and I put my arm around his naked back and I drew the pants up his naked leg and I groaned and deep, deep in my soul I groaned. We hurt, he and I. But his was the sacrifice beyond my telling it. In those moments I came to know a certain wordless affection for Arthur Forte.

(*Now* read me your words, "ministry," and "service," and "discipleship," for *then* I began to understand them: *then,* at the touching of Arthur's feet, when that and nothing else was all that Arthur yearned for, one human being to touch him, physically to touch his old flesh, and not to judge. Holy Communion: in the most dramatic terms available, the old man had said, "Love me.")

When I came to him in the last week of August, I found Arthur prone on the floor. He'd fallen from his chair during the night, but his legs were too swollen and his arms too weak for climbing in again.

I said, "This is it, Arthur. You're going to the hospital."

He was tired. He didn't argue any more. He let me call two other members of the congregation. While they came, I dressed him — and he groaned profoundly. He groaned when we carried him to the car. He groaned even during the transfer from car to wheelchair: Douglas and Clarence and I had brought him to emergency.

But once inside the shining building, his groaning took new meaning.

"I'm thirsty," he said.

"He's thirsty," I said to a nurse. "Would you get him a drink of water?"

"No," she said.

"What?"

"No," she said. "He can ingest nothing until his doctor is contacted."

"But, water—?"

"Nothing."

"Would you contact his doctor, then?"

"That will be done by the unit nurse when he's in a room."

Arthur, slumped in his chair and hurting, said, "I'm thirsty."

I said, "Well, then, can I wheel him to his room?"

"I'm sorry, no," she said.

"Please," I said. "I'm his pastor. I'll take responsibility for him."

"In this place he is our responsibility, not yours," she said. "Be patient. An aide will get him up in good time."

O Arthur, forgive me not getting you water at home. Forgive us the "good time," twenty minutes waiting without a drink. Forgive us our rules, our rules, our irresponsibility!

Even in his room they took the time to wash him, to take away the stink, before they brought him water.

"Please—call his doctor," I pleaded.

"We're about to change shifts," they said. "The next nurse will call his doctor, sir. All in good time."

So: Arthur, whose smell had triggered much discussion in the halls, finally did not stink. But Arthur still was thirsty. He said two things before I left.

He mumbled, "Bloody, but unbowed."

Poetry!

"Good, Arthur!" I praised him with all my might. Even a malicious wit was better than lethargy. Perhaps I could get him to shiv a nurse or two.

But he turned an eye toward me, gazing on this fool for the first time since we entered the hospital. "Bloody," he said, "and bowed."

He slept an hour. I sat at bedside, my face in my hands.

Then, suddenly, he started awake and stared about himself. "Where am I? Where am I?" he called.

"In the hospital," I answered.

And he groaned horribly, "*Why* am I?"

In all my ministry, I have wept uncontrollably for the death of only one parishioner.

The hospital knew no relative for Arthur Forte. Therefore, at eleven o'clock that same Saturday night, they telephoned me. Then I laid the receiver aside, and I cried as though it were my father dead. My father. Indeed, it was my father. Anger, failure, the want of a simple glass of water: I sat in the kitchen and cried.

But that failure has since nurtured a certain calm success.

I do not suppose that Arthur consciously gave me the last year of his life, nor that he chose to teach me. Yet, by his mere being; by forcing me to *take* that life, real, unsweetened, barenaked, hurting and critical; by demanding that I serve him altogether unrewarded; by wringing from me first mere gestures of loving and then the love itself—but a sacrificial love, a Christ-like love, being love for one so indisputably unlovable—he did prepare me for my ministry.

My tears were my diploma, his death my benediction, and failure my ordination. For the Lord did not say, "Blessed are you if you know" or "teach" or "preach these things." He said, rather, "Blessed are you if you *do* these things."

When, on the night in which he was betrayed, Jesus had washed the disciples' feet, he sat and said, "If I then, your Lord and Teacher, have washed your feet, you also ought to wash one anothers' feet. For I have given you an example, that you also should do as I have done to you. Truly, truly, I say to you, a servant is not greater than his master; nor is he who is sent greater than he who sent him. If you know these things," said Jesus, "blessed are you if you do them."

Again and again the Lord expanded on this theme: "Drink to the stinking is drink to Me!" One might have learned by reading it. . . .

But it is a theme made real in experience alone, by doing it.

And the first flush of that experience is, generally, a sense of failure; for this sort of ministry severely diminishes the minister, makes him insignificant, makes him the merest *servant,* the least in the transaction. To feel so small is to feel somehow failing, weak, unable.

But there, right there, begins true servanthood: the disciple who has, despite himself, denied himself.

And then, for perhaps the first time, one is loving not out of his own bowels, merit, ability, superiority, but out of Christ: for he has discovered himself to be nothing and Christ everything.

In the terrible, terrible *doing* of ministry is the minister born. And, curiously, the best teachers of that nascent minister are sometimes the neediest people, foul to touch, unwuhthy, ungiving, unlovely, yet haughty in demanding—and then miraculously receiving—love. These poor, forever with us, *are* our riches.

Arthur, my father, my father! So seeming empty your death, it was not empty at all. There is no monument above your pauper's grave—but here: it is here in me and in my ministry. However could I make little of this godly wonder, that I love you?

IT IS NOT INSIGNIFICANT THAT my first apprehension of the love of God was granted in an experience with my father. Nor is it generally uncommon that God is apprehended in experience. Nor, in fact, can the divine and human meeting happen any other way. God is not a God of the pulpit, though the pulpit proclaim him. He is a God in and of the histories of humankind.

What *is* significant is that I should have to say so.

We, the professional faithful, the preachers so earnest for our responsibilities, have measured the arena of God's activity by our own; and the people, glad to be led in definitions, have allowed us to noose the mighty God and to remand him to a tiny space. To a tiny space, a discrete time, and a handful of particular, prescribed exercises. Because *we* meet the people formally from the chancel and the pulpit, there it is that God most evidently meets the people. Because we must necessarily schedule our time, sometimes serving, sometimes not, it is assumed that God operates also on some sort of schedule. Because we make much of pious or liturgical procedure, implying some form, good form, some formula, some proper votive attitude as needful for the manifestation of God, so the people assume that there are rules and requirements governing God's good will and his appearing, and that certain people possess the rights of propitiation, while others do not—but that God is circumscribed by them nonetheless. Moreover, because our own most usual apprehension of the Deity is by a noetic labor—studying, reading, analyzing, classifying, theologizing, propounding and providing *doctrine*, teachings—because our preaching is largely teaching, explaining and instructing, so the people may assume that God is a matter of the mind (or the heart, in more emotional deliveries), but not of the whole human in all its parts. We say, of a text, "This is what it means." And we imply that God comes present in the understanding of meanings, *even though these meanings be pointing to events!* Our manner communicates more than the matter we would deliver, because it is subliminal and qualifies every word we say.

Despite what we may think, and despite the freedoms we experience in so many areas of our culture, we remain, where religion is concerned, a people of the priest. By those singled out for the office we meet and perceive our God: the meeting is a conscious desire; the perception is an unconscious shaping; the consequence, except the priest be careful, is the contraction of God and then God's abstraction from the whole of life.

Contraction has through the ages been an effect of the priesthood, and often a desired effect. The first three strictures mentioned above—to place, time, and the special rites of propitiation—have always bound God to temples, festivals, and ceremony. Evil priests found power in controlling the All-Powerful. And frightened people were happier not bumping into an arbitrary god unawares. But even when fraud and fear were *not* the motives, people believed that the Limitless had found limits and *therefore* was approachable. The priesthood was an order within greater society: God was less than the whole; he was contracted.

Abstraction, on the other hand—an effect of the fourth stricture mentioned above—the removing of God from experiential life and permitting him truly to dwell in the analysis alone, is a present-day problem. To be sure, the Greeks of the fifth century B.C.—those who poo-pooed the historical value of their myths, re-interpreting them and worshiping the wisdom which triumphed over story—had mentalized their gods as well; but these were a clear minority and the rest of the culture continued to offer sacrifice. Today the trouble's more pervasive for two reasons: first, we are less honest than they. We pretend God's presence in the whole of our lives, and we believe the pretence, though in fact we honor understanding. Second, our priests themselves participate in the problem. Because they are also preachers; because so many of us consider preaching to be their most significant function; preaching seems to us the clearest access to the divine. Therefore, the shape of preaching most shapes our God. And what is the shape of so much preaching today? Why, it is the shape of the classroom: teaching. And teaching is always (in

our consideration) one step removed from experience and from the
"real." It is an activity of the mind. It prepares for what will be; or
it interprets what has been; it is separated from both. The God who
is met in doctrines, who is apprehended in the catechesis, who is
true so long as our statements *about* him are truly stated, who is
communicated in propositions, premise-premise-conclusion, who
leaps not from the streets, nor even from scriptural texts, but from
the *interpretation* of the scriptural texts—that God is an abstract,
has been abstracted from the rest of the Christian's experience.

O Priests, by the will of the people!

O Preachers, by the patterns of this age!

O Teachers, by thine own choosing—you have severely belittled
the Deity! Though your intent was kind and holy, your manner was
mousy. Though you brought extraordinary intelligence, a fine education, and assiduous study to your office, you reduced that office
to intelligence, its training and its application alone, and this you
made the temple of the Lord.

But the province of God is all creation, all space and time, all
things and all events, all the actions of humankind, and all the whole
human himself!

Nor does he watch these things and care about them only; he
acts within them! He uses them as instruments, the experience of
the people. He participates most fleshily. No abstraction, he! He is
not only transcendent; but by his own will and power he cracks into
our histories and there he works his works.

Or what does the psalmist mean when he sings, "He utters his
voice, the earth melts"? Or Amos: "The Lord roars from Zion, and
utters his voice from Jerusalem; the pastures of the shepherds
mourn, and the top of Carmel withers"? That the word of God is
more than mere instruction: it has manifest power before the eyes
of the people and hard against their hearts. It created. It continues
to shape creation in a most palpable way.

Or what does the psalmist mean when he sings, "When thou
hidest thy face, they are dismayed; when thou takest away their
breath, they die and return to dust. When thou sendest forth thy
Spirit, they are created; and thou renewest the face of the ground"?

Or John the Divine: "And I heard every creature in heaven and on earth and under the earth and in the sea, and all therein, saying, 'To him who sits upon the throne and to the Lamb be blessing and honor and glory and might for ever and ever!'"? It means that both the rule and the necessity of God are presently over and through *every living thing,* visible things, classifiable things, analyzable things—but it is not in the analysis of these things that his power works; rather, in the things themselves.

Or what does Jeremiah mean when he calls the pagan Nebuchadnezzar "the servant" of the Lord? Or what does Isaiah mean when he claims the pagan Cyrus to be anointed of God? They take for granted that the finger of God is in the affairs of *all* humankind, that it requires not somebody's faith to be touched by God, but God's will, God's choosing alone. God chooses *both* to be manifest in human history *and* to direct that history as well, for discipline and for mercy.

Or what, for heaven's sake, is the incarnation, if it doesn't announce God's personal immersion in the events—the bloody events, the insignificant and humbly common events, the physical and social and painful and peaceful and daily and epochal events of the lives of the people? In their experience! And isn't the coming of the Holy Spirit the setting free of that immersion, so that it be not restricted to any sole place, time, or people, but breathes through *all* experience and temples in *every* faithful breast?

Of course. Of course. It is not hard to argue the immanence of God. Why, it is one of our doctrines.

One of our doctrines. There's the sticking point. So long as it remains a doctrine alone, a truth to be taught, immanence itself continues an abstraction—and is not immanent. God abides not only in the church, but in the books in the church, and in the minds that explain the books, and in the intellect.

What then, Priests? Preachers, what shall we do that the people's perception of God not be so much less than God himself?

Make something more of our preaching. Allow the preaching itself a human—and then a divine—*wholeness:* that the whole of the preacher be presently active in proclamation, the whole of the hearer invited to attend, and God will be seen as God of the Whole.

Or, to rush the point: tell stories.

The preacher is not a mouth alone, self-effacing that God alone show through. (When that is the case, then God is a mouth alone, and that is *all* of him which shall show through.) The preacher in all of his parts is the proclaimer of God: his wonder, his humor, his faith, his body, the tone of his voice as well as its words, his *experience!* The entire drama of his own relationship with God, both in sinful enmity and in holy forgiveness! Her husband, if she be a woman, is part of that proclamation, and her children. His parents, his wife, the leaks in his roof, his surgery, his pains and his pleasures, his troubles and their resolutions. Three times in Acts the story of Paul's conversion appears, twice in his own mouth. It comes again in Galatians. His aggrieved experience threads the letters to the Corinthians: the message of Christ is proclaimed not only by Paul's intellect or teachings, but by his very being and in wholeness! He may be embarrassed by boastfulness; but he does it anyway, and so God is seen in lashes, in prison, on a ship, in dreams—everywhere immanent.

I tell you of Arthur Forte, and behold! God's in the squalor; God's in a hospital; and by a naked, obstreperous man, God is shaping me like a clay pot. I tell you of Joselyn Fields, and God explodes in the common language between a man and a woman. I tell you of the day my Matthew forgave me, and Jesus Christ walks through the doors of one man's study, to ease his burning guilt in the cool blood of the cross. Doctrine may judge the rightness of my perceptions; doctrine may name the details of the event and caption them like pictures: "sin," "repentance," "forgiveness," "justification." But I stand before you in flesh and blood; I risk the disclosure of myself and my experience; I present you with the very stuff itself of the events which have shaped this person before you, and so reveal the Shaper shaping. By these stories I am sinfully, gracefully *whole,* and whole may be the drama of God in me. (I do no more than St. Augustine, then, do I?) Like Cyrus to the Jews, Arthur Forte is anointed of God to set me free. Like Isaiah of the Scriptures, I *say* so: and God appears immanent in human events. I am more than a preacher. I am myself the preaching. For God chooses to touch me whole, not only in my mind.

Oh, no! There is no pride in such personal revelation—not unless it is sinfully conceived. For the complete drama of God begins with my rebellion and ends with his forgiveness. Remember St. Paul's repeated story? How could either Paul or I find personal glory in what amounts to confession—confession of sin, confession of faith?

Tell stories, ye preachers of God. Humble yourselves to make of yourselves a parable.

Because when you do that, you invite, as well, the wholeness of the hearers. Then not only their analytic minds, but their laughter shall be in the pew; and by laughter, their lungs and their consternation; their bodies, their sympathy, their emotions, their distress, their inadequacy, their male- and femaleness, their parenthood—their experience! You will be inviting them as *people* (not only as students) into a relationship with you. For if once they laugh, or cry, or remember their own past week, or nod—just nod—then they are using more than their minds, seeking more than understanding. To you, who offered your Self, they are returning their Selves. A teacher calls to students, and intellect to intellects. But a whole person calls to people, and to answer is to allow wholeness, too, in that relationship. There's the word: such preaching encourages human *relationship,* and so, love.

And then—if it is in such a relationship that God takes up his dwelling, he dwells in the wholeness of the people's histories. His temple is their experience. They shall know him immanent, indeed. Nothing is not the stuff of a story. All of the senses participate. Then the pulpit is only a place to stand, and the whole world is seen in a word, and the Word in the world.

I told stories in university classes—
—and football scholarships cared to hear what I had to say.

I told stories to my children—
—together we named their bogeymen, their wordless terrors,

and we were allied against them, since my children listened while I spoke, and so they were not alone; and they dealt in imagination with the hazards of their imagination—it is where they live and solve problems; and they laughed; and the story *became* the power! And the story became the vehicle not just of an affectionate love, but of a medicinal, transfiguring love. And my children triumphed.

I told the story called "Lily" to my congregation—

—Mary Ellen Phillips, who heard it then, told it to her niece in Nevada, who suffers from muscular dystrophy, and the niece chuckled to hear it. But when that niece's friend died in a cruel accident—a boy sixteen, as she was, with whom she was in love—none could comfort her, not her parents, not her pastor, none. But Mary Ellen went into the bedroom where the child was crying, and prayed God for words to say, but had none. But then her niece said, "Tell me 'Lily'—"

If the story of Jesus Christ took place among the people, then the preaching of Jesus Christ must also find place among the people; and since story involves the people whole—enticing personal commitment by the desire to hear the ending—it is story that can plant it there. It is not doctrines that comfort us in crisis. Nor are crises like examinations in school, attention to one isolated problem divorced from reality. It is Jesus himself who comes to comfort us, and crises are the dramas that swallow us down whole, as the fish did Jonah. The stories *of* experience (themselves becoming experiences for the hearers) prepare the people to see God approach them *through* experience.

"I don't want the doctrine of resurrection. I don't even want the promise of resurrection. Please: I want the *calmness* of resurrection. Tell me 'Lily.'" Or one might say, she wanted the kiss of resurrection, which was, just then, the kiss of Jesus, the hand of him who bestrode two worlds at once, the one in which she had to dwell, and the one which had taken her friend. "Remind me: Tell me 'Lily.'"

What were the Saints' Tales in medieval tradition but a high and finely popular form of preaching? And story.

And what were the stained glass windows, and the stations of the cross, and the biblical paintings (all in the dress and the landscape and the face of the times *in which they were crafted*) but visible forms of preaching, and the translation of the Christ into their own experiences? And story.

And the finest Black preaching of this century and the previous three does precisely the same thing—tells the stories of Christ in black-face, and of Israel according to Black experience. Or else, volte-face, it tells the story of its own people, and behold! Jesus walks in. No mystery to that: Jesus *is* the mystery.

Martin Luther King, Jr., begins his proclamation "I Have a Dream" by referring to a small experience he had with a small girl; just as St. Peter begins his sermon to Cornelius with reference to the experience he's just had among Gentiles; just as Jesus seats little children on his lap or remembers a traveler from Jerusalem to Jericho—

Out of experience rises the Word in order to lodge in experience once again. And story is experience communicated. Story is Word and experience abiding each within the other.

If Jesus began a sermon by saying, "There was a man who had two sons"—

—O Priests! Why mayn't we do the same?

Now, this is the truth: I first knew the love of my God in the love of my father.

I used to get dreadful cases of poison ivy. Angry red dots spread my limbs, erupting in bunches like mountain ranges. On my face the pustules ran an amber fluid that scabbed in amber crust. And it went into my hair, my nostrils, the backs of my hands, and so forth. Fierce cases and most debilitating itches. I was miserable.

I was also convinced that scratching the stuff spread it; so I schooled myself in stillness. Awake I could hold a position before the TV set for hours at a time. Sleeping, however, I lost control and would wake both scratching and on fire. So I conceived a plan. I had my brother tie my hands behind my back before I went to bed—with ropes, belts, the bathrobe cord, tape, anything. But nothing worked. I was Houdini in my sleep, slipping the most intricate knots of my brother and scratching hell out of my flesh, I, my own assassin!

So, my mother conceived a plan. She'd heard somewhere that Fels Naptha soap was a warrior against the itch. She had *not* heard that laundry soap is supposed to rinse the skin of ivy oils within an hour of touching it; rather, she considered it a lotion. Therefore, my mother, who didn't do things by halves, worked wonderful lather of Fels Naptha and applied it to every mass of rash on my body, and so it dried, and so it caked, and so her son was mummified. It's hard to sweat under a cast of Fels Naptha. Worse, the stuff was stiff against my skin, so every move I made irritated a thousand dots, which all set up a jubilation of itching and drove me to a pitiful distraction.

More than ever, I schooled myself in stillness. I lay on my bed all the day long and thought that this was the way I would end my life.

On a particular afternoon, when I'd brought my flesh to quietness, was lying perfectly still abed, my father came into the room and sat beside me to talk with me—matters of the world, and so forth, before the dinner I would not share with the family, and so forth.

It was a nice talk. He is a kind man. I didn't move or look at him. But I could hear his voice.

Now, there are certain places on a boy's body which, try as he might, he can't keep still. On that place on my body, there was, at that time, one poison ivy dot. And that bodily part began to move. So that single poison ivy dot began to itch.

This was more than I could take. In a moment, all the plans of the world and all the remedies failed. Life was very bleak. Without turning my head, without so much as a sob or a moan, I began to cry. The tears trailed down my temple and pooled in my ear. I thought that I would die soon.

But then I heard a strangled sound to my left.

It was my father. He'd risen to his feet. His hands were up and empty. His face was so full of anguish, seeing my tears, that my own heart went out to the man. He turned, turned fully round in the bedroom, seeming so helpless; and then he bolted for the door, crying "Calamine lotion!"—hit the wood and left.

Calamine lotion. I was experienced in the ways of poison ivy. I knew that calamine lotion was utterly useless even if it could get to the rash; but *my* rash was covered by a rind of Fels Naptha soap. No good. No good.

Nevertheless, when my father appeared again with a giant bottle of the stuff; when my father knelt down beside the bed, uncovered me, and began so gently with his own hand to rub it on; when my father's eyes damped with the tears of suffering, so that I saw with wonder that my pain had actually become *his own pain* and that it was *our* pain that had sent him rocketing to the drug store; when I saw and felt that miracle, a second miracle took place: the ivy did not itch.

Calamine lotion did not do this thing!

My father's love did this thing—and I knew it! Oh, my heart ached to have such a father, who could enter into me and hurt so much that he took my hurt away.

I was a special child that day, abed and still and watchful. For this was the love of God, incarnate in a man with a receding hairline and a patch of whisker on his chin and a smell I shall never forget.

Whom was I naked before? Whose hand made miracles against my skin? God. God's.

It was here I first began to discover the mercy of God and such magnificent preachments as "Vicarious Suffering." And it was here

I learned that love was no word, but an event, a sacrifice. But as yet I knew none of the phrases, nor the *theou logoi*.

Simply, I had experienced the power of God.

I tell you the story, dear brothers and sisters, to say—
—tell stories. It is the fullness of witness.

A CHRISTMAS PASTORALE

CHILD, YOUR MOUTH IS TURNED DOWN. There are weights at the corners of your lips. And something's squeezed your forehead together; your brow is plowed as deep as the soil, and the winter has frozen it so.

What are these weights? What makes you frown?

Ah, look at you. Your shoulders sag, and hands droop, and knees are bent. Deep sighs, I hear them. Deep sighs blow from the basement of your soul—

Come. Sit. Talk to me.

And, lo: you talk. You shock yourself with talk. You roar.

I think you did not know how visible was your sorrow nor how great the pressure within you, so my sympathy ambushed you; my eyes dropped your defenses. And since my eyes do not look away, grief rushes out of you—words, words, memories, accusations, reasons for your desolation, reasons by the score whirl like blackbirds in the room, making you dizzy with their number: you did not know you had such reason to be sad. You did not know you were so full of complaint. In spite of yourself, you cry. You roar on account of your tears, angered by them as well as by a God-damnable world— until the tears choke you and you jam your face into toilet paper, because I had no Kleenex, and now you don't wish to show your face again—

And I listen.

What I do, I make you a cup of coffee, very slowly, clacking the spoon on crockery to let you know that I am busy *not* staring at you. You need the time and a hollow space in which to meet yourself. This cup of coffee is my gift to your dignity. Here. Sugar? No? Then, here.

You take the cup and do not drink. You press it against your cheek—for the warmth, perhaps: it is a bitter winter. Your elbows on your knees, gazing at the floor, you begin once again to talk— humiliated, I think, for having lost control. I notice that you make whole sentences, now, attempting some popular psychoanalysis for yourself. I do not smile at you. You are no psychologist, so your explanations ring cheap and partly pompous; but the effort is earnest and touching: you are struggling to prove self-mastery after all. I do not smile.

I listen.

My Lord, how carefully I listen, for when will I get this chance again? I don't know. In a thousand ways I signal listening: I nod. I purse my lips. I say, "Oh." I squint recognition of a trenchant point. I cover my mouth, pull at my chin, lean forward, watch closely the dark, flitting center of your eye which steals glances at me—

I listen. And I hear, finally, that all of your sorrows are one sorrow only.

Oh, it is a terrible sorrow, to be sure, and fierce and able to hurt you horribly. But it is only one. You have divided the one into many, because it shows itself in a thousand forms, all of them hiding their source. And you have accepted the *many* as your problems because you do not want to acknowledge that single source. And why? Because the source is in you. No, the source *is* you. And that would be a hell of an admission. With all my heart I understand that: we would rather suffer a hundred troubles caused by other people than admit one for which we alone must bear responsibility. That would be suicidal, wouldn't it? Then nothing whatever of worth remains. But the suicide, don't you see, occurred at the beginning of sorrow, not at the end of it—

And I love you, child. I love you.

Therefore, when you have finally fallen silent and are liking the silence I lend you, when you sip once or twice my cardboard coffee and sigh and wonder whether the pastor minds cigarette smoke, then I take a breath fearfully and I begin to speak.

Fearfully: because I do not take your side against dogs and the bulls of Bashan. In fact, I'll seem somewhat to set my eyes against *you*. Fearfully: because I am going to tell you the truth which you've been so diligent to hide. It's a surgery. But now—right now while the thing is warm between us, and all the evidence is on the floor—you are vulnerable to the truth. Right now, before you lid your eyes against the cigarette smoke and forget that you cried and dress yourself in hard habit again; right now the pain might trigger change instead of anger. And when will I get this chance again?

I draw my breath and say, "Oh, why did you ask the Lord to leave your life?"

You shoot me a glance, as though I'd changed the subject a little too violently; but I haven't. Your nostril flares, as though you sniff a dangerous tack; there you are right.

"Don't you understand?" I ask. I am whispering. "When you sent Lord Jesus away, you sent your strength as well." You lower your eyes to my chin. I've said the name twice, now. Had you hoped I was a pastor above pastoring? Real people?

I speak very low and very fast: "When you dismissed the Christ, you denied the Cause for Joy. Therefore, you lost the cause for honest smiling (though the smile still clutched your face awhile, so you didn't connect his leaving with your losing it). That's where your shoulder's droop comes from, old friend, and the weights at your lips and in the heart of you. Friend of mine—why did you choose to become your own law, your own Lord, Master of your own existence? You are no good at it. Look at you. Look how you have failed. If the pitch goes bad, don't blame the bleachers. Blame the—"

"Pitcher!" Your word: snapped to show I'm not ahead of you. But the second cigarette's too quick upon the first. Your soul is squirming. I suspect that you are seeking reasons to dislike me, to judge me, or, at least, to scorn me. You could devalue my words that way. Or else you are pitying my poor preacherly ignorance, my unworldly idealism, making me too inexperienced to know the truth.

But I love you, child, and I persist.

"Not me," I say, "but the Lord. It is the Lord himself who is unsettling you right now. Not me, though you can't look me in the eye. Not me, who seems to be betraying our years of friendship by God-talk. It is the Lord you wish to avoid. Perhaps you're scared of his return? You think he'll come to judge you? No, it's worse than that: you think that you will die at his coming, see all the furniture of your life destroyed, the delicate balance against the void. Well, in this last," I whisper, leaning forward, "you are right. Masters die at the Master's coming—"

Now you are absolutely silent. Your gaze has jelled, like cataracts; and though you look toward me, it's nothing of me that you focus on. You are making no commitments, not with your eyes, not even the least of commitments, which is that you might be listening. Commitments, I think, terrify you. They wear black hoods and hide their faces and could, in the end, behead you.

Oh, I want to cry for you—so tough, you! You swagger like the children mimicking their elders; but *you* are the elder, mimicking children! You, your only, foremost enemy. You, you, for *your* sake, won't you look at me?

This is the hardest time for me. I truly do not know whether I am winning the moment or losing it. Your face shows nothing: no sorrow any more, for that was vulnerability (dear to me, to you so dangerous), no hope, nor joy, nor pain, nor friendship. Nothing.

I want to cry for both of us. Because I love you—

Therefore, in a voice as clean as its message, laundered of my feelings, I persist. (Lord, let my words be like the snow to him!)

"For God's sake, do not be afraid," I say. "His coming is going to lay you waste, yes. But it will not hurt you in the way you think. He'll come into you the same as first he came into the world: Christmas, old friend! A baby conceived and growing. That's how he enters you.

"Hush, hush, hear me," I say, but I do not touch your knee. You've made it a block of wood. Are you cursing yourself for confiding in me? "It begins in delight," I say, "as when a man and a woman make love together, only, it is God and the people together—"

You mutter, "Penetration," and I laugh out loud. That you talked at all is something. And I'll take your word as a joke. You can't demean my metaphor, because that's precisely what it is—

"Penetration! Right. And you, old friend, are the woman who can do nothing but cease to deny it. You drop your arms, two weapons once against the Love, both muscle and bone. All unprotected you lie before the mighty God, helpless under the Holy One. Penetration: I like that. And then the life introduced by this sweet joining is small and hidden in the depths of your being. But it is there, there, independent, powerful, alive inside of you, and growing.

"And then your mind will sometimes go inward to the baby's turning. 'Ah,' you will sigh at odd moments, grabbing your heart, 'something kicked.' You'll close your eyes to comprehend the miracle: God in you. And the world that watches you will wonder at your silent wondering. They'll say, 'What's come over you?'

"See? This is the first stage of his coming into you again. Christmas.

"But then the parturition, the birth, old friend. Not forever can the Christ stay hidden inside of you, but he will be born into your open life—with labor and pain on your part, to be sure; but with the shock of joy as well: He is! He lives! This is what he looks like, whom I have loved silently, who was in me, but who was ever before me.

"He will live visibly in your deeds and in your doings. Baby pieties will receive from you a trembling attention, a worried, yearning watchfulness. Your language will change. The people will look at you and see a new thing and demand its name, and you will say, 'Jesus,' and they will go away wondering still; but you will smile as any mother would.

"This is the second stage of his advent here: Christmas.

"Finally, he will grow as children grow. He will mature until he is revealed as stronger, broader than you and wiser. Then, old friend, the pain is past, when him you *thought* the infant stands before you as the Lord, and you admit *yourself* the infant once again. Then the pain is past, when you confess how asinine you were to master your own life with such another Master by. Then it is he who lifts your hands and strengthens your weak knees and straightens out your walking, who smoothes your brow and gives you life again and raises up your slack lips to a smile. If first you died in his conception. If you surrendered to the dreadful penetration—"

I am leaning forward. I do not want to stop talking, because, when will I get this chance again? But the words are gone out of my mouth, now, and next I'll repeat myself, but my heart is hammering the repetition already: did I say it right? I'm a little breathless. For two minutes together I struggle to control that, then notice that the intensity of my stare embarrasses you.

That's wrong. I shouldn't embarrass you.

Like a lover compromised, I drop my eyes. I put my hand on my mouth. The snow is stroking the windows. Your cigarette has made a two-inch ash that droops like an eyebrow. It's dead against the filter; the filter's between your fingers. It's quiet here. There's an empty sanctuary outside my door. *Shoosh* says the snow. And you are saying nothing.

It's up to me to set you free, one way or the other, *one way or the other.* That is to say, I have to signify when our conversation's done. You won't. You wait. You've chosen only to endure.

Dear God! What have I done to you?

I whisper, "*Christmas,* child."

And that is all.

You rise immediately. "Merry Christmas to you, too, Pastor," you say, and "Where do I put the cup?" It's full of coffee. You thank me. You are very much collected, now, and no one would know the rip in your soul that I knew one hour ago. Did I get through before the stitch? You are blank. I can't read past the blankness: snow in a frozen field. You shake my hand, and then you leave me, and I hold your cup.

Ah, I pray as you go. With all my heart I pray that you are *not* giving me a fine show of independence, that you have *not* chosen to "deal with my problems alone," the master of your soul and well shed of the wimp, religion. Earnestly I pray that you are going out to meet your Christmas, that acute conception, that laborious birth, life—

But I don't know, after all. I can't tell. All I've got right now are your boot tracks in city snow, and even those are filling. I have to wait long, long, to see the evidence of Christmas in your face. But I will wait. I will wait. Child, I will wait a lifetime. Because I love you.

I SAW ZEPHANIAH KOMETA FOR the first time in the lobby of a Seattle motel, where I'd been waiting for the car that would take both of us up to a mountain retreat. We were scheduled to lecture. We might have been equals, except for our races and his great-hearted humility.

Zephania (he pronounces it Zeph-*AHN*-yah) appeared in the door of the tiny lobby, paused smiling, then stepped to the registration desk and spoke. It was curious—it would have been painful, except for that smile—how the clerk reacted to him.

The Reverend Kometa is African, a pastor, a theologian, a citizen of Namibia. He is black in every respect except one: his skin is white. He was born an albino. So his kinky hair is straw-yellow, and his eyes are hurt by sunlight, and his flesh shows the scars of sun-sensitivity. He stands tall and angular. He keeps his head bowed to the ground. Gently does the man smile; gently does he move; and gentle is the timbre of his voice. His accent is soft and African, requiring of his American listener a particular attention for understanding him.

Zephaniah Kometa asked the clerk for a newspaper, smiling, casting his half-blinded face down to the counter.

The clerk raised her own eyes and uttered the first half of the word "What." The clerk said, "Wha—" saw Zephaniah's face, snapped her mouth shut, and began rapidly to blink her eyelids.

Zephaniah repeated his request more clearly, nodding in order to send it to this woman with gently nudgings.

The clerk popped her mouth open and began to giggle.

She broke sight from the man before her. "I," she said. She frowned at her fingernails. "I, hee-hee, hee-hee."

"Nyews-pepah," Rev. Kometa said.

The clerk peered anxiously about the little lobby, seeking help. And there was I. Her faced suffused friendship and familiarity, and in a whisper shouted: "What did he say? What's he trying to say?"

But I had never met the man before.

The African reached, touched the back of her hand, and pointed to the magazine rack: the newspapers.

His touched snapped her still. His gesture triggered understanding. In a sudden haste to grab the paper, she swept her pen and registration papers to the floor. He bent to help her. He served her.

And I wondered who the man might be, so restrained, refined, patient, dignified, and kind.

And, at first glance, so odd: a black man white; a white man black.

The clerk—relieved when our car arrived—never would know. But I had a week with this remarkable minister. I came to know.

Presently Dr. Zephaniah Kometa teaches at a Seminary in Namibia. In those days he was the Pastor of a parish under South African rule, if indirectly. In those days South Africa's rule was hard, by apartheid distinguishing fiercely among Blacks and Mixed and Whites. Both the pastor and his people knew oppression in their flesh. They suffered arbitrary "detainments," imprisonments without formal charges; suffered impoverished opportunities and circumstances; suffered the severe restrictions of their freedoms, their travels; suffered the fears and the hatreds of a ruling white minority. They had few rights that they could count on, plan upon, build a future and hope and identities upon.

Rev. Kometa himself, as a leader, lived daily, consciously, with the knowledge that he could be murdered. He is younger than I am. In those days he was younger than I was—and I was forty-one.

After the lecturing, after chats at mealtimes and pipes in the evenings—in the night before we would descend the mountains together and part and return to our separate ministries—I sought him out. The wonderment that had begun for me in the lobby of a Seattle motel had in six days only grown the deeper. I knew what he was about to do. But I didn't know quite why. I wanted to know his motives, and something of his heart.

Therefore, I met him late in the evening, in the dark that made similar colors of us both. We sat outside on a high porch, he in a chair, I on a step. And the great starry sky was the ceiling above us.

"Zephaniah," I said.

"Walter," he responded. *Well-tah.*

It was, I thought, not unlike the conversations of the Old Testament which begin "Samuel," and continue, "Here am I."

I said, "You're going back, of course. It goes without saying, doesn't it?"

"Going . . . back?"

"Yes. I mean to Namibia."

Zephaniah's eyes are wide open at night. If he ducks his head then, it is out of habit, not for any need of protection.

"Namibia," he said, looking directly at me; then he tossed his head up and laughed. "Well-tah," he said, "what would my wife say if I did not?"

I, of course, was thinking of the circumstances into which he would return, and I spoke the next words almost as if they were a confession: "You are," I said, "a brave man. A courageous man."

His laughter turned into a hoot. As if I'd told a right fine joke.

I cleared my throat.

Zephaniah bent and touched my shoulder.

"Oh, no," he said. "Oh, no, there is no great courage in me, Well-tah, I assure you. Listen: where we live, our houses are not so tightly closed as yours. Animals come creeping in at night, sometime for the warm, sometime for the crumbs. But if it is for the warm, then I hear them, you see. I hear them rustling under our bed. And *then*, Well-tah. . . ."

The African paused, shuddering with laughter, patting my shoulder in clear indication that I was not the cause of it.

"And *then* I pretend with all my might to be asleep. Oh, yes, so deeeeeply asleep. For you know, Well-tah, that soon my wife will wake up. And she will hear the slippery creature under our bed.

And she will say, 'Zephaniah! Zephaniah, get up and kill that thing!' But me, oh, I am sleeping, sleeping, and can no one wake *me* up— because I am scared to death of little creatures at night. Nooo. No, my wife would have a big argument with you, Well-tah, about this assessment of her husband: courageous."

"Then, Zephaniah," I asked of his laughter, I think, and of the pure melody of his humor, "then do you go home with some fear? Or with none?"

He sat back in his chair, a presence above me.

"Fear," he said soberly. "I go to my home and my congregation always alert with fear, which is a good and necessary fear. But it is a much more dreary fear I carry within me quietly."

I commented on fear then, since I felt it likewise in my own inner-city ministry. But I drew comparisons and simply could not find words for the oppressions that caused his. My life was not in danger.

"But you go home," I said, as if no conversation had passed since my first comment and this.

Zephaniah suddenly raised his right hand high above the both of us, blotting out a thousand stars.

"For my friends," he said.

I was quiet. It was not unreasonable for me at that moment to envision the members of his congregation, his colleagues, his relatives, the "friends" for whom he put himself in harm's way, being a leader—and my sense of friendship was enriched thereby.

But I was wrong.

"My friends," said Zephaniah Kometa, "are in desperate need, are in the soul's need, and perhaps none but we, black and Christian, can save them."

"Your friends, Zephaniah," I said.

"Yes?"

"Your friends are . . . white?"

"Yes. Of course. White."

"They . . . your . . . I'm sorry, but do you mean that these friends are your *oppressors?*"

"Who are themselves far more oppressed than I. Far more imprisoned and miserable."

Rev. Kometa spoke these brief declarative truths without drama. They were the facts of his existence. His ministry. And mine.

"Well-tah, they may be the ones who oppressed me and my people. But they are visible, you know. It is the invisible that oppresses them. It is sin. And who shall set them free from sin?"

"Zephaniah, can you tell me truly that you don't hate those that hurt you? Truly? You are scared of them, but you don't hate them?"

At that question—that appeal, really—my friend slipped from his chair on the porch and took a seat beside me on the step. He bowed his head, and now it was the cloud of his hair that caught starlight and the stars themselves in fiber like a crown.

"You see," he said, "they are not the enemy. They are threatened and wounded and killed by the enemy of everyone. This enemy is killing their souls. He can only take my body, not my soul, not my life. So they are under the worst oppression. I do not hate them. I pity them."

"Then who is the enemy?" I asked. Yes, I knew the answer to my own question; but I had never before met the minister who could utter the answer with the whole of his being, his body and his choices and his actions and his will and his faith—not just with his mouth alone.

"Who?" I asked.

"Evil," he answered. And he gave evil a name, for it had in Africa a personal presence, a power, and a violent purpose: "The enemy is the Devil."

In Africa. In America. Wherever souls might be divided between life and death, evil is not people! Evil is not our first and final kin, the grand scattering of the children of Adam and Eve. Our deepest enemy never was, nor ever will be, those who kill the body, but after that have no more that they can do. "But I will warn you whom to fear," said Jesus to those he called *friends:* "Fear him who, after he has killed, has power to cast into hell. Yes, I tell you, fear him!"

The servant of God, therefore, is sent by God to serve whom?

Joseph served those that had sold him into slavery.

Jonah (in spite of himself, my colleague-ministers!) served the city of the "enemies" of his people, Nineveh of Assyria. In the name of God, he served those who would murder Israel; and by God his ministry was successful, for these people repented that they might be saved.

Hosea served her who had left his marriage bed to share her prostitute's bed with many instead of one.

Jeremiah served those who scorned him, despised him, imprisoned him in a muddy cistern.

The servant of God is sent, therefore, to serve whom?

Jesus Christ ministered unto all people.

In Jesus there is no division of the peoples. For didn't he supercede enmities by urging his disciples, salt and light, to replace the old command, "You shall love your neighbor and hate your enemy," with his new command: "But I say to you, Love your enemies and pray for those who persecute you, so that you may be children of your Father who is in heaven."

And though the Christ of God approached his most horrible act of ministry with fear, praying the Father to remove the cup from him, he nonetheless finished the act and saved the people.

For the enemy is the Devil, the Father of lies, that Evil which would bind the souls of us all and cast them into Hell.

God and the Devil make, between them, a unity of us all! And the true war is cosmic, after all, whether we serve in Africa or America or the city or the ghetto, in wealth or in poverty, in one or the other of the nation-states that have declared (a lesser) war on each other.

In the Reverend Zephaniah Kometa I met a model of the minister who serves the human population *wherever* there are divisions: a minister unto the nations, yes, though his most focused ministry is to the patch surrounding his house. For don't the nations meet there? Right there?

And right here?

And if any should say to me, "But the task is impossible! Enemies will never eat together," I will answer with the story Zephaniah told me, whence his very particular (and most common) method of service.

He said that one day he saw two white children wandering through his neighborhood, obviously hungry and lost and helpless. He did not know how they came to be in a territory altogether black, but he surely recognized their hunger. Spontaneously, he invited them into his house and into his kitchen for food.

Now, Zephaniah's wife was a strong-willed woman who harbored in her bosom a fiery anger against white people. She had many proofs of why the blacks *should* be angry. She was also the only cook in the Kometa household.

When her husband entered the kitchen with the two little white children, she was facing away from them, busy with a soup.

He said to her, "You must give these two small people something to eat."

Still without looking, she said, "Okay. Sit down, all of you," and she ladled soup into two bowls, and then three, and then (Zephaniah was glad to note, for it meant that she, too, would sit with them) four. Except for her anger, she was a woman of kindness.

When she turned holding two bowls, she saw that the children were white.

Zephaniah told me that he ducked but kept watching her face.

"Oh, Well-tah, it was *then* I felt fear, fear in the gravest category."

The woman's face snapped shut like an iron pot. With shaking motions she set the bowls down, one before Zephaniah, one before an empty chair, none before the children. She turned back to the soup and paused a while. Then (Zephaniah said it was for no other reason than civility) she took another bowl and turned and placed it at the chin of one white child, turned again and again did the same for the other.

She did not sit.

But already the children were spooning the soup into their mouths, fearlessly, sloppily. They were so hungry that they took no notice of the drama occurring about their heads. They wanted only to eat. They made much noise, slurping, breathing, sucking.

And as the children ate—by the very act of their eating, the simple human need being satisfied—Mrs. Kometa was softened. She could not watch these hungry children, whom she herself was feeding, and remain angry. The hunger made them citizens of her own country, for its name *was* Hunger, and she had lived there a very long time. Moreover, it was her hand and her soup which now was nourishing them, which made them, too, the children of her own motherhood.

Before they were done, Zephaniah saw his wife touch the corners of her eyes with her sleeve.

This is why the African theologian would stoop in the lobby of a Seattle motel to serve a baffled, belittling clerk.

"When someone serves some other one out of kindness alone," he said, "the first one cannot hate the second one for long. When a woman feeds the children of her enemy, she discovers in her heart that they are of her flesh too. She discovers that she has shared motherhood all her life long with the mothers of these children. And then how can one find the fires for hating still?"

FINALLY, I AM CONVINCED THAT we are not called upon to succeed at anything in this ministry. We are called upon to love.

Which is to say, we are called upon to fail—both vigorously and joyfully.

For the sake of ten righteous people, God does not destroy the world. These are the Lamed Vavnik. They live scattered, in any nation under heaven, are members of any class, of any profession which may be imagined; and they are invisible to the world. Lo, not even they know the significance of their lives. Such ignorance *is* their righteousness. They merely live, so they suppose, as other people live. But Heaven knows the difference.

And this is the mercy of God: that when one of the Lamed Vavnik dies, God raises up another.

I heard this from my friend. He said it was an old Hasidic legend.

I believe it.

THE BODY OF CHRIST

RACHEL

"I'M JUS' LOOKIN' for my grandbabies. And maybe you seen my grandbabies?"

The old woman's voice whines in my mind at odd times, grieving me, urging me, who can do nothing, to do some little thing after all. Oh, the humble supplications are the most horrible, since they enlist the conscience, and it is the conscience that echoes forever until I bend and put it to rest. "Woman! What, what between me and thee?" Conscience. Common humanity. The heart's language commonly spoken, and you speak it, and I understand it, though I do not always choose to understand, but we are members of the same Body, various extremities, and I am commanded to understand—

Woman, hush!

I will do something.

I will name you Rachel; and I will magnify your cry by writing it; and with it I will fill the ears of the people.

At eleven o'clock on a Tuesday night I left and locked my office, then stepped into dark night and a thin drizzle. Oily concrete in the close and cratered city. When I slid into my truck, both my hair and my feet were damped—and my spirit. I sat utterly still awhile, tired.

It is not unusual, at the end of the day, quietly to wish for endings absolute and to nurse the dream.

But then I heard what sounded like a wailing outside the rain's whisper: "Hoo-ooo. Hoo-ooo."

Cat's call?

No, it was a high, broken, desolate voice, as though someone cried "Please, please" without words. Two simple notes, high and low, one simple song. But I saw no one, and I would have thought it the noise of my own weariness, or distant brakes, except that it became insistent, and when I opened the truck door, I heard it the louder: "Hoo-ooo! Hoo-ooo!"

It came from the alley that dead-ends at Gum Street. Louder, and yet infinitely patient.

"Hoo-ooo!"

Then a bent figure emerged from the alley, stood at the mouth of it, and the wailing turned to words: "They ain't bad boys. It ain't that they is bad, oh, no," she said. "I'm jus' lookin' for them, you know. But these old eyes is dim, and I cain't seem to see them no ways." She turned aside and raised a hand: "Hoo-ooo!" She turned to the other side, like the poor picture of an orator: "Hoo-ooo!"

Talking, she was. But there was no one, absolutely no one, near the woman, neither companions to hear her talk, nor grandbabies to come at her call. She was alone.

I stepped from the truck, winking against the mist.

Street-light glinted on her face, gnarled, wrinkled, deep-dark and harder than black walnut. She wore a man's vest and a man's shoes. Her eyes jerked left and right, so intent on the search that she didn't see me. She was a tiny bit of woman.

"It ain't no time," she said full reasonably, "it ain't no place for them to be about. And it's a dirty, weathery night. Hoo-ooo! Hoo-ooo!"

Who was she speaking to? God? The eyeless night? But her purpose was so inarguably right that I couldn't leave her now; and it was clear that love and yearning together had driven her into the rain.

I coughed.

"Hey, Mon!" She saw me. "I'm jus' lookin' for my grandbabies."

She came immediately and clutched my arm in a bird's claw, her head at my chest. I smelled her tight, neat hair. Raindrops hung from earlobes pierced and ripped a long time ago. She was not ashamed to look me in the eye. "And maybe you seen my grandbabies?"

"No, I don't think so," I said, though I wished with all my heart that I had. I thought of brown infants potching in puddles. "How old are they?"

"Oh, they be strapping big boys," she nodded, holding my eye.

"Each of him could give a head to you, Mon." I'm six one. So they were big, these boys. They didn't need me.

My wish to assist her melted in the chilly drizzle.

But the lady was earnest. Her fingers had sunk between muscle and arm-bone. "How long," I asked, "have they been missing?"

"You gonna look?" she demanded, bright old eyes drilling mine. She reached her other hand to my cheek.

"Well," I said lamely—she was buying me by touching my cheek—"yes—"

"Ooo, God bless you, child!" she said. "They been gone two lonely years, now, and I'm thinkin' they hurt, Mon, and I'm feared they be troubled. Oh, Mon, you help me to find them!"

Two years! I spluttered in the manner of educated people whose education is meaningless before the bare, forked animal.

"Mon?" She drew down my face so that I had to look at her.

"Yes, ma'am?"

"It's a promise? You use the powers Jesus given you? You be helpin' me to find them?"

She had no teeth. Gums black and a darting red tongue and lines at her eyes that enfolded the soul.

I said, "Okay."

Immediately she released me, forgot me standing there, and limped down Gum to Governor, a tiny and tinier bit of woman: "Hoo-ooo! Hoo-ooo!"

Mad, I thought driving home and dripping in the cab of my truck. Ho, ho, crazy lady! Midnight's citizen!

And despite my vow I tried to forget her desperate, patient, weary search for grandbabies.

But I can't, you see, forget it. Like spasms of conscience her voice keeps recurring inside of me. Certain sights, certain sounds trigger the cry, and I groan to remember her face, black walnut shell. Neither rain nor the late, exhausting nights do this to me, though one would think so by association. Rather, it's a moral memory.

Listen, and I'll tell you when I hear the pleading song, "Hoo-ooo."

When I see young strapping men slouch into Bayard Park beside my house—

They carry beer cans low at their sides, and bottles in packages. They drink, they laugh unmindful of anyone else, they gaze with vacant eyes to the void-blue skies, they leave a most unsocial mess behind. And compulsively I wonder with the crazy lady's sweet irrationality: Are these her grandbabies? These, the handsome, strong, and lost? Do they know what they have done to her? Can't they hear the old woman's call, "Hoo-ooo?"

So much for intellect and my education. The woman's infected me with madness.

Or, when I smell the strapping young men in front of my house—

Smell, because their car windows are open, and the acrid smoke of marijuana cannot be disguised. "Hoo-ooo!" And they gather in front of Doc's Liquor Store, those who could give a head to me, those beloved of an old and searching woman. And they park at the Eastland Mall; and they ride wild on the North Side, the East and West sides in loud careless cars; and they live in a thousand homes throughout the city, great weights upon an already crippled system, strapping youths who have chosen to live according to their own desires alone, full of their own boredom, forgetful.

"Is that old lady your grandma?" I want to say. "Don't you know that every private choice which you make for yourself is not private at all, but hurts her? Don't you know that she still is looking, a singular figure in the night, still is looking for you? There are no private choices. There is no such thing as 'your own thing'! All selfish action damages those in love with you!"

No. The lady is not mad. She simply has a love that will not quit against reality—and that only looks like madness. She is Rachel.

"A voice was heard in Ramah, lamentation and bitter weeping. Rachel weeping for her children, and she would not be comforted, because they were not."

Oh, go home again, you strapping, slouching youth, so full of promise, so full of yourselves! Bow down before mad, merciful Rachel. Ask her forgiveness. Then give her love for love.

CLARA SCHREIBER

1.

I RECEIVED BY MAIL A formal invitation, a careful calligraphy written on pasteboard and signed with a flourish: "Walter Wangerin the Third," it said, "be pleased to lunch with me in my home, sir." A date and a time were attached, and the whole was signed, "Clara Schreiber."

Sir? To whom was I anything *like* a "Sir"?

I knew the woman, of course. She attended the church where I functioned as an assistant to the pastor. She was old, and older than I knew—a woman of dignities toiling up the aisle toward the chancel on the arm of her daughter, which woman herself was more than sixty years old. At her left hand, then, her daughter Ruth; with her right hand, however, Clara Schreiber leaned on the walking stick she alone controlled; and motion caused her joints to tremble; and a vagrant air caused her white hairs to wave, so silken were they; and I, sitting in the chancel mere minutes before the worship service began, I could see the front of the woman, poor eyes peering through corrective lenses as heavy as lake ice. When she sat, when we sang, she would fix her vision upon some mote in the middle distance between herself and the cross behind me, and she would sing and she would pray and she would confess with the rest of the congregation all from memory.

These are the things I knew about Clara Schreiber, all of it gathered from the public encounter.

What I didn't know was why she would invite me—or why she would make such a to-do about it. If she wanted my ministering, a phone call would have done as well. But she had requested nothing at all of me during the whole year I had been serving Redeemer. I was young. I had not yet finished my seminary training. In fact, my service at Redeemer was fulfilling the internship year required for my graduation—after which I would be ordained. Not me: it was Pastor David Wacker who ministered to Mrs. Schreiber.

Me? I was responsible for education in the church, for the youth, for a host of lesser duties, necessities in a large congregation but mostly invisible. By day I did my job with competence. By night I gave myself backaches, hunching over an old upright Underwood typewriter and writing stories and rewriting stories. . . . This for me was a compulsion. Forces deep within me drove me to write, to improve my writing—"forces," you see, which, since I could not control them, caused me to feel secretive and ashamed.

Once, several years earlier, I'd sent my parents what I considered to be the manifesto of my future and my purpose: *I have decided,* I (a graduate student in English) divulged with some fear and trembling. *I want to be a writer.*

My mother was the one who responded. *Good, Wally!* she wrote. *Write greeting cards. There's money in greeting cards.*

It was the formality of Mrs. Clara Schreiber's pasteboard invitation which confused me—and which assured my obedience—for it implied some honor, some value in the young intern which he himself could neither discover or believe in.

I was surprised by the house. Perhaps the invitation had put me in mind of something stately and Victorian. Instead, the Schreibers lived in a small bungalow, green shutters framing the two windows, one to the right and one to the left of the front door.

Ruth met me, smiling, took my "wraps," and led me back from the tiny front room through a hall into the kitchen.

Ruth was afflicted with a muscular malady. She walked with stiff concentration and slight noises in her throat. She carried my jacket in the crook of one arm and with the other gestured to her mother, Clara Schreiber, crouching on the far side of a little table. "Vicar Wangerin has come to see you, mother," she said, and I saw the older woman's head snap in my direction. It was unnerving. Ruth withdrew with the jacket, while her mother pierced me! The blind old woman under silken filaments, weightless waves of white hair, pierced me with an ancient, milky eye.

I sat.

She never took her eye from me.

Even sitting, she leaned right-handedly on her cane. She crouched, exactly as she did walking, and I realized that age had broken her upper spine like a reed, that the woman crouched perpetually, of necessity.

"I am so pleased," she said, "that you agreed to visit me in my home. Are you comfortable, Walter? Are you content, sir, in every particular?"

Sir: spoken as well as written.

I said I was content, though her blindness made me feel as if our conversation passed through a glass of mystery and that she, after all, set the terms of it.

Mrs. Schreiber said, "You have met Ruth?"

"I—" I began.

But Ruth herself startled me, having returned without my knowing. Standing at the stove she said, "Yes, mother. We have met."

"Then these are my introductions," Mrs. Schrieber said. It felt as if we were ambassadors gathered at some high summit together. "First, Ruth. She is my amanuensis."

I had never in all my studies met that word before: *amanuensis.*

"She sees and reads for me. She is my hands to write my words on paper. Second, Walter Wangerin, Junior. You, sir, are an author."

Wait! What had she said? Shivers shot up my back. She said that I was an *author.* I did not, nor had I ever, felt worthy of such a title. But how did she even know? . . . .

Mrs. Schreiber didn't even pause.

"You, sir, are an author," she said. "And as for the third member of our small communion here, I will introduce myself in a moment. Please, let's eat."

We ate. Rather, I ate. Ruth served. Blind Clara watched. It was a full German meal at noonday. But how could I, under her bluish eye, say no to second helpings of mashed potatoes?

With dessert, Clara Schreiber spoke again.

"I have invited you here for three particular reasons." Her bird-claw-like fingers clutched the knob of her cane. "One," she said, "I am renewing old acquaintances. I knew your grandfather, sir, and I loved him much. In the 1920's Reverend Walter Wangerin was the pastor of the same church where my husband was principal of the parochial school. Lombard, Illinois. Your father was but a boy. You see, sir?" She produced a wintry smile. "I stride across the years to greet you from your generous and gentle grandfather. He and my husband respected one another. They labored well together. If you are half the first Walter Wangerin, you'll be twice the measure of most."

When people spoke well of my grandfather, I was always inclined to sink to my knees and pray profound thanksgivings unto God for such an ancestry. But that feeling was immediately superceded by the stunned rush of joy which Mrs. Schreiber's next revelation caused in me.

"My second reason," she said, "consists of my own introduction. As I have published a small volume of my own, I am an author like you. I wish you to know this regarding me. It is good for those of a common interest to recognize one another."

An author! Oh, this took my breath away. I knew no authors in those days. Authors dwelt in my hungry Olympus, reverenced but out of reach. Yet here! Why had no one told me this marvelous thing about Clara Schreiber.

"You—" I whispered.

"Patience," she interrupted my admiration, "for my third reason demands that we be realistic—and requires of you, sir, level-headed thinking."

She paused. It was only then I realized that the trembling of her joints had been increasing. Her cane twitched for the bending of her elbow.

"Walter," she said softly, "I offer myself to you as a mentor. If you wish it, if you will accept it, I would walk with you a while. But please," she held up a cautionary hand to my grinning enthusiasm. "Please, take time to decide. An elder author can perhaps inure a younger to difficulties before they arise."

Did she truly mean *inure*? To prepare me to meet things undesirable? It's like inoculate. What possible wrong could come of publishing a book?

Clara Schreiber suddenly leaned forward, piercing me to the seat of my trepidations with her gaze and her next comment:

"But do accept, Walter, for you should never, never be forced to dance in the dark. No one should. No, not ever."

And so our first meeting came to an end, and I was dismissed, my latter mood somewhat more subdued than my other moods had been: so premonitory her yearnings that none should "dance in the dark." I had no idea what she meant.

She gave me two books upon my departure. Neither was hers. One was, rather, a biography of Mozart, and the other of Chopin.

And of course I accepted her proposal. That which ratified my secret life?—which brought legitimacy to my private compulsions?—how could I *not* graduate to this next level in my education?

But, as much as I admired the woman, I confess I did not accept the proposal with the veneration it deserved. It was only as the weeks went on and we worked more closely together that she began to disclose herself to me. I learned her story piecemeal, and only then realized how extraordinary was my good fortune. What Mrs. Schreiber (the "Writer," as the German name implied) knew of writing, I quickly came to equal. But what the woman knew of charity and sanctity and sheer endurance, I shall never equal. Great Church, we ought to canonize such women for their outrageously loving spirits, for their suffering, and for this: that they could translate pain not into vengeance, but into blessing.

I give you my Matron Saint, whose mentoring was my epiphany.

2.

Even from her childhood Clara Schreiber was compelled to write. This was no choice. It was what she was. And while she was young, in the last decade of the 19th century, people generally tolerated her curious hobby. They could, you know, tolerate the fancies in a child which adulthood and marriage would finally shake from her. She would soon be schooled in the more proper duties of a woman. She would conform to the role society prescribed for her.

And Clara was no fool. She knew precisely what these expectations were. But neither (she reasoned) did she have to cease doing what still could be done in secret—so long as her church, her community and her family were kept content by her happy accomplishment of every other duty. Therefore, even after marrying Teacher Schreiber, Clara continued to write. But no one read what she was writing.

She raised her children. She protected her husband's reputation and her own. And she did dearly respect my grandfather's person and his ministry. Her daughter Ruth went to school with my father Walter. And all was well. There were no scandals.

Clara wrote when the children were sleeping. When they grew old enough to attend parochial school, she wrote in the afternoons while she had the house to herself. She wrote in perfect solitude, however deeply the writing longs a reader.

For these were the presumptions on that society: that writing was fine for students and essays and sermons and postcards; but *creative* writing, so-called, was a frivolity. And for women—conscientious women, Christian and Lutheran women, pious women—creative writing was considered vainglorious, a vanity to be censured, a self-centered dereliction in wives and mothers, a sin or else the sign of that womanish malady: hysteria.

This is not to overstate the case. For though the church could be as civil as a Sunday suit, it knew exactly what pieties were required of its people, and in a thousand ways how to shame the impious.

But Clara Schreiber wrote, and that's a boldness of spirit I can scarcely comprehend. She wrote. She must have been like Spanish Moss, surviving on air. She survived, though her identity was buried inside of her. She wrote; and what's more, she began helplessly, devoutly to write a book.

This is what the old woman told me about her younger self: that in the autumn of a particular year, after having spent much time in her own researches, she began with deliberation to write an actual volume.

In the mornings she finished the housework. All the chores that were hers to do she cleared from her lists and from her conscience. In the afternoons, then, she sat at the dining room table and produced—page after page in a flourished longhand script—a biography of Katherine Luther. The wife of a Lutheran school teacher was honoring the wife of the fifteenth-century reformer. She described this work to me by the image of fire. "Some coals," she said, "I kept bright in my soul for Kitty and the book. Although the greater fire burned in the furnace of our house, a part of me was always dwelt in the closet of my work."

By the following spring, Clara finished.

She had been storing the written pages in the box that had brought them blank. Now, she told me, she sat at the dining room table sealing that box and (she giggled over the memory) wrapping the box with a delicate blue ribbon. She packaged the whole and sent it off to one of the few publishers she knew, Muhlenberg Press in Philadelphia, Pennsylvania.

And then she waited.

Quietly she passed the summer, hearing nothing, saying nothing—but she could not douse the coals.

Then came September. And then October. And then the letter.

The thin envelope arrived from Muhlenberg Press late one afternoon, too late for a woman to sit and read it because her children were already halfway home.

Clara could have plucked her anxiety and her excitement like the strings of a violin, astonishing her household by a Godawful noise. She didn't, of course. She waiting the evening out, and the night. In the morning she made a point of cleaning the kitchen. And only when she was done with that did she sit down at the dining room table for this: to read the letter.

She slit the envelope. A single folded sheet was inside. This she withdrew, spread open before her, and read.

Mrs. Clara Seuel Schreiber, the publisher had written her. *It is a fine manuscript. We will be pleased to publish it.*

"Walter!" Clara Schreiber said to me, "I wanted to cry tears, just as though they had written, *No.* I wanted with all my heart to rise up laughing.

"Oh, Walter, I folded the letter with two folds again, and I slid it back into its envelope, and I touched the envelope with the tips of my fingers, and I thought I would pray a thanksgiving, but I could not! I could not! Instead, I stood up. And I pressed my hands hard on the top of my head to keep it from exploding. And then I started to turn around. Round and round I twirled, faster and faster, until my skirts ballooned and my arms were high in the air, and I was dancing! I was dancing! Oh, Walter, my hair flew backward and I cried for joy to God in heaven—and I danced that day as I had never danced in my life before!"

Suddenly Clara paused in her glad recitation of this joy, and she was old again in front of me, trembling upon her walking stick and blinking rapidly.

Softly, she said, "But before I allowed such dancing to overtake me, Walter, I went to the dining room drapes, and I pulled them closed so that no one would witness my joy. No, no one should witness such vanity."

In consequence, Clara Schreiber, author, splendor, God's bright eye—she danced. . . .

"I danced," she told me. "But I danced in the dark."

3.

"I offer myself to you as a mentor," Mrs. Schreiber said.

And I accepted her offer. And I thought it was in the craft that she would mentor me. But in was in the spirit, after all. In the Holy Spirit. And in the deepest sense and practice of the Gospel.

For the woman had every right to judge the church for its sins against her: the unconscious sins, the sins of the character of the times and of the people being its worst sins, since there is neither recourse nor repentance then. None dare blame this woman if she had fed her survival with a strengthening anger, or else preserved her soul by a contemptuous separation. In my generation I have witnessed such actions as the genuine liberation of women from these nearly killing oppressions. For them salvation was surely in Christ and through Christ in God, but not in the visible church.

But Clara Schreiber handled the sins against her differently. She was never descended into ignorance. Blind, she never blinded herself to the truth of her situation. And what she did, she did by *choosing* it, not by fear or forcing or capitulation.

In the last chapter of Genesis, just after their father has died, the brothers of Joseph are filled with fear that he will deal with them the same as they dealt with him years earlier, binding him and selling him out of the family into the hands of slave-drivers. Joseph has become powerful, second only to the Pharaoh in Egypt. The brothers fall down before him, begging forgiveness.

Joseph says, "Fear not, for am I in the place of God? As for you, you meant evil against me; but God meant it for good, to bring it about that many people should be kept alive."

Let me be clear: God did not cause the sin that severed Joseph from his family. Neither is God responsible for the oppressions which society and the visible church have imposed upon women such as Clara Schreiber. Nevertheless, it is through the actions of these persons, a Joseph and a Clara, that God comes most truly present to people like me, for in them the sin stops cold and mercy goes forth like warm coals instead! And this is an act of pure grace, since it is not required of Joseph or Clara Schreiber—is not required of any whom the church or this society oppresses—to forgive their oppressors! They are under no *obligation* to transfigure sin into mercy; if they were, it would simply be one more oppression upon them, the oppression of a *law* which commands them (forces them, threatens and frightens them) to obey by forgiving.

"So do not fear," Joseph finishes his response to the brothers. "I will provide for you and your little ones."

Which is precisely what Clara did for me! What a holy conundrum! A marvelous contradiction: rather than spend her life in bitterness, she chose to provide me with companionship and with knowledge. She preserved this young and callow writer from the effects of the sin that had buried her; she preserved a mere stripling from the greater blindness of our heritage. Is not this a wonder?— when all the world expected otherwise from her?

Here, then, is the genuine Body of Christ! Here is the Spirit of the resurrected Redeemer active and breathing among us, in this woman, in this saint!

Surely, great church, in the brightness of such saints we can see and confess our sins against women, our demeaning of any who do not fit our easier categories, our dead-weight pressure upon lightsome spirits. Surely, in the sunlight of my Matron's epiphanies we need not darken others hereafter. Surely we will recognize the personhood of each and each, for then and there is the body of Jesus made visible. In God's name, surely!

And when I was, finally, ordained; and when I was installed as the pastor of little Grace Lutheran Church in the central part of the city; after the blessings had rained down upon my head from fellow clergy, pastors, Bishops (in those days mostly male), I looked up and saw, sitting in the back-most pew of this little sanctuary, Clara Schreiber, piercing me still with her milk-blue eye, piercing me as with the point of a spear.

She saw me then too; so I say, laying my hand upon my heart. Nothing in me was hidden before me. In fact, this ordination placed me outside of that church denomination in which I had grown up, the church body in which Redeemer and all its members, including Clara, held membership. I was now in violation of the express demands of the Lutheran Church Missouri Synod. All that is another story for another time, of course—except for the following detail.

After worship, as people filed past me down the steps of the narthex, there, at that crack beginning of my ministry in the city, Mrs. Clara Schreiber appeared, stopped, turned, took hold of my hand, and held it long in both of hers.

"Walter," she said softly, so softly I almost could not hear her. "Walter, whatever else you leave, you must never, never leave our good and perfect God."

THE PAIN OF CHILDBEARING is not one and once.

It is twofold; and it comes twice; and I am astonished by the love revealed in such a miracle.

Twofold: There are two kinds of suffering which attend the physical bearing of children into this world. The first is that a woman must make space in her body for a baby; and doing that, she sacrifices a host of personal goods: her shape, hormonal equilibrium, energy, her freedom to sleep in any position, beauty (so she sometimes feels) and, with these, her self-esteem.

Did I call such sacrifice a suffering? Well, it is, I suppose. But the wonder is that such suffering also contains the sudden spasms of joy, and that both should come together. The woman who groans is the same who laughs to feel life within her—and I am astonished.

Then, the second suffering of bearing children is the opposite of the first. Having made space for the baby, she must now empty the space. It does not matter how much she has invested in carrying the child. At the end of nine months she's asked to give it up, to separate herself from it, to deliver it whole and squalling into existence. "Go out of me," her muscles say, her womb, her leaning forward, her very self says to the infant: "Go out of me, in order to *be*."

And this is suffering. (The work is so hard.) Yet this also contains the sharp spasm of joy. (Here is life!) And I am astonished that two such things can be together.

Twice: Any reasonable person might think that once through this curious drama of love were enough. Once to labor at making room; once to labor at emptying it. But the mother is asked to do it all over again.

For now the child is not in her body, but in her life.

Again, she sacrifices a host of personal goods to give the child the space in which to grow. Her schedule is broken a thousand times by his untimely needs. Her energies are divided. Her sense of accomplishment is shattered every time she does the laundry without gratitude, because it is an endless task endlessly taken for granted. ("Hey, mom! How come my pants aren't ready yet?") Her hair hangs in her face so often that she sees herself unbeautiful; and when she puts it up, she is still not called beautiful; rather, she is called to question: "Why did you do that? Are you going out tonight? Who'll watch over us?" She grows tired. She goes to bed early, and her husband says, "What's the matter? You sick or something? Don't you want to be with me any more?" And so she makes space for her children. Beauty she sacrifices, and freedom, and with them, self-esteem.

Suffering, did I say? Certainly. Yet at the same time—and this is too high for my understanding—it contains the sudden spasms of joy. She laughs to see her child's emerging life, his walking, his talking, his raking the leaves, his baking cake alone. How is it she can do both?

Then, for the second time, comes the second suffering.

At the child's maturity, she must birth him not out of her body, but out of her house and into the world, an independent being.

It doesn't matter how much she has invested in raising him. By stages, now, she labors to let him go. By degrees she loosens the reins, knowing full well the dangers to which she sends her child, yet fearing the greater danger of clinging to him forever. And now her hurt is the hurt that *he* will encounter on his own. (Will he survive in a careless existence, and thrive?) And beside that, her hurt is loneliness. To *be*, he must be *gone*.

This is childbearing at its most laborious.

On my first day in the first grade, I panicked and cried and raced back to the car where my mother was, ran top speed before she drove away from me.

"Mama! Take me home!"

I thought she would be so happy to see me and to discover my undiminished need of her presence, her love and her protection. I sat smiling in the front seat and heard the car's ignition even before she turned the key. She never turned the key.

Only now do I understand her own tears as she took my hand and walked me back into the school again.

"Mama, do you hate me?"

"No! No, not at all. I love you—"

What she was saying was, "Go away from me—in order to *be*."

So here I am, all done with first grade and writing books like any independent adult, and it is done. My mother sorrowed in the separation; but I am, by miracle, her joy and her accomplishment. Both. It is an astonishing act of love.

They made the Divinity male, and according unto that gender I experienced him. But when they spoke of the creating and the re-creating love of that Deity, their words slipped to the abstract and degenerated into thin, analytic theologizing. *That* love was left to my intellect, but my heart could find no handles for to hold, and my heart hung helpless in a void. I thought of a potter, and I was a pot. I thought of the dust of the earth, and I was still a pot. It is hard to imagine life as a pot, impossible to experience it.

On the other hand, they allowed the Church to be the Holy Mother—and there they struck a chord, and there they found warm-blooded memory. This story I know very well by experience—

God mothered me into being in the first place: "This Great God," sings James Weldon Johnson,

Like a mammy bending over her baby,
Kneeled down in the dust
Toiling over a lump of clay
Till He shaped it in His own image.

The "He . . . in His own image" is a chilly calculation; engineers and sculptors do the same, and the result is steel or stone. On the other hand, the "Like a mammy bending over her baby"—*that* I remember! I have been the object of such love. And the result is blood and bone. At my mother's breast do I discover more wholly the creating love of God.

And then, within the Church I was protected for growth, nourished, fed on supernatural food, clothed in a white robe, and, on my confirmation day, freed to speak my personal faith in God, in a voice not the Church's but my own. It was *urged* that the voice be my own! So the Church made space for me. And then the Church delivered me face-to-face to God. In-and-out of my mother's house do I discover more wholly that re-creating love of God.

What other story should I tell to convince the people of the generative love of God than that which is told by my presence and my being? For I was born of the womb. And what other story would strike more nearly the root of their deepest memory than that which speaks of arms and the babe? They were *all* babes, once.

Body of Christ—though Christ in the flesh was a man—you, you I remember as a woman, and my mother!

I suppose that it is the Lord's prerogative to make his Body also his own Bride—an androgyny so startling as to be difficult, frightening, and therefore ignored.

THE SELF TO THE SELF, AND THE FUSION

(Strophe)

The trouble with atomic bombs
    Is lethal egocentricity:
When one remarks upon himself
    There goes the near vicinity.

(Antistrophe)

But let me tell you this: my vanity

Build bulwarks all around my sanity.

THIS URINAL CAN'T SWALLOW the cigarette someone flicked in it.

Saddest, wettest, shreddingest cigarette butt I ever hope to see, for the moisture that swells the tobacco's not water alone. And the filter's a sponge. And tendrils of brown bleed across the porcelain.

Sad cigarette, indeed. Sadder, however, the poor soul who must twitch the foul thing out again. I know that soul. I call her by name. She has children and tired feet and bills and a blessed capacity for friendship. The custodian here at the Holiday Inn attends my church.

Sad cigarette. Sadder custodian . . .

Yet saddest of all, I believe, is the man who first *dropped* his butt here in a public place. This one is benighted. This one cannot—or will not—comprehend the consequences. Can't see that at the end of even his slightest act there always stands another, one whom he will scorn and trouble and cut, or else will love, by the act.

This fellow, this contemptuous flicker of cigarettes—however well he dresses, however solemnly he sits in his own church pew, however commanding, powerful, arrogant, smiling, self-satisfied, well-married and prudent—can nevertheless *not* claim before God that he loves his neighbor as he loves himself, for he did not love my friend. He visited upon her a moment of moist, unnecessary misery.

This is the acid test. Do you love Christ Jesus? (Which question embraces this next one): Do you love the real manifestations of the Christ in the world around you? (Which question is the same as asking): Do you love the Body of Christ, the people whom Jesus loves? (Which question is made sharpest and purest in the following): *How* do you love the ones you do not meet, who cannot punish or reward you, blame or praise you, or in any way make the action anything more than the unvarnished (spontaneous) revelation of your natural self?

True love arises from the self alone, yours and mine, unqualified and free. Is it love when some threat drives me to it, or some payoff persuades me? A goodness given for a goodness gotten is a business transaction. No blame in that. No love either.

At the end of our least act, still affected by that act (for the world is shaped much more by the million little gestures than by the more glorious *res gestae* of human accomplishment) stands another. Always. And that human was made in the image of God.

It is a radical truth that the Christ identifies much more with "the least of these" than with those of weight and repute in the world. "Radical," I say, because such a downward identification is a flat reversal of the way *we* choose to identify: upward, to those admirable, to those whose station flatters ours, whose power might empower us. We would be heroes. Jesus *is* the stranger. He *is*, in our common existence, the sick and the imprisoned.

How do we (as we will so often proclaim we do) love Jesus? With what attention and genuine love do we attend to the invisible people?

When I lean on the car horn loud and long, whose peace do I destroy? And how do I justify my anger now? Do I know the rules of the road better than the gentlewoman driving precisely the limit in front of me? And which of us is nearer the heart of Christ at this moment? And where is love?

When I neglect to signal a left-hand turn I neglect the driver behind me who might have gone forward in the right lane, had he known of my intention. But he has snuggled up to my back bumper, as has the driver behind him, and so *all* must now wait with me the oncoming traffic, drivers and drivers and Christ as well. (Or did I suppose that holiness rode in my vehicle alone?)

When I break the myriad little promises I make in a day (many of them made just to get *rid* of some persistent person) I break faith. I break my word. And though my word meant nothing to me, to my lessers it was the food of hope. Yes, and if in the littlest things I drop my bond and word thoughtlessly, like a butt in a urinal, in the greater, more "important" things that word will still be stinking of the urinal.

Laugh once at a "nigger" joke, and I've laughed at the skin of the Son of God, who chose to come enfleshed.

O man! When you speak of your wife as a fool, a ditz, a smiling second to your own great self, you shoot out the lip at your Savior. Do you not yet know that Christ both approaches you and tests you in your spouse? Woman, you cannot diminish his native interests without reducing his Creator (and yours) to the bozo you think your husband is.

If, by loud sighs and significant looks and angry gestures, you declare the old man ahead of you in the grocery line—tearing too slowly his food stamps from their packet—you have lost patience with Elisha, the bald-headed prophet of God.

Complain about the children in your neighborhood whose noise unnerves you—or about your own children, whose energy leaves you both angry and exhausted, febrile—and you have complained about those whom Jesus suffered into his presence, saying, "Of such is the kingdom of God."

And what of your father and mother when they descend into their dotage? (Teenagers often suspect that their parents have already entered the *Fuddy* stage, prelude to *Duddy,* by far the worse of the two.) If you despise them because of your vaster knowledge, your greater experience, your more contemporary ethic, your cooler view of life, you despise the instruments by which the Creator created *you.* Can you risk chopping the tree on which you are the fruit?

And surely you wouldn't assume that the only way to rate an employee is by her efficiency. Surely you would not cancel all the rest of this human by the stroke of your executive pen? But "cancel" means "kill" in affairs of the spirit.

Do you recognize that your mood at work is the very air your co-workers breathe? By which, in eight hours, in weeks and in the passage of years, they may thrive or else may suffocate?

So, then:

Toss your fast-food wrappers on the highway.

Toss beer cans in the river.

Toss trash, the detritus of your burned-out desires; toss the very souls of those you use and lose; toss these wherever others do not see you, in the dark, in the night, in your unacknowledged solitude, away.

Toss a cigarette butt in a urinal, and you have made my dear friend miserable one more time, and she is the least of these, the sisters of Jesus.

And shall you rise in church tomorrow protesting your love for the Lord?

But we are more accurately revealed in the unconscious, habitual act than in acts we plan and pay for. In the former our truer nature dwells, and by it is made most manifest.

I am not writing of democracy. I'm not begging a political equality of all individuals. I am begging rather the coming of the kingdom of heaven, whose citizens we are when we elevate the least to that same citizenship.

I am writing of love.

For at the end of *every* deed stands the Master—cleaning urinals.

PALLID NEED

When you come to me biting your lip
Like linen and remorse, when you
Emerge from the darkness
And stand in my doorframe,
Beseeching ease
For the thing that brought you near
But fled you at the coming, when
You are a white Christ-candle here,
Scented of the sanctuaries,
Silent, robed and pale and still,
And waiting,
Oh, what word . . . shall I give you then?

TO JOSEPH, AT HIS CONFIRMATION

JOSEPH, MY SON, I AM PROUD OF YOU.

Tomorrow, before a smiling community of the faithful, the people who have hugged you half your life, you will confirm your own personal faith in Christ. A bold move, child, exciting and frightful all at once. You can't be the same person after it, nor can your relationships with others remain unchanged.

Child, with your confirmation tomorrow, you begin to be my child no longer.

You start in earnest the painful, private, personal and finally triumphant toil of "growing up." You enter that which, when you will emerge from it, shall have made you an adult. The chrysalis, my Joseph, is something which prosaic souls call "adolescence," but something which demands of sons and daughters such heroic efforts that this father is moved by it now—now to tell you my pride in you.

You hardly know: to acknowledge yourself a child of God is to declare your independence from these earthly parents. You take your leave of Mom and me. And parts of you shall sink into yourself for no one's knowing but your own. Like creatures in a deep sea, when you are yourself that sea, certain thoughts and feelings shall never surface at your face; but you shall soon spread smiling over secret pain, and over some of your most blessed pleasures set a frown. In hiding, both Freedom and Anguish shall be born; and each shall feed the other till they grow into Leviathan and you're astonished that one so gentle, Joseph, could produce such monsters.

Oh, my son, what a task you begin! I'm thrilled to see it; I am terrified—both at once.

Well, it's a heady joy to watch you learn your legs, to see you engaged in the most consequential contest of all. No sport is more important or dramatic than this one, this *coming to be*. I groaned and clapped when you shot baskets successfully; how much louder

I cheer you now at the graver game of *being!* Joseph, I am and I shall be your audience, and my spirit shall always applaud you—

But soon my pride shall seem so far away from you, and my cheering most distant (though it won't be any less), and you will feel so lonely, and you will have a right to that feeling, because you will be lonely indeed.

Ah, Joseph. Here is my fear at your chrysalid growing: that I can help you in this labor less and less until I help you not at all. I've no choice in the matter; and sometimes you will understand and demand that I let you alone (when independence will hurt me). Other times you will cry for a father to catch you, but I *will* let you alone (then independence will hurt you). No choice! This is the very index of the act. This *is* the act. Your "growing up" means needing to need me less, dear Joseph; and until you need me not at all, the labor remains unfinished, and my son remains merely my child.

It is this backing-off that scares me, this letting you into yourself. For neither of us knows what shape shall arise from private change. Will he, Heavenly God? Will my son succeed?

More than that, I choke, being all unable to share with you the storehouse of my own wisdom and experience, do choke, seeing you make the mistakes which I by a word could prevent.

And worst of all: I suffer with you the suffering of your loneliness. It's a one-way window. I can see, but in silence. You see only the mirror of yourself. I remember my own past pain, and I see its signs in you; yet the nature of your growing shall disallow my saying so or your believing it. You simply will not accept that I could know what you are going through. Irony, my son! For though your estimation of me shall be wrong, yet your action shall be right: You must struggle alone toward your majority.

How faint my cheering shall seem to you in those days, Joseph, how strengthless my support, how hollow my words of pride and love. That, precisely, is why I tell them to you now—right now, while you are at the slap-beginning of the process. I think that you still hear me.

And you'll feel such a rush of accomplishment tomorrow with your confirmation. I ride that rush with you. And you've the innocence still to see me here.

Oh, and there's one other reason why I cry my pride so loudly, now. . . .

Too often the parents make absolutely nothing of their children's coming-of-age. They let it happen, as it were, by accident. Ho! They took more time over potty training than they take over training toward adulthood. They imply, then, that it is nothing, this "growing up"—or else that it is a distinct hazard in the household, a problem, a sin, a sickness, something that wants correcting. In consequence, the adolescent, unprepared, is shocked by the maelstrom which he has entered. Next, he feels an abiding, unspoken guilt at the changes occurring in him. And when he most needs resources to fight this good fight, he least has them. Indeed, the fight seems anything but good and heroic when his voice breaks, her cramps come, but the family (neither parents nor society) has given no dignified name or place to these profound and exhausting efforts.

At the age of twelve I had to approach my father myself, myself to ask him whether he was proud of me. He'd neglected to mention it. It was a yearning question, and it stung that I had to ask it.

Listen to me, Joseph. Fold this letter. Put it away for reading again, when we've allowed each other our separation and you your quarantine. For this is the truth: I love you, son.

I am so proud of you.

MOSES SWOPE

Moses Cornelius 'Tality Swope
had a problem.

The problem wasn't with his eyes, his ears, or his nose.
These things worked very well on him.
When he saw a table, or a tiger, or a ghost, well,
he *saw* these things both big and clearly.
When he heard a bird, a train's whistle, or the devil's laughter, ho,
he truly *heard* these things, in his ear-hole, on the back of his neck.
When he smelled smoke or vinegar, popcorn or his mother's love,
    say, say,
he *smelled* them and his feelings turned in their breezes.
The problem wasn't with Moses' brains, either.
They could think so fast his head got hot.
Numbers went buzzing like bees through those brains, and words
    like butterflies,
and books and food and Bigfoot and heaven and hell and God,
a dizzy unstoppable storm.
He had good brains.

And he had a good mouth, too.
Everything that he saw, or heard, or smelled, or thought about
he also talked about.
Three million words were in the mouth of Moses Swope.
That's more than ten, to be sure,
and his family would say, "Oh, Moses, be quiet."

Nope. The problem was not with his mouth.
The problem for Moses Cornelius Swope, well, well,
the problem was his FAITH.
Poor Moses *believed* most anything anyone told him.
And worse than that, dear Lord,
most everything Moses believed
came true!
Moses Cornelius Mortality Swope
had a very hard life.
"Don't eat candy! Don't suck sugar!" the dentist said.
"And most especially, stay away from chocolate, cookies, cakes and
    taffy apples!
Because otherwise all your teeth is gonna fall out!"
Well.
But on Hallowe'en, like any other kid, Moses went trick-or-treating,
and he popped a bubble gum into his mouth,
and before he remembered, he hammer-chewed that wad to death,
and then he remembered: "Oops."
But sure enough—that night
all of his teeth fell out.

"Now, don't be playing with them white kids, Mose," said his
    brother, Junior,
and he shook a hair-pick in the face of Moses and he nodded.
"Because one day one of them's gone to touch you.
And look here. Just one touch from a white boy's skin,
and *your* skin gone turn white as leprosy. How 'bout that?"
Well.
Moses, he called up his white friends on the telephone
and told them to leave him alone. "Just lea' me alone!" he said.
Moses, he went to school with his head down,
and he sat in his desk with his head down: he said,
"Don' look lef' and don' look right. Be tiny, Mose."

Because he was a-scared of leprosy.
So here came the teacher, and what did she say?
She said, "Moses, are you sick?" He shook his head.
She said, "Moses, are you sad?" He put out his lip.
So here come the teacher, and what did she do?
She put her hand on Moses' shoulder, Lord, Lord!
And sure enough—that shoulder
got leprosy, turned white as the teacher's hand.
Moses, why didn't you listen?

Moses' sister, she frowned when she pulled the sheets from Moses'
    bed.
Serious frowning, smoky-o face, no man in the lady's life to speak
    of,
but laundry forever and ever.
"Boy!" she said, and why were the tears in her eyes?
"You, boy!" Because Moses had done something terrible?
"You pee in this bed just one more time," she said,
"and you know what God's gone do to you?"

Moses Cornelius 'Tality Swope shook his head.
"He gone to cut your trigger off, and you ain't never gone shoot
    again!"
Well.
Moses had but one trigger, willful altogether!
He went to bed with everything tight,
and he prayed to God for no pee-water in his belly.
"Spit a lot, ole Mose! Go spit it out!"
And this is the way he went to sleep;
but he peed in bed,
and sure enough—God

cut his trigger off.
Ain't gone to shoot no more, poor Moses. No more shots in you.
Moses Cornelius 'Tality Swope,
no teeth, no trigger, no friends on the street,
and leprosy down from his shoulder, well.
It's what you get when you don't listen, Lord.
It's what you get when you be bad.

But the harmfulest thing of all was the word of his Mama to him,
and the hurtfulest thing of all, on account of *she* figured to suffer
for the trouble poor Moses he caused in the world,
and she was so weary so most of the time,
cause who was there worked in the family but her,
cause where was her husband? Where was his father?
Got none. No, never did.
"Can't stand it no more, my Moses," she said,
wheezing and leaning against his doorway.
"If you don' be good, my Moses Corn," she said, "it's goin' to kill
    me,
child.
If you don' pick up behind, if you don' be home on time, if you
    don'
come and run and mind, your Mama is just goin' to die.
You'll be the death of me yet, Moses Corn."
Well.
Who was softer than Moses after that?
Who done the dishes more carefuller than him?
Who swept the kitchen, carried trash and tucked his Mama into
    bed?
And who broke his window with the handle of the broom?
It was a very loud crash. The gates of heaven broke.
His Mama lumbered into his room. She looked at the glass.
She opened her mouth. She raised her hands.

And Moses wished that he would get a switching,
but sure enough—
she died instead.
Moses, he started to cry.
Moses, he patted his hands together, because, why didn't some-
    body switch him?
Moses, he put one foot in front of the other,
which was the same as walking,
and out of the house he went,
and this is what Moses Cornelius Mortality Swope did:
he ran away.
He ran away as fast as he could go,
little Black boy, turning white.
So he took whatever sidewalk was in front of him, Jesus, Jesus.
He ran so blind, cause he was running nowhere, don't you know?
Was *from* that he was running: huff a block, puff another;
From the house
and *from* his Mama on the floor
and *from* his thousand miserablenesses
and *from* his own rotten, run-down *self*.
And maybe he would find a hole, black to the bottom of the earth,
and maybe he could fall into it—
"Moses, you a curse on yourself!
Moses, you a murderer!"
Then, where did the boy run out of his breath?
Under the bridge.
A thousand cars going over; life going over the river; rumbling talk
of the city, mindless of Moses down by brown water and thinking
that when he got his breath again, he would go into the river and
    float away
forever.
Who cared if somebody peed in the river?
A voice said, "I care."
Instantly, Moses pretended that he didn't hear any voice.
There was no one else under the bridge, nowhere around.
Therefore, if he heard a voice, that meant that he was crazy.

The voice said, "Oh, I am *so* holy. And I'm *so* busy runnin' this bad
  old world.
But you know what, Moses my man? I got the time anyway, and I
  care."
Moses rolled his eyes to the water, cause that's where this voice
seemed to come from.
He whispered, "I cain't see you."
The voice began to laugh. "On account of, I'm a spirit, ho-ho! Ho-
  ho!"
The voice had a coughing fit, right over the water.
Moses said, "I'm crazy."
"Insane, my man, completely insane," said the voice. "Lookee here:
  Do you want to see me?"
Moses said, "I want to die."
"All in good time," said the voice. "Moses," it said, "you got a
  mouth?"
"Yes," said Moses, and the cars and trucks rumbled over his head.
"Good. And you got words in your mouth?"
"Three million," said Moses.
"Good. Then say this: say, you got skin, old man.
And when you say it, listen to your miserable self.
And when you listen, believe it."
Moses Cornelius Mortality Swope, the boy beneath the city bridge,
  whispered, "You got skin, old man."
And there before his eyes appeared a skinny old man, black as the
  Bible, bent and naked, except for a loin cloth, walking, walking
  on the flowing river in order to stay in front of Moses.
And look-ee here: the old man was grinning.
"See what you can do?" laughed the old man. "Here I am! Oh,
  you been a sucker, boy, for the words of every con around you.
  Hoo, you been crazy, all right. Didn't you never think that
  maybe *you* could do some of the talking and maybe believe in
  some of the things *you* said?"
"But my Mama is dead," said Moses Corn.
"Now, that's what *she* said," said the old man. "What do *you* say?"

Poor Moses only stared at the trudging individual. "Who are you?" he said.

The old man picked up one foot and hopped on the other.

He showed his foot to Moses. The bottom looked wood-stained and shiny.

Moses saw a hole in it.

"Does that tell you something?" asked the old man.

"You was hurt?" said Moses. "Did I hurt you?"

"Hallelujah, child! You've a slow wit but improvin'. I'm Jesus, don't you know. This here's from my crucifixion, a left-over scar. Did you ever hear tell of anyone else who walked on the water?"

"No."

"Well, amen, then."

"But, is Jesus so old?"

"Sucker, you done *made* me old! Done put me to pasture with your foolishness. Now, look-ee here: I heal bodies, right? And I forgive the sins of the children, right? It's been my business, lo, some goin' on two thousand years. But did you ever *say* so to believe it? Where's your amen? And I'm the one that goes raisin' folks from the dead. Can I have an amen to that, too?"

Moses said, "Amen."

"Now you talkin', child! And be you listenin' to your miserable self?

And can you believe the thing you say?"

Moses said, "But I thought Jesus, he was young."

"Thought?" said the old man.

"Think," said Moses.

"*What* you think, boy? Say it!"

"I think that Jesus, he was young."

"Was?" cried the old man at the top of his lungs. "Was, boy?"

"Is," said Moses.

"*Done!*" cried the old man, and he clapped his hands,

and where the skin hit skin a lighting bolt went out,

and thunder ripped the river,

and Moses covered his face with his hands and trembled,

and when the thunder rolled away, he peeped out again,

and there was the man, still walking on the river,

still grinning with all of his teeth stuck out,
still wearing nothing but a loincloth, and black as the Bible, still—
but young, young, the most handsome, purebred stallion of a man
that Moses Swope had ever seen.

Oh, he held his head so high, and the pads of his feet flashed pink
when he slooped them from the water, and his hands was *dancing!*

"Jesus?" Moses said.

"Amen to your miserable self," said Jesus. "Amen to your mouth,
  Boy," he laughed. "Amen, amen to my own mos' holy name,
  ho, ho!"

Moses stood up on the river bank and began to grin. "Jesus?"

"Now, don't you be trying the water-walkin' trick," said Jesus. "I
  be catchin' one too many no-counts from the drink. Go on; stay
  put. The way it is, is: I come to you." And he walked to shore.

"Jesus!" cried Moses Cornelius.

And when the muscular Black man stepped ashore, the boy threw
  his arms around him and laid his face against his chest and began
  to cry so hard that the big man stroked his head.

"Shoosh. Shoosh. You see what you done, don't you?" Jesus whispered. "Done thought it, done said it, done believed it, done
  done it. Here I am, boy, young and so pretty to knock your eyes
  out. But I was always here. So what you listen to suckers for?
  What for you give them your beliefs? Don't you know, Moses
  my man, oh brother, brother Moses—I care for you?"

"Jesus?"

"What?"

"O Jesus, my Mama is dead," said Moses, his head so down in misery that he seemed a brown puddle.

But the big man grabbed that boy by both his ears, like a jug, and
  lifted him off the ground, stared at him eye to eye. "Dead. Hum.
  So she says. And what else? Come on, boy—what else?"

"Well," said Moses floating, "and I ain' got no teeth."

Toothless. Hum. So the dentis' say. And what else?

"Leprosy?"

"Hum. A damn ignernt disease—so the brother say. And what
  else?"

"Well," said Moses, hanging like a sack, embarrassed.

"Well?" said Jesus.

"Well, and I ain't got no—trigger," said Moses.

"Triggerless! Ho, ho! Triggerless—so the sister say. Oh, ho, ho, ho!"

Jesus took to laughing hard. Horse-laughing. Laughing, he laid the boy aground.

Laughing, slapping his knee with one hand, he scratched in his loin-cloth with the other. Laughing till the tears ran down his cheeks, he pulled out a yellow grain between two fingers. "Oh, little brother, *triggerless!* Them things do grow, don't you know? Look-ee here," he said, and he kneeled down next to the boy, and he skewed Moses' lips apart, and he planted the grain in Moses' gum. "I'll help you with the teeth. This here's a mustard seed, don't you know, better than teeth. You talk with it, you talk with faith. *Faith,* man!"

He slapped the boy on his shoulder.

Moses coughed.

"Now," said Jesus, "it's my profession to be raisin' people from the dead. And I don't shirk, and I don't shuffle. But what I do, I delegate. I send folks to be doin' for me. Moses, brother, go for me. Go talk to your Mama. Go tell her the truth. You big enough, now. Shoot," said Jesus, "you a *man,* now!"

The big man, sleek as a horse, walked out on the water again, and sat down, and floated away.

He bowed his head, and his shoulders were shaking, because he was laughing.

And the last word that Moses heard before the bend in the river was

"Hee, hee! Triggerless! Hee, hee, hee!"

Well, when he heard the cars and the trucks on the bridge again, the first thing that Moses Cornelius 'Tality Swope did was to say,

"In my pants," and he giggled a little like the Lord, "is a proud and pretty trigger."

And he peeped into his pants,

and there it was, a fine fresh trigger, well, amen!
And then he laughed *exactly* like the Lord: Ho ho's all over the
    place.

The second thing that he did,
was to say, "Moses Corn, you can touch yourself as well as any-
    one can!"
And he said, "Skin to skin. Mine to me!"
And he tore his shirt, and he took the rich back of his hand,
and Moses touched Moses, and Moses was Moses again.
Amen!
The leprosy peeled right off.
Amen, amen to that!

But the third thing that he did
was the most important thing of all.
He ran home, and he burst into the house: "Mama? Mama?"
He found his Mama lying on the floor, huge as a mountain.
And he said into her little ear,
"Oh, Mama, this is the truth: I love you!
And Jesus said, you ain't dead, really."
He wet his lips, and onto her shiny cheek he put a fat and drippy
    kiss,
and into her hair went a tear,
and he said, "No, Mama, I ain't the death of you.
What I am is, I'm the life of you on account of how much I love
    you.
Oh, Mama, Mama."
Moses Cornelius 'Tality Swope hugged his poor Mama,
until she sat up, and rolled down her stockings to the ankle,
and sighed, and patted his cheek,
and went to make him dinner.

And Jesus said, from the air around him, "Well, finally, sucker. And
     amen to that!"
And his Mama called, "Boy, you watch your mouth."
And Moses burst out laughing.

MATTHEW, MY SON, how far we have come together. How much we have raised each other. How good it has been.

I first saw you in a crib—thick neck, enormous eyes, compact brown energy, fine amber hair, and I thought, "Can I love this one?"

You were three months old then. You kept your body stiff as a stick the whole way home from Indianapolis. Mom felt she had firewood on her lap. You didn't sleep well that night, stranger in a strange bed; nor did you sleep easily the year thereafter. You were a wakeful babe in every way. And I thought, "Can I love this one?"

Well, I'd been a father one bare year; Joseph was the first, but you were the first we adopted, so I had little experience at the job and no knowledge at all whether a parent loves the ready-made child as much as the child that comes from his own loins. I wondered if we missed some mysterious ingredient since you arrived of a mental decision and not of the physical love of your parents; and you were brown and I was white. Where was the love to come from?

Here is the miracle: my love for you came out of you! You came with printed directions. You trained me.

At first it was a foolish love, aggressive, fierce, protective. When we carried you to the grocery stores, we gathered the stares of the people. Our family was a riddle they couldn't solve. My ears would burn at their ill restraint; I'd grab you to my heart and stare back to shame their eyes. My face said, "*Mine!* He's mine, you little minds!" And so you were.

There was a neighbor, in those early days, who said that you couldn't play with her daughter. She'd seen the two of you holding hands, and she said, "Black and white don't marry." Nip it, I suppose, in the bud: you were four years old. I sat in that woman's kitchen and in a low, choked voice declared you were my son and she should think of me precisely as she thought of you. Curiously, she acted as though she and I were the buddies and you the odd-boy-out, since she and I were white together. But to me her kitchen was alien territory, and she the foreigner, and I despised her stainless steel complacency; I hated her hatreds, and I hugged you hard when I went home again, but you didn't understand that nor the burning love begun in me, half angry, half apologetic. You took my love for granted. You were the wiser, and you trained me.

Baby boy, you gentled that love.

And you expanded it.

Hungry, hungry for all experience, you attempted anything life offered, and my heart went with you. In you I knew a wild existence; without you I was too shy to try it.

One hour after you had learned to ride a bike, you built a ramp at the bottom of a hill: Evel Knievel! Down that hill you hurtled. You hit the ramp at top speed. The bike stopped cold, and you flew over it. When I held you, then, I said, "Don't cry, my adopted son." In dear moments I used the word "adopted" so that it would seem a good word to you and a good thing.

In winter you climbed the ice, stranding yourself on the overflow waters of Pigeon Creek. Oh, wailing boy on a rocky ice-island!

Like the "Six Millions Dollar Man" (your hero before Terry Bradshaw, Franco Harris and the Steelers) you tried to open the bedroom door with your foot. "Ha-YAAA!" I heard through the house, and then a splintering crash, and the pictures on the walls slid sideways. I ran. I found the door still shut, but a foot stuck through it; and when I pulled the door open, a boy dragged out on his back, smiling. Such committed loyalties you made, O my adopted son. To the ones you honored, you gave yourself completely, totally.

You trained me.

But the second miracle and the second source of my love for you was marvelous, holy, and indestructible, the greatest of them all. I came to understand, through the years, that it is in the very image of adoption, and thus divine, that God participates—

The last time ever that I spanked you, you barked your pain and stiffened on my knees and pierced me to the heart: I had hurt you. I sat you down in a chair and left the room. I went out, and I myself burst into tears.

It was a terrible, thwarted thing—for me to cry.

I said, "God, how can I know if I'm a good father to this child?" I said, "God, please, *you* be father for him—"

And quietly I understood: in fact, God *is* your father, and a better one than I. But God and I both became your fathers in exactly the same way. Matthew, God also adopted you! You were not born his son, either. It was something that he chose to do for you. But his adoption contains a love unspeakably sweet and powerful, far beyond my poor, fumbling efforts. I'm in extraordinary company! Therefore, I went back into the room and held you, at peace in this wisdom that he is the source; and you, by the grace of God, you held me back.

Oh, my adopted son! My love for you and my fatherhood both I hide completely in the remarkable love and fatherhood of God for you. *There* is where this wonder comes from. *He* patterns and empowers it. For a little while he allows me to experience the selfsame joy that he has loving you. For a little while he lets me be your father—just like him.

But tomorrow, Sunday, he begins to take over; the real is revealed, and I diminish. You are growing up.

Tomorrow, before the entire congregation, you will proclaim your personal faith in him, because it is your confirmation day. You will say "Yes!" out loud and consciously: "Yes!" to confirm the adoption he began. "Yes! I am a child of God!"

How glad I will be to hear that, because my love is strong, but my strength weaker than my love, and I do sin, but then the Holy Father will be holding you, and nothing, nothing can pluck you from those hands. How relieved I will be to hear that.

Who says adoption makes a lesser relationship than blood or the will of the flesh? Let him contend with the Almighty! And let him be ashamed.

Can I love this one—brown thunder after my white lightning?

Ah, my son, my son! By God, I do. By God, I shall love you forever.

THE ASHES OF WEDNESDAY,
FOR THIEVES AND FOR PREACHERS ALIKE

I THINK I THOUGHT I had solid reasons for moral superiority. I was not a thief. I was not an extortioner. I was no citizen of the night, but of the light. A pastor, in fact, was I—responsible for this church and its building, both: *this* building (slap the brick!) This very one.

It was Tuesday night late February. Lucian Snaden and I were standing alone on the east side of the church, watching for his mother and her car.

Earlier I'd been teaching my adult confirmation class a lesson in the Christian faith . . . until the thunderstorm outside had finally grown too violent for continuing. The interior lights flashed. I went up the stairs and stuck my head into the night: under hard swipes of rain, the streets were already a rashy flood, the sidewalks submerged. In a hubbub, then, the folks of my class covered themselves and fled to their cars. Lucian and I pushed several of these to higher ground before they would turn the ignition key. We lent our backs to the beautiful Rita Cooksey, bearing her dry-shod to her vehicle. He telephoned his mother to say that the class was over early, could she come. And then we two were left alone, outside, under a little shingle of roof, watching. The wind had not abated, but the rainfall had turned to mist and we were already wet. We'd see his mother at a distance. He would run to keep her from the nearer inundations.

The entire Grace Church facility sat relatively high on the corner of Eliot and Gum, both the sanctuary and the parish house immediately west of it. That neat, small house had once been a parsonage and then a rental. A year ago we'd moved our offices into it, gaining a little, losing a little in the exchange. We surely were glad of the extra space; it represented the healthy growth of this congregation. But we gave up a little income; and, what was the heavier loss, the house itself was often empty and vulnerable, therefore, to burglary. This was the inner city. Drugs and guns and various dangers strolled the midnight streets. Twice in the last three months we'd had to repair and replace windows and equipment stolen.

"Coming back tomorrow evening?" I asked Lucian in order to pass the time. "Seven o'clock?"

The wind cut round the corners like an army, but it was from the west and we stood up against the eastern doors.

Lucian didn't answer immediately. In this young man never lived the itch of haste. He studied on a question as though it were a vocation—and sometimes found no proper answer at all.

Lightning scored the heavens, igniting the thousand droplets in Lucian's hair like a sky of stars; then it dropped a *BOOM!* of terrible weight. My skin tightened.

"Ash Wednesday," I said. "It's a good way to start observing Lent—by worshipping, I mean. Tomorrow evening. A person can confess his sins, all his sins, and Jesus forgives him. I'll touch the tip of my finger to ashes and mark your forehead with a cross, and—"

CRASH! I paused a moment, listening.

Glass. Some sort of glass had shattered on the far side of the church building.

"Lucian, just a minute." I raised an index finger, then stepped down from the porch, going to investigate what kind of damage the wind had done. Into its spitting face, I circled the northern side of the building, turning left and coming up to the narrow passage between the church and the parish house.

Lightning stuttered above, suddenly illuminating the dark corridor—and there; slickly, suddenly outlined; crouching against the house-wall; actually *reaching* his arm through a broken window into *my* office: was a thief! Was an idiot robber!

"Look at me!" I bellowed.

Our third break-in, and I went straight to rage.

But it was the crass stupidity of the act that split my brain with the rage. The lights in the church were *lit!* The pastor was *here!*

"Let me see your face," I thundered. "I will remember you!"

The thief started at the sound of my voice, snatched back his arm, turned for a frozen instant toward me, then whirled away and clattered south, out the chute between the buildings.

His image stuck to the back of my sight: thin, young, gaunt, terrified. It sent a perfect thrill of fury down my legs and I, too, ran.

He went slipping down the southern lawn. I did not slip. I was a lion of rectitude, a deer of marvelous grace!

Lightning flashed. The thief was casting a backward glance. He blinked rapidly. His wiry legs wound together like a braid.

BOOM! commanded the thunder, and the fellow careened head-forward into the floods at the banks of Gum Street.

He squirmed round to his back—even as I leaped and flew and fell bodily upon him. Lightning flashed: huge were his eyes, and white, and wild with an uncomprehending horror.

Oh, what power this granted me! I put my left hand flat against his chest, pushed my torso upward from the waist.

BOOM! said the thunder. And again, *BOOM!*

Raising my right arm high to the sky, I kept my furious gaze upon the thief and roared out above him: "THE THUNDER IS FOR YOU, FOOL! THE VOICE OF GOD! THE VOICE OF THE LORD IS SAYING *LEAVE THIS CHURCH AND NEVER, NEVER COME BACK!*"

So said I without a moment's thought or preparation. It poured with high drama from my mouth, from my blazing mind, from my heart.

And I felt wonderful. At one was I, attuned to the universe!

When the thief, gone skeletal, wriggled and twisted and shot like springs from beneath my body and over the waters, I was not disappointed. I had, I thought, accomplished the thing of primary importance: protected our stuff.

Seldom in my life have I had such opportunity (and such immediate ability) to experience winged victory in my own mortal chest.

I returned to Lucian smiling.

But of course, in the aftermath of storm he could not see the smile nor note the triumph in my eyes.

So I said, "Guess what I just did?"

And he, peering steadfastly up Eliot, said, "What?"

And I: "I caught a thief. I drove a thief away."

Then, replaying the scene within me, I added: "Young fellow. Pitiful idiot. I said that God said never to come to this church again!"

Lucian Snaden stopped looking for his mother's car. I felt his dark face angle down toward mine. And the lightning flashed, and I saw the dreadful knot of a frown on Lucian's brow.

He said slowly, in the form of a question, "Told someone? Not and never? To come to church? Pastor?"

Dutifully, the thunder said, "Boom."

And Lucian concluded the question of his confusion: "But you asked me. To come tomorrow. Evening at seven. Didn't you?"

"Memento, homo," say the pastors to every penitent that comes and kneels in the chancel. There is a continuous line of the faithful rising in their pews, processing forward, and another line returning to their pews, darkly marked.

This is the Wednesday of the Ashes.

"Memento," the pastors say, pressing their fingers into bowls of soft ash, then striking two dusty lines, one across the other, on the brows of the men and women still kneeling here: *"Memento, homo, quia pulvus es, et in pulverem reverteris."*

Listen, children: during the worship service this Ash Wednesday, before I touch your foreheads with the signs of our Lord's death and of his forgiveness, let someone touch mine first.

Before I murmur the terrible words to anyone else, let them be murmured in my ear and deeply to my heart: "Remember, mortal: dust you are, and to dust you shall return."

Let me be so persuaded of my own mortality that never again do I seek righteousness or life within me. Such arrogant presumptions make of preachers and leaders the greater thieves after all; for they would keep as theirs the grace God gives to *every* other.

Who among us will claim a moral superiority? Who can? Who is able, or else has the right?

There is but one in all this universe superior to sin, in whom is life and immortality; and he falls down from heaven like light upon the places here below. His is a thunder of mercy, and his love is a storm.

TO MARY, AT HER CONFIRMATION

MARY, GOD LOVED YOU FIRST. Please, dear child, remember that.

Before Mom and I fell in love with you (and we were two of the first to fall in love with you), God loved you.

Before we even met your chunky self or knew what kind of child was living behind those gazing-blue eyes, hungry-blue, curious and laughing-blue eyes; before you grabbed my finger the first time; before you came somewhat shocked and blood-streaked into the air of this world; before you bulked in Mom's womb, lying on the inside, protected; before you wriggled secretly in the deepest regions of her being, when none on the earth knew that there *was* a you about to share the earth with us—in that most solitary time when you had just come to be, but had no name yet, no face, no human shape or thoughts or dreams or fears or fancies; when, like the primal cell, you had but being only and all the rest was possibility, then, Mary, even *then* God loved you.

Yes, yes, it is impossible for anyone to remember back that far. I know it. But that is precisely my point: God remembers. God it was who formed your inward parts, who knit you together in your mother's womb. Your frame was not hidden from him when you were being made in secret, intricately wrought in the depths of the earth.

Before we knew you, God knew and loved you very well.

I tell you that, Mary, in order to prepare you for the difficulty buried in your confirmation day tomorrow, Sunday, May 26, 1985.

But you have a beautiful dress to wear, don't you? And high anticipations for the day. Laughter turns your round face pink! On your own legs, in your own voice, according to your own sole faith, you will declare before the people that Jesus is your Lord and your

Savior. Neither Mom nor I will say this for you. *You* will say: "I believe. This is who I am now: I believe in Jesus Christ, who suffered and was crucified and died and was buried and on the third day rose from the dead, and all this, all this for me."

I will listen to you, and I will draw my breath in a sweet sharp pain, seeing that my daughter has grown up. With your confession you become an independent person. In spirit, an adult. And so it should be: you have been yearning for your independence many long years now, flying up the stairs and into your bedroom, wailing: "Why can't I do the things *I* want to do?" You have chalked a purple make-up on your face, designing that face as *you* imagine it, creating your very self, then flying up the stairs when I told you to wash it off. "Nobody understands me! I am *suffocating* in this house!"

You have flown high-minded, Mary, reaching for such a supernal justice that my plain pragmatism seemed to you as heavy as lead, cold and reprehensible.

Joy in you lifts your very heart to the heavens. Joy in you is a kestrel's flight, straight into the wind, the perpetual dash.

It is, isn't it, your nature to fly?

And there is the difficulty, hidden to you but visible and inevitable to me.

For one day in your soaring freedom you will chance to look down, and suddenly you will see how high you've gone, then various realities will seize your soul: how lonely is such flight! How far the fall! How hard and heartless the rocky world below.

In that day you will cry out for me, but I won't be there as I have been.

"Daddy!" you'll wail. "Catch me! I'm falling!"

And the fact that I do not answer will horrify you. It will seem such a betrayal of our love, though it was *you* who took flight, remember? And it was right when you did. Remember?

Well, Mary, in that terrible moment of reversals, remember this too: God loved you first. God has always loved you. God formed you in his love, and by his love sustains you still.

My love had a beginning. Mine is human, and though I love you to the end, that can last no longer than *my* end, my limits and my death. Moreover, to me you cannot be forever a child.

But to God you are forever a child. And wherever his child chooses to go, there is the Holy Parent beside you. As early as God's love preceded Mom's and mine, even so long shall his love last after ours.

Therefore, however frightful the fall may seem, cry out for God. As once you threw yourself with dramatic abandon upon your bed, so throw yourself still on the bosom of Jesus.

I have a photograph of, my Mary, in which you are sitting and reading a book. Your head is bent; your hair hangs down on one side, lower than your neck, but breaking at your ear; you are soft in a striped and flannel nightgown; and you are deep in meditations. It is as though your spirit has flown out of you, into the story that had already stolen your eyes. You are beautiful—and you are gone, both at once.

When I look at this photograph, my heart is troubled.

I think, "Where has the gentle child gone?" Not for you, now, Mary, but for me is my fear: "I don't even know the direction she's taken. I don't know what world she has gone to inhabit." And— precisely because it *is* a photograph, fixed and impenetrable—I feel somewhat abandoned. "The world she knows, it is not mine."

This picture of you instructs me *too* of the future, when you shall fly where I can't follow. When my love for you can no longer flood you, feed you, be so fully expressed to you.

But then I, like you, will take dear comfort in this, that God loved you first. I am earthbound, indeed; but the Spirit of God is not. And in my loneliness I shall say, "But my Mary is not alone."

For wither can you go, my darling, from the Spirit of the Lord? If you mount to the heavens on a giddy, deceitful joy, God is there. If you make your bed in the pit of the dead, God is there. If you take the wings of the morning and dwell in the uttermost parts of the sea, even there God's hand shall lead you, his own right hand shall cover you.

Tomorrow, Mary, I give you to God.

When you sturdily confirm the covenant you have with God, then you leave me. And then I let you go. These are two distinct acts, performed (when it is well) by the child and the parent as one and at once. Yours is a boldness, mine an obedience. Yours loves the future toward which you rush; mine permits that future, losing you for love of you. These are the twin gestures of growth and letting go: when they happen together, freely, willingly, they are as divine as Noah's dove, the third time he sent her forth and she did not return.

But these gestures would be neither divine nor good nor possible if you left God as well, Mary, or if God should choose to let you go. In fact, at leaving me you go *to* God. And he will not let you go. Not ever. No, never! He soars with you. He wraps you in the rainbow—and I am content, for you are safe, my daughter. He who loved you first shall love you always, always. Always. . . .

FOR MY BROTHER GREGORY
ON THE OCCASION OF HIS MARRIAGE TO LIZA LACHICA

ALL THE BLESSINGS OF GOD, my brother, upon this thing which you and Liza are beginning! He took time and care and mercy to create no other human relationship but this one. That relationship between parent and child; or that between ruler and ruled, between neighbor and neighbor, brother and sister, or that between the co-laborers—none of these received the same creative attention as the one you and Liza are now compacting with each other. Thus the depth of his concern for it: it is holy, Greg. It is different. It bears a divinity. The consequences of its rightness or its wrongness are more profound, more blessed or hurtful to you and others than the consequences of any other relationship between people, for it shall shape you and Liza and your children in all these others.

God's blessings, brother, on your marriage.

Your heart convinced you of this decision. You love Liza. Her heart agreed. She loves you. It is an exquisite meeting between the two, and a sweet harmony greatly to be wondered at, for this conjunction more nearly strikes the image of God than either one of you alone.

But please permit me, Greg, to caution you.

Love may begin a marriage; but love does not make a marriage. You will ride a wild sea, if you think you can build your marriage upon your love. In fact, it is exactly the other way around: your love, eventually, shall be built upon your marriage.

Well, look. If marriage depends upon love, what will you do tomorrow when you discover that Liza's feet stink? Or when you discover that she's got a stubborn streak well hidden during courtship which, behind stiff lips, is as silent as the tomb and puts her a thousand miles away from you, even when you're sitting across the table from one another? Or that she pouts? What will you do with such post-connubial, bedroom revelations?

I tell you, these cold shocks can freeze a love as fast as the northern wind. And then, lacking love, what will you do? Divorce her? (I don't mean merely legally, since divorce can be written on thin lips and in the flashing eye as well as on a legal document.) Shall marriage die when love does—expire on the closer battlefields of bathroom, kitchen and the bunker bedroom? And when love warms up again, what? Are you married again? No, Greg. Such sea-changes would cause a confusion from which the both of you would finally seek release.

But marriage should be itself the solid thing to hold an evanescent love. Marriage is the arena in which love comes, acts, goes, and comes again. Marriage is the house to hold your unpredictable hearts. Marriage, ultimately, is the soil from which a finer love—a sacrificial love—may spring and grow. Marriage itself, by your conscious decisions, is the thing, the bedrock, the reality, that which is to be trusted. And love is the blessing on that marriage.

You do not love in order to have a marriage. You have a marriage in order, sometimes, to love.

Well, after that fusillade of opinion, dear younger brother, I'd better define the thing I'm calling "marriage" in better terms than metaphor, right? Fine.

Marriage is a common act between you, common for two reasons:

1. You both perform, independently, the self-same act. You promise your lives to one another, wholly, daily, and without end. Publicly you pronounce oaths (this though neither of you knows exactly what you're getting in the bargain; that is discovered only in the doing).

2. You both trust absolutely the promise of the other (even though the oath has not yet truly been tested, since trust is commitment without all the facts to hand). Marriage, to be brief, is the vows of two, faithfully given, faithfully received, and binding despite both time and ignorance.

Neither whim, nor life-circumstances, nor stinky feet, nor even the sins of either of you dissolves these vows. Nor love lost. For what in fact does a vow have to do with any of these things? (Which is, of course, the whole point of a vow, something immutable in mutability!) Since death alone cancels the votary, death alone cancels the vow.

I suppose that seems almost cruelly rigid to you, Greg? It is. Houses are built of a wise rigidity. And I recognize that if this were all, it might squeeze your changing, spontaneous selves to death. For how, says all the world, can one make an everlasting promise in ignorance? And what of the hurts and the mistakes that each of you shall surely deliver the other?

Well, but there is one other essential element to your marriage which makes the house-building possible (which makes the house a living thing, not stone alone), and which shall permit you not to break under the sinful hurts, but rather to heal and grow the stronger. This is the element which ultimately plants the highest form of love in the soil of marriage. This, my dear brother Greg, you cannot do without:

Forgiveness.

That you can forgive one another the sins which shall surely come is the growth and flexibility of a rigid house. It is the one single thing in all the world which saves marriages and fosters their maturity. Even the much-vaunted "communication" is only a tool, good in a good hand, bad in a bad. Communication often magnifies a sin. Forgiveness alone puts that sin away.

You smile. You say, "Oh, we knew that. People sin, people forgive, and people go on."

I smile. I say, "That's only the game-plan, but half of the truth, and none of the power. Let me finish your sentences for you. People sin—infinitely. People forgive—only finitely. And given that crippled equation, people cannot go on."

Now hear me, Greg. You can forgive Liza a little. Love's a firecracker, all right; but it is not the sun. You alone cannot forgive her forever, nor ever to the measure that she can sin against you. You will say, with all of the men of the world, "There's a limit!" or "I can take only so much and no more!" or "I'm tired, Liza, worn out. I quit." And she would say the same to you. Humans die, don't you know. Human resource is sadly quantifiable. And human relationships are no greater than the souls that feed them—may die as well.

Your marriage, then, would be doomed to a limited existence, either in its time or in its depth—except for this: that Jesus Christ forgives forever and infinitely!

I'll say it straight. Without his resource to alpha and omega it, I could with my small mind span your marriage from its beginning to its end. It is Christ whom you must, each of you, draw upon. You make the marriage; but he doth heal and nourish it. His is forgiveness without end.

Therefore, Greg, for Liza's sake, acknowledge most earnestly that for your infinite sin against Christ, Christ pours infinite forgiveness into you. (It must, first, be personal and Liza-less, this act.) That establishes the relationship of faith and makes, in you, a bottomless well of the Lord Jesus. *Then* turn to Liza. Christ's forgiving you, Greg, enables you, Greg, to forgive Liza in the same measure as she needs forgiveness. And his forgiving of Liza, Greg, will make his infinitely merciful face to appear in *her* face for you. You will look at Liza, and behold! You will see Jesus. And then— then, for God's sake—will you be able to believe in *her* word of forgiveness for *your* measureless sin.

Do you see, dear brother? Christ, the life of your vows, is himself the life of your marriage!

So build a house, Greg and Liza. Of the vows and of forgiveness, build a mansion for your hearts.

BEHOLD THE STIFF-NECKED, the hard-hearted, the dummy!

Observe the camel, blind to one of the most useful gifts of the Lord God—which is that he arranges opportunities for confession and forgiveness between warring individuals, that they might smile and love again. He does so squarely in their day's experience. Yet note well how fierce can be the pride of this blockhead, and learn from him: it's a damnfool practice, to ignore the armistice which God keeps staging.

Behold me, when first my wife and I were married.

Lo! I am the dummy.

We used to fight, Thanne and I.

Well, it was always a "sort-of" fight, on account of, it was all one-sided. I did the talking. She did the not-talking. And then what she did was, she would cry.

I would say, "Thanne, what's the matter?" Real sympathy in my voice, you understand. And caring and gentleness in abundance, and great-hearted love. Dog-eyed solicitation: "Oh, Thanne, what is the matter?"

And she would only cry.

So then, I had my second stratagem. So then, I would sigh loudly in order to indicate that I have troubles, too, not the least of which is an uncommunicative wife—and how are we going to solve anything if we don't *say* anything? (I was skilled at the sophisticated sigh.) And I would ask again, allowing just a tad of aggravation to bite my voice, "What *is* the matter, Thanne?"

For all of which I might receive a head-shake from the woman—and crying.

Now, silence is a saw-toothed tool of the devil. It's also excellent for self-righteous fighting, because it permits the other to imagine the myriad sins he must have committed to cause such tears. He stews in his own juice, as it were. It's the microwave stratagem of attack.

But I was intrepid. And despite the explosions of my imagination, despite paroxysms of guilt in my belly, I would move forward to my third maneuver, which was to *accept* her attack so willingly that it would throw her off her balance. Guilty, was I? Guilty I would be.

"Okay, okay," I would cry with my hands up and my head down, the picture of remorse, "What did I do now?"

But all I got was crying.

Which left me mindless, frantic, and past control:

I would press her, and she would turn away.

I would touch her, and she would shrink from me.

I would stomp about the room to indicate immeasurable pain, cold loneliness, stark confusion, together with the fact that I had seventy pounds on her—

And finally she would cease her tears, finally look at me with blazing eyes and open her mouth—

And then poured forth such an ocean of wrongs, such a delineation of sins in such numbered and dated detail (whether I had intended any of them or not!) that I would stand shocked before the passion in one so short, plain drowning in her venom, aware that things had gotten out of hand, but speechless myself and very weak.

Well, then there was no help for it. I was forced to my final weapon and unapologetic for its power, having been so iniquitously provoked. Without another word I'd jam my arms into my overcoat, bolt down the stairs of our little apartment, and pitch myself into the cold St. Louis night, there to roam the sidewalks three hours at a stretch, wondering whether our marriage would survive, but confident that I had dealt guilt to Thanne's solar plexus and had caused the desperate question in her heart of, Was I being mugged?

Take that.

But then it happened that the Lord intervened, and one night there should have been a different ending to the battle.

(But consider the camel.)

On that particular night (my birthday, as I remember, and Thanne had strung that fact in large letters from wall to wall of the living room, dear woman) we had followed the usual script of our non-fights letterly, through solicitation, tears, pressure, tears, stompings, undeserved accusations and the basset hound look in my face, and tears—

Indeed, all went well, right up to the jamming of my arms into the overcoat, the running downstairs, and the dramatic leap into the night. But then God piddled on the affair.

When I slammed the front door, I caught my coat in it.

Mad and madder, I rifled my pockets for the key, to unlock the damn door, to complete this most crucial tactic against Thanne's peace of mind. Take—

But there was no key. My tail was truly in the door, and the door was made of oak.

I had two alternatives. Either I could shed the coat and pace the night unhoused, unprotected. There was real drama in that, a tremendous statement of my heart's hurt—except that Thanne wouldn't know it, and the temperature was below freezing.

Or else I could ring the doorbell.

Ten minutes of blue shivering convinced me which was the more expedient measure. I rang the doorbell.

So then, my wife came down the steps. So then, my wife peeped out. So then, my wife unlocked the door—and what was she doing? Laughing! Oh, she laughed so hard the tears streamed down her face and she had to put her hand on my shoulder, to hold her up.

And I could have smiled a little bit, too. I could have chuckled a tiny chuckle; for this was the gift of God, arranging armistice, staging reconciliation between a wife and her husband, a gift more sweet than all the rains of heaven. Laughter: extraordinary forgiveness!

But what did the dummy do? Well, he batted her hand away, cried "Hmph!" and bolted to stalk the night more grimly than ever before. *Then* he should have wondered about the survival of his marriage, not by fights distressed, but by his stupid, blind, inordinate and all-consuming pride.

For he had denied the manipulations of the Deity.

Oh, learn from the dummy, ye husbands and wives, ye children and parents, ye politicians so often so unbending from your former policies. Learn, all ye who suffer fallings-out with one another and ye whose inclination is to lick your wounds in cold proud isolation! God doth constantly prepare the way for reconciliation, even by his gimmickry, if only pride don't blind you to the opportunity.

TWO GAS STATION ATTENDANTS.

One met at a self-service pump, the other at her desk.

The first in rain on a chilly night. The second in the afternoon, but there was no sun in that building.

What caused their differing attitudes, I won't pretend to know. There may be a host of reasons why the latter attendant was so bitter, and much sympathy might be excited by each one. But that isn't the point, right now. Edification is the point, a Latin way of saying "building up." The power to build up other human beings, or else to tear them down, no matter how menial the circumstance nor how quick the meeting—that is the power possessed by each member of the Body of Christ, and a mighty power, indeed.

I had my collar up against the rain. I hunched at the rear of the Nova, had screwed the gas cap off, and was running gas into the tank. My hand was numb.

Beside me, suddenly, stood the attendant, his hands in his pockets. His presence was not rushing me because it was at peace. He said, "Hello," and a smile flicked across his face. Nor was he some chill stranger, though I did not know him. When he spoke he looked directly into my eyes—without fear, without embarrassment, with neither judgment nor haughtiness nor threat. I, whoever I happened to be; I, whatever my family or my profession; I was there for him in that particular moment.

He was lean. Dark hair streaked his forehead with the rain. He shook his head slowly when he saw the brown face of my kid looking out the window, and raindrops spilled from his chin. I think he laughed. The fill-up seemed to take a long time.

Now, I ran on no crisis then. I hit seventeen bucks on the penny, capped the pipe, handed him the bills and watched while he folded them into his roll. He did not solve some terrible trouble of mine. Nor did he save me from disaster or fix some thing I couldn't fix. Nevertheless, this attendant did the extraordinary.

He shook my hand.

He smiled one more time, and to *me* he said, "Thank you."

I admit it: this is a minor and nearly forgettable incident. And it should be unworthy of book-print. Except that when I slid back into the Nova, I stopped a moment before turning the key, and Thanne said, "Why are you smiling?" Drip, drip, and a slowly spreading smile.

The fellow had built me up. He had edified me.

I never saw him again.

Neither did I ever see the other attendant again. But I remember her, too.

She kept her separated seat while I filled my thirsty car. No matter to that. Most attendants don't pop out of the station for every Jack that jerks the handle. But when I entered the building, still she kept the seat and her eyes she kept downward, gazing at the top of her desk. There was no book there. She was not reading. She was simply staring.

I held out my money.

"Whadda-ya want me to do with that?" she said.

"Well, take it," I said. "I'm paying for the gas—"

"So how much was it?"

"Seventeen—"

There were lines from her nose to the corners of her mouth. Sullen lines. Anger, from some reason or other. And I was, it seemed, an intrusion in her life. She snapped the bills from my hand and bedded them in the slots of her register. She was chewing gum. It cracked like biddy-whips. She was whorling her hair with a forefinger.

I stood there too long, I think. She said, still without looking at me, "Your car stuck? You waiting for something?"

"No."

I slid disquieted into the car and sat a while. Demolition.

Sadness had made me sad. The day had been torn down utterly.

You say: "But how can I serve the Lord? I'm not important. What I do is so common and of little consequence. Anyone can do what I do."

But I say to you: "Every time you meet another human being you have the opportunity. It's a chance at holiness. For you will do one of two things, then. Either you will build him up, or you will tear him down. Either you will acknowledge that he *is,* or you will make him sorry that he is—sorry, at least, that he is *there,* in front of you. You will create, or you will destroy. And the things you dignify or deny are God's own property. They are made, each one of them, in his own image."

And I say to you: "There are no useless, minor meetings. There are no dead-end jobs. There are no pointless lives. Swallow your sorrows, forget your grievances and all the hurt your poor life has sustained. Turn your face truly to the human before you and let her, for one pure moment, shine. Think her important, and then she will suspect that she is fashioned of God."

How do you say Hello? Or do you say Hello?

How do you greet the strangers? Or do you greet them?

Are you so proud as to burden your customer, your client, your neighbor, your child, with *your* tribulation? Even by attitude? Even by crabbiness, anger, or gloom?

Demolition!

Or do you look them in the eye and grant them peace?

Such are the members of the Body of Christ, and edification in a service station.

1.

"TALITHA! TALITHA!"

The tone of that cry, both yearning and terrified, is what I most remember from this experience—that and the final comment with which Talitha ended it all.

"Talitha!"

It went to my soul immediately. But is was my son Matthew who was shrieking at his sister, urging her to get inside the gates.

"Oh, please, *Talitha!*"

From the first pop, like a firecracker or a stick striking a picket, all motion suddenly slowed, as though events had begun to dance deep in a greening sea. Another pop went off outside the house, and then the screaming started.

Thanne said, "That's a gun."

Two years earlier I would have disputed her. The sound would have seemed too innocuous. And who would have been shooting in daylight, thirty minutes after the children had come home from school? The world was too bright and ordinary for gunfire. But I walked to the front window, drew back the curtains and looked into the street.

Everything outside was, indeed, thick with a mortal circumspection—and I saw a spurt of flame as orange as a number two pencil, and I heard the third pop, and there was a fat woman at the curb directly before our house, her mouth smeared in screaming, her right hand waving the pistol of peppery flame.

I whispered, "Oh, Thanne!" How could the world, how could the world. . . .

I leaped for the front door. I tore it open, leaped into the porch, then hung on the steps. Two events were unfolding slowly, each with an idiot's script and danger. Two people were screaming, one furiously, one fearfully.

The fat woman screamed in a perfect, self-righteous rage, purely careless of the neighborhood and any audience. She stood facing west down Chandler Avenue and stomping her great right leg: "Come back here! Come back here! You come back here, bitch, I kill you. Watch, watch, I be waiting for you!"

She put period to her threat by taking her fourth shot—*pop!*—wild down the street.

A second woman was running as fast as she could, her skirt riding high on her thighs, barefoot—the two shoes standing side by side behind her as if she had ascended angel-like leaving them neatly empty. This woman was not screaming.

My son was.

Matthew crouched half-hidden by the gate at the side of the house, his hands pressed to either side of his face: "Talitha!"

While his sister, my daughter, was standing on the sidewalk slope of the front yard, straight up, sucking a purple lollipop, and with innocent eyes watching this madness as if it were a movie. Nothing but a line of grass divided her from the shooting gun and this crazy woman.

Matthew knew the danger. His heart was failing on account of it, and he was paralyzed. Terrible was the anguish in his voice, because he loved his sister: "Taliiiiiiiitha! Run!"

But Talitha did not know the danger. She was not afraid. Ignorance, on the other hand, was no protection. Ignorance could kill her.

"Oh, please, Talitha!"

So I sailed from the porch and ran to the child. There was a fifth pop, but no pain. No bullet wound. Just an irritable tingling all over my flesh. Then what gave my little girl grief that day? What caused her to cry? I did, I guess, with snatching her up so suddenly, and bundling her roughly behind the gate, inside the fence and safety. Matthew stood gaping at the two of us, trembling like weeds in a high wind.

Talitha, when I set her on her feet again, deigned to give me a baby shove. She stomped one little foot.

"Daddy!" she scolded me, "you lost my lollipop! You," she paused, seeking her harshest accusation: "You ruined my whole day!"

Talitha. Oh, Talitha. You were five years old that day, already capable of a godlike blame.

2.

Today, Saturday the 3rd of May, 1986, you are twelve years and four months old. Talitha *duravisti!* Thou hast endured in spite of all, and thou art astonishingly lovely: *pulchra es, pulcherrima!*

You are nearly a woman, yes? The days of your independence are at hand. And you are my daughter; and you shall ever *be* my daughter, yes. But oh, how hard I had to work to earn this fatherhood and also to win for me your daughterhood. You do not, you need not—but I do and I must—remember.

In one sense, the legal and the divine sense, you became our daughter the moment we adopted you in an Indianapolis courtroom. That covenant was binding from the beginning, requiring no knowing whatever on your part; for all the knowing, all the nourishing and all forensic responsibility became your mother's and mine simply by our promising it. Like the grace of God, this covenant bore altogether upon us and not at all on you.

Binding, I say, as soon as the judge approved. Now no one could snatch you out of our hands. We clung to you as tightly as any mother clings to her children in a crowd: fiercely, protectingly, proudly, cutting a way for you through senseless and self-centered humanity, making a space in which you could dwell securely. You were ours by adoption, and we were yours by loving commitment.

But in another sense, the real and the relational sense, it took a long, long time to earn your willing daughterhood and to find my fatherhood in your eyes. I had to make a space for me in your heart. You see?

Your father I might be in fact; but it's a cold fact which is merely enforced and has no love in it. The legal covenant creates, as it were, a hollow house. This livelier covenant between us must bring that house to life and make a home of it. But that takes the exchanges of love. And love begins in trust. And trust begins in knowledge, and this second covenant, child, absolutely requires your knowing who I am in order to determine whether I am *worthy* of your trust. Worthy to hold your tender life in my two hands.

In a sense, then, I had also to be adopted by *you*, and that adoption had to be voluntary. No judge could decree it by saying: "The child shall hereby adore her father heart to heart, or said father shall have the right to bring suit against her in court, demanding affection by the power of the state. . . ." Surely, no parent is so juvenile as to *presume* love, or so mean-minded as to command it.

Well, and this parent never had the opportunity to be presumptive with you, Talitha. You exploded any such illusions at the very start, the moment you set eyes on me.

You do not, but I remember. . . .

I remember the day when the director of the adoption agency led Mom and me into a small, sunlit, institutional room to meet you, child. Upon entering, I saw a crib to my right. Within that crib lay a peanut, sleeping. Eight months old: your huge eyes closed and fringed with a rich black lash, your whole head shaped like a light bulb, soft scribbles of hair on the dome, your mouth a cupid's bow, your chin a diminishment. Girl, your color was a caramelized butter! And you were not so much snoring as make snozzle-noises in your nose—which shot me dead. I loved you straightaway and painfully.

So I bent my big frame down and brought my face low, closing the inches between us that I might smell your baby breath and next that I might kiss you.

What rests inside your slumbering mind? I wondered, balancing my sight between your well-etched eyebrows. Your birth-mother had initiated this adoption just two weeks ago; but she and all her decisions were as hidden from me as the dreams of sleepers are hidden from the wakeful. The agency said that you had begun to recognize the name this woman gave you (a name we did not know); for that reason they had hastened your placement.

By what name do you know yourself? And what sort of self, I wondered, dozed below me now?

I puckered. I was just about to mark your nose with the kiss of my fatherhood, when those huge eyes flew open. For just an instant you focused on my great, overhanging face; then your mouth grew wide; and then you screamed.

Oh, child, you screamed and screamed until I fell backward, out of your vision. Then you sobbed, staring wide-eyed everywhere around the room, and I knew! I knew you were looking for some familiar thing, some familiar, consoling human—but we were all strangers, and you were alone, and utterly strange to *me* was any image you held in your mind as a touchstone of peace and food and home and wholeness and security. I had no idea what parental countenance you could not find among us. I could not help you. I was helpless, and this was the pain of my love.

Thanne could help, though.

This new mother went to you and gathered you from the crib unto herself, and you wrapped your arms and legs around her as though never to let her go, and so your sobs subsided. And so, as we drove home from Indianapolis to Evansville, you sometimes drifted; but you never let go of your mother.

Thanne named you *Talitha*. She was thinking of Jairus' daughter, whom everyone said was dead, except that Jesus took her by the hand, saying, *"Talitha cumi"*—little girl, arise—and she arose and was hungry.

Even at home, even after weeks and then months, however, you didn't like me. No, let me be clearer: you were afraid of me. If I drew too near to you, your eyes widened and you held your breath a moment, and then you would break into the most desolated wailing.

When I preached on a Sunday morning and you, in your mother's arms, came to realize it was me, was my peremptory voice, wow! How you howled! And how swiftly the congregation ceased listening to me, listened to you, rather, and stayed daggers at me for troubling so sweet a child.

And sometimes you cried so hard you'd swoon. And the silence that followed your sudden faint was cavernous.

No, I could not presume your love. I could not command your trust. I was the father of the baby, but the baby's heart was kept from me; the baby's heart was filled with suspicion toward me; and I remained a stranger to the memories that still could trouble her. I knew her not, as she did not know me. Beauty cannot love the beast in the beginning. I was the father, but the baby was not yet my daughter.

I remember—

Once you backed bare-butt against the cold porcelain of the toilet, then jumped away as if it had been fire, shrieking in a genuine pain. But I could not comfort you (how filled with yearning I was to comfort you!) because I could not know the deeper cause of this wounding.

You were passive. So passive that for more than a year you did not play as other babies play.

Thanne remembers—

Your mother remembers the day she left you in the living room alone and went into the kitchen. Suddenly, out of the silence came a tinkling sound. Mom recognized that sound: a toy, a plastic ball which rang small chimes when it was rolled. Ah, Talitha, your mother ran to the living room door, then paused and felt the tears rising behind her eyes. *You* had pushed that ball! For the first time since coming to us, you had initiated a little game of your own. You were playing.

In precisely this way, love watches. Nothing escapes the eyes of love and the mind that might make sense of what it sees. For to be loved in return, love must earn the child's trust; and to earn trust, love must first learn the child's language, to speak in the language she knows.

And so I remember—

I remember one evening when the whole family sat at supper, Matthew round the corner to my right and Mary beyond him, Joseph round the corner to my left and you in your highchair by him with Mom beside you. Your face and that beautiful head were covered with a vegetable smear. You were doing some glad thing, like kicking your feet beneath the tray. And then, by merest chance, we glanced at each other, you and I, at precisely the same instant.

And you spontaneously lifted your eyebrows.

Love watches!

The love in me responded in kind: I lifted my eyebrows exactly as you had, to the same angle and the same expression.

You gaped. You never turned your eyes from me, but slowly, assessingly, you raised those well-etched brows again—while I mimicked the move.

You made your eyebrows leap. And I, with mine, took flight!

Oh, Talitha, you grinned at me then. I had learned the language. Eyebrow language. And I could speak it with flair, for next I raised a single eyebrow, and you rewarded me with a belly laugh!

Soon we were telling jokes to one another, whirling our brows, sending signs like semaphores. "What's that stuff on your face?" I said. And you said, "It ain't for eating!" And we laughed. "How are you?" I asked more sincerely. "Are you well, my child?"

And before we were done, with my eyebrows I said, "I love you." And you with yours responded, "I know."

It was, perhaps, another year before you offered me your cupid's kiss, by which you said, "I love you, too." But in the meantime you let me touch you and hug you and feed you and talk with you and learn your mind and make that space within your heart.

3.

So there came the day when you trusted me to save you from dangers you yourself had not perceived. (Of *course* I'd never let that blood-lusty woman shoot you, girl!) Yes, and you trusted me so much that you could scold me without fearing to lose me. ("Daddy!"—stomping your pretty foot—"you ruined my whole day!")

And now has come the harder day . . .

Cheap love, cheaply given and lightly received, cracks in the crisis. It isn't built to bear the weight. But expensive love, carefully sold and dearly bought, grows like the oak. The crisis cannot break it down. This is our love, Talitha.

Tomorrow, the last of our four children, you will speak publicly your independent faith in the Lord Jesus Christ. *You* do this thing, not I; it is your initiative, not mine—though I have long prepared you for it. You will use the language of adults, and none shall speak for you; and those who listen, besides your mother and me, are the greater community on earth, and the communion of saints in heaven—and God. No longer do you move oblivious of the enmity around you; nor need you mistake whom to trust and thereby whom to love hereafter. It must be the One who best knows the images and the secrets of your heart, He who has saved you from sin and from death itself and from the Devil.

But still, love watches. My love, I mean: I will watch with joy the continuing acquaintance you are making with yourself and your growth; I will watch with an unexpressed trepidation the boldness that must pitch you forward. . . .

It is a happy crisis, tomorrow, but a crisis nonetheless, when the child leaves childhood and her home. It will change the both of us—for how much of parenthood is left to me, when the youngest finally takes her leave? I'm like you in your infancy: I want to cling to you, Talitha. I want to keep my old values, my old worth (with such difficulty proven to you) by clinging to the old you here.

Yes, but neither one of us is an infant now.

And, I will not cling.

Because you, my strong daughter, have endured. *Talitha, duravisti!* And because our oaken love can still continue to grow and to change as it has changed through the last twelve years. Love, as slowly learned and earned as ours, is durable too. It can develop into its own adulthood.

And what beauty, Talitha, you shall shed on the world, now that you go unshadowed by me! *O pulcherrima!* Most beautiful, beautiful daughter of mine! Go in peace.

SARAH MOREAU MAKES A DIGNIFIED, unfaltering presentation of herself. Not that the woman is, in fact, so self-confident; nor that she is aggressive in her level-eyed look at you. Her voice is as soft as raiment. And she will admit, in moments of utter privacy, to a personal sense of inequality before the natural shocks of this world. But the pride in her eye is the little territory that she has marked for herself and for her family within this world, and is her means for meeting it. It's something like the wall around a city: a needful and altogether proper defense. But it is neither hypocrisy nor estrangement in Sarah. It *is* Sarah.

Therefore, when Sarah left the church, one Sunday morning, unable to raise her eyes to mine, when her face gave the appearance of weakness and wilt, I felt the difference deep in my chest. The walls were down, and that from the inside.

I touched her shoulder to indicate that it was no little question, and asked, "How are you?"

She said, "I don't think I can handle it," as though I knew what *it* was.

I said, "Will you come talk with me?"

She shivered and said, "Yes."

Three days made no change. As handsome as this woman is, light-skinned, grey-eyed, a broad forehead and a perfect widow's peak, she sat sunken in her sorrow, and the tears were not lovely; she apologized for them.

She had spent a month with her daughter in Atlantic City, she told me. Justine was dying of cancer, a child of thirty-eight years and beautiful to her mother's heart. Yet, as grievous a trial as that was for Sarah, there was a deeper grief—the *it* she could not handle.

This: Justine had not yet acknowledged what Sarah knew; the child was still clinging to life. So there had been a moment, before Sarah returned to Evansville, when she sat on the sofa holding her daughter, her daughter crying, "Help me," and Sarah so full of the things that she *wanted* to say, words of love and completion, but which she could *not* say because Justine was unprepared to hear them: the mother's heart was bursting from within, and the walls, which always held the enemy without, cracked before the internal attack, and all she could do was to cry in her helplessness, "I'm here. I'm here. I will always be here—"

And to me dear Sarah said, "Nobody wants to name the terrible thing. But I don't think I can do this alone."

"Well," I said, "now there are two of us, and these ears will hear you." And it seemed to me that a long and double-filed gauntlet stretched out in front of us, and so we prayed.

But I was wrong.

See how speedily, how impossibly quickly the cruel events can run, once they have begun. On Friday of that same week, Bram called me to say that his and Sarah's daughter had decided to come home, both she and her husband; and once she was settled, her husband would return to Atlantic City. But Bram couldn't say, "Come home to die." He busied himself with the details, and he sighed often.

On Saturday I visited the mother and the father in their home, and she was silent before the thing to come, and he was restless, and I said, "Please, please, let Justine direct you: don't impose on her either your sorrow or your anger or your painted and strained happiness. Listen to her. Find out where she is at, then measure your own expressions according to hers. Do you understand? This is her moment, her time. Do you understand?"

"I'll be her servant," said Bram. "I'll cook whatever she wants. I'll wash her. I'll make her bed. She'll be the princess. I wish I knew how to get her from the St. Louis airport. Well, I'll rent a van. She'll be glad to be home. She won't have to lift a finger—"

Sarah bowed her head silently.

On Monday Justine came into Evansville.

By Tuesday she'd been admitted to the hospital in order for the local oncologist, they said, to make his own determinations before she was released to home; and most of the family had gathered by then, two of her sisters from Louisville—Irene and Eve—and a brother, Peter, and children, her three sons; and on Tuesday I saw her for the first time, and her husband Herman. I went to Deaconess with the elements for Holy Communion, and the air was thick with difficulty, and I wondered severely about my own strength—

In the first chapter of John, the last verse of that chapter, the Lord Jesus Christ makes a promise unto his fresh-faced disciples. It is a promise that seems to lean upon the Old Testament for interpretation, and therefore draws its shape and its reality out of the past; and though promises by nature focus on the future, this one is so backward-looking that its future remained for me unfocused. For myself, I could not grasp what goodness Christ was offering.

"You shall see greater things than these," says Jesus. "Truly, truly, I say to you, you will see heaven opened, and the angels of God ascending and descending upon the Son of man."

It's a marvelous prediction. It echoes Jacob's experience at Bethel. And since it places the son of Man at the bottom, while we remember that the Presence of the Lord God was at the top of the ladder of messengers, it seems to be a characterizing promise—one solely directed to Jesus, identifying him and given to us for our instruction, but *not* one given to us as actual beneficiaries of the promise. It seems to say, "By this you will know," and not, "you will yourselves receive." Thus, it seems a closed-circuit sort of promise between the Father and the Firstborn, and we get to look on. That's all. The image of ascending and descending angels is so symbolic—so much a backward allusion—that I could apprehend no reality for it in my own experience and in my future. It could be a doctrine of mine. But how ever could it be for me a breathless expectation, with these two eyes to see it?

So, I thought casually, don't be Nicodemus with these words, demanding fleshy what the Lord meant spiritually. You'll look the fool and you'll reveal a dreadful lack of insight.

But twice the Lord said "See" after he himself had given a demonstration of seeing, "seeing" Nathanael under the fig tree, "seeing" the guileless character of this Israelite by spiritual eyes, to be sure, yet with fleshy and factual objects for his sight. Such "seeing" was not divorced from experience. Rather, it saw and then saw more deeply the true nature of experience. Thus, spiritual insight was not "other than" fleshy sight, but "through and through" it, interpreting it!

Why couldn't I expect, then, to "see" these angels, if not in my experience, then *behind* it? Ah, but how, how, with a promise so vague?

Moreover, the Lord's promises in John are never to be taken lightly; nor are they kept in a merely instructional or doctrinal manner, something to be learned, as it were.

Does he promise the Holy Spirit? Well, and then he gives the Holy Spirit by the experiential event of a resurrection appearance, and a breathing upon disciples, and a clearly evidential *changing* of them. A spiritual occurrence, to be sure; but not one invisible to the eyes of flesh.

Does he promise peace unlike the giving of the world's peace? Well, and then in the same appearing he makes good his promise and delivers unto them his peace.

Likewise, joy.

Likewise, "I will come to you."

In John, promises find their fulfillment, are *not* forgotten. And in John that fulfillment is inclusive (not just between the Father and the Son, but also involving the disciples) as well as transfiguringly real (and not just spiritualized to a teachment).

So: then where did I come in? And how would *I* see the angels?

A friend of mine, an exegete named Robert Smith, helped me. He pointed to a possible remembrance of this first promise of Jesus, one that followed the same pattern of promise-keeping as I've touched above, because it came post-resurrection, was inclusive, and was fleshy sight on its way to spiritual insight. And when I looked at this keeping of the promise, I found not just the backward allusions to Jacob, but the configurations of experience which

I myself knew and could know in the future; I saw the fleshy objects of seeing, common details, through which, by the grace of God, I might hereafter "see" angels!

Bob pointed to what Mary Magdalene saw, but could not yet see *through:*

"But Mary stood weeping outside the tomb, and as she wept she stooped to look into the tomb; and she saw two angels in white, sitting where the body of Jesus had lain, one at the head and one at the feet."

Ascending and descending upon the Son of man.

"They said to her, 'Woman, why are you weeping?' She said to them, 'Because they have taken away my Lord, and I do not know where they have laid him.'"

No knowledge, yet, that these are angels. No, not until Jesus himself calls her by name and sight turns to insight, flesh *through* flesh to spiritual truth, and death to resurrection, desolation unto joy.

But listen: whereas I hardly know Jacob's experience, I do most certainly know the experience of Mary Magdalene! And though I've never slept with my head upon a stone, I *have,* dear God, stood in places of death and have myself been riven with sorrow, blinded by it, broken by the loss. These details I know by the bone. Now, don't you see, the promise takes on the flesh it must have ever before it reveals unto me its Truth, its spirit. Now it finds focus in *my* future, too. O Mary Magdalene, you are my sister; I know where to look!

Bob Smith, dear friend of mine, I have a good thing to tell you.

Though not at the head and the foot, but rather on the left side and the right, I have seen the angels. Seen them, and after that, "seen" them deeply, and I was blessed.

Justine turned and turned in her hospital bed. She kept drawing her knees to her chest, then thrusting them down again as if the first motion had stabbed her. This aggravated the catheter and the I.V. But she was in pain.

She was wasted. The skin was sunken at her temples; her cheeks were scooped to her teeth. Her eyes were thick with a milky, occlusive rheum. No. No. Sarah was righter than any of them: Justine was dying.

Bram said, "Well, how does she look to you?" A bright, heroic gambit. "Isn't that some girl of mine? Oh, she's a fighter, all right."

Eve, the youngest of them all, was close to tears. She was trying to explain herself to Justine, leaning over the bed. "I'm only trying to help you," she said. "You know that I love you."

Because Justine had said to her, "Don't worry me, girl."

But the girl was worrying her.

Her husband grinned when he met me, reminding me of a sermon I had preached a thousand years ago and acting like a gracious host in his own living room. He hadn't shaved. Improbably, since we didn't know each other well, he hugged me and hung on—but was grinning again at the release. "Do you want some coffee?" he said.

Sarah sat silently by.

I told them that I had brought communion for Justine. Could I give it to her now?

Sarah said to Herman, "Do you mind?"

Herman blinked at her, a blank surprise in his eyes.

"No," he whispered, and he left, although he was the husband.

Only later did I learn that he thought she was asking him to leave, and later he said, "Why wasn't I wanted there? What's the matter with me?" But that isn't what Sarah had meant at all.

The air was thick with difficulty. The healthy were having a horrible time even talking to one another, because disease had changed the world completely.

Whether Justine could understand me or not, I spoke to her as though she could. I explained that I would dip a tiny fraction of bread into wine, then put it upon her tongue, and this would be Jesus come into her, for strength, for faith, and for consolation. I said that she could pray with me in her mind. And then I prayed.

Kneeling beside the bed, while she twisted and others agonized about whether to hold her still, I spoke the words of institution, and I gave thanks (O Lord, what a mockery!), and I broke the bread, and I damped it with wine, and I held her poor head, and I touched the fleck of body to her tongue.

Suddenly she went still.

I was so grateful.

And then I was grieved.

For what she did, she considered this intrusion in her mouth. And then she rolled her tongue round and round, and she scraped the sticky bread from her jaw, and again and again she thrust it forward, but she hadn't the strength to spit. She didn't want it!

With a failing heart, I explained to the family (but what did I know of the mysteries?) that even if she hadn't swallowed, yet she'd eaten of the Lord's Supper; and sadly, with my forefinger, I scoured her mouth and brought the bit out again, and there it stuck to my flesh, and what was I to do with it then? Wash it down the drain? But it was the body of the Lord. Eat it myself?

The air was so thick with difficulty. Death damns all our healthy habits.

"Auuugh," moaned Justine, and there was Herman again.

He put his ear to her mouth. He understood that she was thirsty. And then this man who hid behind his grin effected a communion where mine had seemed so ineffectual.

He sucked water himself from a straw. He kissed his wife. She held still. This was a holy kiss, for he fed her water, and this she drank.

Now his own face broke.

"Can't you do something for her?" he pleaded with the nurses. "She's hurting. She's hurting so bad."

They gave her morphine.

The poor woman relaxed.

There were moments on Wednesday when she opened her eyes and spoke clearly. Everyone rejoiced in these moments, and they told them, word for word, to one another. They squeezed them for every drop of hope that wasn't in them. I came to pray, and in the visit heard of Justine's extraordinary progress. "She slept last night." "My girl's a fighter. She's rallying. Would you believe it? She said, 'Don't worry me, Papa.' She said, 'You kiss me one more

time and I'll beat you.' So, I'm listening to her, just like you said."
"She wants her nails done." This was Eve. "Don't you think we
should do her nails? She always liked the way her hands look."

Whether she heard my prayers, I didn't know.

Whether she accepted the blessings which my hands put upon
her forehead, I didn't know. What good was I in this place? I didn't
know.

Late, late Thursday night—no, two A.M. on Friday morning—
Justine died.

All Thursday she lay in a coma, with her eyes open.

I declare unto you that when I came to her that evening, she was
beautiful. The irises and the pupils were clear, now, though seeing
nothing we could see. The deep brown flesh of her face had taken
every depression of bone; and with her mouth ajar, as though at
the first part of a word, she seemed like nothing so much as a saint
of the early church, aggrieved by a treacherous pain, yet holy and
otherly in her peace.

She was so thin. She was sticks arranged beneath the blankets. I
could tell that she was breathing only by the pulsing underneath
her jaw.

Sarah sat in a chair to her left. Something was wrong. The
woman's silence was angry and her lips were pinched.

Bram, too, was silent, now—his back to the wall. He couldn't
sit. And Herman constantly came and went. Peter was in the
lounge, working on penciled figures, a Sony Walkman at his ears.
He told me what was wrong. While Sarah was sleeping for a few
minutes in the afternoon, Eve had followed instinct and the
request that she'd heard Justine to make; she'd invited a manicurist
into the hospital room who was only half-done with Justine's nails
when Sarah returned. Sarah, then, was not pleased by the
stranger's presence at such a personal affair, and tension flashed.
Therefore, between Sarah and her youngest daughter, at this

precious and terrible moment, there stood a wall, and the silence was hurtful to them both—and there was so little time left.

Difficulty. Dear Lord, the air was hard with it. And what was I to do? And how to open the gates between? And you, God—*where were you!*

They've taken away all the powers of healing in this world, and I don't know where they have put them—

When, past eleven o'clock, I returned to her room, Justine lay center in a little falling light. Right and left of her, each at a distance, were her father and mother, one against the wall and one in a chair by the curtain. Left and right of her, on the sides of the bed, holding her hands, were her sisters Irene and Eve—and the slender fingers of her hands and the deep red of her long nails were lovely beyond words. And I stood at the foot of the bed, hollow and unable.

But look at these sisters, and see what they were doing.

Eve had a linen handkerchief, with which she rubbed the tips of Justine's cuticles, over and over again; and I thought, What a ministration! The girl is serving the earthly need of her sister, even now making her beautiful, and how that must feel to Justine and what a comfort to know that this yearning need is being cared for when otherwise she might feel so unlovely! She's holding her hand; but she is also *serving* her in the grasp with a most peculiar love.

And—though she did not seem to mind whether anyone heard her or not—Irene was talking. Low, throaty, absolutely confident, Irene was speaking her faith.

"I know," she said, "that the Lord Jesus is in this place. I know he has not let you fall, Justine. I know the long, abiding love of our Savior for you, because I have felt it in myself—" For nearly twenty minutes Irene sang on and on in the ear of the dying, never a sob, never a broken note, but altogether assured.

And I gasped.

These were the angels! *These* were the ministers of the Lord, one accounting for an earthly need, the other for a heavenly one, moved unknowing by the presence of the Almighty, sitting side to side of a tomb going empty between them. I leaned far, far forward, not to miss a thing that the Lord was doing, nor a word of his love in

Irene's mouth, and this is the time when I wept, but for gladness. He was not absent. He was here in these two. And I saw them fleshy at the loss, soft in the sorrow; but through them I saw the descent and the ascent of the messengers of God and heard angelic motion toward a resurrection.

"Greater things than these will you see—"

I saw the love of God at work: "Rabboni!" I have seen the Lord.

It is no small thing to say that then the difficulty of death passed out of the air, and I was free since I was no longer alone.

Both free and empowered, permitted to act.

Later, while I sat in the lounge, Eve came sobbing helplessly; no longer the angel in descent, she was simply a very sad daughter. I knelt before her and let her speak her anguish at a mother that seemed to have cut her off—the walls of emotion at death.

Then, soon after, I went back to the room where Justine lay and began conversation with Sarah.

"How are you?"

"I'm making it," she said.

"You're no longer shaken?" I asked.

She changed my word and answered, "No longer shaking. I can stand, now."

So I turned the talk. "This puts everyone to a strain, doesn't it?"

"Yes," she agreed.

"And it's easy to miss the living in the dead."

"Yes."

"Sarah, I think that Eve is very stretched out, just now."

Quietly, "Yes."

"Since you have the strength in you, now, would you watch for the chance to give this daughter some of your time and some of your love? She feels very lost, now, and maybe more lonely than you. She needs her Mama."

And then this is the truth.

Even while we still stood speaking, Bram and Eve came down the darkened hallway, and Bram was chattering of arrangements for the night, but Sarah moved immediately to her daughter and put holy arms of motherhood around her and held her tightly, tightly, and Eve wept with other tears outside her sister's room, and neither was alone any more.

Bram hardly knew what miracle was taking place. He kept talking of the arrangements. So I took his hand and walked him away from the two as though he were a child, and he came with me. It was a bold move on my part. But I could make it peacefully, now, because I knew—and I knew because I had seen it with my spiritual eyes— that God was in this place.

For hadn't I been promised that low, at the bottom of the ladder, in these circumstances, in the tears of death, would be the Son of man?

THE BODY OF CHRIST—SET FREE!

FOR MOST OF THE JOURNEY, as we drove west and then west and finally south, our bus was filled with noise. We were a choir, after all, and young, and busy about ten concerts in ten days. Bus time was petcock time; we blew steam together.

But now the bus was silent. We were thoughtful and not a little frightened.

We were thirty-four bodies all together, a patchy collection of personalities, progressions, colors, classes and inclinations— though all of a single inner-city congregation and of the self-same Lord. Some were struck poetic by the Kansas sunset; others ignored it, singing songs of love in falsetto voices. Some nigh choked on the size of the Rocky Mountains and their whiteness; some stared at the heat gauge of the bus, anxious that the engine might overheat on a seven-percent grade; some ate; some slept; some played Uno and laughed; and the children did their home-work, while others stayed oblivious, singing songs of love in falsetto voices.

Yet, for all our scattered concerns, our purpose was common and the same: through four states and eight cities we bore the Holy God upon our lips, his love in our voices—the Sounds of Grace, gone singing its Thanksgiving.

Only now, on the afternoon of Thanksgiving Day itself, did all our moods become one mood, and we gazed forward grimly. Tense, silent, and uncertain. Songs of love had ceased. Falsetto throats had thickened. We were scheduled to sing within the Colorado women's penitentiary.

Holy, holy, holy. Who suckered us into this?

"No pocket knives, no matches, no metal of any kind."

Thus we were instructed by one John Beltz, an admissions officer who had boarded the bus to direct us out of Canon City and then to authorize our entrance.

"No handbags, nail files, and no photographic film, because they can make bombs out of that."

Bombs?

"What kind of criminals are in this place?"

"All kinds," said John so airily, acclimatized, we supposed, to the scruff side of humanity. "Mostly lesser offenders, credit card fraud, prostitution. But there are murderers here, too. Infanticide, in the parlance. But don't worry. Passion-killers go quiet in prison."

But—

But we were to be the strangers in a strange, oppressive cage. We swallowed. And we worried.

Holy, holy, hold the throat of him who suckered us—

By no hand that we could see, the bars of the front gate slid open. Down a hall; past a glassed control center (guns there?); and into a waiting room set with tables and chairs, bright-colored like a restaurant. Here we met the Matron, a woman in plain clothes, smiling, respectful and composed.

"The girls are free to listen to you or not, as they please. Line up in two rows, male and female. Raise your arms. Thank you."

One by one, male and female, we were patted down while our arms drooped out like chicken wings: pits, waist, back and stomach, crotch and legs. I was the first man frisked. The first woman came forward shivering as though she'd swallowed a raw and living fish. "Ohhh! That was terrible!"

Down another hall, fluorescent-lit, this time passed knots of women whose cigarettes hung at the lip, very few of whom returned our smiles. (Holy, holy—) They were slippered or bare-foot (as they pleased?), undershirted, braless, or, at best, dressed in jeans and a flannel shirt. We struggled to act businesslike. "We've got good reason to be here." But we couldn't wipe the silly smiles off our faces. And we swallowed.

The auditorium was a great cement room in which all sound was as alive and clean as a guitar string. Folding chairs, a pool table, a huge wooden box (in which the piano was locked) and a little kindergarten stage.

Hollis began to set up the amplifier for his bass.

Brenda plinked at the freed piano.

There was some giggling and little humor.

Cheryl, louder than she intended, called the choir to position and to practice in its little space—

But who would listen to us? And of those who did, what would they care? Would they scorn us? Sneer in the face of our earnest offering?

Well, we were free to come and go. They weren't. That's a burdensome knowledge. We were soft as the civilized belly. These were hard, slouching and experienced. They walked like men and swore like mercenaries, with absolute, silken conviction. Yep: they could make bombs of film—and bullets out of toilet paper, for all we knew.

Cheryl raised her arms before our parti-colored choir, intending to practice a piece, to measure the sound of the place. Hollis hit a chord.

And then the stark wonder began.

Sloppy was our singing at first, but very fast and punctuated by our clapping. Nerves are an excellent upper. "Good!" shouted Cheryl as voices came together. "Good!"

She hardly saw behind her an entering band of women, hard eyes gone curious—but Hollis did. By the fourth and the sixth contingent of the inmates' entrance, hot, black Hollis was smiling like he never had in church, and his guitar had discovered a new certitude, new rhythm that flirted with the unholy, holy, holy—

It wasn't even time, yet, for the concert to begin. No introductions had been made, either by voice or music, and this was *not* our program. Yet the women were coming, and the practice piece drew a spattering of applause, and Cheryl was lost. By fitful habit she led the choir into another piece for practice, "Soon and very soon, we are going to meet the king." Oh, the choir swung hard and speedily against its beat, and Timmy simply hid himself in the solo, and the women laughed at our abandon, and behold: the song itself, it took us over! The nerves left us, and we too began to laugh as we sang, as though there were some huge joke afoot, and we were grateful for the freedom in our throats, and we looked, for the first time, on one another, nodding, slapping another back, singing! And the women took to clapping, some of them dancing with their faces to the floor, their shoulders hunched, and they filled the place with their constant arrival, and somewhen—no one knew when—the practice turned into an honest concert, but there was no formality to it, because we were free, don't you see, free of the restraints of propriety, free of our fears, free to be truly, truly one with these women, free (Lord, what a discovery!) *in prison.*

Song after song, the women stood up and beat their palms together. And they wept, sometimes. Timmy can do that to you. And at one point the entire auditorium, choir and criminals together, joined hands and lifted those hands and rocked and sang, "Oh, How I Love Jesus."

My God, how you do break the bars! How you fling open the doors that prison and divide us! This is true, for mine eyes have seen it and my heart went out to it: You are so mighty in your mercy.

The last song sung was not ours at all. Some thirteen of the inmates demanded that we sit while they took the stage. Then, in shaky voices and in nasal Spanish, embarrassed as schoolgirls but arms around each other for support, they sang:

"De Coloris! De Coloris! The sun gives its treasures, God's light to the children. . . . And so must all love be of every bright color to make my heart cry."

They sang, braless and holy, so holy: "Joyfully! We will live in God's friendship because he has willed it, pouring outward the light from within, the grace of our God, his infinite love—"

They sang. And we answered, "Yes." And the mountains themselves said, "Amen."

BOOK TWO:

LITTLE LAMB, WHO MADE THEE?

THE LAMB

Little Lamb, who made thee?
Dost thou know who made thee?
Gave thee life, and bid thee feed
By the stream and o'er the mead;
Gave thee clothing of delight,
Softest clothing, wooly, bright;
Gave thee such a tender voice,
Making all the vales rejoice?
Little Lamb, who made thee?
Dost thou know who made thee?

Little Lamb, I'll tell thee,
Little Lamb, I'll tell thee:
He is callèd by thy name,
For he calls himself a Lamb.
He is meek, and he is mild;
He became a little child.
I a child, and thou a lamb,
We are callèd by his name.
Little Lamb, God bless thee!
Little Lamb, God bless thee!

From *Songs of Innocence* by William Blake, 1789

A DEDICATION: FOR MY OWN FOUR CHILDREN—

1.
Tell me, girl: how is it you can rust
At three? The talk scrapes in your throat
Like hinges like to bust;
Idle joints lock and loose on a corrosive note;
Tiny flecks of oxide make your glances bold—
How is it, girl, that rust on you is just
Another brown more beautiful than gold?

2.
Jack Ketch, my sons have seen you!
On a tight October morning have
Seen you gibbet a million rattled leaves—
Each leaf a sinew
Popped, each fall a potter's field and grave—
Have seen you, Jack, and laughed at you!

3.
My sons heard rhythm in the falling leaves.
A rhythm's always an occasion for
The dance, so they danced! They danced like the poor;
They thumped it like berries in a metal pot,
Harrowed together a mountain of compost gore,
Excited the wind to a deeper declarative roar,
Went down with a laugh they had not laughed before—

4.
Make three angels in the snow,
Ageless, cold, and hollow;
Remind me once before you go
You, too, were here—then follow.

LET THE CHILDREN LAUGH and be glad.

O my dear, they haven't long before the world assaults them. Allow them genuine laughter now. Laugh *with them*, till tears run down your faces—till a memory of pure delight and precious relationship is established within them, indestructible, personal, and forever.

Soon enough they'll meet faces unreasonably enraged. Soon enough they'll be accused of things they did not do. Soon enough they will suffer guilt at the hands of powerful people who can't accept their own guilt and who must dump it, therefore, on the weak. In that day the children must be strengthened by self-confidence so they can resist the criticism of fools. But self-confidence begins in the experience of childhood.

So give your children (your grandchildren, your nieces and nephews, the dear ones, children of your neighbors and your community)—give them golden days, their own pure days, in which they are so clearly and dearly beloved that they believe in love and in their own particular worth when love shall seem in short supply hereafter. Give them laughter.

Observe each child with individual attention to learn what triggers the guileless laugh in each. Is it a story? A game? Certain family traditions? Excursions? Elaborate fantasies? Simple winks? What?

Do that thing.

Because the laughter that is so easy in childhood must echo its encouragement a long, long time. A lifetime.

But yesterday, even in my own community, these are the things I saw:

I saw a man walk toward me on the street, leading two children by the hand. His mouth was as straight as the slot of a mailbox, his eyes drawn tight as ticks. He wasn't looking at me. I greeted him. He did not answer. I greeted the children by name, the boy and the girl, and although these are our neighbors, I saw an instant and marvelous duplication: the children's mouths sucked in, as straight as mailbox slots; their eyes contracted, tiny and hard, like ticks. And I saw the cause of the change: the man, never yet glancing at me, had clamped their hands to silence.

Now, there may be many reasons why my neighbor would harden his heart against me. And some of these reasons may be reasonable. And perhaps it is not *un*reasonable that he should harden his children as well. But, while he has always carried his face like a cuttlefish, the boy had laughed quite blithely in my front yard the day before yesterday, and often the girl had made beautiful blushes of affectionate giggles when we spoke. They are changing. They are mimicking their elder.

And I saw a woman picking at her child, a baby no more than two years old. She was picking at him, pinching him, pushing him, prodding him forward as she walked and he trotted down the center of the mall. But the woman was scarcely aware of her own behavior. She was enjoying a conversation with another woman, friends out on a shopping trip.

But the baby couldn't maintain their adult pace. So she kept pushing his shoulders faster, faster—while his eyes grew huge with the fear of falling. Her eyes were fixed on her friend. Without looking at the kid, without ever losing the thread of her conversation, she interrupted herself to admonish him:

"Tad," she said—*poke, poke*—"keep moving."

"Go!" she snapped. *Poke!*

"Move it, dummy!" *Poke, poke, poke!*

Finally the woman stopped and, with her hand on her hip, actually looked at the kid. "Tad, what is the matter with you anyway?"

Well, he had sprawled face-forward on the ground. But he had gone down in perfect silence. Unto whom should he call for safety or support?

His mother was granting herself her own golden days—but at the expense of her son's. No one was laughing.

I saw a well-dressed man—a professional man, a man of success and genuine repute in our community—speaking in cool, indifferent tones to his daughter. His language was precise, articulate, intelligent, and devastating. No one could match his ironic contempt—least of all this adolescent. I think he thought he was being funny, that he was dealing with his daughter as an equal: two adults. Straight talk. No sentiment. No wishy-washy indirection. I think he thought his manner wonderfully restrained and civil; thus he could speak in public without embarrassment: "We communicate. We don't prevaricate. We tell the truth. We can take it." *Bang!*

But the truth he was imparting concerned her dress, her friends, her taste, and therefore herself. *Bang!* While his truth displayed his own self-confident intelligence and even his excellent, progressive method of parenting, it shot dead the child inside his daughter. An early death. Who was laughing then?

I heard inside a house two voices shouting. One belonged to an adult: "Brat! You never listen! I cook for you, I work for you, I bust my back and all I ask for in return is a little cooperation. Do I get it? No! What do I get from you? Nothing! Nothing! Oh, no, you don't! Don't you go rolling your eyes at me, baby brother—"

Two voices, but the one that belonged to the child was crying.

And I have heard the smack of human fury on human flesh.

And I have heard the laughter that children create on their own when their elders do not care. *That* laughter is bitter and sarcastic. That laughter declares with their parents: *Don't care. No, we don't care. No, nothing will get at us—*

And I've seen parents who, after seven years of not caring, suddenly rise up and fight on their child's behalf *against* the teachers, *against* some judgment of the educational or legal systems. These parents appear like heroes on the horizon, come to save their kids from systems which have, in fact, been trying to save the same children for the same seven years of parental neglect. This sudden, heroic passion on behalf of their kids is meant to prove parental love. It arrives too late. It looks too much like wrath to allow for laughter now. And these particular children ceased to laugh when they ceased to know their golden days—about seven years ago.

Sorrows such as these shall surely come—but surely, parents, not through us! Haven't we ourselves suffered the same abuses? Even as adults? And weren't they a misery more than *we* could stand? Isn't that motive enough to stop our tongues and stay our hands when we might wound our children? Do we need more?

Then hear this:

Children do not exist to please us. They are not *for* us at all. Rather, we exist for them—to protect them now and to prepare them for the future.

Who is given unto whom? Are children a gift to their elders? No—not till children are grown and their elders are older indeed. Then they are the gift of the fourth commandment, honoring hoary heads which have begun to feel past honor. But until then, it is we who are given, by God's parental mercy, to the children! And it is we who must give to the children—by lovely laughter, by laughter utterly free, and by the sheer joy from which such laughter springs—the lasting memory: *You are, you are, you are, my child, a marvelous work of God!*

THE CHILD OF HIS PARENTS

SPRING CLEANING

CURIOUSLY, I've never thanked my mother for cleanliness. But I should. And I do.

Here comes the spring of the year. Here comes an air so laden and loamy, breezes so sweet I want to weep. Here come some of the purest colors of the earth: jonquils of unsullied yellow, the rouge of the redbud like the red breath of the forest itself, the white of the petaled dogwood like explosions of pillows. Here comes that scent after thunderstorm that is so like the warm, clean scent of wind-dried bedsheets against my cheek.

It stormed last night. For several hours there was a full cannonade of thunder and the heavy rain—and then the air had a dark, sparkling quality in my nostrils. Intoxicating. The night streets shined. All the earth was washed. Today the soil is shrugging toward rebirth.

And all this reminds me of my mother.

One particular gift of hers to us was cleanliness. The experience of cleanliness, of becoming clean. We took it for granted; but it was a way of life, maternal virtue and holy consolation.

My mother kept cleaning, kept reclaiming territory by the act of cleaning it, kept redeeming her children therein.

And spring was always that fresh start of the faith and the hope in cleanliness, of the forgiveness of cleanliness, actually, since everything old and fusty *could* be eliminated, allowing the new to take its place—or better yet, the old itself could *be* the new again.

My, my, I haven't realized till now—sinking into a thoughtful old age—how dearly I loved spring cleaning.

Mom was happy, cleaning. She sang the winter away. She cracked old closures. Everything grievous and wrong and knotty and gritty and guilty was gone. Life returned, and sunlight and laughter and air.

She was a priest. This was her sacramental ritual. We children would wake in the early morning to a sudden bluster of wind through the house. Mom had thrown open all the windows upstairs and down, front and back, living room and our own bedrooms. The curtains blew in and clapped above us: *Get up! Get up! This is the Day of Atonement!*

We stumbled up to find that Mom had propped the front door open and the back door and the basement. We sailed through windy hallways.

Mother herself never paused the day long. She bound her hair in a bandanna blue with white polka dots; she wore weird pants called "pedal-pushers" and rubber gloves and a man's shirt and red canvas shoes with rubber soles: silent, swift, and terrible was she!

Rugs came up and were hung on lines outside for beatings. Her right arm got victories that day. Rugs coughed dark clouds into the yard, and then the hardwood floors were waxed with such power to such a marvelous shine that we, in sock-feet, slipped the surface, surfing. Clean is a feeling beneath your feet.

The curtains came down to be washed. The naked windows squeaked under Windex and newspaper. Mom's dust rag made the Venetian blinds clatter and complain. Bright light flooded the rooms. They seemed to inhale, these rooms, and so to enlarge themselves. Our house was growing. The furniture had to be moved back. In the huge, gleaming living room our voices echoed. Lo, we were new creatures, laughing with a louder sound and singing a sweeter treble than before.

Out with the old, then! Out with the bad. My mother was a purging white storm, focused and furious. Out with the sullen, germ-infested air, colds and flus and fevers. In with the spring! In with lily breezes!

In buckets Mom made elixirs of Spic and Span. She shook Old Dutch Cleanser on sinks as if it were a stick to scold. Throughout the house went ammonia smells, pine smells, soap smells, sudsy smells that canceled sweats and miasmas.

Winter clothes were washed and packed away. Summer wear appeared. Our very bodies lightened, brightened, beamed in newness and health.

I loved to be in my mother's house on such spring days.

Dresser drawers got new paper linings.

The closet hung straight and true.

By evening we ourselves were bathed, the dust of the day removed, leaving a creamy me.

And this, finally, was the finest comfort of the sacred day: that when I went to bed that night, I slipped my silver self between clean sheets. Sheets sun-dried and wind-softened and smoother to my tender flesh than four white petals of the dogwood tree. Delicious above me and below, blessing me and holding me at once: my mother's cleanliness. Such a sweet fastness of sheets declared the boy between them to be royalty for sure, chosen, holy, and beloved—the son of a wonderful queen.

Understand: the blessing embraced more than the house. The whole world seemed ordered and good in that day. My mother's feats of cleanliness persuaded me of universal kindness. I liked the world in which I dwelt, and I assumed it liked me, and I trusted it therefore.

Well, she sang when she cleaned. Her eyes flashed gladness. She had a plan, and she never doubted that she would accomplish it. Morning to night, I knew exactly where she was because her presence was a music, like birdsong, like the laughter of water.

What then? Why, then for me my mother *was* the springtime. She inaugurated it. She embodied it. She gave it her own peculiar and personal character. When she swept her right arm up, the firmament was made balmy and blue, and winter was over.

Never, never should children take so cosmic a gift for granted. "Cosmic," I say, because it defines our world for a while, and it teaches us whether to meet the real world hereafter with confidence and glad anticipation—or else with fears, anxieties, suspicions. We children inhabit twice the worlds our mothers make for us: first when that world is no wider than a house, a yard, a neighborhood, and then again when that world *is* the wide world—because her smaller world teaches us how to see and interpret the real world when we shall travel into it.

My mother made my infant world a clean, well-lighted place. Now, therefore, in spite of wretched evidence to the contrary, I continue to trust in the ultimate purity of God's universe.

My mother taught me the goodness of order and brightness. Now, therefore, I seek order in friendships and offer a bright unvarnished truth in return.

My mother assured me annually that newness has a right and a reality, that error can be forgiven, that the sinner can be reclaimed. In springtime she surrounded me with the immediate, primal light of God. Now, therefore, I trust renewal. Resurrection. Easter!

Surely, then, it is time to thank her.

With all my heart, Virginia, I thank you for the theology of your spring cleaning, the vernal sacrament. And how often, while we sat at worship in church, didn't you cock an eye at some smudge on my face? And how often didn't you spit on your handkerchief and with that most private cleanser, your personal scent, wipe the smudge away? Well, for that too, thank you.

I am washed within and without. I am myself the gift that you have given me, and all the world is the wrapping.

EARLY IN MY CHILDHOOD I suffered a spiritual crisis.

I can't remember now *how* early this was, but I was young enough to crawl beneath the church pews, small enough to be hauled back up by my mother one-handed, yet old enough to wish to see Jesus. I wanted to see Jesus with my own eyes. Ah, but I was also child enough to admit that I never truly had seen my Savior face-to-face. Never.

That was my crisis. Every Sunday everyone else who gathered for worship seemed so completely at ease that I was convinced they had seen God in his house. Everyone, that is, but me. They sang without distress. They prayed without regret. They nodded during sermons without a twitch of anguish, and I stared with envy into their peaceful faces. It was a party to which I alone had not been invited—in the Lord's own house, don't you see?

So who was it not inviting me?

I wanted desperately to see Christ Jesus strolling down some aisle in a robe and a rope and sandals, eating a sandwich, maybe, since I would catch him off guard, just being himself. I spent all the time between Sunday school and worship peeking into every room, the pastor's study, the roaring boiler room, seeking the signs of his presence. Nothing.

Do you think he'd hide from me? Well, I knew he knew his house better than I did. He could hide. Do you think I made him mad by some sin I couldn't even remember now? I promise, I tried with all my might to remember. But I couldn't remember one *that* bad. As soon as I thought of it, I was right ready to confess and be forgiven. Until then I tried to surprise the Lord in hiding.

During services I would slip down from the pew to the floor and peer among ankle-bones and pants-cuffs and shoe-laces. So then, that's when my mother hauled me one-handed high onto the pew-seat again and clapped me to her side with a grip incontrovertible.

She's a very strong woman, my mother. You don't cross her. Once a forest ranger said, "If you meet a bear, you give the bear the right-of-way. Get out of there." Yeah, but my mother could silence whole congregations with a single, searing, righteous glance—so when she *did* meet that bear she beat two pans together until the bear backed down. "Woof," said the she-bear, astonished. "Not with *my* kids!" snapped my mother, uncowed. A very strong woman. Therefore I could not drop to the floor any more during worship.

But my yearning, imprisoned, increased to something like a panic. *I wanted to see Jesus!*

The heart of a child is capable of great desolation and thereby of great cunning. The more I felt abandoned, the sharper became my baby wit, trying to figure where Jesus was hiding.

During one worship service, while the pastor stood facing a long wooden altar and chanting the liturgy, it dawned on me that the voice I heard was too rich to be his. This was a pale, thin preacher, but that chant charged the chancel like the King to Kings. Ha! Of course. The pastor was pretending. It was really *Jesus* who was chanting—Jesus, lying on his side in the altar-box, which was the size of a coffin, after all.

So, as soon as the final hymn was over and my mother's hard arm released me, I snuck forward, eyes ever on the altar to catch anyone else who might be sneaking away. Up the steps I went, right to the altar itself; and then I crept around to the side, and *YA-HA!*—I let out a loud shout to surprise the Lord in his tiny bedroom.

But nope. No Jesus. Nothing but dust and an old hymnal and a broken chair. And the angry arm of my mother, who hauled me home and caused me to sit on a bench for exactly the time of one more worship service.

The heart of a child can grow heavy with sorrow and loneliness. Why was Jesus avoiding me? Why did he take flight whenever I came near? Maybe it was my cowlick. I was not a pretty child. I knew that. Moon-faced, someone would say. Moony, generally. A daydreamer who frustrated folks who'd rather go faster. But—

But I really wanted to see Jesus.

Couldn't I see Jesus too?

Which room had I never checked? Was there any such room in the church? Was there somewhere all the rest of the saints made sure I didn't see?

Yes!

Oh, my, yes! Yes! My mother didn't know how helpful had been my time on the bench. It ended in pure inspiration. There was indeed one room into which I had never gone, nor ever so much as peeped—a sanctum of terrible mystery and terrible charm. It horrified me to think of actually entering the place. It tightened my loins and made me sweat all week long, every time I contemplated venturing that door. But I would. I wanted to see Jesus, and I was convinced that this room did above all rooms qualify for a Holy of Holies. Surely he was in that place where, if a boy came in unworthily, he would die on the spot.

And so it came to pass that on the following Sunday morning I wagered my entire life on chance that I knew where the Son of God lurked. That is to say, I risked my mother's wrath. During the sermon I flat slipped from the pew, ducked her reach, skipped down the aisle and tiptoed downstairs to The Dangerous Door, The Room of Sweet Folly and Holy Violence:

Breathlessly, I approached The Women's Bathroom.

The girls' *toilet,* you understand. Boys don't ever pass it without spasms of awe.

But I was determined. And the need had made me very bold. As bold as my mother.

I knocked. I nudged the door inward.

"Jesus? Are you in there, Jesus? Jesus?"

So then my life was over.

Nothing mattered any more. I was so hopeless when I returned to my mother in her pew that I felt no fear of punishment. She could do to me as she pleased, and it would mean absolutely nothing. Jesus wasn't in there. Mirrors and wide tables and weird smells were there; but the King of Creation did not dwell in the women's bathroom. Mom could kill me for all I cared. I had looked in the last place, and the last place was empty. There was no more.

Well, no, she didn't kill me. She froze me with a glance, blue-eyed and beautiful and severe: *Just wait, young man.* So what? She pointed to the front where the pastor in black was intoning: "This cup is the New Testament in my blood. . . ."

Blood. I guess she was indicating an ominous future for me. So what? What did I care?

"Do this in remembrance of me," said the gaunt, white, ghostly preacher, and then people began to move forward, pew by pew. They sang and they filed up the aisle.

My mother got up. She walked forward with them.

Surely I must have seen the ritual often before, but it never had had so curdling an effect on me before. I was stunned by what my mother proceeded to do.

She acted docile! In a strange humility this strong woman knelt down before the pastor. She bowed her head. And then—like a child, like a *baby*—she raised her face and let him feed her! Yo! My mother can handle me. My mother can handle the neighbors. My mother can handle black bears in the Rockies—and my mother can surely handle herself. Yet now, as meek as an infant, she accepted a cracker from the preacher's hand. Then he gave her a little drink, and she didn't even touch the cup with her hands. She sipped at his bidding. My mighty mother, brought so low! What power could have stricken her so?

Yet, when she came floating back down the aisle and into our pew, there was nothing of defeat in her face. There was a softness, rather. Pliability and private smiling. She was different.

She smelled different, too. She came in a cloud of peculiar sweetness, a rich red odor. When she sat and bowed her head to pray, I stuck my nose near her nose, whence came this scent of urgent mystery. She felt my nearness and drew back.

"Mama," I whispered, "what's that?"

"What's what?" she asked.

"That smell. What do I smell?"

"What I drank," she said.

I wanted to pull her jaw down and look into her throat. "No, but what *is* it?" I begged. "What's inside of you?"

"Oh, Wally," she shrugged, reaching for a hymnal, "that's Jesus. It's Jesus inside of me."

Jesus?

My mother started to sing the hymn. I stared at her. Her profile, her narrow nose, her perfectly even brow all suffused with a scent of bloody sweetness. *So that's where Jesus has been all along. In my mama!*

Who would have guessed that this was the room in the house of the Lord where the Lord most chose to dwell? In my mama. Strong woman, meek woman, a puzzle for sure. My mama.

Well, I clapped my own small self smack to her side, and I took her arm and wrapped it around me to be the closer to them I loved, and we sang, and I grinned. I beamed like sunlight.

And I know we sang a heroic *Nunc Dimittis:* "For mine eyes have seen thy salvation. . . ."

. . .in blood, in a rich red smell, in the heart of my mama.

Amen!

MY FATHER'S FATHER DIED YOUNG, almost four years younger than I am now. He left this earth at fifty-five. Last week Wednesday, I reached the fifty-eighth year of my own age.

Until bare months before his death, Reverend Walter C. Wangerin had been a Lutheran pastor in Grand Rapids, Michigan; but a hellishly high blood pressure so embrittled his body, so endangered his life, that the church council chose to lighten his load in spite of himself: they removed him from active pastoral service, hoping sincerely that the action would be temporary and beneficial. I visited Grandpa during that enforced vacation. To me he seemed no different than he had been before; he was the same man that had taught me one year earlier—at his dining room table on a drizzling afternoon—to pray as a mealtime prayer: "Oh, give thanks unto the Lord, for he is good, for his mercy endures forever." The heart was the same. And it's the heart the young child sees. He knows nothing of the explosions of blood pressure—and shortly after my departure, Rev. Walter C. Wangerin was admitted to the hospital. That was in February, 1948. On the thirteenth day of that month, in Chicago, Illinois, I was unwrapping presents given me for my fourth birthday. From my mother I received a set of Lincoln Logs wherewith I began to build whole villages. Grandpa, however, lying in his hospital bed, was coming to realize that this bed was his last bed.

As my Aunt Clara wrote me years and years later: "He lived less than two months after that trip."

That trip: Aunt Clara (my father's younger sister, whose warmer name was and is "Tante Teddy") had accompanied me on the train from Chicago's Union Station to Grand Rapids; she and I and Grandpa and Grandma Wangerin then drove north together, to the Straits of Mackinac and the Upper Peninsula. This is the trip my aunt refers to. A most sacred journey, so it seems to me even yet today; for while we sailed the islands between Lakes Michigan and

Huron, my grandfather bequeathed unto me the source and the name of our power over that ancient serpent who is called the Devil and Satan, the deceiver of the whole world.

When it was all done—the bequest, the trip and its return, our last night's sleep in the parsonage—Tante Teddy and I boarded the train in Grand Rapids and rode the rails home to Chicago, and my Grandpa died. I never saw him again.

So I exhort the elders among you, as a fellow elder and a witness of the sufferings of Christ, writes Peter the Apostle: *Tend the flock!* Grandpa Wangerin the Pastor tended his congregational flock, indeed. But Pastor Wangerin the Grandpa tended that single lamb, his oldest grandchild, just as well and yet more lovingly.

Peter defines the quality of such tending: *not by constraint, but willingly, not for shameful gain but eagerly, not as dominating those in your charge but being examples to the flock*: to that grandkid of swallowing eyes and a vulnerable heart.

Cast all your cares on him for he careth for you.

Be sober, be watchful.

Your adversary the devil prowls around like a roaring lion, seeking someone to devour. . . .

The train still belched smoke in those days. "Choo-choo," to the children.

The train still jerked its starts, because the engine wheels first spun hard and the chuffing grew frantic before metal caught metal, rim caught rail, and the unspeakable weight of the long train finally rolled slowly forward.

When we achieved speed in the sunlight, batting through the small towns, climbing swells of farmland, I kneeled on the seat and pressed my cheek to the window; I nearly gnawed the glass in my hungry desire to see the engine ahead, the great-hearted creature that whistled and roared and clickety-clacked the million little wheels beneath us, drawing us toward our destinies. But the engine stayed hidden in mystery, as impossible to see as to see my own face without a mirror.

And having arrived at the farther station, we stepped down from our coach, Tante Teddy and I, onto a long concrete island that ran between tracks and trains to a terminal I could not yet see. Noises, hootings, hissings, hollerings; the scents of metal heat and steam heat and the acrid coal smoke; dramatic changes of light and darkness—the great, grinding climate of the railroad station made an alien of me, small and profoundly cautious. Several tracks away an engine started up, sending a series of hard bangs down its entire length from the choking head to the caboose. Trains still concluded with cabooses in those days.

"Wally?" My aunt adjusted her glasses to see me the better. "Wally, are you all right?" She put forth her hand, and though I didn't take it—my arms being full of a cardboard carrying case—I produced a smile, and so we began to walk. We walked toward the distant terminal, passing along the carcass of our own particular train: the dining car, the lounge car, sleeping cars, the mail car, luggage car, coal tender. . . .

In those days a locomotive still relieved itself by blasting great clouds of steam from lower valves into the paths of oncoming boys, terrifying them.

"Yow!" I cried, jumping backward.

"Wait!" Tante Teddy started to reach for me, "It's okay—" Then, in mid-motion she reversed herself, turning back toward the steam-cloud and murmuring: "Dad?"

Behind the sound of hissing steam I, too, heard a low roll of gentle laughter, and I looked, and a form took shape in the cloud, and the features of a familiar face began to gather there, brown eyes grinning, silver hair enwrapping the sides of his head: Grandpa!

Grandpa Wangerin came striding out of the mist and into the clear air. Straightway he slipped his hands beneath my arms and lifted me. He swung me high above his face, then caught me and held me to himself, my case, my squeal, my bones and all.

And so in a twinkling we were through the terminal and in his car; and I beside him was no alien, was a citizen, after all; and the sunlit weather felt very good.

I knew Grandpa. I knew him by sight and by smell and by the texture of his chin and by the timbre of his voice when my ear received it straight through his bosom. Of *course* he was familiar to me: I remembered him with the mind of a four-year-old child, whose memories seem taken not from mere months passed, but rather from that perpetual and primal past in which God creates heavens and earths and gardens of savor and sweetness. And I trusted my grandpa, whose presence stretched backward forever, in whose presence I was at peace.

Forever and forever, then, Grandpa Wangerin had been a preacher, for I had seen him preach and that was my memory of him. He was noble in the pulpit, splendid in his black cassock and a surplice as white as his own silver hair. Grandpa had a baritone voice as comforting as the Paraclete. My father once told me that Grandpa had been offered a position with the Metropolitan Opera in New York City, but that he'd chosen to become a pastor instead. He did sing, of course. All his life long he sang in public, gladly—until the last years when his voice was torn ragged by a persistent cough, and even his preaching was disturbed. Dad said that Grandpa would always tuck two Ludens cough drops under his upper lip before he preached, hoping by the drizzle to suppress that cough until the sermon was done.

"But those cough drops destroyed his front teeth," Dad said, "and he lost them."

I don't remember that. I didn't see teeth-gaps. It's Grandpa's softly puckered smile I most recall.

Forever and forever, then, the man had smiled, his brown eyes steadfast and tender. He smiled when he shook hands at the church door after worship. He smiled with anticipation when, in the mornings, he crossed the lot between the parsonage and the parochial school in order to lead the children in a matins devotion. He smiled a private, unattended smile when, in the evenings after supper, he sat down in his study to inscribe the day in his diary. Grandpa had begun this practice already during the first days of the ministry. When one book was full, he closed it and began another, saving the whole series of books against some future reckoning. *My Grandpa writes books,* I thought to myself, watching him from the darkened doorway. *My Grandpa writes stories down on paper for people to read.* But the diary was not, in fact, a journal of his private thoughts. I doubt he ever considered his personal notions worthy of preservation, except as they served the greater good of the Gospel.

Just a few years ago I had the opportunity to see the diaries again for the first time. Yes, they told stories. Or perhaps it is truer to say that they only hinted at ten thousand stories while Grandpa repeated the same daily tale over and over: he was keeping the accounts of a common cleric of uncommon obedience. *Who then is the faithful and wise servant, whom his master has set over this household, to give them their food at the proper time?* My grandfather's diaries record plain facts and calculations: the dates and times of every visitation he made to members of his congregation, whether to serve communion, or to pray with them, or to visit folks who had fallen away. The diaries remember every appointment the pastor made and kept for marital counseling; for the weddings themselves; for baptisms and funerals. They note the Scripture lessons which he chose for occasional services. They are a record of Rev. Wangerin's external duties, not of the thoughts of his internal heart—except as the very keeping of every duty, preciously and faithfully, *was* his heart and his life, being his deepest vocation: *Blessed is that servant whom his master, when he comes, will find so doing.*

Yet, if I cannot now read my grandfather's heart in the words he left behind, I did and *could* read his heart in the lines written on his face while he sat in his study writing in the diaries. With a fearsome clarity I see the man's silver head bending lightly above his desk; the lamplight plays upward over his face, his smile appearing and vanishing by turns, unattended. I hear the short strokes of his fountain pen as he moves it across the page, bright in the darkish room. I think that Grandpa doesn't see me in the doorframe, watching. I am the oldest of his grandchildren. My name is Walter, too. I am named after him, though he is Walter Carl and I am Walter Martin, like my Dad. One day I will write just like Grandpa, words spilling from my fountain pen upon pages and pages. My face, too, will work like sunshine and clouds in skyborne exchanges; my face will show the sadness and the gladness of the stories I am writing. And, just like my Grandpa, I won't even be aware that these expressions are revealing my secret heart to someone beloved who is lurking nearby and watching me. But Grandpa screws the cap to his pen (the cap flashing a tiny white dot) and, rising, begins to sing in his slightly ragged baritone:

> *"Du lieber, heilger frommer Christ,*
> *der fur uns Kinder kommen ist . . ."*

Kinder! That means—as even then I know—"children"! Not looking at me, switching off the desk lamp, Grandpa is nevertheless singing about me. I can hardly stand it:

> *"damit wir sollen weiss und rein,*
> *und rechte Kinder Gottes sein."*

"Unfortunately," Tante Teddy wrote me forty-six years later, when I was fifty, "Dad discontinued writing in his diary early in February 1948, the day before he entered the hospital because of his soaring blood pressure. You and your grandma, I fear, did not realize that your grandpa's illness was terminal. He lived less than two months after that trip . . ."

That trip.

The car we drove in seemed full of talk to me. My young aunt was highly verbal then, as now she swims the English language, written or spoken, as smoothly as a porpoise. Into most pauses she introduced sentences of endless delight.

Grandpa himself commented on every passing thing: "The solid line's to keep us in our places; the broken lines allow us to scoot." And: "Look, Wally—windmills!" He read all the roadside signs out loud: "Burma Shave!" with a smiling triumph. And sometimes he broke into song. Hymns, actually. *Wachet Auf.* The bass lines of German chorales. "Come, *mein Enkelsohn,*" he urged. "Sing with me!"

Once, while driving between the tall pines, Grandpa took his eyes from the road and squinted sententiously at the side of my head. "*Kinderschrecke!*" he whispered, not looking back to the road: "*Mir gruselt auf Kinderschrecke. Dir auch?*"

And I nearly yipped that my formal, controlled, obedient Grandfather kept his eyes fixed on me, allowing the car to drive itself.

Grandma raised a harsh complaint.

But "*Dir auch?*" Grandpa repeated, looking at me. *You, too?*

"Yes, yes, yes, yes," I said, in order to save us alive. Yes to whatever quiz the man was giving me.

Well, well: that quick flash of wickedness passing again from his face, the Reverend Walter C. Wangerin lifted his eyes once again to the road, smiling gravely and uttering his next words with a pulpit clarity: "Bogeymen give my grandson the creeps. Just as they do me. My grandson and me, why, we are the same. Two peas in a pod."

Apart from her various admonitions, I remember my grandmother chiefly by her silences and the marvelous revolvements of hair piled upon her head.

I must have lent my own chatter to the talk as we drove. The car and my relatives invited it.

And then, at the peak of our journey, the four of us were gathered on the deck of a sightseeing boat, sailing from island to island, nudging near the shores. It was a flat, canopied vessel, set with rows of chairs like pews on the deck. It was populated by people as white-haired as my Grandfather, though older than he was, truly, and wrinkled and grateful to be sitting beneath a canvas shade. I recall two tin speakers attached to the forward wall, crackling now and again with an impossible monologue. I knew that they were issuing words, that someone somewhere was saying something; but I had no idea *what* was being said.

Grandpa drew me near to him and murmured translations for my sake, and then I understood that a guide was describing the sights to be seen ashore; and as Grandpa pointed his finger, I too began to see the sights. Most of them. Not all of them.

To me the scene spread all around was an Eden, raw wood, creation undiscovered: tall trees and a vernal undergrowth, the sudden sweep of eagles in the air, wheeling on a soundless wing. And the air itself was a sun-splintered crystal, a breathless, dimensioned clarity. And through the trees strong rays shone slantwise earthward, splashing the needles and the foliage below.

The speakers crackled, *There! Do you see*—? But I lost the next words.

Grandpa translated, "Two deer on that spit of land," he said, pointing. "See them, Wally?"

"No." No, I couldn't see them, but was suddenly filled with desire.

"Their heads are down. They're feeding."

"Grandpa, no! I *don't* see the deer."

"Okay," he said. "Come."

And so it was that Grandpa led me to the very back of the boat. He put his hands beneath my arms and lifted me up. But the canopy covered the entire deck; so Grandpa leaned backward over the stern and swung me out, bodily, above the boil of propeller-churned water. My feet dangled down. I regarded the white confusion some ten feet below, but I did so only glancingly, without fear, because Grandpa's hands were gripped around my chest, and Grandpa himself was raising me higher and higher until I could with my own eyes see over the canopy.

"Do you see the deer," he called.

And I looked. And, yes! Yes, I saw the two deer, both of them, one with its head bent down in a spray of green fern, the other with its head lifted up and looking directly back at me.

"Yes, Grandpa! I see the deers. I see two deers."

Tend the flock, not by constraint but willingly, not dominating those in your charge. . . .

And so I hung above my death, and I was not afraid. In fact, I was sweetly oblivious of every emergent danger—not, mind you, because the dangers were not real, nor yet because I could not know them. In a moment I'll show you how desperately susceptible the boy at four could be to peril and its mortal terrors. No, I was oblivious because I was experiencing—was even in that moment *receiving*—my Grandfather Wangerin's sacred bequest: power over Satan and every deadly evil.

But it's a child's manner first to experience some new thing with a mindless subjectivity—and only later to learn the thing, to think *about* it with an analytic objectivity. On the boat I received and had what I did not know I had. It was only later, on the railroad train as it hurtled home to Chicago, that I learned what had been bequeathed me, and whence it was and how to call it by name.

I sat by the window on the right side of the coach.

Again, I was suffering the hungry desire actually to see the steam locomotive that pulled us forward—to see it, you understand, *while* it was active and living, belching smoke and directly affecting me by its monstrous speed.

I climbed to kneeling on my seat. I pressed my right cheek against the glass and, one-eyed, peered ahead.

It was late afternoon. The sun, standing off my side of the train, had descended nearly to the horizon, giving the country fields and forests a golden hue, as if the trees and the chopped corn glowed with their own sanguinity.

And then the miracle began to happen so reasonably that I in my heart said, *Of course! This is exactly the way it always happens.*

The long train began to curve into a lazy right-hand turn. I peered, and saw a flattened black shape racing in the forefront. The engine! Bending into my view! And soon I saw the tight blow of smoke into the streaming air, and the cloud torn backward, developing over the engine—and then the stretch of that dark metallic snout, and yes! Yes! There it was! There was the force itself, the cause of my rocking here on my seat, the thunderous muscle that even now was drawing cars and cars and a thousand people round a big bend to Chicago.

Almost I turned to tell my aunt of the wonder—but just then the engine's window flared with a bloody red reflected sunlight. I gasped, terrified. To my child's mind, this was a living, angry, glaring *eye*. And all at once I knew the danger: that our engine was the iron head of a serpent, and the entire train was its body, and all we inside the train were in the serpent's belly, and now the serpent was staring straight back at me as if it *knew* that I knew the horror which no one else had realized.

Do not dismiss this experience of cosmic discernment as the foolish imaginings of a child! It is at the promptings of such symbols as these that the child leaps past the slow processes of logic and in an instant understands the presence and the grandeur of wickedness in the world.

Mute, too terrified to let *anyone* know (and so to suffer) the truth that had been imparted to me, I bore alone the conviction that we had been consumed by evil. The serpent, that devil wandering the earth seeking someone to devour, had devoured us. . . .

Grandpa? Grandpa Wangerin?

Spontaneously I called to him in my mind. I did it before I knew that I was doing it: *Grandpa, why aren't you here?*

And then with a spiritual swiftness I learned. I held in my two separate hands these two separate experiences and all in a wordless flash considered their differences.

I am afraid. Because Grandpa is not here.

It was that simple. Grandpa was back in Grand Rapids.

But the very thought, the remembering of the boat and the dangers then and the fact that I was *not* then afraid because my Grandpa's hands then bore me up—that very thought, I say, brought ease into my situation now. Not that Grandpa had come upon the wings of my own memory. No. But rather that Grandpa had bequeathed me something that followed me then and ever. The source of our power over evil was in us. In *us*, the being together, you see, even when we were not together. And this was the name of that wonder: Love.

I sat down on the train seat. I kept my own counsel. I held my breath until we made Chicago. But I had begun to trust that we *would* make Chicago. And when we did, Grandpa's bequest had become a tangible thing within my breast.

And now that I am a man—and a grandfather too, in my own right—I can declare as a sacred fact, that this manner of being together outlasts every trip we take, even the final journey into death.

Shortly before my Tante Teddy wrote me her remembering letter, I had published parts of the story as you've read it above. She read those parts as well and dearly wanted to add several things and to correct several things.

I recall, she wrote, *that you and your grandpa had some pretty extensive conversations throughout that trip. Grandpa loved to explain how things worked. Grandpa said, "Look, there's a windmill," and you, Wally, four years old, you said, "I call them caffy-caps." Apparently Grandpa didn't repeat your word correctly, because you said, "No, Grandpa, watch my mouth: caffy-caps."*

The boat ride was indeed spectacular. My 22-year-old self was not into scenic appreciation, but I remember being awestruck by the lush virgin timber, the rare wildlife up close and personal, the rushing, gorgeous waters of the river. And I was right there next to your Grandpa when he lifted you out over the railing to see the deer, with your Grandma fretfully admonishing behind us, "Oh, Walter, be careful!"

I don't recall all the towns we saw.

Unfortunately, Dad discontinued writing in his diary early in February 1948, the day before he entered the hospital because of his soaring blood pressure. So what's the tribute?

He lived less than two months after that trip, but oh, what warmth and joy and contentment you showered upon those last two months! You recognize so eloquently his love for you, Wally, dear Wally. You gave as good as you got. For the rest of his life your Grandpa basked in your love and your trust and your irresistible four-year-old wonder at the world around you. Whenever he'd seem in pain or feeling sad during my hospital visits, I would mention a few catch-words from the Upper Peninsula trip, and he'd be instantly diverted to those happy memories and ultimately to peace of mind and of soul.

Thank you for making that visit with me and for doing so much to enrich your Grandpa's life.

It becomes even more evident, then, how in the being together we constitute a power against the greatest evils of this existence, Satan and desolation. And death. And the name of such wondrous being together even when we are no longer together is itself tough, enduring, and scarcely sentimental: Love.

In a postscript Tante Teddy concludes her letter:

I submit reluctantly to your poetic editorial license, but ding-dong it, Wally! There's no way I'd let an iron-headed serpent swallow my nephew down!

IN THOSE DAYS HOMESICKNESS seemed to curl in me like a little creature deep in my bowels. When it stirred, I suffered a sweet abdominal pain, like having to go to the bathroom. If it only stirred and stayed put, well, then I was okay. No one needed to know what was going on inside me. But if my homesickness grew worse and worse, that creature seemed to climb through my stomach into my chest. In the chest it was a suffocation, and I would puff and puff and suck air, and this would look like sobbing, but I wasn't sobbing, exactly. No, I was not crying. I was fighting the tears. I had not yet lost control.

But when the homesickness rose all the way into my throat, then it was a plain pain at the root of my tongue, and *then* I was crying. Then my sobs were huge gulps. And then almost nothing could console me, and everyone knew there was a problem with Wally.

I was often homesick, is how I understood the process so well.

But I had good reason to be.

I feared death. There was a lot of death around me.

Well—how does a kid know, when he has left behind him his home and his mother, his brothers and everything he loves, that they might not die while he is away? He wouldn't be there to save them in the event of disaster—and a kid just at the age of entering school can conceive of countless disasters.

Or who's to say the kid himself won't die away from home? And who would be there to hug him then, when his mother's absent?

Or, worst of all: what if his family just didn't care? What if they forgot the kid while he was gone? What if they finally decided that he was just too much trouble to put up with, so they all packed and moved away and he would find a shining empty house at his return? Well, whom would he go to *then* for help? The principal? Principals don't love small boys. He'd have to live on his own, forever sad that the thing he had feared actually happened exactly as he feared it.

Or what if he got lost on the way home? His mother would just cry her eyes out, so sorry, so sorry to lose her eldest, most precious son. So how could the boy live with himself, imagining the great grief he had caused his dear mother?

You see? All this is death. Different kinds of dying. But any one was a possibility.

That's why, on the first day of kindergarten, surrounded by strangers of various levels of confidence, the boy put his head down on the floor and cried. He feared death, and it made him unspeakably homesick.

That's why, when he was left with his Aunt Erna in St. Louis while his mother was in Chicago, he cried for two days together.

And again, the first day of first grade, he made it almost to lunch, but not all the way, and he put his head down on his desk, and the rest of the people looked at him. *Something's wrong with Wally.*

Yep. Something. The little creature of sorrow was clawing raw the back of his throat; his tummy felt completely empty, but his face was all full of sadness.

Death. He always lost, the kid did, when confronted with this lonely skull-bone of abandonment and death. But how could he defeat it? He was just a kid, a little one, weak, not strong. Not strong at all.

Yet that's exactly what my mother asked of me: "Oh, come on, Wally! Are you little or big?" she demanded, and I knew the answer she wanted, and I knew the truth. "Are you weak or strong?" she said.

I sighed and whispered, "Strong."

"Right!" she said. "Let's go."

Go our dusty ways to death, lonely, lonely on the way.

In the spring of my second-grade year, several months before the school term concluded, my whole family moved from Chicago, Illinois, to Grand Forks, North Dakota. My father had accepted a call to serve Immanuel Lutheran Church as its pastor. This church also maintained a parochial school, eight grades and kindergarten, though classes had to double up in rooms, one teacher taking several.

This meant that a little kid might meet some very old kids even in his classroom.

So, then, here we were in a completely new environment, a new neighborhood in which every face was strange, and even a new house, a huge house, a three-story house that made odd sounds in the night, keeping me awake with wondering.

So, then, I was completely unprepared for my mother's plans for me. *Surely,* I thought, *in the midst of so foreign a territory we need not increase the strain by dividing the family just now.* Surely she knew that the potentiality of death at separation had just shot up to plague levels.

They told me that tornadoes could come straight up from South Dakota and hit Grand Forks directly on the nose, just like that. They said, "Watch out!"

But my mother said, "I think you ought to go to school."

I said, "School's almost over for the year."

She said, "All the better to go now. Meet classmates now and they'll be your friends by next year."

I was aghast. Already now, even at this distant early stage, I felt the small creature stirring in the cradle of my loins. Sweet pain.

I said, "What about the tornadoes?"

She said, "What *about* tornadoes?"

"They'll probably come while I'm gone."

"Oh, Wally, that's utterly silly."

"I don't think so."

"Well, you don't know what's best. The sooner the better."

I said, "I don't feel very well."

She said, "Oh, come on, Wally! Are you little or big? What will your brothers think of you?"

So, then, in spite of the clear probability of death by disaster, my mother prevailed. She's a strong woman.

So, then: three of us drove on the following morning to the white wooden, two-story structure, Immanuel Lutheran School. Three of us. My mother, myself, and the creature deep within me, tickling the lower parts, stirring, stirring, threatening. Homesickness. But I said I wouldn't cry.

Mom took my hand and led me from the car into the building, up the stairs, and into a classroom. She introduced me to Miss Augustine, who was to be my teacher. This woman was beautiful beyond description, lithe and soft and tall, but she was a teacher. I hoped she would forgive me, but teachers by nature can be frightening, and even the smells were strange in this room, and the sunlight seemed cold and northerly and unkind. I felt a serious spasm of homesickness below my stomach. Therefore, as soon as Mom and Miss Augustine fell to talking together I slipped out of the room, down the stairs, out the door, and into the car, front seat. There I sat and waited for Mom to come back.

I persuaded myself that my mother would be delighted by my decision, as relieved as I was to find that I would be going home with her after all today.

Well—no.

When she found me in the car, my mother opened the passenger door, put her hand on her hip, and demanded, "What's this? What's the matter with you? Wally, Wally, are you little or big? Are you weak or are you strong?"

I sighed and whispered, "Strong."

"Right! Let's go."

I huffed a little. I puffed a little. Things were swelling in my chest.

I sat in the back with the W's. Wangerin. A kid named Corky Zimbrick sat behind me.

I didn't talk. I didn't move. My face was already warm. My mother had driven away some time ago. I was alone. Danger zone. Homesickness had made itself felt in the regions of my chest. I *had* to hold completely still.

The beautiful Miss Augustine was saying something, teaching something to someone—but which class it was, mine or those older than me, I didn't know. All sound was like waterfall in my ears: a roaring.

Corky Zimbrick whispered in my ear, "Who are you? Are you the preacher's kid?"

Oh no, I was known! Someone actually knew me. It was like being snatched from hiding. I started puffing and puffing, sucking huge chestfuls of air. Homesickness was coming higher, almost too high to be controlled.

I raised my hand.

Miss Augustine saw it immediately. Extraordinary woman! Without a word she nodded full recognition of my request and permission thereto.

I got up and rushed out of the classroom, down the hall to the bathroom. I unzipped and stood up to the urinal, pretending to pee. All I wanted was to be alone for a while, to control the great grief rising within me—to stand perfectly still, to concentrate my energy on not crying. I said I was not going to cry this time.

Those were big urinals in those days. Big as a kid. Big as a closet. Intimidating. You stared straight forward at concave porcelain that seemed to be waiting for proof you belonged there.

Suddenly the door behind me banged open. With thunderous energy there entered an eighth-grade teenager, huge fellow. He recognized me.

"Hey, Wally," he shouted, bellying up to the urinal beside mine.

I recognized him, too, and I burned to be in his presence. This was Dicky Affeldt, the principal's oldest son. This was a man of the world, a wild and sinful sort. Just last Sunday I saw him in a deserted Sunday school room with an eighth-grade woman named Marcia. She had so many freckles all over her body that even her eyes were flecked with freckles. Well, Dicky Affeldt had her bent backward over a utility table and was kissing her on her freckled lips. And she laughed! She had actually laughed.

He said, "Hey, Wally," but I didn't answer him. I stepped closer to the urinal to hide that I was not peeing.

He started to whistle, making a torrent against the porcelain.

Then he looked at me. "What color's yours?" he asked.

I hoped he didn't mean what I thought he meant. This was becoming as frightening as I expected the world to be.

"What color's your pee?" said Dicky Affeldt. "Mine's clear," he said. "That happens when I drink lots of water."

Yep! Yep! He meant what I thought he meant. I was in the world, all right: treacherous, immoral, dirty, strange, and dangerous.

I zipped and raced out of there before I became the more involved. My mother should *know* what obscenities I had to deal with here.

Back in the classroom, back at my desk, I sat violently still, biting my teeth together as hard as I could. That little creature, homesickness and horror, had crept higher on account of the lewdness of Dicky Affeldt. It was nearly throat-high. It was almost uncontrollable. I breathed deeply, deeply, blowing air out at the nose, staring directly at the bottom left-hand star on the American flag— not crying. I said that I would not cry.

But then the worst thing happened, and I lost it.

They sang a hymn.

Hymns'll kill you.

All the kids in the classroom started to sing, "Blest be the tie that binds/Our hearts in Christian love—," and homesickness clogged my throat and squirted out my eyes. I burst into tears, sobbing, sobbing. I put my head down on the desk and tried at least to cry quietly. But I was crying, now. Nothing could stop it or console me. Nothing.

Miss Augustine called for recess. Kids began to rush outside.

"What's the matter with him? Isn't he coming?"

"Never mind," said Miss Augustine. "Never you mind, Corky Z."

So, then it was altogether still in the room. So I allowed some boo-hoos, some genuine shuddering sobs, all with my head down on my arms, down on the desktop.

Suddenly I heard humming beside me.

I peeped out underneath my arm and saw Miss Augustine sitting at the desk across the aisle from mine. She was huge in the little seat. She was grading papers. She glanced at me. Straightway I covered my face again.

"Walter Martin?" she said in soft voice. "Walter Martin, do you mind if I sit here?"

I shook my head.

"Oh, thank you," she said. "Sometimes I like to sit here when I do my work."

She began to hum again. Soon the humming turned into a little song, with words: *Jesus loves me, this I know—*

But then, in the middle of a line, she stopped. "Walter Martin?" she said. "Walter Martin, do you mind if I sing?"

I shook my head.

"Thank you," she said. "Sometimes I like to sing when I work."

—for the Bible tells me so—

Then she said, "Walter Martin, do you know this song?"

I nodded. I did. I had learned it last summer.

She said, "Well, then, do you want to sing it with me?"

Forever and ever I will recall with admiration that Miss Augustine was not offended when I shook my head, meaning no. It was in this moment that I began to love my teacher. Somebody else might have gotten mad because I wouldn't sing with her. But Miss Augustine, in her soft voice, said, "Oh, that's right. Little boys can't sing when they're crying, can they?"

She knew that she was not the problem, that I was.

She said, "Well, but do you think we could shout the song together?"

So then the children of Immanuel Lutheran School who were playing on the playground for recess heard two voices roaring through the windows, one fully as loud as the other:

"JESUS LOVES ME, THIS I KNOW! FOR THE BIBLE TELLS ME SO—" And I screamed as loud as I could, blowing the creature of homesickness out of my throat, dispelling sorrows and fears and mournings together:

LITTLE ONES TO HIM BELONG!

THEY ARE *WEAK,*

BUT *HE* IS STRONG.

YES!

JESUS LOVES ME. YES—

Yes, yes, yes. Jesus loves me. Yes.

Ah, Miss Augustine, teacher of natural skill and native insight into a kid's horrific fears: together we met death; we outfaced that specter together; and never have I forgotten the triumph. Once, while still I was young, death did not defeat me, but by a brazen shout and an expression of perfect faith, death itself—and homesickness too—was whipped. *Whupped!*

You shaped a boy, and forty years passed, and the boy became a man, and even today I declare the simple truth of *who* is strong after all, and who is weak, and in whose weakness power is made perfect.

Dear teacher, I heard recently that your smile is lopsided because a stroke destroyed the strength on one side of your face. Do you still shout your faith in the time of trial? The signs of dying? I do.

Last month my friend and my doctor, Stephen Ferguson, died suddenly and altogether too soon, leaving behind him two young children. No, three: his death reduced me to a child again. Homesickness stormed in me. I preached his funeral sermon—and I would have wept then except that first I had gone striding through a deep wood, roaring at the top of my lungs:

> JESUS LOVES ME, HE WHO DIED,
> HEAVEN'S GATES TO OPEN WIDE;
> HE WILL WASH AWAY MY SIN,
> LET HIS LITTLE CHILD COME IN.
> YES, JESUS LOVES ME!
> YES, JESUS LOVES ME.
> YES, JESUS LOVES ME—
> THE BIBLE TELLS ME SO.

IN THE SUMMER OF my seventh year I found an electrical cord in the kitchen and was immediately dazzled by its potential for wild, destructive power.

My mother was in the backyard mowing grass. She used a pushmower in those days, a clattering metal machine whose blades spun only when one drove the wheels forward with fierce energy. My mother possessed such energy. Brave, she was, strong enough to hit a softball farther than my father could, strong enough to punish a child with such rectitude he knew he'd met the forehead of the Deity. Whatever he'd done before she chastised him he would never do again. God had spoken in the arm of a mortal woman.

Clunk-whirrrr, went the mower outside. Thus I heard the power of her matriarchal arms: *Clunk-whirrrr! Whirrrr!*

Why I happened to be alone, I don't remember. I was the oldest of five and should have been baby-sitting. Dad was at church. Mom was busy. The children were my responsibility. Yet the kitchen was altogether mine, and I was alone.

And there was that black electrical cord. I drew it out of its drawer and pinched it as you pinch a serpent's neck, just behind the plug. The blinkless head. Two prongs like venomous fangs would strike and bite any socket in the wall.

The tail of the cord was a plume of naked copper wiring. The cord attached to nothing.

So, if I stuck this plug in a socket, there in the mild reddish metal would be such violent force that it could kill at a touch. *Yow!* Heaven and earth could collide at the command of a seven-year-old boy. My tummy tightened at the thought.

Well, and I knew the potency of electrical outlets. At the age of four I had managed to stick my right thumb into a living-room socket and had suffered a rapid, pulsing shock. It snapped my teeth shut and threw me backward across the room. My mother greased my poor thumb with butter, her healing of all horrors.

But here was a serpent that could suck juice from the wall and hold it in the bright ends of its tail—for *me! For* me rather than against me. This snake could strike with true authority where *I* willed it. I myself could hold a cobra of inestimable damage in my own two hands—

—if only I would, you know, plug it in—

Clunk-whirrrr! My mother labored in vigorous oblivion outside. I was alone. Nothing stopped me from arming my rattler. So I did. I thrust the teeth of this *Blitzschlange* into the socket by the refrigerator and stood back, pulling the cord out to length, staring at the copper scream of tail beneath my face—so close, so close to disaster! I began to grin. I could scarcely breathe because of my audacity.

But what good is the possession of power unless there's some evidence of it?

I began to wave my hand back and forth, swinging the snake's tail left and right, up and down in front of me. But nothing happened, of course. So I increased the speed, giggling, panting. Oh, I was scaring myself! Soon I was whirling the cord above my head like a lariat, barking a harsh, frightened laughter on account of such daring. I was so rash. Such a wild kid—

Suddenly, *crack-BOOM!* Copper wires struck the white refrigerator; yellow flame flashed forth; an explosion sent me backward, snatching the snake from its socket, and throwing me down on my butt against the far wall.

I held my breath a moment and surveyed the situation. I was alive. Not wounded. I had dribbled a little in my pants, but that dark shadow would pass. Here was the black cord dead across my legs. I—

Oh, no! Oh, *no!* Suddenly I saw that the refrigerator door had been scorched black by my sin. That yellow flash had burned white metal to a filthy char! Oh, no!

Clunk-whirrrr! Mama, what are you going to do to me when you see this? *Clunk-whirrrr! Whirrrr!* I began to whimper. I dribbled a little more. Now I felt the fear I had not felt before, my mother being more deadly than a whole nest of serpents. My life was in jeopardy. Before nightfall I would be dead.

Clunk-whirrrr!

Well, then this wet child arose from the kitchen floor and minced toward the refrigerator and put forth his thumb and touched the black patch of his personal wickedness—and lo! Where he touched, he wiped it clean!

"Jesus, Jesus, thank you!" This child experienced a sudden honey-spurt of gratitude in all his muscles, so that he trembled and he lifted up his heart unto the Lord in joy. Black patches from electrical shocks can be erased after all! Sins and error can be canceled!

He ran for a rag and rubbed the mark away altogether, rubbed the white door white again, rubbed iniquity clean.

And so it was that at seven I did not die, neither from the bite of the serpent (which could have killed me, body and soul) nor from the wrath of my mother (which, far from desiring my death, desired my life, loving with an angry love, a dreadful love, a mother love alone).

I have since myself become an adult. And a father. A man who prays for his children with loud cries and tears, since his own experience has shown him how closely all children do creep toward the dangers. They could die! Even my beloved sons and daughters, unprotected by my love when I am outside and oblivious, could by their own hand die!

I pray: *O Lord God, save the children from danger, from the cunning of the Evil One, and from the disasters of their own stupidity!*

How often have they covered some sin to keep it from me?—my child, my children, in the fond notion that they could save their lives thereby, though it is the sin itself that can kill them!

Christ, let terror check them!

I love my children. Even in my sometime anger—especially then— I love them and beg your mercy upon them. Amen. Amen.

FIRST OF ALL THE LOVE of God is a terrible thing. It begins by revealing unto us such treacheries and threats in the world that we know we must die soon—and until then (we are sure) we shall live in continual terror of the end to come.

The first act of divine love is to persuade us of the reality of death. We shudder and doubt that this can *be* love. We hate the messenger. We loathe such lovers. But it is a dear, necessary act nonetheless, because without it the second act of God's love would be altogether meaningless to us.

The second act is mercy. An absurdity of mercy. It is that God himself enters the same reality he first revealed unto us; he bows down and joins us under the same threat of death—and those whom he taught to fear he leads to safety. But those who do not fear do not follow. See? We had to suffer extremest fright in order to know our extreme need.

We who are under death must admit the peril; we have no other choice—except to die. Except to die.

But God, who exists above death, who knows no need at all, had the choice which we did not have. If, then, he emptied himself of power and humbled himself to death—even to death on a cross— this was purely an act of mercy on our behalf.

Then who can measure the love of God, to be thrice sacrificed: first, to be despised for declaring the terrible truth; second, to descend by choice into this treacherous and transient world; third, to save us by dying indeed the death he had revealed, dying it in our stead? Or whereto shall we liken so violent, valiant, and near an approach of the kingdom of heaven unto us?

Well—

The coming of the kingdom is like the coming of my father to my brothers and me when we sat fishing, blithely fishing, from a ledge twelve feet above the water in a stony cove in Glacier National Park.

In that year of sudden awakening, 1954, I was ten. My brothers, grinning idiots all (for that they followed a fool) were, in descending order, nine and seven and six.

Just before our trip west, I had furnished myself with fishing equipment. A Cheerios box top and my personal dime had purchased ten small hooks, three flies, leader, line, a red-and-white bobber, and three thin pieces of bamboo which fit snugly into one pole. Such a deal! Such a shrewd fellow I felt myself to be.

A leader of brothers indeed.

On a bright blue morning we chopped bits of bacon into a pouch, left the tent on high ground, and went forth fishing and to fish. We sought a mountain stream, though we ourselves did not depart the trail down from the campground. Fortunately, that same trail became a wooden bridge which crossed furious roaring waters, the crashing of a falls from the slower bed of a stream.

A mountain stream! There, to our right, before it dived down into the rocky chasm below this bridge, was a mountain stream. Filled with fishes, certainly. We had found it.

But the bridge joined two high walls of stone, and even the slower stream came through a narrow defile.

But I was a shrewd fellow in those days, a leader, like I said. I noticed that a narrow ledge snaked away from the far end of the bridge, that it went beneath the belly of a huge boulder and therefore was hidden from the view of lesser scouts. If we could crawl that ledge on hands and knees through its narrowest part, ducking low for the boulder, why, we'd come to a widening, a hemisphere of stone big enough to sit on, from which to dangle our legs, a sort of fortress of stone since the wall went up from that ledge a flat twelve feet and down again from that ledge another twelve feet. Perfect. Safe from attacks. Good for fishing.

I led my blinking brothers thither. None questioned me. I was the oldest. Besides, I was the one with foresight enough to have purchased a fishing pole.

"You got to flatten out here," I called back, grunting in order to fit beneath the outcropping boulder. They did. One by one they arrived with me in a fine, round hideout. Above the sheer rock some trees leaned over and looked down upon us. Below our feet there turned a lucid pool of water, itself some twelve feet deep.

And so the Brothers Wangerin, Sons of Gladness and Glory, began to spend a fine day fishing.

We took turns with the pole.

The bacon didn't work, but—as a sign of our favor with all the world—the trees dropped down on silken threads some tiny green worms, exactly the size of our tiny hooks. We reached out and plucked worms from the air, baited the hooks, and caught (truly, truly) several fingerling fish. Oh, it was a good day! All that we needed we had.

Then came my father.

We didn't see him at first. We weren't thinking about him, so filled with ourselves were we, our chatting and our various successes.

But I heard through the water's roar a cry.

Distant, distant: *Wally!*

I glanced up and to my right—where the water dropped over stone, where the bridge arched it—and I almost glanced away again, but a wild waving caught my eye.

WALLY! WALLY! WALLY!

"Dad?" Yes!—it was Dad. "Hey, look, you guys. There's Dad leaning over the bridge."

They all looked, and straightway Philip started to cry, and then Mike, too. Paul dropped my pole into the water twelve feet below. And I saw in our father's eyes a terror I had never seen before.

WALLY, HOW DID YOU GET OVER THERE?

Over here? I looked around.

Suddenly *here* was no fortress at all. It was a precipice, a sheer stone drop to a drowning water, and *that* water rushed toward a thundering falls far, far below my father. With his eyes I saw what

I had not seen before. In his seeing (which loved us terribly) I saw our peril.

He was crying out as loud as he could: *WALLY, COME HERE! COME HERE!*

But the ledge by which we'd come had shrunk. It was thin as a lip now. The hairs on my neck had started to tingle, and my butt grew roots. I couldn't move. Neither did my brothers. I didn't even shake my head. I was afraid that any motion at all would pitch me headlong into the pool below. I gaped at my father, speechless.

He stopped waving. He lowered his arms and stopped shouting. He stood for an eternal moment looking at us from the bridge, and then his mouth formed the word, *Wait*. We couldn't hear it. He didn't lift his voice. Quietly under the booming waters he whispered, *Wait*.

Then he bent down and removed his shoes. At the near end of the bridge, he bent down farther, farther, until he was on his stomach, worming forward, knocking dust and pebbles by his body into the stream, bowing beneath the enormous boulder that blocked our freedom.

"Dad's coming. See him?"

"Yep, Dad's coming."

"I knew he would."

He pulled himself ahead on the points of his elbows, like the infantry beneath barbed wire, his face drawn and anxious. He was wearing shorts and a long-sleeved flannel shirt. Red with darker red squares. I remember.

When he came into our tiny cove, he turned on his belly and hissed to the youngest of us, "Mike, take my heel." Mike was six. He didn't.

"Mike, *now!*" Dad shouted above the waterfall with real anger. "Grab my heel in your hand and follow me."

You should know that my father is by nature and breeding a formal man. I don't recall that he often appeared in public wearing short-sleeved shirts. Nor would he permit people to call him by his first name, asking rather that they address him according to his position, his title and degree. Even today the most familiar name he will respond to is "Doc." Dad is two-legged and upright. Dad is organized, controlled, clean, precise, dignified, decorous, civil— and formal.

What a descent it was, therefore, and what a sweet humiliation, that he should on his stomach scrabble this way and that, coming on stone then going again, pulling after him one son after the other: Michael, Philip, Paul.

And then me.

"Wally, grab my heel. Follow me."

It wasn't he who had put us in these straits. Nevertheless, he chose to enter them with us, in order to take us out with him. It was foolishness that put us here. It was love that brought him.

So he measured the motion of his long leg by the length of my small arm, and he never pulled farther than I could reach. The waters roared and were troubled; the granite shook with the swelling thereof. But my father was present, and very present. I felt the flesh of his heel in my hand, leading me; and I was still in my soul. I ceased to be afraid.

That stony cove had not been a refuge at all but a danger. Rather, my father in love bore refuge unto me; my father bore me back to safety again. So I did not die in the day of my great stupidity. I lived.

Thus is the kingdom of heaven likened unto a certain man whose eldest son was a nincompoop—

I REMEMBER THE DIFFICULT ritual of my confirmation—when at the age of thirteen I stood in front of the whole church and confirmed my faith in my Lord Jesus.

It felt that it happened wrong for me.

In fact, it happened right; but that feeling of personal terror was a measure of the personal, important, and public step this infant took toward adulthood. Spiritual and communal independence is, when it is real, a scary thing.

My confirmation class consisted of five students. There were two girls, sisters, who commonly pulled my hair on Saturday mornings, protesting in thick accents that they liked me, they *liked* me, then falling absolutely silent when the pastor arrived and the lesson began. They were Dutch immigrants, strong as to muscles, weak as to English. There was one boy who truly did befriend me but who could memorize nothing and who likewise subsided into an unteachable silence when actual class work began. There was a boy who set himself in direct, perpetual competition with me, a glittery-eyed bird of a fellow, a crouching raptor-bird of a fellow. And then there was me—bespectacled, small of stature, grotesque as to hair in which I suffered explosions of cowlick on the back of my head, and as to intellect, passable. I could memorize. Well, and I *had* to memorize, didn't I? In those days my father was the president of Concordia College in Edmonton, Alberta, Canada, a Lutheran, Christian institution. His reputation, therefore, would be affected by my public performance of matters faithful and pious—and that's exactly what was coming: confirmation started with an examination in front of the whole congregation and all my family and God and everybody. Dad is "Walter." I am "Walter." I am his oldest child. I had to uphold the name. I memorized. I memorized everything in the catechism. I memorized *both* the answers *and* the questions *and* the Bible passages that proved those answers to be right.

I ate that book like Ezekiel.

Grim.

I had to.

So on Saturday mornings Pastor Walter Schoepf said to one boy, "What does this mean?" And that boy always said, "Umm. Umm." He didn't know.

So the pastor turned to the two sisters and said, "What does this mean?" Well, but they remained serenely innocent of questions and answers and reputations and English, too. No fears of failure in them. No pressures on their pretty heads.

So then the pastor—all he had to do was say, "Wally." He didn't even have to say again, "What does this mean?" because I memorized questions. Just looked at me and said, "Wally"—and I popped up and recited: "I believe that Jesus Christ, true God, begotten of the Father from—"

All at once (but so regularly that I grew gun-shy in my recitations, waiting for this attack) the competitive fellow, unable to contain himself longer, erupted knowledge, trembling and shouting: "ALSO-TRUE-MAN-BORN-OF-THE-VIRGIN-MARY-IS-MY. . . ."

There was much to wrack my nerves.

So much depends, so much depends, so much depends upon Wally. . . .

The day of confirmation drew near. One week away.

My mother took me downtown to shop. We got me new underwear, new shoes, a shirt, and a new blue suit. Expensive raiment. All this made my heart pound, thinking, thinking: *They're putting money into this thing!* They loved me, of course. They expected me to do well—and to be worthy of a new blue suit.

Would they, then, in the actual event, be proud of me?

On Saturday—our last class, the day before The Day—the Dutch sisters pulled my hair. Routine. But it hurt. And it made me think about my looks for tomorrow. I decided that they pulled my hair because the cowlick invited exactly such scorn. The cowlick, as it were, deserved it.

So that night I took a careful bath, cleaning everything with a scrubbing brush. Toenails. Ears. My whole unbeautiful body. My mortified face. It's too bad I didn't have good looks. But maybe I didn't deserve good looks. *That raptor-bird boy had a certain glittering intensity and dark grooming that made him good-looking.* I thought of my competition, and I thought: *Well, but there is one thing I can do,* and I did—

When I got out of the tub, I didn't dry my hair. I combed it dripping wet. Then I got a nylon stocking from my mother's drawer and rolled it up into a tight hat and put it on my wet, straight hair and rolled it down again over my ears. I wore it to bed. I planned to have perfect hair tomorrow. That's what I could do for my mother and her expectations and her expensive blue suit, for my father and his reputation and our name. At least I could have one perfect thing.

So much depends upon a Wally beautiful with learning—

I lay perfectly still. I prayed a lot that night. Mostly the Lord's Prayer, though, because I kept losing my place in the middle and had to start over and over again. Pastor Schoepf kept coming in and saying, *What does this mean?* Somebody would quote part of the Apostles' Creed, "—And in Jesus Christ, his only Son, our Lord," and then Pastor Schoepf would interrupt and say, *What does this mean?* So I kept losing my place in the Lord's Prayer—which I wasn't saying from memory so much as really trying to pray it.

Well, at that time I was already the oldest of seven sisters and brothers. My confirmation was the first. And Aunt Erna had come all the way from St. Louis because she was my sponsor at my baptism, and she told me that she had a present for me, and she even told me what it was: a King James Bible with onion-skin pages, a very delicate thing; but she also said that she wouldn't give it to me until after my examination, so I better do well in this examination.

So much depends upon. . .

On the morning of the Sunday of my confirmation I put on my new underwear and my new shirt and my new blue suit. I went into the bathroom. Standing in front of the mirror I rolled up the nylon stocking, careful not to muss a hair on my head. The front looked flat, wispy, obedient, very nice—

But suddenly there shot up from the back of my scalp a whole rooster tail of a cowlick! Oh, no! Oh, *no!* It was like a broom sticking up. It was huge and waving and happy to be there, like it wanted to come to the party, too. I pressed it down with the flat of my hand, and that actually hurt the roots. It just jumped up again. *Oh, no, dear Jesus, no! No!* What would people say about me now?

I took a brush. I flooded it with water. I slicked and slicked my hair until the cowlick grew too heavy to rise again. I was, with great perturbation, drowning a cowlick, killing it. I wanted it dead on the Sunday of my confirmation.

So, then, my father drove me to church, his grim and dripping Ezekiel. I got to sit in front. Mom sat in the back seat. They let me out first.

So, then, I was walking up the path to the church door, my back to the car, wondering whether they were watching me and whether they were proud of me now, whether maybe they were even mentioning out loud to one another that this was their oldest son about to engage in an act of extraordinary courage—when I felt one single cowlick hair pop up: *Ping!* Immediately I reached back and yanked it out and kept on walking.

So, then, all five of us dressed in white robes behind the pastor—the confirmation class—processed up the aisle of the sanctuary while the congregation stood on either side singing a hymn. The church was absolutely jammed with people. I kept my eyes properly forward, but I couldn't sing. There was no spit left in my mouth. I was the shortest confirmand—so how was I to maintain dignity and uphold the family name? A hair popped up. With one hand I covered my mouth to cough; but the cough was a fake to hide what my other hand did; it plucked that hair out of my head.

Finally we sat down upon five chairs that were arranged like a little U in the chancel, our backs to the congregation (but we could hear and we could feel the overwhelming weight of so many people leaning forward to listen and to judge). Pastor Schoepf stood up in front of us rubbing his hands. About to begin. He had the questions on a sheet of paper. We were supposed to have the answers in our heads. A hair popped up on the back of mine and began to wave to the congregation. This time I didn't try to hide the gesture: I pulled it out.

Today as an adult, a father and a pastor too, I declare that my terror in that moment—caught, as it were, between the millstones of responsibility and fear—had its holy purpose. Our present society has few true rites of initiation by which a child can leave childhood and enter, through the valiant accomplishment of a significant task, adulthood with all its rights and responsibilities.

How is he to know that a change has taken place, both in him and in the community's regard for him? How is her very soul to recognize that she must—and can!—shoulder a new role? And how is the community itself to be persuaded to treat the individual differently hereafter? Such a radical shift both in self-awareness and in communal relationships requires an event to mark the change and actually to effect it. It doesn't always happen by unconscious development. In fact, precisely because we *don't* attend as well to such rites of initiation as cultures foreign, primitive, and past, we are a society infested with grown-ups stalled in their childhood, people of age still stuck in immaturity, people unable or unwilling to take responsibility for themselves, people as self-absorbed as children because they are, in spirit if not in body, children.

Their chrysalis never broke nor opened. They never emerged completely whole and capable of high, frightening, independent flight. There never was a rite.

But such ritual must be, as all rituals are, an *event*. And that event must involve a *task* to be accomplished by the initiate. The task, then, must be a personal *experience,* not merely some received piece of information or money or status without the fear and the possible failure of personal action. It must be an experience which relies on the self and God alone, so that the initiate can truly feel the new definitions of her being and the change they represent. Such persuasion comes not so much by words and teaching as by crisis and survival. The task must be *significant,* not some safe parody of adult duties, not a "cute" conferring of honor upon children for no deserving except that we love them. If it is significant—crucial to one's future, so difficult as to threaten failure and, at the same time, to honor success with an honest praise—then passing the test is a genuine entrance into adulthood. Finally, the task must be *public.* The whole society might then honor and admit the change of one individual, receiving noisily a new adult within itself as a responsible citizen.

Confirmation was my initiation.

I can conceive of nothing more significant than that I should, of my own heart and strength and mind, confirm that God is God and is my Lord. This was not some childish entertainment for my congregation. This was in fact a matter of life and death. I knew so by the great burden placed upon me, father and mother and aunt and people. I know it better now for the greater consequence of faith. Life and death: this was no cliché. I would live or die by this divine relationship. Lo, I was crossing into a maturity of faith. In baptism Jesus claimed me. Confirmation, now, completed that holy moment as I independently and with full knowledge claimed him: my Lord.

Terrible, terrible, beautiful! Filled with anxiety before the task, because of the task, because of its monumental importance; trembling, swallowing, standing here at the edge of adulthood, standing here on the precipice 'twixt heaven and hell—

Pastor Schoepf glared at the Dutch girls with a sort of haggard fear. He had already endured three *Umms* and silence from the poor boy who could memorize nothing. The pastor now said to one sister, "What does this mean?"

"*Vass?*" she said, blinking.

He turned to the other sister, "And in Jesus Christ, his only Son, our Lord. It's the second article of the Creed. What does this mean?"

The second sister smiled blithely, showing two stalactites of teeth, monsters of white indifference. The pastor swallowed, glanced at the heavy ocean of folks behind us, and said, "Wally, please, what does this mean?"

I stood up.

That small motion caused a bush of hair to spring up from the back of my head, nodding and grinning at the congregation. I was tempted to tear it out in tufts and handfuls, furious that the one thing which I had hoped would be perfect turned out to betray me. That laughing cowlick! That uninvited idiot! That ugliness—

In the minute while I stood hesitating and Pastor Schoepf's expression grew more and more desperate, my competitive classmate started to answer in a low hiss: "I-believe-that-Jesus-Christ-true—"

And a marvelous thing occurred.

I thought, *I can do this myself,* and straightway, at the top of my lungs, I began to bellow: "NO, NOT YOU, GERALD—*I* BELIEVE THAT JESUS CHRIST, TRUE GOD—"

Such a rush of holy energy blew through me that I *loved* the thing I was saying. I was not reciting. I *meant* it. I meant it with so complete a joy that I forgot about my cowlick.

"—JESUS CHRIST, TRUE GOD, BEGOTTEN OF THE FATHER FROM ETERNITY—"

Oh, I boomed the affirmation. I shouted sweetly oblivious of anyone else's opinion or judgment. I had broken *through!*

"—AND ALSO TRUE MAN, BORN OF THE VIRGIN MARY—"

While I roared forth the words of my own stout heart, I truly forgot about my father and his reputation, my aunt and her gift, the pastor and my classmates and anyone else whom I was supposed to represent except God, except my God. Was my mother proud of me?

O let her be proud forever of this (for by this I rose on my own strong legs and took my stance among the saints), that I turned to the church and shouted with baby abandon:

"THAT JESUS IS MY LORD!"

CRY

NOT LONG AGO I saw a small girl squatting by a rack of coloring books in the narrow aisle of a grocery store. Altogether absorbed, she touched a tiny forefinger to the staring paper eye of Raggedy Ann.

The kid and the picture: each was lost in the eyes of the other, until I approached them pushing a cart whose right front wheel flapped ridiculously. The sound awoke the child, who glanced up toward me.

At first her face was composed with gladness, ready to chat. I think she thought I was her mother coming.

But then her eyes widened. She peered left and right, starting to stand up and murmuring, "Mommy? Mommy?"

There was no one else at all in the aisle.

When she stood, I saw that the hem of the girl's skirt had gotten caught in the band of her underpants. That small lapse and my complete inability to do anything about it (though this mustachioed man is himself a parent and would have unmussed his own daughter easily) caused in me a sharp sense our alienation, one from the other.

I *felt* the panic in the poor child's eyes, the slackening of her lips. Raggedy Ann hit the floor. Gaping at me, the girl gulped air and shrieked at the top of her lungs: "MOMMY! MOMMY, WHERE ARE YOU?"

Little girl abandoned. That fear, when we are suffering it, overwhelms every other consideration. Neatness, social graces, how we are seen or how we *seem*, reputation, physical hunger, nakedness, even, and dangers—these all are diminished by the greater dismay of our personal abandonment, complete alienation. This may be, in fact, the central horror of dying, that we shall be left all alone in the universe.

We all suffer this fear; but children are the quicker to express it. Children are shameless, screaming, *Don't leave me! Come with me! I might never find my way home again!*

Actually, her mother was only an aisle away, right here, but out of sight. At her baby's shrieking she came running, grinning apologies, embarrassed by the outburst and her public association to it. She kept nodding and smiling at me as if I were standing in judgment on her parenting.

The girl, on the other hand, straightway drove her face into her mother's stomach and boo-hooed sobs of immense relief. No, *she* was not embarrassed. She knew and she would pursue her priorities until comfort had come and she was content again.

As for myself, I left the episode still bearing her fear in my bosom. The feeling is altogether too familiar. As a child I suffered terrible bouts of homesickness. I bore the pain of abandonment within me as if it were a bowl filled with water: too swift a motion, too sudden an emotion, and the water would slop out, and I would find myself weeping, helpless to stop the flow of my tears. So I learned to walk with fierce restraint and a perpetual circumspection. I would keep all things balanced within me. I would maintain a sober expression always, whatever befell. I would not cry.

What I learned young, I have practiced for much of my adulthood. I am controlled. I will not be put to shame. If I showed such fear as openly as the child does, why, I would burn with humiliation, compounding the primary terror with this secondary loss of face. Therefore I tuck loneliness behind a measured sobriety, wherever I go.

I am not afraid. I am strong.

I—

While I was a student at Concordia, an all-male boarding school which prepared youth for the Lutheran ministry (while I was, I mean to say, at a middle point between childhood and early adulthood) my mother once drove me back to school at the end of a summer's break.

It was just the two of us alone in the car. For most of the trip she said nothing. Neither did I, sometimes pretending to sleep, most times just staring out the window and suffering the initial twists of homesickness deep in my abdomen.

That same morning Mom had completed laundering my clothes. For much of the morning, in fact, she had helped me finish my packing—and all had been done in a terrible rush, because I had awoken unprepared. *(I did not want to go.)* But Mom wanted to drive both to the school and back again in a single day. She had planned for an early departure—until she saw her son's great unreadiness.

While we worked, then, and while she watched time tick away, my mother had grown more and more angry with me. She stood in slippers at the ironing board in her bedroom, slapping the hot metal to my shirts, pinching her lips, and with a stentorian silence— with the coldness alone—scolding me every time I brought another shirt for ironing.

I was miserable at our departure.

And long before we arrived at school, then, solitude embraced me like ropes around my chest, crushing the talk within me. Homesickness, as I am now convinced, is related to the fear of abandonment, that primal fear, the infant fear perpetual. If I didn't talk to my mother during the car ride to Concordia, it wasn't because I chose not to talk. It was neither pouting or punishment on my part. I did not talk because I *could* not talk. And if I had tried, I would have cried.

But I am strong. . . .

Then, just as we entered the city, my mother spouted forth an unbroken run of language. Intense, frenetic, gazing hard at the streets ahead, she questioned me regarding common things: type-writers, sheets, my courses, church, food, exercise, underwear, when was I coming home again.

We parked in front of my dormitory, and still she talked. We carried my stuff up to the second floor. Classmates also arriving greeted us with a wave or a word, but Mom persisted, oblivious: she'd make my bed for me this once, she'd show me how to arrange my clothes in the closet, she wanted to know if the dining hall published menus in advance.

And then, when all was unpacked, and the car was empty again, and we stood outside the dorm on the sidewalk awaiting the moment of her return, my mother fell silent again.

We stared down at the ground. At our feet. At the black soil on either side of the cement walk, where a green haze of newly sown grass seemed to float above the dirt. Here and there sprouts of sturdy dandelion had taken root and flourished among the baby grasses.

It must have been a full five minutes that we stood staring downward, saying nothing. I couldn't break the silence. What would I say? I didn't know my mother's thoughts. What if I said the wrong thing?

All at once Mom moved. She stepped onto the soft soil and dropped to her knees and began to yank the dandelions out, one by one.

"How *could* they?" she wailed.

Her gestures were choppy with outrage. She crawled forward, her skirt hiking up her calves, and tossed dandelions into an angry pile.

"How could they," she wailed, "let the lawn go to weed like this? Disgraceful!"

Ah, Mother! You suffered the same as I did, no matter your age! You knew too the wretched desolation of abandonment....

It wasn't the weeds, of course, that hectored her so terribly. It was the mess of human existence. It was separation, initiated by our own human moods, perhaps, but experienced like the abandonment of God, which is called Hell.

And what prolongs the separation? What keeps us homesick, yea, though we are standing side by side and thinking the self-same thoughts? Why, pride. And that, too, is a purely human attribute.

Well, no. Let's be absolutely clear: pride is the attribute of the human *adult*. Very few children know such restraints upon the full expression of their feelings.

Sad, the child will cry. Afraid, the child will scream. Abandoned, the little girl shrieks unto high heaven, and any parent in between will hear her, and come, and comfort her. For this, too, is a human attribute: to comfort those we love.

Oh, I wish we had been children, my mother and I, able to cry and to hug and to heal the dying between us.

Or what shall any of us do when we confront the Last Abandonment?

At that extremest of confrontations, surely, and in all the time between then and now, it is no shameful thing to cry. To plead aloud with those beloved:

Please.

It terrifies me when you walk away.

Let us—please—repent and make a home together again.

A Preface to "Kinder- und Hausmärchen"

The following sonnet sequence constitutes a genuine investigation into the shared sufferings of mother and son.

This is the nature of poetry: I did not write this material as a remembrance or a record of some separate activity, mental, emotional or spiritual. In fact, the creative process was ITSELF the investigation of my past—to probe, to understand it, and by poetry's formal principles to give form to experiences which otherwise had been too disturbing for either a shape or a name. At the same time (like crossing the waters stone by stone) I moved from poem to poem into the future, reaching toward a genuine reconciliation of the conflict and the sorrows caused by those past experiences. To name them is to know them; to know them is to gain some power over them, and thereby to creep beyond their control toward healing and the hope of renewal.

And this too is the nature of poetry: it can take the poet by storm. I had not planned these sonnets the way I plan a novel, researching it first, sketching outlines, preparing myself to execute the piece. Rather, the first poem appeared of its own accord and demanded me, my full attention and my following.

In those days, at my publisher's request, I was putting together a manuscript of poems already written, revising some, arranging them all for publication as a book. The second part of this manuscript was entitled "My People" and contained pieces written for and about the members of my families. I intended to include an acrostic sonnet dedicated to my father (see the poem at the end of this preface), and suddenly felt an imbalance. There was no comparable piece dedicated to my mother. One spring morning, therefore, just as Thanne was leaving for work, I told her that I would write Mom's poem that day.

When she came home, Thanne found me gaunt and tearful. The poem to my father is a gentle conceit, more mental than emotion, an affectionate game. I had thought to do something like that for my mother. But by its third line I realized that her poem was refusing to be tame. It would, by God, utter truths that never had been uttered before. It would name a cruelty, and it would cry out that name in anger and grief. And so it did.

And so when Thanne came home she found me frightened by my own feelings. Something had been released to prowl around, roaring without restraint or conclusion. We both recognized, then, that this single poem started a process it could not end. The accusations in it left me sodden with guilt—some of it inappropriate, some of it perfectly appropriate.

I said to Thanne, "I have to write another." Just one more, so I thought then. It behooved me, having given voice to my own experience, now to write myself into my mother's experience with equal candor and force.

On the following day, alone in my study I wrote a second poem. But neither did this one complete the process.

This poem only sought my mother's personal point of view, and only as she was an adult, the woman I'd known since infancy. Sought her point of view, I stress, because it did not wholly find it. Nevertheless, the last two lines presented themselves so suddenly and so spontaneously, that a surface seemed to crack, and I met my mother's anguish face-to-face.

This second poem/stepping stone, then—though mostly intellectual— had become necessary by bearing me forward (and backward) into my mother's formative experiences. By pure imagination I moved into the third poem and its discovery, which was the terrible similarity of our experiences, my mother's and mine. In the boil of that poem, too, an astonishing new kinship sprang up between us—yes, though I was entoiled in the drama altogether alone in my study. It is the nature of poetry truly to reveal what had not been known before, and so the world is altered slightly; and it is the nature of the poetic imagination in truth to dialogue with persons not bodily present. Afterward that truth remains, even though the absent one has yet to learn it—for it has become eminently learnable.

The truth of the kinship established in the third poem now gave me the right to repeat my initial accusation, this time under the dear hope that it might be received and understood. Thus, the fourth poem.

Next, in consequence of the third and the fourth, the fifth poem took me backward to find in our common troublous experiences (to find this for the first time, for the first time in my life to name it and know it) a sacred, abiding goodness in spite of all: that the child had contrived to love his mother in, with, and under the conflicts between us. Or that love itself had found a way even through the maze.

And upon THAT recognition, I had marked a concluding change in me. Through poetry I had evolved enough to make a further declaration of love, even in the midst of a living story still unresolved: the sixth piece was the last, had every right to be the last of this episode, this sequence. Thunne agreed. My hollow anguish had been somewhat filled with a healthier food. A personal hope, if not yet a paired reconciliation.

Altogether, the first draft of this sequence took me about a week to write.

SOME NOTES: This little cycle of poems uses the world of Grimms' collected tales as a contextual metaphor through all six sonnets. There is an old-world German flavor throughout, especially established in the first poem:

—Ungesammelt *refers to the subtitle of Jakob and Wilhelm Grimms' book of stories: they were* gesammelt, *that is, "collected, gathered together." The main title was "Kinder- und Hausmärchen," that is, "Children and Hearth Stories."*

—Recchelees *is a Middle English word for "reckless, heedless, negligent—careless, lacking care."*

—Dodgson *is Charles Dodgson, who wrote* Alice in Wonderland *under the pen name Lewis Carroll.*

—The Mother Hölle *in poem v also entitles her own tale among the Grimms' collection.* Hässliches *means "hateful."*

—Poem vi is based on the Grimm tale, "Jorinda and Joringel." *In the German version, the unarticulated sound is not "jug," but "zickut."*

Here is the poem written to my father, which triggered the formal outpouring to my mother:

Father, See Me Seeing You

W hen have we seen our changings in a glass?
A rrest me in your mirroring eye, and I will
L oose my habilimental privacy
T ruly to smile at you; smile back at me.
E ncounter my laughter; laugh back . . . remarkable!
R emark it: me, you, is, to be, and was!

W hen has anyone seen new wrinkles screw
A round his face, or watched age grace him, till
N ow? And mere reflected smiles are spectral, thin;
G lassy smiles fade as soon as guilt or sin
E rase the smile progenitor. But MY guilt,
R eflected in MY progenitor—in you—
I s atoned, and lo! One smile remains.
N o, two: but two's one in the glass of our singular names.

Kinder- und Hausmärchen

i.

My mother's tongue was wooden, straight, a broom
Projecting from her mouth, her hair the brambles.
She cleaned house like the north wind, cold, white, grim—
Jakob! Wilhelm! You found her *ungesammelt*
In God knows what thatched *Bauern* cottages:
What did it serve, putting her back together?
Philology? *Recchelees* sciences!

My Mother's tongue was wooden. Write that after
You've written how she licked my skin the way
The medieval bear licked cubs to shape.

My mother's mouth was wooden. Dodgson may
Have met her peppered, yes; but he escaped
To *clepe* her "Duchess." I (my mother's face
Was Teuton) lived the tale as commonplace.

ii.

Blame, so we blame her—but who thinks the tale
Which tells his childhood governed, too, his mother?
What could she choose to do?

    If she were frail
The work would kill her: *Storm, then, through another
Summer!*

    If she were passionate, they'd damn
Her for a gypsy; passion, though, was proper
For rearing proper, upright children: *One
Became the other.*

    If she wept at color,
Words, dusk, the lark, or thought, they'd cluck and sing
Of Bedlam; if she laughed too longingly
Or loose, her uterus was wandering—
So rage found reason in her progeny.

    Peter, Peter! You made that woman wild
    You kept inside the pumpkin of your child.

iii.

I remember your cellar, now. Do you?—
Clean concrete tubs, a glass-ribbed scrubbing board,
And a smell—(Grandma had dry buttocks, bald
Armpits, leather intestines, a mouth that chewed
Blasphemies silently, although the Lord
God still issued commandments she still heard,
Adding them chunk by chunk to the coal pile,
Stirring a Sinaitic dust)—the smell
Grandma wore was the odor in your cel-
Lar, remember? It was the house you grew
Up in. So here's my question: had you, too,
For lies, to bite Fels Naphtha soap, and chew?

    Mother, Mother—Gretel! We had one mother
    After all. I'm Hansel! I am your brother.

iv.

Yes, there were giants in those days and in
Our world. Yes, they despised you. And Yes, they'd
Kill you if they could. But you couldn't slay
Them, so it was a standoff, stick for sin.

Giants: Sweet Acid Gossip, gross as air;
You smelled your name in breezes like scorched hair;
Outdoors you grew fearful, but indoors you
Grew furious, fumbling for what to do.

Giants: those women all were members of
One body, like a ball of bees, a fist
Of snakes, or Jesus. To assault or to love
Them singly killed no more than cut a mist.

Giants! So you sent me forth, full of rage—
Your rage, though it felt like mine; full of rage—
For them, though it felt like me; full of rage,
Like a knot stick thrust down my throat, a rage

To beat your giants with: *Stick, beat! Stick, beat!*
The stick said, *whom?* But I (a child) said, "Me."

v.

Mother Hölle, do you know how much I loved you?
Under the well and in its meadows—do you know?
It was I who shook down red ripe apples when they begged me,
I who shook your feather ticking, making snow.

Under the well, in sunken meadows, in the cottage
Where you dwelt dreamly, Mother, I obeyed you well.
In the glare light of common day we were another
Pair, *hässliches,* perhaps—but my yearning cast such spells!

I rose from the well wet with gold (all this is true)
And I, flushed with obedience and its reward,
Came home: *"Unser goldener Junge is wieder hie!"*
You rushed to me, you lady longing rich young lords. . . .
Never (I breathed submerged, I breathed through large eyes,
        through
Wish within that well) *never* did I not love you!

vi.

And now I search the bloodred rose
Whose center cups one pearl (a dew
Drop, beautiful and trembling) whose
Charm is the *Schamir*, to undo

The doors, to set the captives free.
I dreamed you were a nightingale.
Zickūt was all you croaked for me.
A wire cage kept you, and travail—

I dreamed the bloodred rose, its touch
Alone, would spring that cage and hush
Your grief and shift your shape, all three.

The bloodred rose, too, grows encaged.
Bones are its bares—but I will break
My breast to break you, Mother, free.

THE PASTOR OF CHILDREN AND PARENTS TOGETHER

Give us, O Lord, clean eyes, uncomplicated hearts, and guileless tongues.

Make us like children again!

Here is an irony: when we are still children, we might be the best that we're ever to be—yet we yearn to throw off childhood. We rush to teenagerhood, a worser state in every way, all the while thinking we're getting better.

Let me explain. . . .

When we are children we're likelier to be kinder because we are small in an overwhelming world, and smallness keeps us humble. We identify with them the world considers inferior, helping the helpless and the infirm.

But children wish they weren't children. Smallness is itself a bafflement, a vulnerability. Children rush, therefore, toward the biggerness and the blunt authority of their betters, the teenagers.

Again. . . .

When we are little children we're likelier to be honest. That doesn't mean we're likelier to be *right;* but the honesty alone—our inability to say anything except what we ourselves see of the world—is wondrously effective and refreshing. "But the king has no clothes on!" cries the kid, an observation both honest and right and therefore revolutionary in a kingdom where politics means sucking up and where favors are earned by flattery.

Ah, but that same kid wishes he were older. Soon enough, then, he learns to dissemble, and soon he is buttering his peers, if not his elders—and then he's a teenager surely.

And again. . . .

When we are wide-eyed children the world is filled with things both visible and invisible, things material and immaterial. We make no distinction between the two. There are ghosts. There is also God. These are as real as the walls of our bedrooms and the mouths of our mothers. And that which is real we honor by obeying, by accommodating its presence in our lives and our behaviors. We fear the ghosts. We pray to God.

And we ourselves are spiritual beings too, therefore: small bright bundles of body-and-soul. There is a glory around our heads of which we're unaware but which renders us radiantly lovely since those who see angels do shine as well an ethereal light.

But children are soon ashamed to be children. They're dazzled, rather, by the cold (and self-protective) cynicism of punk teenagers for whom nothing is honorable, by whom nothing need be obeyed (or else one loses one's rep, one's rap, and one's glory). The world of the teen seeks matter and sensation, sound and color and clothes and spasmodic satisfactions—and everything spiritual proves to have been a conspiracy of elders to keep their children on chains.

So we rush to throw off the best we might ever be and to put on instead the dead-slouch, know-it-all, hard-as-steel, lank-lipped sneer of the cynic.

So we are children no longer. This wish is always granted slower than we would and sooner that it should—but this wish is always granted.

Yet, when we were children we laughed without embarrassment. We hooted and giggled and roared till our sides cracked and our cheek muscles ached. The unselfconscious laughter rang very true, like bells in a blue sky, and therefore taught our elders themselves how to laugh again.

When we were children we could gasp with delight at a sudden, beautiful thing, yearning to touch it. We didn't worry whether our notions of beauty were naive. We didn't pretend sophistication. We were not proud; therefore, we could not be humiliated. But our unsullied joy was itself like leadership to all God's creatures, a call to be at peace together.

When we were children our loving was given immediate expression. We *said* it. We *showed* it. We would throw our arms around beloved people and kiss them and purr to be kissed in return. No one had to guess whether we loved. Nor did love seem either a weakness that must be hidden or else a physical desire that must be gratified. Love made us happy. We liked to be happy. And so we were leaders even of whole countries into the image and the command of God—Who *is* Love.

When we were children we accepted forgiveness completely. It truly did—when it was truly given—ease us and allow us to begin again, *anōthen,* as new as one just come down from heaven. We could bounce back from the most grievous sins so quickly that adults wondered whether we had truly repented. Oh, we had repented. Children can move to sorrow instantly and instantly to gladness again, yet feel both moods profoundly. This is the emotional nimbleness of those who have not yet sickened their feelings with self-analysis nor thickened their motives with ambition.

Those who fly swiftly to delight, who fear not to express their love, who believe completely in forgiveness—well, they are fearless. And so it is that the sucking child plays blithely on the hole of the asp, and the weaned one scares her elders by putting her hands on the adder's den.

But then—children don't want to be children.

They want to grow hair in smooth places, immediately to cut it off again.

They want to smear outrageous colors on places God had painted pink and to punch holes in places God had made smooth. This is called "style."

They pretend to love the things they don't and feign indifference for things they love unspeakably. This is called "fashion."

Because their peers do, they walk in streets instead of on sidewalks; they wear jeans beaten old before the purchase; they do not lace their tennis shoes; they congregate on corners like lemmings going nowhere, doing nothing. This is called "doing my own thing."

They laugh when it isn't funny and do not laugh when it is. This is called "cool."

When they don't feel something, they act as if they do, and they exaggerate the act for fear that someone may notice it's only an act. They fear to be different from peers. When, however, they feel an emotion deeply (whether rejoicing or love or repentance) they mask the mood and gaze wanly into the distance.

They are not what they are; and what they are they strive to hide. This is called "teenager." It is considered an advance over childhood. It's the rush from innocence into society. It's a determined dispersal of the clouds of glory which we trailed when first we came from God.

It is a pity.

"Give us clean eyes, uncomplicated hearts, and guileless tongues, O Lord!"

That, immediately, was my prayer when I found among my letters the following, unselfconscious "summery" by Erica Ulrey. Her grandmother had read to the child a book of mine. The book was about Jesus. Then Erica took pen and printed on paper and mailed to me these words:

SUMMERY JESUS STORY

Well it all started out when an angle came to mary and told her that she was going to have a baby, it would be a boy, a boy name jesu. He would be the son of the Lord. They traveled to drusilem. They knocked on inkerp's door but know one had room. So they went to a stable. She had the baby. Jesus grew older when he was 20 or 30. He went and told stories. He got bapties because he wanted to have sins. He told Peater that his enimes would kill him. Jesus arived in drusilem on a donkey. Children were waving palm limes. Jesus went in two the Temple and open the cages of animals tiping taples. His enimes came and hung him up on a cross. After three day's his desiples came to his grave, and angle stood in front of his grave. He was not in the grave. They found Jesus. They thought he was a gost but he had the holes in his hands. Then one day Jesus said I will be up in hevan. The End.

O sisters and brothers (so often so teenish in spite of our years, because we desire the approval of peers) if we would turn and become like little Erica, then such fearless and faithful contemplations of the gravest mysteries need never end for us as well.

No, not ever: for it is as little children that we shall enter the kingdom of heaven.

I LOVE THEE, BABY B

BRANDON MICHAEL PIPER. What a sober name for a two-year-old! It sounds senatorial. It seems an executive's name.

But you bear the big name well, my little godson. You've a stalwart constitution and a sweetness of spirit that softens me when I hold you. No, the name is not too large; rather, you make the name foursquare and strong.

Dear Brandon:

Perhaps you won't remember in the years to come (but I will always remember) that I am the one who holds you these Sunday mornings during Bible class. Your mother and your father both have duties; but I have two arms free and a large heart, and I am your godfather, and I love you.

You cling to me, child. Stump-arms soft on pliable bone, you grip my neck. You lock your legs around my body. I couch your butt on my forearm and press you to my chest and feel the deep warmth of your trusting infancy. Oh, Brandon! You hallow me with such trust! You make me noble and kind.

They call you "B," don't they? "Baby B." A lighter, lesser name than the one you'll carry into adulthood but one conferred by affections. I remember when I was trying to distract you in Bible class and happened to draw that letter. You read it. You astonished me by the recognition. "Beeeee," you murmured with wonder, gazing at yourself. Then, "Ef," you said when I made an *F*. And "Ay" and "Eeeee."

This kid's a prodigy, reading at two! This kid is my godson.

Perhaps in the years to come you will also forget that your baby bones were not always stalwart or so strong. You limped. No complaint. You seemed to take this particular development for granted.

But you began to favor one leg over the other, and walking became a difficulty.

In fact, it was on a Sunday morning that I first became aware of trouble. Your leg came too close to my coffee cup; I shifted it, and you whispered, "Ow," so fleetingly—but then without a sound you started to cry. You gazed at me with a sort of pleading through the tears that shined in your Brandon eyes, and I saw again that astonishing trust. You trusted your godfather somehow to help. Oh, Baby B, how could I? I didn't know what hurt you. Too deep. The trouble was hidden too deeply in your tiny body.

But your parents were ahead of me. They had already planned to take you to the doctor.

And this is a thing I hope you will forget completely: the X-rays revealed a growth high in your leg, near the hip, against the thighbone.

Your mother and father listened as the doctor enumerated the possible problems, from a cyst to a malignancy. Then he explained which procedures he would advise. But his language was indirect and faintly patronizing. He described "windows" into your leg—until your mother fixed him with a baleful eye and said, "If you don't want a hysterical mother here, you'd better speak clearly to me." The doctor blinked and began in a more respectful tone to use the word "biopsy."

You have bold parents, B. They are patient and faithful. Their patience may—as with silly physicians and sillier children—come sometimes to an end. But never their faith.

They said to the doctor, "Yes, schedule a biopsy. Schedule a biopsy. But we, in the meantime—we will pray for our son."

We all prayed for you, then, Brandon Michael Piper. You won't remember. But the aunts and the uncles, your parents and grandparents and godparents and the whole congregation of Grace commended to heaven both your big name and your little leg.

Someone worried about the intensity of your parents' praying. He said, "But what if the boy's too sick? What if he doesn't get well? Doesn't it scare you that you might lose your faith if God doesn't answer the prayer?"

But your parents said, "We will pray for our son."

You see, Brandon, this was their faith: not that they felt God had to heal you on account of prayer, but rather that they wanted never to stand apart from God, especially not now. Yes, they were scared for you. But they were never, never scared of God, nor ever scared to lose God. They took their Baby B to the steadfast arms of the Father so that *whatever* happened, the love of God would hold it. Might there be a healing? Then give glory to God. Must there be a worse hurt? Then let the dear Lord strengthen everyone when strength would be most needed.

Their prayer was meant neither as a demand nor as magic, neither an ultimatum nor manipulation of the Deity. It was love. It was their highest expression of faith—not faith in your healing, Brandon (though they yearned that) but faith in God.

This is an important distinction which, in the future, you must remember. Your parents' faith did not depend upon God's "correct" answer to their prayer. Instead, the reality of their prayer depended upon their faith. With prayer they encircled you as tightly as you do hug my neck on Sunday mornings—and behold: that circle of faith was the arm of the Almighty.

And then there came the night when you could not sleep because of the pain. You cried, not silently this time. You broke your mama's heart. So that was when the patience of your parents (but not their faith!) came to an end. They bundled you to the hospital, and the biopsy which had been scheduled too many weeks in the future was immediately rescheduled.

Dear Brandon, whatever else you forget in the future, remember this: God loves you.

I was there, my godson, when they signed the love of God upon you—as if God himself wrote his name across your forehead, saying *I own this one; this one is mine.* I was there when they gave you *your* sober, senatorial name, and it became the name of you forever. I was there when they washed you thrice with a purging water, and

I with my own ears heard them say, "Brandon Michael Piper, I baptize you in the name of the Father, and of the Son, and of the Holy Spirit." That's how I became your godfather. That's how the mighty God became your own most holy Father, your final Father after all. That's how the magnificent name of *Brandon Michael* got written into the Book of Life. And that, child, was a healing for any hurt which you shall ever encounter, because it has overcome death itself.

Of course your parents would not lose faith if you weren't healed of this particular problem in your thighbone. They might be very sad for you, but they would not despair—because your baptism had already declared the rising of all your bones in the end.

Whatever else you do in the future, Brandon, hold to the God that now holds you. Pray always as your parents prayed for you. Cling to the body of Jesus more tightly than you do to mine on Sunday mornings. And the God who signed you will love you infinitely, finer, and longer than ever I could—

As it happened, the biopsy proved the growth benign. It shall be removed, together with all memory of a falling limp and the nighttime pain.

And I will continue, Brandon Michael Piper, a little longer to let you sleep on my shoulder in church. But you will grow. You'll pull back from such dependencies upon earthly fathers, godfathers first, flesh fathers second. Even then I will pray for you, my godson, my Baby B.

And this shall be my prayer: that you never pull back from the God who, since your baptism, is your Father forever.

AN INSTRUCTION:
THE DIFFERENCE BETWEEN PUNISHMENT AND DISCIPLINE

SHOULD THE PARENT PUNISH or discipline the child?

Prisons punish. By most accounts, that's all they can do. Some parents punish too, but that's not all *we* can do, nor is it what we're charged by God to do. Nor is it healthy.

Rather, it was for discipline that we were set above the children and the children under us.

Punishment administers pain for pain and hurt for hurt. If it is meted in an ethical manner, it makes the pain the criminal gets equal the pain he gave. It balances the social books of righteousness. And if it loves anything, it loves the law. Or vengeance. Or, at its best, society as a whole. But it does not love the criminal. Simply, he is made to pay *post factum* the debt his crime incurred; and the social order is, by an eye and an eye, a tooth and a tooth, preserved. Society receives the benefit. Except that he will be restrained hereafter, the criminal is scarcely affected or changed: correctional facilities do precious little correcting.

On a level more rude, punishment is merely the expression of someone's discontent, irritation, anger—and then nothing is loved so much as that one's thwarted desires and his own power to say so. Again, nothing changes.

But discipline loves the criminal.

And though discipline also gives pain, unlike punishment it seeks to change the child at the core of his being.

Note, please: the benefit of punishment is for the person or the system administering punishment; but the benefit of discipline is for the one who is *being* disciplined. It is, says the writer to the Hebrews, "for his good, that he may share in holiness." A supernatural benefit!

Moreover, it is a gift of the discipliner to the disciplined, both of whom will suffer the pain of the process: "For the moment all discipline seems painful rather than pleasant; later it yields the peaceful fruit of righteousness to those who have been trained by it." But if a parent says that the pain is "for your own good, you little———," and punishes to relieve himself—for anger's sake or for vengeance or because he's lost control, but in no wise to plant in his child *the peaceful fruit of righteousness*—he lies in his teeth, committing a double treachery and multiple sins in a single swat.

Does the parent seek tears? It is punishment. Does the parent grow frustrated when there are no tears? When there is no sign of pain? It is punishment.

And punishment is not the charge God gave the parents.

Another difference: discipline is an extended and carefully managed event, not a sudden, spontaneous, personal reaction to the child's behavior.

I sat with a mother in her kitchen, visiting. Her daughter toddled in, whining, and yanked the woman's skirt.

"Don't. We're talking," said her mother. She gave the kid a cookie and continued to talk.

But the cookie lasted only a little while. When it was eaten, the child was back, whining again and yanking her mother's skirt.

"I said don't!" She nudged the kid and kept talking.

A third yank earned a vague wave of the hand.

The fourth yank earned a swat on the butt.

And when the child began truly to cry, the mother in exasperation stood up, hoisted the girl, and hauled her from the room. "When will she ever learn?" she said. She punished the kid by dumping her in her crib and closing the bedroom door.

"Punished," I say, because this was in no way a careful event for the child's sake, in love with the child. It was altogether for the parent's desire, peace, and ease.

An event . . .

Let Jesus teach us.

Even as he disciplined Simon Peter, so may we discipline our children—seeking, as he did Peter's, the children's righteousness that they might share in holiness.

The end of such a process is that they know the love of God and their place within it.

It has three steps and a peaceful response to the child's sin. She is of our flesh and we are sinners. She is not different from us. Therefore—

1. Anticipate the sin

Right clearly and with sufficient sadness to indicate the wrong, Jesus said, "You will deny me, even before the rooster crows the morning in." He didn't argue it. He said it. He prepared Peter to recognize the sin when it would occur—for he couldn't change Peter's soul if the sin had never surfaced, nor could he change Peter's mind if the disciple didn't see and acknowledge the sin when it did.

It must be the same for the parents. Choose a few significant rules to be kept in your household (not countless numbers, stirred up by your own continual frustration in the face of having kids around). Choose rules that touch upon the child's deepest righteousness. Consider the two most elemental commandments: loving God, loving others. Let your rules define *this* behavior in the child.

Declare them clearly. Post them if necessary so that the child surely is aware of them. There is no need to argue them. They are not here to restrain the child right now (for our own peace) but for training her when she breaks the rule.

She will break the rule.

That, in fact, is the point. It's her nature. It's the "Adam," the "Eve" you seek to change by discipline. If you anticipate the transgression as much in your emotions (peacefully), as in your planning (this is just step 1), you won't explode at the sin ("You rotten kid! Oh, where did I go wrong?"). Rather, you will be glad that her sinful nature surfaced and gave you the opportunity to teach and revise it. Also, you won't act in anger (punishment) but will in cool love discharge the duty God gave you as a parent.

2. In the very instant of the sin, shine a light on it

Call it wrong and painful to others and self-destructive.

Peter did, of course, deny the Lord exactly as the Lord had said, exactly as the Lord expected. In that instant two things happened: the cock crowed to remind Peter of Jesus' prediction, to apply the name of the sin which Jesus had given it earlier, to persuade Peter that Jesus was, in fact, superior. Peter could not *not* see himself as Jesus had seen him now. He had not kept his promise: "If I must die with you, I will not deny you." Jesus was right (so Peter knows by the predicted rooster crow) and Peter was wrong.

Moreover, in the moment of his denial, Jesus "turned and looked at him." The sin was not antiseptic. It was very personal. It hurt someone whom Peter loved. And Peter must see that in Jesus' wounded eyes. This is *shining a light* on the sin. This is, in the same gesture, shining a light on the sinner. Peter saw himself more clearly now than he had when he boasted.

He went out and wept bitterly.

The pain he caused in someone else is the pain he felt in himself (this is what guilt—a good thing!—accomplishes), so for Peter sin was no longer an abstract concept, but an act both real and dangerous and his own. His personal pain communicates better than any argument, any rational discourse. Such awareness comes in experience.

Let it be the same for the parents. When your child breaks the rule, immediately communicate the wrongness of the act and its painful consequences and the child's responsibility for it. In terms she can understand, define it for her. Speak to both her mind and her soul that she and you—the both of you—have been wounded.

In a special place of the house (rooms define our actions) by a repeated and recognized ritual (for she shall not sin once, but often) name the rule again and mark the details of her breaking it (as Jesus used the rooster to remind Peter of what he'd said in the past). *Do you remember, child? This is the rule. And this is what you did. Do you remember both, child?* So and so: the sin as a sin becomes real unto her in the conversation of your relationship.

Do none of this in anger. Be sad. You love her. You can survive as you are, but she must change for her survival. You have been hurt. Now the hurt must communicate itself to her. For finally it is not your hurt but the child's of which she must be persuaded. Therefore, (ah, me!) let pain define both the general effect of sin and the kid's responsibility—and the ultimate personal suffering of that effect (for destruction circles back, in the end, upon the destroyer). What she feels will speak to her more than rational discourse: you may (though many may not) choose a careful spanking.

"Careful." Act *after* you've named the sin and reminded the child of its consequence—not immediately or passionately.

"Careful." Adhere to the consequence prescribed for any infraction. If it's two weeks' grounding, keep to two weeks, no more, no less. If it's five swats, then let it be five swats, no more for anger, no less for tenderness.

"Careful." Any spanking must hurt the parent equally to the child. A flat hand on a covered butt. Flesh absolutely must feel flesh. I mean that no instrument can come between to increase one's pain and decrease the other's. And there can be no true wound. It is the tactile communication the parent seeks, not punishment. Not punishment. No, not punishment.

And this parent will recognize her love in her own pain. If there is no parental pain, there must be no such discipline. Choose something else!

3. Heal the hurt

This must follow or else what you have done is merely punishment. Please read John 21:15–19.

After the sin Jesus took time and patience to repair the relationship between himself and Peter. More than that, he called Peter to greater faithfulness and mightier action, proving his trust both in the strength of his (Jesus') forgiveness to change the man and in the reality of his (Peter's) change. Thrice Peter had denied the Lord; thrice, therefore, did the Lord ask him to declare his love (and by the third declaration Peter clearly saw the effect of his sin, because he was grieved—reminded and grieved); and thrice Jesus showed confidence in Peter's ministry thereafter, in Peter's worth, in Peter:

"Feed my lambs. Tend my sheep. Feed my sheep." *All is well,* the Lord Jesus said by repeating then the words with which he had called Peter in the first place: "Follow me."

All is well.

Once again let it be the same for the parents. There are three necessary gestures at this point, all modeled upon Jesus' gentle ministrations.

When the child's tears subside, speak again the sin in such a way that your love is proven unchanged; speak again the rule that had been broken; speak again the child's personal responsibility in breaking it—but cast your entire talk in the gentlest of terms: love, love—"Do you love me?" Jesus asked in order to give Peter opportunity to prove that he no longer denies but loves.

The sin is not hidden now or else forgotten; you do want the child to change, to move beyond this iniquity, and so you both must from a new vantage confront it. But love outlives the sin and its consequence.

Next, touch the child. Physically. As physically you communicated her wrong, communicate your love. Touch her now not for pain but for gentleness and in soft caress. The touch communicates. Hold her. Hug her. This is critical for finally changing her. Tell her her worth and your abiding, unchanging affection.

Finally, affirm her worth (and prove your renewed trust in her) by giving her specific responsibilities in the household, as Jesus right easily called Peter back into discipleship: *Feed my sheep.* Make the responsibility real, something which, if she does it well, benefits others—benefits *you!*

If you punish only, the spanking shall have satisfied you and there you cease—abusing your kid. If you discipline, this loving satisfies her need for spiritual growth, for it announces her share in holiness, her newness, and your trust.

Now, love is not flaccid.

Parents are not appointed to be the buddies of their children, seeking their affections and praise, seeking ever and ever to keep the kid happy. Parents, rather, are called to be instruments of God for the children, seeking their holiness.

Love does not neglect to discipline. That's negligence. But neither is love the plain demand for obedience by pain. That's punishment.

If we love our children as the Father loves us, that is parenting indeed.

WE CALLED IT CONFIRMATION CLASS when I was young. (See chapter 7 above.) In the Lutheran Church we call it Confirmation Class still, now that I am old and have myself spent years and years as the Pastor who taught it. Other churches have other means for introducing children and youth to the teachings and the commitments of the Faith: Sunday school, youth groups, Pastor's classes, Baptismal Instructions. But all churches acknowledge the responsibility some-how to communicate our most important Christian truths to the next generations, the sons and daughters of our mothers and fathers. And the question becomes: how do we do it? Do we do it well?

Age to age—generation to generation, in fact—our educational methods have changed. Have we lost effectiveness in the change? Or found a method more effective? Or exchanged one strength for another, different strength? One weakness for another?

Under the methods of the previous generation, I learned sternly. All was conducted with a solemn lawfulness (for these matters *were* grave, weren't they?—consisting of life and death.) So: I conned by heart the meaning of the Lord's Prayer, the meaning of the Apostles' Creed, the Commandments and the Sacraments and the Christian Table of Duties—conned, I mean, word for word Martin Luther's explanation of all these things. There was little joy in the exercise; there was, rather, great anxiety to . . . Get. It. *Right!*

PASTOR: "The Fifth Commandment."

WALLY: "Thou shalt not kill."

PASTOR: "What does this mean?"

WALLY: (Standing erect, his thumbs upon his pant-seams) "We should fear and love God that we may not hurt nor harm our neighbor in his body, but help and befriend him in every bodily need."

Therewith, we memorized biblical proof passages to support these meanings. I have these things by heart even still today.

Indeed, there *was* value in the severity of my training. But a faith without joy is a faith that knows *about* the Savior, but never yet has *met* him or felt his steadfast gaze upon its face.

During the years of my ministry, on the other hand, new methods of education have risen up to ease us all. And joy might now find voice in the instruction—especially since severity is less and less commended in any "extra-curricular" training which depends upon the youth's own willingness to come and learn at all. This generation must not feel (as, cruelly, I did feel) burdened. Therefore, the giddier spirit and the contentments of the youth themselves have shaped the atmosphere of their religious schoolrooms.

And therefore it is with some dismay that I've watched how this tendency to Good Will has replaced the genuine gravity of these matters (which *do,*—don't they?—train the student in the difference between life and death). No longer need they know the Bible with close familiarity; no longer memorize great portions of Holy Scripture, that the words be handy in circumstances yet to come; no longer need they give a good verbal account for the basic, most important tenets of their Faith and Salvation.

Instead, after classes which have spent more time in personal discussion than in significant instruction, entertaining every thought as equally valuable to any other, requiring teachers to devolve into mere facilitators and thereby allowing the students to lead and to shape the substance of the material—after, I say, even energetic and satisfying discussions, comes something like a public examination. And for this spiritual Rite of Passage the students are asked to prepare themselves. Not, mind you, to gird themselves with the accumulated insights and wisdom of the elder generations; but rather to sit down and write, each student, his and her own statement of faith; in her own words; according to his own lights. And *these* statements, then, are offered to the congregation as proofs of . . . of what, really? Not of the youths' advancement beyond themselves and their own callow experience; proofs, rather, of juvenile sincerity as evidenced by a thirteen-year-old's concept of the Deity: how God Almighty and the Lord Jesus Christ—the Judge and Savior of the world—seem when seen through the eyes of teenagers.

But in many Christian traditions, this instruction accompanies the most transfiguring decision a boy or a girl can make: to accept Jesus, to be baptized into his name, to drown the old and to rise anew. Such instructions are the plans for an entire life to come. And baptism is reserved until a child has attained the age of reason precisely *because* a personal understanding of one's choice and of its consequences is considered essential for a true and faithful participation in the act.

In my tradition, too, confirmation is connected to Baptism. And though, in earth-terms, time has elapsed between the act of Baptism and the instruction of the Baptized, in God's time the two events are one: God initiates the sacramental act, and the child finishes it. God acts in Baptism to establish a relationship with the child, and then the child (having attained the age of understanding) of his own will acts to say "Yes!" to the relationship.

In the waters of Baptism, God says, "You are my child!"

Which word the youth personally confirms by answering, "And you are my Lord!"

In all Christian traditions, then, Baptism elevates the purpose and the practice of the training of our youth in the faith. It should never, therefore, be diluted or diminished, never dismissed as of lesser importance than, say, the glad contentment of our teenagers. Likewise, it should never fall upon the youth as a grim and heavy imposition, crushing the love, suffocating the joy in an entire generation—and thereby diminishing the Church itself.

I think there is a middle way. A third way, actually, as old as story and as new as the weekend movie. I commend it to pastors and teachers, to anyone responsible for passing our culture and our covenant to the next generation.

Some History

My own first year in the parish, during which I undertook the Confirmation Class, was a dismal experience. This was a small congregation in the inner city; and though adults had strong hearts for the faith, their children were altogether undisciplined in religious ritual. I could count on no one's regular attendance. Homework simply did not occur. I could make friends with the kids—and did. But I could not of my own authority persuade them that the topic I taught mattered more than basketball or (in those days) Run DMZ or Nintendo.

By the end of the teaching year, I took the hard line, seeking to establish with *everyone* how seriously we must take this learning, and no one was confirmed. I invited them all back for a second year.

During that year two events happened to shape my confirmation classes ever thereafter.

The first was formed of my Pastoral desperation. I decided to teach each student in his or her own home, under the required attentions of the adult who was raising that child. *I* would go to *them*. And I would make the parent/grandparent/older sibling as much my student as the kid, establishing relationships with both and expecting the older to oversee the younger's personal homework.

But in order to set up *that* labor-intensive program, I first went to each home seeking promises! I wanted a contract in hand by which to encourage (or enforce) the commitment when kids or parents lagged in interest or energy.

So I sat with the whole family. According to my plan, we *all* spoke of our individual readiness to embark on confirmation classes. The atmosphere was completely democratic: if any one of the three of us (child, pastor, guardian) felt unready or unable—or if a parent truly thought the child unready—that single veto moved the question of confirmation on to the next year. But if we all three said "Yes!"— why, I had both the promise and individual good will to go.

The fact that I ended up with five students made possible the regular home visitations. But everyone will recognize how inefficient such a scheme must be. I did not in the following year repeat that part of the performance.

On the other hand, I had learned how crucial is this common covenant. And it would *not* be a covenant if it lacked true choice.

It was the seeking and the saving of the three-way covenant that I continued ever thereafter.

The second event happened Easter Sunday morning that year . . .

I'd come to the church in the wee, dark hours of the morning, in order to pace up and down the central aisle, conning my sermon by heart. This was my Sunday habit: preparation for preaching was as much emotional and spiritual as it was intellectual.

After the sun had arisen, about an hour and a half before worship was to begin, children started to arrive. Without their parents. And since our building had only two large rooms (the fellowship hall below and the sanctuary above) the kids chased through them both, heedless. No parents; no Sunday school teachers either. No adult besides myself! I couldn't think. The sermon dying inside me. I was veering toward panic and schemes of bloody assaults. Where were the teachers? Why were these kids here *now?*

I did not know that the children were not here for Sunday school at all. I did not know that the teachers were *not* here because there was no Sunday school planned. I did not know (no one had told me) that the refrigerator downstairs was filled with cartons of colored eggs. Of *course* the kids were antsy: they were looking for a good time and gifts.

All shot out of patience for the want of a sermon, I shouted to the children, "Sit down!"

They froze mid-run and looked at me. *Sit? Why?*

"Sit down," I said, and the next thing popped unbidden out my mouth: "And I'll tell you a story!"

I'll tell you a story. It was the most natural thing for me to say. And it had its natural effect: the kids sat. All ages sat down in the pews, facing me, filled with anticipation, *ready* for a story. (Well, the inner-city does tend more toward oral communication than to written.)

And because no other story was so immediately to hand than this one, I began by saying, "Jesus was eating supper with his disciples, and he was soooo sad."

The littlest faces fell straightway into lines of deep sorrow. They knew sadness, and with my next words, they *felt* sadness: "Because one of his disciples, one of his friends, was going to go out and rat on him. . . ."

For the next forty minutes I told them the story of Jesus' suffering. I watched them closely. I said that the hero was going to die. They did not believe me! Heroes never die! And they were identifying tightly with this hero. They *liked* Jesus.

When, therefore, I described in detail his arms and hands being nailed to a cross-piece of wood; described in detail how they lifted the cross-piece and Jesus' body up to a stout pole and dropped the whole onto a peg there; when I raised my arms to show the great weight that pulled on them, closing Jesus' chest, causing his own body to suffocate his lungs—why, some ten pairs of children's arms were unconsciously up in the air, same as mine. And faces filled with an unspeakable sorrow. Because I said, "He died. He died. Jesus really did die . . ."

A marvelous thing was occurring in that little sanctuary: by story, twenty-five children had been transported straight back to Jerusalem and to Golgatha.

And then the adults started arriving at church, chirping welcomes back and forth, bringing with them a daffodil morning, and smiting the eyes with their bright Easter finery. The adults entered the sanctuary . . . and found their children all gloomy in the pews. Well, he died! No, there was no joy in the hearts of the children at that moment.

Shuffling mostly, the children moved to sit with their families. They did not sing "Jesus Christ Is Risen Today."

And I was very clear about my sermon now. There was no choice. How could I *not*, for my children's peace of mind, finish the story?

"But that's not all," I said directly to the children. And then I said, "Mary Magdalene was crying. . . ."

I spoke of the early Easter events through Mary's eyes. But when that moment comes when Jesus addresses her by name, I looked straight at Larry Thomas and I said, "Jesus said, 'Larry!' And Jesus said, 'Dee Dee,' 'Charlotte,' 'David.'"

And I saw then, and I testify now to, their genuine wonder and transfiguration. Those who had truly experienced the death of their hero now truly rejoiced in his resurrection. It was no self-manufactured emotion; it was the genuine thing! And it was not in response to the holiday, no; it was in response to the living Lord Jesus Christ.

Out of my weakness and the mistakes of the day emerged this simple (and at the same time ancient) conviction: that story telling conveys the realities and the relationships of our faith better than almost any other form of communication we have, for in story the child does more than think and analyze and solve and remember; the child actually *experiences* God through Jesus and through Jesus' ministry. The whole of the child is involved in the faith.

Out of these insights the following program was formed.

1. Covenant

This first step into the confirmation class is essentially the same as I have described above, with a few refinements.

—I encourage the teacher/pastor to meet with the candidate and her family in their own homes, not in a large group at the church. These matters must actually *be* personal from the beginning: eyes looking into eyes, the prayers of the pastor embracing the child by name.

—Yes, begin with prayer. Conduct the meeting with formality. This is not a time for cookies or adult laughter and conversation; nor should the child feel in any way patronized. On *her* account is this gathering gently serious. I encourage, if possible, the presence of her Baptismal sponsors as well, especially to establish the relationship between her Baptism and what is about to be.

—Meet *twice* with the candidate and her family, expecting everyone to be at both meetings, since each will be of equal importance. During the first meeting simply discuss confirmation, its meaning in the candidate's life, its practice, what it requires. All this will be under the question: "Are we ready, the three of us, to begin confirmation this year?" But that question is not to be answered at the first meeting. It is too important for swift responses (even if the parents have already discussed it). The space of time between this meeting and the next will surely persuade everyone of the gravity of the class, and make the covenant more felt and thereby more binding.

At the second meeting, after prayer, the pastor/teacher receives the answer. Honor the "no." Open pathways to the repeat of this discussion next year. And for the "yes," have cookies. *Then* a celebration is in order.

—Sometime early, the child should be invited to pick her own confirmation-sponsor from among members of the congregation, for a continual interaction throughout the next two years.

2. The First Year: Meet God

Yes. Two years, not one. But, by making each year its own good experience, the students do not count this a woeful waste of time.

And this is how that first year is spent: by telling the stories. By weaving them, week after week, together, and *thereby* telling the whole story of faith after all.

Listen: religions have and do exist without doctrines and theologies; but no religion has ever existed without a story at its core, not as an *illustration* of some doctrine, but rather as the very truth, the evidence and the testimony of God's action for the sake of the believers.

But a story that goes untold lacks life. It becomes a puzzle to be solved by intellectual analysis alone. And a religion whose story is untold, likewise, lacks life!

For if we never have, by means of the sacred story (the Gospel!) *experienced* the presence, love, activity of our Christ, then we will fall back upon lesser experience; we will fulfill our natural need of religious experience with mere sentimentalities and silly diminishments of God. And so our religion, too, will be diminished.

On the other hand, if all we have of God is our own religion's doctrines, well, then we will begin to worship the most subtle idol of all: our own words *about* Jesus, as if they were the Christ, the Word of God! Such a blindness will never recognize that it *is* blind.

When I was a child, we went Satur-daily to the YMCA where, for a dime, we watched two films. One was a full-length feature (Ma and Pa Kettle; Abbot and Costello), and the other, often a cowboy movie, was a cliff-hanger. We had to come back the next week to see how the Lone Ranger got out of his desperate fix.

When I taught confirmation's first year, I did essentially the same thing, with essentially the same results.

From September to mid-December, while the students sat before me in the pews of the sanctuary, I told key stories of the Old Testament. Each new week I quizzed them on the events of last week's story—both as a test and as the summary that would carry us into this week's episode. I promise you: it is astonishing how much of what is experienced is retained, as opposed to what must be seized and held by intellect alone.

I used "Covenant" as the theme for that half the year: God's first covenant with humanity, in the stories of the creation and the fall; God's second covenant with humanity through Noah; God's third covenant with a single individual, Abraham, then Isaac, then Jacob; God's covenant with a single people at Sinai, after leading them out of Egypt; God's renewal of covenants with Joshua; God's peculiar covenant with King David and his heirs; and the cries of the prophets against those who break covenant with God.

This theme granted me an unbroken thread through the Old Testament by which to choose the most important stories *and* still to keep them (cliff-hanger-like) in the sequence of a single story which finally must lead to the dramatic new and concluding covenant in the Lord Jesus Christ.

So the stories moved naturally (and carried the confirmation class easily) to the events which the whole congregation was to celebrate in the rest of the year: I told the birth stories through Christmas. I told the stories about *who* Jesus, the Hero, is—and what his ministry looked like—during the weeks after Christmas up to Ash Wednesday. Between Ash Wednesday and Palm Sunday I showed Jesus fighting against all that would kill us: the devil and sin and death. (You see how powerful by *any* standards this story of ours is? Evil things want to kill us.) We walked, those days, through darkness, and hatreds were real, and fears found form and a name.

But then, just as I learned one early Easter Sunday, all things came to a climax at the cross—after which I told of Jesus' resurrection appearances and his entrance into Heaven.

When I speak of this program to other pastors and teachers, they often object: "But we can't tell stories. There's a special skill to telling stories."

I reply that they are right: there *is* a special skill to the craft. But it is both learnable and findable by nearly everyone who can speak in front of children to teach them.

In this case, method follows motive. *How* you tell stories will depend upon *why* you tell stories, and if your personal reasons are right, you will surely tell stories effectively.

There are two rules.

(1) If the story that you are telling is of profound importance unto you—unto *you;* if the tale communicates that without which you could not live, that which seizes your whole heart and mind, then you will find the method and manner by which you personally communicate most important things.

My father-in-law, Martin Bohlmann, was a farmer, not an orator. He listened in church and scarcely spoke. He was the father of fourteen and the grandfather of that village that raises children. When *he* had something to say which he considered of first importance, he would lean slightly forward in his chair, would lower his voice and look folks directly in their eyes; and folks (dozens and dozens of folks) would fall quiet to hear him.

It shall be the same way with you: if it is of the Lord God that you are speaking; and if you love the Lord your God with all your heart with all the strength with all your mind, well, your delivery with have authority and power, though your method be different from every one else's method.

(2) And the second rule is like unto the first. If you do truly love your neighbor; if you love the children unto whom you speak; if you love *them* particularly, by name, desiring him and her and him to know of Jesus and to be brought under his wing, then you will speak *to* them. You will look them in their eyes. You will shape the story to include them, sometimes using their names. But you won't do these things because this is how stories are told, as if you were practicing a craft (and so paying more attention to a right method than unto the living kids before you). You will do these things spontaneously, *not* even thinking of them, because you have the hearts of these children upon your own pastoral heart.

Work with your strengths. Use music or drawings. But understand and honor the ancient oral tradition, since this has ever been the primary means by which one generation prepared the next to bear the mantle unto the third.

3. The Second Year: Know God

This was the year of hard work. But by this year we had established and nurtured a genuine partnership in the faith. So much of what it means to be human had already passed between us, so strong had our bonds become, and so common now was the base upon which our hard work would stand, that we were ready for the hard work.

During this year I expected and received serious study: they memorized the biblical words which last year had been biblical stories for them; so they were not memorizing in the dark, as it were, isolated portions of Scripture. They were memorizing things already beloved and familiar.

I taught them according to Luther's Small Catechism—yes, just as I myself had been taught. But as we discussed a particular doctrine (say, the commandments) I would ask *them* to tell *me* the Bible story that supported our lesson (say, the story of the Golden Calf as example of idolatry). Their participation delighted the both of us, and I could praise them, and joy *did*, you see, prevail in these classes, even when learning was most difficult.

I went through the teaching material twice that year. First, for two-thirds of the year, teaching by means of homework, responsory activities, testing, methods common to any schoolroom.

Such labor required a truly communal support. Now, therefore, I called in the covenants of families and Baptismal sponsors, sending them a second set of the materials which the child was working on, asking them to set regular periods for working together at home.

The confirmation sponsors which each child chose I had installed in a public worship service in September. But to empower their support, I met with them as a whole group three times throughout each year, teaching them *how* to be sponsors; how, for example, to listen to memorization and comment on homework; how (especially!) to take their charges on private excursions during which the adult might share his or her own faith with the child, explaining by personal example *how* the faith is woven into the daily life of the adult.

After Easter of the second year (confirmation classes always continuing to Pentecost Sunday) the students planned, prepared, and served a fancy dinner in thanksgiving to their sponsors; for it was now, through the last third of the year, that we were reviewing the catechism material for the second time, studying furiously for the public examination.

4. Public Examination

Now, finally, came crunch time and the genuine rite of passage into spiritual adulthood: the moment of confirmation.

The nervous fear that preceded the public examination was good! It was necessary for the catechumen's sense of personal achievement.

An initiation ritual is only as real as the task is real, as significant as the task is difficult. If it's free—or else made easy for the poor child—that child remains even in her own estimation a child still, and dependent. Moreover, expressions of faith that require no labor will carry no weight. To love and to honor the Lord will seem a light thing indeed—and shields so lightly constructed can protect against no weighty enemy after all, nor sin, nor death, nor the Devil.

So I gave them a genuine question-and-answer exam, seeking the doctrines now in their own words, from their own mouths.

But by now they did not see me as the cruel task's *master.* I was their helper! I, together with their sponsors, worked and worked the material into their hearts by saying: "We won't let you fail in front of so many people. We are on your side. You will strike them with astonishment by your great learning!" I became the managing coach. Their chosen sponsors worked individually with each. We made confirmation day into something like the final game of a long season.

At the same time we prepared the families likewise to take seriously the event to come. Plan parties, we begged. Invite relatives even from far away. This event must supercede birthday celebrations. It must be of greater moment than the prom (or what are we saying to our children about the things that truly deserve their hearts?).

In our church the public examination took place on the Saturday night before the Pentecost. All those supporting the confirmands attended. Family, sponsors, the officers of the congregation, all the teachers and every member who wished to come.

We chose an evening in order to have time for true questioning and careful answering. Everyone dressed up, for this was a formal affair, after all.

And when the confirmands had succeeded in their answers, when all teaching and all questioning were finally at an end, the adults who loved and honored the children now burst into a downright jamboree of laughter and applause. Always! Every year they whistled and stomped, though in each new year the applause was completely spontaneous and offered to that year's group alone.

Only once in all the rest of my tenure at Grace (from 1974 to the late 80's) did a student *not* pass.

On Pentecost Sunday itself, the final act of Baptism/Confirmation took place before the entire congregation.

"You are my child," the Lord had said, and made it true in the saying. Now that child, having come to understand the meaning of so celestial adoption, declared before the witness of the whole church, but unto none but Jesus himself, "And you are my Lord!"

No fears this Sunday morning. Only the joy of a sacred ascension, the self-confidence of personal accomplishment, the security of a new covenant uttered and established—and *well* established, given the difficulty of the task that brought the child to this first level of adulthood.

For salvation is free indeed. But discipleship has ever been a costly thing.

Pastors! Teachers, instructors in the Christian faith: soon the child before you will be my own, my grandchild, I mean, fresh and ready to be shaped by your training. I trust you with this bone of my own, that you shall not crush the joy in him, that you shall not merely entertain her. I expect the language of salvation to be as sober and as lively as is the business of salvation itself.

Please: do well by my children. Grant them adulthood in the Church that as adults they may be citizens of the Kingdom.

A Preface to "Little Lamb, Who Made Thee?"

I sat with the daughter and her father in the lounge of the youth and children psych ward in Wellborne Hospital. We occupied a corner, the father and I side-by-side on a short sofa, his daughter's chair at right-angles to ours.

The girl, however, could scarcely keep her seat, wriggling, wreathing her arms, tucking her legs up under her. She was a sophomore in high school, plain, roundish, with a Victorian abundance of brunette hair. I will call her Sharon here, though any other name but her own seems strange to me, and somewhat sad. It should not be that in public places I cannot call her by the name she knows for herself and herself inhabits.

Sharon dropped from her chair as if suddenly falling out of it. I made a spontaneous reach. Her father sat impassively. But Sharon had dropped to her knees, in fact, and was shuffling toward her father smiling brightly: all is well! All is well, and the daughter loves her daddy very much.

The man beside me did not move as she approached him. He wore a full beard. He sat like Lincoln, staring forward—staring still when Sharon lay her chin upon his knee and gazed up at him. In a moment she giggled and twisted around to sit on the floor with her back against his shins.

The lightness of her manner and the sweet persistence of her chatter—altogether as if they were cuddling of an evening in the living room—hardly fit the circumstances, unless of course she had recovered with wondrous speed and the cause of admission to the hospital were truly an aberration.

Sharon's father moved. He leaned slightly down to his daughter and reminded her that they were in a public place.

"Sit in your own seat," he said.

The man had eyes so intensely blue, they seemed to flame like gas jets.

Sharon jumped up, twirled on one toe and dropped hard into her seat.

These were almost the only words this father had for his daughter. He leaned back into his Lincoln stare, and I wondered whether he were profoundly disappointed in the child for her wretched carelessness. Sharon herself showed no disappointment whatever, neither in herself nor in her father's silence.

But she had only this morning, in the bathroom of Bosse High School, tried to kill herself.

The family had moved to Evansville only a few years earlier. Sharon's attempted suicide suggested to me that there may be certain interior stresses for which they may one day be willing to receive some help. So Thanne and I made a point to befriend them all, the parents and their two children.

But at that particular crisis, it was explained to me that Sharon was by nature high-strung and troubled. (Hence, I supposed, the serenity with which the father visited his daughter in the hospital.) She had, they said, been undone by the move from one state to another at about the worst time in her adolescence. She felt alien among the students at Bosse, bedeviled, belittled, terrifically unhappy.

Thanne's relationship with Sharon's mother took a true root; friendship bloomed between the two of them then.

My relationship with Sharon's father, although warm, remained rather formal. He was the pastor of a small congregation. It was perfectly natural for us to discuss professional issues; it gave me good cause to be near him, offering support without seeming to demean his own independence. The weight, the difficulties of his ministry presented themselves as complaints and criticism rather than as problems seeking thoughtful solutions or as weakness seeking companionship. Colleagues I think we were, or so I characterized the relationship. We never did, however, relax into the honesty of friendship. We never did become friends.

And then, when his daughter was a junior, the man announced to his wife and to his congregation that he was filing for divorce. Within a week he had moved out of the house into an apartment. I still met with him, but only in the pastoral office at his church. And Thanne, who in those days managed my writing and speaking affairs, offered his wife work in the office on the second floor of our home. It granted the woman a communal shelter and some money of her own.

And then, bare months after her father's departure, Sharon tried in bloody earnest to kill herself a second time.

Again the father and I met his child in the hospital. In no lounge, however. Beside her bed. And the girl bore bandages of comic thickness. But there was no coquetry in her face or in her manner. There was, rather, a pleading and a piteous sorrow.

And still the man was no more to her than a stone-white monument of the dead cerulean gaze. I bent to take the child's hand. I knelt to put my presence on a level with hers. And so it was that someone took her hand, but it was not the one she wanted, and it did not brighten her eye with life.

I left the hospital with a throat-full of suspicions.

That night I told Thanne what I was fearing.

And Thanne confirmed the worst.

Sharon's father had abused his daughter sexually. The move to Evansville had been the family's effort at a new beginning. The results of that effort were now sadly manifest. All these things Thanne had learned from Sharon's mother—because Thanne had recognized the symptoms long before I did, and had questioned kindly, softly.

How furious I felt that night! How dear to me was Sharon's broken self. With what tenderness I yearned to protect her deep, submerged and sacred beauty—to raise it up and praise it and persuade her of its truth.

All my life I've wished I were less passionate. Perhaps New York would not have dismissed me as a babbler then, or San Francisco as merely "emotional." Writers as uncontrolled as I lack the distancing irony that saves them from the world's contempt. Compulsively we do, and then we're forced to suffer what we did.

On the night of Sharon's second attempt, my passions governed me, and I wrote the letter printed below. I meant to give it to Sharon as soon as she was healthy enough to read it, and then I would offer myself as flesh and spirit to stand by the words, to stand by her.

Come the morning, however, and I repented of my plans. On the one hand, the letter seemed too brazen, too direct; on the other, it seemed too complex for a teenage mind. So I put it on Thanne's desk upstairs, hoping for her cooler opinion. If she feared its effect, I'd trash it.

Thanne did not read it. I mean, she was not the first to read it.

Having come in for work that afternoon, Sharon's mother found it. And though I had neither named her daughter nor specified the letter's intended recipient, as she read it the woman knew. She knew it belonged to Sharon. Without a word, then, and without my knowledge, she took the letter to her daughter.

Who read it herself.

And who, through her mother, sent serious thanks back to me. Sharon hadn't the words, yet. Abuse steals the most personal languages, and someone has to learn how to speak truth and truths and truly all over again. But Sharon had the experience, the effect, of an epistle that brings the better Shepherd to that one lost lamb; and of that experience she knew thanks, and these she sent to me.

In less than three months, while Sharon was still a teenager, but when she began to reveal signs of an uncommon maturity, she herself suggested that I publish the letter. Except for that it would have remained Sharon's own forever.

But I did. I published it in the regular column which I wrote in those days, for The Lutheran *magazine, which had a circulation then of some three quarters of a million readers.*

I published it thus:

Little Lamb, Who Made Thee?

Secretly beaten.

Sexually abused—

O child, it's not your fault. You do not have to earn the approval of your tormentor—no, nor his forgiveness either!

Is it strange that a victim thinks she caused the wrong and must right it again? Well, not so strange when we consider her helplessness. She's looking for leverage. She needs some principle by which to control her horror. And if *her* sin caused the punishment, then *she* might prevent it by a confession. See?

So the victim seeks her own iniquity—and the Christian faith is made grotesque thereby, allowing the guiltless to suffer guilt. And the abuser's become a Destroyer therefore, both of the body and the soul.

No, child—it was his act.

He was its cause. He was its doer. He took the wretched benefit. He must own it now, not you, not you.

He did it!

But because of your native innocence (which your tormentor encourages, since it shifts his guilt to you), and because you crave order in dangerous chaos (some ethical order anyway), you see a connection between one's behavior and one's fate. The good get goodness back again; and the bad get hurt—and look what a mess you're in; therefore you must be bad. Is that how you think? It saves the world from absurdity, doesn't it? It argues a certain rationality in human affairs. Good is rewarded, evil is punished, right? And your punishment proves evil in yourself, right? *WRONG!* Absolutely, unequivocally wrong.

If you've suffered abuse, the one who abused you sinned.

Sin is an uncaused evil. Responsibility sticks with the sinner. The sin came from him. He is the source. He bears the blame. His is the shame. Not you! Not yours! Do you hear me?

You, my child; you, dear lamb—you are beautiful and clean.

This sin occurred because a fool considered himself superior to you. He considered his whim superior to your health, his desire superior to your body, his mood superior to your peace. But you were made in the image of God, so his action condemns him: he demeans the creature whom God exalted; he attacks the child whom heaven loves. Listen: such spiritual blindness, such bestial selfishness, such a pitiful lack of self-control, declares this fool your inferior after all. You needn't seek kindness from him. No, no, and you need not forgive him either! For the Church that tells you you *must* forgive has burdened you with your sinner's sin, has laid a more terrible law on you, for you are not God, and you need not prove your Christianity now. You need prove nothing, not now when healing is the holy thing.

Let this fool seek forgiveness where it may be found; let him confess to the One against who he sinned most and most wickedly; let him confess unto Almighty God, for it is God who speaks for you now, child. And it is there that he can no longer excuse himself or compromise the force of his sin. It is there—and only there, finally—where he must strip his spirit bare and fall utterly on heaven's mercy and so be deeply and radically converted.

You need not, because you cannot, transfigure this fool.

God will, if the sinner wills. And the sinner must will! For *somewhere the sin must stop!*

The sinner tells me that it was his parents' fault in the first place. His father did him the same way. His mother was silent and critical.

He didn't (he tells me) have a chance. He can't help his breeding and his personal shaping.

But if this is true, then we're all a cosmic landfill for every sin that ever occurred; they fall on us from the past generations, all the way back to Cain. Such a weight of sin (everyone else's fault except our own) must crush our innocent souls. Such an undeserved history must kill us.

But it hasn't killed us. In other words, there must be some break in this chain of responsibility, sinners causing sinner to sin—abusive parents turning their children into abusive parents.

And there is: it is the acceptance of responsibility *by the sinner,* by none other than the sinner himself, so that when divine forgiveness transfigures that one, the sin and the sinning are canceled together, and the chain breaks.

No, sir, it doesn't do to blame another, neither the parents before you nor the child behind you. You, sir, as perpetrator of a vile abuse, must with a contrite heart confess.

And you, the child whom he ravaged, must not call yourself ugly. You aren't. His action does not define you.

You, child: you are as soft as the blue sky. Touch your cheek. Do you feel the weft of life there? Yes: God wove you more lovely than wool of the clouds, smoother than petals of lily, sweeter than amber honey, brighter than morning, kinder than daylight, as gentle as the eve. Listen to me! You are beautiful. You are beautiful. If you think you're ugly, you've let a fool define you. Don't! Touch your throat. It is a column of wind and words. Stroke your forehead. Thought moves through its caverns. Imagination lives in there. You are the handiwork of the Creator. You are his best art, his poem, his portrait, his image, his face—and his child.

And if the Lord God took thought to create you, why would you let a sinner define you?

God caused the stars to be, and then bent low to make you.

God wrapped himself in space as in an apron, then contemplated the intricacy of your hands; he troweled the curve of your brow; he fashioned the tug of your mouth and the turn of your tongue; he jeweled your eye; he carved your bones as surely as he did the mountains.

God conceived of time and in that instant considered the purposeful thump of your heart—and the blink of your eyelid.

God made galaxies and metagalaxies, the dusty infinitude of the universe—then filled your mind with dreams as with stars.

You are not an accident. You were planned. You are the cunning intention of almighty God. Well, then, shall you think ill of yourself? NO! You shall think as well of yourself as you do of any marvel of the Deity.

Please, my sister, do not allow a sinner to steal you from yourself. You are too rare. No matter what filth has befouled you, your soul is unique in the cosmos. There is none like you. Whatever thing you admire—a leaf, a little cup, a sunset—you are more beautiful.

Sleep peacefully, you. God loves you. And so do I. And so ought you in the morning light, when the dew is a haze of blue innocence. But sleep now, child, in perfect peace. You are God's, who spreads wide, holy wings above you now.

A Postscript to "Little Lamb, Who Made Thee?"

Within days of the publication of this letter, I began to receive mail from readers. I had never received so many responses to a single piece before. A rule of thumb is that one angry letter represents three angry readers; but one letter of agreement represents 10, nine of whom did not write.

Evening after evening, Thanne and I stood in our kitchen while I read the letters aloud. And we wept.

For there were more than a hundred letters in the space of three weeks.

And all but one were from women; and only one of those took issue with the column.

They told their stories, these women did in letters addressed to me. Handwritten, typed, printed from a computer. Countless stories of personal grief, the willful destruction of their persons and their personalities. They had BEEN the nameless. Yes, and it was their stories that made us cry.

But more than that, it was their courage.

For not one letter was sent nameless to me!

Woman after woman poured forth her terrible secret, then signed her name to it and did no longer hide. That gesture, so fearless, overwhelmed me with the sense of their resurrections.

No, I am not nor ever shall be ironic. Objective. A mind above the mass of human entoilment and experience.

Still, therefore, even now as I recount the deep entrenchment of this sin and its sorrow among us, I am borne down by the weight of it all.

And still I am dumbfounded by the valor of those who did not die.

My dear, dear friends: I take my own hope and courage from you.

From Sharon, too, who lives her life today in the company of her husband and their three children.

i.

If you were not so frightened, child,
　　As I am gentle, or . . .
If *I* were crouched, wide-eyed, defiled,
　　And *you* the comforter,
　　Then I would touch you.

But since it is that you've grown scared
　　Of men, and since it is
That I have seven years, now, cared
　　For you, I will not kiss
　　You, child. Let that be true.

Let that be true along with this:
　　That when you fall asleep
I wonder if an old man's kiss
　　Would wake you. Oh, I'll keep
　　That wish still unfulfilled—
But still will wonder, wonder still—
Oh, grandchild!—what a touch would do
If it were mine for touching you.

ii.

No. Sing another song.
Tell her a certain line
Between her brows ("a Rubicon
For deepness") is a sign.

Tell her you know how cruel
The grief within her is.
But you'll conclude it with a jewel:
And on that line, a kiss.

THE PARENT OF HIS CHILDREN

SNOWBOUND

IT WAS THE SNOWFALL of '76 (though I confess I'm fuzzy on dates and it might have been in '77).

January. The children were small, four of them, ages two to six. We lived in the country on two acres with chickens and fruit trees and large gardens. We were bordered by woods on the east and the south; to the west lay a farmed field; we shared the northern border with a neighbor who kept horses.

To this day the children remember a beautiful mare who slipped into a ditch and broke her leg. She had to be shot. They were the ones who discovered the accident. They stood at the edge of the ditch and watched the poor beast whinnying, lying like an eighteen-wheeler on her side, throwing her head up as if to snap her great body upright, rolling her eye so that the white showed terror.

This was new and horrible for my four young ones. Horses should not be helpless. Hugeness should not lie down and die. They came to the house with a look of awe in their faces. And then we heard the gunshot.

But that was a summer sometime after the winter of '76.

And that winter was kinder altogether, bequeathing unto us a snowfall of memorial proportions. It shut down the city for a week. Us it kept isolated for a full two weeks.

The storm began as a true blizzard, wind and a straking of snow straight out across the land. Our house leaked air, so it whistled and shuddered all night long. The boys, the older of the four, kept their eyes wide open. They had high, piping voices in those days. I heard them talking off and on about the relative strengths and weaknesses of the house.

"Joe? Joe? Is it goin' t'blow the baf-room away?"

"No, Matt, 'cause how would we pee then?"

"Oh."

By morning the wind had relented, but the snowfall itself continued down and down, and the world was utterly white. Cloaked, Siberian, forgiven. *(Though your sins be as scarlet, they shall be white as snow.)* All the ruddy, rotting colors of an exhausted autumn, all the blackened, unraked leaves, the shivering stalks in the beanfield, the corrupted melons in my garden—all was covered in a smooth white purity.

The children knelt at the window, transfixed.

God had called forth a new Eden.

"Can we," they whispered.

Their tiny voices were hushed by holy things. It sounded as if they were praying.

"Can we go. . .out?"

Going out, of course, was not without danger. Pigeon Creek snaked through the woods east and south on its way to the city. Hunters prowled the wooded banks, banging at living things. Not in January, though. Other months, other days. One once mistook my dog for something wild and free.

And once, after the creek had—in a quick succession—first flooded and then frozen, the boys snuck into the woods to explore the dazzling ice-world.

That afternoon their mother in her kitchen slowly became conscious of a distant sound, a faint cry, a sort of creaturely squeaking like fox kittens caught: "Mommy?" one voice mewed. "Mommy, mommy, mommy!"

The other voice barked, "Mop!"

Well, in those days Matthew was testing toughness. Tough kids don't say Mommy, and he never got the hang of Mom.

MOP!

Thanne ran down the hill and into the wood and found her sons stranded on a single circle of ice fixed like a tutu round the trunk of a large tree. The flood had begun to retreat. The rest of the ice, hollowed now, had broken under the boys' weight. "Mop?" They genuinely thought they would drown, tender adventurers paying for their boldness. Who knows how long they stood on the frost-island, crying?

But that was another year, another time.

Now they gazed upon a white paradise, soft, untroubled, a bosom mounded, maternal, abundant. Lo, as far as the eye could see through textured air the silent snow still coming down, the world was religious in serenity.

"Can we go. . .out?"

My chickens found the drifts impossible to negotiate, too deep for their legs, too high for flight. The effort defeated them. They were plumped here and there like marshmallows in milk, their wings having made angel-wings in the snow at their sides. If I had not myself gone forth, booted and gloved and blowing clouds, to bear them back to the coop, and if I had not then shut the door against their next escape (well, to them it was day, and day demanded foraging, and the instant they were returned to the dry coop they forgot the trouble with snows), they would have starved and frozen and died.

"Dad? Dad, can we?"

"What?"

"You know—go out?"

"Why?"

"To play."

In that same blizzard of '76 certain cattle were caught out in the fields, enduring alone the long night and the terrific blowing cold. They turned their backs to the wind; they packed themselves side-by-side together; they drooped their great heads. By morning the hoarfrost of their breathing had grown big and joined the earth, trapping their snouts in heavy columns of ice. Such silent, obedient monuments, bowed down, locked to the frozen ground, patiently dying.

But that was far west of us, out on the plains. Cattle in Southern Indiana are always closer to barns; and children are safe. The children are safe. Their parents protect them and keep them safe.

"Well, can we, Dad? Is it okay to go out and play?"

My oldest son ran away from home once. He slipped out the back door and headed west on a dusty road. He got as far as the bridge over the creek. A neighbor spotted him and drove him home again. He said afterward that he was looking for us because we had left and left him with an uncle who truly frightened him—so he lit out, though he was only four years old.

Even the little ones know of danger. And I think they suspect that something like death can descend on the living. They can be frightened. Their parents, of course, do more than suspect. Parents know in the cold part of their hearts that children can die.

"Yes," I said. "Yes, you can go out to play."

Grins bloomed in four faces, four little foxes whose expressions should never freeze in fierce grimaces—no, not these bounding and beautiful kittens.

"Wait!" I said. "Wait for me!"

Oh, my children, my children, so wonderfully young that winter! Oh, the radical magic of your innocence! In those days what you did *not* know transfigured the world I *did* know into something generous and kind and joyful and motherly and good after all.

This, then, is what I recall of the snows of '76: that we stomped a huge pie in a white field and chased each other down trails three feet deep and fell and laughed and blew clouds in frigid air and no one was hurt.

I remember snow forts in our snowbound days, each fort confronting the other, and snowballs stacked like cannonballs, and dusty throws of soft ammunition, and no one was hurt, and every-one felt the safety and the dearness of family.

I remember an ache in my wrist from the snow that crammed my mittens.

I remember an ache in my heart.

There was a snowman so huge that both my sons could stand on his hips to have their picture taken, their arms spread out like Hollywood stars, laughing, fearing nothing.

We ice-skated on Pigeon Creek.

For two full weeks we went out and played every day. And I loved my children until I wept. And not one of them was wounded. Not one.

But that was a very long time ago.

I WATCHED YOU SWIMMING, Mary. You were as unconscious of me as you were of yourself; but I was exquisitely aware of you—and then of myself as well.

Mary! You're not a woman yet, but womanhood is in you.

And suddenly, by slow degrees, the quality of my fatherhood is changing: new demands upon my soul, new dangers, revelations, new moments of the primeval quiet—and sometimes I'm a mumblin' fool with you, and sometimes I gaze in wonder like Balboa when he stood on an escarpment and contemplated the Pacific.

Mary, what are you doing to me?

What is happening to you?

The changes come slowly, to be sure; but we poor parents wake to them as though in surprise, and then we seek sympathy from companion parents, some consolation for the bewildering transformations of our children—while you children sometimes seem to take the whirling world so easily that we feel Paleolithic beside you. Sometimes, I say. For there are times when your limber spirit stiffens and brittles and breaks, and then you are like a figurine shattered, and no one can glue you, no, no one can put you together again.

Yesterday I watched you swimming in a blue Wisconsin lake— you, seabird, all alone. I sat some twenty feet above you on a bluff and so could see Olympian, as it were, could see through the lake to its bed below you, whose stones you never touched: you stroked too well and lightly through the element. Child, you were delightful, flicking the water like a trout with liquid, familiar assurance—

But I caught my breath and leaned forward, the better to see. Mary! Your legs are so long! And strong. And they churned the water with luxurious competence. And the crystal water gave them a pale, aquatic cast—dreamlike, it seemed to me, and absolutely beautiful. Mary! When did you come to be so beautiful? There are true hips at the ascendant curve of those legs, and a slender waist where once a child threw out her belly, and brown and lithesome arms, and bold shoulders. And when you toweled yourself, your wet lashes joined together like black starbursts, radiating glory round your eyes—blue eyes, shooting lashes, and a laughing child! Oh, Mary, when did you come to be so beautiful?

And when did you begin to stop to be a child?

When did that woman commence whom only now I notice?

All at once! By slow degrees.

There was a period, five or six years ago, when your older brothers received more letters than usual from aunts and uncles who addressed them in formal terms: "Master" Joseph and "Master" Matthew Wangerin. Talitha was perplexed by a title she had never heard before.

"If boys are masters," your younger sister asked, "then what are girls?"

You solved the puzzle straightaway, as easy as swimming.

"Masterpieces!" you declared.

And Mom laughed at the aptness, since you are a piece of work yourself; and I laughed for three or four seasons; and you—you laughed for the pure pink pleasure of it all, the center of attention, a round cheesecake of a child, dumpling cheeks, not a cloud in your blue sky.

Well, now in these latter weeks I realize, sweet Mary, variation in that laughter. The weather's less stable than it used to be, isn't it?— and could change upon the instant.

Or, the laughter's eager still; you grin so hard, and your eyes desire to swallow the one you're laughing with, and you clasp your hands at your breast (like any Victorian) never, never to let the sweet sensation go—

But suddenly, these days, a single word can change your aspect altogether. One frown from another can collapse the happiness and spill true tears down cheeks still formed for grinning. And the harder you laugh, the likelier are these tears to fall. High and low emotions are one with you, exultation and despair: you take offense as quickly as the snail's horns withdraw, and then my offended daughter, with her long strong woman's legs, storms up the stairs, wailing (a Victorian perfection of grammar), "You do not understand! No one understands me! I could just die—" And the bedroom door slams for punctuation, and you sail (in a graceful trajectory, surely) through the air and to your bed of bitterness, there to weep, "I could just die."

A woman nearly, nearly you are, a woman of complicated, intense, and profound emotions. No, you are not acting. This isn't pretence. Nor do you try on moods as people try on dresses to buy. The moods are painfully real in you, and life is less simple than it was. Relationships for you are in fact divine. Or else disastrous. And the divinity or the damage *does* last forever, until tomorrow. (I'm serious. I am not teasing you, my daughter. Today is forever in your baby woman's heart, and tomorrow is ever your wonder, unexpected when it doth come with healing in its wings.)

A woman you nearly, nearly are. But to me what are you truly, Mary?

My lover. (Oh, yes!) You comfort me in a manner most mature, having learned since childhood to read my moody meditations. Your eyes are perceptive. You see me truly, and quick to the heart; and your hand consoles me, even when lightly you pass me in the kitchen and pause in the passing; and you are beautiful in compassion. A woman. Such a woman.

But what are you to me?

A thunderstorm! A headache. (Oh, yes! So changeth the weather.) Suddenly things are not hard for you, nor merely difficult: they are "*impossible,* Father!" Anything I ask you to do, when you're convinced that you cannot or should not do it, causes you trauma—and formalizes me in the process, refusing me my more intimate names and freezing me with "Father." Then how do I reason with one who declares with creedal conviction that I "hate" her? One tormented by loneliness, lovelessness, as forlorn as the poet at the fading of his nightingale? One who sees me as the Ogre, the Ancient, both stony and hateful, the Judge, the Warden, and the Executioner?

I don't. I'm smarter than that. I do not try to reason with such a one. Simply, I wait for tomorrow, which, though you dispute the turning of the times, shall most surely come. I wait for tomorrow, when I shall be your intimate again, and your tender friend.

Ah, Mary, when did you begin to stop to be a child? It's a difficult business, isn't it, this adulthood. You yearn it and you curse it, woman.

When did you begin to cover yourself and lock the bathroom door against us? When did you begin to take yourself and all the world (and right and wrong, and justice and international oppressions) so seriously? And when did you become so beautiful?

All at once! By creeping, slow degrees.

God gave us a sky of infinite and wild variety, storms and the imperial blue, scudding clouds and the symphonic sunset and lightning too. But the sky never touched me lightly to say, "I love you." Nor could that sky receive my little love in return.

So God gave us daughters—

—more wonderful than the sky, lights for telling the seasons by.

Ah, Mary.

Masterpiece!

NO FIELDS OF YELLOW FLOWERS ANYMORE

i.

When our neighbor informed us that our small son could no longer play with her daughter, I was sorry, but I didn't argue. Rather, I took the opportunity to school him in self-restraint.

Even from infancy Matthew had been an exuberant child. Life and every desire were matters of gladness for him. He was up with the morning sun, loud and laughing and out the door, racing the fields like a sheepdog, loving the grass and the speed and the freedom. Oh, Matthew! He was three and free—never, never the slave of anyone or of anything.

We lived in the country in those days. I raised all sorts of fruits and vegetables. Matthew tended to the sweeter crop always—and when strawberries fattened in the green patch, he did not, as he said, "Think two times." He flew on wings of an aching hunger faster than anyone else, landing on hands and knees, ramming his face among the leaves.

I yearned to delight in life as he did.

At the same time I wished that he would learn self-discipline because he could hurt himself. He could hurt others, too—and he did, and he always felt remorse thereafter, and that was perhaps the worst way of hurting himself, but he did it again. He always did it again.

Ah, the wild child! There was such a splendid joy in his satisfactions. Unrestrained in action, he was also unrestrained in gladness—and then again as unrestrained in sadness when his natural self would wound another. It all went together, you see? Desire and delight and a native skill gave Matthew the edge: so he got there first; he ate it first; he ate it *all*, thinking of nothing but the fat red strawberry bursting its sugarjoy against his palate—until there was none left for others. Nothing for his family. Nothing for his three-year-old friend, who may have felt frightened by such energies both going and coming.

So, then, I didn't argue when her mother announced the new rule: "Your son is out of control," she said, and she ended the friendship. The children were forbidden to visit. No more playing. No talking, no whispering secrets. Nothing.

Matthew was suddenly very sad when I told him this law. He really liked the girl, this tiny porcelain person so different from himself, small-boned, wispy-haired, blue veins in a milk-white skin. His eyes grew large and silent in sadness, and I took the opportunity to teach:

"You've got to think of other people first, Matthew," I said, "or look what happens. People go away." We stood in our backyard, he gazing across the new, invisible wall, I gazing down at him. "Matthew, give before you take. Walk before you run. Listen before you talk, and whisper before you shout."

But he kept gazing next door.

He murmured, "Now but she don't have a friend too, either."

"I guess not," I said.

"My fault," he whispered.

I held my peace.

He looked up at me. "Daddy, can I take her a bowl of strawberries?" *Daddy, can I fix the friendship?*

"Not now," I said. "We don't have any ripe strawberries left, remember?"

He kept looking at me. "Well, maybe later," I said, thinking that Matthew's lesson might honestly change him, and the change in him might change our neighbor's mind. Maybe she'd relax her law in the future.

I was wrong on every count. Worse: I was deceived, and when the truth appeared I saw in it the dangerous intransigence of the imagination of the human heart.

Within the month my wife telephoned me at the office. "Come home," she said. She was crying. Thanne seldom cried. "Please come home right now," she said. "I found out why Mrs. Duvall cut Matthew off from her daughter—"

"Because he's hyperactive," I said.

"Please," Thanne sobbed, "just come home."

I did. I drove home. I listened for ten minutes to Thanne's explanation, hearing how wrong I could be. My blood rose up in fury. I went straightway to the house of our neighbor and, with restraint, confronted her. She answered in civil voice. In fact, she spoke in a smiling conspiratorial tone, as if two intelligent adults such as ourselves would agree on a matter like this. She felt no need to explain nor to apologize—no, not even to feel guilty. But Thanne's information had been absolutely accurate. And the way this woman accepted so serenely my burning accusation, the complete ignorance of any wickedness in all of this, astonished and aggrieved me—which dead-sorrow of soul I have not forgotten even to this day.

I came home and looked for my son. I found him downhill behind the house in a field full of yellow flowers, his arms flung out to some interior melody, turning circles. Actually, the flowers were a kind of weed in poor soil, profuse that summer; but to me they seemed most terribly beautiful for that my son was in their midst, and my heart was smitten thereby. The yellow field seemed a sort of grounded sunlight, a glory around his dark complexion.

Oh, Matthew!

I descended to him, then knelt in the field, and gathered the boy in a hug so tight he grunted.

"Daddy? Daddy, what's the matter?"

"Well, let's keep our strawberries here. We'll eat them together. But I don't think we should take them next door. Not now. Not ever."

Matthew had huge brown eyes. "Why?" he said. "Don't they like strawberries?"

He didn't understand. Nor, at that age, could he. In time he would, of course; but then he would be more than sad. The boy would be confused and wounded personally; and by then he'd know that he was suffering the assaults of a most iniquitous world.

ii.

Parents, we teach our children fairness; and we do well.

The selfish child is a danger. The self-centered child grows into a marauding adult whose sins are justified by that same grim idol, *Self.*

We wish our children to be good, and so we teach them to be just; to be selfless themselves; to do to others as they would have others do unto them. We teach them to be fair.

We do well.

And we do it (don't we?) out of deep parental fears and affections. We train them in fairness for their own protection, because we do not want them to suffer blame or slaps hereafter, do we? In a world both bigger and badder than they are, selfish children are dangerous mostly to themselves.

So we take every opportunity to say: "Don't be selfish. Share with your friends, and they will stay friends with you." Cause and effect, right? While buttoning their coats for school, we say, "Play by the rules, kid, and others will learn to trust you. They will *like* the one who knows right from wrong and acts upon it." Connections, right? Good people do good; good invites good friends; goodness gets goodness in return. We drive our youth to college, repeating the fine and fundamental ethic: "Be fair, son, even when I'm not near to watch you. O my dear daughter, out of your own soul, be fair. This is moral independence. This is maturity. When you practice fairness, you are on your own finally and surely. Be fair."

In this way we imply that they have a personal control over their destinies: certain behaviors will have certain consequences. Choose the right behavior for a righteous future. All we teach them is based upon the presumption that there is a reasonable law at work in the world—reasonable and feasible and universal and impartial: *The Law of Fairness.*

Its positive expression is this: Good behavior earns a good reward. Good gets goodness in return. This is a most consoling logic, both for the parent and the child.

Its neutral expression is: If you do not misbehave, you will be left in peace.

And its negative: But if you break the law, the world will punish you according to your deserving. Ill deeds bring an ill response. This may be a cold logic, but it is orderly withal and necessary.

The Law of Fairness does not pretend to love people; rather, it loves stability in the community, and everyone benefits. It maintains a structure that all can understand, within which every individual can choose good or evil for himself. Its very rigidity, therefore, permits a moral liberty person by person, gives ethical independence to child and child, no child excepted.

See? In any game—in this game particularly—it's good that there are rules, and good to know the rules, and good that the referees are watching the rules. Each individual may now play heartily, and the winner *is* a winner after all.

So we teach our children *The Law of Fairness* as carefully as we can, both to know it and to obey it. And we do well thereby; and all should *be* well therefore.

And all *would* be well—if the world itself obeyed that law.

But what if the world the children encounter tears fairness to shreds? What then?

iii.

At ten-thirty on a Saturday night Matthew was just coming out of a gas station door, his head down, counting change, when he heard shouts by his car.

He looked up. Two police officers were pointing stern fingers in the faces of his friends. His friends were backpedaling, helpless.

One of the officers shouted: "Get in the car! Get in the car right now!"

This, Matthew knew, was not possible. By habit he'd hit the button that locked the doors. Even as he broke into a trot toward the gas pumps, he heard the cop continue: "Get in, boy, or you're going to jail!"

Exact quotes (though not unlike other quotes he has heard often and often). Matthew doesn't forget what he meets with emotion. His mind and his heart are strong.

He pulled the car keys from his pocket as he approached the scene. The officer saw him and redirected the order. To Matthew, now, he yelled, "Open this car. Get in and get out of here, now, *now!*—or you're the one going to jail!" Matt's the one. My son is the one.

He was seventeen years old. (But it happened when he was sixteen. It has happened every year of his driving life.) He had by then developed a flat manner for precisely this sort of situation. That is, he blanked his eyes and slacked his face and slowed all motion until nothing in him suggested threat, aggression, or flight. He stared into the air. He neither grimaced nor smiled nor said, "Sir." Any such gesture is dangerous.

Deliberately Matthew began to unlock the four doors of the car—

And the uniforms exploded: "Not fast enough. I don't like your attitude, boy! In fact, show me ID. Now, now, NOW!"

Just then a friend whom the police hadn't seen stepped round the car, surprising them. "Yow!" They both leaped backward snatching their sidearms. Embarrassed, they yelled, "Oh, yeah! Oh, yeah, you are going to jail!"

Matthew stood absolutely still, now *not* giving back what he was getting nor getting what he had ever given; now *not* invoking fairness nor anticipating it nor even believing in it—for he had learned, Lord; he had learned beyond my teaching him; he had learned that the best posture in a crisis like this is not to be. Vanish.

Matthew had learned by cruel and redundant experience.

I do not lie. I declare it as an objective fact that my son has regularly been harassed by officers of the law for no ill that he has done and in spite of the good that he has sincerely chosen.

My son is adopted.

He is black.

His color alone is, in this world, the cause of his harassment.

iv.

We live now in a black neighborhood, in the center of our city, where there is the congeniality of community for our children.

The police here are mostly white.

But we were not wrong to move here. Here most of the people suffer the same derisions of *The Law of Fairness,* and here we can talk of the trouble to folks who understand it in their bodies as well as in their minds.

While we still lived out in the country, we experienced the cold, white eye alone; and we, at first, were inclined to accept guilt. Well, we hadn't yet learned. We didn't recognize the depth of human prejudice nor the bland face it wore. We thought it was we and our children who were somehow at fault. We (Thanne and I in our own belated ignorance) were still assuming fairness to be an active principle of human relationship—

—until our neighbor spoke the truer motive of her mind.

That's why I hugged my son so hard and why he looked so terribly beautiful and tragic in the field of yellow flowers. The mother of his young friend had just said to me, without anger but with a complete and creedal conviction: "They won't never talk again 'cause black and white don't marry."

That was the reason for the separation.

She said, "I don't want them touching or holding hands or whispering secrets. It's unnatural. You go on and keep him hobbled and at home, away from my girl, 'cause black and white don't—"

don't marry, she said, when these two children were no more than three years old. And she smiled as if I would surely understand the long weight and history of her truth.

But this was truth: that *The Law of Fairness* crumbled in the face of such mindless, murderous racism.

The Law of Fairness was a far less effective ward in the wicked world than the "trick" that Matthew had learned thereafter, which is not to trust anyone, which is the blank expression, the slack face, and vanishing. Do nothing. Say nothing. Be nothing.

That night, when he was still seventeen, it worked. He seemed to the officers sufficiently subservient. He did not go to jail. He came home. He shrugged and told me the story, by then a very old story. No big deal. This is the way things are. Cops harass young black males.

But I wish he were three again, dark and lovely in a field of yellow flowers, laughing as once he laughed when he was innocent, when desire and delight and satisfaction and life were all one with him. Fairness was a good law then. And my son could hope and be happy then—

v.

All of our children must suffer the loss of that good law. Do you understand? The world is not, after all, fair.

So what do we do when it is the world and not our children which proves selfish in the real encounter?—selfish and unrepentant and unpunished after all?

Teachers will deal unfairly with our daughters; coaches will scream at our sons, pink and popeyed; friends will trash our children at the pleasure of other friends; bosses will play favorites; the marketplace will not love our children as we do, but will rather love itself at their expense; countless promises will be made and, though the children count on them, will then be broken. Politicians will lie. Police will obey the imagination of their hearts more than the cool and equable law. So what do we do when bad people possess power while good and goodness are crushed as wimp and weakness?

Injustice, in this fallen world, will certainly strike the child both bluntly and personally.

Listen, parents:

If we do nothing, if we do no more than communicate *The Law of Fairness* strictly and only, then our children will change to protect themselves, but the change will break our hearts.

One young man may react with an anger so radical that all our teaching—all of it!—shall be compromised and lost on him. He may then mimic the world, exchanging laws of fairness for laws of brutality: might makes right. The strong survive. Look out for number one, since you have no better friend than yourself.

Or one young woman, having been deceived, may never trust another person again. To the degree that she was burned for her faith in fairness, to that same degree she shall now doubt promises altogether and dread the motives of other people. Scared child! If hurt came from the place she had considered safe, then hurt can come from anywhere. And love itself becomes the ultimate personal risk—too dangerous ever to take. Lonely child, unfulfilled and frightened.

Or the saddest change within our children is this, that they never let go of *The Law of Fairness,* that they accept therefore the guilt and consider themselves deserving of all the hurt the world gives unto them. A harsh twist: they believe themselves evil precisely because they have had to suffer evil. And if they cannot perceive what wrong they did to cause it, soon they conclude that it is the wrong they *are.*

If, when this good law breaks in a broken world, we do nothing new for our children, they shall begin to die various early deaths.

vi.

At Bosse High School Matthew played the point position for his basketball team. He had the spirit of a leader. Even off the court he wove his players together by driving them hither and yon in his car, by giving them haircuts in our basement, by gathering the team together at our house before a game. I remember with pleasure the laughter bubbling from the basement, and I cooked suppers for them, and I felt a parent indeed.

All but two of the Bosse players were black.

I remember, too, how nervous the team would become on the days they had to be bused from the city into the counties of southern Indiana to play small-town high schools in all-white communities.

These plain folk in their own gymnasiums enjoyed a joke or two. When they met a team as black as Bosse's, their fans would enter the stands carrying hubcaps. Humor. Matthew and his teammates simply expected it. Students wore watermelon patches, red, green, and seeded. "Fun! It's all in good fun!" Yet, though he expected it, Matthew genuinely did not understand why this was considered funny, why folks laughed, why parents rocked backward on their seats amused. Oh, he knew that whites think that blacks like watermelon. But why such an unsubstantiated notion of one people regarding another should make the first people laugh, he had not a clue. But he tolerated these milder forms of foolishness. All the Bosse players did. Part of basketball. Hoosier hysteria. We live in Evansville on the Ohio River.

But then in the dark midwinter of 1988—just as the bus and its basketball team were slowing down to turn off Highway 231 into the parking lot of a rural high school—there flared beside the windows a sudden fire, a bright ascending yellow flame. Suddenly, boys could see boys' faces in the firelight, and the bus driver gunned his engine. Matthew's eyes went as wide as when he was young. The entire team fell silent, watching.

This was the first time any of them had seen a cross afire.

Matthew (he later told me) had such tightness in his chest he couldn't breathe. It occurred to him that a fire near a high school was unsafe. Even the building might burn.

So, then, how do you exit a bus in front of strangers? How do you strip and change clothes in foreign walls? How do you enter the glaring light and loud sound of a basketball court when your own mood is so filled with confusion? Well, the act had seemed so obscene to Matthew—that someone should burn the cross of Jesus. What had Jesus done? He couldn't make sense of it. His stomach was knotted. His face felt hot. Something was dreadfully wrong. But how do you walk on court when everyone else is happy, laughing, and ordinary?—though somebody in this place just torched the wood of the Christian cross.

Well, you enter stiff. Wooden-legged. You put on the blank-eyed mask of not-caring, the impenetrable wall and the slack-faced declaration that nothing matters. You pretend indifference even while your heart ticks so quickly you feel the pulse in your throat,

and your ears are so acute that they hear the whispers, *Nigger,*
nigger. But the word registers nowhere in your expression. You take
the ball. You shoot. You warm up. Stretch. Avoid looking at the
stands. Shoot. Shoot. Shoot.

vii.

There is another law. The laws of fairness and brutality are not
the only ones a child might learn. Against these two—or against
lawlessness altogether—the third is absolutely essential.

This is what we do when the children suffer the failure of fairness
in the world: with all our hearts, for the health and the blessing of
the children forever, we model before them and for them enact *The
Law of Forgiveness.*

Parents, if we love them this is not a matter of choice. It is
necessary for the life of the children. Without it, they shall be
caught in a killing society, dying. Moreover, it is at the core of our
Christian faith: a loving God knew the need long before we did. . . .

We who have been appointed parents by the most Holy Parent
must in all our action image the forgiveness of Christ himself—and
must name Christ Jesus both as the Lord and as the source of what
we are doing. No secrets here. His forgiveness must pattern the
children's. His forgiveness must empower theirs. And as their spirits
more and more reflect the Spirit of God, they shall more and more
be *free of the world*— neither to be ruled nor to be crushed by it.

This is not merely an abstract doctrine to be conned.

This is wholly pragmatic.

This is a daily shield, the children's best protection after all.

Even as we train them to eat and to dress and to perform some
sustaining skill, so we must train them to sever themselves from the
hurt and the powers of the world (though not from the world itself)
by a true and holy pardoning.

Sinner, I do not hold this thing against you.

No, the children do not say such a thing simply on their own.
They must know (by your guidance) that Jesus said it first to them

from the cross, and that Jesus says it thereafter *through* them to the world before them.

Whisper their sins to their souls until they ache in sore repentance; but then quickly sing to them the measure of the mercy they have received from the dear Lord. Their sins are gone. In place of sin is righteousness and the love of God. The Spirit of love then lives within them. God is there, and from the God in them truly, truly comes this miraculous power to forgive the people who do not in fact deserve forgiveness.

But forgiving inverts the powers. Evil cannot control those who do not fear evil; and those who forgive it do not fear it; they are above it, gazing *down* upon it in pity. Nor can evil rule those who are themselves not evil. Those filled with grace are filled with God.

Children of forgiveness are liberated, therefore, from this world, utterly free, making choices altogether on their own, unpressured, unthreatened, unambitious, unpersuadable. Such children enjoy partnership with the almighty God. The world can indeed destroy *The Law of Fairness,* but it cannot destroy that which dodges its tooth, *The Law of Forgiveness.* Why, it cannot comprehend the premise at all. Forgiveness is a puzzle before it.

Again, the world can destroy any child committed to *The Law of Brutality,* since the greater power may always kill the lesser. But it cannot destroy the Holy Companion of the child of forgiveness, nor else the child that this dear Companion keeps.

And look at the marvelous accomplishments of such children of the Spirit: they become the means by which God enters the world; for their forgiveness is the coming of Jesus again and again.

Is there a higher calling than to be the bearer of the Lord?

viii.

They won. Matthew's team won.

No razzle-dazzle, no slam dunks, no show—just a steady game, a solid and solemn, respectable win. The fans in the stands were not happy.

Neither was Matthew's coach, despite the triumph. He was nervous, tense—and finally furious.

As both teams were leaving the court, a heavy-set man sitting half-way up to the ceiling bellowed something about a "nigger win," and the coach of Bosse's team blew up. With a strangled shout he began to mount risers, clearing a path by short chops of his arms, preparing to crack the skull of a fat fan who was suddenly very frightened. Friends of that fan started to converge around him, balling their fists.

But immediately both basketball teams swept up the stand together, like sea waves.

And amazingly, Matthew was not afraid. He was the first to reach his coach. He tried to pull the short man backward and got tossed aside for his effort. But he wasn't scared, and he truly did not expect a fight—because of what had happened during the game.

The first half ended in a grim stand-off, a balanced score and an equal suspicion on both sides.

But near the beginning of the second half, Matthew (by habit, I think, a spontaneous act) complimented his opposite for a good shot. Just a nod, an acknowledgement between equals: "Hey, man."

And "Hey," said his opponent.

And suddenly Matthew realized the potential of the gesture. Several times by glances and touches he praised the white point guard. Since he himself was known as a good player, the compliment carried weight. And the opponent, not bad himself, smiled back, grinned back, praised Matthew in return.

So, then, there was a mutual relationship here, independent of the noises in the gym, shaped at first by a common commitment to the same game. So, then, Matthew's mask cracked and his hot face cooled. So, finally it became a conscious gesture on his part to forgive: to honor the humanity of the other, permitting the other as fully human also to return relationship.

The rest of the team observed in two point guards the lack of fear and vengefulness. They saw in Matthew a weird, uncaused behavior (except as God causes things that otherwise would never have happened, as God makes miracles through his children), and so they hunkered down and played basketball. Both teams shut out the idiocy of sinful fans and apoplectic coaches. They played the game they liked; and within this pale of forgiveness they liked the players they faced.

It was a good, close game.

That's why Matthew wasn't afraid when his coach arose in a rage and he himself went after him. It was a single team that swept up the stands and interposed itself between the Bosse coach and the friends of a fat fan—a single team composed in equal measure of white and black players, rural and city, Bosse and Bosse's opponents.

You see? *All* the players were, by the benefaction of the forgiveness of one, perfectly free.

ix.

Yesterday I said good-bye to my son all over again. He was on his way back to college. He is twenty. I feel a heartbreak homesickness for him.

He has, of course, changed. Innocence is gone. Likewise, his exuberance is much tempered—or else he'd get into trouble much more than he does. He is cautious now. And I am altogether helpless to protect him. No more. I cannot attack the attackers any more.

The sense of general fairness and universal beauty in this world has been compromised for both of us. Various sorts of worldly authorities accomplished that destruction.

Matthew departs this home of his parents for a difficult life, my dear one does. I hugged him. I hugged him very hard, but I could not hug him long, as once among the flowers. There are no fields of yellow flowers anymore.

I hugged him and let him go, and he is gone.

And now I console my loneliness in prayer:

O Holy Father of my son, he bears in your forgiveness his veriest strength. Forgiven, he can forgive—and forgiving, he shall survive this world unto eternity. Never let my boy forget this best of lessons. Never.
Amen.

I WISH THE FISH took my bait as quickly as my daughter takes the ring of the telephone.

One ring and that child has burst from the bathroom, scorched through the kitchen, and snatched the receiver: "Hello, this's Mary."

One ring! Evidently there are no joys Mary will not forego for the phone. Certainly a long, contemplative, comfortable crouch in a little room is no match for a chat.

Mary doesn't like to be alone. My daughter's gregarious by nature and gladdest when gossiping.

Listen: the other night while she was sleeping—in her bedroom, an hour into her slumber, the door being closed where she lay—the telephone rang. Even before that first ring finished, Mary—sleeping still, her pupils as tiny as pinpricks, smiling in dreamy expectation—Mary went floating down the hallway: "I'll get it," she murmured.

I do not lie. I woke her before she embarrassed herself by sleep-talking.

Ah, but over the telephone that girl *never* embarrasses herself. She's a TJ for skill and aplomb, *Telephone Jockey,* liquid language, opinions on any matter, grace under pressure.

When Mary receives the heavy-breathers' call (as she has), she holds her own cheery conversation until *he* hangs up. "Hello? Hello? Hello?" she chirps. "Oh, poor pitiful-little-mute-man, what's the matter? Asthma? Can't you talk? You think maybe I'm nine-one-one?"—and so forth.

She is undisturbed even by the mentally disturbed, as long as her weapon is the telephone. Mary's an expert.

She's tireless, too.

Howcanateenagertalkforhoursandneverrunoutof*words*? Or out of breath either?

And are both of them talking at once? I mean, is the father of the daughter at the other end *also* hearing endless, breathless, uninterrupted news reports about nearly nothing at all? Or when does Mary's interlocutor get to speak?

Well, I believe these children have perfected a method of talk/listening whereby they do both at once with equal energy. I think there's a detachment within the head of the mouth from the ear. Just as, when teens do homework while watching TV, there's an obvious detachment between brain and face. It's an evolutionary phenomenon.

Progress.

Moreover, with the talk/listening method it is possible to attend to five, ten, twenty topics all at the same time. This is why teenagers can discuss seventeen significant issues while flying through the kitchen and out the back door: unkind teachers, no homework again, friends in life-and-death situations requiring immediate visits, don't wait up, and good-bye. While the poor parent, pop-eyed, is still emerging from the consolations of the bathroom and wondering if he heard the telephone ring.

Now, then, the posture for telephone calls will vary according to the caller and the urgency of the call.

They are as follows, depending on who's at the other end:

Girlfriends: Lie on the floor, feet propped on the walls, hair in disarray. Gesture with the free arm. No matter the clothing, no matter the lighting. This is the posture for gossip.

Girlfriends, pastime: Watch TV with the girlfriend on the line—two phones, two TV sets, two running sets of opinions, two bloody shrieks for brothers who, mistaking a phone call for a phone call, switch channels. Also, while watching TV and talk/listening, do one's nails—and blow on them too.

Girlfriends, serious: Sit up, hunch over, hang the hair around one's head as if in private, but speak dramatically, even explosively—especially if discussing some personal insult.

Boyfriends: Laugh a lot. Stand up. Prance, swinging the free arm wildly. Good lighting for glancing in mirrors.

Boyfriends, serious: Sit in a chair. Doodle with pencil or the forefinger. Button all buttons as if dressing well. Low light is preferable. Music too—but not MTV.

Boyfriends, very serious: Absolutely no one else in the room. If a parent should skirt too close to this lair, a hissing will indicate his danger.

Boyfriends, very, very serious: Perfect silence. Weeping.

This last posture the father will notice. He will wait until the call is concluded, and then he will offer his daughter a hug. She has run out of words. No TJ now, no longer tireless, no expert at anything—she is desolated. Her father holds her very tight and hates the phone right now. He hates anyone and any thing that hurts his daughter.

On the other hand, there is no punishment worse than being grounded with telephone silence.

Ask Mary.

For it is on the phone that she renews her spirit again, laughing. Oh, this child laughs at the fleetingest joke and, having started, cannot stop. Tinkling laughter runs into boisterous laughter swells into mighty Mississippis of laughter, till my Mary is left gasping and streaming tears over some fool thing one of them said, which is, of course, not funny in the retelling but which, in fact, is friendship anyway. Plain friendship. Whole and healthy, holy friendship.

And in such moments I love the telephone very much. I appreciate anything that makes my baby lovely again.

But I wonder, as I pass the poor kid squealing on the floor: are these two friends just moaning in one another's ear, saying nothing, yowling like animals? No words? No worthy communication on this expensive and advanced device, but inarticulate giggles and woofings as if they never learned language at all?

Is this what the phone has returned us to, the primitive grunt and the Mary-onic burble?

Actually, no: it's not the invention, it's the daughter. She'll do it off satellites and halfway round the globe; or else by wire; or face-to-face, if she has to. She'll do it cheap or dear—all's one with her.

She *must talk,* whether in words her parents recognize or in noises more expressive of the subtler teenage spirit, burps and barks and purrings.

However complex, however progressive technology may get, it is the daughter that does not change. For which pertinacity, saith this father (from within a small, locked, porcelain room, his only throne in a house inhabited by a Princess): *Praise the Lord after all.*

DELIBERATE, DEVOUT, AND BEAUTIFUL, the woman walks to the altar and places there her precious gift and watches while it is consumed—

How long has this been going on? For eons.

How many people have done it? Myriads. But mostly women.

Then why haven't we been astounded by such holiness? Well, I think we are by nature blind to sacrifice. Even the receivers of this outrageous love don't truly know its depth if they have never felt the wound of it, have felt the sweet blessing only. Perhaps we have to suffer sacrifice in order to understand it.

Perhaps that's why I didn't know my mother well. I mean: I didn't know the quality of her love until I myself experienced her circumstance and did myself make a mother's choices—

Children, honor that woman who for your sake placed on the altar of motherhood some core part of her precious self. Honor and do not neglect her!

In 1985 Thanne and I switched household duties. She went to work full-time, and because mine was the more mobile work, I brought it home. Writing had become my primary profession. Now housekeeping became my primary obsession. From that year forth I took over the cooking, the shopping, the kitchen, the bed, and the bedroom—yea, and the children.

Through the winter and spring of 1985 things went swimmingly. By eight in the morning I was alone in the house, busy in the kitchen, to be sure, but at the same time thinking through the day's writing ahead of me. By nine, dinner was in a crock and I was at the typewriter. For six solid hours thereafter, the writer wrote.

At three in the afternoon the children came home. So writing was done. The writer turned into a father, and the father emerged from his study ready to usher his children everywhere. I cheered their games, I refereed their arguments, I disciplined and pitied and talked and cooked and set the table and timed our dinner to begin at six, when Thanne got home.

Thus the noonday writer and the afternoon father thrived, both of them—so long as they stayed separate.

But then came June. And my dear children came home to stay.

Now, I had committed myself to completing a book length manuscript that summer, but I trusted my ability to organize and I intended to accomplish the same amount of work now as I had when school was in session. I established a schedule to occupy the kids (with an equal mix of chores and recreation) while I wrote. Of course I would write. There never was a question about such a thing. I was a writer. That was my core *self*, my purpose for being.

But the telephone was suddenly seized with a thousand fits of ringing a day. And the children ate meals whenever the mood took them. And friends came over, shouting, fighting, laughing, interrupting the sweet symmetry of my schedule (chores and recreation). Okay, so I had to stop writing, come out of my study, put limits on the use of the phone, dismiss kids who were not my own, remind my own (over and over) to clean the kitchen after their meals, and stab my finger for emphasis at the schedule on the refrigerator: "Do, do, *do,* you fools!"

Back to writing again. Whew.

Ah, but even when I didn't rush out of the study, every time a kid raised his voice I had to stop. To listen. To figure out what was going on. Or any time the kids lowered their voices, I had to stop. To listen even harder. Silence is dangerous. And if you can't hear it, you have to go *see* it. So up and out I went after all.

And you cannot schedule arguments. And you can't plan tragedies. So? So I stopped writing. I burst out of my room. I yelled. I arbitrated. I held my poor daughter till she stopped crying. Ach, I stopped, and I stopped! I brought kids here, I drove them there, I answered their questions, I filled out their forms, I took them swimming, and I blew up:

"LEMME ALONE! JUST LET ME ALONE! I'VE GOT TO WRITE!"

("Shhh, Daddy's going crazy.")

Okay, so I stopped writing altogether. That is, I decided it was time for a whole new start, for all of us. I took a week's break from writing, calmed my spirit, jettisoned all that I had (so miserably) written during the first days of summer, quietly instructed the children in the necessities of my job ("It feeds you, sucker!"), and sat down to start all over again, refreshed—because, of course, I *would* start over again. I would surely write. It's who I am, you see—

Can anyone explain to me? Why, if you have told your children never to interrupt you, do they interrupt you with little whispers as if whispering were better? As if whispering proves them obedient after all? I HATE WHISPERING! IT DRIVES WRITER-DADDIES MAD!

Okay, so then why *don't* children interrupt you when they're about to take off for parts of the city you've never yourself had the temerity or the stupidity to enter? And why must the writer-daddy come out of his study to find the house as dead as marble? Wondering where his children have gone? And whether his previous rage is the cause of their present danger? Dumb, dumb, dumb, Daddy!

Three times that summer I stopped, cooled, smiled, gathered my forces, and started all over again. Three times my children slew the book in me. Three times!

But these kids were not bad kids. No, they were just plain kids who needed a parent. It's the order of things. They needed a presence. A mother. But I am so slow to learn. And finally, only experience itself teaches me. By bending me to the right will, the holy way.

Finally, I bowed my head before my children's natural need. Finally, I confessed in my soul, *This is right. These children of mine must take precedence—because they are children and they are mine and they come first—yea, though it consume me—*

Then, then I discovered my mother's mothering and the astonishing quality of her love. Then: when I chose. When I sacrificed
the writer-self and consciously renounced my book and offered my
children, completely, a parent. I had to do the former to allow the
latter. These were the same act after all. I had to let the core of me
die—for a while, at least—that they might properly live.

Ah, Mother, every summer since then I have thought of you and
of all your sisters through the ages. I see you, darling, distinctly—
as in a vision. I see deep, and I see this: that once there lay in the
precinct of many mothers' souls some precious personal thing.
Some talent, some private dream. The characteristic by which they
defined their *selves* and their purpose for being. To write? Maybe.
To run a marathon? Or to run a company? Yes. Yes.

But then the baby came home, and then you and others like you
made a terrible, terribly lovely choice. You reached into your soul
and withdrew that precious thing and lifted it up before your breast
and began to walk. Deliberate and utterly beautiful, you strode to
an altar of love for this child and placed there the talent, the dream,
some core part of your particular *self*—and in order to mother
another, you released it. There came for you a moment of con
scious, sacred sacrifice. In that moment the self of yourself became
a smoke, and the smoke went up to heaven as perpetual prayer for
the sake of your children.

And when it was voluntary, it was no less than divine. Never,
never let anyone force such a gift from any woman!—for then it is
not sacrifice at all. It is oppression.

But never, either, dear children, take such an extraordinary love
for granted. It is holy. For this, in the face of such women, is the
mind of Christ, who emptied himself for us. And then again, for us.

Ah, Mother, I am so slow to know, but now I know—and out
of the knowledge wherewith my own children have burdened me
I thank you. From an overflowing heart, I thank you, Mother, for
your motherhood.

COMMENCEMENT

OUTSIDE MY STUDY WINDOW, just this side of Bayard Park, sit two boys on the hood of a cream Camaro—in the process of becoming men.

How old are they? Well, their backs are to me. I see an occasional profile: sweet, smooth cheeks on the one boy, an innocent twinkle in his eye, rather chubby. The other is leaner, with broad, capable shoulders and a low brow. Athletic, obviously. God has given him a quality body. But how old? Seventeen? Eighteen at the most. Boys.

But they're speeding toward manhood with grave purpose.

And I grieve at the process. I am sick at heart for the men they wish to become and the means whereby they intend to achieve it.

Jekyll drank something, and Hyde sprang forth. These, too, begin by drinking—although their ritual is much more elaborate and clearly rehearsed. It smacks of tradition. It's been handed down to them. And watch! In thirty minutes they shall be men. Men after the image of . . . someone. There is some model in their minds according to which they are shaping themselves.

Men.

Okay, so lean child hands chubby child a pint, the flat bottle shrewdly concealed in brown paper. They exchange a bolder bottle of orange juice. They suck. They stare across the park, unspeaking yet. They are thinking great thoughts, obviously. They are, at this point, discovering that they have as much right to think great thoughts as any president of the United States, and the capacity, too. Or else they are merely waiting for the warm transformation of their minds so that the great thoughts already thought, already lodged above, might be released and descend. They suck. A car drives by. The bottles slide down between their thighs, but neither child ceases his stare. This is a solemn moment. They suck.

A little conversation now begins between them. I can't hear it; but by the nodding and the pursing of lips, I know: they consider their words to be uttered in wisdom; and they are in agreement together, lean kid and large kid. The great thoughts are coming down, now, like a sober rain. Manhood is arising. It is not just that they are beginning to feel good, but that they are feeling good *about themselves,* in every respect children of this progressive world. Aye, the smiling world should be proud of two who learn so well. Moreover, each of these feels he's in fine company.

It's time for the second agent of their maturation.

While lean fellow stretches his marvelous spine, hunches his athletic shoulders, and rolls his neck (gazing forever across the park), chunky fellow produces a Ziploc plastic bag. The shreds of dried vegetation inside are most carefully shaken onto white paper, the which is balanced on a finger, licked, rolled, and twisted at the ends. Sealed. Skillfully shapen and sealed. I am impressed by the earnest attention to ceremony given this act. There's more than mere practicality in chubby child's gestures; there is symbol and meaning and obedience, as if he were priesting at an altar and handling sacred elements. There is, clearly, a "right way" to roll a roach. And he who does it "right" is an initiate. He's passed some test. He is a man.

The white twist, now, is lit with fire. It burns. The round cheese-chunk of a fellow sucks on it. Then, with sacramental care—not looking at his brother, keeping his own face passive, gazing across the park—he passes it to the bean beside him, who performs the same rite: sucking. They are sharing.

Conversation develops a new weight. It becomes louder.

Lean kid slips from the hood of the Camaro. He begins to wave his arms, to stab the air with a pointed forefinger, to snap his head back at particularly critical strokes of rhetoric.

Lean kid is preaching.

Great thoughts, thoughts first conceived in an alcoholic fume then passed from mind to mind in devout conversation, thoughts consecrated by Mary Jane's numb benediction, these thoughts have now become *opinions.* Lean boy has opinions. He has, by the flash of his eye and the crack of his delivery, judgments to pass on many things within the world. Clearly, he feels he has a calling and the right to make them. Even so, he is above the world he criticizes. Even so, he has arrived. He is a man.

See him strut and frown? He's a passionate fellow. Do you see him beat his chest? Lo: *he* is the sweeter substance of all his thought. He has elevated *himself* by the elevation of his mind. There is no doubt, now: he can do great deeds. And do you see how he receives the approval of his brother, who roars and thumps the hood of the Camaro? He is not only wise, he is right! Hear him shout, despite the glances of more conventional passersby. Not only right: yo!— he is free.

Lean baby and chubby baby, they are men now. They possess a certain swelling self-importance. They've found their places in the universe.

And I grieve.

Where are the other men, the men who served as models for this travesty? Where are the true adults—by years, adults—who considered their lifestyles to be their "own business" and did not notice younger, watchful, malleable eyes desiring to make it *their* business, too? Where are these heroes and teachers of the children, these failures in plain responsibility, these liars of the good life, these fathers, older brothers, uncles, friends? Frauds! Around their necks should be hung the millstone Jesus described. Carve in that millstone the epitaph, *Just doin' my own thing. Ain't hurtin' no one.* Then cast them into the depths of the sea for having tempted little ones to sin.

Little children, strutting men!

God help them all.

In the end these two step away from their Camaro and perform a final rite of virility. They reverence the tree.

Lean fool and chubby fool stand side by side in silence, facing the trunk of a huge oak, their legs spread, their hands hidden below, their heads bowed down, peeing.

Then they zip. And then they drive the Camaro away to confront their destiny somewhere in the humdrum traffic.

P.U.T.T.

I DON'T WANT CEREAL on my kitchen floor. Does anyone? Is there anywhere a rational person who is not distressed by cereal on the kitchen floor?

Well, it grinds the no-wax floor I've just no-waxed. It murders the shine and my good mood. At night it hectors my sleep with dreams of a house buried in Cheerios. In the morning it sticks to my socks. It blackens dried dribbles of orange juice.

So what? So am I a lunatic to ask my children not to spill cereal on the kitchen floor? Is this a law too difficult to bear? No, this is basic and reasonable cleanliness.

It's unarguably healthy.

Then why, when hopping on one foot and declaring myself unhappy about cereal on the kitchen floor, do my children gape at me as if I'm countermanding some previous command that they *should* spill cereal on the floor, together with milk and a little orange juice? Why do they indicate my insanity then? And why do their wounded eyes call me the only warden in the world upset by a little cereal?

O fathers and mothers of the world, unite!

And what about homework? Does my daughter do her homework to benefit *me*? Am I enlightened by her learning? Will my name appear on the report card? Will I get a job thereby? Well, of course not. I am myself not a whit improved by her endeavor.

But then why, when I require of her the work that shall reward none but her, does she groan? Why does she pout and glower at me as if I've just ruined her life for my own satisfaction? I HATE GLOWERING!

Why do my children, in the best of moods, humor me—and, in the worst, act punished, imprisoned, unjustly troubled by a mindless giant?

Yours too?

O parents, unite!

My second son, whose back ripples with quick strength on a basketball court, is suddenly crippled by the mere mention of the lawn mower. It is his job to walk the dog. He has never walked a dog in his life, poor troubled soul.

And I have considered the regular series of emotions that cripple *me* when that same son is late for his curfew:

1. Mild annoyance (the kid is snitching minutes, though he promised to be home on time);

2. Anger, hotter by the hour;

3. Earnest worry, laced with guilt (is he hurt?—why did I blame the innocent child?);

4. And finally, crashing rage at his return and the explanation he offers, words meant to calm me by their reasoned and weighty consideration: "Uh, I forgot."

Every night, Matthew?

And can anyone explain to my own mother's son how it is that the lack of clean clothes is my fault?—when the cracker-jack kid neglected to throw her dirty clothes into the laundry?

Is it written somewhere that children must dress slowly, making everyone late for important occasions? Late and angry? I HATE TO BE LATE!

And who said that my cologne (and my socks and my razor and my room and my car and my wife's whole wardrobe) is theirs just because they inhabit the same house with us?

And did you know that TV is a teenager's constitutional right? Actually, noise is the right—any sort of noise: booming, strumming, shrieking, giggling.

And did you know that teenagers regularly detonate clothes-bombs in their bedrooms? The quicker the mess, the gladder the kid.

What do they do with our money anyway? Eat it?

O parents, one and all, what manner of thing have we sheltered all these years? What have we taken to our soft bosoms, which sprouted thereafter a vulture's beak and a taste for the flesh of progenitors? Teenagers! A breed apart.

It's a relatively new creature, this teen. For most of the world's history teenagers didn't exist. Until the last few hundred years, children ceased dependence upon their parents at fourteen, fifteen, sixteen, then shouldered their own apprenticeships, their labors and land and families. That wasn't considered too tender an age then; it certainly is no tender age today, but rough-cut and ready and stronger than I!

Parents, I have two proposals to make:

1. That once again we abolish teenagerhood; offer our fourteen-year-olds all rights of maturity, all the freedoms, and therewith all the responsibilities as well; throw them a *true* come-out party and give them luggage as a gift and mean it. If such a ritual of transition is universally observed, it'll benefit the nation whole. Think how much energy would be converted to solid work and taxable income—the which is now spent in malls on walking, talking, preening only. Think how we might augment the military, allay the national debt, and regain our place as first among industrial countries. Think of one father who will sleep unhectored by dreams of cereal on his kitchen floor.

Or, if my first proposal proves impossible, consider my second:

2. P.U.T.T. An organization entitled *Parents United To Tolerate Teenagers.*

Teenagerhood is, in fact, the kid's leave-taking from the family— extended over a longer period than in generations before. It is a normal process after all—a time when she learns independence and practices it, even while she is yet physically dependent upon her parents; a time of strife, then, and of inherent contradiction, but not of anything sick or sinful or wrong. The tension between independence and dependence causes violent shifts in attitudes. It confuses parent and child alike. The rules of relationship change daily; so what is a parent to *be* from Sunday to Tuesday?—A companion? A confidant? A cop? A teacher? Zoo keeper? Cheerleader? God?

Precisely during this period, dear parents, unite.

The process of separation is good and necessary, already defined in Genesis chapter two: *Therefore shall a man LEAVE his father and his mother, and shall CLEAVE unto his wife: and they shall be one flesh*. For any proper cleaving hereafter, there must be a true leaving now. The irritation, then, the pain of separation, the emotion and the provocation, the trouble and the break itself cannot be abolished, and it should not be avoided. It will be. Teens will bug us. And we them.

But we, their parents, might regularly support one another. Let's find stability with those who have managed (or who are managing) similar challenges, rather than demanding stability from the teens who, by the nature of their present passage, are as unstable as water. They simply cannot give it now.

Parents, let us laugh together by telling tales of the idiocy of these tall children. Laughter diminishes problems by granting a blessed release and a realistic perspective. Let's talk seriously, too; exchange advice; discover how very common, after all, is all that we thought bedeviled our family alone. And let's pray out loud. For each child by name. And for the parents. Because God is God of teenagers too. God is the one parent who shall *not* be superseded. And God will work internally in the confusing kid, using ways we can't even see.

For now we must love at a distance; but God never departs the intimate heart of the child. Never.

Ah, parents, attend to your own consolations now when the job of parenting *is* a job, an assignment, not a pleasure—and you will become a consolation for the teen who is as bewildered as yourself.

It's been two seasons now since I saw her, but because of the tremendous respect she inspired in me (and then, as well, the pity) I can't forget her.

It picks at the back of my mind, over and over again, asking: *What does she remind me of?*

Something remarkable.

Last spring a duck entered our backyard journeying eastward, eleven little ducklings in file behind her. It was an outrageous appearing, really, since we live in the midst of the concrete city. The only waters east of us are the pools at the state hospital, four miles away, which distance is an odyssey! Between here and there are vast tracts of humanity, fences, houses, shopping malls—and immediately to our east, Bayard Park of tall trees and lawns.

Yet this duck moved her brood with a quick skill as if she knew exactly where she was going.

Buff brown generally, vague markings on her wings, a smooth pate with a cowlick at the back, she and her name were the same: blunt and unremarkable. The ducklings were puffballs with butch haircuts, obedient and happy. Big-footed, web-footed, monstrous-footed, floppy-footed, the children followed their mother as fast as drips down windowpanes, peeping, questioning, keeping together, trusting her judgment.

And she, both blunt and busy, led them into our yard, which is surrounded by a wooden palisade fence. Maybe she came this way for a rest.

But we have a dog. He rose to his feet at the astonishing sight. He raised his ears and woofed. The duck backpedaled to the wall of the house and turned eastward under the eaves' protection and waddled hard, her ducklings in mad zip behind her. But the dog is leashed and could not reach the wall. This part of the passage, at least, was safe. The next was not.

Without pausing, the buff duck spread her wings, beat the air, and barely cleared the fence, landing in the middle of Bedford Avenue between our yard and the park. There she set up a loud quacking, like a reedy woodwind: *Come! Come!*

Eleven ducklings scurried to the fence, then raced along it till they found a crack: *Plip! Plip!*—they popped through as quick as they could, but their mother must have been driven into the park. By the time they gained the wider world she had disappeared. The babies bunched in confusion, peeping, peeping grievously. One bold soul ventured down Bedford to the alley behind our yard. The others returned through the fence.

Immediately the mother was back on Bedford, the one bold child behind her, scolding the rest like an angry clarinet: *Now! Here! Come here now!*

Well, in a grateful panic ten ducklings rushed the crack in the fence, thickening there, pushing, burning with urgency, trying hard to obey their mother—

Not fast enough.

A car roared south on Bedford. Another. The duck beat retreat to the farther curb. Joggers came jogging. A knot of teenagers noticed the pretty flow of ducklings from under our fence and ran toward it. The tiny flock exploded in several directions. The mother's cries grew hectic and terrified: *Come! Come!*—her beak locked open. She raced up and down the park's edge, and there was but the one puffball following her.

The simple unity of twelve was torn apart. My city is deadly to certain kinds of families.

Five ducklings shot back and forth inside our yard now, but the hole through the fence led to roaring horrors and they couldn't persuade themselves to hazard it again—though they could hear their mother. That unremarkable duck (no!—intrepid now and most remarkable) was hurling herself in three directions, trying to compose her family in unity again: eastward she flew into the park, south toward violent alleys, then back west to the impassive fence. *Hear me now, hear me and come!* Her children were scattered. She was but one.

I saw a teenager chase one duckling. He was laughing gaily in the game. He reached down and scooped up the tiny life in his great hand and peered at it and then threw it up into the air. The baby fell crazily to the ground. The youth chased it again.

"Don't!" I yelled.

"Why not?" the kid said, straightening himself. "What? Does this duck belong to you?"

But where was the mother now? I didn't see her anywhere. And now it was bending into the later afternoon.

I poured some water into a pan and placed it by the back wall of the house for those ducklings still dithering within our yard. They huddled away from the dog. But the dog had lost interest. They crept sometimes toward the hole in the fence. Now and again a duckling looked through. Their peeping, peeping was miserable. What do you do for innocents in the city—both the wild and the child? By nightfall they had all vanished.

No, not all. I can tell you of two.

The next day we heard a scratching in the vent pipe of our clothes dryer. I went down in the basement and disconnected the shaft and found a shivering duckling who must have fallen down from the outside opening. Perhaps it had sought cover and didn't know the cave went down so deep. It had spent a long dark night alone in its prison.

And then at church on Sunday a friend of mine said, "Weirdest thing! I saw this duck crossing highway 41—"

"What?" I cried. "A duck? Alone?"

"Well, no, not alone," said my friend. "I almost ran over her. I guess she didn't fly on account of baby ducks can't fly, and she was protecting it."

"Michelle," I said, "what do you mean *it?* How many ducklings did she have?"

"One. Just one."

There have passed two seasons, I say, since I encountered this blunt, buff duck—and still in my heart I whisper as I did then, *Godspeed* with honor and pity. *Godspeed, remarkable creature, tenacious and loving.*

And now I know what she reminds me of.

Of single-parent families in a largely indifferent world.

She reminds me of that impoverished mother (Oh, my culpable country!) who has small means to nourish and raise and protect her children. I have met that mother far too often with far too little to offer her. Mighty is her love. Illogical, absurd, and marvelous is her love for the children. And terrible is her sorrow for the loss of any one of them. The world may not enlarge her love or else diminish her sorrow. The world may in fact begrudge whatever little thing it gives her. Worse: the world can be dangerous to the family whole and to her children in particular.

But she loves. This mother knows from the beginning that the children will be chased, harassed, scorned, beaten, belittled—both by raggedy folks and by the upright and civil people of her city. She knows that one child may tumble down black shafts of a blatant disregard and another into drugs and another into crime and another into despair. From the beginning their prospects must wring her heart with a tight anxiety. She labors to give them a life for a while and some esteem and safety—and against desperate odds, marvelously, she loves.

To this one I say, *Godspeed, good parent, all the way east to the pools of Siloam and your children's maturity.*

And to the holy community of the church I say: *Help her! Surround this single parent, mother or father, with love and a service equal to her own. No: with a love equal to God's, whom you are sent to represent!*

In God's name, help her.

i.

My daughter's father's name is Carter.

Until Talitha was in college, I didn't know his name. Well, I didn't know the man. I knew only that some such person must exist. Because my daughter existed.

Often when we sat at supper, I would look across the table at Talitha and seek in her features the faces of her begetters. They seemed always to hover ghostly behind her, their faces indistinct, blurred versions of her own face. Her father, I knew, was African American, her mother white. And because Talitha, who has been our daughter since the eighth month of her life, was growing older among us, so were the presences of these two anonymous souls.

But they were the blank part, the root of this child still deep down in the soil. Talitha's birth parents had made her in their image, and I sought those images in her: a slant, receding jaw, softly curling hair, high cheeks, an aggressive personality. Would I recognize either one if I met the mother or the father on the street? How much is our daughter *ours*, after all, and how much theirs?

The man and the woman were ghosts in the family, not because they were not, but because they were not known.

Now Joseph was a righteous man. He obeyed the word of God, whether written in the laws of Moses or else uttered in dreams by angels. He obeyed, and obedience made a marriage where there might have been divorce. Obedience saved his son from Herod's hatred. Joseph's obedience took him to Egypt and then again to the security of Nazareth, where it shaped the daily life of his family by offerings and sacrifices and the keeping of feasts.

The more I think of this man in whom meekness was a strength, the more I honor him. Unlike Zechariah—who mistrusted the word of God—Joseph was not made mute. Yet the Bible records no word spoken by Joseph. Most folks involved in the events of the Nativity talked. They sang and chattered and expostulated. Everyone! Kings, priests, scribes, relatives, neighbors. Even the shepherds. But not Joseph. He didn't talk. He obeyed. Silently and steadfastly his word was ever his deed. He acted. He served.

Yet the man was no one's puppet. And his heart was kind. Joseph chose to temper righteousness with tenderness. Whether the law accused her or not, he would never put Mary to shame. Nor would he leave her behind when he, as head of the household, went to the City of David to be enrolled. He might have. He could have. Most husbands would have left the matter of childbirth behind them, at home, in the hands of women, since this was women's business, surely.

But Joseph took Mary with him. And in Bethlehem a babe was born which was not his own, even as he knew beforehand that it would not be. In the face of this infant he would never find his older face reflected. Nevertheless, kindly, righteously, Joseph adopted the child.

Perhaps you are already aware that Joseph is the patron saint of the fathers of families. I think he stands as a model for all parents, in fact, because the ghostly unknown that hovered behind his adopted son—the Begetter of *this* boy, in whose features was the First Father's image—is also the Primal Parent of every child ever born in the world. And God's heavenly parenthood makes all mothers and all fathers the adopters of their children.

But I feel a particular friendship for Joseph. Our fatherhoods are so similar that I cannot but learn from his plain response to the glorious task of raising the Son of Another: his faith, his obedience, his tenderness—and finally his willing release of the child. The child was his but a little while. . . .

ii.

In May 1993 Thanne and I were driving Talitha back home from college. We had just passed through Louisville on Interstate 65 and were crossing the Ohio River into Indiana when Talitha leaned forward from the back seat, held her face between our faces a moment, gazing at the road ahead, then spoke.

The van was full to the roof with of her stuff, so the rear view mirror was blocked by boxes—and now by my daughter's earnest brow. I recall how like logs the ladder-like shadows of the bridge's top-structure fell across the windshield in quick rhythm: *Poom, poom, poom, poom—*

Thanne had begun to turn her attention toward Talitha, opening her mouth around some pleasant word, when the girl abruptly declared: "I want to stop in Frankfort."

That declaration has fixed the moment in my memory forever.

I glanced at her in the mirror. She was not looking at us. I returned my gaze to the road, saying, "Really? Are you sure?"

Frankfort is a small town about thirty-five miles northwest of Indianapolis. For all the years we'd lived in this state, both south and north of little Frankfort, we had never stopped there before. We had, of course, known its name. For us the name had borne a peculiar significance. In me a certain emotion attended the speaking of it, because we had her birth records, and we knew: this is the place where Talitha was born, nineteen years ago.

She said, "Are you challenging me?"

I was about to say, *No, of course not.*

But Thanne spoke to me directly: "Yes, she's sure."

I glanced at both women.

"What?" I said. "Have you two been discussing something without me?"

Thanne said, "Wally."

I frowned.

Again, urging me to look at her, Thanne said, "Wally."

And when I did glance at her, with emphasis she said, "No. We have not been talking."

I said nothing then, but entered a private bewilderment and continued to drive north. Frankfort was still more than a hundred and forty miles away.

Two days earlier Talitha Michal Wangerin had finished the final exams of her first year at Spelman. This is a historically Black women's college, an excellent institution, free in the faith—and God's merciful answer to prayers her mother had been praying for Talitha's salvation and her safety.

My child! My daughter in high school had been grimly rebellious—almost as though rebellion were the job of the proper teenager. Talitha is and ever will be a fighter, a swashbuckler: fearless, willful and willing to fight for her rights as she perceives them. It's a marvelous, martial collection of characteristics; but lacking maturity, it had also lacked the wisdom to distinguish which rights were worth the fight, which were merely whimsical, and which were plain selfish. Thus the drama and the trauma of her adolescence.

Thanne went toe to toe with the girl. If Talitha screamed, my gentle wife screamed back, word for word and hoot for hoot. I knew even then it was the parent's job that Thanne was herself accomplishing. And it produced in her daughter astonishment early and her admiration late. But this particular display of parental love took my breath away. Mute before a screaming match, fearing I might hit something or someone, I would hurl myself bodily into the dark nights to walk long and lonely and far away, considering the talents of these two women against my perfect helplessness.

Actually, I stood in awe of this youngest of our children on many counts: she could schedule herself to the fractions of a minute, studying, playing, eating and *sleeping* according to her own clock. Talitha did conscientiously shape herself into a student! She was willing to "try out" for everything, expected to fail at some things in order to find her aptitude for a few. She chose independence. Independence was for my daughter a religion. Woe, therefore! Woe to anyone, sister or father, who woke the girl from sleep earlier than her schedule had planned for waking. Why, she came up from her cave like a she-bear, claws extended.

Well, so Thanne and I watched while state schools offered Talitha scholarships, watched and prayed that somehow she would choose Spelman, watched and prayed and *never* argued for Spelman (because her independence would on principle reject such parental persuasions), watched and praised the dear Lord God when she, choosing Black—choosing to *be* Black—chose Spelman.

Approaching the south side of Indianapolis I formed and I asked the question that would at least entitle Tabitha's present determinations.

"Why," I said, "do you want to stop in Frankfort?"

And she said, "I want to find my birth parents."

Yes. Yes, that had been my own wordless assumption. But at the speaking of the matter, things felt suddenly and vastly reversed: all at once I, the adoptive father, had become the ghost; *my* fatherhood was the fatherhood invisible. For my daughter had begun to peer through me, seeking the features of her begetters. And though I may have been a tool, a means to that end, theirs—those primary beings, flesh-and-blood at her conceiving—was the substance Talitha desired. In *them,* now, she sought her identity and her self.

What should I do in the next fifty miles? What word should I obey, now? Tabitha's? Or that different word which hovered behind my lips as I slowed for Indianapolis?

Or else some deeper murmurings of Almighty God?

Such a moment, I believe, also occurred for Joseph.

Jesus never challenged his adoptive father's authority the way Talitha did ours. Luke says he "was obedient to" his parents. Yet, there were intimacies in which this father could not participate. For he likely would sit at a Passover meal and look into his son's face and find there absolutely no characteristic of his own.

Mary's eyes, perhaps, the curve of *her* jaw. He could see a mother-son relationship, but he could only watch. It was a parenthood beyond his reach.

Someone else dwelt in his son's face. Another source governed the boy's behavior. Indistinct, completely different, strange to Joseph, a ghost in the household.

Training up the child of one's own loins has a deep spiritual and genetic appropriateness. One doesn't question one's right and the instinctive rightness of one's methods. Communication is as deep as the chromosomes. Thanne and I have raised children born to us as well as children adopted, and we've experienced the difference. Unto one's born children, for example, a raised eyebrow can speak powerfully, because they *feel* the command in the lift of their own eyebrow and, internally, in the sense of such a gesture. External behavior speaks to internal emotion, when the speakers share the both together.

On the other hand, in order to train up the adopted child, one must also learn *her* language, since communication needs must begin at the surface of things. One must never assume a complete knowledge of this child—except as watchfulness reveals her to the hungry love of her parents. And very early the adoptive parent realizes that the methods of training *this* child must obey a greater source than flesh and natural conception.

I'm speaking for Joseph, as well as for myself. He must have trained Jesus with a more conscious loving, a more patient searching of his son in order to learn the character of the stranger placed into his care. And I am convinced that Joseph founded his right to raise this child upon the word of God—the immediate message of the angels, and the covenantal law, the righteousness required of all faithful fathers. Joseph sought the source of his authority in God, and he accomplished it by obedience to God and by faith.

In the regular day-to-day labor of raising children (all our children, those adopted in the flesh *and* those adopted in the spirit), Thanne and I have stood in the shadow of this common, quiet man.

But then comes the frightening moment, the vast reversal when present parenthood grows ghostly and invisible because the child is seeking his identity in Another. . . .

Joseph and Mary and Jesus took a trip. The little family traveled from Nazareth to Jerusalem. All was well. They went to celebrate the Passover, and since Jesus was twelve—an age of transitions not unlike the eighteenth year of our children today—this may have been his first experience of the feast. This was the year when the Law required his father to acquaint him with the duties and regulations that he would assume as a thirteen-year-old male.

So Joseph did what was required of him. He bought a lamb. He took Jesus to watch the priest's ritual slaughter of the lambs. He showed his boy the Temple itself. They went together through the Gates Beautiful into the court of the Israelites, where they stood less than fifteen meters from the High Altar itself. Joseph faithfully enacted parenthood, and then the little family began to travel home again.

Suddenly, late in the journey, the parents realized that their child was absent. He was nowhere among the pilgrims, and because their love was genuine, they rushed all the way back to Jerusalem in a panic.

When was it that Joseph suffered the prickly feeling that he was seeking a stranger? When did he admit that he didn't know his son well enough to guess where the lad would hang out in Jerusalem? They spent three days searching everywhere *except* in the temple. And when they found Jesus sitting there, they were, says Luke, "astonished" by his ability to amaze even the teachers: a stranger!

The boy's mother was upset. Mary took it personally: "Why have you done this to us?" she said. "Your father and I have been so worried, looking for you!"

As Luke records the scene, the adoptive father was quiet.

But then occurred the moment of vast reversals, when Joseph became the ghost past whom his son was peering to see his Real Father, in whose substance was his self.

"Why were you looking for me?" Jesus said. "Didn't you know that I must be in my Father's house?"

Let no one ever diminish the depth and the complexity of Joseph's response. It is right now that faith and obedience and mercy and a parent's personal choosing all had their most significant effect!

Joseph obeyed.

Whose word did he obey? No word nor wound in his own heart! Neither pride nor self-pity controlled him, for he continued as before—never changing—to be the father of this boy, taking him home again to Nazareth.

Joseph "did not understand the saying" that Jesus had spoken to him. Intellectually, the plain man was ignorant. Yet he acted nevertheless, because obedience is always possible—even, and especially, without knowledge! Joseph acted by obeying the words God had already spoken to him. And though he did not directly submit to the saying of his son (which would have given the child rule of his household), he did obey the deeper meaning behind the saying—for there it was that God dwelt.

Here, then, is the saint of parenthood and the model for Thanne and me: this father, not comprehending all that was going on around him, receiving the lesser respect of his own son—this adoptive father chose mercifully still to *be* a father. By faith! In obedience. Already now he ceased to covet his child's first love and praise and honor. The quiet man was also a humble man. In fact, he could best fulfill his parental role precisely because he did not do it for his own benefit.

Thus a plain man accomplished a task of terrible glory, raising a child who was born in the image of God. Has any parent a different task than that?

Luke writes that Jesus was "obedient" to Joseph and Mary thereafter. In their household he "increased in wisdom and in stature and in favor with God" and with the neighbors.

By loving God, Joseph loved Jesus rightly. And by following God, Joseph led his son out of the house, into adulthood and into the purpose for which he was born. A righteous father raised a righteous son, then released him finally to the righteousness of his greater ministry.

iii.

We stopped in Frankfort. We found the courthouse where birth records were kept, and the Lutheran Church where Talitha's birth mother might have attended, and the high school, and the hospital where our daughter was born.

The town was altogether white. It seemed to us that the presence of a Black man nineteen years ago might have caused a stir. Perhaps it might be remembered by someone.

And because Talitha's first mother had kept her for eight months before giving the baby up for adoption, we believed that the birth had not been a secret. We also felt that those eight months must have made the infant dear to the young mother. These things persuaded Thanne and me to agree with our daughter's desires and not to discourage them.

We chose Joseph's way: to parent in humility, allowing our child a self-discovery which must take her beyond our own spheres and influence, yet continuing to parent her even during the search, and forever praying her Heavenly Father's benevolence upon her.

Be born, Talitha. Be born a second time, this time into a knowing and a heritage and an identity.

Obeying the Lord, who gives us children for a little while before they must enter their independent lives and purposes completely, we chose to help her seek her source. If things grew destructive, we would be there. If things developed unto goodness, we would stand by, watching. But if we had denied her this choice in the first place, we'd have canceled not her looking but ourselves, and would ourselves have missed everything thereafter, whether troubled or glorious.

So our sassy, pushy daughter returned to Frankfort that summer. And Thanne's spirit more than mine hovered over her entire adventure. Of course it did: she told me that she had, during the last several years, been expecting Talitha to initiate this search. For once they had been watching an Oprah Winfrey show wherein birth parents met their children for the first time. Talitha got up and went into the bathroom, Thanne said. When she came out again, Thanne saw that she had been crying. It was a clue.

"So," Talitha said, standing in the secretary's office at the high school, "do you remember a Black man about town nineteen years ago? Did he have a baby by a woman here?"

She and Thanne talked with administrators of the county, of the hospital, of the newspaper. They kept notes. One or two people remembered details of the past. By midsummer they had nosed the family name of the woman who had brought Talitha to birth.

And then they learned the woman's first name. Mary.

The old ghosts were growing evermore present. And I was feeling evermore ghostly. I wondered: the closer Talitha came to *that* mother and father, would she travel farther and farther from us?

But, in ignorance and in humility, faithfully, we parents obey. We seek the wholeness of our children as God conceived that wholeness from the beginning. We hunt their identities in the past, in order to uncover their purposes for the future. Clinging can kill these things, surely!

Early in September, after Talitha had returned to Spelman, she and Thanne finally learned the first name of Mary's father, and that he still lived in Frankfort! He was their link. They discussed how best to approach him and to ask the address and the telephone number of his daughter.

How much could be gained! How much could be lost in this single telephone call.

"You do it," Talitha said. "I can't."

Thanne agreed. But she swallowed hard before the doing. And she prayed and she trembled. She told me that she absolutely would not lie. How could she seek truth by false means? Yes, but if she misspoke her request, if she suddenly raked up old odors and emotions, the man might well hang up, and the link would break.

She dialed Frankfort from our home in Valparaiso.

A woman answered.

Thanne asked for Mary's father by name.

When he came on the line, Thanne said, "My daughter knew your daughter years ago. But she has lost contact. Can you give me her phone number and address?"

There was a distinct hesitation at the other end of the line. Then the man said, "Wait." He returned. Slowly he gave Thanne the information, and he hung up without a question.

Immediately Thanne called Talitha.

"She lives in Dallas, Texas," Thanne said, panting.

And then she hung up. But she stayed by the phone, scarcely moving. Talitha was, as that same moment, dialing the number in Dallas. Such union in these women's hearts and goals! This adoptive mother dwelt in the terrible excitement of her daughter as the younger one sought to talk with another mother completely.

The phone rang.

Thanne snatched it up.

Ah, but a mother almost weeps with her daughter's disappointment. She and Talitha spoke softly a while, and then went each to her own business. The number in Dallas had been disconnected, and they were at a dead end.

It is precisely here that I believe her Supernal Parent to have intervened. God the Father joined the search. For Talitha took a trip to Evansville. There she visited friends. Among the people she stopped to see was a family in our old neighborhood, where she used to baby sit. On their tea table was a copy of the Frankfort High School yearbook.

"Did you," she asked the husband, "go to that high school?"

"Yes," he said. Ach! And they had known each other for so many years!

Talitha asked, "Did you know a Mary W____?"

"Only by name," he said. "She was several classes behind. Wait— but they had a reunion last year, and I know who has a list of names and addresses. . . ."

This man obtained that list. And Mary W____'s telephone number, still in Dallas. He passed the information to Talitha, now back in Atlanta.

Late that same night, Talitha called Thanne, screaming, "I have it! I have it! I know Mary's telephone number—"

Thanne didn't scream. She became the voice of reason: "Talitha, it's late. Don't call her tonight. You know how much *you* hate it when someone wakes you up."

That night neither Thanne nor Talitha slept. Restless, restless, the ghost was taking flesh. The ghost was *there*, waiting for the telephone to ring.

By seven in the morning, Atlanta time, Talitha could wait no longer.

She dialed the number. She heard the pulse of the ring in Dallas.

Then the connection was made. A woman's voice came over the lines: "Hello? What?"

Talitha tells me that she had planned to ask just two questions, and then to make a statement.

She said, "Is this Mary W--?"

The woman said, "Yes."

And then Talitha asked, "Did you have a baby girl on January ninth, nineteen-seventy-four?"

There was a breathing pause. Finally the woman said, "Yes. I did."

Talitha made her statement: "I have reason to believe," she said, "that I am the baby that you had."

Now there stretched between Dallas and Atlanta a silence too weighty and too long. But Talitha did not hang up. Finally she spoke into the silence, saying, "I can call you back later."

And the woman answered.

Mary W_____ said, "I always knew you would call—[pause]— I just didn't think you'd call at six and WAKE ME UP!"

My daughter's father's name is Carter. He is very short and very dark. He lives in North Carolina. So does his mother, our daughter's grandmother, Trula.

After Talitha had taken a trip from Atlanta to her house, Trula called Thanne. The elder woman was in tears.

"The baby called me Grandma!" she said to Thanne. "The baby called me Grandma."

This woman had been praying for that "baby," she said, ever since the child had been swallowed into the darkness of adoption.

And we have visited with the Frankfort side of Talitha's family. Her white birth grandfather knocked tears out of his eyes when he met her for the first time. "You are a part of us," he said with a rough-hewn formality.

Sitting in his living room, he looked at Thanne. "You called me up, didn't you."

She admitted it.

He said, "I knew this call was different. It was her." He pointed at his wife. "She reckoned the difference too. She pushed me. She said to give you the number."

And we have met Mary _____, whom we now call "Mother Mary" to distinguish her from our daughter, Talitha's "Sister Mary."

The ghost has flesh! She is no longer ghostly. And I was not wrong all those years to seek the face of the begetter in the child's face. Mary has precisely the same slant to her jaw, the same high cheekbones, the same aggressive character. They laugh alike, talk alike, aggress alike, bear their bodies quite alike, since the bodies, too, reflect each other. They are good friends, now. And Talitha has learned both her own infant history and the histories of her families. She hath a bloodline and a heritage!

But neither have Thanne and I been rendered invisible. We are flesh and blood, still, and parents of our child.

Simply: we, too, see her face in the faces of *all* her parents: Mary and Carter and the Almighty, dear and loving Creator God who stands behind all and collects all in his everlasting union.

The ghost in Jesus was holy. In him all the fullness of God was pleased to dwell. This is what Joseph by his plain, faithful obedience was granted to see: Immanuel, God with us.

In all our children's faces is the image of their Creator. When parents, by loving God, love their children right; and when, by following God, parents lead their children out of the house, into adulthood and into the purposes for which they were born, then in the fullness of their grown children they, too, will find the face of God the Father—who had lent them the children in the first place. And for a little while.

Gently, gently, parents, stand aside, even as a grandmother named Trula once stood so long aside and did her duty by praying.

After the nativity stories, Joseph's name appears again, on the lips of those who are trying to place the identity of this Jesus from

Nazareth. But the man himself finally decreases almost completely, as his adopted son increases, and the greater Father is glorified by the increase.

iv.

In those days we learned that Talitha's birth name had been Cassindra Marie. It was for "Cassindra Marie" that Trula had prayed on every holiday and on every ninth day of January, trusting her to the care of the Father.

("And see?" Trula said to us while we sat beneath Stone Mountain, celebrating our child's graduation from Spelman. "See? God heard every one of my prayers! You," she said, looking significantly at Thanne and me, "you were God's answerings all along.")

"Cassindra Marie." Talitha cherished the name as a living contact both to who she was in the beginning and to those who nursed her then.

And now our daughter has children of her own, grandchildren in triumph unto these aging adoptive parents, Ruthanne and I.

But here's a circle so cosmic it is beyond my own poor comprehension: that Talitha named her firstborn daughter by the name first empties and now made full again:

Her daughter's name, our granddaughter's name, is Cassindra Marie.

Oh, my children! What can I bequeath
You more than stories? Lips don't last: they dry
Soon, tremble soon, and die; but that they breathed
Warm words against your hair and kissed your eyes—
That will remain in memory a story.
All of the goods I leave you you will use
Up, digging out the goodness as they quarry
Carrara: I can't stay in what you choose
To change—and you *will* choose when I cannot.
But stories deep as fairy tales, as searching
As poetry, as hoary, unforgot
And vulvar as the *Heilsgeschichte,* cursing
And blessing at once—these stand mining (whether
I'm dead, ye delvers, or alive) forever.

THE PARENT OF HIS PARENTS

THE COMMANDMENTS HAVE NOT expired. Nor have the holy promises that attend them been abolished.

When, therefore, I am asked regarding the future of some human community, some family, some nation—or the church, the visible church itself!—straightway I look for obedience to the commandments of God. Particularly I wonder regarding the one which urges honor for the parents: I look to see whether someone is singing songs to his aged mother—and if I can find him, I say, "The signs are good."

This is no joke. The best prognostication for the life of any community—whether it shall be long or short—is not financial, political, demographic, or even theological. It is moral. Ask not, "How strong is this nation?" nor "How many are they? How well organized? With what armies and resources?" Ask, rather: *How does this people behave?*

See, there is always set before us life and good or death and evil. If we walk in the ways of the sustaining God and obey his commandments, then we have chosen life—for the Lord *is* life and the length of any nation's days. This is flat practicality. How we *are* defines whether we shall continue to *be.*

Do we as a people honor our mothers and our fathers? Do we honor the generation that raised us—especially when it sinks down into an old and seemingly dishonorable age? When our parents twist and bow and begin to stink, what then? When they harden in crankiness, what then? Do we by esteeming them make them sweet and lovely again? The question is not irrelevant to our future, whether we shall have one or not. Its answer verily prophesies of *That it may be well with you and you may live long on the earth.*

The Hebrew word here translated *earth* may also be translated *land,* meaning more than just soil, meaning *country.* The promise attached to this commandment is precise: so long as the Israelites

honored their parents, they would continue to live in the land that
God had provided for them. If ever they began to neglect their
parents or, worse, to scorn or in some way to hurt them, that break
between the generations would break the people from their land
as a sick tree breaks at the trunk and dies.

Even so we—as long as we sing to the mother who bore us the
songs she heard in her youth, the same songs once she sang to us
in lullaby—we may live long in the land.

I have seen the signs. In Wisconsin. In quiet obscurity, where I
went to visit a friend of mine who lives with his mother in the farmhouse her father built one hundred years ago. She has a wasting
disease. My friend cares for her.

M. is a studious man. In the evening he reads by a low lamp in
the corner of the parlor. The light casts shadows on an ancient florid
wallpaper, on heavy furniture, on the bed in the farther darkness
where his mother sleeps. He reads through half-glasses, his head
bent to the page, fingers at his chin. He reads very late because his
mother may murmur softly—too softly to be heard from any other
part of the house—and this is his signal to serve her.

But when he welcomed me to the farmhouse, it was daylight. He
opened the door and grinned with thin lips his genuine pleasure at
my coming and immediately invited me to the parlor.

The house smelled sweet and brown with cinnamon, tart with
apples.

"Your mother's baking?" I asked as we walked.

"No," he said and ducked his head a bit, an angular apology.
"No, she doesn't do that anymore."

"Then who—?"

"Oh, well," he said. Sheepish. "I see to the necessary things."

We entered the parlor, and so I understood.

His mother was sitting up in bed, a shawl around her shoulders,
smiling. I, too, smiled and walked toward her. But M. interposed,

introducing us with a formal civility as if the woman were very rich, as if we had never met before: "Mother, be pleased to meet—"

In fact, I've known M.'s mother almost as long as I have known him. But now it became clear that she had ceased to know me, and I was startled by the change. Her face was round, slack, soft, white, and, except for the querulous smile, expressionless. My dear old friend who once wore an apron and cooked for me, her face had the glaze of a dinner plate. Her watery glance never found my eyes but dribbled down my chest to my hands as if she were a child looking for candy.

M. said, "Shake hands with mother."

I did. As I reached, her right arm rose spontaneously. I took the powder-white hand that hung at the wrist and squeezed something like dough. She never ceased to smile, but questioningly. I stepped back. M. offered her a prune from a dish. She had a wonderful set of teeth. She was munching when we left the room.

We talked the rest of the day, M. and I. We strolled a sharp autumn countryside as the sun descended and the chill came down and the air smelled of crushable things, husks and hulls and leaves and the scented fires that burn them.

All the farmland had been sold, except five acres and the house itself. They kept a small orchard—and that was floating on the cool air too, a winey aroma.

I have always enjoyed the probing intellect of my friend's conversation: soft-spoken, forever undismayed, M. has a natural savvy which he has enriched with his reading. He could, if they would listen, counsel presidents.

Finally it was the night. I praised his apple pie and retired to my room and lay down and slept.

I tell you the truth—that very night I saw the signs:

At two in the morning I was awakened by a cry. I felt my stomach contract. I thought I heard a cat in the house, a lingering, feline wailing, inarticulate and mournful. It was a sort of screamed lamentation.

It seemed that someone was terribly hurt.

So I rose and followed the sound downstairs—through the kitchen to the parlor. A low lamp was lit. I peeped in.

This was no cat. This was M.'s mother. Her head was thrown backward, her mouth enormous, all her upper jaw and teeth in view. She was yowling: *Ya-ya-ya-na-naaaaah!*

M. himself was crouched at her bedside with a pan of water and cloths. He turned and saw me in the doorway. He smiled and motioned me to sit. I sat in his chair, under his reading lamp, granting them the privacy of darkness—but by the odor in the room I know what my friend was doing.

He was honoring his mother, exactly as the Lord God commanded.

He was washing away the waste. He was changing her diapers.

And he was singing to her.

Softly, in his mother's tongue, he was singing, *Müde bin ich, geh zu ruh*—Lullabies. The simple, sacred, everlasting songs.

And she was singing with him. That was the sound I had been hearing: no lamentation, no hurt nor sorrow, but an elderly woman singing with outrageous pleasure at the top of her lungs.

And lo: This old face was alive again. This old woman was as young as the child who first heard the lullaby, innocent, happy, wholly consoled. This old mother of my friend was dwelling in the music of her childhood. This was the face of one beloved, whose son obeyed the covenants and honored her—and kept her honorable thereby.

This boisterous singer is my sign. And the sign is good. Shall we endure? So long as such obedience continues among us, O my people, yes, it may be well with us. We may live long on the earth.

TWO WEEKS AGO I sat in the crowded holding area at one of the gates of Houston's Intercontinental Airport, waiting to board my flight home. First dribblingly, and then wondrously in so public a place, laughter rose up by the door of the jetway. It became a loud, footstomping hoot.

I glanced up.

Two young women were rooting through the enormous purse of a third, an older bonier woman who was obviously nervous, obviously the traveler of the three.

"Where you *got* them Tums?" cried a younger woman, her face and her full right arm deep inside this purse. "You know you need— *Whoop!*" she shrieked. "Lookee here!"

Laughing, laughing till tears streamed from her eyes, she drew forth and held up five magazines, a sandwich wrapped in wax paper, earplugs, small cans of juice, an umbrella—and a new package of underwear entitled: *Three Briefs*.

"Mamma!" she cried. "Oh, Mamma, what you want with these?" The older woman looked baffled. The younger one laughed with a flashing affection. "You got plans you ain't tol' us about?" Maybe the two young women were daughters of their more solemn elder, maybe her granddaughters. "Honey, it's the Tums'll do you most good." She dived into the purse again. "Now where you got... Oh, Mamma. Oh, Mamma," she whispered with suddenly softer wonder: "Look."

This young woman had a magnificent expanse of hip and the freedom of spirit to cover it in a bright red skirt, tight at the waist, wide behind, and tight again at the knee. She stood on spiky heels. Fashion forced her to walk by short wobbly steps, oddly opposite her amplitude of hip and cheek and laughter.

"Oh, Mamma!" Suffused with gentleness, she pulled from the purse a worn leather-bound Testament and Psalms. "Mamma, what? What you thinkin'?" The two women exchanged a silent look, each full of the knowledge of the other. The generations did not divide them.

"Well," said the older, bony woman, "you found the nourishment, but you ain't found the Tums." With a bark of laughter, Young Woman in Red hunkered down into the purse again—tottering on her tiny heels.

At the same time there came down the concourse an old man so gaunt in his jaw as to be toothless, bald and blotched on his skull, meatless arm and thigh. He sat in a wheelchair, listing to the right. The chair was being pushed through the crowds at high speeds by an attendant utterly oblivious of this wispy, thin, and ancient passenger.

The old man's eyes were troubled, but his mouth, sucked inward, was mute. His nose gave him the appearance of a hawk caught in a trap, helpless and resigned.

Now the attendant turned into our gate area, jerked the chair to a stop (bouncing the skeletal soul therein), reached down to set the brake, turned on his heel, and left.

But the brake was not altogether set, nor had the chair altogether stopped. It was creeping by degrees toward the generous hips of the woman whose face was buried in the generous purse of her elder, giggling.

The old man's eyes—the closer he rolled to this red rear end as wide as Texas—widened. He opened his mouth. He began to raise a claw. He croaked. And then he ran straight into the back of her knees.

Yow! Up flew the great purse, vomiting contents. Backward stumbled the young woman, a great disaster descending upon a crushable old man.

At the last instant, she whirled around and caught herself upon the armrests of the wheelchair, a hand to each rest. Her face froze one inch from the face of an astonished octogenarian. They stared at one another, so suddenly and intimately close that they must have felt the heat—each must have smelled the odor of the other.

All at once the woman beamed. "Oh, honey!" she cried. "You somethin' handsome, ain't you?" She leaned the last inch forward and kissed him a noisy smack in the center of his bald head. "I didn't hurt you none, did I?"

Strangers were strangers no longer. Suddenly they were something more.

Slowly there spread over the features of this ghostly old man the most beatific smile. Oh, glory and heat and blood and love rose up in a body dried to tinder.

And the young woman burst into thunderous laughter. "Look at you!" she bellowed. "What yo wife gon' say when she see my lipstick kiss on yo head? Ha ha ha!" He reached to touch the red, and she cried, "You gon' have some explainin' to do!"

That old man closed his eyes in soundless laughter with the woman—two made one for a fleeting moment.

So did the elderly woman, who still hadn't found her Tums, laugh.

So did I, surprising myself. So did a host of travelers who had been watching the episode with me. We all laughed, gratefully. *We,* in the brief event and the silly joke of wives and kisses, were unified.

It wasn't the joke, of course. It was goodwill. It was spontaneous affection. It was the willingness of a single woman, wholly human even in the public eye—in risk and under judgment—suddenly, swiftly to love another, to honor him, to give him something graceful without hesitation or fear, something free and sweet and durable. But she gave it to us all. I won't forget her. I beg God, in such revealing moments, that I might be as generous and good as she.

There was a sanctity in the kiss of that woman.

And in this: that the man was as white as the snows of Sweden, and the woman as black as the balmy nights of Africa.

ONE SUMMER WE TOOK Dorothy to the mountains. It was a risk, but it had become necessary to initiate certain changes in her life.

Soft Dorothy was as citified as they come, though the city she comes from is tiny. She had lived her whole life in the shelter of her parents, who kept that life very regular: sleeping, rising, eating, a little work, a load of ease, and ice cream before she went to bed each night. Almost nothing interrupted the daily round of Dorothy-affairs. She never got caught in the rain downtown. She seldom *walked* to town. She rode everywhere. She had almost never been separated from her parents.

But her father was eighty-nine years old, her mother not much younger—and Dorothy herself was forty. The clock which ticked her day so neatly was likewise ticking the lives of her parents to their ends. It was time that she should experience a real separation from them before death forced the issue and sorrow complicated everything. So we took her with us to the mountains.

But it was a risk.

Round Dorothy was ever exceedingly private. She squirreled money in secret places in her room. More valuable than money were the pictures she clipped from magazines, pictures she hid so well they shan't be found till doomsday. Her eyes would open wide with panic when little children entered her bedroom. Who can control little children? But even then Dorothy said almost nothing. She was private. She buried her thoughts; she muted her basic communication in grunts and grumbles. But she didn't have to talk, after all. Her mother knew her needs, decided her desires, spoke for her—spoke, indeed, even before Dorothy thought she had a thought. It really was time, you see, for Dorothy to step out on her own.

But round Dorothy was also exceedingly—round. The woman stood no higher than my elbow, yet was wider than I am by half at the beam. Cute little ankles, prodigious thighs, and a body as round as a medicine ball. To the *mountains* with Dorothy? Why, she could scarcely climb the stair steps one flight up.

Her eyes are slant behind their glasses; her tongue lolls on the lower lip; her chins redouble backward; her expression is generally benign and vague.

Dorothy has Down's syndrome. She is what people call "retarded." She is also Thanne's sister, my sister-in-law; and since I was to teach for several weeks at Holden Village in the Cascade Mountains of the Northwest, we took Hob in our hands and said: "Let Dorothy come with us."

Her mother swallowed painfully, considered the need, wept with a mother's solicitude, and relented. She packed for her daughter a suitcase the size of Montana (in which *she* squirreled handwritten instructions not shorter than the Book of Leviticus. For example: "Dorothy's bazooka is in her underwear. She likes to play it." Her *bazooka?* What was that? Ah, when we looked in her underwear we found her *kazoo*).

O Holden Village, hold your breath!—here comes Dorothy, the daughter of her mother. Holden, be patient and kind. We can all sacrifice a little to train this woman-child in independence, right?

Oh, and Holden? Please give us rooms low down, on a flat level with the rest of your buildings, because Dorothy is so very . . . round.

So we went to the wilds, the Wangerins six and sister Dorothy of the wide, wide eyes. It was an airplane flight from Chicago to Seattle, a car trip to the town of Chelan, a boat trip for three hours up the lake while mountains rose around us to dangerous sizes, and finally a bus trip up those mountains—miles high in the mighty, remote, foredooming mountains of God.

In Holden Village, then, Dorothy rolled her beanbag body off the bus, looked up at the craggy peaks yet higher than she, patted her bosom, and sighed: "Whew!"

The registrar met us. He pointed to our quarters. He pointed upward at an angle of forty degrees, to the top of a long road.

Whew! We—all seven of us—bowed our heads and climbed.

"Whew!" said Dorothy. She moved as slowly as the moon. *Whew!* This medicine ball expressed herself in a variety of sighs, one for each new height as she struggled upward. And when we achieved the top of the hill—when still we stood at the bottom of the staircase that extended up to the front porch of our house—Dorothy stopped and produced a truly admirable cavalcade of sighs: "Whew! Whew! Whew!"—fanning her face, popping her eyes, and grinning. Grinning! She was Rocky Balboa at the end of his run.

Now I declare to you a wonder: Dorothy was not mute at all! She was profoundly expressive to those who had the ears to hear her.

Later, when she spied the busy ground squirrels, she paused and offered them a series of happy squeal-sighs, as if meeting with glee some long-lost relatives. When deer raised their noble necks and gazed at this round dollop of a woman, she honored them with murmurous sacred sighs as soft as lullabies. When she stepped on a slat bridge over roaring waters—which water we could see between the boards below our feet—she made a bleating sigh, and I realized how brave she was to stand so near the tumbling chaos. And when she lifted her eyes to the ring of mountains around us, and when she grew gravely still, allowing one long sigh, one eternal expulsion of breath to escape her languorous throat, I said in my soul: *Listen, my sister is praying!*

Retarded? Who is the fool that says so? This woman had an apprehension of the universe more intimate and more devout than my own. Her knowing was not troubled by extraneous thought. Dorothy had a language of genuine sophistication and of immediate response. Sighs were her words. Add to that some simple English grunts which even I could understand, and Dorothy was bilingual.

I had been to Holden Village three times before that summer, but I had never seen so well the crown surrounding it, had never seen with primal eyes until I stood with Dorothy looking up and sighing. I took squirrels to my heart, honored deer, and praised the God of supernal peaks—because of Dorothy. She was the quick one. My responses were baffled and slow. She was the one who trained me, both in seeing and in speaking. I, in the high, green tiara of the Deity—I, in simple creation—was the retarded one. How often we get it backward. How much we miss when we do!

On the second night we were there, Dorothy went up on her toes and embraced me in a mighty hug and kissed my chin and murmured, "Whew!"

I, too, said, "Whew!"

Her word meant, "What a good day!"

Mine meant, *Thank you, sweet sister, for taking me to the mountains this summer.*

AT ABOUT NINE O'CLOCK in the evening—a weeknight, as I recall it—my mother telephoned from her home across several states to Evansville. She asked to talk with me.

"Hello?" I said.

She was abrupt. There were the metallic tones of urgency in her voice.

"We leave tomorrow," she said to me. "You knew that? Did you know that, Wally?"

I knew that they were preparing to travel through sub-Saharan Africa, my parents together, but no: I hadn't known that their departure was so close upon them.

"Tomorrow," I said.

"Tomorrow," she repeated. "Flight leaves at eight thirty-six in the morning."

Mom was breathing heavily, as if they meant to run the distance and were getting a head start now. Or else as if she were terrified of the prospect. What time was it for her right now? Shouldn't she be in bed?

But Mom and Dad had already spent a great portion of their lives in Hong Kong, where Dad established a Christian college and Mom taught Chinese children. At various points in my father's career they had traveled overseas, and by many means had they gone. Why would my mother be fearful now?

"Wally? Are you listening to me? Are you paying attention?"

"Yes, Mom. Of course I am."

During this particular journey my father would act as an educational consultant for a host of Christian schools, spending time at each one, assessing, discussing, leading workshops. Preaching. My father preached almost everywhere he went. He considered these assignments late in his career to be "Missionary Journeys." He drew quiet parallels between his labors and St. Paul's.

"Wally?"

"What."

"Do you remember that night—?"

She paused. For an instant she could not continue. But my mother is ever verbal, as quick as scissors with her words, and fiery, too.

"Mom. What are you—"

"Do you remember what you said to me?" she demanded.

"But what night do you—"

"The night in the dining room—" she overspoke my words, denying me any speculation about which night she had in mind. "We were in the dining room. After supper. You, home from school," she rushed to the point. "You caught your jacket on the screendoor. Wally! Do you remember what you said to me?"

Ahhhhh. *That* night.

Our memories are remarkable and immediate, my mother's and mine. And a single detail can pitch us at once and together into the furnace of any past event. We hit the coals walking, as did Shadrach, Meshach, and Abednego.

Do you remember what you said to me?

Yes. Yes.

Mostly, when my mother screamed at me, I was mute, incapable of *any* response, let alone a loud one or a reasoned one. Her force blew language straight out of my head. I couldn't even think a word, let alone utter it, so consumed was I by the guilt of her accusations, so confused by the dizzying, impossible leaps of her logic. She was a square-set woman in those days, a solid physical presence. And her words, under pressure of her emotions, shot like jets of flame into my soul. She was a poet of the thrilling, ripping image, and I was torn, and I burned before her.

But on that particular night I had found my voice. Hoarsely I had shouted back at her. And the thing I said was a thing I had been contemplating for a long time. I suppose it had been packaged and prepared for delivery, though I knew nothing of such internal preparations.

The thing I yelled at her had been born of a fathomless sorrow in me. For it seemed to me that my mother did not truly believe in the grace of God. For she never confessed a sin of her own—not, at least, in my presence nor in our long relationship. And anything that even betokened a personal fault on her part would send her into furies of retaliation and counter accusations. *But,* I thought to myself, *if only she would confess.* She would then be forgiven, and her torments, her internal contradictions could finally be eased. The fire extinguished, the furnace would cool. In fact, she *was* forgiven, could she know it. But first . . .

Ah, mother, the yearning rose from an ineffable love, *God can make you peaceful.*

On that night of screaming, I raised my own voice and the thing got said.

I remember an autumn weekend. Friday evening. Saturday. Most of the rest of the family is absent, out of the house or out of the room. Whatever the case, they do not appear in my memory. There are but the two of us, dirty dishes on the table, Mom still sitting at her place, I standing across the table. I am wearing a light windbreaker. The light seems impossibly bright.

As she scolds me, she becomes more and more agitated. I think we're discussing the amount of time I do and do not spend at home.

I utter excuses. I speak in my own defense.

But every effort on my account bedevils my mother the more. She slaps the table with the flat of her hand. Finally she rises up, screaming, screaming.

And I can't bear the look in her face. Or the cut of her words. And to tell it truly, it is not only the personal assault that drowns me and leaves me breathless, it is also the howling desolations of my mother's soul.

"Mom!" I cry it as loudly as I can: "I have already forgiven you!" I turn. I start to escape the dining room. I can't now recall whether she is screaming still, or else has fallen silent, but I *think* she's screaming, for everything in me yearns to run away. I reach the back door. I open it. I'm clumsy. I can't jerk the screen door open.

"I have already forgiven you!" I shout, scarcely aware of the source of these words. And I shout: "You just don't know it yet!"

The pocket of my windbreaker catches on the screendoor handle. I am so desperate to run, it tears, and I go.

"Do you remember what you said to me?" my mother asked, so many years after that night, mere hours before she and my father took off for Africa, and who knew when they would be home again.

Her telephone voice was urgent, headlong.

Do you remember?

And I—my head lowered, my left hand cupping the mouthpiece of the telephone, my voice subdued, and my heart made vulnerable all over again—I answered in the darkness, "Yes. I remember."

There was a beat of silence. I was in my study. The study door was closed. That's why the room was dark. Thanne was in the kitchen.

"Well," said my mother with this persistent urgency, "did you mean it? Did you mean what you said to me?"

And although I was no longer that boy, trembling in a dining room so brightly lit with lights and fires and feelings; though I could only recall, not actually feel, the mood with which the boy first spoke the words, I said, "Yes."

"Well, then," my mother said. "So, then. Good. Fine. All right."

She hung up. I heard the distant click.

GENUINE LOVE IS DEFINED by this, that it is prepared to sacrifice itself for the sake of the beloved.

Sham love, on the other hand, makes *itself* the motive, the cause and the end of relationship. Sham love may know "sacrifice," but only as a means to reach some goal of its own. It says, "Since I have given up so much for you, now you owe me. . ." There is no giving without some getting, even if that which is gotten is merely public praise or the sweet internal feeling: *What a good person am I!*

Genuine love serves. Neither requiring nor expecting something in return. Its character is, simply, to serve—and those who stumble against these twin axioms of sacrifice and service will likewise stumble against the cross. They will fall down crying, "Scandal!"

Sham love stumbles.

Sham love may *think* it desires to serve the beloved; in fact, it desires only (and precisely) the beloved for itself. It desires his company, her person—some respondent love. So its service is not an end in itself. Sham love may perform the most difficult services, things its beloved shall absolutely need—until she becomes dependent upon them and thereby bound unto her "servant," her benefactor. Do you see? Sham love fulfills itself in the end by possessing the other.

Genuine love has one goal only: the health and honor, the full flowering and the *freedom* of the beloved. It serves her that she might become her own most beautiful self. It seeks the rose within the bud, and then—when all the world sees but a nubble—it nourishes that bud with rain and the richness of its own self. This is holy sacrifice, the outpouring of one self upon another, until that other opens up and blossoms. Genuine love rejoices when the beloved is finally lovely and perfectly free.

Sham love never perceives the image intrinsic within the other. Rather, it makes up its own image of what she ought to be according to its own designs, then imposes this fiction upon her. When she does not conform (well, she can't: she is *herself,* not *his* self) sham love might remain resolutely blind to what she is and pretend that *she* has conformed, imprisoning her within its restrictive lie. Or else it will blame her for the failure: "I'm so disappointed in you!" Thus justified, sham love will try harder to force conformity, or will reject her altogether. In either case, it confesses no wrong. It believes it has *been* wronged.

One of the plainest signs of sham love is self-pity.

Another is fear of freedom.

Since the goal of sham love is itself, it must control the beloved. In fact, it measures her love by the amount of obedience she gives its will. Therefore, though genuine love takes a genuine joy in the free flight of the beloved, sham love is angered by her slightest act of independence; angered first, then threatened; then frightened by the independence that bodes separation; and finally, if she has flown indeed, sham love falls into the despair of the unfulfilled.

Listen to the songs of the world and the language it uses for love. How often the point of the song is the singer! Listen to the wisdom of the world: "Feeling good about myself, yeah! Satisfaction is my birthright, and my worth you must acknowledge, just because I AM." Such a demand—though it makes a worldly sense—is exactly the opposite of sacred love, for it makes a god of the self.

It must always be offended by the cross.

But listen, and I will show you a more excellent way.

More than forty years ago my parents-in-law brought Dorothy into the world—their thirteenth child, an infant afflicted with Down's syndrome. Because of her mental incapacity, they chose to keep her at home; and though she learned much and went forth to work each day, they lavished upon her more service than any other child required. In fact, her presence and her need required her parents to continue *as* parents long after they might have been taking their ease. Martin added ninety years to his age and still was parenting a child; Gertrude added eighty-four. But this is love, that they served with unceasing, uncomplaining devotion for forty-one years.

But this, too, is genuine love: that finally they had to stop serving her.

Dorothy has moved into a group home established for the mentally handicapped. She received her own room, her own place in life. She picked out her own wallpaper and curtains—and all this was pure delight to her. She was free.

But her mother was weeping. And her father, full of love, was solemn. Suddenly they weren't parents any more. They were not needed as they had been. They had sacrificed, for their daughter's sake, their significant reason to *be,* had sacrificed something of their own identities. This is love. The emptiness of the house; the release of its sometime sweet inhabitant, who had been life and focus for old eyes; the farewell of the heart: "Good-bye, good-bye, Dorothy"— this is love.

But Gertrude and Martin knew how close they were to dying. They knew that Dorothy would suffer a double trauma should they die while she was still beside them, since any new home would then be ruined by the reason for going and the grieving that brought her there. So Gertrude and Martin chose to bear the grief of departure themselves, while Dorothy could feel a full, untroubled joy in it. This is a gift she may never comprehend. This is her parents' personal sacrifice. This is love.

Just before she was driven away, they kissed her. Martin moved slowly in a walker. Gertrude, for a weak heart, puffed small puffs of air. Dorothy clambered into the car without a second thought, grinned, and waved brightly. Gertrude rushed back into the house, embarrassed by her tears. Martin bent into the car window. "Be good," the old man whispered. "Be good, Dorothy. Good-bye."

And then he, too, wept.

But he let her go. The bud was becoming a rose. The rains that washed and watered her may never see this blossom blow. They serve, and then they sink into the earth. This is a genuine love.

THE GRANDPARENT, FINALLY, OF MANY

A NOAH TREE

BRAVELY, DRAMATICALLY I DECLARED to the woman at Samuelson's Nursery, "I want to purchase a Noah Tree. Does Samuelson's have a Noah Tree?"

She frowned, not even pretending that such a thing existed.

"He should be a beautiful tree," I fairly sang the description: "straight-stemmed, full of promise for the strength and the height of his maturity. For he will carry me, one day!"

At my approach the woman had removed her gloves to serve me. Now, wordlessly, she began to put them on again.

So I came down from my foolishness. "Forgive me," I said. "I have a grandson, two months old. Our first, you know. And I want to plant a tree in his name." I grinned hard, helplessly. "In the name of Noah Martin!"

And I knew the color of my tree instinctively.

"Do you have," I said, "a flaming maple?"

I bought the tree on Wednesday.

All day Thursday I dug a great pit on the highest ground in the field behind our house. I lined my pit with a rich mulch and a good black earth. I watered both the root-ball of the maple and the soil that would receive it. And then, myself a rain of sweating, I rolled the ball into the pit and filled it layer-by-layer with more black earth.

I delighted in the labor.

On Friday our daughter Mary came to town with her husband John and their child, our grandchild, Noah Martin Sauger. They took a bedroom. I said, "Come outside."

I showed them the tree. Baby Noah was oblivious, but his parents appreciated the work. The Noah Tree stood twelve feet high, its stem two inches in diameter, its red leaves spread like a double umbrella just above our heads.

Friends from Evansville showed up on Saturday—many of these past members of the Sounds of Grace, our remarkable choir. All of the rest of the family—Thanne's and mine—came too: Joseph from Minneapolis with his fiancée, Catherine Preus; Matthew, up from Atlanta; Talitha and her fiancée, Ray Washington from Connecticut. These two were in graduate school together. They had come home to marry.

In fact, their wedding was much the public center of our gathering, this particular weekend in May, 1998. On Saturday afternoon Talitha and Ray were married here in Valparaiso at Christ Lutheran Church. I preached. Oh, how close to the gates I stood that weekend: for under my formal ministrations, and in the rituals of our worship, generations and generations were meeting and weaving together. I was entering the golden age of my vocation with a nearly speechless joy: I preached.

And then, on Sunday morning, I drew fresh well-water into a basin. I bore the basin to a low table in our living room. I set a cross before, and lit two candles on either side of, the water.

And, thus prepared, I called together the whole company of family and friends, to witness the baptism of our grandson, Noah Martin.

Although I've never found it written down, by way of the oral traditions of African-Americans I know a certain ritual observed by grandmother slaves in the deep and humid, long-ago South. Twice the living grandchildren described the ritual to me. And though the details differed between my two story tellers, the human sadness and the grave admiration of their telling was the same.

It was a ritual involving of infants and trees. It was performed on hidden ground in perfect secrecy; the custom was the spiritual use of material things; it was a brave assault on time and space and separations; and it fought the sorrow of a certain loss with a stern, perpetual union—and with a Something Dear To Do.

Here, briefly, is what I heard:

That shortly before a slave woman was to give birth, she was led by the grandmother slaves into the woods, to a clearing in the woods where there grew a tended and nurtured grove of trees, to a tub of water in that clearing. At night under moonlight, the old women washed the younger one in that tub. They saved the water.

That, in the same night, a seedling was planted at the edge of the grove, where trees of every age and species could be found, saplings and the mossy oaks tended well together.

That hard labor brought this woman and all the grandmothers back to the grove and to the tub and to that water, waiting.

That she bore her baby in the tub, and all the fluids of this parturition mingled with the waters of her own washing; yes, and the afterbirth, too.

That the placenta was buried near the root of the seedling planted, and the soup of birthing was poured over all.

And that the infant and the tree bore the very same name together. Not two same names for two beings, one rooted and one walking. No: it was one name, one spirit in two manifestations.

And why would the grandmothers go to such a trouble? And why did they return regularly to this grove, to prune and to mulch, to protect it and to stand in its shade?

Because this was the grove of the generations of their children. Every tree received the same nursing as did the child whose spirit dwelt within that tree; and the love of the grandmothers was fed to the fleshy mouth as to the woody one, both as one. They kissed the baby when he grew a child. They taught the fresh young woman of blood and bearing. They loved the flesh while flesh was with them still. But ever and ever they lived against the day when that sweet flesh would be taken from them and the two would be torn asunder. For the slaves were sold, and these grandmothers had no control over the sale, and the children lost would surely *suffer* the lostness, too—aliens in the universe.

Aliens, except for this: that their spirits still had a dwelling place near the love and the nourishment of home.

For the grandmothers had a Something Dear To Do, by which to keep a fierce, abiding union. Daily they cared for the trees, caring thereby for the souls of their grandbabies. Here were their children's symbols close to hand.

And the young men lost, and the young women sold into Midianite hands—they knew. They had in memory the tree, the place where their grandmothers were rendering service. And they need never doubt the service! Someone still was stroking their souls and begging the Heavenly Father on their behalf. Wherever else they went, their home remained their home. And the hard link was the tree.

Maintaining that grove maintained the family in spite of the knives of time and space, and the strikes of the unkind powers of this world.

Moreover, I learned from a Jewish friend that he and many Jews balance the circumcision of their sons by planting trees for their daughters. It becomes her own placement among the People, as trees in nature are placed. Her life, its life: green beneath the summer's sun, growing, a citizen of every weather—with mountains and hills, with fruit trees and all cedars praising the name of the Lord!

So the Sunday morning living room was crowded soon with our People. I stood at the little table that bore the basin of water, and prayed a prayer.

Catherine Preus sat down at the piano. She made chords sound like falling water, and then we, all of us, sang a hymn together. And because the voices from Grace Church were among us, we were angels hovering at the baby's shoulders.

We sang: *Thy holy wings, O Savior, Spread gently over me.*

Our words were lifted on behalf of baby Noah, who could not utter a word for himself: *And let me rest securely, Through good and ill with thee.*

Noah slept. Asleep, his eyes never opening, Noah stretched and yawned, and the sunlight flooded his mouth, and still we sang: *O be my strength and portion, My rock and hiding place . . .*

Tears sprang up in my daughter's eyes, Mary the mother still holding her baby in arms. I motioned her to stand and come forward. She did. John did. The baby did, while we sang: *And let my every moment Be lived within thy grace.*

Then Mary could not stop crying. Nor could John. And Grandma Thanne's eyelashes sparkled with her gladness. And before all the people, I made floods of water fall upon my grandson's head, saying, "Noah Martin, I baptize you in the name of the Father, and of the Son, and of the Holy Spirit."

Loud clapping exploded in our living room, and it seemed to me that every pair of hands was a pair of wings beating the air as when great flocks of birds take flight.

I lifted the bowl of baptismal water in my own hands. I wound my way through the crowd, then through the kitchen and out our back door, and Mary came beside me, and Thanne was carrying Noah now, and the angels followed as we processed to the field behind our house, and to the flaming maple waiting there.

The people sang spontaneously in the sunlight:

"O let me nestle near thee
Within thy downy breast
Where I will find sweet comfort
And peace within thy nest."

As we approached the tree, I whispered to Thanne to stand beneath its shadow. The tree would protect the baby from the harsher sunlight.

The rest came through the field. They gathered in a circle, singing:

"Oh, close thy wings around me
And keep me safely there;
For I am but a newborn
And need thy tender care."

Thanne elevated the child as high as she could. Noah went up fearlessly. The maple leaves crowned him with fire beneath a cobalt sky. Wind tousled us all. Then Grandpa, the preacher, spoke of the Tree of Life at the beginning of time, that tree which was shut against us when we had sinned by eating the fruit of another tree. Grandpa poured a little of the baptismal water at the roots of the maple.

Next the preacher spoke of the tree at the center of time, upon which Christ hung as the curse of God, upon which Jesus poured his red, red blood, to win us life again. And at the roots of the maple I poured a little more water.

Finally I spoke of the Tree of Life, now awaiting us all at the end of time.

"Awaiting you, my blessed grandson," I said.

I stooped and poured the rest of the water of Noah's second birth at the wooden mouth of Noah's tree.

When I am done writing today, I will get up from my desk and lock my studio door and walk home over the field in which my grandson's tree still stands, still grows, is more than twice my height. There are four such trees in the field, now: a willow, a fir, a blue spruce, and the maple. I pause as I pass them. For not one of our grandchildren lives nearby; and who knows where their parents will take them in the future, or what their destinies shall do to them. And I am growing older. I travel less. I count my remaining years. I keep close to home.

But in these trees are the spirits of my grandchildren invested, and by each tree I am reminded that the time and the space that takes them away cannot finally sunder the cords of my compassion for them. No. And should they go so far from me that I cannot hear their voices at all, yet this relationship shall supercede the unkindness of the slavers of this world, surely. Surely!

For even as I have named the trees, God has named my grandchildren one by one! And the name God gave them, every one, is "My Delight Is In You," and "You Are My Child."

Yea, though Noah should take the wings of the morning and dwell in the uttermost parts of the sea, even there the shadow of the Savior's tree shall find him and cover him.

A PSALM: GOD IN A GRANDCHILD, SMILING

Omnipotens sempiterne Deus!
Almighty God, the Everlasting, Thou!
I cannot look steadfastly at the sun and not go blind. Holiness exceeds my sight—though I know it is, and I know thou art.

Aeterne Deus omnium rerum Creator!
Thou art above all created things.
To everything made, thou art the Other. Greater than thee there is no world; in thee all worlds have being; and I take my trivial, mortal way upon the smallest sphere of all. How shall I hope to see thee and not to die?

Lux Mundi!
But in thy mercy:
Thou shinest down upon the things that thou hast made. They brighten in thy light. Every morning they reflect thee. I wake to an effulgence of mirrors, and lo: I see.

Misericors Deus!
For my sake, for my poor fleshly sight:
Thou changest thy terrible holiness here before me into glory—the visible light, the doxology I can see. I rise and look around, and I cry praise to thee.

Deus, incommutabilis virtus, lumen aeternum!
From thee to me it is a mighty diminution:
Ever the same, thou makest thy presence manifest in things that are both mutable and common. But from me to thee it is epiphany: gazing at things most common, suddenly I see thy light, thy glory, and thy face.

Nobiscum Deus!
Then:
What shall I say to thee but *Deo Gratias?* Thanks be to God!

Deo Gratias!
For the dew that damps the morning grasses is a baptism, always, always renewing the earth. And the air remembers that once it ushered down the dove that was the breath of God. And I myself inhale the rinsed spirit of the morning air and I, too, am renewed.

Deo Gratias!
For dawn, in the chalices of the clouds, brims them with a bloody wine, a running crimson. And this is a sign to me. The sun is coming.

Deo Gratias!
For the sun, when it breaks at the horizon, transfigures every thing. And this is a gift to me. For the transfiguration itself persuades my soul of sunrise.

Jesui filii Dei, gratias!
For I have seen a baby sleeping in a shaft of sunlight, and behold: in the curve of every eyelash was a small sun cupped. And from these fringes tiny rays shot forth to sting me. Wherefore sunrise at the far horizon was sunrise near me in this infant.

Et verbum caro factum est—
For the baby suddenly opened her mouth and yawned. And into that pink cavern rushed the sunlight, trembling and flashing like a living thing. But it was thee, bright God, in the mouth of a mortal infant.

"Ecce ego vobiscum sum—"
For the baby woke to the morning and saw me close beside her, and she smiled.

Ah, God! What an epiphany of smiling that was! My own transfiguration! For this was the primal light, the glory of the morning, thy splendor and thy face before me come.

Deo gratias, cuius gloria!

Then glory be to thee, Father, Son, and Holy Spirit, as it was in the beginning, is now, and ever shall be, *saecula saeculorum*.

Amen.

MY NAME IS DOROTHY BOHLMANN

Dear Dorothy:

Just last Saturday we gathered at Mom and Dad Bohlmann's to celebrate Independence Day. You came—you and all your mates from group home, both the staff and the "handicapped" inhabitants. Thanne and I were there too, of course, with four other Bohlmann "children" and their spouses. They all have spouses. All your mother's children married—except two. Of the fourteen children she bore, only two did not leave home to marry and to bear children of their own. But Raymond died when he was an infant, more than half a century ago.

And you have Down's syndrome.

Dorothy, did you ever stop enjoying the weddings of your many siblings? Did you ever think it was your turn to be given such attention, such a beautiful day, and such a good good-bye? And then did it ever seem that the ceremony everyone else received had been denied to you alone? The last child to leave left nearly twenty years ago. But you stayed. Did you watch and wait in yearning? Did yearning ever turn to envy, and envy into sorrow?

It is my instinct that you did. I think you, too, in the natural course of growing older, wanted to marry. It's only an instinct. You never spoke. For years and years you made your feelings known in tears or smiles or fussy grunts—or sighs. You said "Whew" a thousand ways. But no words.

Well, and it is also my instinct that having been granted no choice in something so universally human, you exercised choice in one of the few areas over which no one had control but you. You could not choose not to eat, of course. And your mother insisted on choosing *what* you ate, *what* you wore, *where* you went, *how* you got there, *when* you would come home. I think you marked off a tiny area of independence by withdrawing into silence. No one could reach you there.

Dorothy, I think there was a part of you that *chose* not to talk.

So, on the Fourth of July last week, we "normal" folks stood on the library lawn in Watseka, Illinois, and watched a parade in which the whole town participated. Your housemates dressed like clowns and strode the street with great solemnity, staring straight ahead—oh, so obedient and so earnest!

Then we gathered in Mom's backyard under a splendid blue Midwestern sky. We gave thanks to God for independence and for freedom. We sang "God Bless America." We prayed. We ate. You sat in state, it seemed to me, receiving the attentions of many friends, the only one related to everyone there—and then it dawned on me how you are the hinge that joins two families, for you are a Bohlmann, and you are the only Bohlmann in the group home. If the Wangerins and the Bohlmanns had gathered, then Thanne would have been the hinge between two families because she married me. Because she left her home and I left mine and we made a new home together, joining two.

I gazed long at you that afternoon, dear sister, and I said in my soul, *No, but Dorothy did leave her mother and her father to cleave unto others, and they have made a new home together—*

Oh, Dorothy, how you have changed!

Look at you, Lady: here comes Donny of the group home, whizzing through the yard (Donny, whose face is as aerodynamic as a 747, is always whizzing); he suddenly stops to hug you and ask how you are doing, seriously searches your eyes for a whole second, then is seized with another spasm of speed, and whizzes on. Donny wears an old World-War-One-flying-ace hat with earflaps. And you? You accept his adoration as something natural to him and due to you. Then you happen to catch me watching you. So you wave a little wind into your face and you smile back at me and you sigh, "Whew, whew!"—as if to say, *That's Donny. He'll take your breath away.*

Do you remember when we went to the mountains together? That was four years ago. You still make the silly sigh you made then, but you scarcely *need* to any more. You've lost roundness! Motion is easier now than before. The new home which you have made with others has made you a healthier woman. Independence. I said in my soul, *No, Dorothy's no different from any child of Gertrude after all.* Independence is the beginning of health, an absolutely necessary thing.

Yet Gertrude suffered when you left her. That was two years ago. And since you were the last to leave of her fourteen, it was, I believe, as if all fourteen symbolically left with you; motherhood itself departed Gertrude when you did. How long did it take her to reconcile herself? She kept appearing in your new home, still making decisions for you, rearranging your clothes in the dresser drawers, still instructing you in what to wear. Well, and then you made silence your privacy: you thrust out your lip and folded your arms, and sometimes you wore exactly what you wanted to wear, though it wounded and outraged your poor mother. For something so wrong as this, someone must be at fault. Well, so she'd blame the staff of the group home for letting you get away with murder. Well, so everyone was upset for a while. Independence is a terrible thing. It tears from those who are left behind their very reason for being. It causes a nearly catastrophic loneliness. It was very hard on Mom. Recently I wrote that she has stopped crying about your absence. She wrote back straightway to tell me I was wrong. She still cries.

She's eighty-seven this year. What a change she had to sustain in her old age! Her heart is weak, this mother of many, this grandmother of multitudes. It cannot be long before she and Martin shall die. They know that. They speak of it, not always peacefully but always, always faithfully. She trembles when she moves too much. Martin is ninety-two. He drags a walker slowly. He had to lean on his son's arm in order to come down the porch stairs into the yard for our Independence Day picnic, and there he sat in a wheelchair making jokes. Both of your parents have minds as lucid as your own heart is lucid, Dorothy. Yes, Gertrude still cries for you. Perhaps she always will. And I think you know that, don't you?

I watched you throughout the length of a long, lazy afternoon. And before the Midwestern sun had set, sweet sister, I saw you do two marvelous things.

One was new and astonishing. It took my breath away. It made me know how much you've grown and how good "marriage" has been for you. The other was natural unto you, no change at all, the same sort of thing you've been doing all your life but no less marvelous for that.

In the midst of the day's activity, I heard something. I heard you. Under the noises of your housemates, who speak a yowling sort of English, who laugh with perfect delight and lolling tongues, who rush hither and yon as if accomplishing some business so urgent the sky would fall without it; under the hubbub of eating and gossip and fire-cracking, the dashing of the children; under the long, slow snoozing of the sun, I heard a murmuring. I looked and saw that your spirit had withdrawn into its private vale, and I thought that the day had become too much for you again. But then I saw your lips move. You were repeating the same soft sentence over and over.

Dorothy, you were speaking! Sister, you were talking—although you seemed oblivious of the loud celebration all around you: talking to yourself, then.

Well, I crept near you to hear you the better but slowly, slowly, so that my coming would not disturb the moment nor destroy the quiet sentence. And then it was you who took my breath away.

With your head bent as if contemplating some complicated thing, gazing into your two palms upturned in your lap, scarcely moving your lips, you were murmuring, "My name is Dorothy Bohlmann. My name is Dorothy Bohlmann. My name is Dorothy Bohlmann—"

I said in my soul, *This woman is free! This woman is whole! No, she is in nothing diminished. She is the equal of any child of Gertrude and Martin, the peer of any child of God.*

Thirteen children indeed did leave to make new homes for themselves and new lives, too. Only Raymond did not. You did. The only difference between you and your siblings is that you were the last to go and bore the greater burden therefore. But now you, Dorothy, are fully adult. Let no one lisp when they speak to you. Let no one simplify speech and exaggerate their tone as if they were talking to a child of small understanding. In that sense you are no child at all.

And in another sense you are more mature than most of my acquaintances.

Near the end of the day, after the rest of the group home had departed, leaving you with us for the night, after the yard had been cleaned and while we sat chatting, entering evening, suddenly Mom cried out in pain and grabbed her leg. All her children rushed toward her. "No!" she said, waving people back and trying to laugh the pain away, but it kept returning in stabs and she couldn't help crying out again: "Oh! *Oh, NO!* "

It had been a hard day. Mom doesn't know how to quit. Moreover the party had been her idea. She wanted to make some gesture of thanksgiving to the staff of the group home. She wanted somehow to say that she didn't blame them any more. Gertrude is making peace. Your mother, Dorothy, is laboring to let you go. I think she is granting you your liberty. It was a day made hard, then, as much by the work of the heart as of the body.

"Ow!" she cried. Tears broke down her cheeks.

Immediately your face twisted with anxiety. You felt your mother's pain. It is your skill immediately to enter another soul and to feel precisely what that one feels.

And you love your mother.

Gertrude allowed Thanne to come near her. It was a severe muscle spasm in her leg; it wanted a hard massage. And you. You crept near your mother, too, patting and patting her leg with your small hand, you and Thanne, sisters side by side: where Thanne's hands went your hand followed, your eyes deep within your mother's eyes—and that, Dorothy, is as marvelous as anything you've ever done, because of the unsullied love it revealed, but then it is exactly what you have done all your life. It is natural to you. Independence has not changed sympathy. Independence does not cancel love. It transfigures it, making it purely a gift.

So your touch eased your mother like a medicine.

And I said in my soul, *No, but Dorothy is different from us after all. She is better. She loves more quickly and with less confusion.*

Ah, Dorothy, I think God honors hearts more than brains. You are the image of God in my world. In you the best of the child continues, while the best of adulthood emerges. Your declaration of independence never stole a state nor severed a nation nor warred against another soul. It only allowed you to return love for love in greater measure than before.

I love you, my sister.

Walt

DUST

I yearn
To curl in the corner
Of death's eye:
Death's deep eye.
When he blinks
I am enclosed,
And I am washed
With weeping.

April 28, 1995:

I've opened a small suitcase on the bed. The window shades are pulled. They usually are, night and day. Their white translucence, though, allows a fine spring light in the bedroom; and as I move from the closet to the dresser, gathering clothes for packing, I feel glad anticipations about the weekend.

It's Friday. Early afternoon. In forty-five minutes I will leave town for Wheaton College in Illinois where one of my stories is to receive its first public performance. As good as that—better than that, actually—I'm to meet one of my best friends there, whose full-length play will also be performed. His piece is the real feature of Wheaton's theater festival; mine's a private excitement.

My friend's name is David McFadzean. The director at Wheaton is Jim Young, soft-spoken, with talent as deep as tree roots.

I'm going to drive. I'll be back on Sunday.

So, then: two clean shirts, fresh underwear, a pair of dark slacks; my shaving kit is in the bathroom. . . .

Just as I burst from the bathroom, Thanne appears at the top of the stairs. She lets me rush past her, then follows into the bedroom. She's moving slowly. Thanne will often suspend her work while I get ready for some extended trip. She'll say good-bye in the driveway.

"You think I'll need my raincoat?"

She doesn't answer.

"Thanne?"

I glance at her. No, her slowness now is not a preparation for "Good-bye." She hasn't sat. My wife is gazing at the window shades as if they were open and the world lay visible before her. Her head is drawn back. There are small bunches of flesh at the corners of her lips.

"Thanne?"

For a moment she stands unmoving. The shades *are* pulled; there *is* no world before her. There's nothing to see. Her face is illuminated by a diffusion of light. I stuff the shaving kit into my suitcase. I will say her name again, with greater emphasis—but then she speaks in a dreaming murmur: "Wally."

"Yes? What?"

Now Thanne turns and turns on me the same wondering gaze she gave the window shade.

"Dad's gone," she says.

"Ah."

There is no explanation for this, but I understand the sense of her words immediately, completely. I don't ask her to elaborate. There is no compulsion in me toward surprise or shock. Rather, I scrutinize the woman carefully, to see how she is herself responding to this . . . this, what? Act of God?

Dad's gone.

But she stands as erect as first I ever saw her, and the cast of her neck and head make her seem a Grecian column to hold the roofs of temples. Except for the line between her eyebrows, her countenance is composed.

"Thanne?"

I'm asking after her state of being. I would add, *How are you?*— except she thinks I'm asking for details, and answers first.

Softly, as if all this were a wonder to her, Thanne draws me the picture in her mind. "Mom says it was just after lunch. They'd come back to their rooms. Dad had shifted himself from the wheelchair into his TV chair. Mom wasn't paying any attention. She was just about to sit, when Dad took three quick breaths . . . and then he was gone."

I step toward her now. I gather the woman into my arms. I take her face against my throat, and we stand still. She is not crying. She is deeply quiet.

My wife's father, Martin Bohlmann, has just died. This is the first of our four parents to go.

Softly, still with that note of awe-ful wonder, Thanne adds one more detail.

"Mom's says it's a good thing Dad took those three breaths, and that they were loud. Otherwise she'd have talked to a dead man till suppertime."

Spring, 1967:

The farmer was not a talky man. Not ever, I suppose—though when I first met him I assumed that the size and the noise of his family didn't permit him time to talk.

At the age of twenty-three I drove west from Ohio to the flat, black farmland of eastern Illinois, there to visit the Bohlmann farm, to seek approval of the Bohlmann parents, and to court the Bohlmann daughter named Ruthanne.

On a Friday evening we sat down to supper in the spacious kitchen. The day had been balmy. I remember that the kitchen door stood open to the porch, so that breezes stole in behind me. The air was warm and rich and loamy. Jonquils and daffodils were in bloom, the tulip beds about to pop, the ground as yet uncultivated. I'd been a city boy all my life. I wanted to weep for the perfect sense of sufficiency which this world provided me.

There were eight of us at the table, though it could accommodate fifteen at least. Martin and Gertrude had brought forth fourteen children. They buried one in infancy and now had watched nearly all the others depart for college. Ruthanne was the tenth child born to them, the fifth from the last.

The farmer bowed his head. "Come!" he said with surprising force, then lowered his voice for the rest of the prayer: "COME, Lord Jesus, be our guest. . . ."

I soon learned that the first word was something like a gong, alerting the rest of his huge family to the sacred duty now begun.

Apart from that commanding "Come," Martin's praying and his manner both were mild. His hair, on the other hand—aimed at me from the bowed head at the other end of the table—constituted a fierce aggression. It never would comb down, but stood up and stabbed like bayonets in defiance.

As soon as the prayer was done, a hard, clattering silence overtook the table, while every Bohlmann concentrated on filling up their plates.

Potatoes and vegetables had been raised in the kitchen garden. Popcorn, too. Milk came from Bohlmann cows. There'd been a time when the hog was hung up on a chilly autumn morning and butchered in the barn door, giving cracklings to the family, hams and chops and sausages and lard. Gertrude used the lard for the wedding cakes she baked to earn spending money. The Bohlmanns owned neither the land they worked nor the house they slept in. They rented. They never paid income tax, since their annual income never approached a taxable figure. For them it was a short distance from the earth to their stomachs—and back to earth again. Thanne recalls the cold two-holer on snowy winter mornings.

Martin ate that meal mostly in silence. But so did he eat all his meals, and so did he live most of his life: in silence.

When he was done, he slipped a toothpick into the corner of his mouth, read aloud a brief devotion for our general benefit, pushed back his chair, stood up, and walked outside.

I followed him. I think I thought I'd talk with him, persuade him of the honor of my intentions. But Martin moved in the sort of solitude which, it seemed to my young self, admitted no foolish intrusions. And once outside, he kept on walking. So I lingered in the yard and watched, following no farther than that.

In twilight the farmer, clad in clean coveralls, strolled westward into the field immediately beyond the yard. He paused. He stood silhouette, the deep green sky framing his body with such precision that I could see the toothpick twiddling between his lips. His hair was as stiff and wild as a thicket, the great blade of his nose majestic.

Soon Martin knelt on one knee. He reached down and gathered a handful of dirt. He lifted it, then sifted the lumpish dust through his fingers onto the palm of his other hand. Suddenly he brought both hands to his face and inhaled. The toothpick got switched to the side; Martin touched the tip of his tongue to the earth. Then he rose again. He softly clapped his two hands clean, then slipped them behind the bib of his coveralls, and there he stood, straight up, gazing across the field, his form as black as iron in the gloaming, his elbows forming the joints of folded wings—and I thought: *How peaceful! How completely peaceful is this man.*

It caused in me a sort of sadness, a nameless elemental yearning.

April 29, 1995:

I am in Wheaton with David McFadzean, sitting at a small table in the college snack bar. I drove my little pickup here, while Thanne drove the mini-van south into the Illinois farm country of her childhood. She's with her mother and her siblings in Watseka, arranging for her father's funeral, which has been scheduled for Monday. Thanne has already contacted our own children, to see which will be able to attend the funeral. They will all be there—at least for the wake on Sunday.

Since there's little I can do for Martin now, and since Thanne herself is surrounded by a small city of Bohlmann's, we decided I should keep my appointments after all. And I have. But I move as something of an alien here. I'm morbidly conscious of my body, the thing I live in, as if it were a bunting concealing my truer self. No, that's not quite accurate: rather, my body is the heavy thing I bear wherever I go, as if it were a prison of severe limitations. And here's the irony: to lose it or to leave it is to die.

Last night the Wheaton College Theater Department performed my story, "One In A Velvet Gown." It's a melancholy piece, based on personal boyhood experience. Watching it, I became a watcher of my past, departed self.

We're going to watch David's play tonight. He tells me it's still a work in progress. He grins, suddenly conscious of what he's doing. He's preparing the both of us to forgive the flaws he fears we'll see.

"How's Thanne," he says. This is a running joke: "I'd rather be talking to her, not you!" His eyes blink flat with a false sincerity.

I swallow coffee and surprise myself by saying, "He can't be gone."

"What?" David tucks his chin into his neck and curls a lip of wry query: "Whaaat?" He thinks I'm giving him joke for joke.

I say, "Thanne's Dad died yesterday," and then I feel terrible. It's a crude, stupid way to announce such a thing. But this is how separate I feel: when David snaps to a confused sobriety, I don't apologize. I don't say anything. I don't even acknowledge his gestures of sympathy—or if I do, I don't *know* that I do.

For as soon as I uttered that sentence of death out loud, I realized I meant much more than Martin's physical departure. I meant the man's entire way of life, his perfect peace in the universe. And now my spirit is breathless at so tremendous a loss. For if *these* are gone, than the world has become a dangerous place altogether.

What? And shall all my fears return again, making me an alien wherever I go?

1900–1950:

Martin Bohlmann was born with the century. His relationship to the earth, therefore, was established long before society developed its ever more complex technologies for separating human creatures from the rest of creation.

Throughout his young manhood, farming was largely the labor of muscle and bone, hoof and hand. The very first successful gasoline tractor was not manufactured until 1892. In 1907 there were a mere 600 tractors in the entire United States.

Thanne can remember the years before her father purchased his first John Deere in the late forties. She watched him plowing behind draft horses, steady beasts with hooves the size of the little girl's head.

"Prince," the farmer called them, and "Silver."

Often it was Ruthanne's task to lead them to water. And this is why she remembers the time and the chore so well: it frightened the child to walk between two such massive motors of rolling hide, her head below their necks. The quicker she went, the quicker they took their mighty paces, until she thought she could never stop them, and they would fly headlong into the pond, all three!

Her father, however, commanded them mutely with a gesture, with a cluck and a tap of the bridle. Silent farmer. Silent, stolid horses. They were for him a living, companionable power. And when Martin and his horses spent days plowing fields—moving with huffs and clomps and the ringing of chains, but with no explosions of liquid fuel—their wordless communication became community. The farmer never worked alone. He was never isolated. And if the dog named Rex ran beside them, then there were four who could read and obey the rhythms of creation, four creatures, therefore, who dwelt in communion with their Creator.

Ah, what a woven whole that world was! How the picture stirs my yearning—and my sadness too, if I could not enter the peace the farmer knows!

Horses plowed. ("Hup, Silver. Hup!") Horses mowed. Horses pulled the rake that laid the alfalfa in windrows to dry—giving Martin's fields the long, strong lines of a darker green that looked, from the road, like emotion wreathed in an ancient face.

And when the hay was dry, horses pulled a flat wagon slowly by the windrows while one man forked the hay up to another who stood on the wagon. This second man caught the bundles neatly on his own fork, then flicked them into an intricate cross-arrangements on the wagon, building the hay higher and tighter, climbing his work as he did, climbing so high that when the horses pulled the wagon to the barn, the man on his haystack could stare dead-level into the second-story windows of the farmhouse. Then horses pulled the rope that, over a metal wheel, hoisted the hay to the loft in the barn.

Martin and his neighbors made hayricks of the overflow. They thatched the tops against rain and the snow to come. The work caused a gritty dust, and the dust caused a fearful itch on a summer's day. But the work and the hay—fodder for the fall and the winter ahead—were a faithful obedience to the seasons and the beasts, Adam and Eve responsible for Eden. Martin Bohlmann knew that!

He milked the cows before sunrise. There was a time when he sat on a stool with his cheek against their warm flanks in winter. Cows would swing their heads around to gaze at him. He pinched the teats in the joint of his thumb and squeezed with the rest of his hand, shooting a needle *spritz* into the pail between his ankles. He rose. He lifted the full pail and sloshed its blue milk into the can; then he carried the cans, two by two, outside.

The winter air had a bite. His boots squeaked on the crusted snow as he lugged the cans to the milk house. The dawn was grey at the eastern horizon, the white earth ghostly, the cold air making clouds at the farmer's nostrils—and someone might say that he, alone in his barnyard, was lonely. He wasn't, of course; he was neither lonely nor alone. His boots still steamed with the scent of manure; his cheek kept the oil of the cattle's flanks; the milk and the morning were holy. They were—the very harmony of them was—manifestation of the Creator. And the work was nothing more or less than Martin's obedience. Of which is peace.

1991–1995:

When Thanne and I moved from Evansville in the southeast corner of Indiana to Valparaiso in the northeast, I was granted the chance to fulfill a personal yearning—a life-long yearning, to tell the truth, but one made ever more intense by the farms of eastern Illinois. I wanted in some modest way to live the farmer's life. We sought more than a lot and a house, therefore. Thanne and I went looking for land. Today we own twenty-four acres, fields and woods, a tool shed, a barn.

Martin himself had retired before we moved to this place; but we were closer to him now, could visit and talk with greater frequency. And I could focus my questions upon practical problems and solutions of my own small farm.

I have learned! In these latter years, I've come to understand the thing I once could only admire.

So, then: in the spring of 1992, I became the owner of a John Deere 5000 series farm tractor. It pulls at the power of forty horses, more than enough to handle the work I do, light plowing, disking. I drag timber from the woods to cut and split for firewood; I mow the broader fields, stretch fence, chip tree limbs, grade the ground and haul earth and stone and sand—all with my little Deere. The machine is perfectly suited to the cultivation of our modest crops, berry bushes, hickory and walnut trees, strawberry hills, scattered stands of apple trees, a sizable vegetable garden.

For decades before our relocation north, my family and I had lived in the inner city. We were hedged in on every side. True safety (or so it seemed to me) existed only within the walls of our house. I lived in suspicion of strangers. My children's new friends—the boy-type friends especially—might-could bring the threat that I could not protect against. After nightfall folks regularly gathered across the street from our house to drink, gamble, smoke dope. I *slept* tense.

I drove my car with such distracted anxiety that Evansville Police Officers knew me by sight: the pastor with a rap sheet. Well, I was not felonious; but I'd gathered my share of driving tickets and accident reports.

Once we came to the land, however, and once I'd learned to listen to its rhythms, I've felt a dear sense of expansion—yes, and the beginning of peace: I plant and pick, harrow and harvest generous crops in their due seasons.

My tractor is nothing like the modern behemoths that cut swaths as wide as avenues through dustier fields, machines wearing double tires on every wheel, pulling several gangs of plows and disks and harrows at once, while the operator sits bunkered in an air-conditioned cab, watching the tracks of his tires in a television monitor.

Me, I take the weather on my head. I mow at the width of six feet. And mine is but a two-bottom plow.

But Martin's wisdom makes of small things true sufficiency.

Summer, the late '40s:

My father-in-law purchased his first tractor—a John Deere exactly as green as mine, but smaller and less powerful—at the only price he could afford, something less that two hundred dollars.

"Billig," he judged the sale, which could be translated from the German as "Cheap," but which in his mouth meant, "Such a deal!" He bought the tractor used from one of his neighbors. The machine wasn't even two years old, but it kept stalling, driving the neighbor crazy. In the barnyard, in the field, pulling a wagon or plowing, the tractor would quit and refuse to produce the spark for starting again, however hard the poor man cranked.

That farmer figured he was selling aggravation.

Martin, on the other hand, sought to buy a sturdy servant, not only with his cash but also with his spirit. The dollars bought the cold equipment; but patience and peace bought time to examine it with complete attention, his mind untroubled; and mother-wit brought the tool to life again.

In those days tractors used a magneto generator. My father-in-law opened it and discovered a loose washer inside. The washer had shifted whenever the tractor bumped over rough ground, shorting the coils and killing the engine. Martin simply removed that washer. Thereafter he had a dependable tool for as long as ever he farmed. It was there when I came courting his daughter. It was there when he finally retired at the age of seventy and was forced to auction off his farming equipment.

Autumn 1993:

Near the western boundary of my acreage, the land descends to a low draw through which my neighbor's fields drain their runoff waters. For several years, the only way I could get back to the woods—and to the writing studio I'd built there—was through that draw. But every spring the thaw and the thunderstorms turned it into a wide stretch of sucking mud.

In order to correct my problem (to me it *was* a "problem") I laid a culvert west-and-west over the lowest section of the draw, then hired a man with a diesel earth shovel to dig a pond on the east side, then to pile that dirt over my culvert. I built a high bank, a dry pathway wide enough to take the weight of my tractor. I seeded it with grass, and the grass grew rich and green. Had God given us dominion over the earth? Well, I congratulated myself for having dominated this little bit of earth.

Congratulated myself and used this elevated path, that is, until the following spring, when severe storms caused such floods that the earth broke and my metal culvert was washed backward and submerged in the pond.

I tried again. I paid several college students to help me re-set the culvert, re-dig and re-pile the earth upon it. I walled the mouth of the culvert with rock and stone in order to teach the water where to go. I re-seeded the whole, yes. Yes, and during the summer months I watched miserably as little runnels of water found their ways beneath the culvert. By spring these runnels had scoured out caves, and the caves caused the culvert to slump, so that my draw returned to its first state as if it had never been anything else: primal mud.

When Martin came to visit, I showed him my new John Deere. He described for me the pattern for efficient plowing, then told me the story I've recounted above, about his own first tractor. We walked slowly across my back field. I took him to my failed culvert. That's what I called it while we stood by soupy pond: "Failed."

Martin turned bodily and looked at the fields west of mine. Even in old age his cheeks still bunched beneath his eyes. He seemed ever to maintain a private smiling. And his nose! That wondrous blade looked Navaho, though the man was German, through and through.

He turned back again and looked down at the flood-torn earth at our feet.

"Take your time," he said to me as if the last two years had been no time at all. "You've got the time," he said. Martin was himself ninety-three years old, and I but forty-nine. Yes, from his vantage I had whole quantities of time.

Finally he raised his eyes to mine and said, "Ask the water what *she* wants, then give her a new way to do it."

My John Deere 5000 makes a low muttering sound. At full throttle it emits a commanding growl. But its voice is muffled, modern.

Martin's first tractor uttered that steady *pop-pop-pop-pop* which, when it called across the fields to the farmhouse, revealed the essential vastness of the earth and all skies.

Pop-pop-pop-pop! Thanne recalls how she would step outside the farmhouse with her father's lunch, cock her eye and listen for that *pop-pop*, then follow the sound to find the farmer. She ran between cornstalks as high as her waist, the flat leaves nodding, whispering, slapping her legs as she passed them by. In the lunchbox were thick beef sandwiches, some cookies, coffee and two toothpicks. Always the toothpicks for her father at the end of his meals.

Pop-pop-pop-pop, and suddenly the child would come out on high ground and catch sight of her father in the distance, mowing between the solitary cottonwoods, creeping the low and golden land beneath the white cumulus giants striding the blue sky above. *How tiny,* little Ruthanne would think to herself, unable to distinguish her father's features. *How little he is:* one man on a tractor, far away.

But *How peaceful,* think I to myself, in spite of Martin's littleness in the universe. And: *How completely peaceful is this man!*

For during these last years, I've learned to know the nature of his peace, that it is not in spite of his smallness. Verily, it is *in* the smallness, as long as his is smallness under God.

For Martin Bohlmann, the sweet admission of his personal limitations was ever the beginning of wisdom. Only in knowing oneself as *created* can one know God as *Creator.* Otherwise, striving to be in control of our lives, the true Controller must feel like an adversary of massive and terrible force.

I have despised the limits on my own existence, and in that despite have suffered perpetual tensions, seen enemies everywhere. Why, the common act of driving a car can become a contest of mortal consequence. For the streets are battlegrounds, aren't they?

But Martin dwelt in patience and in peace.

Faith and trust and farming were all the same to him. He read the weather as humbly as he read the Bible, seeking what to obey. My father-in-law was an obedient man. This is the crux of the matter: his *obedience* was the source of his peace, because the one whom he obeyed was God of all, and by obedience Martin became one with all that God had made, as powerful himself and as infinite as the Deity with whom he was joined.

Daily the farmer did more than just read and interpret the rhythms of creation (though these he *did* do, these he *had* to do, for his vocation depended upon such readings, or the farm would fail). As Prince and Silver heeded their master's mute commands, so the farmer also obeyed the natural signs of the Creator, entering into communion with God Almighty.

So here was Martin's peace: not in striving for greatness but in recognizing who is truly great. And this was his peace: by a glad humility to do the will of the Creator.

And so this was Martin's peace as well: to bear the image of God into creation.

> Have you not known? Has it not been told you from the beginning? It is he who sits above the circle of the earth, and its inhabitants are like grasshoppers; who stretched out the heavens like a curtain and spreads them like a tent to dwell in. . . .
>
> Lift up your eyes on high and see: who created these? He who brings out their host by number, calling them all by name; by the greatness of his might, and because he is strong in power, not one is missing.

April 30, 1995:

No, but one *is* missing! Martin is missing. My father-in-law himself. He is gone. This man is dead.

I'm driving south on Interstate 57 with a clenched jaw and stark knuckles. Angry. Anxious, really. It's nearly nighttime. South of Kankakee the Illinois farmland stretches east and west of me. More than I seeing it, I feel the cultivated earth as a swelling tide, a heaving of massy weight as of an ocean. It will fall on me soon, and I will drown.

I am about forty-five minutes from the funeral home in Watseka where Thanne is, and my children. And Martin in a box.

I'm driving at sixty-five miles per hour precisely. The speed limit. Cars rip past me, fire-eyed enemies, each one triumphing over me in my pickup. This particular obedience is not my habit. But I'm torn between desires to be with Thanne and *never* to be near the casket of my father. So I'm going at a grim, calculated slowness.

Death and the empty skies consume me now.

I hate this pickup truck! A beaten '84 Chevy S–10, the seat's too low and too hard. It wasn't made for distance driving. My back is killing me. Oh, God, I want to howl! To howl at *you!*

Because all our human limitations may be made easy in obedience—all, Sir, but this last one: death!

I gnash my teeth. I roll down my window and weep with the frustration of it all. *Martin is not here! I can do nothing about that!* This single, final limit makes every other limitation insupportable! And God's infinitude becomes my hell, for it makes my smallness burn like a flesh afire.

I have already left the Interstate. I'm driving east on highway 24, approaching state highway 49. The night is hugely black, endlessly empty above my little vehicle, though once I took the farmer's daughter for rides on county roads nearby, and then the nights were filled with delicious mystery.

I had a VW convertible in those days. When the nightwind grew chilly, Ruthanne would draw her knees up to her breast and pull the sweatshirt down over all to her ankles. That tender gesture stole my heart; her easy intimacy made me a citizen of the night and all that countryside. But there was no death in those days.

The parking lot is full. So I pull out again. I park on a side street and walk back. The funeral home spills light from various windows. I can hear a hubbub within.

I enter at the side of the building, artificial light, heat, a human humidity.

In the hallway I hang up my jacket. With slow steps I move to the viewing room. Martin's name and the dates that round his life are on a framed placard: 1900 to 1995. There is a birthday and a deathday.

I shift my sight to the room and look through the doorway. Many people are sitting. I recognize Thanne's sisters, her brothers.

And then, astonishingly, here is Thanne standing directly before me, looking up into my face.

My wife, my wife: are we okay together?

Her countenance wears a pleasant expression. She has not been crying. She touches my cheek. This is how Thanne will remove dried patches of shaving cream. It's also how she indicates to me by feel what she sees by sight: *my* face does not wear a pleasant expression. Yes. I know how gaunt and anxious I am, my face and my spirit, both.

Thanne takes my hand.

"Come," she says gently. She leads me into the wide viewing room. People glance my way, acknowledge my arrival. They sit on folding chairs all around the walls. Others stand in knots of conversation.

There is the casket, at the far end surrounded by a jungle of flowers. It has the appearance of an altar in church. No one is near it now. We approach, still hand in hand. The room seems (can this be?) to hush a little. I feel a general expectancy. But my role among the Bohlmann's is of no greater stature than anyone else's. In fact, this hush tightens my stomach even more than it was. I don't like to be on display. No emotion could possibly be natural and easy under scrutiny.

But Thanne continues forward to the casket, drawing me with her.

Behind the casket's linen, I see that great sail of a nose now rise up. Yes, it is Martin whom I'm coming to see. Yes: and there is his cantankerous hair. Even in death those spikes will not lie down. His eyebrows, too, are great sprouts of hair. His eyes are closed. His bunchy cheeks are slightly rouged.

Suddenly Thanne lets a little giggle escape her lips. The sound of it tingles inside of me. *She's laughing?* But then I see the farmer's mouth, and I understand her immediately and completely. Sticking straight up from the corner of his lips, causing a little grin to pool there, is a toothpick, straight, bold, erect.

Thanne tries to whisper in my ear, "The mortician . . ."

But the whisper becomes a squeal: "Oh, Wally," she squeals with perfect clarity, "the mortician's mort*ified!*" And then she can't help it. She breaks out in laughter.

That laughter kills me. I mean, it kills my silly anger; and I glance at Thanne's bright, wet eyes and burst into laughter, too.

Martin doesn't move; but his face is not offended by the hilarity, and besides, he was never a talky man. And here are my children, gathering, grinning, all four of them. And now I know what the whole room was anticipating: my taking the last step, my joining them, too.

And so I know exactly what happened after lunch on Friday, April 18, 1995.

Martin Bohlmann, having finished his meal, popped a toothpick into his mouth. He wasn't about to read his devotions. Rather, he was about to *do* them, devoutly and well.

And though he'd mostly been bound to a wheelchair, the farmer got up nevertheless, and pushed that chair aside and strolled out the door and into the fields west of his dwellings. Twilight. Farther and farther west the old man walked, until he came to a place of pausing. He tucked his hands under the bib of coveralls and gazed extremest west and listened to the deepest rhythms of the universe.

Yes, and I know what happened then. In his own good time, Martin Bohlmann knelt on one knee and scooped up a handful of the black earth and brought it to his face and smelled in it its readiness for plowing and for planting.

A springtime breeze got up and blew. And when at last my father-in-law allowed the soil sift from his hands into the wind, why, it was himself that blew forth, ascending. Here was the dust of his human frame and the lightsome stuff of his spirit.

This, then, I know as well as I know any other thing: even his death was an obedience.

Martin died, therefore, in a perfect peace.

LITTLE ONE, are you afraid of the dark?

Is that why you grab my hand and press against me? Because you are frightened?

Well, if we were still in the city I would show you the places where good people live. I'd name them and describe their kindness. Then if we had trouble, we could walk to a door and knock and get help.

In the city I would tell you where the hospital is and how to avoid dark alleys and which streets are well-lit. Or else I would just take you home. . . .

But we're not in the city, are we? And dark is darker where no human lights are. Even the noises are foreign here: no human machinery, no cars, no trucks, no TV, or tapes, or radio.

Little one! You cling to my arm as though the touch itself will keep you from harm, as though I were a good strong guard; and yet you tremble!

Are you still so scared of the dark?

O sweetheart, if we were out in the country now I would teach you the goodness of God's creation, even at night. I'd show you the stars and tell you their tales till they became your friends: the giant Orion (three stars for his belt and three for his dagger), the seven sisters all in a bunch (called the Pleiades, even in Scripture), Cassiopeia (whose shape makes a bent W like my initial). I'd light the star of Bethlehem. I'd talk about the angels, "the hosts of heaven," until the night skies were crowded by kindly spirits and we were not lonely below them.

In the country I'd make you hear the wind; I'd teach you the breath of God therewith, the *spiritus Dei*. God, who made it, keeps it still. The Creator laughs at the bullfrog's burp and loves the mockingbird—melodies, melodies, all night long. The phantom flight of the owl, the cricket's chirrup, the wolf's exquisite, killing harmonies—all these you would hear as the handiwork of God, just as you yourself are God's good handiwork. And then, my dear, you would be consoled. . . .

But we're not in the country, are we?

Little one, you whimper with fear. You turn and you bury your face in my bosom. I hug you with all my strength, with all my love. I rock you and rock you and stroke your thin hair—but still you are scared of the dark.

O my dear heart! O my dear, if you were going blind, if *that* were the darkness into which you descended, I would teach you touching—and feeling itself would be your light.

I'd lift your fingers to my face and let you touch me from temple to chin. Brush my lashes. Brush my smiling eyes. Linger at my cheekbone. Take upon your fingertips my kisses. Then take my hand and let me walk you through the dark world till all its furniture becomes familiar to you.

But. . .but the blindness you suffer is worse than that, isn't it?

Baby, afraid of the dark! Scared of the prison the darkness shuts around you! Frightened because you are soon nowhere at all, in spaces invisible, endless, empty. . . .

O little one, we know what your darkness is, don't we?

It's old age. You have grown old. And now comes the deepest darkness of all: you are dying.

My little one, my darling! The dark is your departure. You are leaving this world altogether, going to that undiscovered country from whose bourn no traveler returns. Yes? Yes.

Yes, and my darkness is sorrow, because I must remain behind.

Hush, old hoary head. My best beloved, hush. Let me hold you a while. Cling to me as tightly as you please, and I will whisper the thoughts that occur to me now.

No. This is not some city through which we travel. Yet there is a city ahead of you. And you shall enter before I do. But I am coming, and then it shall be *you* who welcomes *me* and makes the streets of that place familiar to me.

Because you are dying in faith, my little one—you who always were but a pilgrim on this earth. You're finishing the trip begun by Baptism; you are entering a better country, that is, a heavenly country. Wherefore God is not ashamed to be called your God—for he hath prepared for you this city!

And when you arrive, you won't need me to show you around. God will meet you there. Alleys and highways, God will show you everything—but first he'll take from your vision the crust of old age, the terrors and the troubles of this present world: for God himself shall wipe all tears from your eyes; and there shall be no more death neither sorrow, nor crying anymore.

And no: the dark surrounding you now is not the countryside either, nor sky nor stars nor the woofings and bleats of God's creatures. It is, in fact, their absence, since you are passing away from all this.

Ah, but you go from creation to its Creator! You go to the God who conceived of Eden and Paradise and everything between the two. Better than the handiwork of God, dear heart, is God himself.

But yes: dying is a kind of blindness. It is preparation for deeper sight and dearest insight. Little one, this darkness is not because you cannot see, but because the world cannot *be* seen. The material world is becoming a shadow before you, so that the coming world (bright with divine reality) may not blind you at your arrival. That city is brighter than sunlight. It hath no need of the sun in it. For the glory of God doth lighten it, and the Lamb is the light thereof.

Hush, now. Close your eyes. Don't be afraid. I'll hold you with my lowly love till God receives you in his highest, most holy love. My darling, you are embarking through darkness on your best adventure. Only the start is scary. The rest is endlessly marvelous, eternally beautiful.

But when you get there, wait!

Turn around. Look back through the glorious light, and watch for me. I am coming, too.

BOOK THREE:

MIZ LIL AND THE
CHRONICLES OF GRACE

And those who are good—they delight to hear of the past evils of such as are now freed from them, not because they are evils, but because they have been and are not. With what fruit then, O Lord my God, to Whom my conscience daily confesseth, trusting more in the hope of Thy mercy than in their own innocency, with what fruit, I pray, do I by this book confess to the people, also in Thy presence, what now I am [against what I have been]?

Augustine, *The Confessions* 10.3.4

EASTER-WINGS

Lord, who createdst man in wealth and store,
Though foolishly he lost the same,
Decaying more and more,
Till he became
Most poore:
With thee
O let me rise
As larks, harmoniously,
And sing this day thy victories:
Then shall the fall further the flight in me.

My tender age in sorrow did beginne:
And still with sicknesses and shame
Thou didst so punish sinne,
That I became
Most thinne.
With thee
Let me combine
And feel this day thy victorie:
For, if I imp my wing on thine,
Affliction shall advance the flight in me.

George Herbert

AUTHOR'S NOTE

THE STORIES TOLD in this book are true. They happened. And most of the characters you will encounter here are also accurate portrayals. But I've made an aesthetic and ethical decision sometimes to conflate events, sometimes to create a single fictional character from a composite of many people, and sometimes to invent the detail and the character which the deeper spirit of the story required. In this manner I've tightened the pace of a human life considerably, and I have absolutely rejected using details or identities which would disclose another human life besides my own.

A WANDERING CLERIC was my father.

Wherever he went I went there too, as rootless as he was in this world. But there came a time when I turned and traveled in ways he never chose, and then we were divided for a while.

I was born in Portland, Oregon, the first child of a youngish Lutheran pastor and a woman of eager intensities: dramatic, enthusiastic was my mother's hunger for the world. And she was handsome in those days. One mute snapshot shows an even, intelligent brow, a sparkling eye, and a widow's peak.

Within a month of my birth, my pastor-father baptized me. He prepared for the rite by warning the deacons not to worry if the baby should cry from the shock of the water. "A lusty lung," he said, half joking, "means my son is destined to preach." But I remained serene throughout the ceremony. I uttered not a peep.

After the service—so my father told it—the deacons met him "with faces as long as hoe-handles."

"We're sorry, Reverend," they said.

"Why?" said my father. "What's the matter?"

"Well, your son will never make a pastor," they said.

The baptism took place in Vanport City, Oregon, where I lived the first year of my life. I remember nothing of Vanport City—except that we returned there thirteen years later to view it from a hill, and found that it had been lost entirely to a flood. Nothing built remained, nothing but the flat grid of empty streets and grass.

We moved. I spent my second year in Shelton, Washington. My mother once said that we could see Mt. Olympus from the kitchen window, but I don't remember Mt. Olympus. On the other hand, it is during this period that personal memory begins for me—

sudden, sharp, and seemingly pointless—and I do recall a sighting of the Pacific Ocean.

This memory starts as we are driving a narrow highway through tall, continuous forests of pine. I have made a bridge of my body, my toes on the back seat of the car, my arms and chin on the ridge of the front seat, my face between my parents' faces. They are gazing forward through the windshield. My father drives. My mother is talking—though memory preserves neither the timbre of her voice nor the words; rather, I see the tip of her nose dipping down as her mouth keeps forming soundless sentences. Forever and ever that tiny trick of her nose consoles me when I watch it, proof of my mother's presence.

Then my father says, "There!" I hear the cordwood tone of that command. "Look to the left," he says. "You'll see the ocean."

Almost casually I glance left. The forest is thinning as we speed through it, and a distant water flashes between the trees. Suddenly the pine is altogether snatched away, and I am startled by the sight. There, indeed, lies the monstrous sea, a nearly impossible reach of water, massive, still, impersonal, and infinite.

"I rowed a boat out once," my father says, still looking forward, "and swam in the Pacific."

My mother shudders.

I imagine my father in that boundless water, a dishrag beside a bobbing rowboat, and I shudder too.

This is where my earliest memory ends.

We moved again—to Chicago, Illinois, where my father served the youth organization of the whole church body. His wandering increased in distance and frequency, but he traveled alone. The rest of us spent portions of the hot, hot summers with my mother's family in St. Louis, Missouri.

Dramatic was my mother's hunger for the world, enthusiastic; but the world would not hold still for her; therefore her enthusiasms were forced to turn in upon themselves. And as the forms of my father's religion did not change, however much we wandered, the forms themselves became a sort of moveable stability and structure for our lives; and my mother—deep-hearted, brave, a

warrior for the sake of the homeland, had there been a homeland—
guarded the doors of religious form as though it were the fortress
that kept her family safe. We were the Jews, whose Sabbath and
whose circumcision were bound to no particular place, though their
hearts might long intensely for a city.

We moved again. Before I enrolled in the third grade, my father
had entered the pulpit of a parish in Grand Forks, North Dakota.

Now we lived in a windy old house above the banks of the Red
River. Our backyard ran down a hill of weed to the wood that
bordered the water. In spring this river burst its banks and rose to
cover half our hill, then descended, leaving a blackened vegetable
growth that disappointed my mother's sense of order and beauty.
She waited till the ground grew dry again. She waited while weed
entangled the whole of the hill. And then one day she took an
ancient, clattering push-mower and attacked the ugliness. Back and
forth, back and forth with a sort of fury she mowed and mulched
the humid weed, leveling the growth, by will alone prevailing. I
watched her and said in my soul, *This is a very strong woman.*

By midsummer the weed returned, and rabbits lived in it.

We moved again.

My father accepted the office of president for a small preparatory
school, many of whose students went on to the seminary and then
into ministries like those my father had served.

We lived in Edmonton, Alberta, Canada. The winter shocked us
with its cold, then held us in its everlasting cold. The North
Saskatchewan River, whose valley the front of our house oversaw,
froze solid. And for several years my mother suffered certain chill
indignities which I could not understand. In that place, then, the
fortress of our faith grew stronger, stonier, more embattled; and I
would watch my mother's eyes, sometimes, and marvel at their icy
perseverance: the hard blue guardianship which would, by God,
maintain the protective structures of this family's safety. And I
would want to cry for her.

We moved again. But with this move we separated.

My parents and family returned to Chicago, while I, the firstborn
of my father, attended a boarding school in Milwaukee, Wisconsin,

a high school like the one he had administered, a prep school for the Lutheran ministry.

I too, it seemed, would prove a wandering Aramaean like my father.

And I did go wandering—but not in the obvious, geographic way my father took. In fact, I had already departed from my family several years before I left them for Milwaukee. Nobody knew my leave-taking, least of all myself: the spirit of this nomad was invisible. But quietly—as my family struck camp again and again—secretly, unknowingly, I had decamped the faith.

I lived still within the forms of my father's religion. My mother's fortress still surrounded me. And so far as I knew, there were no reasons why I should not also march the walls of the stronghold of Christendom. It was without a conscious deception that I planned to become a pastor.

But form was form alone; the law alone was real; and I had stolen out-of-doors to wander another sort of waste.

Half of the stories that follow in this book recount that hidden journey of the spirit of a child. Into Egypt, one might say.

And then—despite my silence at the Baptism, despite my distance from the heart of the faith of my parents (but nothing is as simple as that statement sounds, and I was valiantly ignorant even of myself)—I was ordained into the ministry. I did, as a young man, start to preach.

But if my father had moved continually, I would stick in one place only. Early in adulthood I began, as the pastor of a small, black congregation called Grace, to preach; and I stayed there: in the center of Evansville, Indiana, on a northward loop of the Ohio River.

Yet if my father had never deviated from the still center of one consoling creed, his firstborn had. Ever in Evansville, the invisible spirit of this nomad had very far to go. Out of a deep unknowing. Out of his Egypt, learning to walk.

And a frozen river must break before it flows again. But a summer of constant hearts can accomplish this terrible wreckage.

Half of the stories in this book observe that other journey—of the spirit of a young man bound to a particular people, a spirit bound to Grace.

It will help the reader, perhaps, to know that these two series of stories are presented alternatively, first the adult, then the child, the adult again, the child again, and back and forth as once my mother went back and forth to level the tangled weed until her hill was beautiful.

"Petals, Reverend?"

"What?"

The man startled me from my thoughts, though that wasn't his intention. He was frowning into the rearview mirror, watching the line of cars that crawled behind us.

"I'm sorry, what?" I said.

"Petals or dirt?" he said, returning attention to the road ahead. "What's the Lutheran tradition?"

I closed my mouth and looked forward too. I fingered the black book in my lap. Everything was feeling like a test these days, and every test had its trap; and though Mr. Lawrence George was the most civil of men, conducting his business merely, the question embarrassed me. I didn't understand it.

Two cars passed on the left. A pickup labored by, muttering smoke.

We were traveling north on Garvin, a one-way street which, with the parallel south-running street called Governor, gave access through the inner city of Evansville. Mr. George drove at a grave rate, slowly, slowly, never more than fifteen miles per hour. Generally motorists raced these streets, trying to hit the stoplights green, then shooting the stretches between as though the city streets were country highways. Even now the vehicles passed us in clots of two and three at a time. But Mr. George maintained our dignified crawl as the difference between mindless haste and old decorum.

He had solemn reasons for driving slowly. He was a man with a ramrod commitment to ceremony and deep convictions of propriety. The car he handled was a Cadillac, long and low and black. The car behind us was a hearse. And each of the seven cars that followed the hearse displayed a purple flag on its fender. We were a funeral procession: he was the director.

"Reverend?" he repeated, giving his eyebrows a delicate twitch, gazing forward.

Mr. Lawrence George was the funeral director. I was the pastor. And the woman in the hearse behind, she had belonged to Grace Lutheran Church—an old, old soul only lately come into my care. We were at the end of her mortal age and the beginning of my mortal ministry: this would be the first interment for the both of us.

"Petals? Or a handful of dirt? Lumps of earth?" said Mr. George. "You're in charge, sir."

"Ah," I said.

We were approaching Walnut Avenue. Mr. George did not speed up. Neither did he slow down, though the stoplight was red against us. He closed the distance with unshakable serenity, driving, driving, while I trod the floorboard under my right foot.

"I don't," I said, clearing my throat, "I'm afraid I don't know what we're talking about."

Mr. George began to sound his Cadillac horn and entered the intersection against the light. "D'you plan to say 'Ashes to ashes'?" he said over the organ of his horn. The traffic on Walnut, both on the left and on the right, was forced to stop and to stay stopped for the slow succession of cars that followed us. I avoided the drivers' faces. "Do Lutherans say 'Dust to dust'?" he asked, releasing the horn, still gazing faithfully forward.

"Yes, I think so," I said. "Yes, we do."

"So then," he said, "d'you want me to drop petals on the casket then? Or clay? Different preachers have different notions, but I am yours, sir, to see it's done in dignity."

"Ah, yes. Dignity."

Mr. Lawrence George sat erect beside me, the knot of his tie projecting bravely from his throat, the rest of the tie disposed within his vest, a man as dignified as Immortality.

"Yes," I said. But I had never considered the question of petals-or-dirt before. I didn't know that such a question existed. There were suddenly so many questions to consider. What *do* the Lutherans do? What do the blacks do when they mourn? What do *I* do when the cultures collide? People remember these things forever, especially funerals, especially the funerals that failed and gave offense somehow. Oh, Lord! I did not want to be in charge. Maybe

The Pastor's Companion contained an answer to petals-or-dirt. But neither did I want to look like I wasn't in charge by checking the black book in my lap. So then: wing it.

"Wouldn't dirt," I said, "make a sound? A truer sound, I mean? Symbolical—a hollow rattling sound?"

I'm certain that Mr. George would have responded, then, with an opinion—but he didn't have the chance. Suddenly he stiffened at the wheel.

High and whining behind us, screaming in low gear its furious impatience with slow decorum, a stripped-down Buick came passing the entire funeral procession in a single, angry acceleration. It cut in front of the Cadillac, shifted, vomited at the tailpipes, and roared ahead.

Mr. George compressed his lips and allowed his eyes a momentary diffusion; but he did not vary our funereal pace.

He counted cars in the rearview mirror. He stroked the steering wheel with his left hand, and then expelled his breath.

"There was a day, Reverend," he said. He grew more formal with the quiet declaration. "There was a day when folk respected the dead, when they rose up in pity with the mournful." Mr. George had a neat, close crop of iron-white hair: light-skinned, pressed, and proud. He glanced at me a fleeting second, then seemed to make a decision in my behalf.

"I remember that day," he said, gazing forward, nodding. "Reverend, I remember when construction workers on Seventh Avenue stopped their riveting as we drove down the street. They laid their tools aside, they stood in lines on the lofty girders, they covered their hearts with their hats, and they dignified our grieving, yes. I saluted them. They stood like soldiers in the sky." He lifted his chin, remembering. "It didn't matter what day it was when the casket passed. All the days were Sunday for a funeral. And I'll tell you another thing too. It didn't matter what color we were, driving to the graveside, no. Didn't matter what color the folk on the sidewalk sported neither. They paused respectful. Death had one color in those days, sir. Bereavement had one color only." He breathed through his nose a moment. He had elevated his face until the line of his sight went down his cheeks. "Black," he said.

He shook his head. "Everything's changed today."

Mr. Lawrence George fell silent.

I looked out of the side window. I felt my nerves grow tighter in the silence. The gravity of this man's remembering lay burdens on me that I could scarcely bear. Nothing was light. Everything required a heavy rectitude—and I was the pastor in charge. Ah, Lord, the office was so much older than I was. Petals or dirt? And how many people would be affected by the choice I made? I hardly knew these people. Petals or dirt? Well, well—then let it be dirt.

We had driven far north of the inner city by now. Garvin and Governor joined to form a single two-way street called Stringtown. Here on my right was a busy high school, the students pouring forth for their lunch hour, the curious students peering in our windows, mugging. I turned my face forward again. There, ahead of us, was Diamond Avenue, four lanes of a nearly constant traffic, a median dividing the lanes.

But Mr. Lawrence George made no concession to modern thoroughfares. He caught a yellow light at Diamond, sounded his Cadillac horn, and kept on driving, slowly, slowly. He made a left turn, west on Diamond. He drew his sad train slowly through a red light, while on every hand the cars of the city hit their brakes and stopped.

Three young girls suddenly broke from a knot of students, threaded the stalled traffic, and dashed across two lanes of Diamond to the median. For a few moments they raced with us. Then all at once they lined up in a little-maid row and waved and smiled and clapped as we drove by. We were their parade, a noontime entertainment.

"Everything's changed," sighed Mr. Lawrence George.

In the cemetery some twenty men and women gathered quietly beneath a yellow canopy.

The coffin rested on a shining device above its hole. As though it were a confidence between the two of us, Mr. George tapped the end where the woman's head was enclosed. Propriety put me at her head, not her foot. I took my place at that end, then, and waited, feeling sweat on the cover of my black book, *The Pastor's Companion*. A breeze flapped the fringe of the canopy.

Six members of the immediate family arranged themselves on a row of folding chairs to my right. They gave particular consideration to one who was the daughter of the deceased, an elderly woman herself, sagging in sorrow, sagging in all of the lines of her face, leaning on the arms of a nephew and a niece in order to lower herself and to sit.

Two weeks ago we had laughed together, this woman and I. We had laughed at the fact that she had but a single personal tooth in her jaw, more precious to her than a pearl—and when the dentist suggested he ought to pull it, she bit him.

She kept her head down now. It seemed to me that we should look at one another sometime before this mournful day was done. Pastor and parishioner in sympathy together. Perhaps we were avoiding the direct glance. I myself—I think I feared it. I had hardly known her mother, dead at ninety-two. What would I have in my eyes to give the daughter, should she look at me?

But then, none of the bereaved was looking at me now. Arms were folded on their chests, lips pushed out in meditation.

Mr. Lawrence George stepped to the foot of the casket, removed a single marigold from the bouquet, began to crush it in his left hand, and with his right hand saluted me: erect and military, his duty discharged. He meant, *Begin*.

I did. I lowered my head and read from the black book, pinching pages against the breeze.

"We brought nothing into this world," I read, "and it is certain we can carry nothing out. The Lord gave, and the Lord hath taken away—"

My voice lacked resonance out of doors. The wind scooped and billowed the canopy.

When I reached the words, "O Death, where is thy sting? O Grave, where is thy victory," the daughter of the woman who had died began to cry. At first she just said, "Hooooo. Hooooo," and compulsively I read a little faster. But then a great gout of grief broke from her throat.

"Mama!" the woman wailed, throwing her hands to the top of her head. "Oh, Mama!"

I glanced nervously among the faces. No one seemed terribly distressed. The niece and the nephew were patting her shoulders and fanning her with cardboard fans from the funeral home. Others were rocking side to side as if hearing a music.

I ducked and read on: "Forasmuch as it hath pleased Almighty God, in his wise providence, to take out of this world—"

Suddenly the woman drew a shuddering breath and shrieked, *"Mama, Mama!"*

I shot a pleading look to Mr. George; but he merely pursed his lips, closed his eyes, and nodded that I should continue.

Hasty and nervous and gripping the book like a banister, I continued: "—out of this world the soul of our departed sister, we therefore commit her body to the ground; earth to earth, ashes to ashes, dust to—"

"Mama, you gone! Oh, Mama, you—" The poor old woman simply erupted. She rose from her chair. Her mouth gapped black. Her dentures dropped, dead-grinning, to her chin. She made a gurgling sound and passed out backward in her nephew's lap.

In that same instant I saw that Mr. Lawrence George was with unshakable serenity scattering marigold petals on the coffin lid. Not dirt! The skin of my face burst into flame. I felt in the midst of everything a sudden, speechless fury. I thought I had told the man *dirt!*

Driving back to the funeral home, Mr. George cast off his solemn mood and relaxed. He grew talkative, sunny even. I myself—I could not speak. I glared through the side window and fingered my moustache.

When we crossed Walnut southward and entered the inner city again, the mortician grew positively expansive.

"I used to deliver newspapers here when I was a boy," he said, another sort of remembering, I suppose. "See that house down Cherry?" he said. "The two-story house with cornices? That woman never missed a payment, summer nor winter, three years straight," he announced. "But she shot her husband dead with a single bullet while he stood at the top of the stairs. What d'you think, Reverend?" He glanced at me. "Maybe it was passion gave her the aim?"

In the parking lot of the funeral home, I broke out of the Cadillac and strode to my own vehicle, a small Toyota pickup truck, and threw myself inside.

"Reverend! Wait a minute," Mr. Lawrence George sang out, with interminable slowness rising from his longer, blacker car.

I turned the ignition. "I've got to go," I said.

"You'll do all right here," he declared as though I hadn't spoken, as though I wanted his approval. "Stay tender, sir," he called, touching his hand to his forehead in that formal military salute. "Stay as tender for folk as I saw you today, and you will do all right."

I shifted into first. "I've got to get back to the church," I said.

"Oh—wait!" He suddenly bent at the waist and reached into the Cadillac. "Wait!" His voice was muffled in the dark compartment, but I heard him say, "Your Bible!" and I didn't even answer that.

Wrong, sir. I had taken no Bible with me.

I accelerated, muttering Toyota smoke.

I drove west to Governor, then turned left and joined the traffic streaming south. One-way street. I kept in the extreme left-hand lane, my tires eating the pavement just inches from the curb, telephone poles switching past my ear. Go! Go! Go!

Grace Church was on Gum Street, one block east of Governor. But before my turn I had two stoplights to negotiate, one at Lincoln just ahead, the other two blocks farther down at Bellemeade. I sped up. I intended to hit both lights green, because if you got stopped by one you'd certainly have to stop for the other. The sequence was very tight.

Immediately on my right was a silver Chevy traveling at the same speed as I was. Evidently it planned to catch a green at Lincoln too. A race. I sped a little faster. So did the Chevy, vexing me.

But together we did it. We hit the stoplight yellow, in fact, and cleared Lincoln in a double bound. Two blocks to Bellemeade. Bellemeade was waiting green. Go!

But then I lowered my sight and saw an obstacle ahead. I squinted. At the end of the first block was an old man sitting on the curb, his legs and his upper body bent directly in my tires' path. Idiot!

I had two choices: step on the brakes and stop, or step on the gas and beat the Chevy to that fool, veer to the right, and miss him. The old man gave no indication of moving or even of noticing us. I beeped.

In compressed time I saw him with a frightful clarity. He was thin, unkempt, hunched forward so that his head hung down between his knees. What then? Drunk? His clothes were wretched. On the pavement between his shoes lay something vividly red. He was staring at it. I felt enraged by this utter indifference to danger, which forced me in the middle of my busy day to make decisions on *his* behalf. Oh, the indigent are so arrogant! Why didn't the man reach down and snatch the damn bandanna between his feet and get out of my way? I beeped. I beeped. He didn't budge. I chose speed.

All in a hurtling instant, furious for what he made me do, I down-shifted, mashed the accelerator, caused my Toyota to whine ahead of the Chevy on my right, swerved away from the old man's knees, and whipped his pantlegs with my wind. I gave him a wicked, accusing stare as I shot by—and I took, in that stare, a picture that only slowly developed in my mind.

That red bandanna was crawling the ground as though alive. Threads of red were hanging from the old man's chin. The man had just begun to raise his face, and I saw that his mouth was also smeared with red. No, no—this was no bandanna at all. It was blood. The old man was vomiting blood in the gutter. Jesus!

The light at Bellemeade met me green. I took it numbly, then slowed to make the turn at Gum. How was I to know? How was I to know? The silver Chevy blared its horn as it roared on south down Governor and was gone. I didn't respond.

I pulled up in front of Grace Church and sat in the Toyota with my forehead on the steering wheel. Trembling. I couldn't stop trembling. I sat for a long time trying not to tremble, but failing.

For God's sake, how am I supposed to know these things?

Suddenly someone rapped on my window, and I jumped.

Mr. Lawrence George.

The funeral director stood outside my pickup truck, erect and formal in a three-piece suit, serene and smiling. He showed me that he was carrying a black book in his hand. He opened my door and extended the book to me.

"Reverend," he said, bending a bit for a bow, "you forgot your Bible."

"No sir! No sir!" I snapped. "It is not a Bible. No sir!" I grabbed it from him. My hand shook. "It's called *The Pastor's Companion.*"

I stepped out of the pickup and walked toward the church, almost mute with fury because I could not stop myself from trembling.

My MOTHER WAS KNEELING on the floor in the dining room. I stood directly in front of her, face to her face. She was gazing at me, eating me in big bites with her eyes.

"Wally," she whispered, nearly a sigh.

Suddenly she leaned forward and seized me to herself. She hugged me with my arms straight down and printed her tears on my cheek. She had been crying.

"Oh, Wally, Wally," she murmured into my neck. She kissed me. Then she sank backward on her heels and shed a glittering smile upon me. There was a clear drop clinging to the end of her nose. I had the fleeting thought that she would burst out laughing—on account of the pressure of her smile. She didn't. Instead, she said, "You are the spittin' image of your grandpa."

This is the first time I ever heard that expression.

But my poor mother seemed overcome by the thing she had said. Her face dissolved to tears again, even while she kept gazing at me. She whispered moistly, "Yessir, yessir, child: the spittin' image of Grandpa Storck."

So she said—and then I wondered what the "spit" was.

I was six years old, a trooper in the first grade, the oldest kid in my family, and quick at the mysteries of words. I had the immediate sense that "image" meant I looked like Grandpa, which flattered me because I loved the old man. The big man. The man with wild white hair like Moses on the mountain and a face as severe as the tablets of stone. It was good to think I looked like Grandpa, an elevation of sorts.

But I didn't know what the "spit" was. That disconcerted me.

Oh, Grandpa was a wonderful man to "image." Superintendent of the cemetery in St. Louis, he was: master of the green lawns walled around with brick to six feet high; watchman, warder of the scattered stones, the gracious trees, the winding roads, the memorial shrines in which the memories were enclosed; king of the sleeping kingdom was he, to whom I was the green and golden prince—I the huntsman and herdsman as well, and grandly happy. Grandpa shot red squirrels when I visited him in the summers: single shots, most accurate pops in the silence of the cemetery. He skinned them and I watched him hang the pelts in the basement of his house, which was also on the cemetery grounds. And this is how strong the man was: during Prohibition (so my mother told me) he was called to the little illegal saloons that certain Germans maintained in the neighborhood around the cemetery. When Louie had a drunk he couldn't handle, big Bill Storck strode into the oily darkness (ah!) and lifted the drunkard bodily, like a basket of cabbages, one hand at the poor man's collar, one hand at his belt. Then he strode outside again and across the street to the cemetery wall, where, with little effort, he slung the drunkard up and over six feet of brick. And my mother said that Grandpa said: "Let a *Säufer* wake on a grave, and see if he changes his ways."

My mother grew pink with pleasure remembering such stories. And she said I was the "image" of this man, whom she obviously loved, whom I loved and honored with all my heart. It was good to be a little image of Grandpa Storck.

But the *spitting* image of the man?

It made me nervous, thinking what the "spit" was.

Well, Grandpa chewed tobacco.

Was there some custom of which I was ignorant that grandsons must take the places of their grandfathers, to chew tobacco on behalf of the whole family—and to spit? Grandpa spat. Would his spitting image have to spit?

The prospect dried my mouth out. I didn't fancy chewing on the old man's quid.

Besides, I could never match my grandpa for spitting. I didn't think anyone could. Grandpa Storck was an athlete at spitting. 'Twas an admirable, breathtaking thing that he could do.

Moreover, he loved me, did my Grandpa Storck, the solemn Lord of the green lawns and the gravestones. He loved me. And this was his particular way of showing love for me, by spitting. No, I simply could not imagine duplicating the *meaning* of the marvelous act.

Marvelous? It was a spectacle of skill, performed for me alone; and the more skillful he, the more love for me, since the finer was the gift that I was given.

Grandpa seldom smiled. He had an eruption of moustache beneath his nose, like white smoke from the chimney pots of his nostrils. His face was mostly expressive of one mood only: solemnity, rectitude, Lutheran doom. His arms were long and strong, his hands huge, his stride unhalting, his whole body an uncompromising dogma. Moses! Grandpa Storck, his hair like cloud at the top of his head, was an immediate Sinai, grim and untender—but I was not intimidated.

For *this* Mount Sinai could spit.

This old man, he loved me in the spitting.

For we would be sitting in his study, as dark and oaken as Lutheran truth. For he would be massive behind his desk, while I kept silent in the corner, according to his admonition. For he would flick me a sudden, significant glance, and I would recognize a break in the weather, and my heart would leap, but I would strive to keep my face as solemn as his. For he would clear his great throat and creak backward in his swivel chair, backward, *backward* until his face was aimed toward shadows at the ceiling, toward some spot so high above his brass spittoon, itself three miles away from him, that no one would bet a nickel he'd hit it. For I would fight the giggles in me, trying to be worthy of the grand occasion. For Grandpa—angled backward in his chair, twitching his mighty moustache—was Olympian.

And Grandpa spit.

Ha! but there was a splendor in that rising, shining, dark brown spew—and a glory so important that everything moved slow-motion to my sight. Listen: the goober never touched his moustache! It rose from his lip like a darker comet with a long, delirious tail. It ascended the air of his study in reckless daring: he spat *up*, not down. He spat *distance,* not safety. This was no timid dribble. This was the audacity of outrageous skill. High in space that comet would curve into a perfect apogee, then suddenly tip and sail downward with a gathering, giddy speed—till, *Poooom!* it hit the target center-brass, *Poooom!* a ring of triumph. Done.

And Grandpa would flick me another glance from his spit-position in the chair, and that undid me truly. I laughed out loud in spite of myself. I shouted. He had done it, and he loved me, and I acted like a kid for what I'd seen, laughing pure delight and gratitude.

But Grandpa brought his body forward then. He brought down the frown upon his eyes and restored sobriety between us. He would growl, *"Halt's Maul, Junge!"* and I did. I shut up. But I sat with my ears stuck out from grinning.

So we would walk the kingdom together, he and I. And he would stride, but I would run to stay abreast of him; and the summer was hot, but the day was always lovely, and I was happy as the grass was green, oh, I was lordly in the rivers of the windfall light. My grandpa, the Keeper of this cemetery, the rule of all the world, he loved me.

And twice that I remember, my grandfather smiled at me.

Once we stood at a distance from some people gathered beneath a canvas canopy—they in their Sunday best, murmuring words around a coffin, we in our boots and overalls, waiting by the shovels till they spoke a last Amen and we could go to work. I felt superior since those strangers had come at our behest and stood at a hole we'd dug, we and the workmen, six feet deep. This was our province. We would be here when they had dispersed. My overalls felt like a uniform, a privilege outranking their suits and their dresses.

While we waited, Grandpa began to talk. His very voice had whiskers in it. He kept his eyes on the murmurers at the grave, but he gave me his leisure; he chose to disclose to me the mysteries of Death.

"Junge," he said solemnly. *Boy,* he said in the German tongue, pursing his lips so that the moustache dropped a heavy wisdom.

"Grandpa?" I whispered.

He chewed in silence a moment. I knew better than to interrupt even the breathing pauses of his talk. Between the murmurers and

us a mound of earth had been covered by a tarpaulin. Neat squares
of sod were stacked beside that.

"*Junge,*" he said, "did you know that a dead man, he don't die
all at once?"

"No," I whispered.

"*Ja,*" he said, chewing. "It's a *seltsam* fact of nature. I have seen the
proofs of it. I myself have opened the coffins. Little things live on."

I looked up at his eyes, the eyes that had seen. I looked where he
was looking, at all the Sunday people bowing heads around a coffin.
I gazed steadfastly, then, at the coffin itself, curiously wrought with
hinges and handles. A body was in there. "Am I," I whispered, "a
little thing?"

"*Ein kleine Bengel,*" he declared.

"Ghosts live on?" I suggested, feeling the twist of excitement in
my tummy.

"Parts of the body, *Junge,*" he confided. "Even buried, parts of
his body live on." He was calm and solemn, imparting such information to me. But I grew breathless, approaching the mysteries.

He flicked me a measuring glance, then gazed away and grunted.
"I have seen," he said, "the hair of the corpses, long and tangled
in the tombs, still growing in their graves—"

Wow! I began to grin, seeing the same thing.

"I have seen," he intoned, "yellow toenails curled around the
feet like claws. It's the hair and the nails that keep on growing. *Ja.*"

Wow! With my eyes I tried to drill into the coffin over which the
Sunday people were praying. What would those people say if they
knew what I knew now? Intoxicating knowledge! Or what would
they do if I opened the lid? The hair and the nails—wow!

"*Junge?*"

"Grandpa?"

"Do you know the big word *cremation*?"

I did. I felt very proud that I did. "Burning dead bodies back to
dust," I said, more breathlessly than ever. I felt that my face was
shining beside this man, before his exquisite secrets. But he was
keeping his face earnest and professional, his great hands behind
his back, observing the people at their distance. I could hardly stand

this. I put my own hands behind my own back and gripped them hard and tried to frown.

"Well," he said, "when they burn the bodies, they close the furnace doors. And do you know why that is?"

"No?" I peeped.

"Because the dead," he said, "they sit up in the fires and scream—"

"Wow!" I shouted right out loud. That picture popped my eyes with an astonishing insight, and I lost control. *"Wow!"* I bellowed, and all the people at the graveside stopped praying and turned to stare at me.

Instantly I glanced at my grandpa—and there it was.

Though he was watching the Sunday people still, in his eyes there appeared a sudden twinkle, and under his moustache: a smile. It was as suddenly gone; but while it shined, it was a grin of cunning satisfaction. He bowed grandly at the staring people as if to say, *So, have you met my grandson?* and he continued to gaze at them until they turned away again.

"Whisht, whisht, *Junge,*" he said to me with a surprising tenderness in his voice, "there is a perfectly scientific reason for this. Fire expands the air in the lungs, you know. Leftover air, you see. It rushes through their throat-boxes, so they scream. And it tightens their muscles, so they sit. Reflex, ain't it?"

That was the first time that Grandpa smiled for me and bound me to himself. Twice he smiled. I remember them both as treasures.

But the second was not a cunning smile. The second was purely kind.

One afternoon that very summer when the sun grew round, my grandfather honored me by showing me a place which no one knew but him, which no one used but him—and even he reserved this place for extremest need. Near a shed that smelled of oil and hay, in a corner between two fences—one of them wooden and one of them brick—my Grandfather Storck introduced me to the wall against which, when he simply could not wait to get back to the house, he peed.

And thus it was that sometimes that summer we stood side by side, my grandpa and myself, solemnly facing the same wall in a wordless fellowship, bowing our heads as devoutly as though we prayed, but peeing. This was a holy moment, and I knew it. For we were man and boy together, little and large, absolutely intimates, members of a proud society, and in love.

My grandpa's prayers lasted longer than mine. My grandpa's capacities were in every way a wondrous flood, mine but a trickle. No matter. This hard and stolid man, this Moses of the wild white hair, this Lutheran of inflexibilities and spit—he loved me enough for both of us. I know. I know.

For once when we were done, when I had heaved a sweet and shuddering sigh, he turned and looked directly in my eyes. And he smiled.

And then one afternoon in Chicago I returned from school to find my mother in my bedroom, busy, busy, distracted. "We have to visit Grandpa," she said.

She said "have to" as though it were distasteful to her. In fact, she was packing my clothes in a suitcase and all her gestures seemed sharp and angry to me. And because it was my clothes in her hands, the anger seemed aimed at me.

I said, "Why?"

She gave me an angry look. "What's the matter?" she said. "Don't you want to?"

That's not what I meant. I always wanted to visit Grandpa. I said, "Well, but I'm in school now."

"Call it a vacation," she said, punching a wad of socks into the suitcase.

Vacation? My mother never relaxed the rules. Only something extraordinary could persuade her to change patterns or plans already fixed.

But school isn't what I meant either. I think I meant: *Why are you angry?* But that's too hard a question to ask entirely, so I just said, "Why?" I think I meant: *What's wrong, Mama?* And I surely meant: *Why don't you look at me?*

I said again, "Why?" And since I had no other words but these, I said, "Why do we have to visit Grandpa?"

She frowned. She glowered. She said, "Nosey children lose their noses."

"Mama?" I said. "But why?"

"Because he's dying, Wally, all right?" she snapped. "Is that good enough for you?"

"Dying?" I whispered.

"Dying. Yes, dying. Cancer," she said, as though she were answering a stupid question. She slammed the dresser drawers.

But I wasn't asking a question. I was just confused by the word "dying." I thought I knew the word. Grandpa had already taught me about dying; but he spoke wonders and mysteries. Now my mother spat the word like a bile, and suddenly I didn't know "dying" at all. What was this "dying" that my mother should be so angry about it? Something was terribly wrong—and the fact that she wouldn't look at me frightened me, because I feared that somehow I had done the wrong.

"Mama?" I said. This was not good judgment. I probably shouldn't be talking now because I'd make things worse. But I needed to know something and I couldn't help myself. "Mama?" I said. "What's cancer?"

"Tumors," she said. *Whap!* "Sickness," she said. *Whap! Whap!* She was trying to close the suitcase. It wouldn't shut.

"No," I said. "No, but what do you *do* for cancer?"

My mother raised her eyes a hot second and burned me with a look. Once more she tried to shut the suitcase but failed. "Oh, Wally!" she cried. She slammed the lid so hard that my shirts bounced out. "Oh, Wally, just leave me alone!" she cried. She left the room.

So then I understood that I was a guilty person, though I didn't know why. And I knew that dying must be very horrible, though I didn't know now what it was. And I understood above all things that I had better be quiet, had better keep still and do as little as possible, because anything I did might be wrong. Nobody had prepared me: *What is right? What do you do for this sort of dying?* I didn't know.

For the rest of that day I tried to make myself as small as my baby brother, as hidden as the mouse. I didn't like it that I was the oldest. My body felt gross and clumsy in this atmosphere. I wished, in fact, that I could disappear.

At sunrise the following day we were gone. We drove the long road from Chicago to St. Louis in a killing silence. Silence, as I understood it—silence was either parental disappointment or parental impotence before enormous badness. I shrank and shrank in the back seat of the car. But I could not, finally, become nothing. I couldn't make me not be there. I kept my head against the windowglass and closed my eyes and pretended to be asleep.

In St. Louis I watched the city go by. I found that I felt very sorry for all of the people that I saw.

And then the cemetery, when we entered the iron gates, was not the same. It was quiet. It was under governance of a grim adulthood, no longer green nor golden, annexed: the childless land. Cars like husks were scattered around my grandfather's house.

We went in the back door. The kitchen had high ceilings and cupboards with windows so that you could see the dishes inside of them. Aunts and uncles greeted my mother with murmuring, and all were severe, and all of them angry, and nobody noticed me, for which I was grateful. Where was Grandpa? If anyone noticed me, what would I do? How should I behave? The dying I didn't understand was in this house, thick like a smoke, like the smoke of a burned food—shameful. But what it was, and what you do for it, no one had taught me. Where was Grandpa?

With a strict gesture and a meaningful step, my mother led me from the kitchen through a little hallway, through the dining room and into my grandfather's living room. There was a cot in that hallway, covered with white sheets; and a man was under the sheets. At first I thought that it was Grandpa. But there was time for only a glimpse, and then I thought that it wasn't Grandpa because it didn't look like him.

My mother made sure that I sat on the sofa, and then she left me among the cousins, all of us silent. We didn't look at each other. I didn't swing my legs as I sat. I didn't know what they were thinking, but I was thinking this: *If you don't know what to do for dying, do nothing. Say nothing. You'd only make it worse.* Where is Grandpa? What is cancer?

I did not cry. I folded my two hands in my lap and sat in a private trembling, voiding my face of everything.

And then it was that my Grandfather Storck remembered me.

My mother returned to the living room, but I didn't see her. She touched my shoulder, and I jumped.

"Grandpa wants to see you," she said.

I got up and followed her in mute obedience, not even unfolding my hands. We went back through the dining room, into the little hallway. My mother moved behind me and put her hands on my shoulders, positioning me before the cot which was covered with white sheets, and then she left me, and I was standing fixed to the floor, staring at the man beneath the sheets.

My heart beat in a sort of panic, and I thought, *Is this what dying is, that people are not the same anymore? They become—someone else?*

The man before me was bones, old bones and nearly no strength on those bones, but a yellowed sacklike skin.

I could neither move nor speak. I looked. No one had told me what to do.

The man had a moustache as yellow as straw, nose holes huge and black and empty, a yellow face with the cheeks sucked in, the temples sunken, the poor eyes covered with a paper skin, thin, translucent, oh! His long arms were longer than Grandpa's and skinnier. His hands were wider than Grandpa's; they lay on his chest like empty shovels. The breathing whistled in his nostrils. He stank. His hair stood up like a wild, yellow fire—

And then the man moved.

He rolled his head in my direction. He allowed his eyes to open, and he looked at me, and he said nothing at all, but he did this: he smiled.

I drew a sudden breath, and released it in a word: "Grandpa," I whispered. "Grandpa, it's you."

For everything else may change in mortality, everything except this one thing: the smile that love engenders. And then nothing else is important anymore. Grandpa smiled and suddenly this was my Grandpa Storck. And he smiled at me, so I was there as well. In a flood I felt a freedom, I felt me come to be, and I grinned so that my ears stuck out. We were there in the room together, companions, man and boy, little and large, his Moses hair and mighty moustache, my silly, impossible giggling.

"Grandpa!" I said.

"Junge," he smiled.

And then, without another word, he taught me what this dying is; and he taught me what you do for it. He invited me to himself. Having loved me when we walked the green and golden ground together, even now he disclosed the final mysteries to me, and he loved me to the end.

The smile faded. Solemnly the old man raised his right hand from the sheets and reached in my direction. I understood the invitation. I knew what to do.

I walked to him and stuck out my lesser hand. He took it and held it in his—and he did what you do for dying. We shook hands. He shook my little fist with a dignified, sober ceremony, first up, then down: Once. Twice.

I learned. I did not tremble, and I did not cry, since I learned not only what you do for dying, but also what it is. It is leave-taking.

I said, "Good-bye, Grandpa."

And under the cloud of his moustache the old man moved his mouth. He smiled.

All this is right and true.

How long was it later? I don't know. It can't have been more than two weeks. My mother and I were sitting at lunch in the kitchen of our house in Chicago. We were eating soup. The telephone rang, and I looked quickly at her eyes. There are times when you know the message by the ring itself.

My mother stood up and went into the dining room, where the telephone was attached to the wall, shoulder-level. I watched her go. But I knew already what she would hear.

She lifted the receiver and put it to her ear. She said some words, and someone said words to her. She bowed her head while she was talking, and she pressed her left arm against her stomach. When she was done speaking, she kept her head bowed, leaning forward until her forehead touched the wall, and she stood that way, utterly silent, her eyes closed, replacing the phone by habit. Grandpa was dead. I knew that someone had just told her that her father had died. I also knew immediately what to do.

I rose from the kitchen table and walked into the dining room. "Mama?" I said. I stood at her left side. She didn't hear me.

I tugged her skirt. "Mama?" I whispered. She opened her eyes and looked down at me. Then I did what you do for dying. I stuck out my right hand.

Slowly my mother reached down and gave me her own hand. I gripped it in a fine strong grip, and with a dignified, sober ceremony I shook my mother's hand, first up, then down: Once. Twice.

This was clearly the right thing to do. Because with the second handshake, I brought my whole mother down upon my shoulders. She covered me with a pure and holy hug, and she allowed herself to cry on me, softly, softly, and I didn't mind because this was my job now, because I had learned and I knew and was able: my Grandfather Storck had taught me.

In a little while her sobbing subsided. My mother kneeled down and gazed directly into my eyes, looking, searching. She kissed me. She smiled a glittering smile upon me, a rainy sort of gladness, and I thought she might burst out in laughing. She didn't. Instead she said, "Wally, Wally—you are the spittin' image of your grandpa."

And I began to wonder what the "spit" was.

Or whether I had to chew the quid my grandpa chewed before he died.

Some twenty-seven years thereafter I was sitting in another kitchen in another city altogether, Evansville, in the home of one of my parishioners.

The woman across the table from me was Musetta Bias, a strong-boned, strong-hearted woman as capable of love as any of my fore-bears, but nowhere near as stern in Lutheran rectitude. Lutheran she was. German she was not. Musetta was black. Her love had no hard edges.

We drank tea together on that particular day, because we had only recently buried her husband; and, though the committal service had been smooth and gracious and (she told me) comforting, there'd been no chance for personal words at the graveside. Arthur had died of a wasting cancer. He had been a big man, a police officer, a man who liked his green beans cooked with bacon fat.

We were spending a holy moment remembering him.

Suddenly Musetta turned her face to the window.

"Arthur Junior," she said, speaking as though their son were just about to enter the room. "Arthur Junior," she said, "is the spittin' image of his daddy."

No! No, she did not say "spittin'" at all.

I nearly lunged at the poor woman.

"What did you say?" I said.

She blinked at me.

"Musetta, what did you just say?"

"I said," she said, "that Arthur Junior is the spee-it 'n image of his daddy—?"

"Did you say 'spit'?" I demanded.

"No," she said. There was Southern blood in the woman, ancient roots to the language in her mouth.

"You didn't say 'spit'? Spit? Like spittle, spit?"

"No," she said, backing away from my intensity. "I said 'spee-it.'"

Spee-it, dear God! That's the way the South elides its syllables, swallowing Rs in the process. *Spee-it* is *spirit.* Musetta was saying *spirit.* Arthur Junior was the spirit and image of his daddy.

That's what the spit was.

And my mother, whether she knew it or not, had said no less. I did more than look like Grandpa Storck. His spirit, the character and the force of his being, dwelt within me. When I put forth my boyhood hand to touch her, why, it was as well the hand of her father. Her father had come consoling her, not gone at all, not altogether gone, abiding in his grandson, one.

Even so had the child, still young and easy, received like clay the impress of an old man's love. Death was not division in that summer, in the sun that is young once only.

Junge! Did you know that a dead man, he don't die all at once?

And the boy, before he followed time from grace, said, *Yes, old man, I know.*

1.

Douglas Lander drove the mule that pulled the plow that broke the earth to dig the hole on which was built Grace Lutheran Church. They dug that hole twice. The flood of 1937—when folks boated above such streets as Governor and Garvin—filled it in the first time. But Douglas was ever an even-tempered man and would do the same thing six times over uncomplainingly if five times first it failed.

"You can't command a mule," he chuckled even to the end of his days, "until you got its attention. An' you know how you get a mule's attention?" It was a tired joke; but Douglas was so sweet in its delivery, so pacific a man himself, so neat and small a ginger stick, that people grinned on the streets when he told it. He was a pouch of repeatable phrases. Besides, it was understood that he meant more than mules: the younger generation, the government, some recalcitrance in human nature, cocky young preachers—whatever the topic of his present conversation. He could trim a joke to any circumstance. "Hit it with a two-by-four."

He wore oversized glasses with silver stems. He never learned to drive a car. He walked wherever he went, and he paused to talk with whomever he met. And quietly, confidently, as though it were the deeper creed of her soul, Miz Lillian loved him. Miz Lil. She was his wife primevally. Her loving needed no public demonstration. She had been there before he drove the mule that pulled the plow that broke the earth—twice.

Both Miz Lillian and Douglas—and she was as short as he was, though neater, thriftier, quiet, maternal—were fixtures of the inner city neighborhood, as standard as pepper shakers on a table. They *made* the mean streets neighborly. They gave the crumbling streets a history. Douglas could point to a rubble three blocks west of Grace, where the city had demolished some substandard house, and remember: "I lived there. Right over there. And I recall when Line Street *was* a line, black to the west of it, white to the east, and you better not cross 'less you got business takes you across. Now we black on both sides." He grinned. He lifted his sweet eyebrows. "One o' them things," he sang high tenor. "One o' them things."

Miz Lil spoke less of the past than did Douglas. Not because she did not remember, rather because she spoke less than Douglas in all things. She hadn't a compulsion to talk. She watched and kept her own counsel, and her words were weightier, therefore.

But Miz Lil remembered slippers in the Depression, how that Douglas once came home with a box of pairs of slippers, payment for an odd job when jobs were scarce. She remembered the distribution of slippers among their relatives and friends—and chickens, when they got them, and canned goods. And the slippers may not have been terribly warm in winter, but they were a sort of bank deposit, a sort of security, because some relative might earn an extra coat and a friend might find some precious article like long underwear—and then Douglas, who hated the cold as perhaps his only enemy, could dress the warmer in consequence of the slippers.

These were the flesh of the inner city, Douglas and Miz Lil, the living ligatures. For their sakes, do not call it a ghetto. Do not presume it a mindless, spiritless, dangerous squalor—a wilderness of brick and broken glass, brutality, hopelessness, the dead-end center, no! They made it community because they remained in confidence and honor. The *Lamed Vavnik:* the Righteous Ones. They gave it civility, familiarity, and purpose—they caused it to be a good ground on which to raise fat children—because they remembered the names.

"Her grandma's name was Alice Jackson," said Miz Lil. "Come up from Kentucky with her family when the coal mines couldn't support them. Turn of the century. She went to school with me, Alice did," said Miz Lil, remembering, the veil of time upon her eyes. "Bright. She was bright in those days. With stories and plans, all eager for the future. But then she got caught raising children, and then her children had children, and she raised them too. And she suffered to feed her grandbabies. She put on weight.

I remember how Alice Jackson labored to breathe, surrounded by grandbabies. But she suffered to make them good too. Took them to church, yes. Prayed to Jesus for their souls. She did the best she could. A body can only do so much. When you talk about skinny Marie," said Miz Lil, "you think on her grandma, fat Alice Jackson; then you can't help but talk with pity, and you'll be inclined to give Marie a drink of water for her grandma's sake. No, you won't be judging Marie then. She's got good blood in her and the print of love in her poor face. The fat just closed on Alice Jackson's throat, I think. I think it got to be more misery to breathe than not to. That's how she died, I think."

In the context of such remembering, how could the inner city be faceless, rootless, cruel? Concrete and desperation only?

Under the sunlight of such a mercy, how could anyone, smug in the suburbs, fear it as dark and dangerous?

This was no ghetto. Douglas and Miz Lil—invisible perhaps to the outside eye for that they blended in; who were black and short and old, who held no office but had lived there since the beginning of the world, when folks swept not only their porches in the morning, but their sidewalks and their gutters too—Mr. and Miz Lander, they were its citizens.

He wore long underwear, autumn and winter and spring, laughing at himself because his little body could not endure the cold: African indeed.

She trudged to the projects with pies and helped move Mrs. Collier's furniture out on the lawn so they could bomb her place for roaches. Mrs. Collier needed comforting for the incomprehensible disruption of her life. Mrs. Collier also needed a bath.

They wore, did Douglas and Miz Lil, the mantle in the neighborhood. They scarcely knew this; therefore they wore it in a perfect modesty; but perhaps any community with blood ties and past history and present complexities, problems that want a personal solving, contains one or two wise spirits, sages to whom the rest of the people will come when they are themselves at wit's end and helpless. Upon these the mantle has fallen. These Wise Ones are chosen unconsciously, by the mute agreement of the truest members of the neighborhood. They are invested with a silent respect. The community is stabilized—the community is both grounded and elevated also and comforted—just knowing that the Wise Ones are there. Whether one ever takes advantage of their presence or not, one knows he has a place of appeal: *Somebody knows my name.*

But to eyes outside that small society, the mantle is invisible. Who would ever talk about it?

To hearts within the small society, it is a consolation taken for granted. No one would ever talk about it.

Nevertheless, it is nothing other than prophecy. It is the presence—the *bath qôl,* the living voice—of God.

Douglas Lander died while watching "The Lawrence Welk Show" and eating a piece of pie. Miz Lil was dozing on the sofa at the time. She didn't realize that he was gone until the house had filled with a perfect quietness and she saw him slumped all wearily on the floor. Perhaps he'd been coming to tell her something.

His glasses, those wide temples and the silver stems of them, had always seemed too big for his filbert face, too formal for a man so sweetly malleable to all the sudden circumstances of this existence. But when he lay thoughtfully in the casket, the glasses seemed absurdly superfluous. And the suit that they had dressed his body in, it was too big at the neck, excessive at his thin wrists and little hands.

At his wake the people noticed the lack of long underwear and chuckled over homely jokes. "He be warm now, Miz Lil," they said. "He got God for sunlight now, and it ain' nothin' but summer where he gone to."

Miz Lillian barely acknowledged the joke.

She stood at the bier of her husband, rubbing and rubbing her abdomen, a little woman gazing at a little man now lost in thought.

She would have to do the talking now. One pepper shaker stood alone.

In the months that followed, Miz Lil did not interrupt the habits of an old, old life. In the evening she sat behind screens on the porch of her house, facing Bellemeade Avenue, watching the traffic. Watching nothing. Sometimes relatives sat with her. Sometimes not. She gave the impression of rocking, whether the chair could rock or not, because she maintained a slow, perpetual rhythm in her body, a secret drumbeat. In fact, she was rubbing her stomach with one hand or with both.

On Sundays she went to church. She sat in the second row from the back on the left-hand side, the same pew that the Lander family had always occupied since the mule first plowed the ground and the little building had been built. She didn't sing the hymns. Neither did she, who had never been demonstrative of deeper feelings, demonstrate her feelings now: her face was internal, her eyes were like tiles of porcelain.

In this wise did she take her place among the people after worship, and file through the tiny narthex, and shake the pastor's hand.

The pastor leaned down to her and spoke as if no one else were there. He said, with earnest significance, "How are you, Miz Lillian?"

She responded as if no one at all were there, neither the pastor, whom her tile-eyes did not see, nor even herself. "Fair," she said. That was all she said. She proceeded through the double doors outside, holding her stomach with the hand the pastor had just released.

And so the year unraveled.

Douglas and Miz Lillian, complements of one another in character, behavior, and in wisdom, once had worn the mantle together. It was uncertain—though no one consciously asked the question—whether Miz Lil would lay it aside now altogether, or pull it over her head and hide in sorrow, or else wear it for the people's sake alone. If she did not wear it, it would be quietly cast upon another, whom slow time, the passage of a thousand days, would reveal. Or if none other received the mantle, that would be a sure and terrible sign of the breakup of this small society. But if, in time, she lifted her face and smiled again and spoke to someone a consoling word, then God would not have left the inner city without its prophet, would not have left the people without *bath qôl,* the daughter of the voice of God.

The end of this story is this:

On a particular evening the pastor came to visit Miz Lil in her living room. While they sat together, he on the sofa, she in a rocking chair, rocking and rubbing her stomach at once, dark grew darker in the room and the faces of both of them dimmed to the other's sight.

The pastor prayed a prayer. That is what Miz Lil had said he could do for her. But he ran out of prayer before he ran out of yearning on the little woman's behalf; so he sat in silence.

And then she broke the silence. Miz Lil began to talk. The pastor listened without interruption and slowly began to realize, even before she was done, the holy benevolence of her words. In the darkness he allowed himself to cry.

In fact, Miz Lil was speaking of grief. Carefully, touching the subject with infinite reverence, she said that her grief was a stone in the womb. Not *like* a stone, no. It was there—a lump as mortal as an infant between the wings of her old hips, but heavier: a painful, physical presence. "And you pray it would go away," she said. "It doesn't go. You plead to Jesus you can't bear the suffering. You bear it anyway."

She rocked and rocked in the darkness. There was the sound of a whispering fabric: she was rubbing her stomach.

"Finally you understand," said Miz Lil, "that this is the way it's going to be forever till you die. The stone is never going to pass. You're going to mourn forever. But you say, *This isn't wrong.* Finally you say, *This is right and good.*"

The sorrow that started as the enemy, it ends a friend. This is what Miz Lil explained as the night developed. Sorrow had become a familiar thing for her now, and the perpetual pain in her stomach a needful thing. It was there when she woke at midnight, there in the morning. She took it to church with her, and she brought it home.

This particular baby would never be born nor ever leave, but would companion her forever. This was the loneliness that kept a widow from being altogether lonely—because it was, inside of her, a memorial of her husband. It was pain and wanted rubbing. It was sorrow and caused her to sigh. But it was also the love of Douglas—and stroking it was the same as stroking the husband whom you love.

"Douglas is not far from me," said Miz Lil, "nor me from Douglas—" In midsentence, she fell silent. There was only the sound of the whispering fabric. And the pastor in the darkness realized his tears.

More than that, he understood them. For he wept for the old woman whom he loved, whose sorrow affected him, but whose resolution of the sorrow kept his tears from being merely hopeless. For he wept as well for the neighborhood at large, because this marvelous, holy talk of Miz Lillian's was a sign: she had taken the mantle up again; she had found a way to wear the mantle not altogether alone. The voice of God had not departed from the grim streets; the inner city had its Wise One still.

For he wept, most particularly, for himself, because the woman had chosen to speak such intimate wisdom to him, to reveal her inmost spirit to him. He was, therefore, no more a stranger. The invisible was visible before his eyes, and he could see the mantle, and he was made a citizen. *Bath qôl,* the daughter of the voice of God—it had spoken in his hearing, and he was moved to tears because he thought: *Somebody knows my name.*

This, as we said, is the end of the story.
The beginning and the middle follow.

2.

From the first days of my ministry at Grace—when I still wore massive, black-rimmed spectacles, unpolished shoes, unmatching clothes, and a halo—I took a greedy pleasure in the ritual of greeting members after worship, shaking the hands of every soul who'd sat to hear me preach.

There was one main door from the tiny sanctuary, through which all the people had to pass. Down some steps from that was the narthex, where I took my pastoral stand—and then, to my left, the double doors of the church, which opened outside to sidewalks and lawns and the weather.

"Good sermon, Reverent," parishioners complimented me. I grinned. I agreed.

"Glad to have a preacher not afraid of preaching!"

"Wonnerful, wonnerful."

"Very spiritual, Reverent."

"Well, I enjoyed myself today, that's a fact."

"Fellow pumpin' gas at the Mobil station, he said to me, 'Yeah, but can that white boy preach? I mean *preach?*' Well, I was proud to tell him, 'White or purple, my pastor gives as good as he gets, yessir.' I shut his mouth. I told him, 'He can raise the dust.' Amen, Reverent—right?"

"Right," I said.

"Right," said the grinning face in front of mine, one in the file of parishioners greeting me: "Just keep on doin' what you doin'. Right."

They were including me—on their own terms and in their own language embracing me. They were glad I was there, and I was glad to note their gladness. More than glad, I was relieved. Happy days, those early days! I had position and a host of admirers.

Well: the fact that the church was black, and the concomitant fact that it sat in the inner city, caused a sort of contention in me which needed this affirmation. Actually, two separate problems needed this balm in my breast.

First, I was purely flattered that a people not of my heritage received me as one of them and praised me in the reception. That spoke well, it seemed, of my deeper humanity and my ministry; it laid to rest the uncertainty I'd had of whether I might prove prejudiced or meanly provincial. Success in the city must be prized.

So the problem of doubt was eased in a private rush of triumph—
to God be the glory.

As for the second problem, I was (I explained to myself) inexperienced. I was (in actual fact) a stranger on this turf, untutored.
The inner city was altogether foreign to me—and I might have
been a pastor inside the church, with all the rights the office granted
me; but on the street I was alien, ignorant, an interloper notably
white. I was (to put the issue more plainly than I ever did in those
days) scared.

But the more that the members of Grace affirmed me here *and* on
the streets, the safer might be my goings forth—and even the inner
city might be persuaded to accept my pale, improvident presence.

Oh, love me, Grace. But love me out loud, okay?

I was hungry for handshakes in those days to calm my fear. So
much depended on their approval and their praise.

"I'm the kind of person," said Eleanor Rouse, "who brings her
flowers to the living. I don't wait till they're dead. So I tell you to
your face: Pastor, *my* Pastor," she said, "you got my respect."

And Eleanor Rouse had my immediate, complete devotion—
most especially because she, who had called me *her* pastor, was not
a member of Grace. She belonged to New Hope Baptist Church,
only sometimes attending our worship with her parents. Besides,
Eleanor was a most outspoken women and might therefore bruit
my goodness abroad, in the courts of the neighboring kingdoms,
as it were.

She had a vigorous handshake. I returned it with equal energy.

"To God," I said, "be the glory."

"Thank you, Jesus."

"Thank you, Eleanor—"

And then her mother, whom the people called Miz Lil, followed
in her turn; and then her father followed next, both of them shorter
than their daughter, shorter than all their children, it turned out:
shorter than most of the population. But a couple most serene. A
couple, whom to meet and know, was comforting indeed.

This Miz Lil distinguished herself from the common run of
compliments for several reasons. She looked me directly and kindly

in the eye, no embarrassment on her behalf, no qualms regarding me. Her gazing caused a sort of solitude around the two of us which lent her words importance. Nor did those words come tripping from her tongue. A fox eye had Miz Lillian, a canny glance, and a habit of pausing before she spoke. Her thoughts were parceled one by one and personal.

Under the aegis of such a spirit, one remembers what was said, yes, word for word. And one is a bit discomfited if he cannot fully interpret the oracle.

On a certain Sunday Miz Lillian said, "Well, you taught us today."

And then on another Sunday she fixed me with her eyes: "Hooo, Pastor," she said, "you preached today."

Her husband was another matter. Douglas Lander, always equable whatever the time of day or year, wherever the little man turned up, downtown or mowing the lawn of the church or shoveling snow, could talk at an endless length, his sweet voice on and on, his glasses bobbing up and down, his single, final, philosophic observation for any topic he could not otherwise resolve or explain or morally excuse being: "One o' them things." So he sang the tougher problems of life to rest and lived in peace in spite of them: "Just one o' them things." With such a metaphysic, the man was fearless; he could talk on anything, no subject too perilous for him.

But Miz Lil was chary of her words. She knew how she would end whatever she began. She gave infinite space to Douglas, undismayed however far his droning led him; but her own subjects she chose with a watchful care.

Therefore, I began to notice, Sunday after Sunday, that Miz Lil had but two words for my sermons. One was "teach," and one was "preach," and there surely was a difference between the two. But I could not, for all my pondering, guess what that difference was.

Everyone else in the congregation seemed at peace with Miz Lillian Lander, innocent of her effect; they seemed to take her much for granted—like children sporting on the shore of some almighty, rolling ocean.

Me she made nervous.

On a particular Sunday, then, when she reached to shake my hand, I held on and began to question her.

"Miz Lillian?" I said.

The fox eyes, sharp and kindly, gave me more than a moment, gave me the whole day if I wanted it. "Pastor?"

"Sometimes," I said, "you say I teach."

"Mmm?" she said.

"And sometimes you say I preach."

"Mmm-hmm." She said this high in her sinuses. She smiled. She waited.

"Well," I said, "is there a difference?"

The old lady raised an ironic eyebrow, as though she thought an educated seminarian would know of differences. But she kept on smiling. I felt suddenly brutish and lumbering in front of her. And white.

"Of course there is," she said.

"Well?" I said, making a smile myself, embarrassed. "What," I said, "is the difference?"

Now Miz Lillian was holding my hand in hers, which was work-hardened, her little finger fixed forever straight, unable to bend.

"When you teach," she said, instructing me, "I learn something for the day. I can take it home and, God willing, I can do it. But when you preach—" She lowered her voice and probed me the deeper with her eyes. "—God is here. And sometimes he's smiling," she said, "and sometimes he's frowning surely."

I grinned. Her language was elemental, but I chose immediately to take it all as a compliment, for the teaching and the preaching together—but for the preaching especially, which seemed to be the calling of the holy God into our little church. What a mystic power that gave my homiletics, like shining from shook foil! I grinned.

Miz Lillian Lander smiled and released my hand and went out the double doors.

But in the next instant Douglas Lander floated into view, shrugging as though in apology for his wife. He shook his head while he shook my hand. "Just one o' them things," he sang, seeming to ease some little friction, seeming to salve some little thorn between us—as though we men could stand the female nature which we couldn't understand. "Just one o' them things," he said, and I lost my grin.

In my hypersensitive state a prickle went up the back of my neck. Why would Douglas think he had to cover for his wife? What had I missed? How was Miz Lil's compliment one of Douglas's "Things"?

Or wasn't it a compliment at all?

What had the woman said to me, *of* me, truly?

Oh, the more desperate I was to make sense of it, the more foreign seemed to me the language of the inner city. Black talk: teach and preach! Black talk: smilin', frownin'. What exactly did I *do* to make it teaching, or how was I different to make it preaching? *Yeah, but can that white boy preach? I mean PREACH?* What did she mean by "God is here"?

Maybe (I mused alone in my tiny study) I am not, at the bottom of it all, a part of this people. How can I know, if I don't know what I do to them? Maybe Miz Lil is the only honest one among them, though she speaks in riddles. Maybe I'm the dupe of a harmless, necessary deception: because they need some sort of pastor, they'll gladly make this pastor think they like him—*ack!*

And then came a Sunday of revelations. And then came the sermon in which I told a story to illustrate some point. I don't remember the point. But I do, for two particular reasons, remember the story.

First, it was factual. I drew the story from personal experience in the church and in that inner city neighborhood, involving a woman who had been and gone before the telling of this tale. She was a transient. No one, I thought, would recognize her.

Second, when worship was over Miz Lil took my hand in the narthex, and held on, and gripped it until it hurt. She wouldn't let it go. She pierced me with her fox eye. "Pastor," she said softly, "you preached today. Pastor," she whispered in the solitude she caused around us, "God was in this place."

She said this with utter conviction. But the diminutive woman was not smiling. And she would not let me go. . . .

3.

(Herewith, an account of the experience, a portion of which was "preached" on the Sunday when Miz Lillian killed me with a word.)

Marie

All day long she sits in front of her shotgun house, in a cotton dress, on a tubular kitchen chair, gazing at nothing, rocking: the crazy lady, surrounded by a patch of weed she does not mow.

Neighborhood children call her the crazy lady because she mutters to herself. They sneak to the tree behind her; they watch her gesturing to the air; they hear her arguing with no one at all, and their eyes grow wide at the aberration. "Pastor! Look at the crazy lady!"

She does them no harm. She scarcely admits their existence. Perhaps she would deny the existence of any in her world except a few men, and those only of necessity.

One day I said hello to her. Well, that house is right across the street from my office, and I am a pastor, after all. "Hello!" I called with a friendly cheer. She froze midsentence. Her mouth snapped shut, her nostrils flared. She stared at me over her right shoulder. I came halfway across the street. "Hello," I said. "I'm the pastor here. We're neighbors, you see. What's your name?"

No answer.

Her body is a boiled bone, curved like a rib-bone, gaunt. Her eyes are huge, the dome of her head is huger. Her age is impossible to tell.

"What's your name?" I said.

No answer. The skull-gaze only, undecipherable. Which left me in an uncomfortable predicament: how to close a conversation that never started?

But a kid no more than two or three years old came ripping down the sidewalk on a wretched trike. "Marie!" he shrieked at the top of his lungs. "Marie! Yaw-waw-waw! Yaw-waw-waw!" He rocketed over the curb, lowered his head like the bull, and made directly for my suit pants. He wasn't pretending. At top speed this kid meant to run me down. "Yaw-waw-waw-waw!"

So I learned that her name is Marie, and this was her child—though she did nothing to stop him and merely watched me dodge his assault—and that was the last conversation we didn't have together.

And I learned to leave her alone. I could only wish that she left me alone as well.

This kid of hers is an affliction to Christian piety. Nobody disciplines him. Up and down the street he rides like a wandering siren. His mother disappears into her muttering, and no one's there. He shatters the air as though the city's afire. And no one is there. He's a disaster, an act of God, a tight tornado three feet high. But *I'm* there. My office is the tiny room to the right of the chancel, no windows, one outside door to the fire escape—to Gum Street. I am there. And I am forced to choose, when the kid is screaming, between two sacrifices: either I will shut the door and stifle in the still, hot air. Or else I'll open the door and pay for the breeze by enduring the noise of that boy. Either way I pay. Neither way is it easy for me to work in my study.

But I pity the kid. I do not blame him. I've heard him lift his voice in a truly wounded anguish, the poor child wailing in abandonment. I've looked and seen that his mother has locked him out of the house, and then his screaming doesn't frustrate me. It hurts me.

This is what happens: at sundown men begin to come to Marie's front door, alone, in pairs. They knock or they do not knock. They enter. Almost immediately her child is put out like the cat, and he whirls around and he beats on the door and he howls. Finally he sits on the stoop and gives himself over to the tears alone. Time those tears: twenty minutes. Then do not blame the boy.

The crazy lady across the street from Grace Lutheran Church, who lives in a haze the whole day through, who regards me with a rabid eye, who regards her baby not at all, is a prostitute.

So then, this is a serious question of ministry, of Christian and civic responsibility—of charity to the child, if nothing else: what should I do about Marie?

Well, it's a ticklish circumstance, isn't it? Rights and freedoms; contrasting lifestyles; morals, to be sure—but by what authority could I approach a woman who wouldn't talk to me? I'm new in the neighborhood.

I did nothing.

But Marie did something. And this is what happened between us.

One night I sat reading by a small lamp in my study, all the doors being locked to the church (for fear of the lurking inner city?—for safety, for common sense and safety, since the members warned me, "Lock the doors when you're alone"), all the lights being out in the church save mine. One night while I was reading at my desk, someone began to whistle inside the building.

I froze in my chair. A tingling tightened all my flesh. It has been my habit from childhood, when confronted with a fright, first to pretend that the fright's not there. To freeze in whatever position I had when I sensed my danger. But my heart goes ramming against my ribs, and my face may seem indifferent, but my ears are roaring.

Deep in the darkened building, smack in the middle of the inner city, far from any assistance I could in the moment imagine, someone had commenced a weird, a coldly passionless, whistling.

I prayed to God that it would stop. Just go away and release me. It didn't.

I stole a glance into the sanctuary, to the back of the sanctuary, to the door that leads to the narthex and downstairs. No light. No one had switched on a friendly light. There was only the darkness made ghostly by shadow and shapes from the stained glass windows, effigies in glass.

Twice in the past year thieves had broken into the church. But no one else had been here at the time.

Why in God's name would a thief disclose himself by whistling?

Okay! Okay, I'm the pastor. I never figured that ministry meant law enforcement or fights or bloodshed or whatever was about to be required of me—martyrdom!—but I am in charge. The building is my responsibility. I'll see who you are (you idiot!) and what you're up to.

I crept from the warm light of my study into the sanctuary. I crept down the dark aisle toward the back. The floorboards creaked. I froze. And I found in the midst of my terror that I was angry. Furious, in fact, to be sucked into a confrontation I hadn't caused and didn't deserve. I hated this whistling thief.

But hatred wasn't enough to ease my fears. The whistling was below my feet. In the basement. The nearer I crept to the steps downstairs, the more I swallowed. In the narthex, now, I heard it loud in ecclesiastical pits. In the boiler room, which was dark, dark.

Inhuman whistling! I began to notice that it never took a breath. One note, on and on and on—a mechanical sort of whistling.

I burst into the boiler room, crying, "Hey! Hey!" horrifying myself.

But there was not a soul in all the gloom.

And the whistling continued undisturbed. Above my head.

I reached up. I groped what I couldn't see. And touched pipes. Water pipes! Oh, my heart nearly flew in its happy freedom: water! How could I mistake it as anything else? The whistling was running water; the noise was water rushing through the plumbing of the church, ho ho! I could handle water.

Behold: I was bold again, though panting still from a host of emotions. And the conclusion to my private drama seemed clear and evident: find the faucet leaking water and shut it off. Ah.

I went into the men's bathroom right next to the boiler room. I checked the toilet, the sink, the urinal, and found all of them dry. I had almost turned to leave, when a shadow in the window caught my eye. Something outside. This window was at ground level facing the parking lot. I put my face to it—

Some*one* outside!

Lord, there was a thief here, after all.

Under the dusk-to-dawn light, crouched so close to the window that we might have kissed, but busy at the lawn faucet, unaware of me, filling plastic milk jugs with water from Grace Lutheran Church, was Marie.

I jumped backward. For two minutes I stood mute on the near side of the wall, listening to the water go, feeling her presence altogether too close, feeling (instantly) abused, a victim, a sucker. Apparently brick walls did not keep out the corruption of the inner city. Marie was taking our water as her due, no effort to ask us. Geez! the presumption griped me. She was busy stealing. She was reaching into the very heart of the building, even to frighten me in the privacy of my study. I felt very, very vulnerable.

The whistling fluted up and stopped. She'd shut the water off. When she passed the window, I saw her from the knees down, lugging in each hand two plastic jugs of water, and then I was alone again—and full of anguish.

I should do something about this, you know.

I went up into the sanctuary and switched on the lights and began to pace up and down the aisle.

I had no idea what to do about Marie's little theft—or the arrogance of it. Well, well, well: water isn't communion ware, after all. What do you pay for water? Pennies. So let it go. That's what I said to myself. Just let it go. And I thought: if the city has turned off her water, you can bet they've turned off her gas and electricity too. The woman's without utilities. And she's got a kid who needs to drink and wash and use the bathroom. So calm down and call it charity and let it go.

Yeah, but that kid nagged at my mind. What was she teaching her child? That he could take whatever he needed—whatever he wanted, for heaven's sake. Any child, I don't care who or whose it is, deserves better than this poor kid was getting.

And then that's the next thing that nagged: what is the ethic for supporting a prostitute, even by inaction and noninvolvement? This is a church, after all. We have a covenant with virtue, after all, a discipline, a duty, a holy purpose, a prophetic presence. Shouldn't I talk to the woman?

Precisely at that point all my abstract inquiry skidded against reality. *Talk* with the woman? Why, the woman doesn't talk! She stares you a moribund stare. She scorns you with murderous scorn. Talk with the woman? I might as well reason with the moon or argue with the whirlwind. Who knew, if I truly approached her, whether she would flee or fly at me with a gun—or simply stare as though I were some dream that she was dreaming.

"So let it go." I said that out loud in the doorway of my study.

It didn't ease the itch of responsibility in me, fiscal responsibility (Grace pays for its water too, you know, and we have members no better off than this particular profligate), social responsibility (that kid stuck in my mind), moral responsibility, and even an evangelical responsibility. But nothing at seminary had prepared me for such a dilemma as this. I had no wise solution. I simply had no other solution at all.

"Forget it," I said and, as proof of putting the issue behind me, I went into my office, sat down in my chair, picked up the book I had been reading, and bit my lower lip. "It really doesn't matter. It isn't worth the worry. Let it go."

And so it was that I sat glowering at a page of print, in a church ablaze with electrical light, in an inner city that had bested me, at nearly midnight of the clock—when the whistling began all over again.

Sometimes when your neighbor does something to annoy you, you feel compelled to go and watch her do it. You know that you'll learn nothing new by looking. That's not why you need to look. You're angry, that's why. And anger wants to see its cause. Anger wants to get angrier. It is sweet to feel a just and righteous wrath—that's why.

So when the whistling began again I was out of my chair and down the aisle like a shot. I verily flew down the steps and into the basement, into the men's room, flew! I thrust my face to the window and looked into midnight and squinted to make my eyes adjust. I saw the figure beneath the street light. I saw the body bending at our faucet. Two feet from mine I saw a concentrating face—and I let out an astonished yip, and I leaped from the window.

That wasn't Marie. Four more milk jugs at his feet, thankless pomposity in his manner, a skullcap clutching his head—who was this drawing water from the bowels of Christendom? One of the prostitute's *johns!*

I tell you truly, doubt was gone in a flash. I knew straightway what I would do. I had a sudden vision of Grace Lutheran Church, the building itself, rolled over on her side like a helpless sow, while *all* the people of this neighborhood like wriggling piglets were pushing their snouts into her belly and sucking and sucking the poor church dry. "Nip it," I hissed with inspired clarity. "Nip it in the bud!"

I slipped into the boiler room, where the water was whistling one note over my head. I reached up to find the coldest pipe. I fingered along that pipe, feeling for a knob. Found that knob. Turned it to the left, and heard the whistling choke and stop, then covered my mouth and swallowed giggles of glee. For I saw in my mind's eye the john hunched over a faucet that suddenly died in front of him: drip, drip, and nothing.

I had shut the water off.

Even so in the end did a cleric and the church prevail, by cunning, not by confrontation, and no one was hurt, and no one's feelings or reputation was wounded, neither the church's nor the prostitute's. We could coexist on opposite sides of Gum Street. All in a rush of inspiration, a problem had been solved; and I drove homeward feeling equal to the task at hand, as sly as any rogue in the ghetto—a native. I slept very well that night.

To God be the glory. Amen.

4.

Down the steps and through the narthex, making agreeable racket with each other and greeting me one by one, the members of Grace filed out of the church and into the daylight. Worship was over. I was shaking many hands.

I loved the ruckus. I loved the genial disorder. I was at home.

"Pastor. Did that really happen?"

"It happened, Herman."

"Well, you just don't know 'bout some folks, do you?"

"No, no. You never know."

"Takes all kinds."

"All kinds. Say hello to Janey for me, will you? Tell her I missed her."

The next man said, "Just one o' them things."

I almost laughed aloud. "One of them things, Douglas," I said. His observation struck me as perfectly accurate. He slipped from view like trout in a stream, flashing silver at the stem of his glasses.

"Pastor?" All at once, Miz Lillian Lander. She took my hand and we exchanged a handshake, and I let go, but she did not.

"Pastor?"

Her voice was both soft and civil. It was the sweetness of it that pierced me. I think its tones reached me alone, so that it produced a casement of silence around us, and the rest of the people receded from my senses: there was Miz Lil, gazing up at me. There was her shrewd eye, soft and sorry.

"You preached today," she said, and I thought of our past conversation. "God was in this place," she said, keeping my hand in hers. I almost smiled for pride at the compliment. But Miz Lil said, "He was not smiling." Neither was she. Nor would she let me go.

She paused a while, searching my face. I couldn't think of anything to say. I dropped my eyes. *God was in this place.* Evidently she meant more than a spiritual feeling, a patting of feet and gladness. The old woman spoke in velvet and severity, and I began to be afraid.

"Her grandma's name was Alice Jackson," Miz Lil said staring steadily at me. "Come up from Kentucky and went to school with me, poor Alice did. She raised her babies, and then she had to raise grandbabies too. She did the best she could by them. But a body can only do so much. Pastor," said Miz Lil, "when you talk about skinny Marie, you think of her grandma. You think of Alice Jackson by name. You think to yourself, she died of tiredness—and then you won't be able to talk, except in pity."

I stood gaping at the floor, a large man with monstrous glasses on his face. My shoes were skinned at the toes. Look. Look around. Not another member wore such wretched shoes to worship. This was embarrassing. My whole face stung with the humiliation.

Miz Lil continued to press my hand with her large, work-hardened fingers, the little finger forever straight. She would not let me go.

"God was in your preaching," she whispered. "Did you hear him, Pastor? It was powerful. Powerful. You preach a mightier stroke than you know. Oh, God was bending his black brow down upon our little church today, and yesterday, and many a day before. Watching. 'Cause brother Jesus—he was in that child Marie, begging a drink of water from my pastor."

Miz Lillian Lander fell silent then. But she did not smile. And she would not let me go. For a lifetime, for a Sunday and a season the woman remained immovable. She held my hand in a steadfast grip, and she did not let it go.

1.

On Halloween the fireman's wife came walking down the middle of Overhill Street, straight down the center of my street. She was white in the deepest dark. She was singing. Her voice was not lovely. It was shaking and high and old. Yet I caught my breath at the distant sound, which was like wind in the attic or wind in the branches at your window, a fitful, alien wind—and I peered at the floating, approaching figure.

I thought she was wearing the robes of a ghost. I had streaked my own face with charcoal and wore my father's shirt reversed. But she wore no costume at all. She was wearing a full-length slip, low on her shoulders, long at her ankles, and nothing more. She walked the concrete barefoot. Bare were her arms, naked her back to the weather. The shame of it astonished me. And when she passed in front of me I saw that neither was she singing. She was weeping. My heart and all the world fell silent at the passing of the fireman's wife. She moved in a terrible solitude.

"Jesus, Jesus," she was saying. It might have been a hymn. It might have been a nursery rhyme: "Jesus, the demons won't leave me alone."

Her knees kept punching the front of her slip, so that moonlight broke like water on the nylon. The braid of her hair swung like a censer behind her. In all my life, this was the first and the most lasting vision of the awful beauty wrought by human malice in the humans who endure it.

"Ring the bell," she chanted, "I don't care. Fill my house; no, I don't care. Crowd my bedroom. Gather and laugh. Poor Emily isn't there. No, Emily doesn't care, and Emily isn't there—no more, no more—"

Emily. Her name was Emily. I never knew.

Poor Emily. She was, she said, a realist. She didn't have an Alternative of Giants. She never had the consolation of the stories of the mind.

2.

My father taught me how to find my way to school. Late in the summer he put me into a wagon with my brother Paul, and then he pulled us all the way up Overhill Street—and a long way it was, too—until we came to a corner which he told me I must remember.

"See that stop sign?" he said.

I looked at it.

"Now, do you see that house on the corner? Can you remember the two pillars on the porch?"

I said that I could.

"Good," he said, "because here is where you'll make a left turn. Turn left, Wally. This is the only turn you have to remember. But the school is on the other side of the street, so you'll have to cross. Don't cross here. There's a stop light at the school. Cross there. I'll show you."

So then we turned and he pulled us down another street, block after block after block of pulling, and he showed me the stop light and the stripes on the concrete and the brick pile which was to be my school, surrounded by a chain-link fence.

My father was very careful in his instructions, anxious that I should understand them. I was going into the first grade. I was the oldest of his children. And it was appointed that I should walk by myself to school in the mornings, home again in the afternoons.

As long as I sat fork-legged in the wagon, with my little brother between my knees, I felt confident. And as far as the daily journey was concerned, when my father or my mother drove me in the car I managed it without distress.

But when I actually went forth on my own, this odyssey frightened me to tears. Dad said, "Wally, it's only a mile," and I didn't think he lied to me, but neither could I explain to him how treacherous and long that mile was, or what happened to me when I traveled it alone.

It was a mile of foreign territory. The faces I saw were not my people. None of them knew me. They looked on me like a criminal thing. They knew the laws of their lands, but I didn't. In order to get to school each day, I had to pass through valleys of the shadow, unconvinced that I would make it to the other side. I truly believed, each time I went forth, that I might die.

How could I tell my father that?

Or how could I explain to him what happened to my person on the way? I shrank. The farther I went from my own familiar neighborhood, the littler I became. The houses around me, they grew huger, they swelled to tremendous sizes. The distance from corner to corner expanded, because my legs diminished like rubber bands. So I would run faster and faster, my lunch box flying at my hand, but I kept arriving at corners later and later. The whole world seemed vast and pitiless, because I was reduced to a dashing dot with a lunch box. And that's how I imagined I would die: *pop!* By vanishing.

So how could I tell my father that? It was true, of course—but of course he wouldn't believe me.

So I pretended that my breakfast made me sick, and threw it up.

I cried whooping tears, true tears, no pretense at all.

I became recalcitrant, disobedient, tardy. Punishment plus a ride to school was infinitely preferable to walking alone into danger and to death.

But in the end I walked. And that is how I came to know the fireman's wife. Her house, two blocks up Overhill Street, became for me a refuge from the peril. It was by her kindness that I survived.

Until the days I walked to school, my neighborhood *was* the world; nor did I shrink in that place, though it wasn't without dangers itself, because I knew precisely how I fit in it. The people of Overhill Street, they knew me. Therefore I knew me too. I wasn't a big person, but I was a whole one; and what I was, the strengths and the weaknesses together, remained unchanged from day to day. I didn't have to pay attention to identity, then: just be, because I belonged. Such being is freedom, although it is caused by the strictures of being known and by a thoughtless obedience to community.

These are the blessings of familiarity: being and freedom and confidence.

So these are some of the people who granted me a place in the world and a self:

Ross. He lived across the street from my house. We were friends, though we never noticed it to talk about it. We had a fight once which lasted a long time, full of violence and fury, but which ended the instant one of us (I don't remember which of us) threw a punch. Pain was a shock which neither of us had anticipated. Ross's family owned the only TV in the neighborhood. I glanced at it once and saw my first actual death. I saw a close-up of a woman's face. A man was choking the breath out of her. Her eyes swelled and her tongue came out, and so did mine, and I mourned that woman several days, aghast that people could die. Ross's father had a car with a rumble seat instead of a trunk. He took us for rides.

Chipper and Laurie. They were a sister and brother who lived on the corner in the other direction from my school, and who had the remarkable gall to run from their mother when she wanted to spank them. Incredulous, I watched them hide beneath the dining room table. This was a liberty I'd never seen before: outright defiance! Their mother barked her shin on a chair and made a mighty uproar, but she never retrieved the mice from underneath the table. My mother would have cut that table in two. Chipper and Laurie were friendly kids. The world is full of wonders.

Jimmy Newman. Jimmy lived immediately next door. On the Fourth of July he produced a package of black pellets that looked like licorice, and told me he could turn them into worms. He lined them up on the brick of an outdoor barbecue, then lit them with matches. They hissed and extended into long, twisting shapes, exactly like agonized worms. Part of me believed absolutely that they were grey worms. Part of me thought them nothing but ash. But the two parts never argued inside of me, and I accepted both explanations as the truth. I said, "Where do they go after they're worms?" He answered gravely, "They turn into nails." And because he could show me nails—a rusty clutch of nails—in the bottom of the barbecue, I believed that too. The world is full of wonders, but this was not one of them. This I accepted as the natural way of things, a matter of fact.

Jimmy's grandmother came out one day and screamed at me because I was throwing bread crumbs in her yard. She was a short woman, swollen, angry. I thought I was feeding birds. She thought I was wasting food and causing trash. But then my mother came out and screamed at Jimmy's grandmother with a truly stunning arsenal of words, and so began a war which never ended. Jimmy and I didn't play together after that. But I mention this family because, despite the enmity, they were also people of my neighborhood and essential to its familiarity.

Clyde. In fact, Clyde was not from the neighborhood, nor was he a friend of mine. He lived across the alley behind our garage, in a house that faced an anonymous street. Therefore he was something of an alien. But he roamed, Clyde did. And his presence had a powerful, predatory effect. He must be mentioned.

In Clyde there always hummed the deep machinery of violence. His pale, lashless, empty eyes, his emotionless mouth—they were a lie. His easy, liquid stride and the subduing murmur of his voice were all a lie. Clyde was blonde and lean and three years older than I. And evil. The boy could kill.

I had seen him—in my own garage when the car was gone and the door left open to the alley—take by the tail a garter snake as long as a cable. He raised this snake to the level of his vision, holding his arm straight out. He walked from the sunlight into the garage where I was, not a trace of feeling in his face, and dangled the serpent between us. "Watch," he said. The snake kept trying to climb itself, as if its body were a flagpole. Clyde gazed at me a while. I said nothing. The instant the snake relaxed and let its head hang down, Clyde doubled himself at the waist and with a terrible swing of his full right arm snapped that snake like a whipcord—then held it up again. "Watch," he said. The creature was quivering. "Snake's blood is thick," Clyde told me, dead-voiced. "Watch." The serpent's mouth had skewed sideways, its bottom jaw loose like a flap of shoe leather. Clyde was right. Soon, as slowly as syrup, a red drop rolled out onto the bottom jaw and hung there till it was huge. Snakes don't close their eyes when they die. They just keep looking at things, frowning as if in criticism or displeasure. Neither did Clyde close his eyes. But neither did he frown. There was utterly nothing in his face, not pleasure, not displeasure. Merely a pale gaze and murder.

But he was right about snake's blood. It is very thick. I actually heard the red drop hit the concrete of my garage. It sounded like a lump of boiled vegetable.

3.

She began to compliment, and I began to grin—

So I was running very fast one day. I was urging my legs to go as fast as they could go down the strange streets, when a woman made herself apparent on the sidewalk ahead of me. She was watching my approach. I was thinking that my neighborhood couldn't be far now, because my spirit was almost exhausted and I was so miserably tiny.

Maybe my smallness lent the woman strength.

For she said, "Do you know what this is?" and I stopped immediately, as though she had cried a command at me.

But she'd only just spoken it. "Do you know what this is?"

She had iron hair, like a helmet of hair, drawn back from her forehead and tied in a single, hanging braid—the way my grandmother tied her hair for sleeping. Her eyes were hooded with folds of old flesh, so that they seemed to be peering from animal dens. "Well?" she said. "Do you know?" She stood willowy erect, in a posture I would come to regard as Old World gracious; but her chest was caven. Her cotton dress was empty there. Her hands trembled. And glittering: the hooded eyes seemed glittering to me.

I shook my head.

"Child, you're a piece of work," she said.

I thought I might go on now. But her words had not dismissed me. The woman was watering her lawn. The hose wound lazily over the sidewalk like a snake.

"This." She tapped the nozzle, which made the softest wing of a water spray. "This." It was a nozzle as wide as a human smile, two score tiny jets, blameless threads of water. "Do you know what this is?"

I shook my head.

"Why," she grinned triumphantly, "it's a fireman's spout. Yes! My husband brought it home when he retired. He was a fireman. This is the genuine thing. Isn't that a pleasant diversion?"

I nodded.

"Yes, and he gave it to me. And he said I could show it to whomever I pleased." She paused, gazing at me. Evidently I was someone she pleased. I wanted to go home.

"Would you like to hold it?" she said. Her deep eyes glittered with eagerness. "This very spout has put out a hundred fires. Here, child. Here."

She coaxed the lunch box from my hand, then wrapped my fingers round the neck of the hose. "Like this," she said, still holding my wrist. Together we waved the soft caress of water over the lawn. "Good. Good. You are very good. My husband would have been proud of you."

Her hand trembled on my wrist. She smelled of soap. There was a blue vein working in her temple. She kept passing her fingers over her brow as though catching loose tendrils of hair; but there were none. Not a strand of hair was out of place. I really wanted to go home. A dribble of water down my left arm triggered in me the need to go potty.

"What is your name?"

"Walter Martin Wangerin, Capital six six four two oh."

"You go to school, don't you?"

I nodded.

"Yes. I knew you were a scholar. I've seen you serious. I watch you mornings and afternoons in passage to and fro. And there is your little lunch pail, of course. Observation with me is second nature. In my opinion," she said with a gracious sort of laugh, "Dupin was a very inferior fellow, and Lecoq was a bungler. I'm a realist, you know."

"I think I should go now, please," I said.

"Oh!" Her hand flew to her forehead. "To be sure! To be sure, you probably should!" She said this with such a sudden vigor that I feared I'd hurt her. "And I'm done. My little plot is probably drowned. Walter Martin," she said, and then she frowned, snatching invisible hairs at her forehead. "Please, is it Walter Martin?"

I nodded.

"Well, Walter Martin," she brightened, "I have very much enjoyed our conversation together. Who cuts your hair?"

"My dad."

"He does a very good job." She touched the cowlick on my skull. I was holding the hose alone by now. "Tell him for me, sir, that he is an excellent barber. Would you like a Tootsie Roll?"

I nodded.

"Do you smile, Walter Martin?"

I nodded again. And then I made a smile.

"Come. Come, let me shut the water off. No. I'll tell you what we'll do. You shut the water off. Here. Lay down my husband's spout right here. You shut the water off whilst I go get you Tootsie Rolls. We'll not waste time, all right? There. On the side of the house. The faucet, see? All right? Does that sound fine? All right."

Her hooded eyes flashed a sort of fever—so many things to do. She hastened up the little sidewalk by her house, pointed at the faucet as she passed it, then disappeared around the back. I put the nozzle down. It whispered messages to the grass. When I bent I felt a terrible, terrible urge to pee, so I pinched my mouth fiercely. I went to shut the water off.

Even while I was turning the knob, the fireman's wife reappeared beside me, smiling.

"Put out your hand, Walter Martin," she said. And then with great ceremony she counted three wrapped pieces of Tootsie Roll into my palm: "One and two and three. Perhaps you saw the hearse in front of my house this summer," she said.

Hearse. I knew that word.

Suddenly the fireman's wife bent down in front of me. "Why, what's the matter?" she asked, a true anxiety in her voice, her eyes searching mine.

I realized that I had groaned aloud, and I groaned again in spite of myself.

"Walter Martin!" Her eyes were instantly moist with pity and tears. "What's wrong?" She wanted to touch me, but she drew back. "Please. I'm sorry," she said, and I saw that she felt at fault for something. "What's the matter, child?"

I myself felt very embarrassed. But the situation had really grown desperate, and I was forced to speak.

"I have to go potty," I said.

"Potty?" she said.

"Pee!" I nearly cried it. "I think I'm peeing in my pants."

"Oh! Well! Yes, of course. And we can do something about that!" She straightened—erect, concerned, relieved, all at the same time. Smiling and serious. "Follow me, Walter Martin," she said, and she marched up the sidewalk, and I crept after the pendulum braid of hair.

All of the rooms of her house were very dark, except for the bathroom, the sink of which had been scrubbed so hard, I thought, that she'd worn the enamel to black metal in places. This room smelled overwhelmingly of the soap I'd scented on her skin. And beneath that there were old-people odors here, like the nightgowns of my grandmother. I did not feel alien in this place. I wasn't even conscious that I might have felt alien, though this was not my neighborhood. In fact, I was enormously relieved. And the fireman's wife was standing, she promised, guard outside the door.

This is what I sang while I peed: "Never laugh when the hearse goes by, for you may be the next to die. They put you in a wooden box, and cover you up with dirt and rocks." Soon I was bellowing it. I still sat down on the toilet, even to pee, and I took my time. "The worms crawl in, the worms crawl out—" This is a song that Ross had taught me. This is how I knew the word *hearse*. "You shrivel up and turn all green, and pus flows out like—"

The fireman's wife was subdued when I came out.

Silently she led me through a living room of darkness and imposing furniture and massive drapes. She opened the front door, and there was my lunch box on the sidewalk.

"Listen, Walter Martin," she said full seriously. "Any time you wish to use the fire-fighting spout, come visit me. Or any time you long for Tootsie Rolls, come visit me. Or if you like another kind of sweet, please tell me. I'll get it for you. The hearse was for my husband the fireman. Is the water tightly off? Are you consoled now, child?"

I nodded.

"Good. Good. I think you should go now too. Your parents will be waiting. But visit me. That was a real invitation. I am not much given to fantasies, you know. I am a realist. Ring my doorbell." She demonstrated, reaching around the doorjamb. As long as she pressed the button, a persistent ringing sounded within her house. I thought of a fire alarm. "Like that. Good-bye."

I walked down her steps to the front sidewalk. I picked up my lunch box.

"Walter Martin?" she called. She was still standing in the doorway. She swept her fingers past the hairline. "Good-bye?" It was a question.

I said, "Good-bye."

She looked old and formal in the door frame. Her shutters were painted green.

I gave Ross a Tootsie Roll that afternoon and chewed another in front of him.

He said, "Where did you get that?" He meant, Where did you get the money? Ross and I bought bottles of 7-Up with dimes, jawbreakers with pennies, Oh Henry bars with nickels. We found coins in the gutters of the street. We believed that certain gutters were luckier than others—like fishing holes. So he was asking me which lucky gutter had yielded up the money. He had no idea of the marvelous treasure I had discovered.

"From the fireman's wife," I said, grinning, rich with news.

And then I did the poor woman a grievous harm. I told Ross of her grand promise to me. "Just ring the doorbell," I said. "She'll give you candy."

In the days and weeks that followed, Ross did. He rang her doorbell, and he earned Tootsie Rolls for his boldness. And besides that, he told her what other kinds of candy he liked.

So the news was spread abroad.

Chipper and Laurie traipsed from their far corner of the block up Overhill Street yet several blocks farther to the house of my friend and got candy for themselves. Behold: I had expanded the horizons of our neighborhood. Jimmy Newman rang her doorbell. Jimmy Newman ate candy. Everyone came to know of her, and everyone who rang the doorbell ate. But I was the only one who called her the fireman's wife. That piece of her history seemed totally irrelevant to the others. They all called her the candy lady.

Even Clyde learned of our vein of gold: Clyde, who prowled all neighborhoods with a silken, predatory stride; Clyde, whose house belonged in foreign territory, but who was not impressed by custom nor by boundaries or propriety—Clyde, the pale-eyed, rang her doorbell and received the candy he did not deserve.

And my brother Paul went and rang her doorbell when the rest of us were in school. He took advantage of his freedom, and he prospered.

But for me she was the fireman's wife, a genuine friend and a refuge. Her house became an outpost in the wilderness. Whenever I was rushing home from school, terrified of the perils of the unknown world, I set my mind upon that house and those green shutters. The image itself encouraged me.

No, the world between the school and my block had grown no kinder as the autumn grew cool. It was always dark with enmity and threat, and so long as I couldn't see the friendly houses, I was in danger. One false step could kill me. Watch for the stop sign, Wally! Watch for the porch with the pillars! Turn right and run! Run home!

Daily I shrank and prayed to Jesus to keep me alive. Daily, twice daily, I raced so fast, so dreadfully slowly past strangers who stared at me—

Wow!—look at that little boy go! But he has such a grim face.

Of course he has. That little boy is filled with fears of death. He doesn't want to die. But he doesn't think he's going to make it.

Just look at him run! Too bad he's a cripple.

Jesus, save me! Save me, Jesus!

Oh, how grateful I was when I saw the house of the fireman's wife ahead of me, her little porch, her green shutters, her promise of kindness and of candy. I swelled—literally. I jumped to my common six-year-old's size, and my breast was flooded with gladness. I giggled and dashed the last half block to her door, uncrippled and wholly able. I bounded up her steps and rang the doorbell, panting.

I'm here!

It's me!

I didn't die today, isn't that wonderful?

O Fireman's Wife, answer your door and look at me. Let me see the rope of your hair hang down, and let's have candy to celebrate survival.

By the first week in October, I had developed strong feelings for the woman. Perhaps she had in some ways taken the place of my Grandpa Storck.

4.

Cross patch, draw the latch, sit by the fire—

"Walter Martin?" The fireman's wife cracked her front door just an inch. I saw a hooded eye. "Is that you, Walter Martin?"

She never watered her lawn anymore, nor did we talk about the fire-fighting spout of her husband. Dry leaves were clutching her grass. The air had a bite. I wore a windbreaker jacket.

"Yes, ma'am," I said, puffing and grinning at that single, glittering eye. "It's me."

"Because you are the person that I especially care to see, Walter Martin," she said through the door. "Do you understand that?"

"Yes, ma'am," I said.

"You've come for Hershey's chocolate, I expect?" she said. There was an odd, plaintive edge to her voice. I began to wonder whether she was in pajamas, if that was the reason she hid behind the door.

"Oh, it doesn't matter. Well, yes. Hershey's is good."

"And perhaps you'll want to sit a while?"

I nodded.

She began to pull the door open, nodding too. No, she was buttoned to the neck in a dress, not pajamas. And perhaps she had tied her hair rather tighter, since her eyes had a kind of staring appearance. "Because," she said, "I have a topic for our conversation today. I have something delicate to talk about, perhaps."

She led me into her living room, saying, "Walter Martin, I trust you above the other children." It was dark, severely draped. She said, "Won't you please to have a seat?" I sat on the edge of a large, uncomfortable chair and kicked my feet. With an unconscious grace— she always moved, it seemed to me, with an engaging loveliness and grace—she took a settee across from me. I thought to myself, *How odd:* from the outside her house seemed a little cottage trimmed in green. But from the inside the same house seemed a castle.

"No," she said, "no, that's not true. I trust you above all other people," she said. "That's what's true." She stood up. "May I rest your coat, Walter Martin?"

I had begun to unzip it. I shook my head. She sank to sitting again.

"Trust you," she said. "Therefore I can't. . . . Therefore I wish. . . ." Her fingers fluttered at nonexistent hairs on her forehead. "Oh, dear," she sighed. She smoothed the dress on her knee. "Well, first I'm going to tell you what my husband's name was," she said.

"Did you want to eat the Hershey's chocolate now or later?"

"Oh, later," I said, smiling and swinging my legs. "I'm going to share it with my friend Ross."

"Ross?" she said in a voice suddenly faint, fixing her eyes on me.

"That's the name of my best friend."

"Ross? A boy? He lives nearby?"

I nodded.

All at once the fireman's wife exclaimed, "I'm out of candy, it's gone." She stared at me with a surprised expression, as though I had just said this, not her. And then, in a rush of words: "Yes, yes, you are a kind person, Walter Martin, to share your things with your little friends, and heaven knows I would rather die than blame the kindness in you. Does your father cut your hair with scissors? I only just assumed, you know. But I'm clean out of candy now, though I can't tell you why, it's a mystery, and I would appreciate it if you mentioned this new piece of information to him, to your friend—to Ross, to all of the other children," she said, and she gulped air, staring.

Into the silence that followed, I said, "No, but he uses a clippers."

"What?" whispered the fireman's wife, widening her eyes.

"My dad," I said.

I told her that my father cut my hair with a clippers, not scissors, two-handled clippers which had a hundred teeth and which pulled my hair when my father squeezed it. I truly liked to tell her such things. Her face lit up with an enthusiastic interest, and she obviously respected my wide knowledge of the world. Yes, I told her, he cut our hair in the basement. He would tie a bedsheet round my neck so tightly that my vision went pink.

"Pink?"

Yes, the whole world took a rosy hue, and I could see the veins in my eyes. They became a sort of lattice between my seeing and the basement wall. Once I fainted, with a roaring in my ears.

"Walter Martin!"

My father caught me. He has very strong arms. He has a work smell, a flesh scent which comforts me. He calls the haircuts crew cuts. We look like the backs of rabbits when he's done—

"Rabbits?"

"Rabbit-butts, round and furry."

The fireman's wife covered her mouth with the fingers of her right hand and began to laugh. I grinned back at her, vastly pleased with myself. Gazing at me, she laughed almost soundlessly till the tears filled up her eyes. I hadn't intended a joke, just an image. But if she perceived a joke in what I'd said, I wasn't about to argue. I was by nature a sober child. These moments when, by the luck of my language, I caused the fireman's wife to laugh—well, they were rare and wonderful indeed. Lo: in the presence of the fireman's wife I was that marvelous personage, a "character."

I said, "Rabbit-butts"—and together we went off into fits of sinful giggles, delighting in our libertine ways and in each other. O Fireman's Wife, you are a mortal angel, and I love you.

Suddenly a bell began to ring. We both jumped up, confused by the insistent ringing.

The bell kept screaming.

"Oh, dear. Oh, dear," she muttered, her fingers flying to her hairline. She was hesitating. I couldn't understand that. It took me only a second to realize that this was the doorbell, and then I thought that the next thing was, you answer the door. But the fireman's wife had a look of distraction in her eyes. Her iron hair seemed to be gripping her brain, paralyzing her. She wrung her hands. She forced herself to the front door. Just before she opened it, she turned to me and pleaded, "But I'm out of candy."

She opened the door.

The ringing stopped.

It was Clyde, pale-eyed on her porch, who immediately peered past her and saw me standing behind.

"Whatcha got, Wally?" he said.

I squirmed in a great discomfort, saying nothing.

The fireman's wife, still holding the door, said, "I'm clean out of any kind of candy, sir, and perhaps you will go away now." She'd lost her grace. She sounded fretful and old. The braid was Grandma's again, and this whole transfiguration wounded me.

"That's okay," said Clyde, leaning left and right to see me. "I'll take what Wally's got."

The woman whirled around and saw me and gave me an anxious look.

"You!" she said. Then she murmured, "No, um. No, no. No, Walter Martin shares enough. Um." She turned back and stared at Clyde. I didn't like Clyde at all. She said, "Wait." The vein in her temple worked like a crawling worm. She raised a hooked hand to Clyde. "Wait—just a moment, please," she said.

So then, I in the darkness and Clyde in a wide autumnal sunlight— we gazed at one another while the fireman's wife sank deeper into her house, sighing. I was hating Clyde then. He was lashless and impassive. She returned with five Hershey bars in her hand, each of them as civil as a Sunday suit. She gave them all to Clyde, then shut the door on him.

Instantly her fingers fluttered to her forehead. "Oh, dear, I forgot," she murmured. "I forgot to say good-bye to him." She opened the door, but Clyde had vanished. The porch was empty. "Something else too," she said, staring at the lawn and the fallen leaves. "What else did I forget? There were two things—"

Bewildered, tragically close to tears, she began to pull the door to, and then she noticed me. "That's you, Walter Martin! Oh, dear!"

I felt sad to be there. I felt so guilty Clyde had come. I looked around and reached for my windbreaker.

"That's right," said the fireman's wife. "You were about to leave, and here I am, shutting the door. Is that what I forgot? That you were going to leave?"

And then here was my lunch box in my hand. And I had my jacket on by now. But the fireman's wife still stood in the doorway so that I couldn't get by.

Suddenly she seized my one free hand in two of hers.

"Arden," she said.

Under their hoods her two eyes fairly smoldered with that word. Her look pleaded with me to understand that this was a very important word. "Arden, Walter Martin," she repeated. "The thing that I forgot. My husband the fireman, his name was Arden."

5.

Hark, hark! The dogs do bark. The beggars are coming to town—

Precious to me was the little green cottage at the end of my daily race. I rang her doorbell daily. But the fireman's wife was changing. The other children of the neighborhood still rang her doorbell too. But the fireman's wife was different.

She grew shrill. She said that she had no candy, no candy of any kind. Nevertheless, if someone hung long enough before her door—even after she had closed it—she would finally bring cookies instead. A lesser sweet. A sorry second to Tootsie Rolls to everyone's way of thinking, and soon even these came burned. But I didn't mind. I didn't blame her.

"I'm running out of cookies," she said, looking past me to the weather. "Maybe people shouldn't visit anymore. Maybe they shouldn't ring my doorbell anymore. Maybe they should just go away—"

But it truly wasn't sweets that brought me to her house. I had no easy way to tell the lady that I was feeling sad for her and yearned with all my heart for something to give her, some way to make her laugh, some words to comfort her poor, distracted, frightened, grandma's face.

"Can I go potty?" I said.

"Oh, well. Well, yes," she said. No joy. Worry, rather. "Come in."

And then, in mid-October, I did indeed have something to give her, a piece of wisdom nearly magical in power. It had rescued me from death. It could, I was convinced, save her as well. Surely it would delight her and cause her some moments of happy triumph—and she would praise me for the story I had to tell. She would raise her two hands up and laugh. *Oh, Walter Martin, you're such a character, sir. Bless my soul, I never would have considered the Giants on my own without your smartness—*

But this time when I rang her doorbell, she didn't answer. She didn't come to the door at all.

Consider the Giants:

Once upon a time a kid was running homeward with his chin tucked down and his lip stuck out and his grim eye on the sidewalk. Huffing and puffing was this kid, protecting himself from the evils around him by high speeds. He had made a right turn at a certain corner, and now the wind was in his face with dead leaves and malice. Well, with scowls of his own the kid was ignoring the wind.

He was thinking to himself, *Two more blocks to the fireman's wife. Two more blocks, home free.*

He had his fists in the pockets of his jacket, a lunch box under his arm.

At a certain distance past the turning-corner, the kid lifted up his eyes and looked ahead—and then his legs continued to pump, but his heart had almost stopped.

"Fireman's Wife," he whispered to himself, "where is your house?"

He stared to the left and the right. He squinted ahead as far as he could see. Dead trees and sidewalk. Nowhere—not anywhere in his whole field of vision—was there a green cottage or a single stick of familiar wood. But he had measured the mile in his mind no differently today than any other day, and this was the end of it and that's where the cottage ought to be, but it wasn't there.

"Three blocks?" said the kid. "Or maybe four?"

He ran with his eyes wide open now. The wind grew colder and whistled and laughed in the trees and needled his eyes to tears. All of the houses around him looked almost like the houses of his neighborhood, but every one of them was just a little different. No, this was not his neighborhood. He was lost. He ran forward, getting loster and unhappier—but he had done nothing wrong. He had turned exactly as his father had taught him long ago. So the fact was, he could not be lost. This was very bewildering. He ran and he panted through his nose, and his stomach started to cry.

Crash! His lunch box slipped from his arm and hit the concrete and jumped open. The waxed paper from his sandwich flew out and the wind tore it away. Used waxed paper is a private thing, like underwear. The kid felt humiliated. He squatted down below the alien houses, beneath their gazing windows, and he picked up his thermos bottle—but it made a dry, rushing sound inside. The glass had shattered. That was more than the kid could bear. Now his face began to cry. He didn't even stand up again. He found that he had run out of running. There was no more running in him. And he wouldn't know where to run if he could. He said, "I'm not lost!" He sobbed, "I'm supposed to be right here."

Still picking at his open lunch box, still holding the broken thermos in his hand, the kid cried out the terrible truth. "My neighborhood is lost!" he wailed.

And the cold wind screamed and howled, and the windows of the houses didn't even blink. The waxed paper had spiraled higher than the naked trees.

"It isn't funny," the kid whispered. "My neighborhood is gone."

Why it wasn't funny was, soon he would shrink away. He would disappear the same as the houses that should have been here. He felt the coldness creeping down his back, the locking of his joints in preparation for death.

"O Fireman's Wife, where did you go?"

All at once an absolutely unaccountable thing occurred. The waxed paper blew down from the sky and slapped the kid on the right side of his face.

Immediately he leaped up and cried, "All right! All right!" He made fists and a fierce face and he bellowed, "All right now, that's enough!"

Because the waxed paper in his face was *not* unaccountable—not if someone magical was teasing him. And that was the answer, of course, but he had been too dumb to see it before, so the Giants had had a good laugh, you can be sure of that.

The kid was shaking with anger. The anger felt very good to him, warm and empowering.

"I hate you, Giants!" he roared, turning left and right so that they couldn't miss the implications. "I hate you and I spit!" he cried. Free and proud, offended and angry at once, this kid reached down and shoved the thermos in his lunch box and slammed it shut and began to march back in the way that he had come.

Giants had played a trick on him. That's what had happened. Giants had picked up all the houses on his block and carried them probably one block over, then replaced them with dummy houses—just to frighten him. But if Giants had engaged in all that work to trouble a single kid, why, then this was a very important kid indeed.

He stumped in a magnificent wrath back to his turning-corner, glaring fury for the sake of any Giants still observing him.

"Wait'll I tell my mother what you did to my thermos bottle. Just wait."

When he reached the turning-corner he made an interesting discovery: this wasn't the right corner after all. He had turned one block too soon and had been on the wrong street all along. Ah, but that little detail was dismissable, no matter how true it might have been. Truer still, and not to be dismissed, were Giants of malevolent natures, mighty and huge and defeatable. Truest of all, endowing a kid with wizard powers of survival, was the hatred he experienced against those Giants. Both were real, of course: both his mistake and his rage. But rage felt infinitely more precious to him. He believed them both, but he valued the latter the more.

And why? Because the strength of his wrath would keep this kid from ever shrinking again.

So now he was racing in giddy hilarity down the next street one block over, his own full size and twice his strength.

Fireman's Wife! his happy heart was calling. Oh, let me tell you about the Giants! All you need, dear Fireman's Wife—the only thing you need to do—is to hate them!

Up the steps of the porch of the little green cottage Walter Martin flew. He beat on a ginger door. He knocked on a spearmint sash. He pushed a licorice button and made a bell weep deep in the halls of her castle.

She didn't come to the door.

She didn't answer.

Oh, but I had such a story to tell her. I had such a gift to give her—to save her from sadness and fear—that I kept my finger on the doorbell, saying, "Please, please," and bouncing from foot to foot, repeating the story in my mind. *Once upon a time a kid was running homeward—*

Walter Martin, you are a character. You make me laugh and I love you.

"Fireman's Wife, please open the door—"

She never did. She never opened the door to me again. And I began to worry that she had moved away.

In the days that followed, I suffered a sort of stomachache that the fireman's wife had left the neighborhood without first telling me—except that I saw her one more time. And then that was the last time.

6.

The beggars are coming to town; some in rags, and some in jags—

There was a moon on Halloween, which could be seen from my kitchen window even before the dark. A rising moon. Paul and I streaked our faces in charcoal to give ourselves fantastical grace and grimaces. But he said he was a pirate, and though we looked alike I said I was Sir Lancelot, wearing my father's shirt reversed as armor. It came down to my knees. I carried a double-barreled shotgun for protection. We each had pillowcases to gather candy in.

In an exciting darkness, then, we criss-crossed Overhill house to house, ringing doorbells, knocking on doors, and crying, "Trick or treat." The adults, with their living room lights aglow behind them, would bend down and drop wrapped candies into our pillowcases, smiling. The night was cold and windless and busy with the black forms of children, clutches of rushing children. No one was afraid.

Ross was sick.

Jimmy Newman said, "Knights of the Round Table have swords, not guns."

I said, "Yeah, but this is real. It was my grandpa's before he died."

"What difference does that make?"

Calmly I cracked the barrel of my shotgun, closed it, and discharged two loud bangs to prove it lethal. After that Jimmy Newman didn't argue anymore, and I really believed that the gun had been my grandpa's, because I couldn't think of any reason why it couldn't be true. I wasn't afraid.

"Grandpa used to shoot squirrels in the cemetery," I told Paul.

"I knew that," he said.

When the night grew very late, Paul and I ran over to Ross's house so that I could divide some of my candy with him. He was too sick to come to the door, so his mother told me what a terrifying costume I had, and I said that it wasn't pretend at all. She laughed and thanked me for peanut butter drops twisted in orange paper.

Mr. Ramsey was angry when we rang his doorbell. None of his lights were on, not the porch light, not even his living room light. He shouted that we had come a full week too late and we should check our calendars before we did such a stupid thing again. He slammed his door. He was an old man. I couldn't decide whether he actually meant what he said or whether he was tricking us without the smile. For just a moment, despite all the evidence to the contrary, I had the panicky thought that he might be right and that everyone else had participated in a communal mistake.

Paul said, "Shoot his windows, Wally."

And then we stood beneath a street light to check the candy in our pillowcases. The street light was a single naked bulb in a metal reflector suspended from crossed wires. It didn't illumine much. Rather, it made us surer of shadows. But we maneuvered our bags beneath it—smack in the middle of Overhill—in order to peer at the comparative sizes of our loads. So we were standing with our heads down when Clyde slid between us and stood staring at me.

Paul said, "Hey!"

"You're a liar," Clyde said to me. I looked up. He wore no costume. My father's shirt, which hung to my knees, felt suddenly shameful on me. Under the dim light Clyde's eyes were hidden in skull's shadows. His hair gleamed like pewter. He stuck his chin at me and folded a fresh stick of gum into his mouth as though this were a gesture of contempt.

"You're a liar," he said.

"No, I'm not," I murmured, utterly ignorant of his meaning.

"Hey!" said Paul behind him. "I don't like you."

I said, "Shut up, Paul."

Clyde chewed with his mouth open, making a black gap in his face. Juicy Fruit. "You're a goddamn liar," he repeated, his voice silken, his breath pulpy with threat.

I said nothing. Overhill was empty save for us. Why was that?

"I told my brother about the candy lady," Clyde breathed, perceptibly pushing his white face closer to mine, and mine began to burn. "I told my older brother, Bring a truck. I said she's got a house full of candy, and he couldn't carry all the candy she's going to give him." Clyde bumped his chest against me. I stumbled backward.

Paul said, "Hey!"

"Paul, shut up," I warned him.

"On account of you," Clyde said, "I made my brother expect a haul. So you're the liar, not me."

"I never said nothing about a haul."

"So?" said Clyde, raising his eyebrows as if this were a new subject for conversation. His bloodless face peeled into surprise. "So, then—did you go to her house tonight?"

"No," I said softly.

"Oh? Why not?"

"Well. She's out of candy—"

"See? See?—you liar!"

Paul said, "I didn't go either."

I hissed, "Shut *up*, Paul!"

Clyde raised his right hand and placed it against my cheek, which tingled underneath his palm. "Well, we went, Wally," he said. "We rang her doorbell, Wally. And the old bitch!—she never even came to the door. My brother said that I was a liar—"

Compulsively I pushed his hand away. "Don't," I said, and I saw immediately that I shouldn't have done that.

"Don't?" he whined. "Don't? Wally, did you say 'Don't'? Why not?"

"Because," I confessed, "I don't like you to touch me."

Clyde's face twisted. Black shadows knotted in his brow. He drew back his hand and slapped my cheek a stinging blow. "You like that better?"

"Shoot him, Wally!" Paul began to jump up and down. "Take the shotgun, shoot him!"

"Paul, shut up!" I hissed, keeping my eyes on Clyde.

Clyde's face was smeared with rage. "You want to know what we do to people who cheat us?" he screamed.

"No," I whispered. I didn't.

But Clyde went on and screamed this silly thing which sounded savage in my ears.

"We gum them! We gum them!" he fairly shrieked. "We gum them, by God!"

He took the drooling wad of gum out of his mouth and stuck it on the knuckle of his right fist and drew back his arm, his face pure white with fury. I was standing dumb, my hands at my sides, the pillowcase in one, the shotgun in the other. Clyde spun his body and punched me in the stomach. I barked once, then doubled down and knelt on the street, squeaking, trying to get my breath. But I didn't let go the pillowcase or the gun.

"Mom! Mom!" Paul sounded a distant alarm, running away.

"Gum them, by God," Clyde repeated above me, where I couldn't see him. "Are you listening? We jammed gum in that old bitch's doorbell," he said. "And gum in the liar's belly."

There was a moment when absolutely nothing happened. My gut had gone into a spasm. I sweat and simply could not breathe, though I made a cave of my mouth. Clyde's shoes hung before my face, a mystery of patience.

"There, now," he said in a silken voice. "I feel much better." The shoes moved. Clyde walked away into the darkness.

My breath came back in shudders dangerously close to crying. And my eyes were swimming in tears. But I thought that Clyde might be around and I wasn't going to cry, so I made a hideous woofing sound and crawled on my knees to the side of the street, dragging a candy sack and a toy gun in either hand. I managed to sit on the curb.

All my senses were purged in that moment. I saw and heard the night with weird precision and perfect clarity. A mild breeze had begun to rock the street lamp on its wires, so all the little shadows were shaking their heads, and the metal reflector around the bulb was squeaking—chirping, it seemed to me, like a bird. The trees all down the street snaggled the breeze in a whispering sound. Somewhere somebody shut a door. A dog barked.

And then I heard singing far to my left. A night song, high, unnatural, a wandering soprano so lonely and so earnest that it tingled in my scalp. Soon this was the only sound I heard. As soft as it was, it filled the night. Dream-music.

And then a white shape gathered in the blackness a block away. And then it was a figure floating toward me as smoothly as the breeze. And the nearer it approached me, the more aware I was, and the quieter I grew with awe: this was the fireman's wife.

She was walking down the dead middle of the street with unspeakable grace. No spirit she. No ghost.

She was undressed! She wore nothing but a slip, and her shoulders were wasted. She was barefoot on the concrete street.

"Jesus, Jesus," she was singing, "the demons won't leave me alone."

No—but she wasn't singing either. When she passed beneath the yellow bulb, I saw with horror how her hooded eyes were streaming tears. My friend, my fireman's wife, was weeping. She was so old! Her forehead high, but the grandma's braid hung down her back, and the slip was only a slip, after all, and I felt so ashamed for her. Her flesh was as white as flour.

She didn't even see me sitting on the curb.

"Ring my doorbell; I don't care," she wept in a wretched voice. My body shivered to hear her. My face felt her presence as she passed by. "Fill my house; no, I don't care," she chanted. "Crowd my bedroom. Gather and laugh. Poor Emily isn't there." She continued down the street. In the direction of Chipper and Laurie's house. Diminishing. "No, Emily doesn't care. Poor Emily isn't there—no more, no more—"

Emily. Her name was Emily. I had never even thought of the fireman's wife as having a name. Emily.

It was hearing her say her name that broke me down. I bowed my head in my arms and started to cry, and then I couldn't stop. My stomach hurt so bad from Clyde. And the passage of the fireman's wife—Emily—had changed Overhill itself into an appalling place, a street as dangerous and unpredictable as nightmares. But she was no dream. She was no ghost. She was just more sad than any I had ever seen before, and solitary. Where did she think she was going?

I bawled into my arm. And this is the reason why I couldn't stop: I felt ashamed. I felt so guilty.

"Did he hurt you, Wally?"

This was my mother beside me on the street. I accepted her coming without surprise. I stood up and buried my face in her stomach and continued to cry.

She held me. "Did Clyde hurt you?" she said.

I shook my head, but I couldn't answer her. I just hung on.

"Wally? Wally?" she said, stroking my hair. These tears of mine were endless, bottomless. "Wally? Why are you crying?"

Because her doorbell is ringing right now, ringing in an empty house, and her name is Emily.

"Wally?" My mother grew anxious and tried to pluck me from her waist. "What's the matter? How can I help you if I don't know why you're crying?"

Because I am the one who told the other kids about her in the first place. Because there aren't any Giants in the world. There's Clyde. And there is me.

"Wally, for heaven's sake! If you can't get a hold of yourself, I'm going to say I have a baby on my hands—and his name is not Paul."

ROBERT

I WAS WALKING EAST on Gum Street through the sort of rain one ought to have anticipated. Morning had been cloudy; the clouds had bellied low above the buildings; but I had gone forth in a ministerial distraction which took no account of the weather.

Busy, busy: I had already met Helen Alexander on Eighth Street to plan a neighborhood association meeting; she was the president, I was one of two founders, we were concerned that our slice of the city should receive a fair portion of the Community Development Block Grant moneys which the federal government allocated for Evansville. We wanted media coverage to prick the conscience of the director of the Department of Metropolitan Development, so that he could neither deny, neglect, nor dismiss the inner city. Busy.

I had already visited two members of Grace in Welborn Hospital, had prayed before a surgery, had donned a green gown and a mask to sit in quarantine with a young woman whose eyeballs had turned as yellow as gold.

I had already walked over to West Chandler, had mounted stairs to the high, tiny apartment of Dana Varner, who required Communion and conversation. Old Dana, old blind eyes, the endless entrepreneur: his rooms fairly bristled with candles and tiny lanterns, samples of the merchandise he sold to—God knows whom. Dana had talked. I had sat in a pastoral patience, at once suffering and concealing the itch of my busyness.

Busy! But in charge. Eighth Street and Welborn and West Chandler were all in the same general vicinity. I had planned the morning's circuit with admirable practicality in order not to waste a minute on my own account. The rain had begun to fall while I was in Dana's apartment. I strode, therefore, the faster, coming eastward on Gum.

Busy, then; and in control of things—but walking nonetheless. I had resolved to walk the neighborhood as often as possible, and not to drive through it encased in glass and steel. "Hello, Miz Crowe," *sitting on your porch, rocking, nodding, waving back at me—wearing, I see, your workday wig, coal black and functional:* "How are your ankles today?"

"They're fair, thank you, Reverend. They're swole, but fair. I think I'll keep my money this go-round an' leave the doctor alone."

"Glad to hear it. See you later, Miz Crowe."

"Later, Reverend."

Walking: in order to know the neighborhood. Walking: in order to be known. Walking—although I admit it cost me some peace in the beginning, for I grew tense among the strangers and felt my difference when the children stared at me. I still could not walk on Lincoln comfortably, where the young hung out on the hill by the pool, where men stood in knots by Doc's Liquor Store, their spirits feral, their deep eyes veiled and watchful when I passed, like leopards on rocks at the zoo. But I walked. I puzzled the city together for myself, put people in their proper houses, connected children with their mamas, smelled pork and cabbage in the evening air, heard the thumping rhythm of music through the walls, considered my station in this place, smiled at folks and nodded and walked on.

I was a minister, wonderfully busy, truly in control—and personally present.

Therefore (as I said) I was walking east on Gum through a dreary rain toward Grace Church, when I caught sight of a small man on my left, suffering a sort of apoplexy.

As quickly as I saw him, even so quickly did I snap my eyes away from him.

I can be forgiven this dodge: it was Robert. I knew Robert. Robert was trying to hail me in the rain. This would take a while, and longer than I had.

The little man made half a wave, the wave cut short. Half a greeting, half a smile, half a thought—all of them chopped in the middle.

"—because, er, on account of," he was saying. "Say," he was saying: "say you, my man, my man—um—" He wiped his nose on his sleeve and waggled his head. He dipped his face and laughed soundlessly to himself about himself.

I sped up in the direction of the church. I hunched my shoulders and pinched busyness all over my face.

Well, it took true determination and most of the day for Robert to break through the mists that surrounded him. Robert was not a bad man. Just a space man. He lived on another planet. Better yet: he *was* another planet, a wandering globe that had slipped its orbit and swung too near the Earth and—to everyone's surprise, including his own—had taken up residence in a rental room on Gum Street east of the Lutheran church. He stood in his doorway now, a man of indeterminate age, mumbling and chuckling and struggling toward some sort of greeting.

I had almost reached his sidewalk. I was walking now at the speed of hurtle.

Generally one had warning when Robert drew near. Usually one could take precautions not to get caught in the field of his friendly gravity or sucked into his alcoholic atmosphere. *Tippy-tippy-tap-tap:* the little man carried a cane wherever he went, striking the ground with it. Sweet Robert!—it wasn't a cane at all. It was, in fact, an umbrella shaft from which he'd stripped the cloth and the metal ribs. It was a rod so skinny that I had often wondered what was the value of the thing, or what could it support. But *tippy-tippy-tap-tap,* it sounded fair warning; it gave one notice to close the office door, to bury one's face in a book, or else to leave before Jack Daniels became a happy satellite to the rest of one's busy day.

Usually, I say, there was warning. But this time I was walking and vulnerable.

And this time, before I'd gained the safety of the church, gentleman Robert produced an explosion so startling that I stumbled, stopped, and stared at him.

" 'S'HAPPENIN'!" the short man boomed. Birds flew up from the eaves of his house. Robert jumped backward and blinked and then beamed, as though he'd shot a cannon he didn't know he had. And I stood gaping at him—and that was all the weakness that he needed.

"Reverent!" he roared. He'd entered the common world. "Here, Reverent! C'm'ere! Come see what I got. I got sumpin to show you."

I was caught. I was wet. I had no umbrella. Robert's umbrella had no earthly purpose nor protection against the rain. I was the Reverent, obliged to my office and to righteousness. Therefore I was caught and could not decline the space man's invitation into his dry room.

"C'm in." Robert stood back from the door as straight as the bishop of a chessboard, blinking raindrops from his lashes and beaming. "C'm in."

The room was Stygian. It smelled sweet with sweat and with sleeping. All the walls were close. There was a bedframe and a mattress, with one scrawl of a cover on it. There was a wooden chair at a wooden table, a weary hot plate, an aluminum pan with kernels of corn in it, an ancient porcelain sink on two legs, attached to the wall—and under the sink, a cardboard box.

Robert followed me in, took a deep breath, exhaled miasma, and hung his twitch of a cane on a hook on the wall.

"Rest your coat?" he grinned.

I had no coat.

He didn't notice. He rubbed his hands beside me with a slow, most glowing satisfaction. "Awright," he said. "Aw*right!*" He gazed around his room with a beaming, proprietary pride. "Okay, then. Awright."

Two roaches from opposite sides of the wooden table met at the hot plate to discuss dinner.

"Robert?" I said. "You wanted to show me something."

"Isn't that wonnerful, Reverent?" he said with a beaming appeal.

What? What was wonderful?

Suddenly the small man sank down to the floor in front of me. On his knees he shuffled toward the sink. Grunting, then, he pulled the cardboard box out into dim light, pushed it toward my feet, and stood up again.

The box was full of things. Things. Mason jars, a cordless radio, bicycle spokes, aluminum cans, plastic cigarette lighters, a trivet with two legs. Things.

Robert hitched his belt, straightened his neck, then threw his left arm wide in a magnificent flourish, gesturing toward the cardboard box. "Reverent!" he declared, "anything. Anything."

I looked at his box of things and didn't move.

Perhaps he interpreted my confusion as modesty, a hesitation which he, the host, should straightway overcome. He put on a brighter smile. "No, but anything you want," he said, "she's yours." He began some serious nodding of his head now. "Y'all he'ped me in my need," he said, "an' now I wanna thank you. Reverent, I been thinkin' on this a long time, yes. I'm the kinda person pays his dues, and I owe you sumpin." Once more he repeated the expansive gesture, sweeping his arm toward the treasures, and beaming like the sun. "Anything," he said. His chin went up and his eyelids drooped. "Anything."

At last I understood.

For reasons that need no mention here (urgent, personal, ethical reasons) we had established a social ministry at Grace through which the hungry were fed, the destitute were given money for rent and utilities, children were clothed, mothers with dependent children were trained in cooking and budgeting—the poor were supported. We called it The Mission of Grace, and by it discovered levels of human existence we hadn't known before, subterranean souls unlike the stable, Lutheran community of our congregation. We were essentially a healthy people. These were in need. We had a mission. They came in marvelous numbers, once they learned of our goods and our goodwill.

And floating among them from deep space and dreams of his own remembered galaxies, had been Robert.

I bowed my head and smiled a pastoral smile.

"Robert, Robert," I said, "you don't have to give us anything. We do what we do for the love of God, not for payment in exchange." I spoke with a crisp articulation. I felt relieved, now that I knew what the man had in mind, for I could handle this matter. I could lay it quickly to rest and be gone. I was busy. I had business to do.

"How could we call ourselves Christian," I said, "if we turned our ministry into a commercial enterprise? All that we give is free to you precisely because it is the Lord's." What would I do with a two-legged trivet anyway? I patted Robert on the shoulder. His grin was sticking, but his eyes had become unmoored. It was working. I was in control again. "Ah, Robert," I said, moving toward the door, "you owe us nothing at all, no, not a thing. But I thank you all the same for the thought. That in itself is enough. And you know, don't you, that we're always there whenever you need our help in the future—"

I left. I chose rain to trivets. I dashed for my office, to everything left to do that day.

But on the following Sunday it became apparent that I had also left the matter uncompleted, that I had left the little man still groping through the mists for another way to thank us. And he did. Sweet Robert did, in fact, hit upon an excellent method of thanksgiving, a method sure to satisfy his honor and our religion, both.

Ten minutes before the service that Sunday I robed myself in the same white alb that I had used now, Sunday after Sunday and forever. I tucked a long green stole beneath the hood at the back of my neck and hung it down the front of me and caught it in the cincture. My head was bowed; I took the opportunity to pray: O Lord God, dear Father in heaven, I am indeed unworthy of the office and ministry in which I am to make known thy glory—

My shoes were new. Behold the gloss. They shone like the sun, my shoes.

Before leaving my study—one more minute yet alone—I glanced at the bulletin and marked pages in my hymnal so that both the order of worship and the hymns of the day would be right to hand when I needed them. *Alles in Ordnung.*

I was nervous, but not uncertain. I always felt nervous before worship. Well, people depended on me, and people would scrutinize me, so there was a sort of stage fright in the waiting; and God was here, after all, and that's another kind of scrutiny altogether. I preached without notes. That's risky. On the other hand, I was practiced in leading worship; I had a certain dramatic flair which seemed to please the people—and I was Lutheran. We were all

Lutheran. And Lutherans, unlike looser traditions, have a very clear rubric to follow, a controlling ritual which comforted me; and I was in charge. Therefore I could be both nervous and not uncertain. I knew what was coming. No surprises. Amen.

I went out into the sanctuary. Faces, faces, murmuring faces, mostly black. The back pews were filled and so (happy day!) were the middle pews. The only spaces left were down front. Just twenty pews in this little sanctuary. Back and front were not far from one another. Even if the people sat toward the back, they were never far from me.

The murmuring softened toward a decorous silence. I stepped up into the chancel. There was a stained-glass Jesus above our altar, kneeling at his Gethsemanian stone, his nose, his brow, his cool composure all Teutonic. Black may have been the predominant color of our parishioners; but our mood and the prevailing discipline were Lutheran. Everything was done in order and good taste.

"In the name of the Father," I said, "and of the Son, and of the Holy Spirit."

The people, standing, said, "Amen."

I said, "Almighty God, to whom all hearts are open, all desires known, and from whom no secrets are hid: cleanse the thoughts of our hearts—"

And so the worship had begun.

We made common confession of our sins ("—have sinned against you in thought, word, and deed—").

We sang (where the rubric said in red, *The Entrance Hymn is sung*) a hymn.

We intoned the Kyrie, prayed the Collect, allowed a little space for announcements, read the Scripture lessons, sang another hymn. We rose at the *Stand,* we sat at the *Sit,* we honored the *Silence.* We were devout. We were holy, reverential, and devout—and I was not nervous anymore because, as Sunday after Sunday, worship was traveling smoothly. Oh, I loved this trustworthy people, and I, thank Heaven, was in charge of everything.

Nor did I forget my sermon.

I stood in the aisle between the two front pews and hitched my cincture and began to preach. I delivered an introduction of comprehensive clarity, touched upon the outline that would follow, launched myself into the first of three subtopics—and I preached.

The people nodded. I responded. I warmed to my subject. I lifted my voice. I lifted my eyes to the distances, and saw—Robert.

Standing squarely at the back of the aisle, his bumbershoot cane held grandly at his side, his hair picked out so that it stood upon his head in two high peaks, his clothing clean, his coat Goodwill but clean, a shocked expression on his face as though he could scarcely believe the wonderful thing he had done—was Robert.

Oh, the man looked vastly pleased with himself. He had contrived a way to thank us, after all: he had come to church. For what would gratify a Christian better than another body in the pew, another sinner saved? He came offering himself.

Robert. The little man cast greetings left and right by the nodding of his head, the tilting of those tall twin towers of hair. He beamed on people. And finding no seats in the back of the room, he turned his attention forward, toward me, blinking, smiling, and *tippy-tippy-tap-tap:* coming.

But I kept right on preaching. Subtopic two.

We nearly touched, so close did Robert come to me. But he spied a space for himself, the second pew from the front, immediately on my left; and he excused and grunted and nodded his way into that space. He sat. He lay his cane down on the floor, crossed his arms upon his chest, aimed a face of sweet benevolence in my direction, and prepared to hear some preaching.

Me, I just kept on preaching. Points three and four of subtopic two. Something of the wind had gone out of me. I labored more than sailed right now. But I could be dogged, and I didn't forget the sermon. I commenced an illustration for point four in subtopic two. I preached.

Midway through that illustration there arose a mild commotion on my left, second pew from the front. Robert had closed his innocent eyes. But Robert had begun to rock.

Now, I will admit that when I'm straining I tend to raise my voice, that sometimes I overcompensate with a forced, dramatic vigor. This could be dangerous, if someone is inclined to react more to the noise than to the instruction. It is possible that Robert was getting the wrong idea.

Therefore I softened my voice. I modulated my rhetoric. I whispered, but I kept on preaching.

And Robert kept on rocking.

I felt the prickle of sweat in my armpits.

Subtopic three.

By this time Robert's head was low and swinging, side to side. He was lifting a foot and replacing it, lifting the other, replacing it. He was patting his knee with his right hand. There was a rhythm in Robert I didn't recognize. It wasn't from my sermon, Lord. No, not from mine. Robert had another sermon going in his head— and that one wasn't Lutheran.

I kept on, kept on preaching, willing the people to listen to me, forbidding them to glance at Robert, and nearly squeaking when they did.

Up and down those twin peaks of hair went waving. Blissful was the look on his face. And then, in the midst of it all, he began that threatful Baptist practice—clapping.

I raised my voice in spite of myself.

Robert began to stomp.

I sweat. I raced my words. I drove my words with a hoarse command. The end of the sermon was in sight.

But suddenly Robert threw his two arms into the air and shouted at the top of his lungs: "I'M GOING TO PRAY!"

I stopped cold, staring at him.

Robert too was stunned. His eyes flew open. He seemed astonished by this spontaneous promise of prayer.

We were frozen, the two of us, waiting.

But then an angelic expression flooded his features, a radiance, as though he were overwhelmed by the pure, supernal beauty of his promise, and he nodded assent, and he roared it forth the second time: "Yep! I'm going to pray!"

Panic gave me a tongue. *"ROBERT!"* I cried, *"DON'T!"*

But wonder kept him deaf. "Yessir, yessir," he sang, his eyes beginning to droop, his nostrils swelling, all his breathing pumping

toward a prayer, his arms beginning to tremble above his head—
"Yessir, I'm going to pray."

I leaped at the man. I flew at him and grabbed his shoulders,
one in either hand. "Robert," I cried directly into his face with a
desperate authority, "you *can't* pray!"

He looked at me. "Why not?" he said.

"Because," I said, and I scrambled for reasons; dear Jesus, I
needed a reason eyeball-to-eyeball with Robert. "Because," I said,
"we have a *time* to pray."

Silence descended. A frown began to muddle Robert's brow. The
angel-light grew dim in his eye, and by slow degrees his arms came
down. "A *time* to pray?" Robert whispered. Evidently he had never
in all his life been presented with such a concept before. "A time? To
pray?" The little man deflated. The little man grew small again.

By inspiration of the Holy Ghost, I'd pushed the proper button.
I was in charge again. "Yes," I whispered, counselor to counselee
in private discussion together, "a time to pray."

"Oh," said Robert.

Carefully I backed away from Robert, as carefully as parents
depart the nursery after persuading their children to sleep. Carefully
I gathered up my little pieces of Lutheran sermon. Gingerly I
preached. Subtopic three: conclusions.

Ah, me. And while I preached I suffered another commotion on
my left, two pews from the front. Robert was apologizing for his
error.

"Sorry," he mumbled to people on his right, "sorry," to people
on his left. He dipped his ridiculous towers of hair to the people
behind him. "Sorry," he hissed, "I didn't know y'all had a *time* to
pray."

And so my sermon ended.

I crept back into the chancel. I sat. I opened the hymnal because
the rubric said in red, *The hymn of the day is sung*. We sang a hymn.

My alb, I noticed, smelled mightily of sweat. But the serene Jesus
in our stained glass window didn't sweat to pray. I noticed that too.

At the appointed time I rose and went to the altar and faced that
Jesus and reached for the two collection plates, one in either hand.

I turned, then, to the congregation, expecting to see two ushers who would take the plates from me—

—but discovered Robert instead.

He was standing squarely at the foot of the chancel, his hair ascendant like the spires of a cathedral, his posture erect, his face subdued, and in his right hand the cane which was really an umbrella shaft and nothing more.

Again we experienced a moment of silence together. And again he broke it.

"Naw," he said, shaking his head. "Naw, I ain' gome pray for you no more."

For me? That was the plan? For me?

Then he saw that I was holding the collection plates between us.

Were it not true, I would find the following detail too melodramatic to record. But I am bound to the truth.

Robert went fishing in his coat pocket and pulled out a dollar bill as soft as a handkerchief and dropped it in the collection plate, then turned and betook himself down the aisle and turned again and left the church.

Tippy-tippy-tap-tap, gone.

That cane! What could such a cane support, the denuded shaft of an old umbrella? Dignity. And prayer, I suppose. It had carried the supplication meant for me away from me.

Ah, Robert—what do I want with your money?

I USED TO CAUSE myself sweats and panics by my daydreams, by the power of my imagination alone.

I would imagine that I was crouching on a high mountain ledge, on some lonely lip of stone projecting from sheer rock, the distance all dizzy below me and nothing above me to climb. I would, in the daydream, creep to the edge, peer over, and then begin to shake with fear. The height itself was not the problem, however high, however real I made it. *I* was the problem. For heights could always excite in me a perverse and nearly uncontrollable urge to jump; and I sincerely believed that if I relaxed my vigilance a whit, the wilder nature would prevail: I would leap, and I would fall. I would destroy myself.

Therefore even in my daydreams, I crept backward clutching at the ground; I curled with my face to the solid rock and shut my eyes and shut my ears—for the very air would murmur with a thousand sullen voices, "Come. Come. Jump." And my own spirit would answer, "What if—?" and "Why not—?"

So I would waken suddenly in the third grade classroom, trembling and sweating and hoping that nobody noticed the change in me.

Well, there was a certain reality to my daydreams, and there was good reason to doubt that I could resist temptation. I had at least once thrown my body into the blue air and had cracked my arm because of a moment's insanity.

Listen: this is how a boy can destroy himself:

I was swinging in a park in Grand Forks, North Dakota. My entire school had scattered through the park, enjoying a picnic; so there must have been other children around, but I wasn't aware of their presence at the time. I was engaged in a private test of speeds.

The swing had long links, longer than my forearm, and a frame more lofty than any I had ever seen before. I had pumped myself to a remarkable height, forking my feet to the treetops forward, staring straight down on the earth at the backswing, ripping the wind between. I was hurtling so hard and so high that the chains went slack at my extensions, and my buttocks lifted from the seat. I made me go a giddy speed.

From nowhere—from the perversity inside myself—the thought occurred: *What if you let go?* It came as simply as that, in precisely those words. *What if you let go?*

I answered that craziness with honest sense. Right clearly I thought: *I'd hurt myself.*

But I let go anyway.

Rising on the backswing, I simply slipped from the chains and continued to sail higher than the seat itself, watching it tilt without me. Backward, upward, my body stretched straight in the air, and I saw the perfect sky, I saw the blue sky pure, and all my muscles loosened like water, my knees and my fingers filled with floating. I was a balloon. My feet rose into view. I thought: *This is how God feels, touching nothing at all!* Then my legs clocked over my head, and I was staring at the ground, and all at once a massive hand was pushing on my back. It thrust me down with increasing force, with astonishing speed to the earth, so the impact came before I could consider it. I hit and barked and lay still. There was no pain at first, only a dullish saturation, a sense of weight in all my bones. In fact, I felt no sharper pain until the principal had driven me home and I met my father and told him that I had broken my arm. Then it hurt, and then I cried.

But the real instruction of that experience was that I was not to be trusted. There was an evil streak in my nature, and on a high ledge (so I imagined it over and over) against all sense and righteousness, I would probably jump.

It's a dangerous world.

The principal's name was Mr. Affeldt. He visited our house often in the year I attended Immanuel Lutheran School, because my father was the pastor of Immanuel Lutheran Church. They were colleagues with much to talk about.

Mr. Affeldt's ears grew so flat to the sides of his head that I used to consider he had walrus ears. He carried a pouch of flesh beneath his chin, and he smiled by the lifting of his top lip only, revealing a fence of long incisors. So the comparison to a walrus was complete, it seemed to me, except that he was not a fat man. He breathed like a fat man, rather. Through his nose. Even when he was smiling.

Of all the teachers at Immanuel, only Mr. Affeldt occupied an office of his own. Books rose up the walls of this room to the very ceiling, so that you had the sense, when you entered it, of entering the mind of Mr. Affeldt himself—each book a thought, each thought a silent eye inspecting you. To be surrounded thus by the cogitations of Mr. Affeldt (he was a man of cool rationality and legendary intelligence) could factor a child right out of existence.

On the books behind his desk (or else hanging from a hook when it was not in use), he kept a flat piece of wood, varnished and shapen with a handle, and burned across the face of it with the words: *The Board of Education.* I realized that these words constituted some sort of joke, because he lifted his lip when he spoke them and he showed his teeth. So I would shuffle my feet at such times and produce a knowing chuckle. But the joke seemed a bit joyless to me, since he used the wood to administer discipline to a student's open palm, or perhaps to a bending bottom.

Discipline. Regulations. The consequences of transgression. Nothing was hidden in those days. Nothing was particularly complicated. Principals and parents and teachers were not cryptic or tricky, but forthright and trustworthy. "Do this," they said, "and this will happen. Don't do this and the other thing will happen surely." And it did. It always did. They kept their promises. The world was orderly indeed, if a little severe. I knew what The Board of Education was for.

Miss Augustine, on the other hand, was mercy in my world; and I could abide the harshness of the whole world bravely for the sake of my third grade teacher, my Miss Augustine.

Early in the school year she had said, "Don't laugh in class. Please don't disturb the other children when I'm teaching them." It was a reasonable request, since she had to divide her time among three grades, all in the same room, and since at any given moment two-thirds of the students were working on their own. It was also a very persuasive plea, because Miss Augustine herself was a woman inclined to laugh—a pink-faced, musical laughter that stirred my soul when I heard it, a nearly killing benediction when I myself was the cause of that flush of delight in her face for something I had said—a persuasive plea, I say, because she controlled her laughter. She set us a good example. If she could get down to brass tacks, well, so could we.

So I said, "Hush!" to Corky Zimbrick, who sat behind me, and I tried manfully to ignore him.

Corky insisted on whispering jokes in my ear. I didn't understand that. I presumed that every student felt the same dear loyalty that I did toward Miss Augustine.

She had shoulder bones that hunched forward in a cotton dress when she stood by a student's desk. It was like the gentle revelation of internal vulnerability; lithesome and lovely were her shoulders' wings, vouchsafing through the fabric of her dress how tender the private woman was, entrusting me with secrets. And then I could hardly stand their fragility when in winter she pulled a shawl around her shoulders.

"Hush!" I hissed to Corky Zimbrick, not turning in my seat.

But Corky had a hasty manner of speech, a stuttering, breathless delivery that made all his words, however prosaic, nervous and hilarious.

"Ta-ta-ta-ta-ta-ta," he fired the words in my ear as through a peashooter.

That tickled me. I began to frown.

He said, "Shadrach, Meshach, and to-bed-we-go."

I chewed on giggles, like chewing on jujubes.

Corky put his mouth right behind my ear and caught me off guard with an obscenity: "Wally's favorite salad," he said. "Lettuce, turnip, and pea."

I let out a whoop. I said, "Haw!"

So Miss Augustine turned from the blackboard and gave me a look of such wounded disappointment that all my mirth turned sour inside of me.

I wanted, all at once, to cry for hurting her. No, no, but my station in this classroom was to protect her, not to distress her. My face burned with an earnest, genuine repentance.

And Miss Augustine deciphered my soul, I think. She was truly the mercy in my legalistic world. She said nothing at all, but drew the soft shawl tighter round her shoulders and turned to the blackboard again. My eyes lingered on her neck. My spirit swelled with gratitude. She hadn't reprimanded me.

One day I rose up in class and told a lie. I didn't recognize it as a lie—not until the following weekend. It was a story, rather, of sudden, astonishing power. I silenced a roomful of students in telling it; I encoiled Miss Augustine in the filaments of my own imagination, and I caused her almost to cry. Oh, what a wonderful gift I had! And how I relished the use of it.

Kathy Drees had just been telling us about the funeral of her aunt. She had described the open casket and the corpse and the weird chill that the corpse had left on her fingers when she touched it.

"Cold," Kathy said in a low and thrilling voice.

"You mean you actually touched her?" someone said.

Kathy lifted three fingers on her right hand to show us the frost-bites. "So cold I felt it all night long," she said. "So cold I can feel it now." I was moved by the immediacy of her memory. Kathy had a nose like a little rubber ball, a plain sweetness about her that made the death seem cruel indeed.

But I was chiefly impressed by the effect the detail had on the faces around me: they gaped. And Miss Augustine positively melted toward this child who had touched with her own three fingers a corpse.

Well, sir. I could do better than that.

And instinctively I perceived the efficacy of two things: the corpse must be personal to me in order to be real for my listeners (but I couldn't use an aunt, since Kathy had taken that); and the story must bristle with detail. Miss Augustine needed to *see* what I would say in order to be cut by it.

So I stood up by my desk, and I said, "Miss Augustine, it was my sister."

She looked quizzically at me. Sharpen that detail.

"It was," I said, "my *older* sister." Give her a name. "Valery," I said.

I thought at first that I'd let this Valery die in infancy; but I would play no real part in such a story, and the purpose was to excite some sympathy on my own behalf. Therefore Valery was five years old in a twinkling. I was four. She wore thick glasses and walked with a limp. We lived on Overhill Street in Chicago, Illinois.

"She went downtown on a bus one day—"

Amend that. "*We* went downtown together on the Addison Avenue bus," I said. "We didn't get off until it made a big circle and came back to our street again—"

"Wally?" Miss Augustine interrupted with gentle caution. "Really? Would your mother have let you travel alone?"

"Oh yes," I said.

It was a reasonable doubt, I suppose; but my answer was honest. My mother had, in fact, sent Paul and me, not Valery and me, downtown on the bus on a Sunday afternoon; and then it had been me, not Valery, hit by the car. But I had bounced unbroken twelve feet from the bumper. Not Valery. Poor Valery!

"She ran round in front of the bus without looking," I said. "As soon as she was in the street, she stopped and turned. She was going to run back to the sidewalk, but—" Oh, lucky detail! "—Valery limped, you see. A purple car came roaring down the street and hit her—"

"Ah!" said Miss Augustine.

"—and she rolled and she rolled. And the man that hit her had four daughters in the car. He jumped out and ran to Valery and picked her up, and Valery's arm was hanging down, so I started home to get our mother. I ran home all by myself. I was crying."

Miss Augustine covered her mouth and whispered, "I'm so sorry," her eyes beseeching me. I was creating something wonderful. The whole class sat stock still. Oh, I was flying. I wanted never to quit so sweet a flight of pleasure. Miss Augustine, I have touched your heart!

Detail by detail, then, I carried the class to the funeral, not unlike the funeral of Kathy's aunt; but my funeral contained an incident more terrible than the mere touching of the corpse.

"When everyone was looking at Valery in the coffin," I said, "my grandpa whispered that her hair and her fingernails would keep on growing forever—"

"What?" said Corky Zimbrick, appalled.

"But Mom said, 'She's your sister, Wally. You should say good-bye to her.' So we went right up to the coffin, my mom and me, and I said, 'Good-bye, Valery,' because dying is saying good-bye, you see, and my mom, she started to cry. And then she said, 'Wally, you should kiss her.' That's what she said. She said, 'Wally, give your sister a kiss.' So I leaned over the coffin, like this. And I put my lips on her forehead, like this. And I kissed her. Now that," I declared to the classroom, "was cold. *Cold!* Valery was colder than ice. Valery was colder than winter. My lips stayed frozen for six days after that. I couldn't smile on account of, my lips were so cold."

I sat down.

Nobody said a thing.

Miss Augustine was devastated. She had made a prayer of her hands and was holding them at her mouth, gazing and gazing at me, speechless. Her tender eyes were swimming, and her face was pink with feeling, and I was proud. She loved me. I was a sorcerer. I had caused my teacher almost to cry. Miss Augustine, I'll be kind to you.

"Wally," she whispered, "how tragic for your mother."

Mr. Affeldt sat in our living room looking straight at me, his ears so flat that I couldn't see them. Miss Augustine had come with him. She was wearing a print dress with a collar that covered the back of her neck. She wasn't looking at me. So my face was stinging because the principal was, and my teacher was not, looking at me.

Actually they had come to visit my mother. They had spent some fifteen minutes alone with her—and only then invited me to join them. I had accepted the invitation right happily, but no one was smiling at my entrance, and my mother had said, "Sit down."

Miss Augustine kept her head bowed. I couldn't tease so much as a glance out of her, and I wondered if they were blaming her for something.

My mother said, "Mr. Affeldt came to comfort me, Wally. Do you know why?"

I said that I didn't. My mother seemed very strong to me, hardly in need of comforting.

"Well, he thought it would help me if I knew," she said, "that my tragedy is known, that the church stands beside me, that I don't have to keep it a secret any more. Do you know what that secret might be, Wally?" she asked.

I shook my head. I knew so little of adult affairs.

"That I had a daughter," my mother said, "who died four years ago—"

Oh. My face began to sting, my chest to pant. Oh.

"—a grief so grievous," my mother continued, staring at me, while Mr. Affeldt kept his cold gaze on me too, "a guilt so deep that I shut it away and confessed it to no one. I made your father promise not to mention it. So I would never have known forgiveness for neglecting my daughter unless my son had let the secret slip. I am supposed to thank you, Wally," my mother said, "because Mr. Affeldt realized that he should come to speak the grace of God to me. Wally?"

"What."

"Should I thank you?"

No matter how pleadingly I looked at Miss Augustine, she would not raise her face nor return the look. Her flesh was drained white, her slender fingers folded in her lap. My teacher was ashamed of me. I had hurt her. I had told a lie too terrible for mercy.

"Should I thank you, Wally?" my mother repeated.

I shook my head. All of my words had fled me, and now I didn't look at Miss Augustine either. The knowledge rose in a heat around my ears that I was a very guilty thing.

"I think it's fortunate that your principal is here," said my mother, "and your teacher too. Now no one can doubt that the rules of this house are the same as the rules of the school—the same as the commandments of God, Wally. Mr. Affeldt knows that I won't abide a liar. He knows he has permission to punish you if you lie again. *Behold, how great a matter a little fire kindleth! The tongue is afire; the tongue is afire.* Do we all understand that, Wally?"

My face was a perfect fire.

But I was not going to cry. It was horrible enough that Miss Augustine should see what a sinner I was. I would not add to that an abject humiliation. I did not cry.

"Do we all understand that?"

I nodded.

I didn't move when everyone exchanged amenities and left. I was grateful to Miss Augustine that she didn't say good-bye to me, because a word from her might have broken my resolve. I might have wept.

For all his joking in class, Corky Zimbrick was not especially bold. That became apparent when I began to run the schoolyard with a gang of boys at recess: Corky wouldn't. The louder we got, the more he chose to stay in the classroom, he and a handful of girls, Kathy Drees, Lorna Kemble, and a tiny kid named Abner.

Well, and we did more than run the schoolyard. We galloped. We were a black-hearted gang of reprobates who galloped exactly like horses, slapping our thighs and crying, "Giddyup!" and charging the girls on the monkey bars, mocking them, befouling them with names and nasty language before we galloped around the corner: "Hi ho Silver, away!"

I took it for granted, given the changes I found myself making now, that Miss Augustine would reserve her tenderer expressions for someone else. And she did. But I hadn't anticipated that she would shower so much kindness on so many others so constantly. What had been mine seemed given indiscriminately to everyone—smiles and blushings, the murmurous music of her voice, the awful rounding of her shoulders—to absolutely everyone else. Well, so what? I broke pencil points when I wrote at my desk. So what?

And then the news circulated through the school that Miss Augustine was engaged to be married, and that the man intended was Kathy Drees's older brother, a farmer's son. I knew him. Neat hair; pure white temples; a pure white slash for a part; and for a nose, a rubber ball. So what? So gallop the harder at recess and slap my thigh and holler the louder, "Giddyup!" I hated Kathy's brother.

So what? So there came the time that Mr. Affeldt called the lot of us into his office after recess. Seven or eight sweating boys, we stood surrounded by his juridical books and listened to his imperturbably nasal voice and watched him talk by the lifting of his top lip only. When he began to refer to The Board of Education, I felt my bowels turn into water. But Glen Larson dissolved so quickly into wet sobs, and other boys began so shamelessly to wipe their eyes with the heels of their hands, that I stiffened myself and determined not to drop a tear—and didn't. Mr. Affeldt did not use The Board of Education that day. Rather, he lapsed into silence, a watchful, blinkless silence; and then he dismissed us by the merest nod of his head.

While the others were trooping out, he rose and approached me and dropped a hand on my shoulder. "Walter Junior," he said, "this is your last chance. Do we understand each other?"

And then it was that, in the park and urging my swing the higher and higher, I broke my arm.

I lay on the ground a while, aware of my bones and the sick shock inside my chest. My right arm didn't want to hang when I stood. It wanted cradling. So I carried it in my left hand to Mr. Affeldt, where he sat on a picnic bench in sunlight.

"I think I broke my arm," I said.

He twitched his eyebrows up, examined both my face and the protected arm, then stopped looking at me and led me to his car.

He drove me home in a business silence. I kept my face impassive. When I stood in the doorway and saw my father coming toward me through the house, I lost control and I cried. But I kept my right arm to myself.

The doctor called it a green tree break. He distinguished that from a compound fracture, which he described in purple detail while fitting a metal plate beneath my wrist and wrapping it tight.

"Boxing?" he said. This was meant to be a joke. "Fisticuffs?"

"Flying," I said.

So then—what did I get for my rash behavior, my flight halfway to God? A half day home from school. I got a sling for my arm that tied behind my neck. I got assurances from my mother that we would visit an optometrist, though I truly did not understand the connection. I got a flurry of fame when I returned to school the following morning. I got permission to skip phys. ed., together with the command to stay in the classroom during recess.

But these were just candies. What was precious beyond expression, what I got when the recess commenced, was an opportunity I couldn't have planned because I could never have imagined it. I flew again. I flew the third time. And twice I was beloved.

Corky Zimbrick touched my sling and said, "What happened?"

With scarcely a thought to the answer, I said, "I flew."

"You what?"

"Flew."

Corky put on his comic face. "Ta-ta-ta-ta," he said. "Wally, Wally," he chuckled.

That I had said it, and then that he had laughed at it, filled my throat with a thick conviction. "I flew, Corky," I said. Lorna Kemble was in the classroom. So was the tiny kid named Abner. And Kathy Drees, all of us at the back of room for recess. "Kathy," I said, "didn't you see me? Didn't you see me fly?"

Good Kathy Drees of the bauble nose and the wonderful, guttural voice said, "Yes." She corroborated what I said: "You flew."

"See?" I said. "Listen, Corky, I pumped the swing," I said. "I pumped and I pushed and I pulled the swing, so high and higher. You'd think I could circle the top like a bucket of water and not fall out—that's how high I went."

Kathy Drees was nodding. She was watching me, but the flash in her eye was seeing my swing. "It's true," she whispered. I grew excited.

"Corky, Kathy saw it," I said. "At the very highest of the back-swing, I just let go. I just let go, and I sailed into the air. I went out backward, and I spread my arms, and I was staring into the sky, and I flew. I was flying on a soft wind, and looking so high, so high— that I saw God!"

Now Corky Zimbrick was gaping at me. Kathy's eyes were shining a marvelous credence. Lorna and Abner were drawn into the circle. Oh, the sorcery was in me again, sweet, sweet, and the story was very true: in the classroom, on the wing of my words, I was gone again, flying.

Miss Augustine walked into the room and set a stack of books on her desk.

"The reason you don't see God from the ground," I said, "is God is big! Bigger than the sky. And the sky is huge and blue, and the sky is full of clouds, but even the sky is smaller than the eye of God. The sky," I whispered, "is a tear in God's eye, Kathy!"

Miss Augustine had begun to watch me.

Kathy's face was tipped toward me in speechless reverence.

Corky wasn't laughing.

I was king. I began to pant.

"The air makes a shelf in heaven," I said. "You slide that shelf like a slicky-slide," I said. "Airplanes find it and fly and they never flap their wings," I said. "And God said, 'I'll show you that shelf.' God showed me that shelf, and I turned on my belly, and I flew. I soared. I sliced the wind with my arms stretched out, and I looped the loop, and I saw the earth—" I was laughing now, because I was flying. "—I saw the park, and I saw the people, and I saw you there like dots on the grass—"

"Wally!"

"—but Kathy, but Kathy, but God forgot to show me the edge of the shelf, and I slipped right over it—"

"Wally!" This was Miss Augustine. I shot her a glance, and I saw at once that her face was a flaming pink, and my heart exploded with joy, because it had happened again: she was listening, and she loved me. She loved me! She admired the wonderful things that I had done!

"—slipped right over the edge of the shelf," I said with a frantic intensity. "Down I fell, and down in a dive, oh, down so fast that the wind was screaming in my ears, oh yes! I saw the ground, I saw it coming, saw you see me falling down—"

"Wally!" said Miss Augustine. "Stop it!"

"No!" I shouted, panting. "Wait!" I cried. "Wait till I get to the ending," I said—because then she would have such sympathy for me that she would hug me maybe and love me forever. I knew what was coming. She didn't.

"Walter Wangerin—" she whispered, but I raced on.

"I saw everyone," I shouted in the classroom. "The whole school, Kathy and Corky and everyone, and I said, 'I'll miss them all! Won't hit a soul!' And I aimed my body to the empty spaces, falling like a cannonball—"

"Stop that! *Stop that!*" Miss Augustine shrieked. She shrieked it and thumped the desk, and she looked—frightened. I think she looked—

All at once I didn't know what she looked like or what was happening.

Miss Augustine rounded her desk and began to march in my direction glaring at me.

But I couldn't stop. I couldn't stop. I was falling, and I couldn't stop.

"I hit the ground," I cried, staring back at her and rushing the words in order to finish. "I hit so hard I made a hole, and I heard my arm go crack! Crack! It was a compound fracture," I yelled. "The bone, you see, it pierced through my skin—"

In that same instant I realized that my ending wasn't working. Miss Augustine came bearing down on me, her face aflame. There was no sympathy in her face. And still, and still—though burdened with the knowledge of an unspeakable loss—I could not stop.

I lifted my right arm and murmured miserably. "The bone poked through the skin as sharp as a knife, you see, and the blood poured down my elbow too, and I hurt so bad, but I didn't cry, no I never—"

Miss Augustine seized my shoulder and gave it a violent pinch. I put my face down. But I finished my story. "Cried," I said.

"What's the matter?" said Kathy Drees. She was looking back and forth between the both of us. "What's the matter?" she said.

She was pleading her question, in fact, because she was sincerely confused, and I noticed that her chin had started to tremble.

"What's the matter?"

I felt sorry for Kathy. I knew what the matter was. And I wanted with all my heart to be good. I mean, I would have confessed on the spot. I would not have denied, but would have confessed that I had told another lie, a monstrous lie. That was the matter, that was the dreadfulness here.

But without a word Miss Augustine had already yanked my shirt at the neck, the collar and the sling together, so I couldn't say anything at all. She pulled me out of the classroom, and we went walking down the corridor.

Miss Augustine didn't talk to me. She let me go and folded her arms across her chest. She hunched her beautiful, terrible shoulder bones, and drew the shawl so tightly closed that the knit stretched open and showed the print of her cotton dress. I could hardly stand those innocent holes of revelation. I stumbled to keep up with her. Her poor face was mottled sick with the redness. I knew what the matter was. She didn't love me anymore. It wasn't her fault.

It was worse than a lie, of course. I was not ignorant of the truth. In me there was the deep streak of evil, a perversity so villainous and so indifferent to precious, delicate things that it destroyed them—and I simply couldn't control it. Miss Augustine didn't love me anymore. She would never love me again. And this was not her fault. It was mine. No, I was not to be trusted: on a high ledge, even on the cliff of a stone-cold truth, I would probably jump and destroy myself.

It's a dangerous, mutinous world.

"Walter—"

Miss Augustine stopped walking. I froze with my face down, but my heart began to strain the leash on the chance she was about to change her mind and speak a merciful word, would reverse the direction my sin deserved, might love me again.

"Walter—" she said. Oh, her voice in that moment was a music of a thousand incipient vows. I waited, willing myself neither to move nor to cry. But if she intended some further word beyond my name, I never heard it.

I heard instead the rush of her shawl, and her knock on the principal's door.

It is an exacting world.

BAGLADY

I SAID INTO THE MICROPHONE: Robert contrived a frightening way to thank us—

The sound system was good. It didn't echo back at me, though the building was, to my eye, huge, and the walls were far away. I held the mike in my right hand, walked a dais three steps high, drew the loops of electrical wire behind me, and swallowed prodigiously. If I got stage fright preaching in tiny Grace, what would I get in this place? Cataplexy.

I said into the microphone: *Robert decided to come to church*—

The people before me were smiling. Interested and smiling. No one meant me any harm. Yet these people were strangers to me, and they numbered—what? In the hundreds, all lifting their faces, leaning left and right in order to see me.

I swallowed and said into the microphone: *On Sunday morning, bang at the back of the aisle, the little man appeared*—

On the other hand, they weren't strangers truly. They were Americans at worship—no cause for nervousness. Evangelical, nonliturgical, unfanatical, calm and kind and self-possessed, a rational middle mix not even denominated, these smiling people offered me no threat—unless vast latitude and limitless, uncritical goodwill threaten the ortho-Lutheran because he isn't used to so much freedom, because he has to fill it.

I coughed into my left hand. I swallowed and spoke into the microphone: *Sweet Robert stood directly opposite me*, I said, *his hair picked out to double peaks upon his head, a shocked expression on his face, the thin umbrella cane held formal by his side*—

The smiles near me grew broader and heads in the distance nodded. Yes, they said, they could imagine my Robert. Yes, they recognized the irony of the situation and were ready to identify with me. Go on. They liked a story too. Go on.

I began to relax. And I went on.

Well, he couldn't see a seat in the back of the church, I said. *Grace may be little, but Grace ain't provincial. We got big-city ways—we fill the back pews first. So Robert commenced to walk the aisle in my direction—*

"Ha, ha," said the people.

Ah, laughter. I was grateful to these people. I hit a stride, and I went on.

This was the LaSalle Street Church, a congregation in downtown Chicago which I had heard about even before they invited me to come and preach to them. Our ministries were not dissimilar, though theirs was large, sophisticated, and far outstripped the infant Mission of Grace. They had an honest reputation for service. Well— and the territory they served was in itself notorious. Perhaps nowhere else in the country do poverty and great wealth neighbor each other so closely in such extremes.

The riots of the 1960s destroyed whole blocks of the near north side of Chicago in flames; but then the city regenerated itself by building modern structures on the land the poor demolished. Someone had been an opportunist, I thought when I saw the tailored fortresses. Some wealthy someone had reasoned with himself: "If the poor despise it, I will buy it. If the vulgar burn it, I can build." Some wealthy entrepreneurial someone constructed condominiums, impassive, impressive, impregnable in sight of the LaSalle Street Church.

But if you step outside the church and look left, you will also see a nearly unspeakable stacking of poverty: Cabrini Green, high-rise housing, warehousing, the desperate housing of the poor. Down the faces of these grim buildings is a dark, interior cleft, as though Vulcan had slashed each one from the hairline to the jawline with his hammer. But the architect did that. The architect caused this indentation as though some part of every floor in the building should be revealed to the world. "Is it nothing to you, all ye that pass by? Behold and see—" My heart recoiled when I saw that visible shaft. I felt ashamed, partly because I felt as well a fascination and watched for inhabitants to appear in the crack as a boy might watch for ants in an ant farm. I felt embarrassed for the multitudinous poor and for this society which solves them like a problem in structural engineering. Or maybe all my feelings and reflections came from shock at the scale of poverty. I knew the name Cabrini Green. But who knew it was so big, so big? And from this vantage, so globally silent? I was looking at the moon come down and grounded on the earth. I was, I guess, awakening.

And there across the way from me, when I stood on the church steps, rose those stony condominiums, each a mute, blank solipsism; but people lived there too. The contrast was monstrous. People and people, absolutely sundered from one another. I was a baby, waking.

Yet this consoled me: that another people altogether, these of the LaSalle Street Church, had turned their attention and their resources to the poor. They stocked and dispensed food with a practiced efficiency I could learn from; I could take their system back to Grace. They cared for the elderly. They knew about the houseless. With several other churches ("networking"—a new word for me), they supervised a clean, safe dwelling place for black and white together, for those financially dependent and those independent, for the young and the old.

And though they lived in other places through Chicago, though they were themselves a generally middle class collection, the rational middle mix, their language sounded familiar in my ears, and I was inclined to say "We" in the midst of them. "We are engaged in the same kind of ministry, aren't—we? And isn't that encouraging?"

I thought I would tell them of my experience with Robert. It would communicate our common bond: "See? I am your brother, even in Evansville." It might also serve as a sort of warning, in which I was the bad example: "If we grow cumbered about much serving, we might lose a willing humility and lose a world of good besides. Look what I lost in Robert." A cautionary tale, I thought. A sad one because of my fear and my foolishness. But an urgent one because it had been true and Robert, in fact, continued to live on Gum Street close to Grace. I still saw the little man pass on the sidewalk, though he'd never come back to worship with us, and I kept a guilty distance from his tapping cane.

Finally, my story might be some consolation to anyone at the LaSalle Street Church who had grown weary in well-doing: "See how near God is unto you? Angels do sometimes come in the form of the most oppressed. God is here. God is in Cabrini Green, and sometimes he's frowning, but sometimes he's smiling, surely."

They had asked me to preach to them. This is what I intended to preach.

So I was walking in a wide chancel, and the sun was shining in the windows, and a genial sea of faces bubbled and smiled at me, and I had begun to feel a homiletic confidence. No, this congregation need not be a threat or strange to me. See how they understood the story I was telling them?

I said into the microphone: *Robert spied himself a seat two pews from the front on my left-hand side, and he sat, and he laid his ridiculous cane on the floor—*

Even the children locked sight on me and blessed me with attention. I paused and permitted the tiniest twinkle in my eye: the next part of the story would be funny, a joke on myself. The people would laugh.

I said: *Somewhere in my sermon there arose a mild commotion on my left, the second pew from the front.* I affected a look of Lutheran anguish, and I said: *Robert had begun to—*

At that very instant, at the back doors of the LaSalle Street Church, there occurred a real commotion. Three people rushed in a bunch together and exchanged a hissing of words sharp enough that I looked up, even while I continued the story:

—*Robert had begun to rock,* I said. *He was lifting his feet and putting them down. He was patting his leg with his hand,* I said. *His*

eyes were closed. He was hearing some sermon with wonderful rhythm,
but it wasn't mine, and it wasn't—

Lutheran, I was going to say. And people, grinning wide as rakes, were waiting for me to say it.

But the hissing at the back of the church had suddenly stopped. An usher had turned in my direction looking woeful and helpless, while in front of the usher, as bright-eyed, pointed, and determined as a weasel, was a woman beetling forward at a frowning clip.

An old woman; a woman crook-backed, hunched at her shoulders so that her face thrust forward; a woman behatted, but the hat just sat on her hair, because the hair shot out around her head in a white and spiky nimbus, stiff hair, angry hair, hair capable of stabbing. This woman's face was full of the mumble of words. Her mouth was working words as though they were gum. Her eyes were darting left and right, pew to pew as she approached. What was she doing? With a draining horror I understood: the woman was looking for a seat!

The LaSalle Street people filled the back pews first.

"Dear God," I breathed, "who's doing this to me?"

The woman was clutching the handles of a shopping bag in two hands at her stomach. A baglady.

For the flash of a moment I was furious. This was altogether too perfect to be accidental. She was too classic to be true. She was an actress; this was a joke on my Robert story, but a baglady instead of a drunk; and the LaSalle Street Church was having a hoot, strangers to me after all.

I pinched my lips and watched the play unfold.

The woman came straight down to the front. She tucked her body sideways into the third pew on my right-hand side, never casting so much as a glance at me. She thumped to sitting and then proceeded to open the bag on her lap, to root therein all mindless of the place, the time, the worship, the people—and to place her worldly possessions on the seat beside her. She had a glittering eye, precisely like a weasel's.

Well. I raised an angry face to the congregation and only then discovered that they were as much the butt of this joke as I was.

The poor usher, when he caught my eye, literally threw up his hands in apology. Some of the members sent me stricken looks, aggrieved that such a thing should happen in their church. Others raised eyebrows of incredulity. They didn't believe it either. They thought it must be a setup and that I myself had found a tricky way to make my Robert real to them.

Ah, Jesus—nobody's joke, then? A baglady indeed?

No, I wasn't angry anymore. I was plain scared, and all my wretched nerves returned. What was I supposed to do with a baglady here? The story of Robert was a story of my sin, was meant to say, *Don't sin as I did.* How could I continue to tell that story faithfully, effectively, and at the same time ignore this baglady—and so commit the sin again, again? Well, I would be lying in my teeth.

The story of Robert was meant to be a story. An illustration. Not an event. Jesus, please: I had come here to preach, not to be sifted like wheat in public. So what was I supposed to do?

But people all over the church, no longer smiling now, were looking at me, awaiting the next move. I had no other move than the one I'd planned.

Therefore, *I kept on preaching,* I said into the microphone, swallowing prodigious loads of spit, drawing a baleful smile across my face. *And Robert kept on rocking. When I preached quietly it didn't matter,* I said. *He kept rocking. When I preached louder, it mattered. He rocked the harder. And soon he began that threatful Baptist practice—clapping. I felt the trickle of sweat on my spine—*

Nobody laughed. Somebody should have laughed at the humor. That is, somebody would have laughed under other conditions. But Robert was here in the form of the baglady. You can't gossip about the person who is listening to you. Nobody laughed. The people were anxious, rather, discomfited by my talking, which could be slurring her. I was losing them, O Lord. They were repudiating me. Strangers.

Well, then I had no choice.

I had to acknowledge the baglady.

I stepped down out of the chancel, dragging the microphone wire behind me, and walked across the little distance that separated me from the mumbling lady. I approached the third pew, and spoke to the woman herself.

I raised my voice in spite of myself, I said into the microphone, directly to this woman. *And Robert began to stomp,* I said.

The woman narrowed her eyes and pierced me with weasel glances, as sharp as the needles of hair round her head. She hissed a sentence at me, a challenge, in fact. I heard the words but kept on preaching.

All at once, I said, *Robert threw his two arms in the air and roared, "I'm going to pray!" I stopped cold. Robert, too, was stunned—*

The baglady jumped backward and frowned in serious doubt for my sanity. She put her hand to her bosom, which was cased in several layers of shirt.

Robert, I said to the woman as gently as I could, but I boomed in the microphone, *Robert considered the wonderful promise he had produced, to pray, but I stood mute with panic, because his prayer was a threat to me. Do you understand that?*

I meant the question for the people. But the baglady compulsively shook her head.

I was afraid of his prayer, I said. *I didn't want to lose control of things. But things went from bad to worse. "Yessir!" Robert shouted, "I'm going to pray!" "Robert!" I cried, and I dived for him—*

In fact, I reached my left hand toward the woman as though she were my Robert. But even before I touched her shoulder, she trapped the hand and began to fumble for something on the pew.

"Robert, you can't pray," I cried. "Why not?" he said. And I said—

But at that moment in the LaSalle Street Church I said nothing at all. I was silenced, and my story stopped.

The baglady had found what she was feeling for. She snatched it up between us—almost like some talisman against an evil—and she hissed a second sentence with startling clarity, and my neck began to tingle. But what she held was a half-pint carton of milk. And what she was doing was giving it to me.

I heard an expulsion of air, a sigh from the congregation. I interpreted their sigh. The drama around me diminished me, and I was moved, and the microphone sagged away from my mouth.

Behold: the impoverished is nourishing the preacher. Behold: the servant is being served.

I remembered the microphone and lifted it again. My voice continued in an amplified squeak: *"You can't pray because we have a time to pray," I said, and the little man collapsed before me—*

But this woman with spikes of white hair and tiny weasel eyes was willful, insistent. She shook the carton of milk. She wanted me to take the milk. I did. I took the milk in my left hand, then she nodded once, fiercely, as though satisfied with my obedience, and dismissed me by folding her arms across her bosom.

Umbrella canes, twin peaks of a picked-out hair, collection plates, and a dollar bill as soft as a handkerchief—I brought my story to its conclusion. I made whatever points it occurred to me to make. And then I retreated to my chancel seat, which was hidden from the people by a massive pulpit.

Amen, amen, I was grateful to be hidden.

No, I wasn't nervous anymore. A bit overwhelmed, perhaps, that my story had been no story at all, but a holy assault, and that my sermon had been preempted by reality. "Angels in the form of the oppressed"—indeed. God was in this baglady. Whether the LaSalle Street Church was aware of that or not, I was.

And yet I could have explained the awe in me, if awe was all it was.

What I could not have explained—what might have looked like insolence, and why I was glad to be hidden—was that my mouth kept smearing into a grin and my chest kept pumping toward an outright laugh. I wanted to laugh. Every time I thought of what it was the baglady had actually said to me, I covered my mouth to keep from laughing.

Angels, yes indeed! But when angels descend from Cabrini Green and not from condominiums, they don't bathe first; they don't approve themselves with pieties first; they do not fit the figments of Christian imagination: they prophesy precisely as they are and expect us to honor them whole, prophecies and blasphemies together.

I wanted so badly to laugh, because God was roaring a wonderful thunder, surely. The baglady had been a joke, yes—and the joke was God's.

When I had first approached her pew, all crippled with fear, this is what the crook-backed woman hissed at me: "It's damn if I will," she said. "It's damn if I want to, Preacher. You'll never get me to stop my swearing!"

What would the La Salle Street Christians make of that? My ears uncorked to hear her. But I drove my story onward nonetheless.

And when she handed me the carton of milk, when all of the people exhaled their sentimental sigh, she sharpened her weasel-gaze and hissed: "This—is—poison. Hee-hee! Hee-hee!"

The messenger of God was cracked. And so was I, to her shrewd eye. Oh, we were a subversive pair in this rational middle mix, Americans at worship. They had no idea what sedition they'd taken to their bosoms—

And God was pounding his thighs and weeping with the laughter surely.

This is the end of the story of Robert.

I went back to his dim-lit room, and with no embarrassment asked to see his cardboard box again.

He saw nothing strange in my request. He pulled the box from underneath the sink, and he repeated his offer as though nothing at all had occurred between my first and second visits:

"Anything, Reverent," he said. "Anything you want."

I took my time deciding. Finally I selected a trivet with two legs.

We agreed. It was an excellent, tasteful choice.

PAUL WAS IN THE FIFTH GRADE. I was in the sixth. As we had in Chicago several years ago, so here: we walked to school and home again. There was only an open field between the house and the schoolyard, and Mother figured she could police our goings and comings from the kitchen window while she did the dishes.

A practical and obdurately ethical woman was our mother.

She had fought many a brave fight on her children's behalf, and now the bravest of all was for our souls, that we be found righteous in the assizes. That is to say: she kept an eye on us.

If in church on a Sunday morning we could not behave (and she could not reach us), at home on a Sunday afternoon we enacted another sort of church, wordless, spare, and twice as long. The Church of a Perfect Discipline. We sat on a backless bench in sacred silence, our bodies enchained by the eyes of our mother (who could quickly reach us), that our hearts and our consciences might be free.

She had accepted grimmer challenges than ours in the past, and had prevailed: Jimmy Newman's grandmother (remember her?) had bitten a bitter dust; black bear in at least three national parks had woofed and retreated from the pans and spoons of our mother's clangorous ire; blizzards on the plains of North Dakota had not killed nor blenched a child of hers. And the murderous malice of gossip, the cold human enmity in Edmonton, Alberta, where we now were living, our mother outfaced with biblical immobility.

She made a fortress of the forms of our religion. She guarded the doors of that fortress like Peter with a short sword and a key. And though this may seem small to the world at large, to us it was the fate of the children of martyrs—that Mother on a Sunday, when other worshipers were too ignorant to know the proper times for rising, rose, rose grandly, and commanded her children to rise up with her. So we alone would stand in the midst of a whole congregation, gazing staunchly forward, making our stance a lesson to them all, heaping coals of fire, as it were, upon their heads—but suffering the scorch in our own poor foreheads.

Ah, Mother was Amos in Bethel. Mother was Paul in Jerusalem. Mother was Christ in the courts of the Temple. Fearless. And practical. Obdurately ethical. Ours.

We would be found righteous.

Or perhaps we would be found like her for sheer independence and outrageous spunk.

In Alberta, Canada, in the latter part of November, the evenings come cold and early. In the year that Paul and I were in the fifth and sixth grades at Virginia Park School, the cold came dry and mean and snowless; the sky hung low and grey; the earth was bone-hard, frozen, dead.

It was dusk, then, when I hit the crashbars and burst through the door into the schoolyard. It was four o'clock in the afternoon, and I was racing because I was late. There were right and wrong times, right and wrong places to be—and at four o'clock, home was right; practicing the piano was righter; and school was the wrongest place of all to be.

I hadn't even zipped my parka. I had books in both hands. Running at top speed I could be home in less than five minutes.

But when I wheeled around the corner, I saw that the schoolyard wasn't empty yet. Fifteen boys, maybe twenty boys, remained in the dying light, all of them bunched in a circle and making an unholy noise, and in spite of myself my feet slowed down, and my interest was hooked, though none of the boys noticed me since all of them were huddled inward, and I stopped.

It was a fight, of course. A fight always took that shape in the schoolyard, a sort of wandering, swollen centipede, a knot of excited boys that shifted ground as the two fighters in the middle maneuvered to and fro.

Or it would be a fight as soon as one of the fighters threw a punch. As long as the circle was moving, the fighters weren't fighting. They were still circling one another, still threatening horrible things to come, still working their bloods up in talk and taunt, each calculating his reputation against the pain of an honest punch, each hoping the other would fold in fear and quit. As long as the boys who formed the ropes of the ring were screaming and still getting madder, it wasn't a fight yet.

I began to walk around the circle, rising on tiptoe, trying to get a view inside. It was cold out here. It would be hot in there. They probably had taken their parkas off, though they would be puffing clouds of steam.

All at once a silence stunned the air, and a gasp went up from the round animal, the boys in a bunch. Someone had thrown a punch. I wanted more badly to see. I put my books down and started toward the circle.

A head popped up and saw me coming. The mouth opened and formed my name, but I couldn't hear it because of a sudden, bloody roaring. The head belonged to a tall kid named Craig, who started immediately to swim through the mob in my direction.

When he broke free, he threw out his arms to stop me.

"Keep it clean," he yelled at me. "Keep it clean!"

What did he mean, *Keep it clean?* I never fought. I had worn glasses from the third grade on. Marcia Jespersen had told everyone that I walked like a girl, and as humiliating as the observation was, she was right. I was intimidated by your casual comments—forget about your boyhood brawls!

But this tall fork, this fool, this Craig who was freckled past any restraint of conscience, whose neck stuck out all bony like a buzzard's—he was absolutely serious. "Keep it clean!" he yelled at me, a genuine wariness in his eye. Why would I want to make it dirty? Unless—

Oh, my poor heart began to go pipping like the rabbit's, and my sight unfocused, and Craig just disappeared.

My brother was in the middle of this ring! That's why the fight was personal. And Craig's friend Hamilton was his adversary; that's why Craig would expose himself to keep me out. Paul was in the fifth grade, Hamilton was in the sixth. My ears and all my head began a buzzing. This was terrible. The world was terrible. What was I going to do if my brother was in a fight?

I thought just nothing in that moment, but walked mechanically toward the circle of boys. Craig danced at my shoulder. I didn't notice. I dropped my parka. Boys began to open a path for me. I scarcely saw their faces: I was suffering a simple dread, and my whole body was another thing. It didn't belong to me.

When the circle parted to the very center, when I saw Jamie Hamilton astride my brother, drawing his right fist back to hit Paul's innocent eyes, I lost all sense, and I exploded.

Jamie Hamilton, Jamie Hamilton, that rat of a greasy face! Hambones, we called him. Ham-'n-eggs, we jeered between ourselves, my brother and I. He called us "Christians," making bathroom sounds in his armpit: "Chrisssssstians!" He lisped the word and meant that we were fairies. He shamed us in public and forced us in private to doubt the value of a faith that caused such wretchedness, such vile disgrace. Jamie Hamilton—O dear Jesus, how we hated him! And he was going to hit my brother?

No, by God! I simply exploded. I ruptured into something new, Defender of Everything, of Faith and Paul and Truth—

I torpedoed Hamilton with the top of my skull, an inglorious launching of myself, and knocked him off my brother and scrambled to my feet before he did; and the instant I saw his pagan face arising from the ground, I cocked my arm and hit it: *Crack!*

There was a distinct, an almost dainty sensation in that *crack* that satisfied my knucklebone and filled me with an inexpressible pleasure. I'd broken his nose. And then it was breathtaking to me, how suddenly and beautifully the blood bloomed all around his mouth. He gurgled. He touched his lip. And then the eyes of Jamie Hamilton went wide with shock when he saw the blood that he brought away.

That fast, the fight was over.

I stood up with a wild sense of well-being. I hardly heard the bubbles of approval the other boys were popping as they made a way for Paul and me. The delayed rush of adrenaline was glory enough for me, true to the Truth till death. Mock me now, O Jamie Hamilton!

We strode home in a grey light, did not run, did not forget our books, did everything exactly right except, perhaps, the meeting of the deadline. We would be very late, of course; but I didn't think it would matter. Not on my shield, but carrying it, I came.

As it turned out, my mother didn't even mention the lateness of our arrival. Nor did she send me downstairs to practice piano. Nor did she so much as interrupt us, Paul and me, when we recounted in epic detail the battle won and done. We were giddy now, who had been noble on the field.

But if she chose to pass over our tardiness, it wasn't because for once the tardiness was right. Rather, she perceived a still more ominous sin in her son, a greater wrong which wanted immediate and exclusive attention.

"So?" I said when my story was finished, grinning, awaiting some reaction from my Lycurgus. Mother was gazing into a fry pan of potatoes, stirring with her right hand, her left hand on her hip. I couldn't read her expression. She had an even brow and a straight nose upon which I focused when she talked, because the talking always dipped the tip of it. From infancy I liked her nose. It is, in fact, the very first memory I have of her, the pelican's wing of sympathy, the eagle's wing of strength.

"So?" I said.

"You fought," she said.

I said, "I did."

"And you think it's finished," she said.

I said, "I do." More finished than ever before with Jamie Hamilton. The night was black outside the window now.

My mother said, "You're wrong."

Wrong. Obdurately, Mother was ethical. "Wrong" did not mean mistaken or inaccurate. "Wrong" was opposed to "right." It meant "unrighteous." It meant there was a sin abroad, and she had the right to right it.

This was not the direction I thought our conversation would take. I gazed at her profile, which was bright from the light on the stove, and said nothing. Her eyes were intent on potatoes.

"You hit Mr. Hamilton," she said.

"Hambones," I said compulsively. "Jamie," I said more properly. And then, more softly, I said, "Yes." That had been, before this spare interrogation, my triumph. Yes. I hit Hamilton.

"And he bled?" she said.

"Mom, I broke his nose! I told you that."

"Don't take a high tone with me, young man," she said. "You hit Mr. Hamilton. Did he bleed?"

"Yes."

"Wash your hands," she said. "Sit. Eat supper. You and Paul will give him time to compose himself."

All my joy began to drain away from me. I felt weak and weaker, even while I looked at the tip of my mother's nose. A heavier duty than battle was emerging in the kitchen, a dead-load duty. The night outside was cold Canadian winter, and black.

"And then you will go to Mr. Hamilton," my mother said. "You will apologize for the injury you gave him—"

"He's a bully!" I cried out. "Mom, he's always mocking us!"

"He is. He does," she said. "What he does doesn't matter. What you do does."

"Oh, Mom! He doesn't deserve apologies. He deserves exactly what he got. Mother, please!"

"But you did not deserve to give it to him. You fought. You hit him. He bled. Period. You will apologize to Mr. Hamilton. This discussion is at an end."

And so were the potatoes, which she took steaming from the stove. And so was the glory I'd earned that afternoon by blunder and luck. And that was the point: it happened once by accident; it would never happen again. Surely I could have enjoyed my spasm of heroism a while before it vanished. Surely I shouldn't have to destroy it myself. What did she know of the troubles we had in school?

I ate no potatoes, none, that night.

Paul and I walked in parkas down Ada Boulevard, down the middle of the street, because there was no sidewalk there. Neither of us said a thing. There was an icy wind come cursing from the river. My face was stiff, my cheeks were numb, immobile from the cold.

These are the things I hated then. I hated mittens, as opposed to gloves, because your hands were rendered infantile, like penguin flippers. I hated the parka hood tied tight around your face, as opposed to a stocking cap, which everyone who had one called a tuque. I hated parkas generally because they bound your body in a bunting, the way we had to wear them, and made a baby of a boy eleven years old. I hated that your lips chapped in the winter if you licked them. I hated that it hadn't snowed. I hated Paul for pie-faced innocence. I hated fried potatoes. I hated school. I hated rules. I hated this, *this!*

The night sky was a wilderness, mute. The stars had no responsibilities.

You could see the insistent flag of your breathing.

Paul blew steam to the moon. I hated that he wasn't hating anything.

We walked round to the side of Hamilton's house, where there was a yellow porch light shining. I rang the doorbell with an impossibly mittened hand.

In a little while the inner door opened with a suck of air. The storm door was opaque with frost. A darker figure on the inside fiddled with the lock, and then it was Hamilton's mother who peered out, clutching her collar at the throat. She had a modern hairdo like Donna Reed. That shocked me. She looked young.

"We hab to talk to Jamie," I said. I could hardly make my mouth work on account of the cold; but my heart ran hot, an ill-fitted pump leaking blood into my chest. I hated the mumble my mouth made of my words. I hated the way I was feeling right that instant: suppli-cating and scared at once. But Mrs. Hamilton prolonged the distress by saying nothing, merely glaring at me from a haughty profile. No, she didn't look young. She looked put-together. Assembled. Like she bought the pieces in a store.

"You're Wally," she said.

I nodded.

"You fractured James's nose today."

I nodded balefully.

Paul twittered, "Broke it," and I hated him for that.

"I hope you have the goodness to thank God for your mother," said Mrs. Hamilton. "Come in."

We entered a warm landing, stairs to the basement in front of us, three steps up to the kitchen on our right. I was dumbfounded at the cleanliness of the house, and the scent of ginger. I thought Hambones lived in filth.

His mother signaled us to stay put. She went in through the kitchen, and we stood with our arms stuck out, a ridiculous backward tilt to our spines as we watched her go. The parkas put a lock on our necks. I looked like a child. But I was ancient and lean and haggard with a wasting hatred. I hated. I simply, with all my hot heart, *hated*—and I wished to God that there was something truly worthy of the rage in me.

My glasses had fogged. I took them off and began to rub them between the thumb and the shapeless mitten-fingers.

Then Jamie Hamilton darkened the kitchen above us. I tipped my swaddled body back to squint at him. I say, In a parka in order to move your head you must arch your entire body. I say, This is the constraint of humiliation. I jammed my glasses on my face.

Hamilton had a neat bandage taped on the bridge of his nose. Too neat. That made me mad. I wished it were an explosion of cotton batting. But there were bright red scallops under either eye. Good. I had done that.

One of my glasses stems had bent to the outside of my parka hood. Unsettled lenses, they tilted my vision. I let it go.

Hamilton, with a thin face, free in his socks and pants and flannel shirt, said, "What," staring down on us.

Through a cold blubber of lip I declared, "Mby mbom says we got to say we're sorry." And I said, "We're sorry."

"What?" said smarmy Hamilton, smiling, delighted. "You're what?"

Now and forever I will remember that in spite of myself, spontaneously, I actually took a posture of repentance. It had been my mother's command, not my own desire, and therefore not truly my own words. Nevertheless, to say *sorry* caused sorrow to be written in my body, so trained was I in the way that I should go. I bowed my head in apology; and that, of course, bent my whole self down before the egregious Hamilton. Servile. In a humble voice I repeated, "Sorry." And my glasses clattered to the floor.

At once, I reached for them—and I uttered a dirty curse.

Even before I straightened again I heard a sound above me, the hiss of a lisping sound. I squinted upward, tilting backward. I saw that the face of Jamie Hamilton had twisted itself into the ghastly mimic of a smile. And he was whispering, barely audibly, "Chrisssssssstian"—

Heavenly Father, hatred soared in me with a sort of jumping jubilation. And I liked it! Oh, I rejoiced in it. Because all at once I'd found the righteous target of all my rage, the thing that deserved my most violent detestations, a thing of such sturdy repute as to stand my anger:

Christianity!

That is how I endured the humiliation of having bowed to Hamilton, of having manifested any weakness in me. I hated religion with an extravagant hatred. From that moment I conceived and cherished dire convictions against the faith of our mothers, holy faith; and I grew a span in mine own eyes; and I survived the sixth grade with my honor intact.

Joe and Selma Chapman—a retired couple, he with a homburg, she with a stole, he with his white shoes, she with the smile of a Rockwell Madonna, both with the presumptive airs of the successful and the childlike air that everyone knows that they're successful—had their own pew at Grace. Four from the front, on the right-hand side, facing Jesus. They sat by the wall.

They hadn't bought the pew, of course, nor paid some sort of pew fee, nor affixed (as have other traditions) plates with their names to the aisle-side crest of the pew. They just always sat there. It was just known, by any whose knowledge was worth a nickel. Perhaps they'd left their scent on the wood.

Nor were they unique at Grace. Many of the faithful honored ritual and tradition by making possession nearly an eleventh commandment—though no one ever spoke of it: *Thou shalt stick to thine own pew.* Or, since commandments generally take a negative turn: *Thou shalt not trespass on thy neighbor's pew.* There was a practicality in this, and a personal gratification as well, because you could come late to worship without fear of lacking a seat. Everyone had remembered you in your absence, had respected your position in the church, had preserved a place for you. *Come up, come up, dear Joe and Selma Chapman, gentlefolk honored among assemblies. See? We've saved your seat for you. Come, though we've begun the feast. Occupy the pew, which is your due.* Something like that. Even so do Christians, or members of Grace at least, relish the trappings of reputation together with a little modest praise.

And it were best unspoken; that's the Christian characteristic of this praise: its modesty, its pious restraint. Pew space does it nicely, doing it mutely. It is simply, silently *known.* And the less that has to be said about it, why, the deeper strikes its root into the community: "These," no one says unto another, because no one has to; everyone knows, "these are people of repute. Give place to them."

Or maybe Christians need the security of custom. Maybe it merely unnerves them to have to take a different perspective on the pastor Sunday after Sunday. Let sightings be as stable as the faith itself. Let worship be as changeless as God. The world is chancy enough. One room at least, and one community, should fit the Christian as familiarly as the hug of her mother, especially when that Christian has grown old and childlike again.

So Joe and Selma had their pew, though no one advertised as much.

And things went well—so long as everybody knew as much.

But what of the stranger, who would surely come to church in ignorance? Ignorance is a test of Christian virtue. Perhaps we should nail nameplates to the pew-wood after all.

Even ten minutes before the service was scheduled to begin, there sat in Joe and Selma's pew a woman of unconscionable beauty—and a kid of doubtful breeding. The kid had an animal gleam in his eye, and canine teeth, I'd bet, if he opened his mouth and grinned. But the woman had eyes that seized my attention and smoldered in my mind as I bustled about the chancel, preparing for worship.

Her eyes had a catlike slant, a natural black line embordering the lid, a shining white and a steadfast penetration as dark as charcoal, lashes as long as luxury. She gazed at me with direct watchfulness. This was a bit disturbing, to be so brazenly stared at by a stranger—as though some question had been asked and I had left it unanswered, but she was waiting, but I didn't know what the question was. And this was the more disturbing, because she was so beautiful; I couldn't shut her out. Her cheekbones formed an aristocratic V, and her mouth was fine, so fine, *re*fined. Nor could I dismiss her gaze as admiration or curiosity. It was neither of those. It had some particular meaning. Some appeal in it.

So—perhaps five minutes to worship—I walked over to the fourth pew and smiled and offered my hand, introducing myself as the pastor. The kid lit up like Christmas. He grinned. He did not have canine incisors, but a row of tiny, separated teeth and a giggle that hinted insanity. My presence, it seemed, electrified him, and he drummed his heels on the pew, two years old. She never removed her eyes from me nor tempered their intensity. But her mouth said that her name was Jolanda Jones, that you spelled Jolanda with a *J*, even though you pronounced it with a *Y*, and that "this here's Smoke," meaning the kid, that his name was Smoke. Her talk surprised me. It was neither beautiful nor aristocratic. It was sheer street, the aggressive rhythms of Lincoln Avenue. I stumbled on that difference between the dark beauty of her eyes and the flat assault of her speech.

After a moment's hesitation I welcomed her and retreated— nothing resolved. I mean, her eyes still asked a question I had not comprehended. And I had neglected to mention that she could, if she wished, take another pew. Or that we had a nursery where children might be more comfortable. Worship began with nothing resolved.

And if Jolanda Jones caused confusion in me, what do you think she did to the other good people of Grace?

Folks stood up to sing the first hymn, directing their attention to the front. But folks, when the hymn was done and they sat down, quickly redirected their attention to one who was slower at sitting, unused to the up-and-downing of Lutheran ritual: to Jolanda Jones. And then their eyes popped open and church got interesting, and I had a difficult time reminding folks that I was there, leading them in confession of their sins.

Not only did Jolanda Jones possess an unreasonable beauty, but she dressed it (so said their eyes) "like Satiday night on Sunday mornin'!" No skirt, no blouse on her. A dress. But even a pants suit would have been more sanctified than such a dress: low in the back (and most of the folks apprised her from the back), loose on the shoulders, utterly missing below the knee, and as tight on the hips as taste on a minister's tongue. She wore a hat. Well, grant her that—she covered her head in church. But this hat swept left from the side of her head and brushed one bare shoulder with a black feather. Black. That hat was a midnight black. The dress, it was resplendent black. And black were the long Egyptian eyes she never removed from me. Devout were some of the eyes on her, and pious were other eyes; but I don't think it was the absolution which I was pronouncing that caused devotion in certain men and piety in certain women.

I do believe Jolanda Jones felt the force of the piety of those eyes, because her fine mouth pinched. But she didn't blink; and her head and her hat, she held them high. And then—just as I rose to the lectern for the reading of the Scripture lessons—Joe and Selma Chapman arrived at church. If opinions regarding our visitor had been mixed before this, they certainly began to harden now.

Selma came up the aisle first. Joe, her gallant, was hanging his homburg in the narthex. He entered at the back of the church, smiling and nodding, receiving quiet greetings from the deacons and such friends as had their pews in the rear. He shook a hand, he patted a shoulder. But when he was halfway to his pew, he raised his eyes and saw a piteous sight: Selma *confounded*.

Poor Selma was literally circling in the aisle like a hopeless satellite, confused, as though the common world had been transfigured and she didn't know where to go. She looked at her pew and found it full. She turned and looked away, reorienting herself to the whole room proper. Then she turned back to her pew again, and behold: it still was full. People were in it. And what a people they were! A mad little boy was grinning straight at her, and an extraordinary woman was *not* looking at her at all.

Selma Chapman uttered an anxious bleat.

Joseph Chapman rushed to the side of his wife. And since no amount of staring could shame Jolanda from the pew, he led poor Selma to seats much closer to the front, patting her shoulder, comforting her, and contemplating this wonder, that the Earth had tilted on a Sunday morning.

Well, and if the Earth had tilted, then it was not unlikely that storms should follow, a shaking of the elements.

When next I stepped into the aisle to preach, mad little Smoke sat bolt upright, excited by the sudden freedoms my freedom offered his own little self.

It was severely noted by folks in the congregation that this woman, whoever she was, put no restraints upon her child—indeed, paid him no mind throughout the entire time that others were trying to worship God. The kid lacked discipline!

Smoke stood up on the pew while I preached. He grinned at me; then all at once he squatted and flung himself into the air. That child sailed into the aisle, landed belly-flop and loudly, then proceeded to swim a sort of breaststroke up the floor in my direction. Giggling insanely at himself. So we had three noises in the church: my preaching, Smoke's fun, and the hennish sound of clucking in the pews.

But Jolanda Jones did not remove her gaze from me. It grew sharper, more intense, increasingly an act of pure, dark will, a burning as beautiful and stinging as a scimitar.

And when the service had run its course and God had received what praise God could under the circumstances; when folks had arisen and filed out of the church (none speaking a criticism to the woman, such restraint also being characteristic of Christian piety); when that woman herself had finally, the last of all, come down the narthex steps with Smoke at her heels, I learned the question of her deep Egyptian eye.

Douglas Lander had been chatting the idle minutes with me. He caused a pleasant sense of ordinary peace whenever he talked, and for the moment I could almost believe that this was a Sunday like any other. Silver stems to the glasses on his filbert face, a mild and mobile smile, the little man had just begun to tell me the story of a childhood friend named William Quinn. Then Jolanda Jones—like the night of cloudless climes—darkened the steps above us, and Douglas's eyebrows twitched upward in a sort of glee.

"One o' them things," he murmured, and he disappeared, leaving the business to me.

"Good morning," I said. "Thank you for visiting—"

I don't think the woman even saw my hand extended. She prized me with her eye and straightway blurted her question:

"Is there a place for me in this church?"

Well, bless my soul! Well—of course. I assured her that of course there was.

She gazed at me.

I scrambled my answer in two directions. That is, I talked about the wideness of God's mercy, that it embraced everyone, everyone; and "God is in this place," I said. At the same time I gave her a brief description of the steps that anyone could take to join the congregation—urging her (as I did everyone) to go slowly over such an important decision. Come back, of course. She ought to come back often in order to learn what sort of community she might be joining, and whether it was compatible, and whether she believed as we did, and so on, and so forth—

Through it all she gazed at me. When I ran out of words, she said, "Is there a place for me 'n' Smoke in this here church?"

I said, "Yes."

I meant it.

But she did not wholly believe me.

Jolanda Jones did come back again. Not immediately. In fact, there was a longish period when we didn't see her at all; and then, when she did return, it wasn't our welcome but a particular urgency in her own life which persuaded her to come. But she came. And she had made changes which proved that the woman had not been unconscious of the feelings of the people of the church. (How courageous, I thought, to come full knowing! How deep her need must be!)

Changes: she dressed, as it were, down to Christian tastes, down to her shins and up to her neck. No hat. And she sat in the very back pew on the right-hand side facing Jesus (the pew the youth took for themselves). And she wore enormous sunglasses, covering a third of her face.

Those glasses declared her presence, to me at least, the instant I turned to face the congregation and the service began—her presence and her difference, both. Jolanda Jones was trying hard to accomplish that whereof she had no previous experience: to hide like a Christian among the Christians. Never mind the heart. Her style was street-slick. Her idiom betrayed her. She was working with a limited language, not learned in any Sunday school. Sunglasses on a Sunday morning, indeed. And the regal nobility of neck and cheekbone, the beauty that ached in the back of the room, displaced her for sure. Those cheekbones hallowed her face like the wings of the seraphim. So if her style demeaned her, making her less than the normal Christian, her natural splendor exalted her above anything Christians could in good conscience call normal and therefore good. Either way the lady lost.

Changes, I said. She had pulled her black hair back in the bun of a Puritan. My heart went out to her.

But other things had not changed. Lo, the maniacal Smoke, her son! He could, it seemed, discharge himself from one pew as well as another. Down the aisle that gleeful child came swimming on his belly while I preached. Goodwill he offered to every grim Christian that sat on either side of him. Noise, noise the baby made, unaffected by judgments he did not feel. What *did* he feel? He felt himself to be a wonderful show. Obviously the kid lacked training, and his mother had no rods at home. And what did the Christians feel? Impotence. Helplessness in the face of such a rising up to play. Or else, by their expressions, constipation.

And this thing too remained unchanged, the question the woman had for me: *Is there a place for me? Is there room for someone like me in your church?*

"Good morning, Jolanda Jones," I said. I was shaking her slender hand. We stood in the tiny narthex. She had waited this time too until she was the last to leave the sanctuary, sitting as silent as midnight behind her blackened glasses, facing forward—and except for a little Smoke, we were alone.

She tipped her head to the side. The angle suggested she was looking at me, contemplating me. The glasses hid her gaze.

She said, "You called my name."

"Spelled with a *J*," I said. "But said with a *Y*. Right?"

A longer look this time. Smoke was pulling on my cincture as though it were a bell cord. I reached down and scratched behind his ears. The woman watched me do this.

Suddenly, "I wanna show you somethin'," she said, and she took off the glasses, gazing at me.

"Oh! I'm sorry," I said. And I was.

The right corner of her brow was angry with swelling. Blood vessels had ruptured in her eyeball, which was a hot, crimson red.

"Jolanda? You hurt yourself?"

"No," she said. "It ain't because I hurt myself." Her language banged against her beauty. But it fit her injury. "I didn't earn it neither," she said. "It was give me."

My voice grew tentative and low. All at once we were entering private territory. "Someone," I said, "hit you?"

"Hit me? Beat me!" she said, almost belligerently.

But her level eyes were asking, *Is there a place for me—?*

I felt an impulse to touch the wound, like a parent taking a child back home. It made her seem so vulnerable. But her tone was metallic, and her beauty too high for me. Her beauty would make my gesture something else. It stopped me.

"Did you see a doctor?" I said.

"Wouldn't do no good," she said, steady-eyed. "As far as this punch, it heals."

"*This* punch, Jolanda?" She was leading me by careful steps into her life. She was choosing each step as we went. The woman was not a fool. "There are other punches then?" I said.

"They been before," she said. "Why not again?"

Is there a place—?

"Jolanda," I said. "Forgive me for asking: who does this to you?"

"Smoke, behave," she said without looking at the child, probing, probing me with her long Egyptian eyes. "Smoke's bad," she said. And then: "My boyfriend."

"Your—?" Perhaps the woman was seeking some encouragement from me, a push from the preacher in obvious directions. Well, then the matter did not seem insoluble. "Just don't go out with him anymore," I said.

"Go out with him? Out with him?" she said. "*In* with him's more like it, Reverend." She paused. "We live together."

"Oh."

Jolanda was probing my face for every twitch, was weighing me in the balance: *Is there a place for someone like me in your church?*

"Your boyfriend," I said. "Beats you—at home."

"When he gets mad at me."

"Can't you—just leave him?"

"Why?"

For heaven's sake! Because he hurts you. Or maybe she was asking how much religion I intended to lay on her situation. I truly didn't know her meaning, because I didn't know Jolanda. And Smoke had hidden himself beneath my alb. And his mother had incredible strengths, the brazen ability to stare me in the eye without a blink of embarrassment. I was fumbling.

"Leave him," I said, "because he hits you. Isn't that the simplest solution?" If you're asking for solutions, that is. Are you?

"Then, how'm I s'posed to feed Smoke?" said Jolanda Jones. "Smoke ain't his baby—"

I'm telling you me, Reverend. The me that's real. Is there room for someone like me—?

"—and it ain't too many men be willin' to put up with Smoke. He do. He give us a place, and we eat. And besides—we live together," she said as though that explained an enormous thing to me. She closed her mouth with a snap, and it looked so self-possessed, so hard, so elegant again.

What do you say to that, Reverend?

"But you showed me the bruise, Jolanda," I whispered. "But you hid it from the other people. Why did you show it to me?"

At first she gave her shoulders the slightest shrug, as though to say, Why not? Street, street: the flip Jolanda Jones.

But then she said, "Somebody—" and her voice caught, and her face grew tight with appeal. She surrendered a tiny gasp. She was suddenly terribly young, and the rest of her words came out in the sad humidity of need: "Somebody oughta know," she said. And for the first time, she dropped her eyes.

"Well," I said, a little breathless: so much she revealed to me; so moved was I by the intimacy and this sudden softness, the dropping of her eyes; at the same time, so stupid, so helpless! "Well, now I know," I said. "But what can I do for you?"

Immediately the street asserted itself. She popped the dark glasses back on, grew erect, and said, "C'me on, Smoke. We gotta go."

"Jolanda," I said, suddenly hasty, "you know that Jesus loves you, don't you?"

"Hey!" she said with a smirk. "Hey, what? Me *and* poor Smoke?"

"Of course, you and Smoke. Of course. This is Jesus."

"So, then." It was her mouth alone. Her eyes were concealed. "Me and Smoke can come to your church."

"Absolutely."

"And ain' nobody here goin' be tarred by that?"

"No."

"Smoke, he's bad. Smoke, he don' bother the people here?"

"No. Well—no. Well, I'll tell you what, Jolanda. Did you know there's a nursery where little kids might feel more at home?"

"C'me on, Smoke. We gotta go."

And she was gone.

Two times. Maybe three times Jolanda Jones appeared in church after that. But the times were widely spaced, and now she left before the worship was over, so we didn't talk. Once Smoke was with her. Other times he was notably, as they say, absent—and I will admit my relief when I saw the mother without the son. Though I liked Smoke, that thick-necked, grinning libertine, that troubler of Israel.

The fact that we had a nursery began to appear in capital letters in the Sunday bulletin. But the fact that people had pews reserved for themselves, and the fact that they were discountenanced when others sat in their pews, were harder facts to publish. Folks started to come early to church. Jolanda had worked a wonder.

For myself, I thought of her sometimes while I sat in my study. I imagined the scenes I'd never seen, the abuse she must be suffering—and the flat sass with which she was capable of meeting that abuse. Even Egyptian Isis could be shrill, could scrap and scream a fury from the street. But I imagined as well the pain that she hid beneath her marvelous hardness, and I grew sorry all over again and miserable for her. What did she mean, "And besides—we live together"? How is living together, all by itself, a hold to *keep* them living together? Jolanda Jones had remarkable strengths. I had experienced them. Then why couldn't she just walk away from an abusive man? I mulled these things in my study late at night, my books forgotten. I didn't understand them. Or her: that godly comeliness, that grit, that yearning need.

Is there a place for me in your church?

Months after he began it, Douglas Lander finished his story about William Quinn.

He and I were standing on a corner of the church property, he with a rake in his hand, I with a small Communion set. I had been feeding the shut-ins bread and wine. He had been mowing the lawn. He pointed toward Governor Street.

"Used to live there when I was comin' up," he said. "Mmmm. Mm-mm, that's goin' on a long, long time ago." The rake handle touched his jaw. "Had a sister. Had a brother. Had three beds in the bedroom. Had a friend."

"Douglas. A man like you, you had just one friend?"

He chuckled. "No," he said. "A friend in the bedroom. It was my mama could cook like a Martha, you know. Oh, she was magic at the stove. And she was liberal. Any somebody under our roof, that body could sit with us and eat. That's where I got my notions for giving food away, you know. From Mama. That's how we lived through the Depression, Lil an' me—never mind we had a flock o' children to feed. When we had the food, we give it away. When our friends had food, we ate. I lay that to Mama. I used to do some waiting in the dining car 'twixt here and St. Louis in the thirties. Ol' Bill Jones, he let me have the extra food, an' I took it home, and we give it away, yessir, yessir—"

Doug Lander leaned on the rake, remembering. This is how he used to talk, a meandering, peaceable journey through a not outrageous world. His memories were always consolations. His sing-song voice disposed me to patience.

"What was I saying?" he said. "Aw yeah. Mama's cooking. Well, William Quinn, he played at my house most the time when we were boys. He only lived—let me see. There. Just over there. But seemed he liked to come to my house after school. So then, he was there when we ate supper. An' Mama said, 'Sit, William Quinn,' an' he did. Eventually he was there for most our suppers. I said, 'William! Look like you live with us.' He got—I remember this—he got a peculiar look on his face, an' he said, 'Why not?'"

Douglas Lander dropped his head and began to laugh. He raked a stroke, laughing. I smiled with him.

"He had a good mama, 's I recall," said Doug. "Wasn't no nastiness in his house. But we walked on over to his house, an' he told his family he wanted to live with us, and no one said no. So he got a pair of pajamas an' his baseball. Three beds in my bedroom. One for me, one for my brother, and from that day on, one for William Quinn. We grew up together. He was a good boy. Mama said she was goin' to graduation as much for William as for me. But I lay it to Mama's cookin', you see. You feed someone, you make him to home. Just one o' them things. . . . Pastor?"

"What?"

"You goin' to answer that?"

"What?"

Douglas chuckled. "I s'pose somebody's got to get the mule's attention first. The telephone's ringin' in your office."

"Oh!" I dashed for the fire escape and my door.

"Reverend?"

"Yes?"

"This the Reverend of the church?"

"Yes."

"Well, I gotta talk to you."

"Okay."

"No, I mean I gotta *talk* to you. What I mean, I gotta come *over* and talk to you."

"Jolanda Jones?"

"It's a problem, see? I need help on a problem. All right? So— can I come?"

"Of course. What—?"

"I mean right now. So. Can I come?"

"Yes, yes, Jolanda, truly. Come. I'll wait for you."

She hung up. There had been the sound of typewriters behind her voice, a mechanical clatter that didn't appreciate the panic in that voice. Wherever she was, she was alone—or so it seemed to me. Lost in systems that felt like forests full of a tangled undergrowth.

She rushed into my office. Douglas, behind her, smiled and closed the door.

"Downtown," she explained. "I walked. Broke m' damn heel. Oh, Lord!"

Suddenly the world was not peaceable. Jolanda's face had lost Egyptian repose. She was trembling when she sat, and she wrung her hands between her knees. I felt in myself her terror. It was genuine fright—but I didn't know why we were afraid together. I'd have to learn the reason piecemeal.

"Jolanda? What's the matter?"

"I ain't no good," she burst out immediately, "and what's going to happen for it is, he's going to beat me. Lord, he's going to beat me next to death, and what can I say? He's right. There's the beginning and the end of it. He's right!"

"Jolanda, who's going to beat you?"

"Him. My boyfriend."

"Why?"

"Because I deserve it."

"Why?"

"And what's gonna happen to Smoke, O Lord? Smoke's got nothing to do with this. He never had. He just is. He's Smoke."

"Jolanda! Why is your boyfriend going to beat you?"

Her eyes flew to mine, now, for the first time. They fixed on me, as though suddenly realizing that I was there. And then she began to shake her head left and right, and the fear that had sharpened her face turned into utter misery, and the poor face melted. "Jesus, Jesus, Jesus," she murmured, "I made such a mess of things, of everything. O Jesus, *I* am the mess—" but she was looking at me "—an' you can do to me what you want, but what about Smoke? It ain't none of it Smoke's own fault."

"Jolanda, talk to me."

"Is there a place for a baby in this church? Won't nobody laugh at Smoke, will they?"

"Jolanda Jones, there is room for both of you, for Smoke and his mother and both of you, yes! But you've got to tell me what's the matter. What happened to you?"

"No," she said, taking a deep, shuddering breath. "Not *to* me. What was done, I done myself. Reverend, I been to the clinic. I had a test. I think I got the VD." Her eyes on mine. The blazing, beautiful eyes beseeching me, and I struggled not to flinch, to give her a calm gaze of my own, untroubled—though I felt full of her trouble in my breast. She was wringing her hands.

"Well, if you do," I said, "they'll diagnose it. And they can cure it too, with penicillin."

"I know, I know," she said. "That ain't it. They made me tell them who I been sleepin' with the last six months. Reverend, I told them, don't you see?"

"Good." I didn't flinch. For her, sleeping around was not at issue. Well, then, Jesus: let it not be an issue for me. There was room—

"*Not* good!" she said. Her poor face twisted at the difficulties between us: how could she make me understand? "*Not* good. My boyfriend ain't had no one but me in all six months, don't you see? He been faithful to me. Me, I been passionate; and I been mad at him, so I went out on him. So I give the clinic the names of all the men. But I give them his name too, you see? Do you see? Reverend, do you see?"

I nodded because I ached for her. Her terror came in black waves over me. But I also shook my head because I didn't see, and I was so sorry for being such a fool.

"They gone *call* the names," she pleaded with me. "All o' the names. His name too. They gone say, 'Come in for a test, 'cause you might have the VD.' They goin' to say, 'Someone you been sleeping with has got it; you got it from her.' When my boyfriend hears that, who do you think that *her* can be? No one but me!"

Jolanda Jones began to cry, her eyes wide open, still beseeching me for something, something, understanding and—something. The tears tripped over her lids and streamed down her face.

But I had absolutely nothing for her, nothing to say. The world she lived in was outrageously complicated, dangerous.

"Reverend," she whispered, "he's goin' to know I got the VD. He's goin' to know I didn't get it from him. He's goin' to know that I been messin' round with other men. He's goin' to kill me. Oh, Jesus, he's goin' to kill me. And—" She paused. She closed her mouth upon this final misery and lowered her eyes and grew terribly still. "An' he's goin' to be right."

There. That was it. That was all of it.

And I had no answer. Silence filled my little study, and blame came down on me. What solutions did I know that she didn't? None. Or what theologies of Western Christianity could speak a comfort to Jolanda Jones in this particular calamity?

Should I tell her she brought it on herself? You pay the piper? The soul that sinneth, it shall—? She had already said that. So what should I say? Call the police?

Oh, Christian! Go and ask the Street about the police. See what sort of force they are for the Joneses. Good or bad, right or wrong, the Street will only use the Man as it has been used by the Man. Contemptibly. She'd never call the police. She had come to me— Jolanda, Jolanda!

Or what should I say? Leave him? I had said that and had run against a block I could not understand.

What could I say? Saying anything just now would be the same as saying nothing, no matter how right or true or good or godly the words I chose. Jolanda Jones was crying. Words were useless. And I, while I sat across from her, was almost crying too. My skin burned with sorrow for her. No, I was no authority. No, I did not feel like a Reverend. Just sorry. Sorry.

I stood up. I closed the space between us. I took her hand. She gave it to me and stood as well. And then I hugged her, and her bones were small, and there wasn't a scrap of sass, not a piece of street inside this woman. She pressed her face into my chest, and she wept. I stroked her shoulder. We were children together.

Jolanda. I am so sorry.

On the following Sunday I hugged her two times more. The second hug lasted several minutes, and the Chapmans, Joe and Selma, ran out of conversation between themselves, so long did they have to wait to shake my hand. They were reduced to a discourteous, hang-faced gawking.

The first hug was Jolanda's too, but only by indirection. In fact, I hugged her son.

For Smoke on that particular Sunday had come to church with his mother. But Smoke knew nothing of calamities. No, Smoke was as cheerful and unperplexed as ever. That buster launched himself, as ever, headlong into the aisle and swam his giggling breaststroke forward while I preached.

When he got to my feet, he began to yank my cincture. He pulled on the hem of my alb. That was okay. I bent down and gathered the scandal in my arms and rose up and continued to preach. For just an instant Smoke was impressed by the view from my height. He gazed at the valley of faces, while faces gazed doubtfully back at Smoke.

But then he started to grin at my cheek, so close to his. And then he made a cork of his thumb and plugged my nose. And then he began to root through my alb, squealing, "Candy? Candy?"

Preaching became a mite more difficult.

I had no candy for Smoke. But (it dawned on me in a celestial rush of knowledge) I did have food.

Smoke and me, we stepped up into the chancel while I continued to preach. We approached the altar of God. We lifted the lid of a silver ciborium and found therein a secret store of wafers of the thinnest quality. Smoke was entranced. I hefted him into the crook of my left arm, and one by one I fed the child the wafers, the Communion host, the only bread I had to hand.

Once, just once, my hungry Smoke said "Crackers" in my ear, and he kissed me for that, and he settled down to a silent, contented munching.

Preaching came easily then.

And who was to blame my raid on the breadbox if it solaced a child and relieved a whole congregation therewithal?

When we hugged in the narthex, Jolanda said, "You don't hate Smoke, then, do you?" and she clung to me a long, long time. Jolanda herself had begun that hug. She made it last a season and a Sunday and a lifetime.

I said, "I don't hate Smoke. I love the fool."

"He ain' bad. He just a puppy," she said. "He'll hush for the hand that feeds him somethin'."

"No, he's not bad," I said. "And neither are you. And I'm getting smarter myself." Egyptian eyes. The tawny skin of the Cheops. A raven hair, a human soul, an embrace of the lightest bones, and an invitation home: "Jesus loves you, Jolanda Jones. Do you know that now? God loves the whole, bewildered, dreary lot of us," I said. "How else would I know that Smoke is a puppy? Feed the fool, you do make him to home. A smart man taught me that," I said.

Mr. Joseph Chapman coughed. His homburg perched tippily on the very top of his balding head. He coughed again. Selma Chapman got his hint before I did. So then the two of them produced a series of declarative coughings together. Smoke perked up and watched them a moment, then cried at the top of his lungs, "Rowf! Rowf!"

The boy had an aptitude for parody.

Three weeks later I heard a terrific banging on my office door—
a kicking, it turned out to be. Nothing feminine about this sum-
mons. Something horsey, aggressive, imperious. I expected an
angry neighbor or—I didn't know what. Not a woman. Certainly
not the regal Jolanda Jones, in the slant of whose eyes met all that's
best of dark and bright—

But there she was, and she was beaming a refulgent joy. It fairly
took my breath away.

"I did it, Reverend!" she declared. "I did *do* it!"

In one arm she held Smoke, wild-eyed and feral as ever, himself
exploding with her happiness. He laughed with his tongue between
his teeth, spraying me.

In the other arm she cradled a portable television set.

"No VD, no phone calls to nobody—an' I left him!" she cried.
"Hey, I left that sucker flat when he wasn't home to see. Took
Smoke. An' I took my own TV!"

Ah, this was news. I myself began to grin.

"So, what I want to know is," Jolanda grew serious suddenly,
almost devout: "could my own church use a TV set?"

1.

I went to the infirmary twice that year.

The second time was for the closing of a three-inch, self-inflicted laceration of the right forearm. There was no doubt, that second time, why I was there. No doubt, no hesitation, little talk, much action. Blood and worry make a certain breed of people lean, and the nurse belied her size with a quick precision and a dash that surprised me. Part of me admired her sudden command, white sanity, and skill. She'd seemed rather a garrulous woman to me the first time I was under her care, grandmotherly and voluminous. But when she saw the red-soaked rag around my arm, and when she unwrapped it and we watched a fresh emergence of blood from the cave in my flesh, why, she grew lean and deft and quiet, and part of me admired her. The other part was bleeding merely and consumed with shame.

But regarding the first time I went to the infirmary: the cause was less clear then.

I was sick, that's sure. But whether in mind or heart or body first, I didn't know.

I needed a respite. I needed, truly, some sort of hibernation from the horrors of a boarding school I did not love and which did not love me—and something broke down in me, and I didn't argue, and I didn't try to be brave. I simply accepted the week away from everything, from classes, the dorm, the refectory, the gym, the chapel, the harrier faces of the other boys, and I slept.

It is certainly possible that my mind was as troubled as my body. I went to the nurse with a valid fever and spunk water in my veins; and yet, as silly as this sounds, I harbored the notion that the root cause of my breakdown was, in fact, a neon sign—a huge red neon advertisement shaped like a star and stuck in the night sky on the north side of the Twenty-Seventh Street viaduct. The Red Star Yeast sign.

I hated that sign. It was never just still. It was devised of a series of concentric stars which lit up in sequence, so that a single star seemed always to be expanding, always contracting, like a gorge, a bolus in the universe, a red mouth trying to vomit. In the center of the star was a clock, likewise lit in red: time made visible, time made loathsome to me, time in a deadbeat regularity, expanding and contracting with an impassive, purposeless power. No boy could argue with such a sign, with lurid time, because it did not acknowledge boys. It just was. When we drove across the Twenty-Seventh Street viaduct, I always saw it ahead of us on the left-hand side, and I couldn't help but watch it swelling, though it oppressed me. This is what made me sick.

Actually (I know this now), I loathed that sign because it heralded my boarding school.

My family was living in Chicago again; but I was attending a prep school for the Lutheran ministry, Concordia, in Milwaukee; I was a stripling adolescent. We would spend perhaps two hours on the road, my parents and I, driving me back to school after a holiday home. We would breach Milwaukee in the evening, cold city lights and houses and taverns—and even yet there might be twenty minutes' solace before Concordia. But when I saw that star I knew the trip was nearly over, and I despaired. I couldn't pretend anymore that we were going somewhere else. The Red Star Yeast sign was the abandonment of hope.

Reality:

In a very few blocks we would be parking at the dormitory, and my father would help me carry luggage to my room on the third floor while my mother waited in the car; and I would be forced to wear a face of tough camaraderie, to pose as though I liked the banter the boys would fling at me, because my father would be grinning, thinking he understood the feckless ways of boys, but I knew better—I knew the spite and the personal scorn behind that banter, and I hated the impostures I was driven to, and I suffered my father's respect for me because I was a fraud, and I feared deeply, deeply the alienation I would feel the moment my parents drove away: the open contempt of my classmates, the loneliness which was my only refuge from contempt, and the black mood, the melancholia, the heart's paralysis—homesickness. My mother would wait in the car: proud of me? Proud of me? And I would return to her with my father. And we would exchange the farewells that nearly killed me, but we would keep them adult, perfunctory; and she would expend her feelings on irrelevant advice, sounding somewhat angry because advice was her cover for emotion. Proud of me? Sick for leaving me. And then they would drive away. And by the time they were crossing the Twenty-Seventh Street viaduct south toward Chicago, I would be in my room, sitting at my desk, the black mood descending, an utterly wretched child staring at a wall upon which I had hung no pictures, shutting my ears to my roommates, determined, despite the monstrous days to come, not to cry.

So. That's the drill. It happened again and again with minor variations. When I was at home for a holiday, I could actually revise reality and invent some legend for myself, some Camelot. I could make my brother think that I was important, my parents think that I was happy—the standard-bearer for the Wangerins on fields of honor (where my father once had gathered glory, and his father before him). But when I saw the Red Star Yeast sign swelling in the black Milwaukee skies, I failed. Illusion fled me. Fact destroyed me: no, I was not worthy at all, but a squalid boy in grievous circumstance, a byword. I despised that sign, that symbol, that clock, that Bumble, that bloody red specter of a boys' school.

There was a horrid hierarchy of power at Concordia, at the bottom of which—

Actually there were two systems of power at Concordia, one official, the other unofficial, unacknowledged, covert, and cruel. Both were alike in being unrelievedly male. Men and boys in loud community together tend less to mercy than to law; and if the law officially is the imposition of reasonable restraints upon disorder, unofficially it is merely brutal.

OFFICIALLY: Each floor in Wunder dormitory—which housed the freshman and sophomore classes—was governed by two proctors, upperclassmen who had the authority to police and to discipline according to campus rules. (The school was hoary with traditions from the German *Gymnasium.* There is much that could be described about its ranks and subordinations of power, order, and authority, the methods and the language for administration of the same. I could write of its curriculum: Latin, German, Greek, theology. I could write of chapel and the inscriptions on the walls above our heads: *Ora et labora, Ad maioram gloriam Dei, Sola fides,* and so on. I could write of the symbolic seating and the customs that prevailed in the refectory, where boys had and knew their places. But none of that is necessary here. One line alone is enough to draw a picture that otherwise repeats itself.)

In the hierarchy above them, the proctors reported to the dean, a square-jawed man with a rumpled face, a gravel voice, ice-blue eyes, and a legendary reputation, Zeus of the thunderbolts. Below them, the proctors had us. They checked to see that the dorm was cleared for chapel, morning and evening. Attendance was compulsory. They examined the cleanliness of our rooms weekly, and daily the meticulous making of our beds. They satisfied themselves, during evening study hours—also compulsory—that we indeed were studying. They could do this without entering our rooms, because each door had a window through which they peered while standing in the hallway. At ten thirty, lights were extinguished and boys were in bed—and again, the proctors used that window for patrolling. I always had difficulty falling asleep. I gazed at that rectangle of light. I saw the silhouette of the proctor hover there and then pass on. I heard the whip-crack of his heels on the cold stone floor. I heard his walking the hallway of Wunder dormitory. I tried to pray.

The proctors had, too, a certain discretion in creating new rules when they saw the need.

Early in the year one of my roommates sat batting a tennis ball against the wall with his racquet, an innocent pastime, I would have assumed. But the proctor appeared and on the spot laid down a law with such force I was astonished. *"Strafarbeit,* Reinking!" he cried.

Perhaps he'd had a bad day. Perhaps he'd had too much of tennis balls and indoor volleying. Even now it seems an outsized punishment—but then it chilled me with wonder: how powerful these proctors were, how stern their measures, and how terribly careful I must be regarding the rules! I sat at my desk, staring, afraid.

"No sports in the dorm, you got that, Reinking?" demanded the proctor, a fellow with a horsey nose which he thrust forward in his anger. "No knocking tennis balls about! No tennis in your rooms! None! That goes for all of you." His gaze included me. "And you, Reinking—you got two hours *Strafarbeit* tomorrow after classes. See me then." *Strafarbeit:* punishment work. The proctor departed.

Reinking's face was red, though his posture swaggered. "What are you lookin' at?" he snapped at me.

"Nothing," I said, dropping my eyes.

"No, nothin'," he mimicked. "You never mess up, do you? You sit at your desk like Matilda. You girl!" My roommates could make that word sound vulgar, a contemptuous length of burp: *Girl!* Reinking said, "You're not so perfect. You'll screw up. You'll get caught with your panties down, swinging racquets the same as me—see if you don't."

"I won't," I said.

"Oh, kiss off, Wangerin." Reinking dismissed me with a gesture. "Kiss off!" he said.

But my righteousness was the one thing I clung to for salvation. I said "I won't" with serious conviction. Not only did I fear the consequences of "screwing up," the disgrace and the punishment, but I also preserved my self-respect and my identity that way—in my own mind at least. I was good, please. I was good. I was innocent and good. The obedience my mother had schooled me in was the one acceptable characteristic that set me apart from the others. It explained with some honor the suffering I endured in this place: Wangerin in the world, yes, he was different. He was good! No, Reinking, I would not screw up. I would maintain my righteousness, even to the heavens.

UNOFFICIALLY: Bigness and age gave power and advantage to certain boys, to upperclassmen generally. Smallness and childishness had few rights and no defenses. Tears were execrable. Cowardice, damnable. Fear excited the blood of your betters.

Therefore keep a passive face when seniors beat the bones of your shoulders with knuckled fists. This was their privilege. Some-one had done it unto them.

"Wangerin! Hey, Wangerin!"

"What?"

"Wanna play a game with us?"

"What game?"

"Tell us which one hits the harder."

So: *Bang!* on the left shoulder. *Bang!* on the right.

"Okay, Wangerin. Who wins? Who's got a swing he can be proud of?"

A tentative pointing: "Him?"

"Hell, what about me?"

"Well—"

"Rematch! Rematch!"

Bang! on the right shoulder. *Bang!* on the left.

And so forth.

But keep a passive face. The best you can do is file it for the future, when your turn will come and you've earned the right of creative cruelty—

But I thought I would never exercise that right, if ever I got so far. I would remember my hurt and my humiliation; the chain of pain would stop with me, in me. Thus the difference between me and these: I would maintain my righteousness to the heavens. I would never bruise the spirit of another human. But these! Even these, the younger students at Concordia, my classmates: were pitiless. I saw them on an autumn afternoon annihilate a man.

Albert Burns was a mild professor of Old Testament who had never learned the expedience of a passive face. Though he was faculty, his status did not protect him because his mildness was read as meekness, and meekness dropped him to the bottom of the unofficial power structure. My classmates held him in contempt. Was he also contemptible? No, not by nature. He was balding; his arms were thick with a gentle hair; his voice was mild; *he* was mild.

But this is the treacherous, frightening fact which I learned that day: that contempt can make a man indeed contemptible. The action calls forth its own validation. Yes, in the end he was a sadly contemptible figure.

"Burns beats his wife."

While Albert Burns was writing on the chalkboard, his back to the class, George Fairchild lowered his mouth into his hands and began a low and rhythmic murmur, barely audible: "Burns beats his wife," he murmured.

Fairchild sat with the *F*s, in alphabetical arrangement, third row from the front. I sat at the back among the *W*s. The only thing behind me was an upright piano. But I could hear George Fairchild. The words had a wizard effect on me, such cool impertinence. "Burns beats his wife."

Like a running fire the music flew around the room. Boy after boy bowed his head as if in concentration, covered his mouth, and chanted: "Burns beats his wife. Burns beats his wife." Dum, da-da-*dum!* (Pause.) Dum, da-da-*dum!* (Pause.)

Albert Burns froze at the chalkboard, listening, his arm held midstroke. There was sunlight from the windows on the left-hand side; it spilled his shadow long and lengthwise on the board. Suddenly he whirled around and whined, "I do not!"

"Burns beats his *wife!*" (Pause.) "Burns beats his *wife!*" (Pause.)

"Do you—" Albert Burns whined against the waves of chanting, "do you know the meaning of Christian love? Jesus loved the people. Jesus never hardened his heart, never hardened his face to the people. Jesus abhorred—"

"Burns beats his *wife!*" Boom! "Burns beats his *wife!*" Boom!

The classroom jumped to the percussive rhythm. Boys were drumming their desks to the chant. It was astonishing to me how directly they looked into Burns's eyes, unflinching, unabashed, in perfect harmony with one another. Many were grinning. George Fairchild had the gift of high, etched eyebrows, skull-close hair, a totally emotionless face. Nothing in that boy. Nothing. Neither remorse nor delight. He was not smiling. He looked indifferent, rather—and I feared him.

"*Burns beats his wife!*" Boom! "*Burns beats his wife!*" Boom!

"This is wrong," cried Albert Burns. "This is sinful! This is disrespectful! It isn't Christian! You're studying to be pastors! Why won't you listen to me? What's the matter with—"

I remember these words. I remember with dead accuracy his efforts at command and self-esteem. The memory is nailed in my mind by the scene that followed: Albert Burns was annihilated.

He cried, "What's the matter with—" and choked on the last word, *with*. His mouth gaped open, fixed that way. For a moment his whole body seemed a statue. But then it looked as though he were physically assaulted by grief. He sucked air through his open mouth. His face twisted and turned a furious red. His brow crept upward, and all at once his eyesight flooded.

Burns walked toward the back of the classroom. I watched him come. He sat on the piano bench behind me, laid his left arm on the keyboard, bowed his head, and wept. The tears soaked into the thick hair of his forearm.

Burns beats his wife!

He was annihilated, brought to nothing. And all by the words of my classmates. Why hadn't he stormed from the room? But he hadn't. And I had learned the lesson (however tiresome this adolescent slander seems to me now) that contempt can cause the man to *be* contemptible. Moreover, I extrapolated: if they could bring down a full-grown man, what could they do to me? Or what were they doing already, more than I knew, more than I was willing to admit? What sort of figure did *I* cut in this place?

There was some pity in me for Albert Burns, crouched at the keyboard, crying. But only some. I was a boy engaged in survival, and I was thunderstruck at the pure power of derision. Had I feared in the past that I might shrink away to nothing? Well, here were people who could do it to me on purpose, who murdered with malice and smiles, without remorse, by scorn alone. Concordia. My boarding school. My gross environment. The world.

And so it was that after the Christmas holidays that year, precisely as my parents drove me across the Twenty-Seventh Street viaduct, I took sick.

I glanced from the window of the car. I saw the Red Star Yeast sign lurid in the night, expanding, contracting around its clock, and I felt a rush of loathing so strong that I began to shiver. After two weeks in Chicago, surrounded by my family and firelight and carols and the New Year's Eve and safety and security, I was returning to the dorm and to Concordia. The star confirmed it.

Just then the musty smell of hops crept in the car. The brewery odor, fermentation, the warm humus of Milwaukee trickled down my throat. I gagged. I vomited bile. I held this acid behind my teeth and swallowed it by bits, quietly, quietly. But here was a symptom the child could not deny. I was sick.

I said nothing to my father, who helped me carry luggage to my room, or to my mother when we said good-bye. But as soon as they left, I went to the infirmary for the first time that year. The nurse received me. She assigned me a bed, and I fell immediately into a fitful sleep. I slept for three days, dreaming.

2.

I grew conscious of a breathing at my left ear, the steady whistling of nostril hair and narrow sinuses. I was waking up. Someone's face was very close to mine. I moved, and the breathing stopped. In a moment it started again. Then I must have dozed some more.

All at once I was wide awake, and I opened my eyes.

There was a boy beside my bed, sitting on a chair and staring at me. For just an instant he seemed lost in thought; but then he realized that I was looking back at him, and he snapped upright. Guilt stung his eyes. He opened his mouth and produced the most curious honking giggle, his eyebrows flipping up and down as if to say, *See? See? What a silly fellow am I!*

"You're awake," he said, clasping his hands. "Good! Do you know how long you've been out? Oh, a long time, a long time. You'd be surprised at how long you've been sleeping!" Even so quickly did the boy's face shake off guilt. Now it was full of tics and wiggles, animation: it was difficult to read which mood was there, since one followed so quickly upon the other, a frown, dismay, a knowing grin. The boy had a larval face, squirming, bedroom-pale with stark black brows. "I guess you're sick, hey? *Honk! Honk!* Not dodging classes, faking it. No one could fake sleep that long—unless you're a marathon faker. *Honk!* Like the man of a thousand faces. Did you see that movie with Lon Chaney? You talk in your sleep, you know that? Listen, you want some tea?"

Tea? What? Who drinks tea?

I must have frowned.

"No, that's okay. I can make it," said the boy, his face a quilt of apologies, solicitation, pride. "I've got my own electric pot and teabags and cups. You want some tea? It's no trouble, really. You want some? I'll make you some."

He hopped up from the chair and bustled to the bedstand next to mine. He lifted a little pot on high, hanging with a rat's tail cord. He winked. "Water," he explained, and bustled from the ward.

He was wearing two-piece pajamas, creased down the pant leg. Apparently he occupied the bed to my left. There were eight beds altogether in the long room, four facing four; but six were tightly made with fat, unwrinkled pillows. We were the only patients. I think it must have been late in the afternoon; a wintry declining light came through the windows on my right. The single door was to my left.

That boy had said something that stuck in my brain, bothering me. What did he say? A menacing thing. It made me feel vulnerable. It made me want to talk with him some more, to question him—

Oh! He said I talked in my sleep! No, I didn't like that, because what was I revealing to someone I didn't know? And it caused a distressful sense of intimacy with this boy, to think that he had heard my dreams, that he had crept into my sleep. I didn't want to be close to anyone at school. I didn't like that.

On the other hand, there's a powerful curiosity about one's own self, something flattering in a conversation that focuses with interest upon one's subconscious self. I wondered what I said in my sleep.

The nurse came in, stout and starched, Grandma Efficiency.

"Horstman told me you woke up," she said. She came to the side of the bed and placed her hand on my forehead, then her knuckles on my cheek. I liked that. She took a thermometer from my bedstand and shook it. "You brought a bug from home, what?" she said. "But we'll put a little broth in you and you'll be right. Under your tongue, Walter."

"Is it all right to drink tea?" I asked. I cleared my throat. My voice was thick with mucus.

"Tea, what? You want tea?"

"Well—no. I mean, I don't mind. He went to make some."

"Who? Horstman?"

"I guess so."

"Daniel Horstman! He thinks the infirmary's his dormitory, poor lad! Tea? It's as good as anything for a starter. Under your tongue."

I allowed the invasion of her thermometer and bit down. The nurse bustled from the ward. Why did it annoy me that tea was as good as anything? Why did I want this boy—Horstman?—to be wrong? I didn't like his presuming things. I wanted to say—not, "I don't want tea," since that would be too bold—but, "The nurse said I can't have tea." That would be protected by the rules, and Horstman would have run foul of the nurse, not me.

But here came Horstman, *slop, slop,* in slippers, dripping water from his teapot.

"It snowed outside while you were sleeping," he said, kneeling down to plug the cord into the wall. "You're Wangerin, right? Tillie told me."

"Tillie?"

"Tillie Pfund. The nurse. You didn't know? I knew. We're in the same class, you and me, different tracks, but you probably know me since most of the guys know me, and now I know you too. Wally Wangerin." He sat down on the edge of his bed, facing me, smiling, frowning, constantly switching expressions.

He had no right to call me Wally.

I turned away from him. I was beginning to feel sick again, a tingling in dry skin.

"You want me to read your temperature?" he said.

I shook my head. Horstman. Horstman. He was right—I had heard of him before. When? And this skinny restlessness of his seemed familiar, but I couldn't remember the context. I had very little conversation with other boys. I would have had to *over*hear his name. Daniel Horstman.

"You want me to plump your pillow?" he said behind me, and then, to my amazement, he reached right over my head with his left arm—so close that I could smell hair tonic—and began to squeeze my pillow between his hands.

This caused a storm of feelings inside me. "Don't!" I cried, shrinking from him. "Don't do that!" Spitting around the thermometer.

"What?"

"Don't. I'm all right."

"What?" said Horstman, his voice suddenly so tiny that I looked at him. His face, too, was tiny. He was pinched right down to a miserable blister. He had snatched his hands behind his back.

I must have shouted at him. In spite of myself, I felt sorry to be cruel to Horstman.

"Now, now, Horstman, let the poor lad rest," said the nurse, returning to the ward. "Here, Walter, let me see that." She took the thermometer from my mouth. "Um-mm. One oh one. Not bad, not bad. But you'll be with us till it's normal. One full day without a fever, and then you go. Rest. Rest. I'll bring you broth and a bit of Jell-O in a while."

She left. She was snow-light and cleanliness. I would have to go to the window and look at the snow outside. I liked snow. I took comfort in the bed of winter and the purging cold. But I wouldn't get up now. I didn't want to give this Horstman some signal for talking after the nurse said, "Let him rest," meaning me.

Horstman.

Was sitting straight up on his bed, staring forward. Pouting, I think. Or else was truly wounded and suffering.

Daniel *Horstman!* Yes! I remembered him!

Several weeks into the fall term there had been a banquet in the refectory, a gathering of students, all strangers in dark suits. There was beef and potatoes and corn, labored, rhetorical speeches—all of it heavy, oppressive to me. I, too, wore a suit and a choking tie. Someone had played the piano during the meal. He played a long, dramatic piece which descended from sweetness to declarative force, then rose to a lush and nearly impossible sweetness again. I had paid attention to that music. I let it make a space for me in the refectory, and I marveled that one so young could play with such dexterity, that he could play all by himself in the corner of the room while no one, apparently, listened, while everyone was talking and eating. That musician had been Daniel Horstman.

The teapot whistled on his bedstand. The boy in bed, pianist's hands in his lap, didn't move.

"Horstman," I said.

"What." He stared straight forward.

"The tea."

"Well, I expect you don't want any."

"The nurse said it's as good as anything for a starter."

"You mean Tillie Pfund."

"Yes."

"You want a cup of my tea, Wally?" He looked at me, such naked appeal breaking his face that I turned my eyes aside, to the wall, to the singing teapot.

"That'll be fine," I said.

"Orange Pekoe?" he said so tentatively—as though Orange Pekoe might be another mistake—that I couldn't tell him I had no idea what Orange Pekoe meant.

I said, "What was the music you played at the banquet in September? What kind of music was that?"

The boy burst with a radiant light. "See? See? I told you most of the guys know me. And that's a reason!" He bounded from bed, unplugged the pot, shook teabags from their packages, and poured steaming water over them in separate cups—all the while grinning with enormous pleasure, frowning clouds of meditation, twisting his face in spasms of worry, grinning again.

He handed me a cup on its saucer. "Rachmaninoff," he said politely.

"What?"

"Rachmaninoff's 'Rhapsody on a Theme by Paganini.' That's what I played at the banquet."

Reinking came to see me in the infirmary. I was shocked. I hadn't even imagined my roommates noticed my absence. That one of them should actually visit me was a charity so unexpected that it flustered me. I blushed and couldn't speak well.

"What," I stuttered. "What are you doing here?"

"Brought you assignments," said Reinking, sizing up the room, the ward. "Somebody had to. Professors are saying, 'Where's Wangerin?' We're saying, 'Who knows? He don't tell us where he goes.' But I figured it out you were sick. How you doing, Wangerin?"

"Not bad. Not bad." I was embarrassed by the intensity of my gratitude. In that instant I loved Bob Reinking—or felt something approaching love, though this athlete, this tennis player with his bowlegs and rolling shoulders would snort and drop to locker-room language if he had the least idea what I felt. *Girl,* he'd say with a distancing sneer. Therefore I struggled for the impassive face, protecting myself, experiencing fear and pleasure all at once. "Tillie Pfund says my temperature is going down. Two days, maybe three days yet."

"Well, it's five days now."

"Wow."

"Freedom, Wangerin. We got freedom without your gloomy puss in the room, criticizing everything."

"Reinking, I don't—"

"Relax. Just joking. You're all right. But he's not—hoo, boy!"

Reinking was referring to Horstman, who had just left the ward.

Horstman had sat bolt upright at my roommate's boisterous entrance, and then had fixed his face toward the far wall, controlling the tics and wiggles with a mighty effort, his lips gone white. Suddenly he'd thrown back the covers, put on his slippers with grave formality, and gone *slop, slop* from the ward. Grim.

"How can you sleep," hissed Reinking, "with that fairy next to you? I'd watch it, Wangerin. I'd keep a careful eye on those greasy hands if I were you," he said, shifting weight from foot to foot.

My stomach constricted at Reinking's opinion. My face strove for slackness, the passive, noncommittal expression, cool unconcern. "Oh yeah?"

"Oh yeah," said Reinking on the balls of his feet. "Why do you think he stays up here all the time?"

"I don't know." Oh no! Guilt by association. But I really am sick, Reinking.

"I don't know either. All I know is, his roommates don't want him flitting round *their* room in the night. I think," leered Reinking, "they make life difficult for him. Ha, ha! I've seen him sit with that stone face on his bed two hours at a time. Ha, ha! Poor Danny Horstman. We don't do you like that, do we, Wangerin?"

By the time Bob Reinking departed, my feelings of gratitude had turned to water and fear.

Then Horstman returned to the room and sat on the side of his bed, staring at me—the same, I thought, as he must have stared while I was sleeping. It unnerved me. I pretended to be reading. But my ears were hot.

"You talked in your sleep last night," said Horstman, staring.

"Hum," I said, reading.

But I felt a rush of anger. To bring up that intimacy now, just now, seemed to me simply perverse.

"You want to know what you said?"

"No."

"You said, 'Look out! Look out!'" said Horstman. "You shouted it. You sounded scared."

"Hum."

"What do you suppose was scaring you, Wally?"

He had no right to call me Wally.

"Do you remember any dreams from last night?"

"Uh-uh."

He had no right to call me Wally, and he had no business in my fears *or* my dreams. This was private. This was the desperate preservation of myself at the boarding school, Concordia. If I cried *Look out* in my sleep, then I was revealing a weakness I wanted no one, no one to know about—least of all Horstman. I didn't want to join my weakness with the weak. And Reinking's opinion—

"Aren't you going to talk to me?" said Horstman coldly, staring at me.

"Well," I said. "I'm reading now, you see—"

"Wally! *Wally! Wally!*" he shrieked.

This jolted me. This was a purely anguished wail. Horstman had actually clasped his hands before his breast in a begging gesture, and his face was swarming with tics of appeal. He stunned me, so blatant was the pleading.

"Wally, talk to me!" he cried. "I'm on an all-campus blackout. I am! I know I am! And what was Reinking doing here? He told you to black me out too. Talk to me!"

Daniel Horstman was suffering—so undisguised a suffering that it frightened me. The reality might have been exaggerated, but not the feeling. This was no hypocrisy. This was uncontrol.

"I don't," I whispered, "I don't know what blackout means."

"Silence!" he cried, jumping up and beginning to pace the middle of the room. "Nobody will talk to me. But I had to do what I had to do. Wally, you're sensitive, you're good. You can see that?"

"Dan, I don't know what you did."

"You don't?" he roared almost angrily, lifting his lip with suspicion. "Then you're the only one."

"I promise you, I don't. I don't know what you're talking about."

He stared at me a while, then dropped his face into his hands. Long fingers. Trembling fingers, and white. He took a deep breath, then threw himself to pacing again and poured forth his miserable story.

On the Tuesday before Thanksgiving, he and a boy named Bucknell—a massive boy, a jock as big as his father; I remembered both the father and the son—had gone to Sherman Park, some distance from campus, and had met a girl there in the night. Bucknell had arranged the meeting. Bucknell had plans.

After some talk, during which Bucknell was running his hand up and down the girl's arm and bumping his body against hers, he invited her into the trees alone with him. "Horstman, you stay here," Bucknell said. "If anyone comes strolling by, you whistle."

"Whistle," Daniel Horstman said to me. "That's exactly what he meant, that I should whistle." He shook his head. "I don't even know how to whistle, but he didn't ask me that. I didn't know what they were going to do."

But what they were doing soon became terribly audible to Horstman. The girl was giggling among the trees. Bucknell was murmuring. Leaves began to crunch. Then came a breathless silence. And then came moans that disemboweled poor Horstman, who realized that he was standing watch for the act of sex.

That's how he characterized it: the act of sex. Horstman was truly miserable as he told me this.

Well, Bucknell came out of the trees alone.

"She's yours," he said to Horstman. "It's your turn now."

Daniel Horstman was unmanned by the thought. He said something formal and inane, like "Thank you, no thank you." And he fled. He literally took to his heels and raced the whole way back to Concordia as though the devil with a blackened tongue were after him. And then he spent Thanksgiving in a moral, emotional tumult.

"What could I do? What could I do?" Daniel Horstman pleaded with me. "What else could I do? Nothing else and still be right. Do you understand that, Wally? Please, please, understand that."

Upon returning to school from the holidays, Horstman had gone to the dean, the square-jawed, crease-faced bull of a dean, and reported the "act of sex" in Sherman Park. He named Bucknell.

Bucknell's father was a Lutheran pastor. And this is why I remember the two of them, father and son: early in December half of Wunder Hall was hanging out the windows, a silent audience of boys' heads, full of awe and watching. We were watching the sidewalk that traveled from the administration building, past the front of the refectory, to the downstairs doors of Wunder. And then we saw them coming, side by side, saw one of them stern as Jehovah, the other abashed and lacking his swagger. Bucknell and his father, coming to get Bucknell's luggage. The boy had been expelled, and I remember waves of sympathy in me for him, because he was walking to the execution. The man beside him looked capable of a great rage.

"You did that," I said.

Horstman nodded. "I didn't know what else to do. I wish I hadn't. But I did."

This boy was thin, not sturdy. This one was pale and twitching with incessant tics, not full of strut as were the jocks. This one, Horstman, was desolated, and I felt something for him too. Pity. A squeamish sort of pity. Not the awful sympathy as for the heroic fall of Bucknell. Pity like worms in my breast, and at the same time irritation that I should have to feel this way—and, at the same time, fear to be so involved. Something about Horstman seemed dangerous to me.

"Daniel," I whispered. I didn't say, *I'm sorry.*

He sat down on the edge of his bed and stared at me. "Wally," he said. "Can I make you a cup of Orange Pekoe tea? You liked the last one, didn't you?"

Poor, pitiful Daniel Horstman. Behold: I was larger than someone else on campus. Someone was according me a sort of stature.

"Yes," I said.

"Good!" cried Horstman, leaping up, grabbing the teapot. "Good! Good! Good! And I'll tell you what. When we get out of here, I'll play you Rachmaninoff's 'Rhapsody', and I'll give you the music if you want it. Good!"

Well. Maybe. Maybe not.

For the rest of that day, Horstman and I talked. Horstman did most of the talking. He distressed me more than he knew by describing his roommates' abuse of him, distressed me because I feared the same for myself—had, in fact, suffered some of the same and hated the reminder. He chattered passionately about his interests, his music, his home where he lived alone with his mother (for whom I felt compassion, wondering whether she knew the reputation her son had on campus—then that made me think of my own mother, and that too distressed me) because his father had died. His hands flew when he talked. He seemed miles past misery, exhilarated, breathless, bursting with goodwill toward me. I kept a wary physical distance. But I did not discourage the talk. Poor, pitiful Daniel Horstman.

He hardly slept that night.

I did. Deeply.

By morning the nurse announced that I was free of fever and would be dismissed the following day, Saturday. I ate a large breakfast.

But then I began to think of returning to my dorm room and classes, and I grew quiet. It wasn't exactly on me yet, but I felt the black mood coming. The fear of the wars, and the weariness of constant shelling. I ate very little lunch. And I made one critical mistake.

"What's the matter?" Horstman said to me, returning compassion and fellowship for all that I had given unto him.

I said, "I don't want to go back"—and instantly regretted saying anything.

Horstman pulled a long and knowing face, as though to say, *I understand,* and, *We two suffer the Philistines together.*

No! We do not suffer together. No, we are different, you and I. I am not like you.

In that same moment Nurse Tillie Pfund pumped into the ward, followed by a student.

"Well," she said. "Here's three of you together, and all from the same class. I approve, what? It helps to keep each other company."

When she left, the student undressed, gazing at the both of us— at Horstman and me—from underneath high, etched eyebrows, from a totally emotionless face. He took a bed opposite and slid between the sheets in shorts. No pajamas. He gazed at us with a sort of effrontery. George Fairchild.

"We were just saying," said Horstman, ticcing geniality all over his face, "how Wally is nervous about going back to his dorm room—"

Oh! My face blazed. From that instant onward I despised Daniel Horstman. I was appalled by his flat stupidity, his outrageous presumption, his destruction of all I had labored for—and I hated him. I would not say another word to him.

And I didn't. I turned my back to him.

Ice came down in the ward. Winter paralyzed the room for the rest of the day.

George Fairchild, his small, nasty mouth, his close-cut hair, said nothing. His nature was to be cold, superior to any whom he met. He was serpentine.

Horstman attempted conversation a little further. I heard him say, "Well, Fairchild. The news is out. You guys sure stuck it to Bertie Burns, *honk, honk*. What did you say? Bertie hits women? Something like that? *Honk, honk*. I heard he broke right down in class—"

But Fairchild never answered.

Horstman tried the topic on me. "You're in that class, aren't you, Wally? You're in the same class with Fairchild. What happened?"

Neither did I answer. Enough damage had been done. I had no idea what Fairchild was thinking this very minute, thinking of me. Neither did I care. I despised Horstman with all my heart. I didn't move. I didn't speak. I was scared. Fairchild was gazing at me.

Burns beats his wife. (Pause.) *Burns beats his wife.* (Pause.)

In a little while Horstman beached himself and stopped talking too. So then it was the icy silence.

I noticed, when the nurse brought us our suppers, that Horstman had assumed the frigid position, sitting upright on his bed, his hands upturned in his lap, staring straight at the wall across from him, his lips bloodless. He didn't once touch the food that Tillie had placed in front of him, nor even look at it, so far as I knew.

Fairchild slept through supper.

I pushed my food around the plate.

We went to sleep in silence. I was getting out tomorrow.

I heard the whistling breath at my left ear. I felt body warmth. Someone was staring at me in my sleep. Someone had his face bare inches from mine.

I opened my eyes. A wintry moonlight cast shadows over everything in the ward; the moonlight on snow is a luminance. I could see Horstman beside me, kneeling at the bedside, staring. His eyes were mica.

"Wally," he whispered. "You awake?"

I looked at him, then turned away.

"Wally, please," he hissed. "Don't black me out. Please. Talk to me."

I said nothing. His breath was sour. His heat was like disease.

"Wally, whatever I did, I'm sorry. What did I do? I'll play the rhapsody for you. Is it Fairchild? We don't have to talk in front of Fairchild. And we can go off campus when we're out of here."

I said nothing. Daniel Horstman seemed incapable of not being intimate. This was horrendous language to use, perilous in a boys' school—like making dates. I set my face like flint.

"Wally," Horstman hissed directly in my ear. "For Jesus' sake! Please, please, please, please, Wally, talk to me!"

He put his hand on my shoulder then, and I rose up in revulsion, the blankets sliding off of me. In deep shadow across the room I saw the face of Fairchild, sitting up in bed and watching us, his cold eyes sunk in two black holes—and a horror shot through me.

"Kiss off, Horstman!" I cried out loud. I pushed him. He stumbled backward and fell to the floor. I shouted with a shaking passion: "Just kiss off! You hear me?"

3.

It had been a heavy snowfall—what? A week ago. The tennis courts had vanished in a smooth depth of two feet; the nets had caused drifts like windbreaks on a Canadian plain. The sidewalks had been shoveled. *Strafarbeit.* I walked between two embankments higher than my knees. The world was white, a windless white; I was assailed by whiteness.

And the air, so crystal cold, was a shock to my nostrils. To all of my features. It seemed to me that my eyeballs contracted in the cold, grew smaller, rounder, more accurate—hard marbles of a flawless glass. For one thing, they ached in the daylight. For another, I was granted in this frozen air a vision of eagle clarity. I could see each individual brick on the face of Wunder dormitory, and the texture of the mortar, and the blue sky to a distance of infinitude, and the very edges of the starched cloud lingering in that sky. I am nearsighted. Clear vision is a miracle. I felt lean in my face, austere, like Anthony in the desert. But the world was white, and the only smudge on the pure, cold atmosphere was my own breathing, which rose from my mouth in clouds.

I truly believe that I walked from the infirmary to the dorm that day with nothing in my brain, no remembering, no old knowledge, nothing. I was merely a record of immediate impressions, reflecting the world around me: white, cold, blue, brick, sky, air, snow. I made elementary deductions: the campus seemed deserted. I was the only figure laboring through the winter stillness. Why was that? Because it was Saturday. The day of my return was everyone's day of liberty, home again or trips downtown or some personal employment or study or recreation. Whatever. Administrative offices were closed. School business stalled on a Saturday. And the holidays were past, of course, the air of expectation gone, replaced by nothing, by the season of ascesis. Winter.

Wunder too was cavernous and empty. Its halls seemed vaulted to me in those days. My steps echoed on the stairs. I was neither happy nor unhappy. Let me see; I carried my books and papers under my left arm, the stuff that Reinking had brought me. The notion flitted through my mind that I might check my mailbox in the administration building. Or else—I hadn't had a decent shower in a week. Whatever. My legs were trembling from three flights of stairs. I was unused to physical exertion.

My room was 314, halfway down the hall.

It was clean. Even through the window, as I unlocked the door, I saw sunshine skimming the tiled floor, beds made to the bounce of a quarter, blankets squared at the corners. Between my bunk and my desk sat all my Christmas luggage, still unopened. I'd forgotten about that. There was a metal packing case, in which laundered clothes would be neatly folded, and a box of Heath toffee bars, which my mother always included as a gift, a surprise (*don't think*

*about that! It'll kill you! Evidence of your mother's love—here—you're
not prepared yet! It'll kill you with pity!*).

I decided I wouldn't unpack the luggage till later. When there was
some noise in the dorm. Some other life. Boys would be returning
in the dusk before supper. They'd switch on a warmer light and shout
or sing. Whatever. I took my coat off and dropped it, feeling rubbery
in my knees.

My room too was deserted. I said it was clean; but Reinking,
whose desk was in the opposite corner from mine, always left some
junk on the floor. He had a constitutional inability to put everything away—like the child who *must* leave two swallows at the
bottom of the glass, four beans, and a bite of meat on the plate.
Like a dog's scent, maybe. Like a signature: mine. Me. I am here.
Or like one stubborn infraction to prove you're not completely
subject to the law: I'm my own man! Boy. Reinking was a boy,
fourteen years old.

I opened his closet. A whole gymnasium of junk fell out of it.
Leather mitts. Plastic shoulder pads. Jerseys. Balls of various sizes
and composition and bounce. A hockey stick, for heaven's sake! Ice
skates. I picked up a tennis ball and bounced it against the door. It
came back to me. I bounced it again, and it came back. I rooted in
Reinking's junk and found his tennis racquet. When I held the
racquet straight up, it just brushed the ceiling. So I swung it
underhand and popped the ball toward the door. When it came
back I hit it again. I was trying to find the "sweet spot" of the
racquet, where, when you hit it right, you feel no torque at all, just
the perfect *thock* of a well-placed ball, no waste of energy. But you
can't swing timidly to find the sweet spot. You have to risk speed
and a solid hit. I swung hard. I caught the ball squarely in the
center of the netting, barely felt the weight of the ball, leveled it
straight toward the door—

—and smashed its window.

I gaped at the thing I had done.

My Savior!—I'd shot that ball dead center in the hallway window, that's what I'd done. I'd punched a raw hole in the window.
The glass had rained outside the door, a tinkling music on the stone
floor, chimes inappropriate to the horror that spouted inside of me.

"Oh no!" I whined. "Oh no!"

Now there was thought. Now my brain was afire with thought. I was wide awake and wild with remembering: *No tennis in the dorm room! None!*

I do not remember dropping the racquet, but I must have.

Thought: that I had done it. Thought: that I had, yes, screwed up! Thought: that I was no better than any iniquitous, leering student on this campus, dear Jesus Christ! Thought: that I was a liar, a liar, in every way a liar, unworthy of my parents' trust in me, a craven, unrighteous, and damnable liar. My work was in ruins, all my goodness gone. And the fact of it all was before me—the shattered window.

It couldn't have been five seconds before I heard a door open and then shut down the hallway. I wasn't alone. I listened to the whip-crack of the shoe heel coming. Thought: that I was about to be caught, accused, and punished.

I broke my stance and ran forward. So little time, so little time. I thrust my right arm through the window hole, shut my eyes, pierced the flesh on a point of glass, then jerked the whole arm sideways. A clean cut. A deep and easy cut.

And then I stood there with my head down, my heart racing to death, awaiting the proctor with my arm through the window as though through a sling.

I was not wrong, and I was not surprised. It was the proctor indeed who came strolling down the hall unhurried. I saw his horsey nose approach the splintered glass, heard his shoes grind glass. He just looked at things without a word. He looked at me.

"I," I offered. "I," I explained with swallowings and sand in my voice. "Tripped."

The proctor nodded, noncommittal.

A flow of blood had sprung from my arm. Corroboration. It encouraged me. There wasn't the slightest sense of pain. In fact, I hadn't considered that there might be pain.

"I ran," I said. I pointed behind me. "I was coming from—"

Lord! There was the tennis racquet, lying in sunlight on the floor. So my story was false in my teeth. But I was a liar, a liar. I told it anyway.

"I ran," I said with hopeless flatness, "sort of in this direction, and tripped on the way. And my hand went through the window—" I just shut up.

Standing on the other side of the door, the proctor took my wrist and turned the arm to see the laceration.

"But it's cut across," he said.

I was bleeding a lattice of blood down the glass, stripes of a running blood all down the wood of the door. That ought to count for something. Punishment. Compassion. I was grateful he chose to talk about the cut and nothing else.

And I wanted dearly to agree with him, whatever he said. "Yes," I said, missing his implication. "The cut's across."

He nodded. Wordlessly he opened the door. I drew my arm away and held it in my left hand. All at once the blood began to embarrass me because it didn't magically stop. It potted the floor, making a mess. It streaked my pants, ran down the toes of my shoes. Wordlessly the proctor pulled a T-shirt from Reinking's junk and wound it round my arm. He put four fingers over the laceration and squeezed so tight I thought this was his anger at me. But wordlessly he walked me down the stairs and out the dorm, along the sidewalk in snow to the infirmary.

By the time we found Tillie Pfund, the T-shirt was soaked, bright as a red bandanna. And I was humiliated to be returning so soon—the second time that year, the same day I had left the place.

"I thought I discharged you," said Tillie Pfund. Then she saw the bleeding and she said no more. She became lean with efficiency and speed.

"Oh!" she murmured when she had unwrapped the T-shirt.

I had done that too—that cut. She said, "Oh," and I was mortified by shame.

But it is required that I record the entire truth—and this story is not true until it's done. One more emotion seized me in that day.

While Tillie Pfund was cleaning the wound, bent close (since I was too embarrassed to tell her she'd find no slivers of glass in there), George Fairchild came and leaned against the doorjamb of the examination room. He watched for a dead five minutes, his lifted eyebrows, his drooping lids, his cold, emotionless face. I spent that five minutes feeling as though I sat on a toilet under scrutiny. I blinked furiously.

But then Fairchild folded his arms across his chest and spoke.

"I guess you know you did it to him, Wangerin," he said.

I didn't understand.

"You did it right and tight," he said. "Danny boy took his teapot. Know what that means?"

I didn't.

"He left," said Fairchild, as impassive as the sky.

"Without permission," Tillie Pfund said to my arm. "Lads are growing too big for their breeches these days."

"I'd say he took off," said Fairchild. "I'd say Horstman's sneaking home this minute. What do you think, Wangerin? You should know," he said. "You are the nemesis of Daniel Horstman, erstwhile student of Concordia."

All at once I felt a rush of a new blood in my face.

Whether or not George Fairchild had the gift of reading human nature, this is the emotion such high talk caused in me: pride. A swelling pride that seemed more healing than medicines. I sat the straighter under Tillie's ministrations. I closed my right hand into a fist, expanding the forearm muscle so that my wound split wide like a red mouth smiling.

For this was the first time Fairchild had ever chosen to speak to me directly. And oh!—with how exalted a language had he acknowledged me!

"Is Jon coming later, then?"

"He's here."

I looked around. No one was there. "Where?"

"In the car with Hannah. He'll bring her when she wakes."

"Or when the people wake her. Or when the service starts."

"Hum."

"I'm going to put a long table in front of the fireplace. Was it a late night, Cheri?"

"Late night all night long."

"You look tired."

"She cried and I nursed her every two hours."

"Are you all right?"

"Hum."

"Did you get a good breakfast, Cheri?"

"Hum."

I should control myself. This mother resisted being mothered.

In wide arcs I dragged a table from the wall to the space in front of a great stone fireplace. The legs bratcheted on the concrete floor, filling the whole picnic shelter with an industrial racket, and Cheri winced. This table would serve as an altar. Cheri spread a bedsheet over it while I moved wooden backless benches around. I arranged them one behind the other in two sections, so they looked like the ribs of a skeleton. I tried not to scrape them on the concrete. Cheri seemed so wan. She put a jug of Mogen David wine on the sheeted table, a chalice, a paten, a tube of wafers. She paused a moment at the tableau, her head tipped to one side, pondering. Gentle Cheri.

I went to the extreme back of the shelter, climbed a chair, and inserted a three-pronged plug into its electrical outlet. *Tappa-tappa-tappa-tappa.* The picnic shelter was enclosed with windows on all four sides; and though the roof was high enough, and though the shelter itself stood in open country some distance from the woods, yet the bodies of the members of Grace would humidify this place uncomfortably. It wasn't well built for breezes. Wherefore the huge, belt-driven fan installed in the back, which turned not fast, but batteringly: *tappa-tappa-tappa-tappa*.

Besides, I wanted the sweet scent of the morning air to greet the people when they came. Dew and green shoots. The fireplace had left a taste of lingering winter, char and cold ash.

"Do you mind if I block the door open?"

"No."

"It won't chill you?"

"No."

"Cheri, are you all right?"

We were preparing the place for the annual picnic of Grace Lutheran Church. And since our picnics, always scheduled on a Sunday, began with worship, we were preparing for worship. Cheri and I were dressed alike, both wearing black shirts with clerical collars; or else you might say we both wore black blouses with clerical collars. Pastor Cheri Johnson. Pastor Walt Wangerin. The ministers of Grace. We shuffled furniture. We gathered old Coke cups from windowsills and paper trash from corners. We pushed brooms and wiped tables and broke ice into a cooler and measured grounds into a coffeepot and chose a board for potluck dishes and generally attended to matters most sacred, as ministers of minor parishes are called to do.

And then the people began to come.

"Mornin', mornin'!"

"Hoo, what a pretty day!"

"Where do y'all want this?"

"Herman, did you bring the softball bats?"

"I told him, you turn at the F.O.P. sign on the highway, but the old boy never listens. He'll be here by the time we eat."

"Kyle, sit! Sit! Sweat this afternoon!"

"*—was blind but now I seeeee*. What? No piano in this place?"

"Pastor Cheri! Where's Hannah?"

Cheri was bowed at a small stove, fingering water in a pot and finding it warm. Now she poured the water into a glass salad bowl.

And now she carried the bowl to a pedestal in front of our makeshift altar. Her face was long and as solemn as an icon.

But I wondered whether her heart wasn't beating harder than normal as she bore the water altarward. I think so. Her face is long by nature, a slender nose, an even brow, a contemplative, slow-blinking eyelid, a nunnish droop to the corner of her mouth: she has a face composed against such excitements as the harder beating of the heart. And she has a long and slender body, calm, unrevealing of heartbeats. Nevertheless, I'll bet she felt a shiver as she set the water on its pedestal—because this water was meant for a baptism.

In this particular worship service, on this particular Sunday morning, Pastor Cheri Johnson was going to baptize her baby, her firstborn child, her Hannah.

'Twas grace that taught my heart to fear—
The skeletal ribs of the benches were ribs no longer, but wonderfully, colorfully, fatly fleshed. We turned Shaker austerity into jambalaya—we black, demonstrative, broad, declamatory people! We sat and sang without piano, without our hymnals, by memory and by faith alone. Grace had gathered. Honey, shut your eyes and open your mouth. Worship had begun.

—and grace my fears relieved—
Herman Thomas Sr. sang leaning forward with both elbows on his knees, his bulk and all his round contentment hanging down between his thighs. This is a peaceable man.

Miz Lillian Lander sang from a position perfectly upright. Her face looked older than when first I met her, yet she needed no back to her bench. Her back was staunch enough. It had borne children into the world, and grandchildren, and great-grandchildren. It had borne me. It had borne the death of Douglas, and bore the memorial of her husband still. Miz Lil had a back like the rod of Moses. And she sang like Miriam.

How precious did that grace appear—

Dee Dee Lawrence, Bridgette Hildreth, Scott Tate, Rena and Michelle Gilbert, the youth of the congregation sprouted at the rear of the shelter like an unmown patch of grass.

Joseph Chapman sang with his chin tucked into his throat, on a deep bass note. Selma smiled rather more than she sang. Jolanda Jones didn't know all the verses of the hymn, but did not mind. Smoke barked like Bowzer in her lap. Tim and Mary and Herman Moore; Margaret Wiley; Linda Hudson, the mother of Kyle; Ken and Debbie Stewart, whose countenances were ethereal with spirit; Aida and James Robnett, Cherokee and Larry Johnson, Elfrieda Churchill, Gloria Ferguson, Harvey Chandler, Rita Cooksey, Sylvia Davis, all the Malones, all the Outlaws, all of the people, a goodly company, a chosen generation, a holy nation: Grace! We sang like the sigh of the dusty stars of heaven.

And Jon, the husband of Cheri—he sang softly in the ear of baby Hannah, whose head was like a wheel of cheese, who had a birthmark in the middle of her forehead, who was this morning to be baptized in the midst of the congregation.

—*the hour I first believed.*

When the hymn was done and the people focused forward, Pastor Cheri moved to the altar, and we proceeded through the familiar ritual, the worship that named and shaped us.

We prayed.

She said, "Let the people say—"

And the people said, "—Amen."

We read three lessons from the Holy Scripture, from Genesis, from the Epistle to the Romans, and a portion from the Gospel according to St. Matthew.

Quietly, Cheri said, "The Gospel of the Lord."

The people turned a country shelter into holiness. They answered, "Praise to you, O Christ."

We sang again.

I rose and preached. The people listened, laughed and frowned and blinked and listened.

We gathered an offering. ("Kyle, what did I tell you before?")

We sang. We know how to sing.

And then (was Cheri's heartbeat faster than usual?) Pastor Cheri walked to the pedestal, its bowl and its waiting water. Wraithlike, her face. Pale, it seemed to me. Solemn below the cheekbones.

"In Holy Baptism," said Pastor Cheri Johnson, mother of the infant, "our gracious heavenly Father liberates us from sin and death by joining us to the death and resurrection of our Lord Jesus Christ—"

So the Rite of Baptism had begun.

Jon was gazing steadfastly forward. Baby Hannah raised her wobbly head and rolled her eyes to the left and the right. Maybe she was trying to find the source of her mother's voice. A host of people in her vicinity noticed the motion and turned smitten smiles upon the child.

"We are born children of a fallen humanity," said Cheri. "In the waters of Baptism we are reborn children of God, inheritors of eternal life—"

She spoke softly, formally. One could hear the click of her saliva. Perhaps her tongue was dry and tacky on the roof of her mouth.

At the appropriate moment, Jon stood. Hannah was presented—blinking over the people—as the one to receive this imminent baptism.

Cheri acknowledged the presentation by a single nod. The two of them might have been strangers.

Cheri prayed a long prayer regarding waters. "And let the people say—"

The people said, "—Amen."

And then the child came forward. And the father. And the sponsors of the child. All of the sponsors. A munificence of sponsors. Thirteen! They decimated the congregation, leaving gaps on the benches. Jon and Cheri, generally restrained in their behavior, had been prodigal in planning Hannah's baptism, bestowing on their daughter more godparents than Jesus had disciples: young and old, male and female, black and white. Sponsors surrounded the pedestal in front of the altar. Sponsors hid from view the bowl, the baby, and the mother-pastor, Cheri.

So I heard, thereafter, what I couldn't see.

I heard Cheri's voice arise from the tight wall of bodies: "Do you believe in God the Father?" The congregation responded with the creed; the whole body of people confessed belief with tiny Hannah, whom they couldn't see. "Do you believe in Jesus Christ?" said Cheri. "Do you believe in God the Holy Spirit?" Yes, yes, they did. We did.

There was a pause. I imagined someone shifting the weight of the baby, gingerly holding her head above the water. I imagined that Cheri dipped her own slender hand into the water. And I must have been right, because she began the formula for the baptism itself.

Cheri said, "Hannah, I—"

But she paused there. She stopped right there. All she had said was "Hannah, I—" and she stopped.

We waited for the next words. We all knew the next words, so it felt like leaning forward midstride: *baptize you in the name of—*

But she'd only said, "Hannah, I—"

A silence can last a while unquestioned, but only a while. In the middle of a ritual, that is a very short while. But this silence continued, and I became aware of the fan in the back of the shelter, chattering foolishly, *tappa-tappa-tappa-tappa.*

What was the matter? I stared at the close knot of bodies around the stalled sacrament. None of them were moving. Cheri? I glanced toward the congregation. Herman Thomas, his experience slung low between his legs, smiled back at me and shrugged. He didn't know, *tappa-tappa-tappa;* but he was content to wait. Miz Lil gazed straight forward, too wise to worry what she couldn't see, blessed with an endless patience. But the youth in the back of the room were like me, awake to the silence and frowning, halfway standing to see, and seeing nothing but sponsors. *Tappa-tappa.*

I began to feel excessive urges of leadership, that I should do something, walk over and cut through the crowd and learn the trouble and correct it. Do something. I grew very uncomfortable. All she had said was, *Hannah, I—*

Cheri! What is the matter?—

Just then she spoke. I heard her voice rise up. The words were exactly the same, but her tone was different, stricken.

"Hannah," Cheri said. She had to fight to pronounce the word. It came through a constricted throat, and when it did come it was tiny as a wren, a piteous peeping.

"Hannah," she squeaked, "I baptize you in the name of the Father—"

Oh, Cheri! I understood.

She was crying.

Pastor Cheri had stopped to cry. Mother Cheri could not talk for a while because she was weeping over the baptism of her baby.

All at once I saw her—as if there were no sponsors between us at all. I saw her, crimson-cheeked and moist, her hand below her baby, her hand still sunken in the water, but her face split open with its love above the child.

Of *course* Cheri would be crying. She loved this infant whom she washed. It was hers, hers, the bursting and the blood of her own body—Cheri's. Of course she would weep at Hannah's second birth. Cheri knew birthing. She had birthed the baby the first time, and she was not ignorant of the meaning now.

Again—I saw her as if there was nothing between us, neither sponsors nor space nor time. I saw in detail that first birthing of the baby Hannah, for Cheri had entrusted me with the experience.

I saw the bedroom.

Cheri had delivered Hannah at home. She and Jon had been guided by the ministrations of a midwife. But the labor was long, and she told me that she suffered uncertainty at how the baby ought to come. She didn't know what position she should take to accomplish this holy thing.

For a long while she leaned on Jon, and they walked up and down the bedroom. The contractions made a monument of her belly, hard and hard and heavy. She groaned.

Then she kneeled at the side of the bed, like a girl-child in prayer; but the position didn't feel right.

She climbed on the bed. She lay on her back, panting and gasping her breath. The baby was coming, oh! She brought her knees up. Where do the pillows go? No, this wasn't right either. Too low. Not all of herself was in the thing. Restless, rearing Cheri! Laboring mother, trying hard in all things to be right and right for the sake of the baby—and the baby was coming.

Suddenly (so she told me and I saw it) she rose up on her knees on the bed, her knees apart to make a space for the life inside, sheets below to receive it: and she pushed down, she bowed down with all her might, and this is the way the baby was delivered. This was right. Milkweed splits its pod to send its seed adrift. Cheri burst her womb. Hannah slipped headfirst into the world. Hannah was born through the tearing pain of her mother, in a rain of Cheri's blood, but the mother never considered the pain impossible nor the blood wrong. Blood, then: blood had bathed this baby first!

And now the water of baptizing.

Which was a sort of sacred blood, washing Hannah whiter than snow.

Hannah, I—

Of course this mother would weep at the baptism of her child, her heart. She was weeping in gladness for her beloved, whom she loved not merely in sentiment, but in most holy doing, with her bones and her blood and her muscle, her womb and her suffering. She was weeping in knowledge—for this was a birth that no one could snatch away from Hannah, a life forever; and this time no one suffered pain but the Savior, no one bled but the Christ; but Cheri knew what sort of pain that was.

Of course she would cry. Me too. Herman Thomas too, and Jolanda Jones, and Dee Dee Lawrence. And Miz Lil. We turned shining eyes on one another and grinned and began to cry with mother Cheri, Pastor Cheri: *Hannah, I baptize you in the name of the—*

But again, again—I saw Cheri as if there was nothing between us, neither time nor space nor flesh nor worlds, and I recognized in that same moment a most celestial thing:

That *I* was the baby Hannah.

That Cheri was the figure of my God, and God was weeping.

And this is what my heart sang: Holy God, how you have mothered me!

For the crying voice of Reverend Cheri Johnson was precious, was the voice of the Holy One, *bath qôl,* daughter of the voice— of God! Divine the words that she uttered at this second birthing: she was the authority of the love of God, effectual and effectually there. Oh, this was no metaphor nor some image of my mind. This was sacred fact, present and immediate—and I saw how the weeping God had birthed me.

I saw the restless God, pacing and pacing the empyrean, suffering the contractions of my bulking incompletion, my unborn presence, suffering in the deeps and the very elements of uncreated being. I saw God searching for and finally finding the holiest, most merciful posture for bringing me to birth—

I saw the mighty God kneel down.

God knelt in utter humility for a tender parturition, tender to me, hurtful to the tender parts of God. God sank into this world, humble to all of the laws, bowed down to all of its pain. The Word became a flesh that could bleed a human blood.

And having knelt, God groaned and bore me my second time. In pain. I was born in a rain of godly blood: blood that I had caused, for I burst my God, the brow and the palms and the heart of God, in order to be born; but blood my God did not begrudge me, for this was the very life of God upon me. Wash me! Wash me clean.

And even now the maternal God remembers my delivery. I am not lost in the multitude. What mother does not remember the single deliverance of every single child she bore? What mother doesn't whisper the baby's name, remembering? So God loves me and calls me by my name.

At my own baptism, did my mother weep? Did the dear God weep when my human father, then my pastor, baptized me in Vanport, Oregon? And were the waters that washed me, head and soul, perhaps the tears of God? Is that the virtue of those waters?

So much that has fallen between that time and this—the sickness of my youth, the rude cure of my congregation, the hyssop of Grace—so much has been a cause for weeping.

Do you weep for me even now, my God, my God?

Tappa-tappa-tappa-tappa. The fan turns neither faster nor slower but louder, filling another pause in the picnic shelter. Cheri is at the long table, our makeshift altar, where I can see her now. Wan. The woman is, yes, plain and pale as a medieval saint, her nose and her whole face elongated, her body spare and unadorned. But that baby of hers is fat. Hannah is full of a sweet juice, as swollen as some imperial strawberry: rub her, and you rub the red a little redder. Pinch her, she will burst, ho-ho!

And the morning scent has filled this place. Green is the color of the smells. We know nothing of ascesces. Grace surrounds wan Cheri with abundance. Fat baby, a fatter congregation, a morning of fatness—I am smiling.

With the tips of her fingers Cheri is touching the birthmark on Hannah's forehead, drawing two lines there while all the congregation stands and waits and watches: *tappa-tappa-tappa.*

Pastor Cheri breaks the silence. She says, "Hannah, child of God, you have been sealed by the Holy Spirit and marked with the cross of Christ forever."

The people nod. Yes, Grace approves. Yes: Grace agrees.

"HE NEVER LEARNED TO drive a car, you know," Miz Lillian tells me, rocking and rocking into darkness. Neither of us minds the darkness. We welcome it, rather. And she isn't looking at me anyway. She doesn't need the light to see.

"He walked," she says. One arm is tight to the arm of her rocking chair. The other is too; but sometimes it steals to her stomach. These memories seem the lading of her womb. She is old. Miz Lil has grown so old.

"He always wanted to walk. Well, and he loved to talk, is the reason. He would talk with anyone he met, dollar-proud or penniless. I hated to send him for something I needed right now, because it didn't matter how much I hurried or harried him, Douglas would always take time to stop and talk to people. Oh, Pastor," she says in a faint, most feminine sigh. "Oh, Pastor."

I sit in the dying light of her living room, recalling her husband. My sight has settled on the dim lines of her face, the rising lids beneath her eyes which seem to float her vision upward. But her conversation is a powerful agent for remembering, and I see Douglas. I see the man in the post office exactly as I saw him waiting in line when I rushed through the door—Douglas, nodding at me as if my arrival were the very reason he'd traveled so many miles from home. I remember how he sang me to a standstill then, the temples of his silver glasses flashing, all the time in the world for his judgeless observations: *Just one o' them things.*

Even today I will sometimes think I see him standing on the sidewalk, talking; and I'll want to beep as I drive by. I don't, of course. That's sad.

Douglas Lander is dead. Miz Lil is in the rocking chair and riding into darkness, remembering him. And I—of all the children of God, I am most favored. For I came to her house prepared to minister to the woman with prayer and Holy Communion; but then she interrupted mine with a ministry of her own. Gently, almost imperceptibly in the creeping evening, she has laid aside reserve and invited me into her privacies further than ever before, further than my deserving.

The wafer between us and the tiny vial of wine are sinking into darkness. All the furniture, the forests of her photographs, the form of the woman herself are growing obscure. One line of moonlight rims her cheekbone, but she is black in blackness: Africa touched by a twilight. Africa descending.

Her voice is real. And the cricking of her chair—these things are real before me, undiminished.

"But he always came home," she says. "Late, untroubled, he always walked into the house again. He hung his hat with me. I never disputed his habits, no. Seems we never had cause to argue. Seems we just got along.

"'Lil,' he said one evening, 'where is that pie you baked for supper?' I said, 'It's in the kitchen, Doug.' He said, 'I think I'll have some more of that pie'—"

Miz Lil pauses a moment. The rocking ceases. "What *was* that pie?" she whispers. "Mm! Why can't I remember what kind of pie that was?"

I think that it would be nice if I could help her, but I can't. I say nothing. Her effort, her blackness swell into the room. Warm.

"I was resting on the sofa, you know," she says, "where you're sitting. Douglas was watching the television from his chair. Well, and the sound of the television always makes me sleepy. I heard him go into the kitchen and open a drawer, for a fork, I suppose—but then I must have dozed a little.

"I woke up suddenly. It wasn't any noise that woke me up. I didn't hear anything at all. That's what woke me. The quiet. I don't know how to explain it. There was such a peculiar quiet in the house, there was such a stillness on my body like I never felt before—but I felt it now.

"Douglas was lying on the floor, perfectly still. I saw the piece of pie on the arm of his chair, partly eaten, and the fork was there. He must've gotten up and was coming to tell me something; but the house was quiet now, so quiet. I can't explain that feeling to you. Between the chair and the sofa Douglas just lay down and died. I was dozing while he did that."

The living room is full of the darkness now. Miz Lil is rocking again: *crick, crick, crick.* Her shoulder keeps catching a patch of moonlight, then dropping it. *Crick, crick.* I can hear another, softer sound as well, an almost inaudible whispering of fabric—ah. She is rubbing her stomach.

"He always came back, you know," she says. "When he worked for the L & N Railroad in the dining car—it took him all the way to St. Louis, but he came back. When he worked at the Vulcan Plow Works during the Depression, he came back. I used to pack a picnic basket and carry the children on over to Sunset Park, and even if we started to eat without him, well, he would come from work. We would enjoy the scenery and then walk home and get there by bedtime. He always came back, Douglas did, always untroubled.

"But he hasn't come back this time.

"And he's left an ache like stone in my stomach.

"Pastor, the aching is always, always there."

Miz Lil falls silent.

And I draw in that same instant a breath of such startled recognition that I shudder and the breath goes out in a groan. She uses elemental images, Miz Lillian does. My hand steals to my own stomach. I recognize her stone.

Miz Lillian says, "I've gotten used to the ache by now. It's all right. It's all right. I call it a friend to me. This aching reminds me all the time of Douglas. Mm. There is a gravestone in Oak Hill Cemetery, on his grave, you know. But it's a sort of a stone in me too. The children and everyone else can mourn by that stone at Oak Hill. This one is mine. The widow's stone."

Crick, crick, crick. She rocks. She rides a gentle memory deeper into darkness.

"The doctor keeps telling me that he wants to operate on my heart," she says. "They always said that I had a poor heart, even before Douglas died. Well, and I do get tired these days, and I have to lie down more often than not. But I keep telling the doctor I don't want no cutting, I don't need no cutting. I can leave this way as well as another. Douglas and me, we got no debts."

The rocking stops. Moonlight shows me her shoulder.

"Pastor?"

"What?"

"Is something wrong?"

I lift my hands, but the darkness hides them. "No, nothing," I say.

There is a little pause before the rocking begins again, and a longer pause for rocking.

"Douglas loved to fish," she says. *Crick, crick.* "He and his friends, you know. He sometimes get a nice catch of cat fiddlers and bring them home, or blue gill, or else buffalo, we call them. Sometimes he had fisherman's luck. Cyrus Garner, George Warren, Charles Hildreth, Harlan Lee—these were some of his fishing buddies, most of them dead now. Pastor?" She has stopped rocking. I think she is leaning forward. "Pastor? Does my remembering worry you?"

"What? No, it doesn't worry me."

She waits a moment in perfect silence. Yes, she is leaning forward: the moonlight makes a doily on the backrest of her rocker, and her dark head makes the moonlight crescent. She's peering at me.

"Pastor?"

"Yes?"

"You're crying."

"Ah, Miz Lil!"

I am. I'm crying, though I hardly realized it. These are easy, easy, relieving tears, altogether right in the presence of this woman, no noise whatsoever. I haven't sobbed. I've only allowed my tears their freedom. Then how can Miz Lil—?

"You," she whispers carefully, "loved Douglas too."

"I did. I do. I do."

"You've come to share the sorrow with me."

"I would take it from you, if I could."

"I cry sometimes even now," she whispers, still leaning forward, her head a black eclipse of the moonlight. "Alone," she whispers. "In my bed at two of a morning. Always alone."

I hear the soft rustle of fabric. Suddenly her hand is on my knee.

"Pastor, why are you crying?"

And as suddenly the truth slips from me: "Because you're talking with me."

"Oh, Pastor."

For just a moment the darkness in Lillian Landers's living room is an amnesty, and it doesn't matter that I speak with appeal, like a child and not like a pastor. "Is God," I plead, "Miz Lil—is God smiling? Sometimes he's frowning, and sometimes he's smiling. Is he smiling on me now?"

Long, long the silence extends between us while the woman must be peering at me. Fox eyes. The moonlight has slid left to the edge of her chair. Then her hand begins to pat my knee—but the patting comes strangely, as though in spasms. And then Miz Lil produces a high, tiny squeek in her throat. And then it is no squeek at all, but an unmistakable giggle. The old woman is giggling. She clutches my knee.

"Pastor! I'm sorry, Pastor," she giggles right merrily. "You make such a pitiful picture. You mean Marie. You mean skinny Marie, don't you? You've been meditating on Marie all these years? Ever since you shut her little water off? Hee hee! I'm sorry. Hee hee! That's a long time to be sitting on the pity-pot. Hee hee hee!"

Miz Lil is trying very hard to control the sudden hilarity in her throat, or else to make it respectful. She fails both ways. She wants to toss her head with the laughter. Instead she grabs both of my hands in her own and squeezes them.

"But Marie is renting in Sweetser now," she cries. "And God quit frowning long before you quit messing up. And me, I just forgot it. Pastor!" Miz Lil is shaking, full of apology, full of delight at once. It's a devastating combination, and I start chuckling too, a rougher sort of chuckle. "Oh, my Pastor!" she squeeks. "What a terrible waste of devotion! I expect you were the only one remembering. Hum! Hee! Hee hee hee hee—"

Miz Lillian purely enjoys the joke a while. She lifts our hands up as though to make a bridge for someone to pass beneath them, as though she is showing something off. She raises our hands in a high jubilation, then drops them and slumps backward in the rocking chair.

"Hooooooo," she sighs. "Hoo, that feels so good."

And then the silence returns. Silence comes down upon us like (I say) a double portion of the Spirit—and with the silence, the mantle on the shoulders of the ancient prophetess.

Crick, crick, crick. Miz Lil is rocking again. The moon has fallen to a pool on the floor. No: the moon has arisen.

"Douglas," she says, "he knew a Jewish man that owned a coal company. He'd fill our basement with coal. If Doug had the money to pay him, it was all right. If not, he accepted whatever money on Doug's terms. I'm talking about the Depression, you know. It was good people everywhere in those days." *Crick, crick, crick.* "Well, and the people in charge of the West Haven Gun Club—they hired Douglas to serve parties. They would bring him home and also bring all kinds of good food too.

"He always came back, Pastor. I think about that. Maybe late, but never troubled," she murmurs, rocking and riding her memory home. "He hung his hat with me."

Crick, crick.

THE CHRONICLES OF GRACE: AN AFTERWORD

OF THE THREE BOOKS in this volume, I distinguish the third, this *Miz Lil,* from the other two.

Ragman and *Little Lamb* are each a collection of pieces (essays, stories, poetry) assembled around certain loose themes. *Ragman* pays its greatest attention to Christ and the Church. *Little Lamb* considers the family in all its ages, infancy to old age, and all the relationships between these extremes. I was not haphazard in the arrangement of the pieces in either book: rhythm, pacing, color, mood, effect, genre, and the dramatic sequence of things all governed my choices and the final arrangements. Yet, almost any *individual* piece could stand on its own. I would rather that people read *Ragman* and *Little Lamb* from first to last, according to the order I chose for them; but the reader can make sense of it all by picking and choosing until the whole has been read.

Miz Lil, however, is a different matter altogether. Here is a life in a little; a spiritual life, mostly; my life, though the particulars of one man's experience become, in such a work as this, universals for every reader.

Miz Lil is not a collection of short stories merely. It must be seen as an artistic unit, every story affecting every other story as the threads of a spider's web join together in a geometric whole; and all the stories are here arranged to honor change and growth and maturation. They are photographs, complex and sharply focused, of crucial junctures in a life that moves from innocence to culpability, and from culpability to a palpable knowledge of God's grace. Let the stories, therefore, be considered *almost* as the chapters of a novel—though not quite that, since I have kept for each the motion, the climax, the sense of a story. Such story-chapters, then, can appear out of chronological order, creating their own order; and the times between each juncture in this writer's "life" need no telling; and the narrative demand for thousands of details conjoining the times and the chapters is simply skipped. Theme, therefore, and image, character and the present moment intensely told bulk larger in the reader's imagination, allowing his and her mind to reach—personally—for the deeper joins between the chapters which are stories.

And here is how the book has been arranged indeed: to move forward with two sets of stories, one set showing the child's "life" from birth to adolescence, the other showing the man's ministerial "life" from its weak beginning even unto his discovery of God again and grace.

But each set takes a contrasting direction to the other. The boy, bit by bit, loses his shining innocence and by the end has entered into a self-preservative sinning. The pastor, on the other hand, finally exchanges his sinful attitude for one of community, and communion with God *through* the community.

Lay these two patterns side by side with their opposing directions (the boy, as it were, descending; the pastor ascending) and you have the form with which I bind the book and all its insights together: it is called a *chiasmus,* from the Greek letter *chi,* which looks like an X. Now—visually lengthen the X as if you could pull it left and right like taffy, and you "see" the shape of *Miz Lil:* a cross, a crossing, for the boy's track and the man's cross one another in this book—even as I believe our true lives and our vaster experiences continue to form such crosses: for, in a sacred manner, we *are* rising and falling both at once, till heaven intervene; and rather than time's shaping the truth of ourselves, why, this pattern of nearness and distance from God, from truth, from one another, from ourselves, actually shapes *time* as though the chronology of external realities were a plastic thing. Our inner life must ultimately be recognized as the authentic life. It cannot lie or dissemble. It cannot be groomed as one's face and hair, nor dressed in clothing that conceals.

And, deeply, quietly, this *chiasmus* has delighted me ever since the publication of *Miz Lil and the Chronicles of Grace,* for its very shape declares the intrusions of grace and the renewal of our souls: it is the absurdest act of God, the bumfuzzlement of reasonable people, the foolishness of those who make public their faith in Holy Inanities. It is the cross and crossing of the Christ.

Read this book for the experience alone. And then read, within yourself, the experiences *Miz Lil* has caused for you. Watch for the themes of growth: how truth is discovered and then communicated among us; how the artist begins and develops, and what society thinks of that; the crucial role of communities; sacramental meanings, baptism in particular, and the wonderful conveyance of the sacred by means of the common.

Indeed, there is a great weaving of many themes regarding the growth of peculiar individuals.

And at the same time this book chronicles in all of its parts but one theme: Grace. Here are twelve and thirteen acts in the pageant of the good Lord's grace.

Which theme, all rounded out in fullness, cannot end in a physical death. For spiritual deaths occur over and over again. But a genuine chronicle of grace can end nowhere else but in contentment.

Crick, crick.

Walter Wangerin
August 2, 2002

A SAINT'S TALE FOR MODERN READERS!

SAINT JULIAN
A NOVEL

WALTER WANGERIN JR.

A stunning spiritual tale about the life of the legendary Saint Julian, who as a cruel hunter in his youth is doomed to a tragic fate, but only through a lifelong learning to perform acts of charity and kindness does he find redemption in his encounter with Christ himself.

In this spiritual allegory, the young knight Julian is an avid—even voracious—hunter and sportsman. But his thrill at taking the lives of his prey becomes an obsession until he one day confronts a mystical deer that prophesies that Julian will murder his own parents. Terrified, Julian travels across the world to make a home for himself as far from his parents as possible. As fate has it, his parents search for him and his wife takes them into Julian's castle and lets them sleep in the master bedroom. Julian returns late at night, enters the bedroom, and thinking he has found his wife with a secret lover, murders them both.

Realizing that the prophecy has come true, Julian leaves home for a lifetime of wandering and seeking penance. Ultimately he becomes a ferryman at a dangerous river crossing. When an elderly leper shows up and makes unusual demands upon Julian's kindness and hospitality, Julian discovers—with his final breath—that the old leper is Jesus himself, come to absolve Julian of his sin.

Hardcover: 0-060-52252-6

ZONDERVAN™

GRAND RAPIDS, MICHIGAN 49530 USA

WWW.ZONDERVAN.COM

AN INTIMATE PORTRAIT OF A
COMPLEX INDIVIDUAL

A   N O V E L

WALTER WANGERIN JR.

Walter Wangerin brings us a dramatic, fictionalized retelling of the life
of Paul based on biblical texts and
extensive on-site research. Readers gain
a new appreciation for the sacrifices of
the apostles and the early believers and
gain new insights into the life of the
early church.

With vivid imagination and schol-
arly depth, award-winning author Walter Wangerin Jr. weaves together
the history of the early church with the life story of its greatest apostle—
Paul. Wangerin begins to unfold Paul's incredible life by imagining the
childhood and early family life of a boy then called "Saul." A fierce pros-
ecutor of Christians before his conversion, Paul never lost his fiery dedi-
cation, boldness, and strong personality. After his shocking encounter with
God on the road to Damascus, he applied his formidable strengths to
spreading the gospel. Wangerin deftly reveals Paul's character through
each stage of his life, and enables us to see Paul the person, living and
complex, viewed through the eyes of his contemporaries: Barnabas, James,
Prisca, Seneca, and Luke. Paul's rich interaction and brilliant dialogue
with friends and foes, leaders and slaves, Jews and Greeks, create a swift
and intense historical drama around the man who spread the seed of the
Gospel to the ends of the known world.

Hardcover: 0-310-21892-6
Softcover: 0-310-24316-5
Unabridged Audio Pages® Cassette: 0-310-23591-X

ZONDERVAN™

GRAND RAPIDS, MICHIGAN 49530 USA
WWW.ZONDERVAN.COM

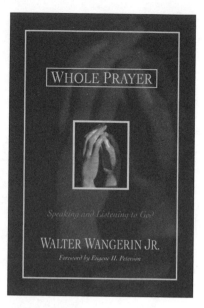

A TRUSTWORTHY GUIDE TO AN INTIMATE RELATIONSHIP WITH GOD

WHOLE PRAYER

SPEAKING AND LISTENING TO GOD

WALTER WANGERIN JR.

Award-winning author Walter Wangerin Jr. gracefully explores the dynamics of prayer—of speaking, of listening, of waiting, and of hearing God's voice. With luminous prose, he surveys the landscape of communication and communion with God—what whole prayer feels like, looks like, and sounds like. He points out that whole prayer is a circle, closed and complete. We pour out our hearts and minds to God, who listens as we do. Then we listen intently for his voice when he speaks. Wangerin encourages readers not to eliminate any part of the circle so we don't cut the conversation short.

Softcover: 0-310-24258-4

GRAND RAPIDS, MICHIGAN 49530 USA

WWW.ZONDERVAN.COM

FOLLOW EVERY DETAIL LEADING TO THE BIRTH OF CHRIST

PREPARING FOR JESUS

MEDITATIONS ON THE COMING OF CHRIST, ADVENT, CHRISTMAS, AND THE KINGDOM

WALTER WANGERIN JR.

In this Advent and Christmas devotional, best-selling author Walter Wangerin Jr. takes the reader day-by-day through the major events and characters leading up to the birth of Jesus in 36 meditations.

In *Preparing for Jesus,* the author recreates verbal images of the events surrounding the Advent of Christ, offering a devotional journey into the heart of the Christmas season. Through rich detail and vivid images, these moving meditations make Christ's birth both intimate and immediate, allowing us to see Christmas from its original happening to its perennial recurrence in our hearts. *Preparing for Jesus* is sure to be a seasonal classic, treasured year after year.

Hardcover: 0-310-20644-8

ZONDERVAN™

GRAND RAPIDS, MICHIGAN 49530 USA

WWW.ZONDERVAN.COM

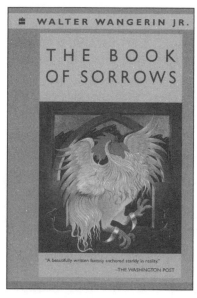

THE BOOK OF SORROWS

WALTER WANGERIN JR.

This sequel to the award-winning *The Book of the Dun Cow* stands on its own as a powerful work of literature. In this absorbing, highly original fantasy, Chauntecleer, Pertelote, and the other familiar characters of the Coop struggle to piece together their shattered lives in the aftermath of the terrible conflict with the dreaded Wyrm. But their respite is short-lived: Into this struggling community, Wyrm again insinuates himself, with dire consequences for all. The reappearance of the dog Mundo Coni unveils a darker mystery yet—and the threat of a final horror when evil yields up its most devastating secrets. Told by a master storyteller, *The Book of Sorrows* is a taught and spellbinding tale that immerses readers in a variety of adventures— heroic, humorous, and touching—moving inexorably toward the final confrontation that decides the fate of the characters and their world. No one who reads it will remain unmoved. It explores the value and goodness of existence, the darker side of reality, and the qualities of love, kindness, courage, and hope that can transform even "this troublous existence." Here is fast-paced fantasy filled with richly drawn characters and gripping excitement, set against a colorful, fully realized world, and with depth of meaning that will draw readers back again and again to ponder the images long after the final battle is waged between the forces of life and death.

Softcover: 0-310-21081-X

ZONDERVAN™

GRAND RAPIDS, MICHIGAN 49530 USA

WWW.ZONDERVAN.COM

A MOVING ALLEGORY OF
THE CHRISTIAN LIFE

THE ORPHEAN

PASSAGES

THE DRAMA OF FAITH

WALTER WANGERIN JR.

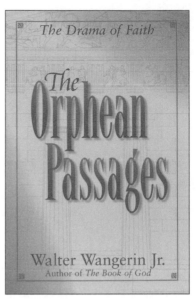

A remarkable weaving of faith, myth, and humanity from award-winning novelist Walter Wangerin Jr. "Faith," writes Walter Wangerin, is "a relationship with the living God enacted in this world." It is ever-changing and inherently dramatic. *The Orphean Passages* is Wangerin's compelling story of a Christian pastor's career and the drama of his faith. Interlaced with the classical myth of Orpheus and Eurydice, this daring and unconventional inquiry into Christian experience ranks among the most challenging of Wangerin's works. Wangerin sees in the ancient myth an extraordinary parallel of the twists and turns individuals follow in their journeys of faith. In the author's own present-day Reverend Orpheus, that parallel is vividly played out—rendering the modern story of one man both universal and timeless. *The Orphean Passages* asserts the truth of a legend that people of all times have experienced. It has the immediacy of a well-wrought novel, driving readers on to the surprising yet inevitable conclusion.

Softcover: 0-310-20568-9

GRAND RAPIDS, MICHIGAN 49530 USA

WWW.ZONDERVAN.COM

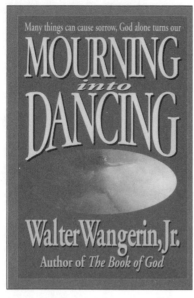

HELP THE HURTING AND YOURSELF THROUGH THIS AMAZING BOOK

MOURNING INTO DANCING

WALTER WANGERIN JR.

"Death doesn't wait till the ends of our lives to meet us and to make an end," says Walter Wangerin. "Instead, we die a hundred times before we die; and all the little endings on the way are like a slowly growing echo of the final BANG!" Yet out of our many losses, our "little deaths," comes a truer recognition of life. It is found in our relationships with ourselves, with our world, with others, and with our Creator. This is the dancing that can come out of mourning: the hope of restored relationships. *Mourning into Dancing* defines the stages of grief, names the many kinds of loss we suffer, shows how to help the grief-stricken, gives a new vision of Christ's sacrifice, and shows how a loving God shares our grief. We learn from this book that the way to dancing is through the valley of mourning—that grief is a poignant reminder of the fullness of life Christ obtained for us through his resurrection. In the words of writer and critic John Timmerman, *Mourning into Dancing* "could well be the most important book you ever read."

Softcover: 0-310-20765-7

GRAND RAPIDS, MICHIGAN 49530 USA

WWW.ZONDERVAN.COM

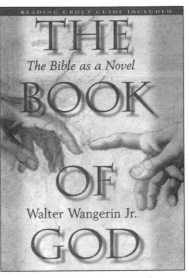

A PERFECT DEVOTIONAL FOR
THE LENTEN SEASON

RELIVING THE PASSION

MEDITATIONS ON THE SUFFERING, DEATH, AND THE RESURRECTION OF JESUS AS RECORDED IN MARK

WALTER WANGERIN JR.

No story has more significance than this: the death and resurrection of Jesus. But somehow the oft-repeated tale of Christ's Passion can become too familiar, too formalized, for us to experience its incredible immediacy. The meditations in *Reliving the Passion,* which received a Gold Medallion award in 1993, follow the story as given in the gospel of Mark—from the moment when the chief priests plot to kill Jesus to the Resurrection. But these readings are more than a recounting of events; they are an imaginary reenactment, leading the reader to re-experience the Passion or perhaps see it fully for the very first time. As only a great storyteller can, Walter Wangerin takes his readers inside the story of Christ's passion. *Reliving the Passion* translates the events into the realm of feeling, image, and experience. In richly personal detail, Wangerin helps us recognize our own faces in the streets of Jerusalem; breathe the dark air of Golgotha; and experience, as Mary and Peter did, the bewilderment, the challenge, and the ultimate revelation of knowing the man called Jesus.

Hardcover: 0-310-75530-1

GRAND RAPIDS, MICHIGAN 49530 USA

WWW.ZONDERVAN.COM

We want to hear from you. Please send your comments about this book to us in care of the address below. Thank you.

GRAND RAPIDS, MICHIGAN 49530 USA

WWW.ZONDERVAN.COM

—